THE BEST
SCIENCE FICTION
AND FANTASY
OF THE YEAR

VOLUME FOUR

THE BEST
SCIENCE FICTION
AND FANTASY
OF THE YEAR

VOLUME FOUR

EDITED BY JONATHAN STRAHAN

NIGHT SHADE BOOKS
SAN FRANCISCO

First Edition

ISBN: 978-1-59780-171-3
Printed in Canada

Night Shade Books
Please visit us on the web at
www.nightshadebooks.com

For Robert Silverberg and Karen Haber, dear friends both, who were kind and generous when they did not have to be, with my thanks.

Acknowledgements

By my count this is either the thirty-third or thirty-fourth book that I have worked on since the chance presented itself for me to edit my first anthology back in the heady Australian summer of 1996. Astoundingly, to me at least, thirty-one (or thirty-two) of those books were edited between mid-2004 and the end of 2009. Five years, give or take. Not one of those books, not a single one, would have been possible without the support, guidance and friendship of the late Charles N. Brown who died this past July. He was a dear friend and his advice was instrumental in guiding this book to publication.

This year has been a challenging one and getting this book done has been demanding. I'd especially like to thank Gary K. Wolfe, whose advice has been invaluable; Alisa Krasnostein, Tansy Rayner Roberts, Ben Payne, Alex Pierce, Tehani Wessely, Jason Fischer and Sarah Parker from *Not if You Were the Last Short Story on Earth* who were my companions on the journey through the year and provided an invaluable sounding board. I'd also like to thank Howard Morhaim, Katie Menick, Justin Ackroyd, Jack Dann, and Gordon Van Gelder. Thanks also to the following good friends and colleagues without whom this book would have been much poorer, and much less fun to do: Lou Anders, Deborah Biancotti, Ellen Datlow, Gardner Dozois, Sean Williams, and all of the book's contributors.

As always, my greatest thanks go to Marianne, Jessica and Sophie. Every moment spent working on this book was a moment stolen from them. I only hope I can repay them.

CONTENTS

INTRODUCTION
JONATHAN STRAHAN

This last year was a good but not exceptional year for short speculative fiction. As was the case in 2008, and for most of this decade really, there were literally millions of words of short science fiction and fantasy published in magazines, anthologies, collections, 'zines, and pamphlets. And, while markets opened and markets closed, there was still enough top notch science fiction and fantasy published to keep any one reader busy, and easily enough to fill several volumes like the one you are now holding.

As is always the case, there were trends that could be readily discerned by any attentive reader. Our fascination with the undead continued through 2009 and looks set to go on for at least another year or two. John Joseph Adams' remarkably successful 2008 anthology *The Living Dead* was followed by several less-interesting books by other hands. Literary mash-ups, of all things (!), gave us the runaway bestseller *Pride and Prejudice and Zombies,* and way too many similar books seem set to follow. The other major trend was a passion for the retro-futurism of steampunk. While Nick Gevers' *Extraordinary Engines* investigated some of the possibilities of the subgenre last year, and Jeff VanderMeer and Ann VanderMeer's fine *Steampunk* laid out its past, 2009 saw major novels like Scott Westerfeld's *Leviathan* and Cherie Priest's *Boneshaker* published which, along with a passel of short stories, made it clear steampunk is here to stay. It's not brave or particularly prescient to suggest we'll be dealing with both of these trends for several years yet. A perhaps longer-lasting trend, though, is our growing interest in the technology of reading. While the enormous, and frankly ominous, Google Book Settlement case continued, it seemed we became more and more interested in electronic book readers. What once was either clunky or dull had, by year's end, become sexy and cool, and was increasingly tipped to become the new iPod. Certainly the 2009 revamp of the Kindle was well received, as was Barnes & Noble's nook, which debuted late in the year. It remains to be seen, though, whether either of these devices, or some as-yet-unreleased competitor, will finally make eBooks a widespread and popular reality.

No single publishing news event dominated the year; instead, people interested in the industry focused on cutbacks and losses, and pondered the future. At various times things began to look grim indeed. *Asimov's Science Fiction* and *Analog Science Fiction and Fact* changed their physical format with their December 2008 issues, which suggested that they would publish less fiction and might even be in some kind of financial difficulty. Then in January Sovereign Media announced that it was ceasing publication of *Realms of Fantasy*, a stalwart of the field since 1994. All of the doomsayers probably felt that the science fiction magazine apocalypse was truly upon us when in April publisher Gordon Van Gelder announced that he was moving the venerable *Magazine of Fantasy & Science Fiction* to a bi-monthly schedule, producing double issues that would be slightly shorter than two of their monthly predecessors.

And yet, as the year moved on it became clear that while every magazine was facing challenges (mostly arising from changes to postal charges), things were not as bad as we feared. Throughout the year, at various times, publishers made spirited attempts to make it clear that, while things were tough, they were still doing okay, assertions that were borne out by the fact that at year's end *Asimov's* and *F&SF* had published pretty much exactly the same amount of fiction they had in 2008 (though *F&SF's* decision to publish a series of classic reprints did mean they published fewer new stories in 2009), with only *Analog* publishing a significantly smaller volume of fiction than in previous years. Then *Realms of Fantasy* was suddenly and unexpectedly resurrected by the enterprising Warren Lapine, with Shawna McCarthy remaining at the editorial helm, and ended up missing just a single issue.

But while things weren't as bad as we feared there still were some genuine losses. In August the publishers of *Jim Baen's Universe*, one of the highest paying short fiction markets in the field, announced that they would discontinue the magazine because of problems finding sufficient subscribers, then *Orson Scott Card's Intergalactic Medicine Show* also announced cutbacks, which was followed by the news that venerable SF media magazine *Starlog* and newcomer *Death Ray* would both be ceasing publication. Even the buoyant anthology market saw cutbacks, with editors Lou Anders and George Mann walking away from their "Fast Forward" and "Solaris Book of New Science Fiction" series to focus respectively on their publishing and writing commitments.

And what of the fiction? Well, as has been the case for the last decade, a lot of excellent fiction was published, and in ever more diverse locations. The seemingly beleaguered major print magazines all had solid if unspectacular years, with *The Magazine of Fantasy & Science Fiction* continuing to set the standard amongst the digests with fine stories from Geoff Ryman, John Kessel, Ellen Kushner, Alex Irvine, Robert Silverberg, Elizabeth Hand, and others. Almost as good was Sheila Williams's *Asimov's*, which published strong work by James Patrick Kelly,

Robert Reed, Nancy Kress, Kristine Kathryn Rusch, Damien Broderick (making a welcome splash with some fine new stories), Holly Phillips, and Rudy Rucker & Bruce Sterling. Williams deserves special note for publishing some challenging newer writers like Sara Genge who had two strong stories in the magazine this year. *Analog* continued very much as it has in recent times, very much being seen as representing an old core kind of science fiction regardless of what it actually published, and featuring excellent stories by Stephen Baxter and Steven Gould. Rounding out the "Big Four" print magazines, if there really is such a thing anymore, was the resurrected *Realms of Fantasy*, which published some solid work by Adam Corbin-Fusco, Cat Rambo and Richard Parks. I remain a little disappointed with it, though, and continue to hope it might be more adventurous. *Interzone* has sat just below the "Big Four" for the last several years, steadily publishing beautifully designed issues (it's easily the best looking fiction magazine in the field), and is a reliable source for good fiction. This year it was a little less impressive than it was last year, but they did publish an excellent story from Bruce Sterling amongst some other good work. There were many, many other print magazines published during the year—far too many to mention here—but I would single out Ann VanderMeer's *Weird Tales* as being especially worthy of your attention. If the magazine can re-establish a regular publication schedule and maintain its high editorial standards it will stand with the "Big Four" within the next few years.

We probably make too much of the difference between print and online magazines: print and online are after all only mediums of distribution and a magazine is a magazine. Under the capable editorship of Patrick Nielsen Hayden, *Tor.com* has very quickly established itself as the best and most reliable source of excellent short fiction on the web, publishing terrific stories by Michael Swanwick and Eileen Gunn, Rachel Swirsky, Kij Johnson, Charles Stross, and others. The only criticism I have of *Tor.com* is that I wish they'd publish *more* stories. Sitting only slightly behind it is Neil Clarke's *Clarkesworld Magazine*, which I think along with *Weird Tales* is one of the most improved magazines in the field. Although it mostly publishes quite short stories, what it does publish is of a very high standard with especially good work this year from Catherynne M. Valente, Kij Johnson, and Gord Sellar. And then there's *Shadow Unit*, an intriguing reader contribution-funded website where writers like Elizabeth Bear, Emma Bull, Sarah Monette, Holly Black and others regularly publish episodes for an unproduced television show, the eponymous "Shadow Unit". The writing is uniformly excellent, the stories intriguing and several of them would definitely be in this volume were they only shorter (almost all of the stories are quite long novellas).

As has been the case for the past four or five years, anthologies continue to be an excellent source of great short fiction. It doesn't seem appropriate for me to say too much about the anthologies I edit myself, so I'll simply note that *The New Space Opera 2* (co-edited with Gardner Dozois) had strong stories by Robert Charles Wilson, Peter Watts, John C. Wright, Cory Doctorow, Bruce Sterling and others, while *Eclipse Three* had good work from Karen Joy Fowler, Nicola Griffith, Caitlin R. Kiernan, Ellen Klages, and Ellen Kushner, amongst others. The two best science fiction anthologies of the year were Nick Gevers and Jay Lake's *Other Earths*, which featured outstanding stories by Robert Charles Wilson, Gene Wolfe and others, and George Mann's *The Solaris Book of New Science Fiction: Volume 3*, which had good work by Daniel Abraham and Alastair Reynolds. The best fantasy anthology of the year was Sharyn November's *Firebirds Soaring*, which included outstanding work by Jo Walton, Margo Lanagan, Ellen Klages, and Marly Youmans. It was very closely followed by Jack Dann and Gardner Dozois's excellent *The Dragon Book*. Any theme anthology is best dipped into, but this strong outing contained a real diversity of high quality work by Diana Wynne Jones, Cecelia Holland, Andy Duncan, and others. I also admired Dozois and George R.R. Martin's *Songs of the Dying Earth*, which also was a book that you had to dip into rather than read straight through. The stories by Dan Simmons, Neil Gaiman, and Lucius Shepard were particularly good. Ellen Datlow continued to show why she is one of our best editors in 2009, publishing no fewer than three fine anthologies. Her *Poe*, *Lovecraft Unbound*, and *Troll's Eye View* (with Terri Windling) were all outstanding and stories from each of them are reprinted here. Peter Crowther and Nick Gevers' *Postscripts* magazine morphed into a quarterly anthology series in 2009. The best volume was *Postscripts 20/21* which had several excellent stories, but the standout *Postscripts* story of the year was Daniel Abraham's "Balfour and Meriwether in 'The Adventure of the Emperor's Vengeance'" from *Postscripts 19*. And finally one or two really interesting books were published back home in Australia this year. Twelfth Planet Press published Peter M. Ball's strong novelette *Horn*, and Tansy Rayner Roberts' highly enjoyable "Siren Beat", which appeared as a double book with World Fantasy Award winner Robert Shearman's "Roadkill", and Deborah Biancotti's excellent debut collection, *The Book of Endings*. All are recommended. Particularly noteworthy, though, was Keith Stevenson's *X6*, an anthology of novellas that is genuinely one of the year's most interesting books. It features an excoriating piece of work from Paul Haines, "Wives", and a terrific fantasy by Margo Lanagan, that make the book well worth seeking out.

It shouldn't be surprising, given the quality of short fiction in recent years, that this was *another* good year for short story collections. It's never easy to pick the best short story collection of the year, but Ian McDonald's *Cyberabad Days*, Greg Egan's *Oceanic*, Gwyneth Jones's *Grazing the Long Acre*, and Charles Stross's *Wireless* all stand amongst the best science fiction collections of recent times, while Peter S. Beagle's *We Never Talk About My Brother* was easily my favorite fantasy collection of the year. A number of excellent retrospectives were published during the year: standouts include *The Best of Gene Wolfe*, *The Best of Michael Moorcock*, and *Trips* by Robert Silverberg. NESFA Press also published the outstanding six-volume *Collected Stories of Roger Zelazny* and two fine volumes of *The Collected Short Works of Poul Anderson*. All of these books deserve your attention.

Finally, a personal note. On July 12, 2009, *Locus* co-founder and publisher Charles N. Brown died in his sleep on his way home to California from a science fiction convention in Boston. I first met Charles in the North American summer of 1993 where we made absolutely no impression upon one another. I did, however, spend time romancing his managing editor, which meant he agreed to suffer through a dinner with me the following year. He was *almost* interested. And yet, because of his managing editor, we both persevered. He let me work for him and eventually, possibly because we spent a lot of time eating dim sum and buying CDs together, he became one of my dearest friends. His advice colored every project I've worked on and his support helped make each and every one of them possible in some way or another. He was, I think, science fiction's best and truest advocate. His passion for the field was deep, profound and perspicacious. He influenced me greatly but he influenced the field he loved far more. When I say you wouldn't be reading this book without him, I say it not just because he influenced me, but because he influenced the field so greatly that the stories here would be different had he not lived. The science fiction field will miss him more than it realizes while I am only beginning to come to terms with how much I miss him.

And now, on to the stories! These were the ones that I enjoyed the most during the year, or found to be the best and most delightful. I hope you enjoy them as much as I did.

Jonathan Strahan
Perth, Western Australia
November 2009

IT TAKES TWO
NICOLA GRIFFITH

Nicola Griffith is a native of Yorkshire, England, where she earned her beer money teaching women's self-defense, fronting a band, and arm-wrestling in bars, before discovering writing and moving to the US. Her immigration case was a fight and ended up making new law: the State Department declared it to be "in the National Interest" for her to live and work in this country. This didn't thrill the more conservative powerbrokers, and she ended up on the front page of the *Wall Street Journal*, where her case was used as an example of the country's declining moral standards.

In 1993 a diagnosis of multiple sclerosis slowed her down a bit, and she concentrated on writing. Her novels are *Ammonite* (1993), *Slow River* (1995), *The Blue Place*, (1998), *Stay* (2002), and *Always* (2007). She is the co-editor of the *Bending the Landscape* series of original short fiction. Her short work and non-fiction has appeared in a variety of print and web journals, including *Out, Nature, New Scientist*, and *The Huffington Post*. Her awards include the James Tiptree, Jr. Award, the Nebula Award, the World Fantasy Award, and the Lambda Literary Award (six times). Her latest book is a limited-edition, multi-media memoir, *And Now We Are Going to Have a Party: liner notes to a writer's early life.*

Griffith lives and works in Seattle with her partner, writer Kelley Eskridge, they run Sterling Editing, helping writers improve their work. Her own works-in-progress include a short story collection, an essay collection, and a novel about Hild, a pivotal figure of the seventh century. She takes enormous delight in everything.

It began, as these things do, at a bar—a long dark piece of mahogany along one wall of Seattle's Queen City Grill polished by age and more than a few chins. The music was winding down. Richard and Cody (whose real name was Candice, though no one she had met since high school knew it) lived on different coasts, but tonight was the third time this year they had been drinking together. Cody was staring at the shadows gathering in the corners of the bar and trying not to think about her impersonal hotel room. She thought instead of the fact that in the last six months she had seen Richard more often than some of her friends in San Francisco, and that she would probably see him yet again in a few weeks when their respective companies bid on the Atlanta contract.

She said, "You ever wonder what it would be like to have, you know, a normal type job, where you get up on Monday and drive to work, and do the same thing Tuesday and Wednesday and Thursday, every week, except when you take a vacation?"

"You forgot Friday."

"What?" They had started on mojitos, escalated through James Bonds, and were now on a tequila-shooter-with-draft-chaser glide path.

"I said, you forgot Friday. Monday, Tuesday—"

"Right," Cody said. "Right. Too many fucking details. But did you ever wonder? About a normal life?" An actual life, in one city, with actual friends.

Richard was silent long enough for Cody to lever herself around on the bar stool and look at him. He was playing with his empty glass. "I just took a job," he said. "A no-travel job."

"Ah, shit."

They had met just after the first dotcom crash, at a graduate conference on synergies of bio-mechanics and expert decision-making software architecture or some such crap, which was wild because he started out in cognitive psychology and she in applied mathematics. But computers were the alien glue that made all kinds of odd limbs stick together and work in ways never intended by nature. *Like Frankenstein's monster*, he had said when she mentioned it, and she had bought him a drink, because he got it. They ran into each other at a similar conference two months later, then again at some industry junket not long after they'd both joined social media startups. The pattern repeated itself, until, by the time they were both pitching venture capitalists at trade shows, they managed to get past the required cool, the distancing irony, and began to email each other beforehand to arrange dinners, drinks, tickets to the game. They were young, good-looking, and very, very smart. Even better, they had absolutely no romantic interest in each other.

Now when they met it was while traveling as representatives of their credit-starved companies to make increasingly desperate pitches to industry-leading Goliaths on why they needed the nimble expertise of hungry Davids.

Cody hadn't told Richard that lately her pitches had been more about why the Goliaths might find it cost-effective to absorb the getting-desperate David she worked for, along with all its innovative, motivated, boot-strapping employees whose stock options and 401(k)s were now worthless. But a no-travel job meant one thing, and going back to the groves of academe was really admitting failure.

She sighed. "Where?"

"Chapel Hill. And it's not… Well, okay, it is sort of an academic job, but not really."

"Uh-huh."

"No, really. It's with a new company, a joint venture between WishtleNet and the University of North—"

"See."

"Just let me finish." Richard could get very didactic when he'd been drinking. "Think Google Labs, or Xerox PARC, but wackier. Lots of money to play with, lots of smart grad students to do what I tell them, lots of blue sky research, not just irritating Vice Presidents saying I've got six months to get the software on the market, even if it is garbage."

"I hear you on that." Except that Vince, Cody's COO, had told her that if she landed the Atlanta contract she would be made a VP herself.

"It's cool stuff, Cody. All those things we've talked about in the last six, seven years? The cognitive patterning and behavior mod, the modulated resonance imaging software, the intuitive learning algorithms—"

"Yeah, yeah."

"—they *want* me to work on that. They want me to define new areas of interest. Very cool stuff."

Cody just shook her head. Cool. Cool didn't remember to feed the fish when you were out of town, again.

"Starts next month," he said.

Cody felt very tired. "You won't be in Atlanta."

"Nope."

"Atlanta in August. On my own. Jesus."

"On your own? What about all those pretty girls in skimpy summer clothes?"

The muscles in Cody's eyebrows felt tight. She rubbed them. "It's Boone I'm not looking forward to. Boone and his sleazy strip club games."

"He's the customer."

"Your sympathy's killing me."

He shrugged. "I thought that lap-dancing hooker thing was your wet dream."

Her head ached. Now he was going to bring up Dallas.

"That's what you told us in—now where the hell was that?"

"Dallas." Might as well get it over with.

"You were really into it. Are you blushing?"

"No." Three years ago she had been twenty-eight with four million dollars in stock options and the belief that coding-cowboy colleagues were her friends. Ha. And now probably half the geeks in the South had heard about her most intimate fantasy. Including Boone.

She swallowed the last of her tequila. Oily, ugly stuff once it got tepid. She picked up her jacket.

"I'm out of here. Unless you have any handy hints about landing that contract without playing Boone's slimeball games? Didn't think so." She pushed her shot glass away and stood.

"That Atlanta meeting's when? Eight, nine weeks?"

"About that." She dropped two twenties on the bar.

"I maybe could help."

"With Boone? Right." But Richard's usually cherubic face was quite stern.

He fished his phone from his pocket and put it on the bar. He said, "Just trust me for a minute," and tapped the memo icon. The icon winked red. "Whatever happens, I promise no one will ever hear what goes on this recording except you."

Cody slung on her jacket. "Cue ominous music."

"It's more an, um, an ethics thing."

"Jesus, Richard. You're such a drama queen." But she caught the bartender's eye, pointed to their glasses, and sat.

"I did my Atlanta research too," he said. "Like you, I'm pretty sure what will happen after you've made your presentations to Boone."

"The Golden Key," she said, nodding. The sun rises, the government taxes, Boone listens to bids and takes everyone to the Golden Key.

"—but what I need to know from you is whether or not, to win this contract, you can authorize out-of-pocket expenses in the high five figures."

She snorted. "Five figures against a possible eight? What do you think?"

He pointed at the phone.

"Fine. Yes. I can approve that kind of expense."

He smiled, a very un-Richard-like sliding of muscle and bone, like a python disarticulating its jaw to swallow a pig. Cody nearly stood up, but the moment passed.

"You'll also have to authorize me to access your medical records," he said.

So here they were in Marietta, home of the kind of Georgians who wouldn't fuck a stranger in the woods only because they didn't know who his people were: seven men and one woman stepping from Boone's white concrete and green glass tower into an August sun hot enough to make the blacktop bubble. Boone's shades flashed as he turned to face the group.

"All work and no play makes Jack a dull boy. And Jill," with a nod at Cody, who nodded back and tried not to squint. Squinting made her look like a moron: not good when all around you were wearing sleek East Coast summer business clothes and gilded with Southern tans. At least the guy from Portland had forgotten his shades too.

They moved in a small herd across the soft, sticky parking lot: the guy from Boston would have to throw away his fawn loafers.

Boone said to the guy from Austin, "Dave, you take these three. I know you know where we're going."

"Sure do," Dave said, and the seven boys shared that we're-all-men-of-the-world-yes-indeedy laugh. Cody missed Richard. And she was still pissed at the way he'd dropped the news on her only last week. Why hadn't he told her earlier about not coming to Atlanta? Why hadn't he told her in Seattle? And a university job: what was up with that? Loser. But she wished he was here.

Boone's car was a flashy Mercedes hybrid in silver. He opened the passenger door with a Yeah-I-know-men-and-women-are-equal-but-I-was-born-in-the-south-so-what-can-you-do? smile to which Cody responded with a perfect, ironic lift of both eyebrows. Hey, couldn't have managed that in shades. The New York guy and Boston loafers got in the back. The others were climbing into Dave's dark green rental SUV. A full-sized SUV. Very uncool. He'd lose points for that. She jammed her seatbelt home with a satisfying click.

As they drove to the club, she let the two in the back jostle for conversational space with Boone. She stared out of the window. The meeting had gone very well. It was clear that she and Dave and the guy from Denver were the only ones representing companies with the chops for this contract, and she was pretty sure she had the edge over the Denver people when it came to program rollout. Between her and Dave, then. If only they weren't going to the Golden Key. God. The thought of all those men watching her watch those women and think they knew what she was thinking made her scalp prickle with sweat. In the flow of conditioned air, her face turned cold.

Two days before she left for Atlanta she'd emailed Vince to explain that it wasn't her who would be uncomfortable at the strip club, but the men, and that he should at least consider giving Boone a call and setting her presentation up for either the day before or the day after the others. She'd got a reply half an hour later, short and to the point: *You're going, kid, end of story.* She'd taken a deep breath and walked over to his office.

He was on the phone, pacing up and down, but waved her in before she could knock. He covered the receiver with one hand, "Gotta take this, won't be long," and went back to pacing, shouting, "Damn it, Rick, I want it done. When we had that meeting last week you assured me— Yeah. No problem, you said. No fucking problem. So just do it, just find a way." He slammed the phone down, shook his head, turned his attention to her. "Cody, what can I do for you? If it's about this Atlanta thing I don't want to hear it."

"Vince—"

"Boone's not stupid. He takes people to that titty club because he likes to watch how they behave under pressure. You're the best we've got, you know that. Just be yourself and you won't fuck up. Give him good presentation and don't act like a girl scout when the nipples start to show. Can you handle that?"

"I just resent—"

"Jesus Christ, Cody. It's not like you've never seen bare naked ladies before. You want to be a VP? Tell me now: yes or no."

Cody took a breath. "Yes."

"Glad to hear it. Now get out of here."

The Golden Key was another world: cool, and scented with the fruity overtones of beer; loud, with enough bass to make the walls of her abdomen vibrate; dark at the edges, though lushly lit at the central stage with its three chrome poles and laser strobes. Only one woman was dancing. It was just after six, but the place was already half full. Somewhere, someone was smoking expensive cigars. Cody wondered who the club paid off to make that possible.

Boone ordered staff to put two tables together right by the stage, near the center pole. The guy from New York sat on Boone's left, Dave on his right. Cody took a place at the end, out of Boone's peripheral vision. She wouldn't say or do anything that wasn't detached and ironic. She would be seamless.

A new dancer: shoulder-length red hair that fell over her face as she writhed around the right hand pole. She wore a skirt the size of a belt, and six-inch heels of translucent plastic embedded with suggestive pink flowers. Without the pole she probably couldn't even stand. Did interesting things to her butt, though, Cody thought, then patted surreptitiously at her upper lip. Dry, thank god. Score one for air conditioning.

New York poked her arm. He jerked his thumb at Boone, who leaned forward and shouted, "What do you want to drink?"

"Does it matter?"

He grinned. "No grape juice playing at champagne here. Place takes its liquor seriously."

Peachy. "Margarita. With salt." If it was sour enough she wouldn't want to gulp it.

The dancer hung upside down on the pole and undid her bra. Her breasts were a marvel of modern art, almost architectural.

"My God," she said, "it's the Hagia Sophia."

"What?" New York shouted. "She's called Sophia?"

"No," Cody shouted back, "her breasts... Never mind."

"Fakes," New York said, nodding.

The drinks came, delivered by a blonde woman wearing nothing but a purple velvet g-string and a smile. She called Boone *Darlin'*—clearly he was a regular—and Cody *Sugar*.

Cody managed to lift her eyes from the weirdness of unpierced nipples long enough to find a dollar bill and drop it on the drinks tray. Two of the guys were threading their tips under the g-string: a five and a ten. The blonde dropped Cody a wink as she walked away. New York caught it and leered. Cody tried her margarita: very sour. She gulped anyway.

The music changed to a throbbing remix of mom music: the Pointer Sisters' "Slowhand." The bass line was insistent, pushing on her belly like a warm hand. She licked her lips and applied herself to her drink. Another dancer with soft black curls took the left-hand pole, and the redhead moved to centre stage on her hands and knees in front of their table, rotating her ass in slow motion, looking at them over her shoulder, slitting her eyes at them like a cat. Boone, Dave, all the guys had bills in their hands: "Ooh mama, I've got what you need." The redhead backed towards them in slow motion, arching her spine now in apparent ecstasy—but not so far gone as to ignore the largest bill at the table: Boone's twenty. She let him tease her with it, stroking up the inside of her thigh and circling a nipple, before she held out the waistband of the pseudo-skirt for the twenty. They probably didn't notice that she plucked them of their bills in order—Boone's twenty, Dave's ten, the two fives. Then she was moving to her right, to a crowd of hipster suits who had obviously been there longer than was good for them: two of them were holding out fifties. The dancer pretended to fuck the fifty being held out at pelvis level. She had incredible muscle control. Next to Cody, New York swallowed hard, and fumbled for his wallet. But it was too late. The hipster was grinning hard as the redhead touched his cheek, tilted her head, said something. He stood and his friends hooted encouragement as he and the redhead disappeared through a heavily frosted glass door in the back.

"Oh, man…" Dave's face was more red than tan, now. He pulled a fifty from his wallet, snapped it, folded it lengthways, and held it out over the stage to the remaining dancer. "Yo, curlyhead, come and get some!"

"Yeah!" said New York in a high voice. Portland and Boston seemed to be engaged in a drinking game.

Boone caught Cody's eye and smiled slightly. She shrugged and spread her hand as if to say, Hey, it's their money to waste, and he smiled again, this time with a touch of skepticism. Ah, shit.

"Sugar?" The waitress with the velvet g-string, standing close and bending down so that her nipples brushed Cody's hair, then dabbed her cheek.

Cody looked at her faded blue eyes and found a ten dollar bill. She smiled and slipped it into the g-string at the woman's hip and crooked a finger to make her bend close again.

"I'd take it as a personal favor if you brought me another of these wonderful margaritas," she said in the woman's ear, "without the tequila."

"Whatever you say. But I'll still have to charge for the liquor."

"Of course you do. Just make sure it looks good." Cody jerked her head back at the rest of the table.

"You let me take care of everything, sugar. I'm going to make you the meanest looking margarita in Dixie. They'll be amazed, purely amazed, at your stamina. It'll be our little secret." She fondled Cody's arm and shoulder, let the back of her hand brush the side of Cody's breast. "My name is Mimi. If you need anything, later." She gave Cody a molten look and headed for the bar. The skin on her rotating cheeks looked unnaturally smooth, like porcelain. Cosmetics, Cody decided.

Curlyhead had spotted Dave's fifty and was now on her back in front of their table. Cody imagined her as a glitched wigglebot responding to insane commands:

clench, release, arch, whip back and forth. Whoever had designed her had done a great job on those muscles: each distinct, plump with strength, soft to the touch. Shame they hadn't had much imagination with the facial expressions or managed to put any spark in the eyes.

Breasts swaying near her face announced the arrival of her kickless drink. She slipped a ten from her wallet and reached for Mimi's g-string.

Mimi stepped back half a pace, put her tray down, and squeezed her breasts together with her hands. "Would you like to put it here instead, Sugar?"

Cody blinked.

"You could slide it in real slow. Then maybe we could get better acquainted." But like the wigglebot, her eyes stayed blank.

"You're too hot for me, Mimi." Cody snapped the bill into her g-string and tried not to feel Mimi's flash of hatred. She sipped her drink and took a discreet peek in her wallet. This was costing the company a fortune.

Boone watched Dave and New York with a detached expression. Then he turned her way with a speculative look. An invitation to talk?

She stood. And turned to look at the stage just as a long-haired woman in cowboy boots strode to the center pole.

For Cookie it was all routine so far, ankle holding up better than she thought it might. The boots helped. She couldn't remember when she'd written that note to herself, *Cowboys and Indians!*, but it was going to be inspired. She flexed and bent and pouted and pointed her breasts on automatic pilot. Should she get the ankle x-rayed? Nah. It was only a sprain. Two ibuprofen and some ice would fix it.

Decent crowd for a Tuesday night. Some high spenders behind the pillar there, but Ginger had taken them for four lapdances already. Well, hey, there were always more men with more money than sense. She glanced into the wings. Danny had her hat. He nodded. She moved automatically, counted under her breath, and just as the first haunting whistle of Morricone's "The Good, the Bad, and the Ugly" soundtrack echoed from the speakers she held out her hand, caught the hat, and swept it onto her head. Ooh, baby, perfect today, perfect. She smiled and strutted downstage. A woman at the front table was standing. Cookie saw the flash of a very expensive watch, and for no particular reason was flooded with conviction that tonight was going to go very well indeed. Cookie, baby, she told herself, tonight you're gonna get rich.

And with that catch of the hat, that strut, just like that, Cody forgot about Boone and his contract, forgot about being seamless, forgot everything. The dancer was fine, lean and soft, strong as a deer. The name *Cookie* was picked out in rhinestones on her hat, and she wore a tiny fringed buckskin halter and something that looked like a breechclout—flaps of suede that hung from the waist to cover front and back, but not the sides—and wicked spurs on the boots. She looked right at Cody and smiled, and her eyes were not blank.

Part of Cody knew that Boone had seen her stand, and was now watching her watch this dancer, and that she should stop, or sit, or keep walking to Boone's end of the table, but the other part—the part that liked to drink shots in biker bars, to code all night with Acid Girls pounding from the speakers and the company's fortunes riding on her deadline, the part that had loaded up her pickup and left Florida to drive all the way to the West Coast on her own when she was just nineteen, that had once hung by her knees from a ninth floor balcony just because she could—that part cared about nothing but this woman with the long brown hair.

The hair was Indian straight and ended just one inch above the hem of the breechclout, and the way she moved made Cody understand that the hat and spurs were trophies, taken from a dead man. When the dancer trailed her hands across her body, Cody knew they held knives. When the male voices began their rhythmic chanting, she could see this woman riding hard over the plain, vaulting from her pony, stripping naked as she walked.

The music shifted but again it was drums, and now Cookie swayed like a maiden by a pool, pulling the straps of her halter off her shoulders, enough to expose half her breasts but not all, and she felt them thoughtfully, and began to smear them with warpaint. When she had painted all she could see, she pushed the buckskin down further, so that each breast rested like a satsuma on its soft shelf, then she turned her back on the audience, twisted her hair over one shoulder and examined the reflection of her ass in the water. She turned a little, this way and that, lifting the back flap, one corner then another, dropping it, thinking, stroking each cheek experimentally, trying to decide how to decorate it. Then she smoothed the buckskin with both hands so it pulled tight, and studied that effect. She frowned. She traced the outline of her g-string with her index finger. She smiled. She stuck her butt out, twitched it a couple of times, hooked both thumbs in the waistband of her g-string, and whipped it off. The breechclout stayed in place. She was still wearing the halter under her breasts.

And the little dyke liked that, Cookie could tell. She smiled smooth as cream, danced closer, saw the stain creeping up the woman's cheeks, the way her lips parted and her hands opened. Professionally manicured hands; clothes of beautifully cut linen, shoes handmade. The men in the room faded to irritation. This was the prize.

One of the men at the table reached out and slipped a twenty between the rawhide tie of her breechclout and her hip, but Cookie barely took her eyes from the woman. Twenty here or fifty there was small change compared to this. *For you*, she mouthed and turned slightly, and tightened down into a mushroom of skin-sheathed muscle, took off her hat, and reached back and pulled the flap of her breechclout out of the way.

She was aware of some shouting, the tall guy with the red face and the fifty but she kept her eyes fixed on the woman.

And then the music changed, and Ginger was back from her lapdance, and she saw Christie was hand in hand with a glazed-looking mark, about to leave for the backroom, and it was time for her to put some of her clothes back on and work the floor.

Five minutes, she mouthed to the woman.

Cookie, Cody thought, as the dancer flicked the suede flap back in place, stood gracefully, and put her hat back on. Cookie. She watched as Cookie left the stage and took all the heat and light with her. She would come back, wouldn't she? Five minutes, she had said.

"Cunt!" Dave shouted again, "my money not good enough for you? God-damned— No, you get off of me." He pushed Boone's hand from his arm, then realized what he'd done. "Shit. That's— It's just— You know how it is, man. But fifty bucks…"

"Hell, Dave, maybe she knew it was counterfeit," Boone said jovially.

Dave forced a laugh, thrust the bill in his pocket. "Yeah, or maybe she just doesn't understand size matters." Boone laughed, but everyone at the table heard the dismissive note.

"Maybe it's time to call it a night, folks."

But Cody wasn't listening because Cookie was standing before her: no hat, buckskins and g-string back in place.

"Okay guys, looks like we lost Cody." Boone laughed, nothing like the laugh he'd given Dave. "Hey, girl, you make sure you get a cab home, hear? Mention my name to the doorman. Come on guys, we're outta here."

"Cody. Is that your name?" said Cookie, and took her hand. Cody nodded dumbly. "I'm Cookie. It's so good to find another woman here."

Another nod. *How are you*? Cody wanted to say, but that made no sense.

"Would you like to dance with me? Just you and me in private?"

"Yes."

"We'd have to pay for the room."

"Yes."

"I love dancing for women. It gets me going, turns me on. I understand what women want, Cody. Would you like me to show you?"

"Yes," said Cody, and was mildly amazed when her legs worked well enough to follow Cookie to the frosted glass door.

Midnight in her hotel room. Cody sat on the bed, naked, too wired to lie down. Streetlight slanted through the unclosed drapes, turning the room sodium yellow. The air conditioning roared, but her skin burned. Cookie. Cookie's lips, Cookie's hips, Cookie's cheek and chin and belly. Her thighs and ass and breasts. Oh, her breasts, their soft weight on Cody's palms.

She lifted her hands, turned her palms up, examined them. They didn't look any different. She unsnapped her watch and rubbed her wrist absently. Cookie.

Stop it. What the fuck was the matter with her? She'd gone to a strip club and had sex for money. It was a first, okay, so some confusion was to be expected, but it was sordid, not romantic. She had been played by an expert and taken for hundreds of dollars. Oh, God, and Boone… She had made a fucking fool of herself.

So why did she feel so happy?

Cody, you're so beautiful, she'd said. *Oh, yes, yes, don't stop, Cody. Give it to me, give me all of it*. And Cody had. And Cookie had…Cookie had been perfect. She had understood everything, anticipated everything. What to say, what to do, when to cajole and goad, when to smile and be submissive, when to encourage, when to resist. Like a mind reader. And she had felt something, Cody knew it. She had. You couldn't fake pupil dilation, you couldn't fake that flush, you couldn't fake that sheen of sweat and luxuriant slipperiness. Could you?

Christ. She was going mad. She rubbed her eyebrows. Cookie was a pro, and none of it was real.

She got up. The woolen carpet made her bare feet itch. That was real. Her clothes were flung across the back of the chair by the desk; they reeked of cigar smoke. No great loss. She'd no idea why she'd chosen to wear those loose pants, anyway. Hadn't worn them for about a year. Hadn't worn that stupid watch for about as long, come to think of it. Cookie hated the smell of cigars, she's said so, when she was unbuttoning—

Stop it. Stop it now.

She carried her pants to the bed and pulled the receipts from the pockets. Eight of them. She'd paid for eight lapdances, and the size of the tips… Jesus. That was two month's rent. What had she been thinking?

We have to pay for the room, Cookie said, *but I'll pay you half back. It's just that I can't wait. Oh, please, Cody. I want you again.*

"God *damn* it!" Her ferocity scared her momentarily and she stilled, listening. No stirrings or mutterings from either room next door.

Give me your hotel phone number, Cookie had said. *I'll call you tomorrow. This has never happened before. This is real.*

And if it was… She could reschedule her flight. She'd explain it to Vince somehow.

Christ. That huge contract gone, in a flash of lust. Vince would kill her.

But, oh, she'd had nearly three hours of the best sex she'd ever had. It had gone exactly the way she'd imagined it in her fantasies. I know just what you want, Cookie had said, and proved it.

But Cody had known too, that was the thing. She had *known* when the hoarse breath and clutching hands meant it was Cookie's turn, meant that Cookie now wanted to be touched, wanted to break every single personal and club rule and be fucked over the back of the chair, just for pleasure.

Cody stirred the receipts. She couldn't make it make sense. She had paid for sex. That was not romance. But she had felt Cookie's vaginal muscles tighten, felt that quiver in her perineum, the clutch and spasm of orgasm. It wasn't faked. It hadn't been faked the second time, either.

Cody shivered. The air conditioning was finally beginning to bite. She rubbed her cold feet. Cookie's feet were long and shapely, each toe painted with clear nail polish. She'd twisted her ankle, she'd said. Cody had held the ankle, kissed it, stroked it. Cookie's smile was beautiful. *How did you sprain it?* Cody had asked, and Cookie had told her about falling five feet from the indoor climbing wall, and they had talked about climbing and rafting, and Cody had told her of the time when she was seven and had seen Cirque de Soleil and wanted to be one of the trapeze artists, and that led to talk of abdominal muscles, which led to more sex.

She padded into the bathroom, still without bothering with the light. When she lifted her toothbrush to her mouth, the scent on her fingers tightened her muscles involuntarily. She dropped the toothbrush, leaned over the sink, and wept.

A blue, blue Atlanta morning. Cody hadn't slept. She didn't want breakfast. Her plane wasn't until four that afternoon.

She'd lost the contract, lost a night's sleep, lost her mind and her self-respect, and flushed two months' rent down the toilet. She would never see Cookie again—and she couldn't understand why she cared.

The phone rang. *Cookie!* she thought, and hated herself for it.

"Hello?"

"Your cell phone's off, but I called Vince back in Frisco and he told me you were at the Westin."

Boone. She shut her eyes.

"Plane's not til four, am I right? Cody, you there?"

"Yes. I'm here."

"If you're not too tuckered out, maybe you wouldn't mind dropping by my office. We'll give you lunch."

"Lunch?"

"Yep. You know, food. Don't they do lunch on the West Coast?"

"Yes. I mean, why?"

He chuckled. "Because we've got a few details to hammer out on this contract. So should we say, oh, eleven-thirty?"

"That's, yes, fine. Good," she said at random, and put the phone down.

She stared at her bag. Clothes. She'd need to change her clothes. Was he really giving her the contract?

The phone rang again. "Hello?" she said doubtfully, expecting anyone from god to the devil to reply.

"Hey, Cody. It's me."

"Richard?"

"Yeah. Listen, how did it go?"

"I don't… Things are…" She took a deep breath. "I got the contract."

"Hey, that's great. But how did last night go?"

"Christ, Richard, I can't gossip now. I don't have the time. I'm on my way to Boone's, iron out a few details." She had to pull it together. "I'll call you in a week or two, okay?"

"No, wait, Cody. Just don't do anything you—"

"Later, okay." She dropped the phone in its cradle. How did he know to call the Westin? What did he care about her night? She rubbed her forehead again. Food might help with the contract. The headache, she meant. And she grinned: the contract. She'd goddamned well won the contract. She was gonna get a huge bonus. She was gonna be a Vice President. She was gonna be late.

In the bathroom, she picked up the toothbrush, rinsed off the smeared paste, and resolutely refused to think about last night.

Cookie dialed the hotel.

"This is Cody. Leave a message, or reach me on my cell phone," followed by a string of numbers beginning with 415. San Francisco. That's right. She'd told Cookie that last night: San Francisco with its fog and hills and great espresso on Sunday mornings.

That might be okay. Anything would beat this Atlanta heat.

Boone didn't want to talk details so much as to laugh and drink coffee and teach Cody how to eat a po' boy sandwich. After all, if they were gonna be working together, they should get to know each other, was he right? And there was no mention of strip clubs or lapdances until the end when he signed the letter of intent, handed it to her, and said, 'I like the way you handle yourself. Now take that Austin fella, Dave. No breeding. Can't hold his liquor, can't keep his temper, and calls a woman names in public. But you: no boasting, no big words, you just sit quiet then seize the opportunity." He gave her a sly smile. "You do that in business and we'll make ourselves some money."

And somehow, with his clap on the back, the letter in her laptop case and the sun on her face while she waited for the car for her trip to the airport, she started to forget her confusion. She'd had great sex, she'd built the foundations of a profitable working relationship, she was thirty-one and about to be a vice president, and she didn't even have a hangover.

The car came and she climbed into the cool, green-tinted interior.

She let the outside world glide by for ten minutes before she got out the letter of intent. She read it twice. Beautifully phrased. Strong signature. Wonderful row of zeroes before the decimal point. If everything stayed on track, this one contract would keep their heads above water until they could develop a few more income streams. And she had done it. No one else. Damn she was good! Someone should buy her a great dinner to celebrate.

She got out her phone, turned it on. The signal meter wavered as the car crossed from cell to cell. Who should she call? No one in their right mind would want to have dinner with Vince. Richard would only want all the details, and she didn't want to talk about those details yet; he was in the Carolinas, anyway. Asshole.

The signal suddenly cleared, and her phone bleeped: one message.

"Hey. This is Cookie. I know you don't go until the afternoon. If you… I know this is weird but last night was… Shit. Look, maybe you won't believe me but I can't stop thinking about you. I want to see you, okay? I'll be in the park, the one I told you about. Piedmont. On one of the benches by the lake. I'm going there now, and I'll wait. I hope you come. I'll bring doughnuts. Do you like doughnuts? I'll be waiting. Please."

Oooh, you're different, ooh, you're so special, ooh, give it to me baby, just pay another thousand dollars and I'll love you forever. Sure. But Cookie's voice sounded so soft, so uncertain, as though she really meant it. But of course it would. That was her living: playing pretend. Using people.

Cody's face prickled. Be honest, she told herself: who really used who, here? Who got the big contract, who got to have exactly what she wanted: great sex with no complications, and on the expense account no less?

It was too confusing. She was too tired. She was leaving. It was all too late anyhow, she thought, as the car moved smoothly onto the interstate.

A woman sitting on her own on a bench, maybe getting hot, maybe getting thirsty, wanting to use the bathroom. Afraid to get up and go pee because she might miss the one she was waiting for. Maybe the hot sweet scent of the doughnuts reminded her she was hungry, but she wouldn't eat them because she wanted to present them in their round-dozen perfection to her sweetie, see her smile of delight. She would pick at the paint peeling on the wooden bench and look up every time someone like Cody walked past; every time, she'd be disappointed. This one magical thing had happened in her life, something very like a miracle, but as the hot fat sun sinks lower she understands that this miracle, this dream is going to die because the person she's resting all her hopes on is worried she might look like a fool. Or doesn't want to admit she had used a woman for sex and then thrown her away.

Cody blinked, looked at her watch. She leaned forward, cleared her throat.

The driver looked at her in his mirror. "Ma'am?"

"Where is Piedmont park?"

"Northeast of downtown."

"Do we pass it on the way to the airport?"

"No, ma'am."

She was crazy. But all that waited for her at home was a tankful of fish. "Take me there."

Without the hat and boots, wearing jeans and sandals and the kind of tank top Cody herself might have picked, Cookie looked young. So did her body language. Her hair was in a braid. She was flipping it from shoulder to shoulder, twisting on the bench to look to one side, behind her, the other side. When she saw Cody, her face opened in a big smile that was naked and utterly vulnerable.

"How old are you?" Cody blurted.

The face closed. "Twenty-six. How old are you?"

"Thirty-one." Cody didn't sit down.

They stared at each other. "Dirt on my face?"

"No. Sorry. It looks…you look different."

"You expect me to dress like that on my day off, too?"

"No! No." But part of her had. "So. You get a lot of days off?"

A short laugh. "Can't afford it. No expense accounts for me. No insurance, no 401(k), no paid vacation."

Cody flushed. "Earning two thousand bucks a night isn't exactly a hard luck story."

"Was I worth it?"

Her smell filled Cody's mouth. *Yes!* she wanted to shout. *Yes, a hundred times over.* But that made no sense, so she just stood there.

"You paid twenty-two hundred. The house takes sixty percent off the top. Out of my eight eighty, Danny takes another twenty percent and, no, he's a bouncer, not a pimp, and I've never done that before last night. And, no, I don't expect you to believe me. Then there's costumes, hair, waxing, make up…" She leaned back, draped both arms along the back of the bench. "You tell me. Would fucking a complete stranger for three hours be worth five hundred dollars?"

Her mouth stretched in a hard smile but her eyes glistened. She put one ankle up on the other knee.

"Does your ankle still hurt?" It just popped out.

Cookie turned away, blinked a couple of times. Cody found herself kneeling before the bench.

"Cookie? Cookie, don't cry."

"Susana," she said, still turned away.

"What?"

"Susana. It's my real name. Susana Herrera." She turned to Cody, and her face was fierce. "I am Susana Herrera. I'm a dancer, I'm not a whore, and I want to know what you've done to me."

"What I've…?"

"I dance. I tease, I hint. It makes you feel good, you give me money, which makes me feel good. Sometimes I give a lapdance, but always by the rules: hands on the armrest, clothes on, a little bump and grind, because I need the extra tips. I dance, you pay. It's my job. But this, this isn't a job! I don't know what it is. It's crazy. I let you—" Her cheeks darkened. "And I would do it again, for no money. For nothing. It's crazy. I feel… It's like… I don't even know how to say it! I want to talk to you, listen to you talk about your business. I want to see your house. I didn't sleep last night. I thought about you: your smile, your hands, how strong it made me feel to give you pleasure, how warm I felt when you wrapped your arms around me. And I'm afraid."

"Me too," Cody said, and she was, very, because she was beginning to get an idea what was wrong with them and it felt like a very bad joke.

"You're not afraid." Susana folded her arms, turned her face again.

"I am. Cook— Susana, do you suppose… Shit. I feel ridiculous even saying this. Look at me. Please. Thank you. Do you suppose this is what I—"

She couldn't say it. She didn't believe it.

After a very long pause, Susana said, "Dancers don't fall in love with the marks."

That cut. "Marks don't fall in love with whores."

"I'm not a—"

"Neither am I."

They stared at each other. Cody's phone rang. She thumbed it off without looking. "My full name is Candice Marcinko. I have to fly back to San Francisco this afternoon but I could come back to Atlanta at the end of the week. We could, you know, talk, go to the movies, walk in the park." Jesus, had she left any stereotype unturned? She tried again. "I want to meet your, your cat."

"I don't have a cat."

"Or your dog," she said. *Stop babbling.* But she couldn't. "I want to learn how long you've lived in Atlanta and what kind of food you like and whether you think the Braves will win tonight and how you feel when you sleep in my arms." She felt like an idiot.

Susana looked at her for a while, then picked up the box at her side. "Do you like Krispy Kreme?"

When Cody turned her phone on again at the airport, there was a message from Richard: *Call me, it's important.* But she had to run for her plane.

In the air she leaned her head against the window and listened to the drone of the engines.

Susana, sitting on the bench while the sun went down, thinking, *Love, love is for rich people.*

A cream labrador runs by, head turned to watch its owner, running alongside. Its tongue lolls, happy and pink. *Dogs love. Dogs are owned.*

She tears the last three doughnuts to pieces and throws them to the ducks.

On Thursday, Vince and the executive team toasted her with champagne. She took the opportunity to ask for Friday and two days next week off. Vince couldn't say no without looking chintzy, so he told her VPs didn't have to ask permission.

VP. She grinned hard and for a minute she felt almost normal. VP. Top dog.

Friday morning she had just got out of the shower when the doorbell rang. She was so surprised she barely remembered to pull on a robe before she opened the door.

"Well, that's a sight for sore eyes."

"Richard!"

"Not that I don't appreciate the gesture but could you please tighten that belt, at least until we've had coffee? Here you go, quad grande, two percent."

She went to get dressed. When she emerged, drying her hair with a towel, he was sitting comfortably on the couch, ankle crossed at the knee, just like Susana in the park.

"I envy you that dyke rub-and-go convenience."

She draped the towel round her neck, sat, and sipped the latte. "To paraphrase you, it's not that I don't appreciate the coffee, but…why the fuck are you here?"

He put his phone on the table next to her latte. "Remember this?"

"It's your phone?"

He took a thumbdrive from his laptop case and gave it, then her, a significant look.

"Richard, I've had a real weird few days and I'm on a plane in four hours. Maybe." Maybe she was crazy, maybe she should cancel… "Anyhow, could you please just get to the point?"

"Drink your coffee. You're going to need it. And tell me what happened on Tuesday night." He held up his hand. "Just tell me. Because my guess is you had a hell of a night with a lovely young thing called Cookie."

She didn't say anything for a long, long time. "Susana," she said finally.

"Ah. You got that far? Susana Herrera, aged twenty-four—"

"Twenty-six."

"Twenty-four. Trust me. Mother Antonia Herrera, father unknown. Dunwoody community college, degree in business administration—oh, the look on your face—and one previous arrest for possession of a controlled substance. Healthy as an ox. Not currently taking any medication except contraceptive pills."

"The pill?"

"What's the matter?"

"Nothing. Go on."

"No known allergies to pharmaceuticals, though a surprising tolerance to certain compounds, for example sodium thiopental and terpazine hydrochloride."

Cody seized on something that made sense. "Wait. I know that drug. It's—"

"RU486 for the mind. That's the one."

"Oh, Jesus, Richard, you didn't *give* her that! You didn't make her forget what happened!"

"Not what happened Tuesday."

Cody, confused, said nothing.

He plugged the thumbdrive into his laptop and turned the screen so she could see the sound file icons. "It will all make sense when you've listened to these."

"But I don't have time. I have a plane—"

"You'll want to cancel that, if it's to Atlanta. Just listen. Then I'll answer questions."

He tapped play.

"*…ever happens, I promise no one will ever hear what goes on this tape except you.*"

"*Cue ominous music.*"

She jumped at the sound of her own voice. "What—"

"Shh."

"*—more an, um, an ethics thing.*"

"*Jesus, Richard. You're such a drama queen.*" Pause. Clink.

"*I've done my research, too. Like you, I'm pretty sure what will happen after you've made your presentations to Boone.*"

"*The Golden Key.*"

"*—but what I need to know from you is whether or not you can authorize out-of-pocket expenses in the high five figures to win this contract.*"

He touched pause. "Ring any bells?"

"No." Cody's esophagus had clamped shut. She could hardly swallow her own spit, never mind the latte. But the cardboard was warm and smooth in her hand, comforting, and behind Richard her fish swam serenely back and forth.

"Terpazine is a good drug. We managed to calculate your dosage beautifully. Susana's was a bit more of a challenge. Incredible metabolism."

"You said you didn't give her—"

"Not in the last couple of weeks. But you've had it six times, and she seven. Now keep listening."

Six times?

"*—the exploration of memory and its retrieval. So exciting. A perfect dovetail with the work I've been doing on how people form attachments. It's all about familiarity. You let someone in deep enough, or enough times, then your brain actually rewires to recognize that person as friend, or family.*"

Pause.

"*There are ways to make it easier for someone to let you in.*"

Clink of bottle on glass.

"*I've told you about those studies that show it's as simple as having Person A anticipate Person B's needs and fulfill them.*"

"*So don't tell me again.*"

She sounded so sure of herself, bored even. A woman who had never thought to use the world *love*.

"*—jumpstart the familiarization process. For example, person A works in a bookshop and is lonely, and when she's lonely chocolate makes her feel better. And one day person B arrives mid-afternoon with some chocolate, says Hey, you look sorta miserable, when I'm miserable chocolate makes me feel better, would you like one? and A eats a chocolate and thinks, Wow, this B person is very thoughtful and empathic and must be just like me, and therefore gets slotted immediately into the* *almost-friend category. It's easy to set something like that up. You just have to know enough about person A.*"

Know enough.

Cody pushed the laptop from her. "I don't believe this."

"No?"

Cody didn't say anything.

"You sat in that Seattle bar, and you listened, and then you signed a temporary waiver." He placed a piece of paper on the table by her hand. It was her signature at the bottom—a little sloppy, but hers. "Then you took some terpazine and forgot all about it."

"I wouldn't forget something like this."

He held up his hand. Reached with his other and nudged the sound file slider to the right.

"Take the pill."

"Alright, alright." Pause. Tinkle of ice cubes. *"Jesus. That tastes vile."*

"Next time we'll put it in a capsule. Just be grateful it's not the vasopressin. It would make you gag. I speak from experience."

He tapped the file to silence. "It really does. Anyhow, a week after Seattle I came here and you signed a more robust set of papers." He handed her a thick, bound document. "Believe me, they're bombproof."

"Wait." She dropped the document on her lap without looking. "You came here? To my apartment?"

"I did. I played the recording you've just heard, showed you the initial waiver. Gave you that." He nodded at her lap. "You signed. I gave you the sodium thiopental, we had our first session. You took another terpazine."

"I don't remember." He shrugged. "It happened." He tapped the paper in her lap. "There's a signed waiver for every session."

"How many did you say?"

"Six. Four here, twice in North Carolina."

"But I don't remember!" The fish in her tank swam back and forth, back and forth. She closed her eyes. Opened them. The fish were still there. Richard was still there. She could still remember the weight of Susana's breasts in her hands.

"You'd better listen to the rest. And read everything over."

He tapped *play*.

"Okay. Think about what it would be like if you knew enough about someone and then you met: you'd know things about her and she'd know things about you, but all you'd know is that you recognize and trust this person and you feel connected. Now imagine what might happen if you add sex to the equation."

"Good sex, I hope."

"The best. There are hundreds of studies that show how powerful sex bonding can be, especially for women. If a woman has an orgasm in the presence of another person, her hormonal output for the next few days is sensitized to her lover: every time they walk in the room, her system floods with chemical messengers like oxytocin saying

Friend! Friend! This is even with people you know, consciously, aren't good for you. You put that together with someone compatible, who fits—whether they really fit or just seem to fit—and it's a chemical bond with the potential to be human superglue. That's what love is: a bond that's renewed every few days until the brain is utterly rewired. So I wanted to know what would happen if you put together two sexually compatible people who magically knew exactly—exactly!—what the other wanted in bed but had no memory of how they'd acquired that knowledge…"

It took Cody a moment to pause the sound. "Love," she said. "*Love*? What the fuck have you done to me?"

"You did it to yourself. Keep listening."

And she did. After she had listened for an hour, she accepted the sheaf of transcripts Richard handed her from his case.

She looked at the clock.

"Still thinking about that plane?"

Cody didn't know what she was thinking.

"Is it refundable?" he said. "The flight?"

Cody nodded.

"Give me the ticket. I'll cancel for you. You can always rebook for tomorrow. But you need to read."

She watched, paralyzed, as Richard picked up the phone and dialed. He turned to her while he was on hold, mouthed *Read*, and turned away again.

So she began to read, only vaguely aware of Richard arguing his way up the airline hierarchy.

After the first hundred pages of *Subject C* and *Subject S*, he brought her fresh coffee. She paused at one section, appalled.

"What?"

"I can't believe I told you that."

He peered over her shoulder. "Oh, that's a juicy one. Stop blushing. I've heard it all before. Several times now. Sodium thiopental will make you say anything. Besides, you don't remember telling me, so why bother being embarrassed?"

She watched her fish. It didn't matter. Didn't matter. She picked up the paper again and plowed on. May as well get it over with.

Somewhere around page three hundred, he went into the kitchen to make lunch. She didn't remember eating it, but when she set aside the final page at seven o'clock that evening, she saw that the plate by her elbow was empty, and heard the end of Richard's order to the Chinese takeout place on the corner. It was clearly something he'd done before. From her phone, in her apartment. And she didn't remember.

She wished there was a way to feed him terpazine so he would forget all those things she'd never said to another soul before.

She tried to organize her thoughts.

He had asked for her permission to use her in an experiment. It would mean she would feel comfortable at the club in Atlanta, that she might even have a good couple of hours, and it would further his work while being paid for to some extent by her expense account. He had traveled to the Golden Key and picked Susana as the most likely dancer to fit her fantasies—and he knew a little about her preferences from that stupid, stupid night in Dallas—and made the same pitch to her. Only Susana got paid.

Twice, Cody thought. *I paid her too.*

And so Richard had flown to Cody's apartment in San Francisco and given her sodium thiopental, and she had talked a bluestreak about her sexual fantasies, every nuance and variation and degree of pleasure. In North Carolina, she had talked about her fantasies again, even more explicitly, encouraged to imagine in great detail, pretend it was happening, while they had her hooked up to a functional MRI and other machines.

Richard put down the phone. "Food in thirty minutes."

Cody forced herself to stay focused, to think past her embarrassment. "What were the fMRIs for, the fMRIs, blood-gas sensors, and—" she glanced at the paper, "—TMS during the, the fantasy interludes?"

"We built a kind of mind and hormone map of how you'd feel if someone was actually doing those things to you. A sort of super-empathy direction finder. And one from Susana, of course. We played your words to each other, along with tran-scranial magnetic stimulation to encourage brain plasticity—the rewiring."

"And," she hunted through the pages for the section labeled *Theoretical Un-derpinnings*. "You gave me, us, oxytocin?"

"No. We wanted to separate out the variables. You supplied the oxytocin on your own, later." He beamed. "That's the beautiful part. It was all your own doing. Your hopes, your hormones, your needs. Yours. We made a couple of sugges-tions to each of you that you might not have come up with on your own: that expensive watch and the loose clothes, Cookie's hat and spurs. But the rest was just you and Cookie, I mean Susana. But you two were primed for each other, so if that wasn't the best sex of your life, I'll eat this table." He rapped the table top in satisfaction.

All her own doing.

"You can't publish," she said.

"Not this, no." He picked up one of the fMRIs and admired it. "It's enough for now to know that it works."

She waited for anger to well up but nothing happened. "Is this real?"

"The project? Quite real."

Project. She watched him gather all the documents, tap them into a neat pile.

"Not the project," she said. "Not the TMS, the fMRIs, the terpazine. This." She tapped her chest. "Is it real?"

He tilted his head. "Is love real? A lot of people seem to think so. But if you mean, is that what you're feeling, the answer is, I don't know. I don't think a scan could give you that answer. But it could tell us if you've changed: your data have been remarkably clear. Not like Cookie's. Susana's." He held the fMRI image up again, admired it some more, then put it back in the pile.

"What do you mean?"

"The data. Yours were perfectly consistent. Hers were…erratic."

"Erratic." Her mind seemed to be working in another dimension. It took an age for the thought to form. "Like lying?"

"She's lied about a lot of things."

"But she could have been lying to me? About how she feels?"

He shrugged. "How can we ever know?"

She stared at him. "The literature," she said, trying to force her slippery brain to remember what she'd just read. "Its says love's a feedback loop, right?"

"In terms of individual brain plasticity, yes."

"So it's mutual. I can't love someone if she doesn't love me." If it was love.

He gave her a look she couldn't interpret. "The data don't support interdependence." He paused, said more gently, "We don't know."

Pity, she realized. He pities me. She felt the first flex and coil of something so far down she couldn't identify it. "What have you done to me? What *else* have you done to me?"

"To you? For you."

"You made me feel something for a woman who fucked for money. Who had her mind fucked for money."

"So did you, if you think about. Just at one remove."

"I didn't."

"So, what, you did it for science?"

Cody changed direction. "Does Susana know?"

"I'm flying to Atlanta tomorrow."

"Do you have her sound files with you?"

"Of course."

"Let me hear them."

"That would be unethical."

Unethical. "I think you might be a monster," she said, but without heat.

"I have a strange way of showing it, then, wouldn't you say? For the price of a few embarrassing experimental sessions you won't ever remember, I won you a contract, a girlfriend and a night on the town."

She stared at him. "You expect me to be grateful…"

"Well, look at this place. Look at it. Bare walls. Fish, for god's sake."

"Get out."

"Oh, come on—"

"Out."

"By tomorrow it will all fall into perspective."

"I swear to god, if you don't leave now I'll break your face." She sounded so weirdly calm. Was this shock, or was it just how people in love, or whatever, behaved? She had no idea. "And you can put those papers down. They're mine, my private thoughts. Leave them right there on the table. The thumbdrive, too."

He pulled the drive, laid it on the papers, stowed his laptop and stood. She held the door open for him.

He was halfway through the door when she said, "Richard. You can't tell Susana like this."

"No?"

"It's too much of a shock."

"You seem to be coping admirably."

"At least I already knew you. Or thought I did. You'll be a complete stranger to her. You can't. You just can't. It's…inhumane. And she's so young."

"Young? Don't make me laugh. She makes you look like an infant." He walked away.

Cookie danced. She didn't want to think about the phone call. Didn't want to think about any of it. Creep.

But there was the money.

The lights were hot, but the air conditioning cold. Her skin pebbled.

"Yo, darlin', let's you and me go to the back room," the suit with the moustache and bad tie said. He was drunk. She knew the type. He'd slip his hands from the chair, try cop a feel, get pissed off when she called in Danny, refuse to pay.

"Well, now," she said, in her special honey voice. "Let's see if you've got the green," and pushed her breasts together invitingly. He flicked a bill across her breasts. "A five won't buy you much, sweetie."

"Five'll buy you, babydoll," he said, hamming for his table buddies. One of them giggled. Ugly sound in a man, Cookie thought. "Five'll buy you five times!"

"And how long did it take you to come up with that, honey?"

"The fuck?" He looked confused.

"I said, your brain must be smaller than your dick which I'd guess is even smaller than your wallet, only I doubt that's possible," and she plucked the bill from his fingers, snapped it under her g-string and walked away.

In the dressing room she looked at herself in the mirror. Twenty-four was too old for this. Definitely. She had no idea what time it was.

She stuck her head out of the door. "Danny!"

"Yes, doll."

"Time is it?" She'd have to get herself a watch someday. A nice expensive watch.

"Ten after," Danny said.

"After what?"

"Ten."

Three hours earlier on the West Coast. She stacked her night's take, counted it, thought for a minute, peeled off two hundred in fives and ones. She stuck her head out of the door again. "Danny!"

"Here, doll."

"I'm gone."

"You sick?" He ambled up the corridor, stood breathing heavily by the door.

"Sick of this."

"Mister Pergoletti says—"

"You tell Pergoletti to stick it. I'm gone. Seriously." She handed him the wad of bills. "You take care of these girls, now. And have a good life."

"Got something else lined up?"

"Guess we'll find out."

There was one bottle of beer in Cody's fridge. She opened it, poured it carefully into a glass, stared at the beige foam. A glass: she never drank beer from a glass. She poured it down the sink. She had no idea what was real anymore but she was pretty sure alcohol would only make things worse.

She made green tea instead and settled down in the window seat. The sun hung low over the bay. What did Susana see from her apartment? Was her ankle better? Contraceptive pills, Jesus. And, oh, the smell of her skin.

She was losing her mind.

She didn't know who she hated more: Richard for making the proposal, or herself for accepting it. Or Susana. Susana had done it for money.

Or maybe... But what about those contraceptive pills?

And what if Susana did feel...whatever it was? Did that make it real? It was all an experiment, all engineered. Fake.

But it didn't feel fake. She wanted to cradle Susana, kiss her ankle better, protect her from the world. The Richards of the world.

She picked up the phone, remembered for the tenth time she had neither address nor phone number. She called information, who told her there was no listing under Susana Herrera in the Atlanta Metro area. She found herself unsurprised.

She got the number for the Golden Key instead.

A man called Pergoletti answered. "Cookie? She's gone. They always go." The music thumped. Cody's insides vibrated in sympathy, remembering.

"—don't have a number. Hey, you interested in a job?"

Cody put the phone down carefully. Sipped her tea. Picked up the phone again, and called Richard.

It was open mic night at Coffee to the People. Richard was in the back room on a sofa, as far from the music as possible. Two cups on the table. One still full.

"You knew I'd call."

"I did."

"Did you program that, too?"

"I didn't program anything. I primed you—and only about the sex." He patted the sofa. "Sit down before you fall down."

She sat. Blinked. "Give me her phone number."

"I can't. She gave me a fake. I called her at the club, but she hung up on me."
He seemed put out.

"What does she know?"

"I talked fast. I don't know how much she heard. But I told her she wouldn't
get the rest of the money until we'd done follow up."

The singer in the other room sang of love and broken hearts. It was terrible,
but it made Cody want to cry anyway.

"How long does it last?"

"Love? I don't know. I avoid it where possible."

"What am I going to do?"

Richard lifted his laptop bag. "I planned for this eventuality." He took out a
small white cardboard box. He opened it, shook something onto his hand. A
grey plastic inhaler.

"What is it?"

"A vasopressin analogue, formulated to block oxytocin receptors in the nucleus
accumbens. That is, the antidote."

They both looked at it.

"It works in voles," he said. "Female voles."

Voles. "You said it tasted bad."

"I've used it. Just in case. I prefer my sex without complications. And I've had
a lot of sex and never once fallen in love." He arched his eyebrows. "So, hey, it
must work."

The elephant whistle hypothesis. *Hey, Bob, what's that whistle? Well, Fred, it
keeps elephants away. Don't be an asshole, Bob, there aren't any elephants around
here. Well, Fred, that's because of my whistle.*

"Cody." He did his best to look sincere. "I'm so very sorry. I never thought
it would work. Not like this. But I do think the antidote might work." His face
went back to normal. He hefted the inhaler. "Though before I give it to you, I
have a favor to ask."

She stared at him. "On what planet do I owe you anything?"

"For science, then. A follow up scan, and then another after you take the
antidote."

"Maybe I won't take it. Give me the info you have. Give me the number."

"Love is a form of insanity, you know."

"The number."

In the other room, the bad singing went on and on.

"Oh, all right. For old time's sake." He extracted a folder from his bag, and a
piece of paper from the folder. He slid it across the table towards her, put the
inhaler on top of it.

She nudged the inhaler aside, picked up the paper. Hand written. Susana's
writing.

"Love's just biochemical craziness," he said, "designed to make us take a leap
in the dark, to trust complete strangers. It's not rational."

Cody said nothing.

"She screwed us."

"She screwed you," Cody said. "Maybe she fell in love with me." But she took the inhaler.

Cody sat in the window seat with the phone and the form Susana had filled in. Every now and again she punched in a different combination of the numbers Susana had written and got the *Cannot be completed as dialed* voice. Every now and again she touched the form with the tip of her middle finger; she could feel the indentation made by Susana's strong strokes. Strong strokes, strong hands, strong mouth.

She didn't think about the grey inhaler in its white box, which she had put in the fridge—to stay viable a long time, just in case.

After a while she stopped dialing and simply waited.

When her phone lit up at 11:46 she knew who it was—even before she saw the 404 area code on the screen.

"Do you feel it?" Susana said.

"Yes," and Cody did. Whatever it was, wherever it came from, it was there, as indelible as ink. She wanted to say, I don't know if this is real, I don't know if it's good. She wanted to ask, Had you ever had sex with anyone for money before me? and Does it matter? She wanted to know, Have you ever loved anyone before? and, How can you know?

She wanted to say, Will it hurt?

Walking through the crowds at the airport, Cody searched for the familiar face, felt her heart thump every time she thought she saw her. Panic, or love? She didn't know. She didn't know anything except that her throat ached.

Someone jostled her with his bag, and when she looked up, there was the back of that head, that smooth brown hair, so familiar, after just one night, and all her blood vessels seemed to expand at once, every cell leap forward.

She didn't move. This was it, the last moment. This was where she could just let the crowd carry her past, carry her away, out into the night. Walk away. Go home. Use the inhaler in the fridge.

That was the sensible thing. But the Cody who had hung from the ninth storey balcony, the Cody who had risked the Atlanta contract without a second thought, that Cody thought, *fuck it*, and stepped forward.

You couldn't know. You could never know.

THREE TWILIGHT TALES
JO WALTON

Jo Walton was born in Wales and emigrated to Canada in 2002. Her first published novel was *The King's Peace*, followed by *The King's Name*. In 2002 she won the John W. Campbell Award for Best New Writer, and subsequently published two more fantasy novels, *The Prize in the Game* and World Fantasy Award-winner *Tooth and Claw*. She then went on to publish her "Small Change" trilogy—*Farthing, Ha'penny* and *Half a Crown*. Her most recent novel is *Lifelode*. She lives with her son and husband in Montreal, Quebec.

1

Once upon a time, a courting couple were walking down the lane at twilight, squabbling. "Useless, that's what you are," the girl said. "Why, I could make a man every bit as good as you out of two rhymes and a handful of moonshine."

"I'd like to see you try," said the man.

So the girl reached up to where the bright silver moon had just risen above the hills and she drew together a handful of moonshine. Then she twisted together two rhymes to run right through it and let it go. There stood a man, in a jacket as violet as the twilight, with buttons as silver as the moon. He didn't stand there long for them to marvel at him. Off he went down the lane ahead of them, walking and dancing and skipping as he went, off between the hedgerows, far ahead, until he came to the village.

It had been a mild afternoon, for spring, and the sun had been kind, so a number of people were sitting outside the old inn. The door was open, and a stream of gold light and gentle noise was spilling out from inside. The man made of moonshine stopped and watched this awhile, and then an old widower man began to talk to him. He didn't notice that the moonshine man didn't reply, because he'd been lonely for talking since his wife died, and he thought the moonshine man's smiles and nods and attention made him quite the best conversationalist in the village. After a little while sitting on the wooden bench outside the inn, the old widower noticed the wistful glances the moonshine man kept casting at the doorway. "Won't you step inside with me?" he asked, politely. So in they went together, the man made of moonshine smiling widely now, because a moonshine man can never go under a roof until he's been invited.

Inside, there was much merriment and laughter. A fire was burning in the grate and the lamps were lit. People were sitting drinking ale, and the light was glinting off their pewter tankards. They were sitting on the hearthside, and on big benches set around the tables, and on wooden stools along the bar. The inn was full of villagers, out celebrating because it was a pretty day and the end of their work week. The man made of moonshine didn't stop to look around, he went straight over to the fireplace.

Over the fireplace was a mantelpiece, and that mantelpiece was full of the most extraordinary things. There was a horn reputed to have belonged to a unicorn, and an old sword from the old wars, and a dragon carved out of oak wood, and a candle in the shape of a skull, which people said had once belonged to a wizard, though what a wizard would have wanted with such a thing I can't tell you. There was a pot the landlord's daughter had made, and a silver cup the landlord's father had won for his brewing. There were eggs made of stone and a puzzle carved of wood that looked like an apple and came apart in pieces, a little pink slipper said to have belonged to a princess, and an iron-headed hammer the carpenter had set down there by mistake and had been looking for all week.

From in between a lucky horseshoe and a chipped blue mug, souvenir of a distant port, brought back by a sailor years ago, the moonshine man drew out an old fiddle. This violin had been made long ago in a great city by a master craftsman, but it had come down in the world until it belonged to a gypsy fiddler who had visited the inn every spring. At last he had grown old and died on his last visit. His violin had been kept carefully in case his kin ever claimed it, but nobody had ever asked for it, or his body either, which rested peacefully enough under the grass beside the river among the village dead.

As soon as the man made of moonshine had the violin in his hands he began to play. The violin may have remembered being played like that long ago, in its glory days, but none of the villagers had ever heard music like it, so heart-lifting you couldn't help but smile, and so toe-tapping you could hardly keep still. Some of the young people jumped up at once and began to dance, and plenty of the older ones joined them, and the rest clapped along in time. None of them thought anything strange about the man in the coat like a violet evening.

It happened that in the village, the lord of the manor's daughter had been going about with the blacksmith's apprentice. The lord of the manor had heard about it and tried to put a stop to it, and knowing his daughter only too well, he had spoken first to the young man. Then the young man had wondered aloud if he was good enough for the girl, and as soon as he doubted, she doubted too, and the end of the matter was that the match was broken off.

Plenty of people in the village were sorry to see it end, but sorriest was a sentimental old woman who had never married. In her youth, she had fallen in love with a sailor. He had promised to come back, but he never did. She didn't know if he'd been drowned, or if he'd met some prettier girl in some faraway land, and in the end the not knowing was sadder than the fact of never seeing him again. She kept busy, and while she was waiting, she had fallen into the habit of weaving a rose wreath for every bride in the village. She had the best roses for miles around in the garden in front of her cottage, and she had a way with weaving wreaths too, twining in daisies and forget-me-nots so that each one was different. They were much valued, and often dried and cherished by the couples afterward. People said they brought luck, and everyone agreed they were very pretty. Making them was her great delight. She'd been looking forward to making a wreath for such a love match as the lord of the manor's daughter and the blacksmith's apprentice; it tickled her sentimental soul.

The little man made of moonshine played the violin, and the lord of the manor's daughter felt her foot tap, and with her toe tapping, she couldn't help looking across the room at the blacksmith's apprentice, who was standing by the bar, a mug in his hand, looking back at her. When he saw her looking he couldn't help smiling, and once he smiled, she smiled, and before you knew it, they were dancing. The old woman who had never married smiled wistfully to see them, and the lonely widower who had invited the little man in looked at her smiling and wondered. He knew he would never forget his wife, but that didn't mean he could never take another. He saw that smile and remembered when he and the old woman were young. He had never taken much notice of her before, but now he thought that maybe they could be friends.

All this time nobody had been taking much notice of the moonshine man, though they noticed his music well enough. But now a girl came in through the back door, dressed all in grey. She had lived alone for five years, since her parents died of the fever. She was twenty-two years old and kept three white cows. Nobody took much notice of her. She made cheese from her cows, and people said yes, the girl who makes cheese, as if that was all there was to her. She was plain and lonely in her solitary life, but she couldn't see how to change it, for she didn't have the trick of making friends. She always saw too much, and said what she saw. She came in, bringing cheese to the inn for their ploughman's lunches, and she stopped at the bar, holding the cheese in her bag, looking across the room at the violinist. Her eyes met his, and as she saw him, he saw her. She began to walk across the room through the dancers, coming toward him.

Just as she had reached him and was opening her mouth to speak, the door slammed back and in walked the couple who had been quarrelling in the lane, their quarrel all made up and their arms around each other's waists. The moonshine man stopped playing as soon as he saw them, and his face, which had been so merry, became grave. The inn fell quiet, and those who had been dancing were still.

"Oh," said the girl, "here's the man I made out of two rhymes and a handful of moonshine! It was so irresponsible of me to let him go wandering off into the world! Who knows what might have come of it? But never mind, no harm done." Before anyone could say a word, she reached toward him, whipped out the two rhymes, then rubbed her hands to dust off the moonshine, which vanished immediately in the firelight and lamplight of the bright inn parlor.

2

It was at just that time of twilight when the last of the rose has faded into the west, and the amethyst of the sky, which was so luminous, is beginning to ravel away into night and let the first stars rub through. The hares were running along the bank of the stream, and the great owl, the one they call the white shadow, swept silently by above them. In the latticework of branches at the edge of the forest, buds were beginning to show. It was the end of an early spring day, and the pedlar pulled his coat close around him as he walked over the low arch of the bridge where the road crossed the stream, swollen and rapid with the weight of melted snow.

He was glad to see the shapes of roof gables ahead of him instead of more forest stretching out. He had spent two cold nights recently, wrapped in his blankets, and he looked forward to warmth and fire and human comfort. Best of all, he looked forward to plying his trade on the simple villagers, selling his wares and spinning his stories. When he saw the inn sign swinging above one of the doors, he grinned to himself in pure delight. He pushed the door open and blinked a little as he stepped inside. There was firelight and lamplight and the sound of merry voices. One diamond-paned window stood ajar to let out the smoke of fire and pipes, but the room was warm with the warmth of good fellowship. The pedlar went up to the bar and ordered himself a tankard of ale. He took a long draft and wiped his mouth with the back of his hand.

"That's the best ale I've had since I was in the Golden City," he said.

"That's high praise if you like," the innkeeper said. "Hear this, friends, this stranger says my ale is the best he's tasted since the Golden City. Is that your home, traveler?"

The pedlar looked around to see that the most part of the customers of the busy inn were paying attention to him now, and not to each other. There were a pair of lovers in the corner who were staring into each other's eyes, and an old man with a dog who seemed to be in a world of his own, and a girl in grey who was waiting impatiently for the innkeeper's attention, but all the other eyes in the place were fixed on the pedlar.

"I don't have a home," he said, casually. "I'm a pedlar, and my calling gives me a home wherever I go. I roam the world, buying the best and most curious and useful things I can find, then selling them to those elsewhere who are not fortunate enough to travel and take their choice of the world's goods. I have been to the Golden City, and along the Silver Coast; I've been in the east where the dragons are; I've been north to the ice; I've come lately through the very heart of the Great Forest; and I'm heading south where I've never been, to the lands of Eversun."

At this, a little ripple of delight ran through the listening villagers, and that moment was worth more than wealth to the pedlar, worth more than the pleasure of selling for gold what he had bought for silver. His words were ever truths shot through with sparkling lies, but his joy in their effect was as real as hot crusty bread on a cold morning.

"Can we see what you have?" a woman asked shyly.

The pedlar feigned reluctance. "I wasn't intending to sell anything here," he said. "My wares are for the lands of Eversun; I want to arrive there with good things to sell them, to give me enough coin to buy their specialties. I'm not expecting much chance to replenish my stock between here and there." The woman's face fell. "But since you look so sad, my dear, and since the beer here is so good and the faces so friendly, I'll open my pack if mine host here will throw in a bed for the night."

The landlord didn't look half as friendly now, in fact he was frowning, but the clamor among the customers was so great that he nodded reluctantly. "You can sleep in the corner of the taproom, by the fire," he said, grudgingly.

At that a cheer went up from the crowd, and the pedlar took his pack off his back and began to unfold it on a table, rapidly cleared of tankards and goblets by their owners. The outside of the pack was faded by the sun to the hue of twilight, but the inside was a rich purple that made the people gasp.

Now some of the pedlar's goods were those any pedlar would carry—ribbons, laces, yarn in different colors, packets of salt, nutmegs, packets of spices, scents in vials, combs, mirrors and little knives. He had none of the heavier, clattering goods, no pans or pots or pails that would weigh him down or cause him to need a packhorse to carry the burden. These ordinary goods he displayed with a flourish. "This lace," he said, "you can see at a glance how fine it is. That is because it is woven by the veiled men of the Silver Coast, whose hands can do such delicate work because they never step out into the sun. See, there is a pattern of peonies, which are the delight of the coastal people, and here, a pattern of sea waves."

When those who wanted lace had bought lace, he held up in each hand sachets of salt and pepper. "This salt, too, comes from the Silver Coast, and is in such large clear crystals because of a secret the women of that coast learned from the mermaids of making it dry so. The pepper comes from the Golden City, where it grows on trees and is dried on the flat rooftops so that all the streets of the city have the spicy smell of drying peppercorns."

"Does it never rain?" asked an old woman, taking out her coin to pay twice what the pepper would have been worth, except that it would spice her food with such a savor of story.

"In the Golden City, it rains only once every seven years," the pedlar said solemnly. "It is a great occasion, a great festival. Everyone runs into the streets and dances through the puddles. The children love it, as you can imagine, and splash as hard as they can. There are special songs, and the great gongs are rung in the temples. The pepper trees burst into huge flowers of red and gold, and the priests make a dye out of them which colors these ribbons. It is an expensive dye, of course, because the flowers bloom so rarely. They say it makes the wearers lucky, and that the dye doesn't fade with washing, but I can't promise anything but what you can see for yourselves, which is how good a color it makes." He lifted handfuls of red and yellow and orange ribbons in demonstration, which were hastily snapped up by the girls, who all crowded around.

The whole company was clustered around the pedlar now, even the lovers, but the landlord was not displeased. Every so often, when he grew hoarse, or claimed he did, the pedlar would put down his perfumes or lengths of yarn and say it was time for them all to drink together, and there would be a rush for the bar. The landlord had already sold more ale and wine than on an ordinary night, and if the pedlar was having his drinks bought for him, what of it? The landlord had bought some spices for his winter wines, and a silver sieve for straining his hops. He no longer grudged the pedlar his corner by the fire.

The pedlar went on now to his more unusual items. He showed them dragon scales, very highly polished on the inside, like mirrors, and rough on the outside. He asked a very high price for them. "These are highly prized in the cities of Eversun for their rarity, and the young ladies there believe, though I can't swear it is the truth, that looking at your face in such a mirror makes it grow more beautiful." Only a few of the village maidens could afford the price he asked, but they bought eagerly.

The grey girl had been standing among the others for some time, but she had bought nothing. The pedlar had noticed her particularly, because she had not paid attention to him at first, and when she had come to watch, he had smiled inwardly. As the display went on and she stood silent, smiling to herself aside from time to time, he grew aware of her again, and wanted to bring her to put her hand into her pocket and buy. He had thought the ribbons might tempt her, or then again the dragon scales, or the comb made from the ivory of heart trees, but though he had sold to almost everyone present, she had made no move.

Now he turned to her. "Here is something you will like," he said, "I do not mean to sell this here, but I thought it might interest you to look at it, for it is your color." He handed her a little grey bird, small enough to fit into the palm of the hand, carved very realistically so you could feel each feather.

The grey girl turned it over in her hands and smiled, then handed it back. "I do not need a carven bird," she said.

"Why, no more does anyone else, but I see it fooled your eye, and even your hand. This bird, friends, is not carved. It comes from the Great North, from the lands of ice, and the bird flew too far into the cold and fell to the ground senseless. If you hold it to your lips and breathe, it will sing the song it sang in life, and they say in the north that sometimes such a bird will warm again and fly, but I have never seen it happen." He put the bird's tail to his lips and blew gently, and a trill rang out, for the bird was cleverly carved into a whistle. They were a commonplace of the Silver Coast, where every fishergirl had such a bird-whistle, but nobody in the village had ever seen one before.

The grey girl raised her eyebrows. "You say that was a living bird of the Great North that froze and turned to wood?"

"It has the feel of wood, but it is not wood," the pedlar insisted.

"Let me hold it a moment again," she asked. The pedlar handed it over. The grey girl held it out on the palm of her hand where everyone could see it. "No, it is wood," she said, very definitely. "But it's a pretty enough lie to make true." She folded her fingers over the bird and blew over it. Then she unfolded her fingers, and the bird was there, to all appearances the same as before.

The pedlar drew breath to speak, but before he could, the carved bird ruffled its feathers, trilled, took one step from the girl's hand onto her grey sleeve, then took wing, flew twice around over the heads of all the company, and disappeared through the open crack of the window.

3

As the leaves were turning bronze and gold and copper, the king came into the forest to hunt. One morning he set off to follow a white hart. They say such beasts are magical and cannot be caught, so the king was eager. Nevertheless, as often happens to such parties, they were led on through the trees with glimpses of the beast and wild rides in pursuit until the setting sun found them too far from their hunting lodge to return that night. This was no great hardship, for while the king was young and impetuous and had a curling black beard, he had many counselors whose beards were long and white and combed smooth. Most of them had, to the king's secret relief, been left behind in the palace, but he had brought along one such counselor, who was believed to be indispensable. This counselor had thought to order the king's silken pavilions brought on the hunt, along with plenty of provisions. When the master of the hunt discovered this cheering news, he rode forward through the company, which had halted in a little glade, and brought it to the king, who laughed and complimented his counselor.

"Thanks to you," he said, "the worst we have to fear is a cold night under canvas! What an adventure! How glad I am that I came out hunting, and how sorry I feel for those of the court who stayed behind in the Golden City with nothing to stir their blood." For the king was a young man, and he was bored by the weighty affairs of state.

The indispensable counselor inclined his head modestly. "I was but taking thought for your majesty's comfort," he said.

Before he or the king could say more, the king's bard, who was looking off through the trees, caught sight of a gleam of light far off among them. "What's that?" he asked, pointing.

The company all turned to look, with much champing of bits but not many stamped hooves, for the horses were tired at the end of such a day. "It is a light, and that means there must be habitation," the king said, with a little less confidence than he might have said it in any other part of the kingdom. The Great Forest had a certain reputation for unchanciness.

"I don't know of any habitation in this direction," said the master of the hunt, squinting at the light.

"It will be some rude peasant dwelling, rat-ridden and flea-infested, far less comfortable than your own pavilions," the counselor said, stroking his fine white beard. "Let us set them up here and pay no attention to it."

"Why, where's your spirit of adventure?" the bard asked the counselor. The king smiled, for the bard's question was much after his own heart.

The king raised his voice. "We will ride on to discover what that gleam of light might be." In a lower tone, as the company prepared to ride off, he added to the counselor, "Even if you are right, and no doubt you are, at the very least we will be able to borrow fire from them, which will make our camp less cold."

"Very wise, your majesty," the counselor said.

They rode off through the twilight forest. They were a fine company, all dressed for hunting, not for court, but in silks and satins and velvets and rare furs, with enough gold and silver about them and their horses to show that they were no ordinary hunters. The ladies among them rode astride, like the men, and all of them, men and women, were beautiful, for the king was young and as yet unmarried and would have nobody about him who did not please his eye. Their horses were fine beasts, with arching necks and smooth coats, though too tired now to make the show they had made when they had ridden out that morning. The last rays of the sun had gilded them in the clearing, touching the golden circlet the king wore about his dark unruly locks; now they went forward into deepening night. The sky above them was violet, and a crescent moon shone silver like a sword blade. The first stars were beginning to pierce the sky when they splashed across a brook and saw a little village.

"What place is this?" the king asked the master of the hunt.

"I don't know, sire. Unless we have come sadly astray it isn't marked on my map," the master of the hunt said.

"We must have come astray then," the king said, laughing. "I don't think the worse of you for it, for we were following a hart through the forest, and though we didn't kill it, I can't think when I had a better day's sport. But look, man, this is a stone-built village with a mill and a blacksmith's forge, and an inn. This is a snug little manor. A road runs through it. Why, it must pay quite five pounds of gold in taxes."

The counselor smiled to himself, for he had been the king's tutor when he was a prince, and was glad to see he remembered the detail of such matters.

The master of the hunt shook his head. "I am sure your majesty is right, but I can't find it on my map."

"Let us go on and investigate," the bard said.

It had been the red gleam of the forge they had seen from far off, but it was the lamplight spilling out of the windows of the inn that the bard waved toward.

"Such a place will not hold all of us," the king said. "Have the tents set up for us to sleep, but let us see if we can get a hot supper from this place, whatever it is."

"A hot supper and some country ale," the bard said.

"There are three white cows in the water meadow beside the stream," the master of the hunt pointed out. "The country cheese in these parts is said to be very good."

"If you knew what parts these were, no doubt my counselor could tell us all about their cheeses," the king said.

They dismounted and left the horses to the care of those who were to set up the tents. The four of them strode into the village to investigate. The bard brought his little harp, the counselor brought his purse, the master of the hunt brought a shortsword on his belt, but the king brought nothing.

The inn was warm and friendly and seemed to contain the whole population of the village. Those who were not there came in as soon as the news came to them of the king's arrival. The counselor negotiated with the innkeeper and soon arranged that food and drink could be provided for the whole company, and beds for the king and the ladies, if the ladies did not mind crowding in together. The master of the hunt pronounced the ale excellent, and the villagers began to beg the bard to play. The rest of the company, having set up the tents and rubbed down the horses, began to trickle into the inn, and the place became very full.

The king wandered around the inn, looking at everything. He examined the row of strange objects that sat on the mantelpiece, he peered out through the diamond-paned windows, he picked up the scuttle beside the fire and ran his hand along the wood of the chair backs, worn smooth by countless customers. The villagers felt a little shy of him, with his crown and his curling black beard, and did not dare to strike up conversation. For his own part he felt restless and was not sure why. He felt as if something was about to happen. Until the bard started to play, he thought he was waiting for music, and until he was served a plate of cold pork and hot cabbage he thought he was waiting for his dinner, but neither of these things satisfied him. Neither the villagers nor his own company delighted him. The villagers seemed simple, humble, rustic; their homespun clothes and country accents grated on him. In contrast, the gorgeous raiment and noble tones of his company, which were well enough in the palace or even his hunting lodge, seemed here overrefined to the point of decadence.

At length the door at the back opened and a girl came in, clad all in grey and carrying a basket. The master of the hunt had called for cheese, and she was the girl who kept the cows and made the cheese. She was plain almost to severity, with her hair drawn back from her face, but she was young and dignified, and when the king saw her he knew that she was what he had been waiting for, not just that night but for a long time. He had been picking at his dinner, but he stood when he saw her. There was a little circle of quiet around the corner where he sat, for his own people had seen that he did not want conversation. The girl glanced at him and nodded, as if to tell him to wait, and went with her basket to the innkeeper and began to negotiate a price for her cheese. The king sat down and waited meekly.

When she had disposed of her cheeses, the girl in grey picked her way through the room and sat down opposite the king. "I have been waiting for you all my life. I will marry you and make you my queen," he said. He had been thinking all the time she was at the bar what he would say when she came up to him, and getting the words right in his mind. For the first time he was glad he was king, that he was young and handsome, that he had so much to offer her.

"Oh, I know that story," she said. She took his ale tankard and breathed on it, and passed it back to him. He looked into it and saw the two of them tiny and distant, in the palace, quarrelling. "You'd pile me with jewels and I'd wither in that palace. You'd want me to be something I'm not. I'm no queen. I'm no beauty, no diplomat. I speak too bluntly. You'd grow tired of me and want a proper queen. I'd go into a decline and die after I had a daughter, and you'd marry again and give her a stepmother who'd persecute her."

"But I have loved you since I first saw you," the king insisted, although her words and the vision had shaken him. He took a deep draft of the ale to drive them away.

"Love? Well now. You feel what you feel, and I feel what I feel, but that doesn't mean you have to fit us into a story and wreck both our lives."

"Then you…" the king hesitated. "I know that story. You're the goddess Sovranty, whom the king meets disguised in a village, who spends one night with him and confirms his sacred kingship."

She laughed. "You still don't see me. I'm no goddess. I know that story though. We'd have our one night of passion, which would confirm you in your crown, and you'd go back to your palace, and nine months later I'd have a baby boy. Twenty years after that he'd come questing for the father he never had." She took up a twist of straw that was on the table and set it walking. The king saw the shape of a hero hidden among the people, then the straw touched his hand and fell back to the table in separate strands.

"Tell me who you are," the king said.

"I'm the girl who keeps the cows and makes the cheeses," she said. "I've lived in this village all my life, and in this village we don't have stories, not real stories, just things that come to us out of the twilight now and then. My parents died five years ago when the fever came, and since then I've lived alone. I'm plain, and plainspoken. I don't have many friends. I always see too much, and say what I see."

"And you wear grey, always," the king said, looking at her.

She met his eyes. "Yes, I do, I wear grey always, but how did you know?"

"When you're a king, it's hard to get away from being part of a story," he said.

"Those stories you mentioned aren't about us. They're about a king and a village girl and a next generation of stories. I'd like to make a new story that was about you and me, the people we really are, getting to know each other." He put out his hand to her.

"Oh, that's hard," she said, ignoring his hand. "That's very hard. Would I have to give up being a silver salmon leaping in the stream at twilight?"

"Not if that's who you are," he said, his green eyes steady on hers.

"Would I have to stop being a grey cat slipping through the dusky shadows, seeing what's to be seen?"

"Not if that's who you are," he said, unwavering.

"Would I have to stop being a grey girl who lives alone and makes the cheeses, who walks along the edges of stories but never steps into them?"

"Not if that's who you are," said the king. "But I'm asking you to step into a new story, a story that's never been before, to shape it with me."

"Oh, that's hard," she said, but she put her hand on the king's hand where it lay on the rough wooden table. "You've no sons, have you?"

"No sons, but I have two younger brothers," he said, exhilaration sweeping through him.

She looked around the room. "Your fine bard is singing a song, and your master of the hunt is eating cheese. Your counselor is taking counsel with the innkeeper, and no doubt hearing all about the affairs of the village. Your lords and ladies are drinking and eating and patronising the villagers. If you really want to give up being a king and step into a new story with me, now is the time."

"What do I have to do?" he asked, very quietly, then she pulled his hand and for a moment he felt himself falling.

It was a little while before anyone noticed he had gone, and by then nobody remembered seeing the two cats slipping away between the tables, one grey and one a long-haired black with big green eyes.

THE NIGHT CACHE
ANDY DUNCAN

Andy Duncan was born in South Carolina. He studied journalism at the University of South Carolina and worked as a journalist for the *News & Record* in Greensboro, N.C., before studying creative writing at North Carolina State University and the University of Alabama and serving as the senior editor of *Overdrive*, a magazine for truck drivers. Duncan's short fiction, which has won the World Fantasy and Theodore Sturgeon Memorial Awards, is collected in World Fantasy Award winner *Beluthahatchie and Other Stories*. Upcoming is a new short story collection, *The Pottawatomie Giant and Other Stories*. He currently lives with his wife, Sydney, in Frostburg, Maryland, where both teach in the English department of Frostburg State University.

I met Destiny Creech during my afternoon shift at the register at a chain bookstore that a 19th-century novelist might here identify with a capital B and a series of dashes but that I am pleased to call Yarns Ignoble. As usual, I was working the register nearest the Yarns Ignoble mall entrance, which compared to the register nearest the parking-lot entrance gets fewer customers but a higher percentage of sketchiness. People who already are angry, needy or neurotic even without chemical assistance toke up on carbs and caffeine at the food court and are propelled straight to my register. So I've had to cultivate a sort of furtive efficiency. I'm the prop girl in black who darts onstage with two inverted wineglasses in one hand and a picnic basket in the other and darts offstage with the previous scene's princess phone and beanbag chair just before the light comes up on the lovers' idyll. I don't make eye contact; I don't tarry; this ain't my show. So I was wholly unprepared when I turned back to the register after rearranging a Nicholas Sparks display to find myself facing a 5-foot-10 blonde with porcelain skin, Cate Blanchett cheekbones and eyes the color of the green flash at sunset that portends good fortune in love.

I gaped. She smiled, plucked at her Hermès scarf and slid a trade paperback a half-inch nearer me on the counter. Her fingers were free of rings. The book was *Best Lesbian Erotica 2008*.

I snatched up the book, clutched it in both hands and blurted: "Oh, is the *2008* out already? Seems I just finished re-reading the 2007!" I felt a junior-high giggle coming on and suppressed it as best I could, so that what came out instead was a junior-high chirp of pleasure abruptly swallowed, like a gnat.

My special guest star, still smiling, closed both eyes and opened them again—sort of like a wink, only doubled—and said, in a throaty voice, "Time flies when we're having fun, doesn't it?"

I pounded the keys one-handed and told myself, Jenny Jenny Jenny get a grip. This is Yarns Ignoble, not *The L-Word*, and Hagerstown is not Showtime, and for the afternoon shift, parental discretion is not advised. I calmed a little when she paid not with an Amex black card but with a tatty twenty on which someone had stamped "John 3:16." "Need a bag?" I piped, my voice cracking.

She shook her head, picked up the book with its pert little white receipt poking out, began to turn away—then set the book back down. With one long burgundy nail she rotated it so the cover faced me—two punk girls locking pierced lips—and pushed it another half-inch toward me. "You read it first," she said, "and then we'll talk." She double-winked and turned and strode around the Dover clip-art rack and into the food court and was gone.

"Ahem," someone said—just like that, not a throat-clearing noise but two spoken comic-book syllables, "A-hem." It was the woman next in line, a girl really in a denim vest, with a crooked grin and a pointed chin and red hair cut short except on top, so that it fell across half her face like a curtain.

"Busted," she said.

"Sorry," I said, my face burning. I dropped my gaze and reverted to the prop girl. I scanned her *Val Lewton Horror Collection* DVD set, rang it up, made her change. "Would you like a bag?" I asked, already reaching for one; those boxed sets are heavy and eight-pointed and awkward.

"She won't be back," the girl said.

I looked at her. She was biting her lower lip and tilting her head like an owl's. She let the lip go, sucked in a deep breath, like a diver bracing on the edge of the pool. "I don't know her?" she said. "Only I sort of do, I mean, from experience? I think maybe she was playing a game? And now the game's over?" She shrugged. "Sorry."

My blush had never quite gone away, and now it flamed anew. "Fuck you," I said, slamming the till on the first syllable and glancing toward Sally the Snitch's register on the second. Score! Smoke break.

"O-*kay*," the girl said. She tossed the hair out of her flashing eyes, and her grin got wider and goofier, exposed big teeth, made her look older and cuter. "Feels good to say that at work, huh?" She looked over her shoulder, smiled at the glowering guy behind her in line. "How ya doin?" she asked. He lifted his wrist and tapped his watch. She pulled from her handmade shoulder bag what looked like a chunky 10-year-old cell phone, which she set on the counter. "Got a pocketknife?" she asked me. "Pair of scissors? Embossed Swiss baselard? Nail file?"

Already embarrassed by my outburst, I silently handed her a box cutter; as she appraised it and winked, I wondered for a moment whether she was going to lunge. Instead, she raked the edge of the package she had just bought, tore back the slit plastic and—despite fingernails down to the quick—lifted out a single DVD case with such ease it seemed to follow her hand, like a card coaxed from a deck by a conjuror. She handed it to me. "To atone," she said. "*The Seventh Victim*. Ever seen it? No? Depressing as the waiting room of hell, least convincing bunch of Satanists that ever flipped a paternoster, makes not two consecutive licks of sense, it's. Fucking. Fabulous."

The DVD case showed a sexy woman in a helmet of black hair and a shape-less fur coat, coolly watching a giant switchblade that may or may not have been moving her way. The redhead before me was watching the screen of her phone, which she held in both hands, punching buttons with both thumbs. She murmured, "Triangulate, damn you. Ah! There you are."

"Jesus Christ," said the next guy in line.

"Listen," I said, "I'm sorry for effing you, and you're probably right, but it's really none of your business, you know. Whether she comes back… or not." Suddenly sure she wouldn't, I slid the erotica volume off the counter, tumbled it into the lost-and-found box, cushioned by an old Betty Boop beach towel.

"Not yet it isn't," the redhead said. She tucked the boxed set under one arm, nodded at the DVD still in my hand and said, "So take a look. Tell me what you think." She headed for the mall entrance. "We can even talk about the book, if you want."

"Hey!" I called. "How do I find you?"

On the way out the door, she held up the phone-thing. "I'll find *you*. I've got your coordinates."

Disgusted, I flung the DVD into the box with Betty and the punk hotties. What the hell movie was I in today, *Let's Tease Jennifer To Death*? I'm not playing this game, I'm not. "Can I help you, sir?"

He slapped down a *Sports Illustrated* swimsuit issue and handed me a black Amex card. "And you don't get to keep this one, honey, if it's all the same to you."

The blonde in the scarf? Never came back. The weird-ass redhead—*that* was Destiny Creech. And what's really interesting about *The Seventh Victim*, I realized that night, the second time through, is the whole point of the movie, right, is supposed to be that Mary is looking for her sister Jacqueline, who's in desperate danger, OK? But once Jacqueline turns up, Mary barely notices. She's too busy hooking up with guys, even with Jacqueline's husband. So Jacqueline, at the end, is left to climb those stairs alone.

Next day the redhead turned up in the Yarns Ignoble café. I noticed her about one, and she sat there much of the afternoon, dawdling over a notebook and a latte, acknowledging me not at all. When the end of my shift finally came, I tore a nail in my haste to clock out, then walked over to her spindly iron table. The notebook pages she studied were filled with cramped handwriting: not words, but numbers.

"A-hem," I said.

She looked up.

"Well finally," she said, and stuck out her hand. "Join me. I'm Destiny."

I hooted. "Well, of course you are," I said. "I'm Jennifer, or Jenny, or Jen, depending on the mood."

"What mood are you in now?"

"Confused. I have your DVD."

She leaned abruptly forward, her eyebrows raised. Her right eye, I saw, ticked to the side. "Isn't it *good*?"

"How do you know I watched it."

"Oh, please." She sat back, looking disappointed. "Let's not *even* pretend. The only question remaining on that score—because there are so many more *interesting* questions, which we'll get to momentarily—is how many *times* did you watch it?"

"Two and a half. I fell asleep, and boy did I dream."

"I bet you did."

"Thanks a lot."

"You're welcome. Here's the first of those interesting questions. You want something to drink? I'm buying, unless you wage slaves eat here free, in which case I could use another latte, thanks."

"Answer another question first. What's that phone-thing in your bag?"

She hefted it, pressed a switch, waited a moment, then handed it to me. "Handheld GPS. Wherever you go, there you are—your coordinates, on screen."

"It says 'Acquiring Satellites.'"

"Isn't that great? That's my favorite part. 'Des, what are you doing out there, the bisque is served.' 'Just a minute, Mom, I'm acquiring some satellites.' Twenty-four medium-Earth-orbit Pentagon satellites, a constellation it's called. The same technology that guides attack drones to Afghan schoolhouses and lures Stephanie Abrams to your bedroom every morning with your local forecast, now turned into your own personal handheld Sherpa guide. Third wonder of the modern age, after the Pocket Rocket and a runner-up to be named later."

I laughed. "Do you *ever* shut up?"

"Yes," she said, with gravity, and then said nothing. I said nothing, either, just watched blue bars appear one by one on the little screen, like on the wireless commercial.

"So what do you do with it?"

Another lunge forward. "Ah! Another interesting question. I'll show you right now. How about a cache and dash?"

"A what?"

"There's a new cache in the north parking lot, a quick one. I got an e-mail update this morning. With luck, ours will be the first logbook entry. Got any treasure in your purse, just in case? Something to leave behind, to replace what we take. Anything will do: an old Metro stub, a Putt-Putt scoring pencil, an expired Nair coupon. C'mon, c'mon, we won't have the light for long."

I jogged alongside her through the café, past my register—where Sally threw me a "What's-the-story?" look—through the food court, around the corner of the Cold Gravy store. Only in the parking lot did she slow to a deliberate pace, studying her GPS unit as a dowser would a forked stick. I couldn't see the screen, so I read her instead, and came to anticipate her pauses, her minute course adjustments. She was wearing khaki shorts, and clearly did a lot of hiking. I heard someone slam on brakes and yell, "Assholes!" but he may not have meant us. Inside her right arm was a long narrow discoloration: a birthmark, or a scar.

Des spoke without looking up from her screen. "When I first spoke to you, Jen, at the cash register? I confess. I had seen you before. Twice."

"Really."

"The first time was about a month ago, out at Antietam. I was tracking a cache that was hidden in the Bloody Lane. I didn't want to be seen when I retrieved it, because the National Park Service, you know. So I had to wait around forever for this damn woman to leave. She was sitting on the bank, sketching in a big spiral notebook."

"I remember that! I was trying to include the observation tower in the distance, and I never could get the angles right."

Des snorted. "I thought you were going to pitch camp and wait on A.P. Hill's reinforcements. I almost said hi to you then, but you were so engrossed. I know *I* don't like to be interrupted when I'm engrossed."

"Are you engrossed now?"

She glanced at me then, and smiled. "What do *you* think?"

"I don't remember you at all at Antietam. I'm sorry."

"No one remembers me, when I'm lurking. I'm good at lurking."

The cars had thinned out. We were headed toward the far corner of the lot, beyond which a couple of windblown shopping carts rested at crazy angles in the scrub.

"And the second time you saw me?"

"That was quicker. You were on the other side of the gas pump at the Sheetz, out on the bypass. I'm surprised that Tracer is still running, by the way. You must call *Car Talk* a lot."

"I'm sorry, but I don't remember you then, either."

"No, well, you're a watch-the-pump person, aren't you, Jen? I'm a watch-every-thing-*but*-the-pump person. It was a windy day, but you just let your sundress blow, you didn't keep clutching at it like those poor timid souls. I always want to yank their hands away and say, 'You bought it short, now *wear* it short, no apologies.'"

"You see a lot, but again, you didn't say anything. How come?"

"Because it was only the second time. You ever read *Goldfinger*?"

"What, the James Bond novel? Is that the one with Pussy Galore?"

Des winced. "Don't remind me. I checked it out of the library in a stack of horse books when I was 12 because a boy at school said it was dirty, and at the end, when Pussy says, 'I never met a *man* before,' and renounces women, I burst out crying, right there in the treehouse. I was years sorting out why. Anyway, that was Goldfinger's motto. 'Once is happenstance. Twice is coincidence. The third time it's enemy action.' So that's my dating rule. The battlefield? Happenstance. The Sheetz? Coincidence. The checkout counter? Time to say something to her, you schmuck."

"So that makes me your enemy?"

"No, it makes you my act—Whoop! Hang on. We've overshot it. Oh, I get it. Must be here." She dropped the unit in her purse and backtracked a few steps, to the last light pole in the lot, a rusty white pillar on a crumbling knee-high concrete base decorated with long-faded gang tags. "We must be talking a microcache," she said, kneeling and clawing at the chinks and cracks in the concrete. Little clots of it pattered to the asphalt like gray cereal. I knelt on the other side and did the same, not sure what I was looking for until I found it: A plastic canister like the ones film used to come in. Several somethings rattled when I hefted it. I offered it to Des, but she shook her head.

"Your first treasure," she said. "Open it, Jen, if you dare. Open it, and there's no turning back."

I popped the lid and shook onto my palm a Putt-Putt pencil, a polished orange rock the size of a marble, a paper clip, and an absurdly small glue-bound notebook, like a doll's. "Damn, two people beat us to it," Des said, rolling the rock between her fingers. "This is Terrapin Dave's. He beats me everywhere."

Inside the notebook was equally tiny writing, in two different hands. The first said:

FEB. 2. 1ST FIND! ALL BOW B4 THE POWER OF MY ROCK—TERPDAVE

The second:

2/2/08—"No man can reveal to you aught but that which already lies half asleep in the dawning of your knowledge."

"Oh, *The Prophet*, fuck me," Des said. She stood, dusted her palms against the ass of her khakis, and said, "Go ahead, your turn. Write something. Anything you like. Be as creative as you want. No pressure. Just make it good. And personality-indicating. A summation of all that you are. And hey—if it's Kahlil Gibran? You and me? We're through."

As she babbled, I looked up at her. The light was going, the wind was picking up, and high clouds were scudding past. Des seemed to stand tall against the sky, hands on hips, the sunset wind rippling her jacket and toying with her long shock of red hair. She looked almost heroic.

I pressed the absurd notebook flat against the light pole, acutely conscious of Des' thigh at eye level, and printed as small as I could: TO CELEBRATE MY FIRST FIND, DES AND I HAD OUR FIRST KISS. When I was done, I just squatted there, one palm against the pole, looking at what I had written. Behind me, I heard a distant zap, like a bug gone a-sizzle, then more zaps, coming closer. The light directly overhead zapped then, and my hand tingled as the pole hummed with power and the bulbs flickered to life, casting a stark pool around us. Our shadows were like cartoons. Des slid the notebook from my fingers. I didn't watch her read it; I watched the concrete instead. "Oh, well done," Des said. "Come here."

"So how long has this hobby been going on?"

"Well, I was new at the high school, and her name was Leah, and soccer practice had just let out…"

"No, you ass." I snatched a pillow off the floor, swatted her with it. Bedding and clothing were everywhere, except on us. We had gone to my apartment, not hers, on orders from Des—"Because," she said, "yours is farther away."

"Not *this*," I said. "Geocaching. Is it new?"

"Oh, that. No, it's not new, not really. Well, the satellites, yes, that's new. But the basic principle, leaving caches and finding caches, that's been done in one form or another, I'm told, since 1854."

"No shit?"

"No shit. Dartmoor was a tourist attraction even then, long before *The Hound of the Baskervilles*. One of the guides placed a bottle way the hell out by Cranmere Pool, so the hardy souls who hiked out that far could leave their calling cards to prove they'd made it. A lonely, barren place. It's part of a missile range, now."

"Why bother hiking out there? The pool must have been lovely."

"The pool, so called, was a dry hole until it rained, whereupon it became a wet hole. The reason hikers went was that it had a story, of course." She twirled a lock of my hair. "You can lead people anywhere, my Jenny Jen, if there's a story attached." She rolled onto her side, facing away from me, facing the wall. "The pool was said to be haunted, you see. Cranmere Benjie, they called the ghost—the shade of Benjamin Gayer, who died broken by guilt because of all the seamen he had doomed. Benjie was a local businessman who had been entrusted a large sum of money, in case it was ever needed for a sailors' ransom. Well, pirates seized a shipload of Dartmoor men, and word was sent home, but was there any ransom to be paid? There was not. Benjie had spent it all, bit by bit—a sailor's right eye here, a sailor's left hand there. So his neighbors came back only in part, and Benjie's neighbors chased him onto the moor, with torches and axes but not with dogs, and so he outran them, wailing with guilt, until he collapsed by the side of Cranmere Pool, and submerged his head beneath the rank waters, and choked himself, and died unsaved and unmourned. And even today you can hear him out there of a night, wailing."

I heard the fan on the dresser, and cicadas, and a distant tractor-trailer on the downgrade. An unfelt breeze stirred the curtains, and the night light burned steady in the hall.

I wriggled closer, threw my arm around her, nuzzled into the back of her neck, which smelled like lavender, like sweat, like her. "If Cranmere Pool is such a dry hole," I murmured, "how did Benjie drown himself in it?"

"Well. I'll tell you how that happened. Things back then were just... wetter, that's all." She snorted, I burst out laughing, and she began to pummel me. "The fuck question is that?" she demanded as we wrecked the bed. "It's a fucking ghost story, OK? Work with me!"

We did lots of things together—not just that, and not just that. And we weren't even together all the time. She was sort of in graduate school at the Appalachian Lab in Frostburg, though at her level it was more of a hike-around-the-woods thing, graphing the connections among forest habitats at Antietam, than a go-to-class thing, and of course I had my job and all its delights, and my parents always after me to visit. Des had no such ties; she said her dad was dead, and she and her mom didn't get along, and that was that. Yet—this was odd—I remember that when I asked what her mom did for a living, she stressed to me that Mrs. Creech was a corporate vice president not of marketing, not some glorified *sales* job, but of product development. Like, she was in charge of actually designing and building the shit, whatever it was; I don't remember, now. Since my sales job wasn't even glorified, it sort of hurt my feelings. But later, of course, I wished I had blown off my own family, spent more time with Des when I had the chance.

We watched every movie in *The Val Lewton Horror Collection*, of course, and certain scenes Des played over and over. Treading water in a basement pool, Alice screams and screams, the echoes drowned by the growls of the thing prowling the encircling tile, claws a-click, a-click. The walls of cane ripple and whisper as Betsy leads Jessica along the bloodied path to the crossroads guarded by the staring dead. Mary sends her would-be protector into the darkness at the end of the corridor, from which he creeps to fall into her arms a corpse. The dropped corn meal sprays across the ground, its thousands of grains an obstacle to vampires but no hindrance to the Leopard Man as the fleeing Teresa leads her pursuer unerringly to her life's last locked door. *Mamacita, let me in! Let me in! Let me in! If you love me, let me in!*

But when I think back on those months now, I mainly remember the caches we found, me driving while she leafed through her marked-up printouts from Geocaching.com, getting us as close as the nearest intersection anyway, or the nearest decent place to park, before heading out on foot. Sometimes the treasure really was a cache-and-dash, like the canister hung on the hook inside the two panels of the big sign outside the ice-cream stand. We barely had to leave the car to log that one. Other times it was a lot harder to find, like the Thermos half-buried in the brambles 20 feet off the C&O Canal trail.

Des was fearless, or simply heedless, when she knew a cache was nearby. The scars on her arms weren't her only scars—some she told me about, eventually—and I wasn't surprised, after watching her in action for a few weeks. She darted across busy highways, looking only at her GPS unit. She clambered up and down steep hillsides, ignoring the trail that offered a safer but less direct route. At the top of the old stone bridge over the Casselman River, she hoisted herself onto the wall and leaned so far out that I grabbed her belt, braced my feet against the base of the wall, and held on, frightened.

"Hey, leggo!" she hollered. "The cache might be in the outer wall, between the rocks. I can check real easy, if you just—."

"You ladies mind coming down from there?"

Behind me, walking up the bridge, left hand hooked into her belt and right hand suspended near her holster, was a Maryland state trooper.

I froze, my legs braced, Des' belt cutting my hands, her feet kicking the air.

"Des!" I said. "The cops!"

Her feet stopped kicking. Her voice was muffled. "Local or state?"

"The fuck it matters? Come back here!"

"Come down, I said," the trooper repeated, planting her feet on the flagstones in a way I did not like at all. She was younger than I had thought, with a spray of freckles across her cheeks, but she spoke with the universal now-see-here-young-lady sternness of her tribe.

"She's coming, officer," I hollered, and so she was, shinnying backward until she dropped down beside me, dusting her T-shirt.

The trooper cocked her head, looked surprised.

"Des?" she asked.

Des squinted at her. The trooper took off her hat, grinned. Des stepped forward. "Terry? Is that you?"

The trooper laughed and ambled up the slope, swatting her thigh with the hat. "Didn't recognize you at first, Des, not from the, uh, angle you were presenting."

"My best side," Des said, walking to meet her. They looked as if they might hug, but at the last instant each raised an arm, and they bumped fists.

"Didn't know you were still around," the trooper said.

"Yeah, well."

"Haven't seen you at the bars lately."

"Been busy," Des said, and then they both looked at me, though the trooper looked first. I was trying to go into unobtrusive prop-girl mode, which is tough on a stone bridge in daylight when you're wearing a bright green LITTLE MISS SAVE THE WORLD T-shirt. Des bought it for me because it matched her hair.

The trooper stuck out her hand, flashed a dazzling smile. "Busy, yeah. Marjorie Terry. Pleased to meet you."

"This is Jen," Des said, before I got a chance. I ignored her.

"Jenny Milledge," I said. Terry's grip was firm and warm and lasted longer than I expected. "Sorry if we gave you a scare."

"No problem. What were you guys up to, anyway?"

"Geocaching," I said.

Trooper Terry looked at Des, a slight crease between her blonde eyebrows. "GPS scavenger hunt," Des mumbled. I never had seen her look embarrassed before.

"Ohhhhh, so that's the latest," the trooper said. She turned to me. "When I met her, it was chess. She walked into Fusion with an ivory Napoleonic set under her arm and said, 'I can mate every dyke in the house!' Then it was, what came next, bartending? Flipping the tumblers behind your back like *Coyote Ugly*? Then you bought that Canon, and hello, Annie Leibowitz."

"I wasn't the one who posted those," Des said.

"I know who posted 'em," the trooper said. "So, it's hidden treasure now." She winked at me. "Clearly you've had some good hunting already. I'll see you around, Des. Find your way back to Fusion sometime. I'm usually on night patrol, but at midday I work on my nine ball. You come too, Jenny. New faces always welcome."

The refusal of Des, thus far, to take me to any of the watering holes west of Baltimore had been a sore point between us. "I'd like that," I said, a little loudly.

In silence, we watched the trooper slide back into her patrol car and drive westward, toward Grantsville. Then Des looked at me. When she really turned on the charm, it was like watching a marquee light up, but the reverse was just as dramatic. Now a full blackout was in effect, and I could hear the air-raid sirens.

"Thanks for all the suckup—I mean, backup," she said.

"Thanks for keeping *me* a secret from all your friends—*if* that's all she was."

"You're projecting." We stomped back to her car. "*I* wasn't the one fogging her sunglasses. It's the uniform, isn't it? And the freckles."

"Shut up." As we climbed in, I slammed my door, so Des slammed hers even louder. The dashboard hula girl wiggled her hips.

"You *wanted* her to slap on the cuffs," Des said, peeling out eastward, toward Frostburg. She was speeding by the time we reached the foot of the hill, and the new Casselman River bridge thrummed beneath the tires only momentarily. We seemed to reach the interstate in mere moments. Time flies when you're not having fun.

"When she walked away just now? You totally checked out her ass. Don't *even* deny it, Jen, I heard you swallow spit and breathe through your nose. Are you familiar with the noun 'tell'? It's a poker term."

"Christ. Poke this," I said, with a gesture. It was true, I *had* checked her out, but would I have realized it without Des nattering on? That made me madder. "Do you tell people *nothing* about yourself? She didn't even know you were a geocacher—which is only, like, your entire life."

"Well, I didn't know she was a cop, so we're even."

I snorted. "Even? No, I'd say a career in law enforcement is harder to hide than a… glorified compass. I think she wins that one." I stopped laughing as my head was thrust back into the seat rest. Des had floored the accelerator.

"She wins, huh?"

"Des, cut it out!" The sound of the air rushing over the never-quite-closed passenger window became a jetlike whine as a distant pickup in the next lane grew impossibly quickly, then hurtled backward past us. "I hate it when you pull this shit! You're scaring me. Des?"

Two tanker trucks were side by side ahead. From their perspective, they were laboring up the grade, barely gaining on the summit. From mine, they were an onrushing wall of metal.

"Tell me who won, then."

Des called them her "black rages," but I thought of them as white. When she was in their grip, her voice was as calm and cool as a marble slab.

I no longer even registered the windshield before me. I saw only the gleaming bulletlike rear of the nearest tanker, on which the reflection of Des' car ballooned like something spurting through a wormhole.

"You won, you won! You always fucking win, OK?"

She laughed and applied the brakes. I lurched forward, palms on dashboard, as the car fishtailed. "And don't you forget it," Des said through gritted teeth as she cradled the wheel and steered the rapidly slowing car over the rumble strip and onto the shoulder, where it shuddered to a stop.

Unable to breathe, I watched the tankers get blessedly smaller as they chugged on up the grade. Then Des' mouth was on mine, breathing for both of us.

Once again, Des somehow had maintained control—of the car, of herself, of me.

I asked Des, early on, if she ever hid any caches herself.

"Yes," she said, "but since I know where those are, what fun would hunting them be? And it's not as if you've finished your current task. You're not half done decrypting those clues."

I had rediscovered my childhood love for ciphers and codes when I realized that many hiders posted not only their cache coordinates but also clues that would help the finder, clues that often were encrypted using this simple substitution cipher:

A B C D E F G H I J K L M
N O P Q R S T U V W X Y Z

A becomes N, B becomes O, and so forth. It was easy to learn, and soon I could just read "vg'f," for example, as "it's," and "gur" as "the." And how Des used to laugh at my indignation when the encrypted "clue" turned out to be the same information already written out above in standard English. "It's like those idiot car owners," I told her, "who buy a personalized plate only to spell out MY MINI, or something, as if that weren't obvious."

"I agree," she said. "People that uncreative shouldn't be allowed to drive."

That was our last dinner together before I went with my parents to visit our Southern cousins over Memorial Day weekend, so I wasn't with her when it happened, had to read about it in the paper that I kicked out of the way when I lugged my mom's latest Tupperware CARE package into the apartment, half-pissed that Des hadn't returned my calls all weekend. I sat at the butcher's block with the unrolled paper and a ham biscuit and a cup of Irish breakfast tea, snapping the newly liberated rubber band against my thigh as I glanced at the local front and wondered—before I had the chance to think about what I was wondering—where they dug up such an out-of-date photo of Des. Her high-school yearbook? Then the story around the photo hit me, not word by sequential word, but at once, like a rogue wave, leaving me gasping among the fragments. Dateline Oakland, Maryland. Fatality. Muddy Creek. Flood stage. Five inches of rain. Lone hiker. Slipped. Apparently. Fell. Waterfall. Fifty feet. Rocks. Body recovered 6:45 p.m. Visitors reminded of danger. Family notified. Services pending. Agencies assisting. Maryland Natural Resources Police. State Park Service. State Police. "Right coordinates, wrong time," Des said into my ear via her apartment voicemail, which she re-recorded frequently in hope of annoying her mom, who never called. "Be careful leaving a message." Southern Garrett Rescue Squad. All to be commended. Oakland Volunteer Fire Department. I set down my cell phone, lifted my teacup by the handle and brought it down hard against the edge of the block. Fragments flew. Hot liquid spattered my chest. Blood welled from my knuckle. I gripped the jagged porcelain handle to gouge my palm, to cut, to hurt, but felt nothing as I lifted the cell in my other hand and speed-dialed again, just to hear Des' voice, and again, and again, the right coordinates but the wrong time, long past the start of my shift, long past sunset, the right coordinates, the only light in the room the microwave time, the wrong time.

The pews were thronged with impeccably dressed, well-coiffed young women, the demurely sniffling products of the best diets, dentistry and tennis lessons that money could buy, as well as, apparently, the latest cloning technologies. Who would have guessed that as an undergrad, Des had been the president of a fucking *sorority*? And here were the sisters, generations of them, what a turnout. Maybe they were earning activity points. I stood at the back of the church with the other latecomers and groundlings, marveling.

And when did they start showing PowerPoint presentations at funerals?

When the world loses its focus, these are the things you focus on.

I looked for Trooper Terry, the only friend of Des I knew, but she was nowhere in sight.

The "ladies of the church," as the gray-mustached pastor put it, had a spread ready for us afterward, in the social hall. I shuffled dutifully past the long table with the rest of the throng, known by and knowing no one, and I put several random food-shaped objects on my coaster-sized wax-paper plate and made arrangements of them. With a couple more corn chips, I might have had a reasonable approximation of the international biohazard symbol. I slid my artifacts off the plate into a trash can and replaced them with two triangular pimiento-cheese sandwiches on wheat bread. Someone had sliced off the crusts. I wondered who she was and whether she thought that trimming the crusts would spare us something, us mourners; or whether she simply had a bread pudding in mind for later; and wondered miserably who in her sorority Des had fantasized about and how far she had gotten with any of them. Or vice versa.

"Ms. Milledge?"

I blurted "Yes" even as I looked up to see Des—an older Des, with crow's feet and smaller eyeglasses, and shorter, and in an expensive black pantsuit. Of course I had been hanging around hoping to get up the nerve to speak to Des' mother; I realized that now. She had been visible throughout the service, enthroned in the beribboned front pew. But what I intended to say to the woman was a mystery ("I knew your daughter, and I mean biblically" and "With your daughter, Mrs. Creech, it wasn't just the sex" both seemed to lack a certain something), and that *she* might approach *me* never had crossed my mind. For all I knew, she'd never heard of me, certainly never would have singled me out in a crowd. She was looking not at me but at my untouched sandwiches. I dropped the plate into the trash, dusted imaginary crumbs from my fingers and reached out a hand—which she grasped with a look of surprise, as if the handshake had been involuntary, like my response when I heard my name. "I'm so sorry," we both said, and then we let go, flustered. I was self-conscious about my own hand once withdrawn, as if I were obligated now to do something with it. I stuck both hands into my jacket pockets.

"May I," she said, sounding hoarse, then swallowed. When she started again, she sounded stronger, more like the vice president of product development. "May I speak to you a moment, Ms. Milledge? In private?" She indicated the nearest kitchen door with a slight palm-up gesture, hand at her hip. Oh shit, I thought as I led the way. She looked like Des, but her vibe was all Mom, and I felt busted, like in the rec room in eighth grade. I flushed, and to my shame, tears welled up; the women in the long, dark, institutional kitchen (trimming more crusts, no doubt) were blurs. Ahead was a welcome oblong of light, a screen door that I pushed open to enter a scraggly little rose garden. In the distance, a buff shirtless boy in denim shorts rode a Toro across the church's vast back lawn.

Mrs. Creech closed both the wood door and the screen door behind us and addressed the yard boy when she said, "Thank you for not making a scene."

"I beg your pardon?"

"Of grief," she said. "A lover's grief." She plucked a pack of gum from her black velvet Christian Louboutin clutch, unsheathed a stick and folded it into her mouth. "I wondered whether you'd be here, and what you would do, but you've been very discreet, and I appreciate that. Juicy Fruit?"

"No, thanks," I said. "I can't chew gum and stifle my flamboyant dyke hysterics at the same time."

"Ha!" she said, and crossed her arms, shivering in the 70-degree afternoon. "I knew you'd be funny. That's what she always went for, smart and funny. Only never quite as smart as her, and never quite as funny, either."

"Is there something I can do for you, Mrs. Creech?"

She stared at me, then blinked and shook her head, laughed. "Forgive me," she said. "Meeting Destiny's… single friends… always brought out the worst in me. Back when she bothered to introduce them, that is. I just want to give you something." I'd seen wallets roomier than her designer purse, but she rummaged as if it were Santa's bag. "I've been boxing up Destiny's—*effects*—and I thought you would like to have this, and this, and this."

A photograph, a locket, a notebook with a zippered cover.

The photograph was of me lying beneath her on my sofa, our lips locked, my hands on her ass beneath her shorts. I had set the timer on the camera and sat next to her; she jumped me just before the flash went off, spoiling what was to have been my ceremonial "This-is-my-new-bestest-friend" photo for my parents. Dad, who is Upstate South Carolina through and through, would have taken this at face value, but Mom would have understood, being from Charleston, and would have appreciated the tact. She's tolerant of almost anything, as long as it's tolerable: neither explicit nor public. There's knowing, and there's *knowing*, as they say.

The locket was cheap and plastic and implausibly green, like something from a Lucky Charms box, and inside was a thumb-sized photo of myself, one I'd never seen. I was looking down, my face so smooth and relaxed I must have been engrossed in a book, or a cipher. This preserved intimacy embarrassed me more than the sofa photo. I thumbed shut the locket and unzipped the notebook.

I recognized it, of course. I had seen it countless times since that first afternoon in the café, but Des never had given me much chance to examine it. It pissed me off, eventually, and I gave up asking. Holding the worn, loved thing—stained not by Muddy Creek, the cover being waterproof, but by coffee and grimy fingers and constant use—seemed like a violation of the dead, especially as it had a permanent curve, having ridden for ages in a well-rounded back pocket. But I leafed through it anyway. Inside were page after page of tiny coordinates and symbols in handwritten rows that spiked across the pages like EKG printouts. Dozens, maybe hundreds, of caches, meticulously recorded.

"Look how short he's mowing this grass," Mrs. Creech said, "and no rain due this week. He's just killing it."

I focused on the numbers until I was over the locket, and able to speak.

"Thank you," I said.

"You're welcome," Mrs. Creech said. "The GPS unit was smashed, of course."

I nodded. "I have my own. A present from your daughter."

"I see. She could be very generous, I suppose, in her own way. Well, they'll be wondering what happened to me in there. Goodbye, Ms. Milledge. You won't be seeing me again." She didn't offer to shake hands this time.

"Mrs. Creech?"

"Yes?"

"How did you know my name?"

She paused on the other side of the screen door; the mesh took 20 years off her age. "You haven't reached the back of the notebook," she said. She closed the wood door behind her, leaving me outside, and I realized I wasn't meant to go back in. I flipped to the back of the notebook and found

JENNY MILLEDGE

JENNY MILLEDGE

JENNY MILLEDGE

written over and over and over in a dozen different inks and pencils, and I cried then, standing amid dry roses at the rear of a Presbyterian church.

I eventually registered that my sobs were sounding louder even as they diminished. The mower had shut off. I looked up. The buff boy was there, a towel around his neck, looking earnest and worried and eighteen, tops.

"Hey," he said. "Uh. Are you OK?"

I dragged the back of my hand across my nose, snorted and nodded. "Oh, yeah. Sure. I'm fine."

He nodded, and we both stood there.

"Thanks for asking," I said.

"No problem," he said. "You, uh, live around here?"

"Hagerstown."

He nodded again. "Cool." He glanced around, leaned in slightly. I could smell sweat and new-mown lawn. "Hey. You want to get high?"

I laughed. "You're cute," I said, "but I like girls."

He tilted back his head, and his mouth slowly formed an O of comprehension. Then he nodded and gave me a thumbs-up sign. "Awesome," he said.

And so I left my girlfriend's funeral, our love ratified by a teenage horndog.

I kept pulling the notebook out of my bedside drawer, turning it over in my hands, then putting it back. Once or twice, I confess, I put it beneath my pillow and slept on it, as if by morning it would have changed into a shiny quarter. Finally, things got so bad that I actually opened it and started leafing through the pages.

All those coordinates, each one checked off with a date. Des was good at finding things. She'd found me, hadn't she? I flipped to the back, looked at my own name for a while, then tossed the notebook onto the bed as I headed for the kitchen. Something out of the corner of my eye as the notebook landed and bounced made me stop in the doorway and look back. It had splayed open, and the visible pages looked funny, had much less writing on them than I would have expected. I picked it up and saw that these pages were new—or new to me, anyway. Same handwriting, but no check marks, no dates, just a single coordinate on the right-hand page with a gibberish row of letters beneath; on the left-hand page, four more gibberish rows.

Des, you ever hide any of these things yourself?

Yes, but since I know where those are…

"Oh my God," I said, carrying the notebook into the kitchen and plucking a pen from the coffee can. This wasn't a cache Des had found; this was a cache Des had *planted*.

I copied the four clues onto a single sheet of paper, one atop the other, and stared at them in a most unproductive fashion.

zmteatuxgfkmi

lmhiahdawtycz

tioxrkiainxzf

fiqieyvmogmuq

Clearly Des had used a key more sophisticated than a simple A=N substitution, otherwise *zmteatuxgfkmi* would decipher into *mzgrnghktsxzv*. Hmph. I stared at the nonsense letters, wondering what to do next, until my eyes unfocused and the rows of letters merged into a rectangular blur. Rectangular? Yes, that right margin did seem mighty regular: Was each clue the same number of letters? Yes, thirteen letters, every one.

So what? So each clue was 13 letters long, which strongly implied that the number 13 was somehow a very strong hint to cracking the cipher. Yes, each row of the geocachers' favorite shift had 13 letters—simply because each row contained half the 26 letters of the English alphabet—but suppose Des had come up with her own grid, the alphabet along one axis, a 13-letter key along the other? I had seen such charts as a kid: Tableaus, they were called.

And for whom could these clues have been meant but me?

I started jotting 13-letter words and phrases, then moved to my laptop to create Excel documents.

First I tried *DestinyCreech*—an obvious 13-letter set—down the first column, the alphabet atop the top row. The other 338 cells I filled in by using the letters of *DestinyCreech* as my starting point and completing the alphabet on each row, starting over at Z, like this:

```
     A B C D E F G H I J K L M N O P Q R S T U V W X Y Z
 1   D E F G H I J K L M N O P Q R S T U V W X Y Z A B C
 2   E F G H I J K L M N O P Q R S T U V W X Y Z A B C D
 3   S T U V W X Y Z A B C D E F G H I J K L M N O P Q R
 4   T U V W X Y Z A B C D E F G H I J K L M N O P Q R S
 5   I J K L M N O P Q R S T U V W X Y Z A B C D E F G H
 6   N O P Q R S T U V W X Y Z A B C D E F G H I J K L M
 7   Y Z A B C D E F G H I J K L M N O P Q R S T U V W X
 8   C D E F G H I J K L M N O P Q R S T U V W X Y Z A B
 9   R S T U V W X Y Z A B C D E F G H I J K L M N O P Q
10   E F G H I J K L M N O P Q R S T U V W X Y Z A B C D
11   E F G H I J K L M N O P Q R S T U V W X Y Z A B C D
12   C D E F G H I J K L M N O P Q R S T U V W X Y Z A B
13   H I J K L M N O P Q R S T U V W X Y Z A B C D E F G
```

I tried solving the first clue. I wound up with shit. I tried *DestinyCreech* across the top row with the alphabet down the side. More shit. OK, so she wasn't so egotistical as to key in her own name. I had no such compunctions, typing in *JennyMilledge* next.

Nada.

I tried catchphrases, names of friends and relatives, breakfast cereals—anything I could think of that we had talked about, laughed about, that would fit into 13 letters. After a half-hour of that, I couldn't see my Excel sheet for the tears, so I moved on to the names of famous people. I never realized there were so many 13-letter lesbians. Alison Bechdel, Barbara Jordan, Radclyffe Hall, Sheryl Swoopes, Aileen Wuornos, Rosie O'Donnell, Camille Paglia, Gertrude Stein, Jodieee Foster. (Hey, a girl can dream.) Neither Ellen De Generes nor Melissa Etheridge has 13 letters, but both *married* 13 letters. Dismissed as coincidence!

When I realized this was just sad, I closed all my Excel sheets, and went for a run.

A run normally helps me think of nothing in particular, just registering the variations underfoot as cement turns to asphalt turns to brick turns to cement again, the dogs barking at me on cue behind fences and inside bay windows, the rolling sweat prickling and reddening my Scots-Irish skin. But of course I kept thinking of Des—her puzzles, her treasure hunts, her games within games. What was the point? What was her big fucking secret? I jogged in place, waiting for a bus to ease around the corner, my reflection sliding across its fuselage and startling me, the way the back of my head always startles me in the three-sided mirror in a department-store dressing room. I thought of Mrs. Creech at the funeral, the way she first spoke to my sandwich plate and not to my face, the way she had to piece me together from clues. Des' big fucking secret had been me.

I lazily cut through the Martin's parking lot. Hunched over a loaded cart, a gray-haired woman with three children in tow—grandkids?—glared at me, or maybe at the world, or at the decades that separated us. I averted my eyes as I sprinted past. I headed uphill for home, the air suddenly damp and cloying, sweat stinging my eyes. Compared to Des, I was the old woman; she had all the kid's enthusiasms: ghost stories, horror movies, treasure hunts, farts, the night sky, the taste on the tongue of stuff that wasn't meant to be tasted. "Arm sweat and leg sweat taste different," she told me the night the AC broke. "I'll show you. And your arm and my arm taste different, and your left arm tastes different from your right arm. See? Isn't that something, Jen? How can anyone ever be bored?" And then she had plucked a dog-eared Norton Anthology from the orange crate beside her bed and stood silhouetted in the window and read aloud, with great drama, while I laughed at her:

From childhood's hour I have not been
As others were—I have not seen
As others saw—I could not bring
My passions from a common spring—

And at that point in my run, just as the humidity and the storm broke, and I plunged into a sheeting downpour like a drowning pool, I realized what the 13 letters had to be.

From the lightning in the sky
As it pass'd me flying by—
From the thunder, and the storm—
And the cloud that took the form
(When the rest of Heaven was blue)
Of a demon in my view—

Back at the apartment, I plugged in *EdgarAllanPoe*, and what do you know? It didn't work either.

"Well, fuck me," I said aloud, sounding so much like Des, on our first meeting, that I had to laugh.

Our first meeting. When a single DVD case seemed almost to float upward and into her hand.

So I filled the left column with *SeventhVictim*, which gave me this:

```
    A B C D E F G H I J K L M N O P Q R S T U V W X Y Z
 1  S T U V W X Y Z A B C D E F G H I J K L M N O P Q R
 2  E F G H I J K L M N O P Q R S T U V W X Y Z A B C D
 3  V W X Y Z A B C D E F G H I J K L M N O P Q R S T U
 4  E F G H I J K L M N O P Q R S T U V W X Y Z A B C D
 5  N O P Q R S T U V W X Y Z A B C D E F G H I J K L M
 6  T U V W X Y Z A B C D E F G H I J K L M N O P Q R S
 7  H I J K L M N O P Q R S T U V W X Y Z A B C D E F G
 8  V W X Y Z A B C D E F G H I J K L M N O P Q R S T U
 9  I J K L M N O P Q R S T U V W X Y Z A B C D E F G H
10  C D E F G H I J K L M N O P Q R S T U V W X Y Z A B
11  T U V W X Y Z A B C D E F G H I J K L M N O P Q R S
12  I J K L M N O P Q R S T U V W X Y Z A B C D E F G H
13  M N O P Q R S T U V W X Y Z A B C D E F G H I J K L
```

I tackled the first clue, *zmteatuxgfkmi*. Z in the first row corresponded with H up top; M in the second row corresponded with I; T in the third row corresponded with Y, and so on until…

hiyanancydrew

"Hi, there," I said aloud, delighted. It was like communicating with the dead, only not in any weird-me-out way. It was more of a collaboration: Jen had written something, and now I was reading it, long after the fact.

Clue No. 2 turned into *timenowforfun*. No. 3 was *betterbealert*.

I started decrypting Clue No. 4, already feeling the process had curdled from a puzzle to a chore. Once you had the key, doing the conversions was pretty tedious, really, nothing but a—

neverforg

Still with my fingertip on Row 9, I stared at the nine letters I had written—or (face facts, Jen) the letters Des had directed my hand to write. For an instant I considered setting down the pen, shredding the tableau, trunking the notebook and moving on with my life. Instead I proceeded to Rows 10 through 13.

neverforgetme

OK, now I *was* weirded out. When had Jen written these pages, anyway? They were in the middle of the notebook, on sheets just as old as the surrounding paper, and just as permanently attached to the spine; the pages, anyway, were not afterthoughts. But if that plaintive request (no, demand)—"Never forget me"—wasn't directed at me, then to whom was it directed?

I looked at the facing page, that single coordinate above that single clue:

xmmwghmztgomz

Gomez, indeed. I stood up, walked across the kitchen, opened the fridge, rummaged for the only thing alcoholic in the house (a single bottle of Mike's Hard Lemonade, left over from a Yarns Ignoble get-together), popped the top, methodically drank it at the sink watching chipmunks scale the neighbor's brick wall, rinsed the bottle, perched it atop the pile in the recycling bin, returned to the dinette table and decrypted the last clue:

firstofeleven

Nearly 6 o'clock. Far too late to start now, and tomorrow a double shift at the store. First thing Sunday, then, I'd acquire some satellites and start connecting the dots, track the multi-cache Des had prepared for me. Perfectly valid reasons for a two-day delay. Nothing whatsoever to do with dread.

I stopped for Sunday dinner at a roadside restaurant where the waitresses wore "plain" Mennonite dresses and the short list of vegetables included applesauce, macaroni and cottage cheese.

"What can I get yez?"

"I'll have applesauce, macaroni and cottage cheese. And a pork chop."

"Onions and gravy?"

"Yes, please."

I flipped my paper placemat—which featured a color photo of the Italian shoreline at Sorrento, oddly enough—and transcribed the messages I had uncovered and decrypted so far.

sorryaboutmom

dontmournmuch

The implied pause before the last word made me laugh.

dontlaughatme

imissyousoido

bestrongforme

yourenotalone

nightiscoming

"What's the point, Des?" I murmured. "What are you trying to tell me?"

"Mighty lot of homework you got there," the waitress said, "and it summer. You want I should set these on another mat?"

"No, it's OK." My handwritten messages from the dead promptly vanished beneath a steaming plate of roadfood, and I was suddenly ravenous. As I ate, the last three messages kept scrolling through my head. Be strong for me; you're not alone; night is coming. As indeed it was. The sun would be below the treeline by the time I got back to the car.

What makes a certain type of cache a *night* cache, as opposed to an ordinary cache that you opt to hunt up at night because you're a night person or contrary or just enjoy making things harder on yourself, is that the coordinates lead you not quite to the cache itself, but to a reflective device, or a series of reflective devices, that lead you to the true location—unlike a will-o'-the-wisp, though that leads you somewhere final, too, I suppose.

The coordinate in the night-is-coming cache had a small symbol drawn at the end, a crescent moon within a circle. My last four destinations would be night caches.

The first was beneath a picnic table near a scarred rock face on Sideling Hill, within a headlight's beam of a roadside floral cross. There I found the next coordinates, and the next clue, which decrypted as:

letgojennyjen

The second of the night caches was in the woods behind the Appalachian Laboratory, within sight of the building where someone else, presumably, was graphing the Antietam ecosystem now. There I found the next coordinates and the next clue, which decrypted as:

youcantjoinme

The third of the night caches was in the rocks along the riverside beneath the Casselman Bridge. There I found the next clue, which decrypted as:

youweremyfind

And of course the next coordinates, which beckoned me into the middle of a swamp.

Even with GPS, finding the Cranesville Swamp by night wasn't easy. It's not what you'd call centrally located—unlike, say, the Everglades—and none of the increasingly obscure crossroads en route was lighted. My quietly hectoring Garmin indicator kept telling me I'd overshot, and I kept turning around in churchyards, where I switched on the overhead and studied my road map, and the driveways of trailers, where I paused as little as possible. It was after eleven by the time I crunched into the shapeless gravel lot, barely large enough for six cars but empty when I got there, thank God. When I opened my door, the surrounding chill filled my car, filled me; I stood, shivering.

I should have expected the cold, even in June. Cranesville Swamp is, after all, a high-altitude pocket ecosystem in the Maryland mountains, left behind when the great Northern forest retreated into Canada ten thousand years ago; the cold is its reason for being. But reading the Nature Conservancy's flyer in my kitchen and being alone in the dark on the edge of the great tangled refrigerated bowl were two rather different experiences.

The lot seemed even smaller than it had been. I flicked my flashlight beam about the surrounding trees, taking care not to look too long into any of the spaces between, until I found the weathered wooden sign marking the trailhead. It was big and misplaced, pocked with old staples and tacks, like the bulletin board outside a college cafeteria, but it was free of messages now. That was just as well; I'd had messages enough. I walked slowly toward the trailhead, my face bathed in the handheld moonlight of the Garmin, and saw the confirming numbers; yep, the final cache was ahead. I may have been taking directions from a ghost, but she hadn't let me down yet. Not in that sense, anyway.

I took a deep breath of skunk cabbage and cranberry and walked into the swamp.

The look of the ground changed in the circle of light before me, became oddly regular, a series of parallel lines in my path: a boardwalk leading into the swamp. I stepped onto it. My footfalls on the planks were hollow-sounding, like a child beating a washtub, or a rowboat bumping against a dock. I walked on, mindful of the boardwalk's sudden turns, sure that a misstep would plunge me who-knew-how-deep into who-knew-what. The bog was doing its best to reclaim the boardwalk. An occasional leafy tendril clutched at my ankle as if hoping to trip me, drag me over and down.

My thumping tread, cautious and measured and regular, now sounded like a heartbeat beneath the boards. Thanks a lot for *that* image. I deliberately varied my step, half-dancing along, as through a minefield.

The breath of the dark swamp was clammy on my arms, and I once again regretted having left my denim jacket at home. I pictured it hanging on its hook beside the front door; I wished I were there with it. My Garmin face tried to reassure me by ticking down the minutes and seconds, not of time but of longitude and latitude. The final cache was only a hundred feet away now, the readout said. Ninety, eighty, seventy-five. I swept my flashlight beam and revealed nothing but level bog all around, trees too far distant to illuminate. If the cache was beneath the boardwalk, I didn't relish mucking about down there bare-handed.

"Jen," called Des.

I froze.

I heard it again, "Jen," then heard it echoed a dozen times from the trees all around. *Jen jen jen jen jen.* Some night bird's call, working on my imagination.

I'm good at lurking, Des had said.

Jeez, what was I doing out here?

Five feet.

Three feet.

Zero feet.

Here we are, said the numbers on my trusty Garmin 60CSX, you're standing on it.

I turned in a slow circle, waggled the flashlight beam around my feet, saw no telltale gleam. I tried again, and again, aiming the beam a little farther out each time, and on my fourth pass was rewarded with a single flash on the boardwalk up ahead, where it angled back toward the nearest shore. The gleam was gone almost before it registered, like the flash of a madman's lantern. Ah, there it was again; now that I had a bead, I trotted along the decking—older here, less resonant, with more give beneath my weight—until I reached it: an ordinary bike reflector at the end of an ordinary wire planted in an ordinary tuft of grass beside the walk. I cast about again with the flashlight. Nothing. This must be the place. I knelt, biting my lip—move away, Mr. Snakey No-Shoulders, move away—and felt beneath the planks on that side. In moments I found it, a cylinder the size and shape of a film canister, sitting in a dry space, a sort of shelf, between the planks and a two-by-four that connected the support posts. A microcache like the one in the parking lot, the first one we found together. I zipped up Des' notebook, squeezed it as if it were a living thing, and placed it beneath the planks where the canister had been.

"Goodbye, Des," I said.

Too aware of the spaces between the planks to sit, I squatted on the boardwalk, suspended in the darkness, surrounded by cold nothing. I popped the canister lid and removed a single slip of paper the size of a Chinese fortune. In the flashlight beam I saw again that scarily familiar handwriting:

dsjooxodvfrwg

OXO, hugs and kisses, farewell. No further coordinates. Number Eleven was the end of the line. I slid my tableau and Bic pen from my shirt pocket and set to work.

l

lo

loo

look

lookb

lookbe

"Damn," I said as my flashlight went out. I twiddled the lens, thumped the casing against the boards, and got it going again, only more feebly than before. Quickly, now, before I lose the light—

lookbeh

How many more letters I needed, I truly can't remember. How many would anyone have needed, in the middle of a swamp at midnight?

lookbehi

I whirled.

Behind me, a few yards across the surface of the bog, in the treeline: a figure.

I sucked in a breath. With no thought, I cupped a hand over my flashlight beam to hide it.

The figure moved nearer, stepped onto the planking ahead of me.

"Hello," she called, and a sudden light in my face blinded me. I recoiled, staggered as if struck in the face, and stepped backward off the edge of the boardwalk.

Have you ever reached for a glass you thought was empty, maybe when cleaning up after a party, or a wake? Not only do you splash yourself, but you feel the surprise in your forearm muscles, which clench, go into lockdown mode, might even be sore for a while. That's what stepping into the bog was like. As one foot went down, my body tensed for a plunge that didn't happen. Instead I stepped onto something solid that gave only slightly, like a rucked-up carpet. My ankle twisted, and in the ensuing little dance step of balance my other foot came off the boardwalk too. Legs spasming from the shock of purchase, I stood in a crouch on the matted surface.

My flashlight had fallen out of reach. It pointed away from the boardwalk, illuminating nothing.

Then my weight broke through, and I began to sink into the bog. A cold like I'd never known sheathed the tops of my feet, gripped my ankles, climbed hand-to-hand up my legs, like softball captains claiming a bat. With a tearing sound my left leg sank up to my thigh, and I fell sideways, clawing for solidity that wasn't there, coming up only with tangled fistfuls of clammy, clutching moss.

As I flailed and gasped at the all-encompassing cold that was claiming my body, I heard rapid footsteps along the planks—strangely solid and unghostly—and a woman, not Des, cried, "I'm coming!"

"Help!" I hollered as I went down again. This time my clawing left hand connected with the edge of the boardwalk, and then strong hands gripped my forearm, hauled on me.

"I've got you," she said. "Stop kicking, dammit. Reach forward with your other hand. That's it, there." When my chest struck the edge, my feet found solid ground, and I levered myself up, was pulled the rest of the way. My legs came free of the bog with an awful ripping sound, and my left foot was bare. Sobbing, gasping, I clawed the spongy netting from my legs. I had no thoughts beyond freeing myself, as if the severed vines could pull me back into the bog. The horrid bright light was in my face again, an industrial-strength flash, and my rescuer's gray pants had a seriously official black stripe up the side. A firm hand kneaded my shoulder. "Jen, hey, don't worry, you're out of it, you're free, you're safe, OK? You're back on the planks. Really. It's me, Trooper Terry. Marjorie. Hey. Look at me."

Back at the cars, she called in my license plate and my driver's license number, to make sure I wasn't infamous. The squawk of her radio was answered by an owl in the trees. I sat, shivering, on the still-warm hood of my Tracer, jeans adhering to my legs as they dried.

Trooper Terry sauntered back over. I guess they can't help sauntering, troopers, with all that crap hanging from their belts. I decided I needed something similar to hold the GPS unit, spare batteries, a notebook of my own.

"Your license, ma'am."

"Thanks."

She kicked gravel. "The Conservancy is worried someone'll set up a meth lab out here, asked us to keep a lookout. You'll understand why I had to check."

"Sure."

She kicked gravel again. "You'll be wanting to get home now, get into some dry clothes, I imagine."

"Yes, ma'am."

"Yes, ma'am," she repeated. She shook her head. "Yes, ma'am."

Long pause.

Then she said, "Let's not make a habit of this, OK?"

"No, ma'am."

Clearly there was nothing more to say, but she seemed reluctant to go. Her face was shadowed, but I saw her take off her hat, scratch her head, replace the hat, sigh, and walk back toward her car. I could tell by the crunch of her footsteps that she slowed, almost turned around, changed her mind and walked on. Climbing into her driver's seat, she abruptly stood, her head cresting the roof, and called:

"I'm sorry about Des. I had court duty that day. So I didn't. You know. Didn't see her."

"Me, neither," I said, which made no sense, but was something to say. A little breeze picked up at just that moment—not that I could feel it, but the bushes were rustling, and I heard a skittering like leaves on the gravel, so I had some evidence—and with the breeze I decided "Me, neither" would be the completely wrong note with which to end the conversation, so I asked, "How's your nine ball?"

In the darkness, the trooper laughed. "Don't ask," she said. "It's a weekly struggle. Every Thursday, at Fusion. That's in Frederick. From noon. I'm sorry. I didn't mean, uh. To imply. Ah, shit. See you." She got inside her car and cranked it up. Her brights came on, and I squinted; the parking lot suddenly looked stark and pitiless, and the surrounding woods very dark indeed. I got into my Tracer and waited, but Trooper Terry clearly intended to follow me out, so I powered up and drove off, jouncing down the gravel road to the pavement, and then zigzagging my way back across Garrett County the way I had come, never missing a turn, the accelerator pedal feeling sort of sexy beneath my bare foot.

"Trooper Terry," I said aloud.

Not until we both were on I-68 did she fall behind. She pulled into a service road, and soon I couldn't see her lights in my mirror anymore.

The Casselman River Bridge: happenstance. The Cranesville Swamp: coincidence? Enemy action…

"Well, Des, we'll see about that," I said aloud. "We'll just have to see about that."

THE ISLAND
PETER WATTS

Peter Watts, author of the well-received "Rifters" sequence of novels and short story collection *Ten Monkeys, Ten Minutes*, is a reformed marine biologist whose latest novel *Blindsight* was nominated for several major awards, winning exactly none of them. It has, however, won awards in Poland, been translated into a shitload of languages, and has been used as a core text for university courses ranging from "Philosophy of Mind" to "Introductory Neuropsych". Watts has also pioneered the technique of loading real scientific references into the backs of his novels, which both adds a veneer of credibility to his work and acts as a shield against nitpickers.

Despite (or perhaps because of) the foregoing, the publishing industry doesn't like him very much.

We are the cave men. We are the Ancients, the Progenitors, the blue-collar steel monkeys. We spin your webs and build your magic gateways, thread each needle's eye at sixty thousand kilometers a second. We never stop. We never even dare to slow down, lest the light of your coming turn us to plasma. All for you. All so you can step from star to star without dirtying your feet in these endless, empty wastes *between*.

Is it really too much to ask, that you might talk to us now and then?

I know about evolution and engineering. I know how much you've changed. I've seen these portals give birth to gods and demons and things we can't begin to comprehend, things I can't believe were ever human; alien hitchhikers, perhaps, riding the rails we've left behind. Alien conquerors.

Exterminators, perhaps.

But I've also seen those gates stay dark and empty until they faded from view. We've inferred diebacks and dark ages, civilizations burned to the ground and others rising from their ashes—and sometimes, afterwards, the things that come out look a little like the ships *we* might have built, back in the day. They speak to each other—radio, laser, carrier neutrinos—and sometimes their voices sound something like ours. There was a time we dared to hope that they really were like us, that the circle had come round again and closed on beings we could talk to. I've lost count of the times we tried to break the ice.

I've lost count of the eons since we gave up.

All these iterations fading behind us. All these hybrids and posthumans and immortals, gods and catatonic cavemen trapped in magical chariots they can't begin to understand, and not one of them ever pointed a comm laser in our direction to say *Hey, how's it going*, or *Guess what? We cured Damascus Disease!* or even *Thanks, guys, keep up the good work.*

We're not some fucking cargo cult. We're the backbone of your goddamn empire. You wouldn't even be out here if it weren't for us.

And—and you're our *children*. Whatever you've become, you were once like this, like me. I believed in you once. There was a time, long ago, when I believed in this mission with all my heart.

Why have you forsaken us?

And so another build begins.

This time I open my eyes to a familiar face I've never seen before: only a boy, early twenties perhaps, physiologically. His face is a little lopsided, the cheekbone flatter on the left than the right. His ears are too big. He looks almost *natural*.

I haven't spoken for millennia. My voice comes out a whisper: "Who are you?" Not what I'm supposed to ask, I know. Not the first question *anyone* on *Eriophora* asks, after coming back.

"I'm yours," he says, and just like that I'm a mother.

I want to let it sink in, but he doesn't give me the chance: "You weren't scheduled, but Chimp wants extra hands on deck. Next build's got a situation."

So the chimp is still in control. The chimp is always in control. The mission goes on.

"Situation?" I ask.

"Contact scenario, maybe."

I wonder when he was born. I wonder if he ever wondered about me, before now.

He doesn't tell me. He only says, "Sun up ahead. Half lightyear. Chimp thinks, maybe it's talking to us. Anyhow..." My—son shrugs. "No rush. Lotsa time."

I nod, but he hesitates. He's waiting for The Question but I already see a kind of answer in his face. Our reinforcements were supposed to be *pristine*, built from perfect genes buried deep within *Eri*'s iron-basalt mantle, safe from the sleeting blueshift. And yet this boy has flaws. I see the damage in his face, I see those tiny flipped base-pairs resonating up from the microscopic and *bending* him just a little off-kilter. He looks like he grew up on a planet. He looks born of parents who spent their whole lives hammered by raw sunlight.

How far out must we be by now, if even our own perfect building blocks have decayed so? How long has it taken us? How long have I been dead?

How long? It's the first thing everyone asks.

After all this time, I don't want to know.

He's alone at the tac tank when I arrive on the bridge, his eyes full of icons and trajectories. Perhaps I see a little of me in there, too.

"I didn't get your name," I say, although I've looked it up on the manifest. We've barely been introduced and already I'm lying to him.

"Dix." He keeps his eyes on the tank.

He's over ten thousand years old. Alive for maybe twenty of them. I wonder how much he knows, who he's met during those sparse decades: does he know Ishmael, or Connie? Does he know if Sanchez got over his brush with immortality?

I wonder, but I don't ask. There are rules.

I look around. "We're it?"

Dix nods. "For now. Bring back more if we need them. But…" His voice trails off.

"Yes?"

"Nothing."

I join him at the tank. Diaphanous veils hang within like frozen, color-coded smoke. We're on the edge of a molecular dust cloud. Warm, semiorganic, lots of raw materials: formaldehyde, ethylene glycol, the usual prebiotics. A good spot for a quick build. A red dwarf glowers dimly at the center of the Tank. The chimp has named it DHF428, for reasons I've long since forgotten to care about.

"So fill me in," I say.

His glance is impatient, even irritated. "You too?"

"What do you mean?"

"Like the others. On the other builds. Chimp can just squirt the specs but they want to *talk* all the time."

Shit, his link's still active. He's *online*.

I force a smile. "Just a—a cultural tradition, I guess. We talk about a lot of things, it helps us—reconnect. After being down for so long."

"But it's *slow*," Dix complains.

He doesn't know. Why doesn't he know?

"We've got half a lightyear," I point out. "There's some rush?"

The corner of his mouth twitches. "Vons went out on schedule." On cue a cluster of violet pinpricks sparkle in the Tank, five trillion klicks ahead of us. "Still sucking dust mostly, but got lucky with a couple of big asteroids and the refineries came online early. First components already extruded. Then Chimp sees these fluctuations in solar output—mainly infra, but extends into visible." The tank blinks at us: the dwarf goes into time-lapse.

Sure enough, it's *flickering*.

"Nonrandom, I take it."

Dix inclines his head a little to the side, not quite nodding.

"Plot the time-series." I've never been able to break the habit of raising my voice, just a bit, when addressing the chimp. Obediently (*obediently*. Now *there's* a laugh-and-a-half) the AI wipes the spacescape and replaces it with

·········· · · · · · · · · · · · · ·

"Repeating sequence," Dix tells me. "Blips don't change, but spacing's a log-linear increase cycling every 92.5 corsecs Each cycle starts at 13.2 clicks/corsec, degrades over time."

"No chance this could be natural? A little black hole wobbling around in the center of the star, maybe?"

Dix shakes his head, or something like that: a diagonal dip of the chin that somehow conveys the negative. "But way too simple to contain much info. Not like an actual conversation. More—well, a shout."

He's partly right. There may not be much information, but there's enough. *We're here. We're smart. We're powerful enough to hook a whole damn star up to a dimmer switch.*

Maybe not such a good spot for a build after all.

I purse my lips. "The sun's hailing us. That's what you're saying."

"Maybe. Hailing *someone*. But too simple for a rosetta signal. It's not an archive, can't self-extract. Not a bonferroni or fibonacci seq, not pi. Not even a multiplication table. Nothing to base a pidgin on."

Still. An intelligent signal.

"Need more info," Dix says, proving himself master of the blindingly obvious.

I nod. "The vons."

"Uh, what about them?"

"We set up an array. Use a bunch of bad eyes to fake a good one. It'd be faster than high-geeing an observatory from this end or retooling one of the on-site factories."

His eyes go wide. For a moment he almost looks frightened for some reason. But the moment passes and he does that weird head-shake thing again. "Bleed too many resources away from the build, wouldn't it? "

"It would," the chimp agrees.

I suppress a snort. "If you're so worried about meeting our construction benchmarks, Chimp, factor in the potential risk posed by an intelligence powerful enough to control the energy output of an entire sun."

"I can't," it admits. "I don't have enough information."

"You don't have *any* information. About something that could probably stop this mission dead in its tracks if it wanted to. So maybe we should get some."

"Okay. Vons reassigned."

Confirmation glows from a convenient bulkhead, a complex sequence of dance instructions fired into the void. Six months from now a hundred self-replicating robots will waltz into a makeshift surveillance grid; four months after that, we might have something more than vacuum to debate in.

Dix eyes me as though I've just cast some kind of magic spell.

"It may run the ship," I tell him, "but it's pretty fucking stupid. Sometimes you've just got to spell things out."

He looks vaguely affronted, but there's no mistaking the surprise beneath. He didn't know that. He *didn't know*.

Who the hell's been raising him all this time? Whose problem is this?

Not mine.

"Call me in ten months," I say. "I'm going back to bed."

It's as though he never left. I climb back into the bridge and there he is, staring into tac. DHF428 fills the tank, a swollen red orb that turns my son's face into a devil mask.

He spares me the briefest glance, eyes wide, fingers twitching as if electrified. "Vons don't see it."

I'm still a bit groggy from the thaw. "See wh—"

"The *sequence!*" His voice borders on panic. He sways back and forth, shifting his weight from foot to foot.

"Show me."

Tac splits down the middle. Cloned dwarves burn before me now, each perhaps twice the size of my fist. On the left, an *Eri*'s-eye view: DHF428 stutters as it did before, as it presumably has these past ten months. On the right, a compound-eye composite: an interferometry grid built by a myriad precisely-spaced vons, their rudimentary eyes layered and parallaxed into something approaching high resolution. Contrast on both sides has been conveniently cranked up to highlight the dwarf's endless winking for merely human eyes.

Except it's only winking from the left side of the display. On the right, 428 glowers steady as a standard candle.

"Chimp: any chance the grid just isn't sensitive enough to see the fluctuations?"

"No."

"Huh." I try to think of some reason it would lie about this.

"Doesn't make *sense*," my son complains.

"It does," I murmur, "if it's not the sun that's flickering."

"But *is* flickering—" He sucks his teeth. "You can *see* it fl—wait, you mean something *behind* the vons? Between, between them and us?"

"Mmmm."

"Some kind of *filter*." Dix relaxes a bit. "Wouldn't we've seen it, though? Wouldn't the vons've hit it going down?"

I put my voice back into ChimpComm mode. "What's the current field-of-view for *Eri*'s forward scope?"

"Eighteen mikes," the chimp reports. "At 428's range, the cone is three point three four lightsecs across."

"Increase to a hundred lightsecs."

The *Eri's*-eye partition swells, obliterating the dissenting viewpoint. For a moment the sun fills the tank again, paints the whole bridge crimson. Then it dwindles as if devoured from within.

I notice some fuzz in the display. "Can you clear that noise?"

"It's not noise," the chimp reports. "It's dust and molecular gas."

I blink. "What's the density?"

"Estimated hundred thousand atoms per cubic meter."

Two orders of magnitude too high, even for a nebula. "Why so heavy?" Surely we'd have detected any gravity well strong enough to keep *that* much material in the neighborhood.

"I don't know," the chimp says.

I get the queasy feeling that I might. "Set field-of-view to five hundred lightsecs. Peak false-color at near-infrared."

Space grows ominously murky in the tank. The tiny sun at its center, thumb-nail-sized now, glows with increased brilliance: an incandescent pearl in muddy water.

"A thousand lightsecs," I command.

"There," Dix whispers: real space reclaims the edges of the tank, dark, clear, pristine. 428 nestles at the heart of a dim spherical shroud. You find those some-times, discarded cast-offs from companion stars whose convulsions spew gas and rads across light years. But 428 is no nova remnant. It's a *red dwarf*, placid, middle-aged. Unremarkable.

Except for the fact that it sits dead center of a tenuous gas bubble 1.4 AUs across. And for the fact that this bubble does not *attenuate* or *diffuse* or *fade* gradually into that good night. No, unless there is something seriously wrong with the display, this small, spherical nebula extends about 350 lightsecs from its primary and then just *stop*s, its boundary far more knife-edged than nature has any right to be.

For the first time in millennia, I miss my cortical pipe. It takes forever to saccade search terms onto the keyboard in my head, to get the answers I already know.

Numbers come back. "Chimp. I want false-color peaks at 335, 500 and 800 nanometers."

The shroud around 428 lights up like a dragonfly's wing, like an iridescent soap bubble.

"It's *beautiful*," whispers my awestruck son.

"It's photosynthetic," I tell him.

Phaeophytin and eumelanin, according to spectro. There are even hints of some kind of lead-based Keipper pigment, soaking up X-rays in the picometer range. Chimp hypothesizes something called a *chromatophore*: branching cells with little aliquots of pigment inside, like particles of charcoal dust. Keep those particles clumped together and the cell's effectively transparent; spread them out through the cytoplasm and the whole structure *darkens*, dims whatever EM passes through from behind. Apparently there were animals back on Earth with cells like that. They could change color, pattern-match to their background, all sorts of things.

"So there's a membrane of—of *living tissue* around that star," I say, trying to wrap my head around the concept. "A, a meat balloon. Around the whole damn *star*."

"Yes," the chimp says.

"But that's—Jesus, how thick would it be?"

"No more than two millimeters. Probably less."

"How so?"

"If it was much thicker, it would be more obvious in the visible spectrum. It would have had a detectable effect on the von Neumanns when they hit it."

"That's assuming that its—cells, I guess—are like ours."

"The pigments are familiar; the rest might be too."

It can't be *too* familiar. Nothing like a conventional gene would last two seconds in that environment. Not to mention whatever miracle solvent that thing must use as antifreeze…

"Okay, let's be conservative, then. Say, mean thickness of a millimeter. Assume a density of water at STP. How much mass in the whole thing?"

"1.4 yottagrams," Dix and the chimp reply, almost in unison.

"That's, uh…"

"Half the mass of Mercury," the chimp adds helpfully.

I whistle through my teeth. "And that's *one* organism?"

"I don't know yet."

"It's got organic pigments. Fuck, it's *talking*. It's intelligent."

"Most cyclic emanations from living sources are simple biorhythms," the chimp points out. "Not intelligent signals."

I ignore it and turn to Dix. "Assume it's a signal."

He frowns. "Chimp says—"

"*Assume*. Use your imagination."

I'm not getting through to him. He looks nervous.

He looks like that a lot, I realize.

"*If* someone were signaling you," I say, "*then* what would you do?"

"Signal…" Confusion on that face, and a fuzzy circuit closing somewhere. "…back?"

My son is an idiot.

"And if the incoming signal takes the form of systematic changes in light intensity, how—"

"Use the BI lasers, alternated to pulse between 700 and 3000 nanometers. Can boost an interlaced signal into the exawatt range without compromising our fenders; gives over a thousand Watts per square meter after diffraction. Way past detection threshold for anything that can sense thermal output from a red dwarf. And content doesn't matter if it's just a shout. Shout back. Test for echo."

Okay, so my son is an idiot *savant*.

And he still looks unhappy—"But Chimp, he says no real *information* there, right?"—and that whole other set of misgivings edges to the fore again: *He*.

Dix takes my silence for amnesia. "Too simple, remember? Simple click train."

I shake my head. There's more information in that signal than the chimp can imagine. There are so many things the chimp doesn't know. And the last thing I need is for this, this *child* to start deferring to it, to start looking to it as an equal or, God forbid, a *mentor*.

Oh, it's smart enough to steer us between the stars. Smart enough to calculate million-digit primes in the blink of an eye. Even smart enough for a little crude improvisation should the crew go too far off-mission.

Not smart enough to know a distress call when it sees one.

"It's a deceleration curve," I tell them both. "It keeps *slowing down*. Over and over again. *That's* the message."

Stop. Stop. Stop. Stop.

And I think it's meant for no one but us.

We shout back. No reason not to. And now we die again, because what's the point of staying up late? Whether or not this vast entity harbors real intelligence, our echo won't reach it for ten million corsecs. Another seven million, at the earliest, before we receive any reply it might send.

Might as well hit the crypt in the meantime. Shut down all desires and misgivings, conserve whatever life I have left for moments that matter. Remove myself from this sparse tactical intelligence, from this wet-eyed pup watching me as though I'm some kind of sorcerer about to vanish in a puff of smoke. He opens his mouth to speak, and I turn away and hurry down to oblivion.

But I set my alarm to wake up alone.

I linger in the coffin for a while, grateful for small and ancient victories. The chimp's dead, blackened eye gazes down from the ceiling; in all these millions of years nobody's scrubbed off the carbon scoring. It's a trophy of sorts, a memento from the early incendiary days of our Great Struggle.

There's still something—comforting, I guess—about that blind, endless stare. I'm reluctant to venture out where the chimp's nerves have not been so thoroughly cauterized. Childish, I know. The damn thing already knows I'm up; it may be blind, deaf, and impotent in here, but there's no way to mask the power the crypt sucks in during a thaw. And it's not as though a bunch of club-wielding teleops are waiting to pounce on me the moment I step outside. These are the days of détente, after all. The struggle continues but the war has gone cold; we just go through the motions now, rattling our chains like an old married multiplet resigned to hating each other to the end of time.

After all the moves and countermoves, the truth is we need each other.

So I wash the rotten-egg stench from my hair and step into *Eri's* silent cathedral hallways. Sure enough the enemy waits in the darkness, turns the lights on as I approach, shuts them off behind me—but it does not break the silence.

Dix.

A strange one, that. Not that you'd expect anyone born and raised on *Eriophora* to be an archetype of mental health, but Dix doesn't even know what side he's on. He doesn't even seem to know he has to *choose* a side. It's almost as though he read the original mission statements and took them *seriously*, believed in the literal truth of the ancient scrolls: Mammals and Machinery, working together across the ages to explore the Universe! United! Strong! Forward the Frontier!

Rah.

Whoever raised him didn't do a great job. Not that I blame them; it can't have been much fun having a child underfoot during a build, and none of us were selected for our parenting skills. Even if bots changed the diapers and VR handled the infodumps, socializing a toddler couldn't have been anyone's idea of a good time. I'd have probably just chucked the little bastard out an airlock.

But even I would've brought him up to speed.

Something changed while I was away. Maybe the war's heated up again, entered some new phase. That twitchy kid is out of the loop for a reason. I wonder what it is.

I wonder if I care.

I arrive at my suite, treat myself to a gratuitous meal, jill off. Three hours after coming back to life I'm relaxing in the starbow commons. "Chimp."

"You're up early," it says at last, and I am; our answering shout hasn't even arrived at its destination yet. No real chance of new data for another two months, at least.

"Show me the forward feeds," I command.

DHF428 blinks at me from the center of the lounge: *Stop. Stop. Stop.*

Maybe. Or maybe the chimp's right, maybe it's pure physiology. Maybe this endless cycle carries no more intelligence than the beating of a heart. But there's a pattern inside the pattern, some kind of *flicker* in the blink. It makes my brain itch.

"Slow the time-series," I command. "By a hundred."

It *is* a blink. 428's disk isn't darkening uniformly, it's *eclipsing*. As though a great eyelid were being drawn across the surface of the sun, from right to left.

"By a thousand."

Chromatophores, the chimp called them. But they're not all opening and closing at once. The darkness moves across the membrane in *waves*.

A word pops into my head: *latency*.

"Chimp. Those waves of pigment. How fast are they moving?"

"About fifty-nine thousand kilometers per second."

The speed of a passing thought.

And if this thing *does* think, it'll have logic gates, synapses—it's going to be a *net* of some kind. And if the net's big enough, there's an *I* in the middle of it. Just like me, just like Dix. Just like the chimp. (Which is why I educated myself on the subject, back in the early tumultuous days of our relationship. Know your enemy and all that.)

The thing about *I* is, it only exists within a tenth-of-a-second of all its parts. When we get spread too thin—when someone splits your brain down the middle, say, chops the fat pipe so the halves have to talk the long way around; when the neural architecture *diffuses* past some critical point and signals take just that much longer to pass from A to B—the system, well, *decoheres*. The two sides of your brain become different people with different tastes, different agendas, different senses of themselves.

I shatters into *we*.

It's not just a human rule, or a mammal rule, or even an Earthly one. It's a rule for any circuit that processes information, and it applies as much to the things we've yet to meet as it did to those we left behind.

Fifty-nine thousand kilometers per second, the chimp says. How far can the signal move through that membrane in a tenth of a corsec? How thinly does *I* spread itself across the heavens?

The flesh is huge, the flesh is inconceivable. But the spirit, the spirit is—

Shit.

"Chimp. Assuming the mean neuron density of a human brain, what's the synapse count on a circular sheet of neurons one millimeter thick with a diameter of five thousand eight hundred ninety-two kilometers?"

"Two times ten to the twenty-seventh."

I saccade the database for some perspective on a mind stretched across thirty million square kilometers: the equivalent of two quadrillion human brains.

Of course, whatever this thing uses for neurons have to be packed a lot less tightly than ours; we can see through them, after all. Let's be superconservative, say it's only got a thousandth the computational density of a human brain. That's—

Okay, let's say it's only got a *ten*-thousandth the synaptic density, that's still—

A *hundred* thousandth. The merest mist of thinking meat. Any more conservative and I'd hypothesize it right out of existence.

Still twenty billion human brains. Twenty *billion*.

I don't know how to feel about that. This is no mere alien.

But I'm not quite ready to believe in gods.

I round the corner and run smack into Dix, standing like a golem in the middle of my living room. I jump about a meter straight up.

"*What the hell are you doing here?*"

He seems surprised by my reaction. "Wanted to—talk," he says after a moment.

"You *never* come into someone's home uninvited!"

He retreats a step, stammers: "Wanted, wanted—"

"To talk. And you do that in *public*. On the bridge, or in the commons, or—for that matter, you could just *comm* me."

He hesitates. "Said you—*wanted* face to face. You said, *cultural tradition*."

I did, at that. But not *here*. This is *my* place, these are my *private quarters*. The lack of locks on these doors is a safety protocol, not an invitation to walk into my home and *lie in wait*, and stand there like part of the fucking *furniture*…

"Why are you even *up*?" I snarl. "We're not even supposed to come online for another two months."

"Asked Chimp to get me up when you did."

That fucking machine.

"Why are *you* up?" he asks, not leaving.

I sigh, defeated, and fall into a convenient pseudopod. "I just wanted to go over the preliminary data." The implicit *alone* should be obvious.

"Anything?"

Evidently it isn't. I decide to play along for a while. "Looks like we're talking to an, an island. Almost six thousand klicks across. That's the thinking part, anyway. The surrounding membrane's pretty much empty. I mean, it's all *alive*. It all photosynthesizes, or something like that. It eats, I guess. Not sure what."

"Molecular cloud," Dix says. "Organic compounds everywhere. Plus it's concentrating stuff inside the envelope."

I shrug. "Point is, there's a size limit for the brain but it's *huge*, it's…"

"Unlikely," he murmurs, almost to himself.

I turn to look at him; the pseudopod reshapes itself around me. "What do you mean?"

"Island's twenty-eight million square kilometers? Whole sphere's seven quintillion. Island just happens to be between us and 428, that's—one in fifty-billion odds."

"Go on."

He can't. "Uh, just… just *unlikely*."

I close my eyes. "How can you be smart enough to run those numbers in your head without missing a beat, and stupid enough to miss the obvious conclusion?"

That panicked, slaughterhouse look again. "Don't—I'm not—"

"It *is* unlikely. It's *astronomically* unlikely that we just happen to be aiming at the one intelligent spot on a sphere one-and-a-half AUs across. Which means…"

He says nothing. The perplexity in his face mocks me. I want to punch it.

But finally, the lights flicker on: "There's, uh, more than one island? Oh! A *lot* of islands!"

This creature is part of the crew. My life will almost certainly depend on him some day. That is a very scary thought.

I try to set it aside for the moment. "There's probably a whole population of the things, sprinkled though the membrane like, like cysts I guess. The chimp doesn't know how many, but we're only picking up this one so far so they might be pretty sparse."

There's a different kind of frown on his face now. "Why *Chimp*?"

"What do you mean?"

"Why call him Chimp?"

"We call it *the* chimp." Because the first step to humanizing something is to give it a name.

"Looked it up. Short for *chimpanzee*. Stupid animal."

"Actually, I think chimps were supposed to be pretty smart," I remember.

"Not like us. Couldn't even *talk*. Chimp can talk. *Way* smarter than those things. That name—it's an insult."

"What do you care?"

He just looks at me.

I spread my hands. "Okay, it's not a chimp. We just call it that because it's got roughly the same synapse count."

"So gave him a small brain, then complain that he's stupid all the time."

My patience is just about drained. "Do you have a point or are you just blowing CO_2 in—"

"Why not make him smarter?"

"Because you can never predict the behavior of a system more complex than you. And if you want a project to stay on track after you're gone, you don't hand the reins to anything that's guaranteed to develop its own agenda." Sweet smoking Jesus, you'd think *someone* would have told him about Ashby's Law.

"So they lobotomized him," Dix says after a moment.

"No. They didn't *turn* it stupid, they *built* it stupid."

"Maybe smarter than you think. You're so much smarter, got *your* agenda, how come *he's* still in control?"

"Don't flatter yourself," I say.

"What?"

I let a grim smile peek through. "You're only following orders from a bunch of other systems *way* more complex than you are." You've got to hand it to them, too; dead for stellar lifetimes and those damn project admins are *still* pulling the strings.

"I don't—*I'm* following?—"

"I'm sorry, dear." I smile sweetly at my idiot offspring. "I wasn't talking to you. I was talking to the thing that's making all those sounds come out of your mouth."

Dix turns whiter than my panties.

I drop all pretense. "What were you thinking, chimp? That you could send this sock-puppet to invade my home and I wouldn't notice?"

"Not—I'm not—it's *me*," Dix stammers. "*Me* talking."

"It's *coaching* you. Do you even know what 'lobotomised' *means*?" I shake my head, disgusted. "You think I've forgotten how the interface works just because we all burned ours out?" A caricature of surprise begins to form on his face. "Oh, don't even fucking *try*. You've been up for other builds, there's no way you couldn't have known. And you know we shut down our domestic links too. And there's nothing your lord and master can do about that because it *needs* us, and so we have reached what you might call an *accommodation*."

I am not shouting. My tone is icy, but my voice is dead level. And yet Dix almost *cringes* before me.

There is an opportunity here, I realize.

I thaw my voice a little. I speak gently: "You can do that too, you know. Burn out your link. I'll even let you come back here afterwards, if you still want to. Just to—talk. But not with that thing in your head."

There is panic in his face, and against all expectation it almost breaks my heart. "*Can't*," he pleads. "How I *learn* things, how I *train*. The *mission*…"

I honestly don't know which of them is speaking, so I answer them both: "There is more than one way to carry out the mission. We have more than enough time to try them all. Dix is welcome to come back when he's alone."

They take a step towards me. Another. One hand, twitching, rises from their side as if to reach out, and there's something on that lopsided face that I can't quite recognize.

"But I'm your *son*," they say.

I don't even dignify it with a denial.

"Get out of my home."

A human periscope. The Trojan Dix. That's a new one.

The chimp's never tried such overt infiltration while we were up and about before. Usually it waits until we're all undead before invading our territories. I imagine custom-made drones never seen by human eyes, cobbled together during the long dark eons between builds; I see them sniffing through drawers and peeking behind mirrors, strafing the bulkheads with X-rays and ultrasound, patiently searching *Eriophora*'s catacombs millimeter by endless millimeter for whatever secret messages we might be sending each other down through time.

There's no proof to speak of. We've left tripwires and telltales to alert us to intrusion after the fact, but there's never been any evidence they've been disturbed. Means nothing, of course. The chimp may be stupid but it's also cunning, and a million years is more than enough time to iterate through every possibility using simpleminded brute force. Document every dust mote; commit your unspeakable acts; afterwards, put everything back the way it was.

We're too smart to risk talking across the eons. No encrypted strategies, no long-distance love letters, no chatty postcards showing ancient vistas long lost in the red shift. We keep all that in our heads, where the enemy will never find it. The unspoken rule is that we do not speak, unless it is face to face.

Endless idiotic games. Sometimes I almost forget what we're squabbling over. It seems so trivial now, with an immortal in my sights.

Maybe that means nothing to you. Immortality must be ancient news from whatever peaks you've ascended by now. But I can't even imagine it, although I've outlived worlds. All I have are moments: two or three hundred years, to ration across the lifespan of a universe. I could bear witness to any point in time, or any hundred-thousand if I slice my life thinly enough—but I will never see *everything*. I will never see even a fraction.

My life will end. I have to *choose*.

When you come to fully appreciate the deal you've made—ten or fifteen builds out, when the trade-off leaves the realm of mere *knowledge* and sinks deep as cancer into your bones—you become a miser. You can't help it. You ration out your waking moments to the barest minimum: just enough to manage the build, to plan your latest countermove against the chimp, just enough (if you haven't yet moved beyond the need for Human contact) for sex and snuggles and a bit of warm mammalian comfort against the endless dark. And then you hurry back to the crypt, to hoard the remains of a human lifespan against the unwinding of the cosmos.

There's been time for education. Time for a hundred postgraduate degrees, thanks to the best caveman learning tech. I've never bothered. Why burn down my tiny candle for a litany of mere fact, fritter away my precious, endless, finite life? Only a fool would trade book-learning for a ringside view of the Cassiopeia Remnant, even if you *do* need false-color enhancement to see the fucking thing.

Now, though. Now, I want to *know*. This creature crying out across the gulf, massive as a moon, wide as a solar system, tenuous and fragile as an insect's wing: I'd gladly cash in some of my life to learn its secrets. How does it work? How can it even *live* here at the edge of absolute zero, much less think? What vast, unfathomable intellect must it possess to see us coming from over half a lightyear away, to deduce the nature of our eyes and our instruments, to send a signal we can even *detect*, much less understand?

And what happens when we punch through it at a fifth the speed of light?

I call up the latest findings on my way to bed, and the answer hasn't changed: not much. The damn thing's already full of holes. Comets, asteroids, the usual protoplanetary junk careens through this system as it does through every other. Infra picks up diffuse pockets of slow outgassing here and there around the perimeter, where the soft vaporous vacuum of the interior bleeds into the harder stuff outside. Even if we were going to tear through the dead center of the thinking part, I can't imagine this vast creature feeling so much as a pinprick. At the speed we're going we'd be through and gone far too fast to overcome even the feeble inertia of a millimeter membrane.

And yet. *Stop. Stop. Stop.*

It's not us, of course. It's what we're building. The birth of a gate is a violent, painful thing, a spacetime rape that puts out almost as much gamma and X as a microquasar. Any meat within the white zone turns to ash in an instant, shielded or not. It's why *we* never slow down to take pictures.

One of the reasons, anyway.

We can't stop, of course. Even changing course isn't an option except by the barest increments. *Eri* soars like an eagle between the stars but she steers like a pig on the short haul; tweak our heading by even a tenth of a degree and you've got some serious damage at twenty percent lightspeed. Half a degree would tear us apart: the ship might torque onto the new heading but the collapsed mass in her belly would keep right on going, rip through all this surrounding superstructure without even feeling it.

Even tame singularities get set in their ways. They do not take well to change.

We resurrect again, and the Island has changed its tune.

It gave up asking us to *stop stop stop* the moment our laser hit its leading edge. Now it's saying something else entirely: dark hyphens flow across its skin, arrows of pigment converging towards some offstage focus like spokes pointing towards the hub of a wheel. The bullseye itself is offstage and implicit, far removed from 428's bright backdrop, but it's easy enough to extrapolate to the point of convergence six lightsecs to starboard. There's something else, too: a shadow, roughly circular, moving along one of the spokes like a bead running along a string. It too migrates to starboard, falls off the edge of the Island's makeshift display, is endlessly reborn at the same initial coordinates to repeat its journey.

Those coordinates: exactly where our current trajectory will punch through the membrane in another four months. A squinting God would be able to see the gnats and girders of ongoing construction on the other side, the great piecemeal torus of the Hawking Hoop already taking shape.

The message is so obvious that even Dix sees it. "Wants us to move the gate…" and there is something like confusion in his voice. "But how's it know we're *building* one?"

"The vons punctured it en route," the chimp points out. "It could have sensed that. It has photopigments. It can probably see."

"Probably sees better than we do," I say. Even something as simple as a pin-hole camera gets hi-res fast if you stipple a bunch of them across thirty million square kilometers.

But Dix scrunches his face, unconvinced. "So sees a bunch of vons bumping around. Loose parts—not that much even *assembled* yet. How's it know we're building something *hot*?"

Because it is very, very, smart, you stupid child. Is it so hard to believe that this, this—*organism* seems far too limiting a word—can just *imagine* how those half-built pieces fit together, glance at our sticks and stones and see exactly where this is going?

"Maybe's not the first gate it's seen," Dix suggests. "Think there's maybe another gate out here?"

I shake my head. "We'd have seen the lensing artefacts by now."

"You ever run into anyone before?"

"No." We have always been alone, through all these epochs. We have only ever run *away*.

And then always from our own children.

I crunch some numbers. "Hundred eighty two days to insemination. If we move now we've only got to tweak our bearing by a few mikes to redirect to the new coordinates. Well within the green. Angles get dicey the longer we wait, of course."

"We can't do that," the chimp says. "We would miss the gate by two million kilometers."

"Move the gate. Move the whole damn site. Move the refineries, move the factories, move the damn rocks. A couple hundred meters a second would be more than fast enough if we send the order now. We don't even have to suspend construction, we can keep building on the fly."

"Every one of those vectors widens the nested confidence limits of the build. It would increase the risk of error beyond allowable margins, for no payoff."

"And what about the fact that there's an intelligent being in our path?"

"I'm already allowing for the potential presence of intelligent alien life."

"Okay, first off, there's nothing *potential* about it. It's *right fucking there*. And on our current heading we run the damn thing over."

"We're staying clear of all planetary bodies in Goldilocks orbits. We've seen no local evidence of spacefaring technology. The current location of the build meets all conservation criteria."

"That's because the people who drew up your criteria *never anticipated a live Dyson sphere!*" But I'm wasting my breath, and I know it. The chimp can run its equations a million times but if there's nowhere to put the variable, what can it do?

There was a time, back before things turned ugly, when we had clearance to reprogram those parameters. Before we discovered that one of the things the admins *had* anticipated was mutiny.

I try another tack. "Consider the threat potential."

"There's no evidence of any."

"Look at the synapse estimate! That thing's got orders of mag more processing power than the whole civilization that sent us out here. You think something can be that smart, live that long, without learning how to defend itself? We're assuming it's *asking* us to move the gate. What if that's not a *request*? What if it's just giving us the chance to back off before it takes matters into its own hands?"

"Doesn't *have* hands," Dix says from the other side of the tank, and he's not even being flippant. He's just being so stupid I want to bash his face in.

I try to keep my voice level. "Maybe it doesn't *need* any."

"What could it do, *blink* us to death? No weapons. Doesn't even control the whole membrane. Signal propagation's too slow."

"We *don't know.* That's my *point.* We haven't even tried to find out. We're a goddamn road crew; our onsite presence is a bunch of construction vons press-ganged into scientific research. We can figure out some basic physical parameters but we don't know how this thing thinks, what kind of natural defenses it might have—"

"What do you need to find out?" the chimp asks, the very voice of calm reason.

We can't find out! I want to scream. *We're stuck with what we've got! By the time the onsite vons could build what we need we're already past the point of no return! You stupid fucking machine, we're on track to kill a being smarter than all of human history and you can't even be bothered to move our highway to the vacant lot next door?*

But of course if I say that, the Island's chances of survival go from low to zero. So I grasp at the only straw that remains: maybe the data we've got in hand is enough. If acquisition is off the table, maybe analysis will do.

"I need time," I say.

"Of course," the chimp tells me. "Take all the time you need."

The chimp is not content to kill this creature. The chimp has to spit on it as well.

Under the pretense of assisting in my research it tries to *deconstruct* the island, break it apart and force it to conform to grubby earthbound precedents. It tells me about earthly bacteria that thrived at 1.5 million rads and laughed at hard vacuum. It shows me pictures of unkillable little tardigrades that could curl up and snooze on the edge of absolute zero, felt equally at home in deep ocean trenches and deeper space. Given time, opportunity, a boot off the planet, who knows how far those cute little invertebrates might have gone? Might they have survived the very death of the homeworld, clung together, grown somehow colonial?

What utter bullshit.

I learn what I can. I study the alchemy by which photosynthesis transforms light and gas and electrons into living tissue. I learn the physics of the solar wind that blows the bubble taut, calculate lower metabolic limits for a life-form that filters organics from the ether. I marvel at the speed of this creature's thoughts: almost as fast as *Eri* flies, orders of mag faster than any mammalian nerve impulse. Some kind of organic superconductor perhaps, something that passes chilled electrons almost resistance-free out here in the freezing void.

I acquaint myself with phenotypic plasticity and sloppy fitness, that fortuitous evolutionary soft-focus that lets species exist in alien environments and express novel traits they never needed at home. Perhaps this is how a lifeform with no natural enemies could acquire teeth and claws and the willingness to use them. The Island's life hinges on its ability to kill us; I have to find *something* that makes it a threat.

But all I uncover is a growing suspicion that I am doomed to fail—for violence, I begin to see, is a *planetary* phenomenon.

Planets are the abusive parents of evolution. Their very surfaces promote warfare, concentrate resources into dense defensible patches that can be fought over. Gravity forces you to squander energy on vascular systems and skeletal support, stand endless watch against an endless sadistic campaign to squash you flat. Take one wrong step, off a perch too high, and all your pricey architecture shatters in an instant. And even if you beat those odds, cobble together some lumbering armored chassis to withstand the slow crawl onto land—how long before the world draws in some asteroid or comet to crash down from the heavens and reset your clock to zero? Is it any wonder we grew up believing life was a struggle, that zero-sum was God's own law and the future belonged to those who crushed the competition?

The rules are so different out here. Most of space is *tranquil*: no diel or seasonal cycles, no ice ages or global tropics, no wild pendulum swings between hot and cold, calm and tempestuous. Life's precursors abound: on comets, clinging to asteroids, suffusing nebulae a hundred lightyears across. Molecular clouds glow with organic chemistry and life-giving radiation. Their vast dusty wings grow warm with infrared, filter out the hard stuff, give rise to stellar nurseries that only some stunted refugee from the bottom of a gravity well could ever call *lethal*.

Darwin's an abstraction here, an irrelevant curiosity. This Island puts the lie to everything we were ever told about the machinery of life. Sun-powered, perfectly adapted, immortal, it won no struggle for survival: where are the predators, the competitors, the parasites? All of life around 428 is one vast continuum, one grand act of symbiosis. Nature here is not red in tooth and claw. Nature, out here, is the helping hand.

Lacking the capacity for violence, the Island has outlasted worlds. Unencumbered by technology, it has out-thought civilizations. It is intelligent beyond our measure, and—

—and it is *benign*. It must be. I grow more certain of that with each passing hour. How can it even *conceive* of an enemy?

I think of the things I called it, before I knew better. *Meat balloon. Cyst.* Looking back, those words verge on blasphemy. I will not use them again.

Besides, there's another word that would fit better, if the chimp has its way: Roadkill. And the longer I look, the more I fear that that hateful machine is right.

If the Island can defend itself, I sure as shit can't see how.

"*Eriophora*'s impossible, you know. Violates the laws of physics."

We're in one of the social alcoves off the ventral notochord, taking a break from the library. I have decided to start again from first principles. Dix eyes me with an understandable mix of confusion and mistrust; my claim is almost too stupid to deny.

"It's true," I assure him. "Takes way too much energy to accelerate a ship with *Eri*'s mass, especially at relativistic speeds. You'd need the energy output of a whole sun. People figured if we made it to the stars at all, we'd have to do it in ships maybe the size of your thumb. Crew them with virtual personalities downloaded onto chips."

That's too nonsensical even for Dix. "*Wrong.* Don't have mass, can't fall towards anything. *Eri* wouldn't even *work* if it was that small."

"But suppose you can't displace any of that mass. No wormholes, no Higgs conduits, nothing to throw your gravitational field in the direction of travel. Your center of mass just *sits* there in, well, the center of your mass."

A spastic Dixian head-shake. "*Do* have those things!"

"Sure we do. But for the longest time, we didn't *know* it."

His foot taps an agitated tattoo on the deck.

"It's the history of the species," I explain. "We think we've worked everything out, we think we've solved all the mysteries and then someone finds some niggling little data point that doesn't fit the paradigm. Every time we try to paper over the crack it gets bigger, and before you know it our whole worldview unravels. It's happened time and again. One day mass is a constraint; the next it's a requirement. The things we think we know—they *change*, Dix. And we have to change with them."

"But—"

"The chimp can't change. The rules it's following are ten billion years old and it's got no fucking imagination and really that's not anyone's fault, that's just people who didn't know how else to keep the mission stable across deep time. They wanted to keep us on-track so they built something that couldn't go off it; but they also knew that things *change*, and that's why *we're* out here, Dix. To deal with things the chimp can't."

"The alien," Dix says.

"The alien."

"Chimp deals with it just fine."

"How? By killing it?"

"Not our fault it's in the way. It's no threat—"

"I don't care whether it's a *threat* or not! It's alive, and it's intelligent, and killing it just to expand some alien empire—"

"*Human* empire. *Our* empire." Suddenly Dix's hands have stopped twitching. Suddenly he stands still as stone.

I snort. "What do you know about humans?"

"*Am* one."

"You're a fucking trilobite. You ever see what comes *out* of those gates once they're online?"

"Mostly nothing." He pauses, thinking back. "Couple of—ships once, maybe."

"Well, I've seen a lot more than that, and believe me, if those things were *ever* human it was a passing phase."

"But—"

"Dix—" I take a deep breath, try to get back on message. "Look, it's not your fault. You've been getting all your info from a moron stuck on a rail. But we're not doing this for Humanity, we're not doing it for Earth. Earth is *gone*, don't you understand that? The sun scorched it black a billion years after we left. Whatever we're working for, it—it won't even *talk* to us."

"Yeah? Then why do this? Why not just, just *quit*?"

He really doesn't know.

"We tried," I say.

"And?"

"And your *chimp* shut off our life support."

For once, he has nothing to say.

"It's a *machine*, Dix. Why can't you get that? It's *programmed*. It can't change."

"*We're* machines, just built from different things. *We* change."

"Yeah? Last time I checked, you were sucking so hard on that thing's tit you couldn't even kill your cortical link."

"How I *learn*. No *reason* to change."

"How about acting like a damn *human* once in a while? How about developing a little rapport with the folks who might have to save your miserable life next time you go EVA? That enough of a *reason* for you? Because I don't mind telling you, right now I don't trust you as far as I could throw the tac tank. I don't even know for sure who I'm talking to right now."

"*Not my fault*." For the first time I see something outside the usual gamut of fear, confusion, and simpleminded computation playing across his face. "That's *you*, that's *all* of you. You talk—*sideways. Think* sideways. You all do, and it *hurts*." Something hardens in his face. "Didn't even need you online for this," he growls. "Didn't *want* you. Could have managed the whole build myself, *told* Chimp I could do it—"

"But the chimp thought you should wake me up anyway, and you always roll over for the chimp, don't you? Because the chimp always knows best, the chimp's your *boss*, the chimp's your fucking *god*. Which is why I have to get out of bed to nursemaid some idiot savant who can't even answer a hail without being led by the nose." Something clicks in the back of my mind but I'm on a roll. "You want a *real* role model? You want something to look up to? Forget the chimp. Forget the mission. Look out the forward scope, why don't you? Look at what your precious chimp wants to run over because it happens to be in the way. That thing is better than any of us. It's smarter, it's peaceful, it doesn't wish us any harm at—"

"How can you know that? Can't know that!"

"No, *you* can't know that, because you're fucking *stunted*. Any normal caveman would see it in a second, but *you*—"

"That's crazy," Dix hisses at me. "*You're* crazy. You're *bad*."

"*I'm* bad!" Some distant part of me hears the giddy squeak in my voice, the borderline hysteria.

"For the mission." Dix turns his back and stalks away.

My hands are hurting. I look down, surprised: my fists are clenched so tightly that my nails cut into the flesh of my palms. It takes a real effort to open them again.

I almost remember how this feels. I used to feel this way all the time. Way back when everything *mattered*; before passion faded to ritual, before rage cooled to disdain. Before Sunday Ahzmundin, eternity's warrior, settled for heaping insults on stunted children.

We were incandescent back then. Parts of this ship are still scorched and un-inhabitable, even now. I remember this feeling.

This is how it feels to be awake.

I am awake, and I am alone, and I am sick of being outnumbered by morons. There are rules and there are risks and you don't wake the dead on a whim, but fuck it. I'm calling reinforcements.

Dix has got to have other parents, a father at least, he didn't get that Y chromo from me. I swallow my own disquiet and check the manifest; bring up the gene sequences; cross-reference.

Huh. Only one other parent: Kai. I wonder if that's just coincidence, or if the chimp drew too many conclusions from our torrid little fuckfest back in the Cyg Rift. Doesn't matter. He's as much yours as mine, Kai, time to step up to the plate, time to—

Oh shit. Oh no. Please no.

(There are rules. And there are risks.)

Three builds back, it says. Kai and Connie. Both of them. One airlock jammed, the next too far away along *Eri*'s hull, a hail-Mary emergency crawl between. They made it back inside but not before the blue-shifted background cooked them in their suits. They kept breathing for hours afterwards, talked and moved and cried as if they were still alive, while their insides broke down and bled out.

There were two others awake that shift, two others left to clean up the mess. Ishmael, and—

"Um, you said—"

"*You fucker!*" I leap up and hit my son hard in the face, ten seconds' heartbreak with ten million years' denial raging behind it. I feel teeth give way behind his lips. He goes over backwards, eyes wide as telescopes, the blood already bloom-ing on his mouth.

"*Said* I could come back—!" he squeals, scrambling backwards along the deck.

"He was your fucking *father*! You *knew*, you were *there*! He died right in *front* of you and you didn't even *tell* me!"

"I—I—"

"Why didn't you tell me, you asshole? The chimp told you to lie, is that it? Did you—"

"*Thought you knew*!" he cries, "Why *wouldn't* you know?"

My rage vanishes like air through a breach. I sag back into the 'pod, face in hands.

"Right there in the log," he whimpers. "All along. Nobody hid it. How could you not know?"

"I did," I admit dully. "Or I—I mean…"

I mean I *didn't* know, but it's not a surprise, not really, not down deep. You just—stop looking, after a while.

There are *rules*.

"Never even *asked*," my son says softly. "How they were doing."

I raise my eyes. Dix regards me wide-eyed from across the room, backed up against the wall, too scared to risk bolting past me to the door. "What are you doing here?" I ask tiredly.

His voice catches. He has to try twice: "You said I could come back. If I burned out my link…"

"You burned out your link."

He gulps and nods. He wipes blood with the back of his hand.

"What did the chimp say about that?"

"He said—*it* said it was okay," Dix says, in such a transparent attempt to suck up that I actually believe, in that instant, that he might really be on his own.

"So you asked its permission." He begins to nod, but I can see the tell in his face: "Don't bullshit me, Dix."

"He—actually suggested it."

"I see."

"So we could talk," Dix adds.

"What do you want to talk about?"

He looks at the floor and shrugs.

I stand and walk towards him. He tenses but I shake my head, spread my hands. "It's okay. It's okay." I lean back against the wall and slide down until I'm beside him on the deck.

We just sit there for a while.

"It's been so long," I say at last.

He looks at me, uncomprehending. What does *long* even mean, out here?

I try again. "They say there's no such thing as altruism, you know?"

His eyes blank for an instant, and grow panicky, and I know that he's just tried to ping his link for a definition and come up blank. So we *are* alone. "Altruism," I explain. "Unselfishness. Doing something that costs you but helps someone else." He seems to get it. "They say every selfless act ultimately comes down to manipulation or kin-selection or reciprocity or something, but they're wrong. I could—"

I close my eyes. This is harder than I expected.

"I could have been happy just *knowing* that Kai was okay, that Connie was happy. Even if it didn't benefit me one whit, even if it *cost* me, even if there was no chance I'd ever see either of them again. Almost any price would be worth it, just to know they were okay.

"Just to *believe* they were…"

So you haven't seen her for the past five builds. So he hasn't drawn your shift since Sagittarius. They're just sleeping. Maybe next time.

"So you don't check," Dix says slowly. Blood bubbles on his lower lip; he doesn't seem to notice.

"We don't check." Only I did, and now they're gone. They're both gone. Except for those little cannibalized nucleotides the chimp recycled into this defective and maladapted son of mine. We're the only warm-blooded creatures for a thousand lightyears, and I am so very lonely.

"I'm sorry," I whisper, and lean forward, and lick the gore from his bruised and bloody lips.

Back on Earth—back when there *was* an Earth—there were these little animals called cats. I had one for a while. Sometimes I'd watch him sleep for hours: paws and whiskers and ears all twitching madly as he chased imaginary prey across whatever landscapes his sleeping brain conjured up.

My son looks like that when the chimp worms its way into his dreams.

It's almost too literal for metaphor: the cable runs into his head like some kind of parasite, feeding through old-fashioned fiberop now that the wireless option's been burned away. Or *force*-feeding, I suppose; the poison flows into Dix's head, not out of it.

I shouldn't be here. Didn't I just throw a tantrum over the violation of my own privacy? (Just. Twelve lightdays ago. Everything's relative.) And yet I can see no privacy here for Dix to lose: no decorations on the walls, no artwork or hobbies, no wraparound console. The sex toys ubiquitous in every suite sit unused on their shelves; I'd have assumed he was on antilibinals if recent experience hadn't proven otherwise.

What am I doing? Is this some kind of perverted mothering instinct, some vestigial expression of a Pleistocene maternal subroutine? Am I that much of a robot, has my brain stem sent me here to guard my child?

To guard my *mate*?

Lover or larva, it hardly matters: his quarters are an empty shell, there's nothing of Dix in here. That's just his abandoned body lying there in the pseudopod, fingers twitching, eyes flickering beneath closed lids in vicarious response to wherever his mind has gone.

They don't know I'm here. The chimp doesn't know because we burned out its prying eyes a billion years ago, and my son doesn't know I'm here because—well, because for him, right now, there *is* no here.

What am I supposed to make of you, Dix? None of this makes sense. Even your body language looks like you grew it in a vat—but I'm far from the first human being you've seen. You grew up in good company, with people I *know*, people I trust. Trusted. How did you end up on the other side? How did they let you slip away?

And why didn't they warn me about you?

Yes, there are rules. There is the threat of enemy surveillance during long dead nights, the threat of—other losses. But this is unprecedented. Surely someone could have left something, some clue buried in a metaphor too subtle for the simpleminded to decode...

I'd give a lot to tap into that pipe, to see what you're seeing now. Can't risk it, of course; I'd give myself away the moment I tried to sample anything except the basic baud, and—

—Wait a second—

That baud rate's way too low. That's not even enough for hi-res graphics, let alone tactile and olfac. You're embedded in a wireframe world at best.

And yet, look at you go. The fingers, the eyes—like a cat, dreaming of mice and apple pies. Like *me*, replaying the long-lost oceans and mountaintops of Earth before I learned that living in the past was just another way of dying in the present. The bit rate says this is barely even a test pattern; the body says you're immersed in a whole other world. How has that machine tricked you into treating such thin gruel as a feast?

Why would it even want to? Data are better grasped when they *can* be grasped, and tasted, and heard; our brains are built for far richer nuance than splines and scatterplots. The driest technical briefings are more sensual than this. Why settle for stick-figures when you can paint in oils and holograms?

Why does anyone simplify anything? To reduce the variable set. To manage the unmanageable.

Kai and Connie. Now *there* were a couple of tangled, unmanageable datasets. Before the accident. Before the scenario *simplified*.

Someone should have warned me about you, Dix.

Maybe someone tried.

And so it comes to pass that my son leaves the nest, encases himself in a beetle carapace and goes walkabout. He is not alone; one of the chimp's teleops accompanies him out on *Eri*'s hull, lest he lose his footing and fall back into the starry past.

Maybe this will never be more than a drill, maybe this scenario—catastrophic control-systems failure, the chimp and its backups offline, all maintenance tasks suddenly thrown onto shoulders of flesh and blood—is a dress rehearsal for a crisis that never happens. But even the unlikeliest scenario approaches certainty over the life of a universe; so we go through the motions. We practice. We hold our breath and dip outside. We're on a tight deadline: even armored, moving at this speed the blueshifted background rad would cook us in hours.

Worlds have lived and died since I last used the pickup in my suite. "Chimp."

"Here as always, Sunday." Smooth, and glib, and friendly. The easy rhythm of the practiced psychopath.

"I know what you're doing."

"I don't understand."

"You think I don't see what's going on? You're building the next release. You're getting too much grief from the old guard so you're starting from scratch with people who don't remember the old days. People you've, you've *simplified*."

The chimp says nothing. The drone's feed shows Dix clambering across a jumbled terrain of basalt and metal matrix composites.

"But you can't raise a human child, not on your own." I know it tried: there's no record of Dix anywhere on the crew manifest until his mid-teens, when he just *showed up* one day and nobody asked about it because nobody *ever*…

"Look what you've made of him. He's great at conditional If/Thens. Can't be beat on number-crunching and Do loops. But he can't *think*. Can't make the simplest intuitive jumps. You're like one of those—" I remember an Earthly myth, from the days when *reading* did not seem like such an obscene waste of lifespan—"one of those wolves, trying to raise a Human child. You can teach him how to move around on hands and knees, you can teach him about pack dynamics, but you can't teach him how to walk on his hind legs or talk or be *human* because you're *too fucking stupid*, Chimp, and you finally realized it. And that's why you threw him at me. You think I can fix him for you."

I take a breath, and a gambit.

"But he's nothing to me. You understand? He's *worse* than nothing, he's a liability. He's a spy, he's a spastic waste of O_2. Give me one reason why I shouldn't just lock him out there until he cooks."

"You're his mother," the chimp says, because the chimp has read all about kin selection and is too stupid for nuance.

"You're an idiot."

"You love him."

"No." An icy lump forms in my chest. My mouth makes words; they come out measured and inflectionless. "I can't love anyone, you brain-dead machine. That's why I'm out here. Do you really think they'd gamble your precious never-ending mission on little glass dolls that needed to bond."

"You love him."

"I can kill him any time I want. And that's exactly what I'll do if you don't move the gate."

"I'd stop you," the chimp says mildly.

"That's easy enough. Just move the gate and we both get what we want. Or you can dig in your heels and try to reconcile your need for a mother's touch with my sworn intention of breaking the little fucker's neck. We've got a long trip ahead of us, chimp. And you might find I'm not quite as easy to cut out of the equation as Kai and Connie."

"You cannot end the mission," it says, almost gently. "You tried that already."

"This isn't about ending the mission. This is only about slowing it down a little. Your optimal scenario's off the table. The only way that gate's going to get finished now is by saving the Island, or killing your prototype. Your call."

The cost-benefit's pretty simple. The chimp could solve it in an instant. But still it says nothing. The silence stretches. It's looking for some other option, I bet. It's trying to find a workaround. It's questioning the very premises of the scenario, trying to decide if I mean what I'm saying, if all its book-learning about mother love could really be so far off-base. Maybe it's plumbing historical intrafamilial murder rates, looking for a loophole. And there may be one, for all I know. But the chimp isn't me, it's a simpler system trying to figure out a smarter one, and that gives me the edge.

"You would owe me," it says at last.

I almost burst out laughing. "*What*?"

"Or I will tell Dixon that you threatened to kill him."

"Go ahead."

"You don't want him to know."

"I don't care whether he knows or not. What, you think he'll try and kill me back? You think I'll lose his *love*?" I linger on the last word, stretch it out to show how ludicrous it is.

"You'll lose his trust. You need to trust each other out here."

"Oh, right. *Trust*. The very fucking foundation of this mission."

The chimp says nothing.

"For the sake of argument," I say after a while, "suppose I go along with it. What would I *owe* you, exactly?"

"A favor," the chimp replies. "To be repaid in future."

My son floats innocently against the stars, his life in balance.

We sleep. The chimp makes grudging corrections to a myriad small trajectories. I set the alarm to wake me every couple of weeks, burn a little more of my candle in case the enemy tries to pull another fast one; but for now it seems to be behaving itself. DHF428 jumps towards us in the stop-motion increments of a life's moments, strung like beads along an infinite string. The factory floor slews to starboard in our sights: refineries, reservoirs, and nanofab plants, swarms of von Neumanns breeding and cannibalizing and recycling each other into shielding and circuitry, tugboats and spare parts. The very finest Cro Magnon technology mutates and metastasizes across the universe like armor-plated cancer.

And hanging like a curtain between *it* and *us* shimmers an iridescent life form, fragile and immortal and unthinkably alien, that reduces everything my species ever accomplished to mud and shit by the simple transcendent fact of its existence. I have never believed in gods, in universal good or absolute evil. I have only ever believed that there is what works, and what doesn't. All the rest is smoke and mirrors, trickery to manipulate grunts like me.

But I believe in the Island, because I don't *have* to. It does not need to be taken on faith: it looms ahead of us, its existence an empirical fact. I will never know its mind, I will never know the details of its origin and evolution. But I can *see* it: massive, mind boggling, so utterly inhuman that it can't *help* but be better than us, better than anything we could ever become.

I believe in the Island. I've gambled my own son to save its life. I would kill him to avenge its death.

I may yet.

In all these millions of wasted years, I have finally done something worthwhile.

Final approach.

Reticles within reticles line up before me, a mesmerising infinite regress of bullseyes centering on target. Even now, mere minutes from ignition, distance reduces the unborn gate to invisibility. There will be no moment when the naked eye can trap our destination. We thread the needle far too quickly: it will be behind us before we know it.

Or, if our course corrections are off by even a hair—if our trillion-kilometer curve drifts by as much as a thousand meters—we will be dead. Before we know it.

Our instruments report that we are precisely on target. The chimp tells me that we are precisely on target. *Eriophora* falls forward, pulled endlessly through the void by her own magically-displaced mass.

I turn to the drone's-eye view relayed from up ahead. It's a window into history—even now, there's a timelag of several minutes—but past and present race closer to convergence with every corsec. The newly-minted gate looms dark and ominous against the stars, a great gaping mouth built to devour reality itself. The vons, the refineries, the assembly lines: parked to the side in vertical columns, their jobs done, their usefulness outlived, their collateral annihilation imminent. I pity them, for some reason. I always do. I wish we could scoop them up and take them with us, re-enlist them for the next build—but the rules of economics reach everywhere, and they say it's cheaper to use our tools once and throw them away.

A rule that the chimp seems to be taking more to heart than anyone expected.

At least we've spared the Island. I wish we could have stayed awhile. First contact with a truly alien intelligence, and what do we exchange? Traffic signals. What does the Island dwell upon, when not pleading for its life?

I thought of asking. I thought of waking myself when the time-lag dropped from prohibitive to merely inconvenient, of working out some pidgin that could encompass the truths and philosophies of a mind vaster than all humanity. What a childish fantasy. The Island exists too far beyond the grotesque Darwinian processes that shaped my own flesh. There can be no communion here, no meeting of minds. Angels do not speak to ants.

Less than three minutes to ignition. I see light at the end of the tunnel. *Eri's* incidental time machine barely looks into the past any more, I could almost hold my breath across the whole span of seconds that *then* needs to overtake *now*. Still on target, according to all sources.

Tactical beeps at us. "Getting a signal," Dix reports, and yes: in the heart of the Tank, the sun is flickering again. My heart leaps: does the angel speak to us after all? A thankyou, perhaps? A cure for heat death? But—

"It's *ahead* of us," Dix murmurs, as sudden realization catches in my throat.

Two minutes.

"Miscalculated somehow," Dix whispers. "Didn't move the gate far enough."

"We did," I say. We moved it exactly as far as the Island told us to.

"*Still in front of us! Look at the sun!*"

"Look at the *signal*," I tell him.

Because it's nothing like the painstaking traffic signs we've followed over the past three trillion kilometers. It's almost—random, somehow. It's spur-of-the-moment, it's *panicky*. It's the sudden, startled cry of something caught utterly by surprise with mere seconds left to act. And even though I have never seen this pattern of dots and swirls before, I know exactly what it must be saying.

Stop. Stop. Stop. Stop.

We do not stop. There is no force in the universe that can even slow us down. Past equals present; *Eriophora* dives through the center of the gate in a nano-second. The unimaginable mass of her cold black heart snags some distant dimension, drags it screaming to the here and now. The booted portal erupts behind us, blossoms into a great blinding corona, every wavelength lethal to every living thing. Our aft filters clamp down tight.

The scorching wavefront chases us into the darkness as it has a thousand times before. In time, as always, the birth pangs will subside. The wormhole will settle in its collar. And just maybe, we will still be close enough to glimpse some new transcendent monstrosity emerging from that magic doorway.

I wonder if you'll notice the corpse we left behind.

"Maybe we're missing something," Dix says.

"We miss almost everything," I tell him.

DHF428 shifts red behind us. Lensing artifacts wink in our rearview; the gate has stabilized and the wormhole's online, blowing light and space and time in an iridescent bubble from its great metal mouth. We'll keep looking over our shoulders right up until we pass the Rayleigh Limit, far past the point it'll do any good.

So far, though, nothing's come out.

"Maybe our numbers were wrong," he says. "Maybe we made a mistake."

Our numbers were right. An hour doesn't pass when I don't check them again. The Island just had—enemies, I guess. Victims, anyway.

I was right about one thing, though. That fucker was *smart*. To see us coming, to figure out how to talk to us; to use us as a *weapon*, to turn a threat to its very existence into a, a...

I guess *flyswatter* is as good a word as any.

"Maybe there was a war," I mumble. "Maybe it wanted the real estate. Or maybe it was just some—family squabble."

"Maybe didn't *know*," Dix suggests. "Maybe thought those coordinates were empty."

Why would you think that, I wonder. *Why would you even care?* And then it dawns on me: he doesn't, not about the Island, anyway. No more than he ever did. He's not inventing these rosy alternatives for himself.

My son is trying to comfort me.

I don't need to be coddled, though. I was a fool: I let myself believe in life without conflict, in sentience without sin. For a little while I dwelt in a dream world where life was unselfish and unmanipulative, where every living thing did not struggle to exist at the expense of other life. I deified that which I could not understand, when in the end it was all too easily understood.

But I'm better now.

It's over: another build, another benchmark, another irreplaceable slice of life that brings our task no closer to completion. It doesn't matter how successful we are. It doesn't matter how well we do our job. *Mission accomplished* is a meaningless phrase on *Eriophora*, an ironic oxymoron at best. There may one day be failure, but there is no finish line. We go on forever, crawling across the universe like ants, dragging your goddamned superhighway behind us.

I still have so much to learn.

At least my son is here to teach me.

FERRYMAN
MARGO LANAGAN

Margo Lanagan was born in Newcastle, New South Wales, Australia, and has a BA in History from Sydney University. She spent ten years as a freelance book editor and currently makes a living as a technical writer. Lanagan has published junior and teenage fiction novels, including fantasies *WildGame*, *The Tankermen*, and *Walking Through Albert*. She has also written installments in two shared-world fantasy series for junior readers, and has published three acclaimed original story collections: *White Time*, double World Fantasy Award winner *Black Juice*, and *Red Spikes*. Her latest book is a fantasy novel, *Tender Morsels*, also a World Fantasy Award winner, and she is working on another novel, *The Brides of Rollrock Island*. Lanagan lives in Sydney.

"Wrap your pa some lunch up, Sharon," says Ma.

"What, one of these bunnocks? Two?"

"Take him two. And a good fat strip of smoke. And the hard cheese, all that's left. Here's his lemon." She whacks the cork into the bottle with the flat of her hand.

I wrap the heavy bottle thickly, so it won't break if it drops. I put it in the carry-cloth and the bunnocks and other foods on top, in such a way that nothing squashes anything else.

"Here I go."

Ma crosses from her sweeping and kisses my right cheek. "Take that for him and this for you." She kisses my left. "And tell him about those pigeon; that'll give him spirit till this evening."

"I will." I lift the door in the floor.

I used to need light; I used to be frightened. Not any more. Now I step down and my heart bumps along as normal; I close the lid on myself without a flinch.

I start up with "The Ballad of Priest and Lamb". The stairway is good for singing; it has a peculiar echo. Also, Ma likes to hear me as I go. "It brightens my ears, your singing," she says, "and it can't do any harm to those below, can it?"

Down I go. Down and down, down and round, round and round I go, and all is black around me and the invisible stone stairs take my feet down. I sing with more passion the lower I go, and more experimenting, where no one can hear me. And then there begins to be light, and I sing quieter; then I'm right down to humming, so as not to draw attention when I get there.

Out into the smells and the red twilight I go. It's mostly the fire-river that stinks, the fumes wafting over from way off to the right before its flames mingle with the tears that make it navigable. But the others have their own smells, too. Styx-water is sharp and bites inside your nostrils. Lethe-water is sweet as hedge-roses and makes you feel sleepy.

Down the slope I go to the ferry, across the velvety hell-moss badged here and there with flat red liverworts. The dead are lined up in their groups looking dumbly about; once they've had their drink, Pa says, "you can push them around like tired sheep. Separate them out, herd them up as you desire. Pile them into cairns if you want to! Stack them like faggots—they'll stay however you put them. They'll only mutter and move their heads side to side like birds."

The first time I saw them, I turned and ran for the stairs. I was only little then. Pa caught up to me and grabbed me by the back of my pinafore. "What the blazes?" he said.

"They're horrible!" I covered my face and struggled as he carried me back.

"What's horrible about them? Come along and tell me." And he took me right close and made me examine their hairlessness and look into their empty eyes, and touch them, even. Their skin was without print or prickle, slippery as a green river stone. "See?" said Pa. "There's nothing to them, is there?"

"Little girl!" a woman had called from among the dead. "So sweet!"

My father reached into the crowd and pulled her out by her arm. "Did you not drink all your drink, madam?" he said severely.

She made a face. "It tasted foul." Then she turned and beamed upon me. "What lovely hair you have! Ah, youth!"

Which I don't. I have thick, brown, straight hair, chopped off as short as Ma will let me—and sometimes shorter when it really gives me the growls.

My dad had put me down and gone for a cup. He made the woman drink the lot, in spite of her faces and gagging. "Do you want to suffer?" he said. "Do you want to feel everything and scream with pain? There's a lot of fire to walk through, you know, on the way to the Blessed Place."

"I'm suffering now," she said, but vaguely, and by the time she finished the cup I was no longer visible to her—nothing was. She went in among the others and swayed there like a tall, thin plant among plants. And I've never feared them since, the dead. My fear dried up out of me, watching that woman's self go.

Here comes Pa now, striding up the slope away from the line of dead. "How's my miss, this noontide? How's my Scowling Sarah?"

Some say my dad is ugly. I say, his kind of work would turn anyone ugly, all the gloom and doom of it. And anyway, I don't care—my dad is my dad. He can be ugly as a sackful of bumholes and still I'll love him.

Right now his hunger buzzes about him like a cloud of blowflies. "Here." I slip the carry-cloth off my shoulder. "And there's two fat pigeon for supper, in a pie."

"Two fat pigeon in one fat pie? You set a wicked snare, Sharon Armstrong."

"You look buggered." I sit on the moss beside him. "And that's a long queue. Want some help, after?"

"If you would, my angel." *Donk,* says the cork out of the bottle. Pa's face and neck and forearms are all brown wrinkled leather.

He works his way through a bunnock, then the meat, the cheese, the second bun. He's neat and methodical from first bite to last sup of the lemon.

When he's done, he goes off a way and turns his back to pee into the lemon bottle, for you can't leave your earthly wastes down here or they'll sully the waters. He brings it back corked and wrapped and tucks it into the carry-cloth next to a rock on the slope. "Well, then."

I scramble up from the thick dry moss and we set off down the springy slope to the river.

A couple of hours in, I'm getting bored. I've been checking the arrivals, sending off the ones without coin and taking the coin from under those tongues that have it, giving the paid ones their drink and checking there's nothing in their eyes, no hope or thought or anything, and keeping them neat in their groups with my stick and my voice. Pa has rowed hard, across and back, across and back. He's nearly to the end of the queue. Maybe I can go up home now?

But in his hurry Pa has splashed some tears onto the deck. As he steps back to let the next group of the dead file aboard, he slips on that wetness, and disappears over the side, into the woeful river, so quickly he doesn't have time to shout.

"Pa!" I push my way through the slippery dead. "No!"

He comes up spluttering. Most of his hair has washed away.

"Thank God!" I grab his hot, wet wrist. "I thought you were dead and drowned!"

"Oh, I'm dead all right," he says.

I pull him up out of the river. The tears and the fire have eaten his clothes to rags and slicked the hairs to his body. He looks almost like one of *them.* "Oh, Pa! Oh, Pa!"

"Calm yourself, daughter. There's nothing to be done."

"But look at you, Pa! You walk and talk. You're more yourself than any of these are theirs." I'm trying to get his rags decent across his front, over his terrible bald willy.

"I must go upstairs to die properly." He takes his hands from his head and looks at the sloughed-off hairs on them. "Oh Sharon, always remember this! A moment's carelessness is all it takes."

I fling myself at him and sob. He's slimed with dissolving skin, and barely warm, and he has no heartbeat.

He lays his hand on my head and I let go of him. His face, even without hair, is the same ugly, loving face; his eyes are the same eyes. "Come." He leads the way off the punt. "It doesn't do to delay these things."

I follow him, pausing only to pick up the carry-cloth in my shaking arms. "Can you not stay down here, where we can visit you and be with you? You're very like your earthly form. Even with the hair gone—"

"What, you'd have me wander the banks of Cocytus forever?"

"Not forever. Just until—I don't know. Just not now, just not to lose you altogether."

His hand is sticky on my cheek. "No, lovely. I must get myself coined and buried and do the thing properly. You of all people would know that."

"But, Pa!—"

He lays a slimy finger on my lips. "It's my time, Sharon," he says into my spilling eyes. "And I will take my love of you and your mother with me, into all eternity; you know that."

I know it's not true, and so does he. How many dead have we seen, drinking all memory to nowhere? But I wipe away my tears and follow him.

We start up the stairs, and soon it's dark. He isn't breathing; all I can hear is the sound of his feet on the stone steps, which is unbearable, like someone tonguing chewed food in an open mouth.

He must have heard my thoughts. "Sing me something, Scowling Sarah. Sing me that autumn song, with all the wind and the birds in it."

Which I'm glad to do, to cover the dead-feet sounds and to pretend we're not here like this, to push aside my fear of what's to come, to keep my own feet moving from step to step.

We follow the echoes up and up, and when I reach the end of the song, "Beauti-ful," he says. "Let's have that again from the very start."

So I sing it again. I have to break off, though, near to the end. The trapdoor is above us, leaking light around its edges.

"Oh, my pa!" I hold his terrible flesh and cry. "Don't come up! Just stay here on the stair! I will bring you your food and your drink. We can come down and sit with you. We will *have* you, at least—"

"Go on, now." He plucks my arms from his neck, from his waist, from his neck again. "Fetch your mother for me."

"Just, even—" My mind is floating out of my head like smoke. "Even if you could stay for the pigeon! For the pie! Just that little while! I will bring it down to you, on the platter—"

"What's all this noise?" The trapdoor opens. Ma gives a shout of fright seeing Pa, and yes, in the cooler earthly light his face is—well, it is clear that he is dead.

"Forgive me, wife," says his pale, wet mouth. His teeth show through his cheeks, and his eyes are unsteady in his shiny head. "I have gone and killed myself, and it is no one's fault but my own." He has no breath, as I said. The voice, I can hear in this realer air, comes from somewhere else than his lungs, somewhere else, perhaps, than his body completely.

Ma kneels slowly and reaches, slowly, into the top of the stair.

"Charence Armstrong," she weeps at him, her voice soft and unbelieving, "how could you do this?"

"He fell in the Acheron, Ma; he slipped and fell!"

"How could you be so stupid?" she tells him gently, searching the mess for the face she loves. "Come to me."

"As soon as I step up there I am dead," he says. "You must come down to me, sweet wife, and make your farewells."

There's hardly the room for it, but down she comes onto the stairs, her face so angry and intense it frightens me. And then they are like the youngest of lovers in the first fire of love, kissing, kissing, holding each other tight as if they'd crush together into one. She doesn't seem to mind the slime, the baldness of him, the visibility of his bones. The ragged crying all around us in the hole, that is me; these two are silent in their cleaving. I lean and howl against them and at last they take me in, lock me in with them.

Finally we untangle ourselves, three wrecks of persons on the stairs. "Come, then," says my father. "There is nothing for it."

"Ah, my husband!" whispers Ma, stroking his transparent cheeks.

All the workings move under the jellified skin. "Bury me with all the rites," he says. "And use real coin, not token."

"As if she would use token!" I say.

He kisses me, wetly upon all the wet. "I know, little scowler. Go on up, now."

When he follows us out of the hole, it's as if he's rising through a still water-surface. It paints him back onto himself, gives him back his hair and his clothes and his color. For a few flying moments he's alive and bright, returned to us.

But as his heart passes the rim, he stumbles. His face closes. He slumps to one side, and now he is gone, a dead man taken as he climbed from his cellar, a dead man fallen to his cottage floor.

We weep and wail over him a long time.

Then, "Take his head, daughter." Ma climbs back down into the hole. "I will lift his dear body from here."

The day after the burial, he walks into sight around the red hill in company with several other dead.

"Pa!" I start towards him.

He smiles bleakly, spits the obolus into his hand and gives it to me as soon as I reach him. I was going to hug him, but it seems he doesn't want me to.

"That brother of mine, Gilles," he says. "He can't hold his liquor."

"Gilles was just upset that you were gone so young." I fall into step beside him.

He shakes his bald head. "Discourage your mother from him; he has ideas on her. And he's more handsome than I was. But he's feckless; he'll do neither of you any good."

"All right." I look miserably at the coins in my hand. I can't tell which is Pa's, now.

"In a moment it won't matter." He puts his spongy hand on my shoulder. "But for now, I'm counting on you, Sharon. You look after her for me."

I nod and blink.

"Now, fetch us our cups, daughter. These people are thirsty and weary of life."

I bring the little black cups on the tray. "Here, you must drink this," I say to the dead. "So that the fire won't hurt you."

My father, of course, doesn't need to be told. He drinks all the Lethe-water in a single swallow, puts down the cup and smacks his wet chest as he used to after a swig of apple-brandy. Up comes a burp of flowery air, and the spark dies out of his eyes.

I guide all the waiting dead onto the punt. I flick the heavy mooring-rope off the bollard and we slide out into the current, over the pure clear tears-water braided with fine flames. The red sky is cavernous; the cable dips into the flow behind us and lifts out ahead, dripping flame and water. I take up the pole and push it into the riverbed, pushing us along, me and my boatload of shades, me and what's left of my pa. My solid arms work, my lungs grab the hot air, my juicy heart pumps and pumps. I never realized, all the years my father did this, what solitary work it is.

"A WILD AND A WICKED YOUTH"
ELLEN KUSHNER

Ellen Kushner was born in Washington, D.C. and raised in Cleveland, Ohio. She attended Bryn Mawr College and graduated from Barnard College. Her first novel, *Swordspoint: A Melodrama of Manners*, introduced the fantasy world Riverside, to which she has since returned in *The Fall of the Kings* (written with Delia Sherman), *The Privilege of the Sword*, and several short stories, including the one that follows. Her second novel, *Thomas the Rhymer*, won the Mythopoeic Award and the World Fantasy Award. Kushner is also the editor of *Basilisk* and *The Horns of Elfland* (co-edited with Don Keller and Delia Sherman), and has taught writing at the Clarion and Odyssey workshops. Upcoming is an anthology of "Bordertown" stories co-edited with Holly Black. Kushner lives in Manhattan, on Riverside Drive, with her partner, the author and editor Delia Sherman.

"He's dead, mother."

"Who's dead, Richard?"

His mother did not look up from rolling out her pastry. They lived in the country; things died. And her son did not seem particularly upset. But then, he seldom did. She was raising him not to be afraid of anything if she could help it.

"The man in the orchard."

Octavia St. Vier carefully put down her rolling pin, wiped her hands on her apron, and tucked up her skirts. At the door she slipped into her wooden clogs, because it was spring and the ground was still muddy. The boy followed her out to the orchard, where a man lay still as the grave under an apple tree, his hands clutching tight at something on his chest.

"Oh, love, he's not dead."

"He smells dead," said her son.

Octavia chuckled. "He does that. He's dead drunk, is all, and old and probably sick. He's got good boots, but they're all worn out, see? He must have come a long way."

"What's he holding?" Before she could think to stop him, her son reached between the old man's hands to tug at the end of what he clutched in the folds of his messy cloak.

Like a corpse in a comedy, the old man sat suddenly bolt upright, still gripping one end of the long pointed object whose other end was in her son's hands. It was the end of a sword, sheathed in cracked leather. Octavia was not usually a screamer, but she screamed.

"Rarrrrrr," the old man growled furiously. It seemed to be all he could manage at the moment, but his meaning was clear.

"Richard," Octavia said, as carefully as if she were back at her girlhood elocution lessons—though this was not the sort of sentence they had been designed for—"put the man's sword down."

She could tell her son didn't want to. His hand was closed around the pommel, encircled itself by a swirl of metal which no doubt had its own special name as well. It was a beautiful object; its function was clearly to keep anything outside from touching the hand within.

The old man growled again. He tugged on the sword, but he was so weak, and her son's grip held so fast, that it only separated scabbard from blade. Octavia saw hard steel emerge from the leather. "Richard…" She used the Voice of Command that every mother knows. "*Now.*"

Her son dropped the sword abruptly, and just as abruptly scrambled up the nearest tree. He broke off a branch, which was strictly forbidden, and waved it at the sky.

The old man pulled the weapon back into his personal aura of funk, rags, hunger, and age. He coughed, hawked, spat, repeated that, and dragged himself up until his back was to the apple tree's trunk.

"Quick little nipper," he said. "'Sgonna break his neck."

Octavia shielded her eyes to look up at the boy in the tree. "Oh," she said, "he never falls. You get used to it. Would you like some water?"

The old man didn't clean up particularly well, but he did clean up. When he was sober, he cut wood and carried water for their little cottage. He had very strong arms. He did stay sober long enough to spend all of one day and most of the next sanding every inch of his rust-pocked blade—there was quite a lot of it, it was nearly as tall as the boy's shoulder—and then oiling it, over and over. He wouldn't let anyone help. Richard did offer. But the old man said he made him nervous, always wriggling about like that, couldn't he keep still for one god-blasted moment, and get off that table, no not up into the rafters you're enough to give a man palpitations now get outta here if you can't keep still.

"It's my house," Richard said. "You're just charity."

"Am not neither. I'm a servant. That's what it's come to. Fetch and carry for madam your mother, but at least I've got my pride, and what does she want all those books for anyway? And where's your daddy?"

It wasn't like he hadn't heard that one before. "She left him behind," he said. "He couldn't keep up. She likes the books better. And me." Richard lifted a book off the shelf. He was supposed to ask permission first, but she wasn't around to ask. "There's pictures. Animals' insides. Inside-out. See?"

He found a particularly garish one. Last year he'd been scared to look too closely at it, but now that he was big it filled him with horrific delight. He thrust it suddenly up into the old man's face.

But the old man reacted a great deal more strongly than even a very horrible picture should have warranted. As soon as Richard shoved the book at him he jumped backward, knocking over his chair, one arm thrown back, his other arm forward to strike the book from the boy's hand.

Quickly the boy pivoted, drawing his mother's book out of harm's way. He had no desire to have his ass handed to him on a platter, the official punishment for messing up books.

The old man fell back, panting. "You saw that coming," he wheezed. "You devil's whelp."

He lunged at him again. Richard protected the book.

The old man started chasing him around the room, taking swipes at him from different angles, high, low, sideways…. It was scary, but also funny. There was no way the old man was going to touch him, after all. Richard could always see just what he was aiming for, just where his hand would fall—except, of course, that it never could.

Not a screamer, Octavia let out a yell when she walked into the room. "*What in the Seven Hells are you doing with my son?*"

The old man stopped cold. He drew himself up, carefully taking deep breaths of air so he could be steady enough to say clearly, "Madam, I am training him. In the art of the sword. It cannot have escaped your notice that he has an aptitude."

Octavia put down the dead starling that she was carrying. "I'm afraid it has," she said. "But do go on."

Richard practiced in the orchard with a stick. His best friend, Crispin, wanted to practice too, but Crispin's parents had impressed upon him that lords did not fight with steel. It wasn't noble; you hired others to do it for you, like washing dishes or ironing shirts or figuring accounts.

"But it's not steel," Richard explained; "it's wood. It's just a stick, Crispin; come on."

The old man had no interest in teaching Crispin, and anyway it might have gotten back to his father, so Richard just showed his friend everything he learned, and they practiced together. Privately, Richard thought Crispin wasn't very good, but he kept the thought to himself. Crispin had a temper. He was capable of taking umbrage for days at a time, which was dull, but could usually be resolved either in a fistfight or an elaborate ritual apology orchestrated by Crispin.

Richard didn't mind that. Crispin was inventive. It was never the same thing twice and it was never boring—and never all that hard, really. Richard was perfectly capable of crossing the brook on the dead log blindfolded, or of fetching the bird's nest down from under the topmost eave by Crispin's mother's window.

He did get in trouble the time he climbed up the chimney, because chimneys are dirty and his mother had to waste her time washing all his clothes out. But Crispin gave him his best throwing stick to make up for it, so that worked out all right. And Crispin's other ideas were just as good as his vengeful ones. Crispin was the one who figured out how they could get the cakes meant for the visitors on Last Night and make it look like the cat had done it. And Crispin was the one who covered for him the time they borrowed his father's hunting spears to play Kings in the orchard, when they forgot to bring them back in time. They never told on each other, no matter what.

Crispin's father was all right, except for his prejudice against steel. He winked when the boys were caught stealing apples from his orchards, and even let Richard ride the horses that were out to pasture; if he could catch one, he could ride it, that was the deal (as long as it wasn't a brood mare) and Crispin with him.

Crispin's father was Lord Trevelyan, and had a seat on the Council of Lords, but he didn't like the City, and never went there if he could help it. Every Quarter Day, Trevelyan's steward brought Richard's mother the money her family sent from the city to keep her there. A certain amount of it went right back to town, to be spent on books of Natural History the next time Lady Trevelyan went there to shop. Lady Trevelyan was stylish and liked theatre. She went to the city every year. She did not buy the books herself, of course, and probably would have liked to forget all about them, but her husband had instructed that they be seen to, along with everything else the estate required from town.

What mattered was that the money came, and came regularly. Without it, his mother said, they would have to go live in a cave somewhere—and not a nice cave, either. "Why couldn't we just go live with your family?" Richard asked.

"Their house is too small."

"You said it had seventeen rooms."

"Seventeen rooms, and no air to breathe. And no place to cut up bats."

"Mother, when you find out how bats can fly, will you write a book?"

"Maybe. But I think it would be more interesting to learn about how frogs breathe, then, don't you?"

So she always counted the money carefully when it came in, and hid it in her special hiding place, a big book called *Toads and their Discontents*. There were some pictures of Toads, all right, but their Discontents had been hollowed out to make a stash for coins.

Shortly after the latest Quarter Day, the old swordsman disappeared. Octavia St. Vier anxiously counted her stash, but all the coins were still there.

She gave some to him the next time he came and went, though. It had been a beautiful summer, a poet's summer of white roses and green-gold grain, and tinted apples swelling on the bough against a sky so blue it didn't seem quite real. Richard found that he remembered most of the old man's teaching from when he was little, and the old man was so pleased that he showed him more ways to make the pretend steel dance at the end of his arm—*Make it part of your arm, boyo!*—and to dance away from it, to outguess the other blade and make your body less of a target.

Crispin got bored, and then annoyed. "All you ever want to do is play swords anymore!"

"It's good," Richard said, striking at an oak tree with a wooden lathe flexible enough to bear it.

"No, it's not. It's just the same thing, over and over."

"No, it's not." Richard imagined a slightly larger opponent, and shifted his wrist. "Come on, Crispin, I'll show you how to disarm someone in three moves."

"No!" Crispin kicked the oak. He was smart enough not to kick Richard when Richard was armed. "What are you stabbing that tree for?" he taunted. "Are you trying to kill it?"

"Nope." Richard kept drilling.

"You're trying to kill it because you're scared to climb it."

"No, I'm not."

"Prove it."

So he did.

"The black mare's in the field," Crispin told him when he'd hauled himself all the way up to the branch Richard was on, by dint of telling himself it didn't matter.

"The racer?"

"Yah."

"How long?"

"Dunno."

"Can we catch her?"

"We can try. Unless you'd rather play swords against trees. She's pretty fierce."

Richard threw an acorn at Crispin. Crispin ducked, and nearly fell out of the tree.

"Don't do that," he said stiffly, holding on for dear life. "Or I'll never let you near our horses again."

"Let's get down," Richard said. He eased himself down first, leaving Crispin to follow where he couldn't be seen. Crispin got mad if you criticized his climbing, or noticed he needed help. The rule was, he had to ask for it first, even if he took a long time. Otherwise he got mad.

Crispin arrived at the bottom all covered in bark. "Let's go swimming first," he said, so they did that. On the way home, they discovered Crispin's little sister unattended, so they borrowed her to make a pageant wagon of Queen Diane Going to War with the garden wheelbarrow and the one-horned goat, which didn't turn out as well as they'd hoped, although that wasn't their fault; if she'd only kept still and not shrieked so loud, nothing would have happened. Nonetheless, it got them both thrashed, and separated for a week. Richard didn't mind that much, as it gave him more time to practice. All that stretching really did help the ache of the beating go away faster, too.

The old man was going back to the city for the winter, where a body could get warm, he said, and the booze, while of lesser quality, was cheaper, if you knew where to go: "Riverside," he said, and Octavia said, "That's a place of last resort."

"No, lady," he gestured at the cottage; "*this* is."

But when she handed him the money, he said, "What's this for?"

"For teaching my son."

He took it, and went his way, just as the apples were ripening to fall. He came back the next year, and the next, and he stayed a little longer each time. He told them he had a niece in Covington, with four daughters ugly as homemade sin. He told them the Northern mountains were so cold your teeth froze and fell out if you didn't keep your mouth shut. And he told them the city was crazy about a new swordsman, De Maris, who'd perfected a spiraling triple thrust the eye could hardly follow.

"Could you fake it?" Richard asked, and the old man clouted him (and missed). They figured it out together.

Octavia gave him more money when he went. Maybe it was a mistake, because then he didn't come back. The old fellow might have just dropped dead, or been robbed, or he might have spent it all on a tearing binge. It hardly mattered. But she had meant him to buy a sword for Richard with it, and that mattered some.

So she went up to the Trevelyan manor, to see what could be done. Surely, she thought, they had plenty of swords there. Nobles owned swords, even if they didn't duel themselves. There were ritual swordsmen you hired for weddings, and, well, guards and things.

The manor servants knew her, although they didn't like her much. They were all country people, and she was a city girl with a bastard son and some very weird habits. Still, it wasn't their business to keep her from their lord if he wanted to see her. And so she made her best remembered courtesy to Lord Trevelyan, who was at a table in his muniments room doing something he didn't mind being interrupted at. Octavia St. Vier was a very pretty woman, even in a sun-faded gown, her hair bundled up in a turban and smudges on both her elbows.

"You've been so kind," she said. "I won't take much of your time. It's about Richard."

"Oh, dear," said Lord Trevelyan good-humoredly. "Has he corrupted Crispin, or has Crispin corrupted him?" She looked at him inquiringly. "Boys do these things, you know," he went on. "It's nobody's fault; it's just a phase. I'm not concerned, and you shouldn't be, either."

"Crispin doesn't really like the sword," she said.

His tutor had taught him about metaphor, but he realized that wasn't what she meant. He also realized that this poor woman knew nothing about boys, and that he should, as his lady wife often told him, have kept his mouth shut.

"Ah, yes," he said. "The sword."

"Richard loves it, though."

"I hear that he shows promise."

"Really?" She said it a little frostily, as her own mother might have done. "Have people been talking about it?"

"Not at all," he hastened to assure her, although it was not true. People did notice Octavia St. Vier's rather striking boy—and the drunken swordmaster talked in the village where he got his drink, pretty much nonstop. But he just said, "Crispin's not as subtle as he thinks he is."

"Oh." She smiled. She really was a very pretty woman. The St. Viers might be a family of bankers, but they were bankers of good stock and excellent breeding. "Well, would you help me, then?"

"Yes," he said, "of course." It was her eyes; they were the most amazing color. Almost more violet than blue, fringed with heavy dark lashes....

"I'd like a sword, then. For my son. Do you have any old ones you don't need?"

"I can look," he said. He leaned around the table. "I'm so sorry. I don't mean to stare, but you've got a smudge on your elbow. Right there."

"Oh!" she said, when he touched her. His thumb was so large and warm, and, "Oh!" she said again, as she let herself be drawn to him. "I have to tell you, I haven't done this in a very long time."

"Ten years?" he said, and she said, "Fourteen."

"Ah, fourteen, of course. I'm sorry."

"It's all right. Yes, he's just turned thirteen. And may I have the sword?"

"You," he said gallantly, "may have anything you wish."

Richard's mother brought him a sword. It was a gift, she said, from Lord Trevelyan—but he wasn't to thank him for it; she had already done so, and it would only embarrass him.

Richard did not ask permission to take the sword to show Crispin. It was his sword now, and he could do as he liked with it. He had already polished it with sand and oil, which it badly needed. Truth to tell, Lord Trevelyan had had a hard time laying his hands on a disposable dueling sword. There were battle swords in the old armory, each with a family story attached. There were dress swords for formal occasions, but he knew Octavia would not be content with one of those. Nor should she be. The boy deserved better. For the first time, Trevelyan considered the future of his unusual tenants. Perhaps he should pay to have the boy trained properly, send to the city for a serious swordmaster—or even have the boy sent there to learn. Richard St. Vier was already devoted to Crispin. When Crispin came of age, he might have St. Vier as his own personal swordsman, to guard him in the city when he took the family seat in Council (a burden Trevelyan would be only too happy to have lifted from him) to fight his inevitable young man's battles over love and honor there, even to stand guard, wreathed in flowers, someday, at Crispin's wedding. Trevelyan smiled at the thought: a boon companion for his son, a lifelong friend who knew the ways of steel….

Crispin was tying fishing flies. It was his latest passion; one of their tenants was the local expert, and Crispin had taken to haunting his farmhouse with a mix of flattery, threats, and bribes to get him to disclose his secrets one by one.

"Look!" Carefully, Richard brandished his blade, but low to the ground where it couldn't hurt anything. It was not as razor-sharp as a true duelist's would be, but it still had a point, and an edge.

Crispin nodded, but didn't look up. "Steady…" he said around the thread in his mouth, anchored to one finger against his hook. "Wait—" With a needle, he teased at the feather on the hook. "There!" He held up something between an insect and a dead leaf.

"Nice," Richard said.

"So. Let's see." Crispin gently balanced his fly on the table and looked up. "So you finally got a real one. Is it sharp?"

"Not very. Want to practice? I'll tip the point for you, don't worry."

"Not now. I want to fish. It's nearly dusk. The pike will be biting."

"I'll let you use the real sword." It cost Richard something, but he said it. "I'll use the wooden one."

"*No*, I tell you! I've been working all day on my Speckled King. It's now or never. I've got to try it!" Crispin picked up his rod, the fly on its hook reverently cupped in one palm.

"Oh, all right. I'll come with you, then."

Richard slung his heavy sword back in the makeshift hanger at his hip, and followed the lord's son out through the courtyard and down the drive and across the fields to where the river ran sluggish, choked with weeds. The afternoon was perfectly golden. He felt that it was meant for adventure, for challenge, for chasing the sun down wherever it went—not for standing very still and waiting for something small and stupid underwater to be fooled onto the dinner table by a feather and a piece of string. Nevertheless he joined his friend on the riverbank, and watched Crispin expertly cast the line.

It was true that the boys had already corrupted each other, in precisely the way that Crispin's father had meant. It was, for them, just another thing to do with their bodies, like climbing or swimming or running races—and with certain similarities there, as well; they experimented with speed and distance, and competed with each other. Fishing was serious, though. Richard prepared to wait. He wondered if it would distract Crispin, or the fish, if he practiced just a little, and decided not to chance it. Crispin fussed at the pole, and cast the line again.

Gnats hummed on the water. A dragonfly mated with another.

"Tomorrow," Richard began, and Crispin said, "*Shh!* I think I've got one." He raised the tip of his rod, and his line tightened. Richard watched Crispin's face—the fierce concentration as he pulled, released, tightened the line again, and gave a sudden jerk as his opponent lashed the surface of the water. It was a pike, a big one, with a sharp pointed snout, its jaws snapping with the hook. It struggled against the pull of the line, and Crispin struggled with it as it raised white water and then rose into the air—it looked almost as if the fish were trying to wrestle him into its own element, holding him at the end of the nearly invisible line, coming toward him, going away, dancing on the wind. Finally it spun in, a writhing silver streak of a pike that landed on the grass beside him with a desperate thud, enormous and frantic for breath.

"Ha!" Crispin cried, viewing his prize as it gasped out its life—and "Ha!" Richard cried, as he plunged his blade fiercely into its side, where he figured the heart should be.

The fish lay still, then flopped once more and collapsed. Richard withdrew his blade, a little raggedly, and fish guts leaked out its silver sides.

"Why did you do that?" Crispin said quietly.

"It was dying anyway."

"You ruined it."

"It was a noble opponent," Richard said grandly. "I gave it a merciful death."

"You don't give a fish a merciful death." Crispin's voice was tight with rage. "It's not a deer or a hound or something. It's a *fish*."

"I *know* it's a fish, so what does it matter?"

"Look at it!" Crispin's fists were clenched. "It looks completely stupid now." The pike's fierce mouth, lined with teeth, gaped haplessly, the hook still in it, the feathers of the fly like something it had caught and didn't quite know what to do with.

"Well, I'm sorry, then," said Richard. "But you can still eat it. It's still good."

"I don't *want* it!" Crispin shouted. "You've *ruined* it!"

"Well, at least get your fly back out of it. It's a terrific fly. Really."

"No it's not. It was, but you ruined it. You like to ruin everything, don't you?"

Oh, no, Richard thought. He knew where this was going, and that there was pretty much no stopping it. It didn't even occur to him to walk away; that would only prolong things. He had to stay and see it out.

"Go away," Crispin said. "You're not my friend."

"Yes I am. I was your friend this morning. I'm your friend, still, now."

Crispin kicked the fish. A little goo ran out of its mouth. Its eyes were open. It did look pretty stupid.

"You said you were sorry, but you didn't really mean it."

"Yes I did. I am. I'm sorry I ruined your fish. It's a great fish."

"Prove it, then."

Here it comes, thought Richard. He felt a little involuntary shiver. "How?"

He waited. Crispin was thinking.

The longer Crispin thought, the worse things were. It would be something awful. Would he have to eat the fish raw? He wondered if he could.

"Give me your sword," Crispin said.

"No!" That was too much.

"I'll give it back."

"Swear?"

"If you do as I say. *I* don't want it," Crispin said scornfully. "It's just a beat-up piece of junk."

Richard put his hand on the pommel at his hip. "Swear anyway."

Crispin rolled his eyes, but he swore one of their oaths: "May the Seven Gods eat my liver live if I don't give it back to you. After you've apologized."

"All right, then." Richard drew his blade, and held it out.

"Not that way. You must kneel. Kneel to me, and offer it properly."

He knelt in front of Crispin in the grass, the sword balanced across his two hands. It was heavy this way.

"All right," his friend said.

"Is this enough?"

"For now." Crispin was smiling the unpleasant smile that meant he'd thought of something else. Richard wondered what it was. It was worth staying to find out. His arms ached, but not unbearably.

"Are you going to take it, Crispin, or not?"

"Give it to me."

Richard held it out a little further, and Crispin grasped the hilt. The weight leaving him was like a drink of water on a hot day.

"Now stand up."

He stood.

Solemnly, Crispin leveled the sword at his chest. Richard looked down at the tip of the blade against his shirt. This was hard. It took almost everything he had to hold himself in check, not to fight back.

Crispin nodded.

"You have passed the first test," Crispin intoned. He put the sword aside. Richard hoped it wouldn't get too wet on the grass. The sun was getting lower. But it wasn't dark yet.

"And now, the second. Are you ready?" Richard nodded. "Take off my boot."

He knelt by Crispin's leg and pulled his left boot off the way he'd seen the valet pull off Lord Trevelyan's after the hunt. Crispin steadied himself with a hand on Richard's shoulder, but that was all right; he had to: the whole thing wouldn't work if Crispin fell.

"Now my stocking."

Richard eased the wrinkled stocking off his foot. It smelt not disagreeably of leather, wool, and Crispin himself. "What should I do with it?"

"Put it somewhere you can find it again. This won't take long."

Crispin's bare foot was balanced on his thigh, just above his bent knee. Crispin was like an acrobat, poised for flight. Or if there had been a tree above them, he might have been about to hoist his friend up into its branches for the sweetest fruit. He could see all sorts of possibilities, but Richard knew from rich experience that nothing he could imagine was remotely like what Crispin would say. And, indeed, it was not.

"Now, put your tongue between my toes."

"*What?*"

Crispin said nothing, did nothing. The foot was there. Crispin was there. The words had been spoken. They were never taken back.

The foot was there. Richard bent his head to it.

Something in his body tingled. He didn't like it. It was just a stupid foot. It should have nothing to do with the way he was feeling.

He tasted essence of Crispin. Crispin's fingers were in his hair, holding tight. He moved on to the next toe. The feeling grew. He really hated it, and he really didn't. He didn't seem to have a choice, actually. He was feeling it whether he wanted to or not. It felt more dangerous than anything he'd ever done, and he didn't hate that, either. He ran his tongue along another toe, and felt Crispin shudder.

"All right," his friend said. "That's enough." But Richard didn't raise his head. "The offense—The offense is purified. The deed is pardoned." Those were the ritual words. Richard should have stopped, but he didn't.

"The deed is—"

Richard went for another toe.

Crispin let himself fall. His bare foot caught Richard on the side of the mouth, but Richard could tell he hadn't meant it to, and let himself fall, too. They rolled on the ground together, struggling against each other for some sort of relief in a fight they didn't know how to win. They pressed their bodies tight against each other, reaching for each other's skin through their clothes, and finally had the sense to tear them off and give each other the release they'd gotten in the past. It felt different this time, more frightening, more uncontrolled, more essential—and more complete, when they had both done, as though they had made an offering to the world they hadn't meant to.

"The offense is purified," Richard breathed into Crispin's ear.

"The deed is pardoned," Crispin whispered to the grass.

They got up and cleaned themselves off, and put their clothing back together, and went home.

The next day, Richard helped his mother clean the loft out. The day after that, Crispin took him riding on a real saddlehorse. They passed through a field with high hedges, but did not dismount to experiment with each other behind them. That particular experiment was over, now. They never spoke of it again.

The old swordsman came back at the end of summer, and spent the winter with them. He didn't say much, and he didn't drink much, either. He was yellowish and hollow-eyed, skin slack on his face, hands trembling when he didn't watch them.

Richard showed him his new sword. The old man whistled low. "That's a real old relic, that is. A pride of ages past. Wonder where they dug that up?" He hefted it, made a few passes with surprising speed. "Wasn't junk once. Nice balance. Length's all wrong for you, boy— 'smeant for a bigger man. Have to work extra hard now, wontcha?"

He wasn't fun to have around. Some days he never got out of bed, a grubby tangle of blankets and cloaks he huddled in a little too close to the hearth and its ashes. On what must have been his good days, though, he'd heft his own blade, or the fireplace poker, whichever was nearest, and smack at Richard's leg or his sword, if either was within reach; he'd growl something in the back of his throat, and then simply go at him as if Richard were some kind of demon he needed to vanquish. Eventually he'd calm down, and start criticizing, or explaining. That was worth the wait. But it was hard.

"I've gotten bad," Richard complained, the fifth time of being smacked along his ribs with the flat of the man's blade. He was waking up bruised. "I've forgotten everything you taught me."

"No, you've not." The old man cackled. "You've grown, is what it is. Arms and legs in a whole new place each morning. Trying, ennit?"

"Very." Richard risked a pass, and was rewarded with a touch.

"Move the table," Octavia said absently, standing at it exploring a bat's insides. They had actually left it on the other side of the room some days ago, but she wasn't paying attention.

"Well, don't break anything, then." She might have meant a bowl, or her son's arm—or probably both.

Nothing got broken. Richard grew all that winter. He was getting hair in unaccustomed places. His voice was not reliable. It made him all the more eager to master the sword.

"You'll be a beauty," the man would taunt him, trying to break his concentration while they sparred. "Good thing you know how to use this thing, because you'll be fighting them off with it."

That was good. The last thing he wanted was people pestering him. This fall the goose girl had started following him around, never leaving him alone—and when he ignored her, she actually *threw* things at him, so he gave her a thrashing—a light one—but still, to his surprise, his mother had given *him* one when she heard, to see how he liked it. She said it was for his own good, but he knew that she was just good and angry. She told him he must never, ever lift his hand against a woman or a girl, not even if they were being very irritating. Not even if they struck him first. Because son, she said, soon you will be much stronger than they. You could hurt someone badly without even meaning to. So it won't be fair. And besides, soon you'll be in a position to, ah, to put them at risk—But we'll talk about that next year, shall we?

"What if her brother comes after me?" Village boys had bullied him a lot when he was small.

She gave him the same answer now that she'd given then to such good effect:

"Oh, him you can try and kill, if you can."

He didn't see much of Crispin that winter. The snows were unusually deep, and Crispin was at studies of his own. His father had sent to the city for a University man to teach Crispin mathematics and geometry and orthography and things. When he saw his friend, Crispin told Richard that this was unquestionably the worst year of his life so far. And he didn't see why he had to learn all this stuff when he was going to have secretaries and bailiffs to do the important writing and figuring for him—which earned him a clout from his father, who explained that if he didn't know how to do those things for himself, he'd be cheated blind and the whole estate go to wrack and ruin. And no, it wasn't a bit like not studying the sword. Some things were indeed best left to specialists; he wasn't expected to be able to shoe his own mare, either, was he? Next year he was to have Logic, and Rhetoric, and Dancing.

"Stand fast," he told Richard St. Vier. "Don't let them teach you to read, whatever they say. Next time she remembers, just tell her you're too busy or something."

"I'll tell her it's bad for my eyesight."

"Whatever it takes. Trust me, it's the beginning of the end."

Crispin was considering running away if things got much worse. But not to the city; that's where all these horrors came from. Maybe he'd jump a boat upriver, if Richard would come with him.

Richard said he'd consider it.

And so they waited till spring.

The old man was better in the spring. He sat out in the sunshine on a bench next to the rain barrel against the wall, like a pea sprout waiting to unfurl in the sun. He dueled Richard up and down the yard, to the terror of the hens, who wouldn't lay for a week. Octavia complained about the chickens, and the old man got all huffy, and said he would go. She was sorry to hurt his feelings, but she was really just as glad to get her cottage back to herself.

They missed him the next year, though. Octavia felt bad, especially as she was pretty sure he must be dead. He couldn't last forever, and he hadn't looked good, even in spring. However, Richard had uncovered the exciting news that Lord Trevelyan's new valet from the city had studied the sword there, as well.

Richard had given up on Crispin as a dueling partner. Crispin said he had too much to study already, and when they had time to do things together, they had better be something fun. Neither of them had to say that Crispin wasn't any kind of match for Richard anymore (except in drill, which even Richard couldn't consider fun).

In an agony of need, Richard plotted how to approach the new valet. Should he be casual, offhand, and only plead if he had to? Or should he abandon all pretense, and simply beg for a lesson?

In the end, it was Lady Trevelyan who decided the matter. Crispin's mother was back from the city, a month early because of an outbreak of fever there, and bored out of her mind. It was her idea to stage a demonstration bout at the Harvest Feast.

By the time Octavia had heard about it, Richard had already gleefully said yes, and it was too late for her to make a fuss about any son of hers displaying himself like a mountebank for the entertainment of people who had nothing better to do than watch other people poking at each other with hypertrophied table knives. It was just as well, really; she had the awful feeling she might have ended up sounding exactly like her mother.

Still, it would have been nice if Hester Trevelyan could have troubled herself to make a courtesy call to explain to Octavia herself that the swords would be tipped, and there would be no First Blood in this duel, the way there was in the city. A mother's heart, after all. Or didn't Lady Trevelyan think she had one? Octavia had Richard's boots resoled, and made sure he had a nice, clean shirt.

Late on the holiday, Octavia braided her hair on top of her head, fixed it with gold pins, and put on her Festival best—not the dress she'd run away in, which had gone to useful patches long ago, but the one she'd stashed to be married in whenever she and her dashing lover got 'round to it: a glittery and flimsy contraption a decade out of date which still fit her perfectly, and made her look like a storybook queen.

When she made her entrance on the Trevelyan grounds, everyone stared. The country folk standing behind the ribbons marking off the fight space sniggered, because they'd never seen anything like it; but Hester Trevelyan, who had worn something very similar at her own coming out ball, looked hard at Richard St. Vier's mother. Then she scanned the crowd for Crispin, and called him to her.

"Your friend's mother," she said; "go fetch her—*politely*, Crispin—and tell her she must come and sit with us."

Octavia had been dreading this. She did not want to sit and attempt to make conversation with Hester Trevelyan in front of or with Hester Trevelyan's husband. Still, one must be gracious. She followed Crispin and arranged herself decorously in a chair on the other side of Lady Trevelyan, and smiled and nodded at everything that was said to her, but that was about all.

Hester found the woman very strange, and not at all appealing, lacking, as she'd always suspected, any agreeable conversation. But she put herself out to be affable. It had clearly been a while since Richard St. Vier's mother had been in any sort of decent company, and perhaps she was worrying about her son. The woman's eyes kept straying across the yard to where the torches were waiting to be lit around the bonfire, and the Harvest tables all set up.

Usually, Hester explained, her dear friends the Perrys held the swordfight *after* the bonfires had been lit. They also brought dancers down from their Northern estates to perform the traditional horn dance beforehand—and that was thrilling to see. But because once the fires were started (and the Harvest drinking seriously begun, though she didn't actually say that) people got a little wild, they'd thought it best here to begin with the duel while it was still clear daylight. She hoped Mistress St. Vier wasn't anxious. Master Thorne, the swordsman valet, was really as gentle as a lamb. She would see.

Octavia had seen Richard running around with Crispin, eating cakes and apples and throwing the cores across the yard at people. She was glad he wasn't nervous. His shirt couldn't be helped; it had been clean when he left the house.

Hester waved a strip of silk at the men with the horns—they were hunting horns, brought into service for a somewhat cracked but nonetheless thrilling fanfare. Richard and Master Thorne entered from opposite sides of the yard.

Master Thorne moved with a smooth elegance Octavia hadn't seen since she'd left the city. He was arrayed—there was no other word for it—arrayed in green satin, or something that shone like it, his breeches without a wrinkle, his shirt immaculate white. He set his jacket aside, and rolled up his sleeves as meticulously as a master chef decorating a cake. It was a treat to watch, the way they folded neatly into place. She stole a glance at Richard, who was both watching the man intently to see if he knew tricks, and fidgeting with impatience. That particular fidget was well known to her.

Crispin had begged to serve as Richard's aide, but Lady Trevelyan had put her foot down; it wouldn't be seemly for the son of the house, not even at Festival. So it was to a footman that Richard handed his sword while he took off his jacket. His mother watched him hesitate a moment before deciding to leave his sleeves as they were. Then he and Thorne advanced to the middle of the field, saluted each other, and began to circle.

It was only a half-circle, really. Richard lunged and struck, and Thorne fell back. People gasped, or clapped, or both.

"Whoops!" said Thorne. "I must have slipped. Shall we try again?"

"Please do!" Lady Trevelyan commanded. She had planned on her entertainment lasting longer than this.

The duelists saluted, and assumed guard. Richard struck Thorne in the chest again.

"Well done!" cried Thorne. He held up one hand for a pause, and then rolled up a fallen sleeve. "You're very quick, my friend. Shall we continue?"

He did not wait for an answer, just went on guard again, and immediately struck at Richard. Richard didn't even parry, he simply stepped out of the way—or so it seemed from the outside. Thorne thrust, and thrust again. Richard sidestepped, parried, parried again, but did not return his blows.

Octavia recognized the drill from her hen yard. He was running Thorne through his paces. He was reading Thorne's vocabulary of the sword, maybe even learning as he went, but it was nothing but a drill to him.

"Stop!" Lord Trevelyan stood up. The fighters turned to him. "Richard, are you going to fight, or just—just—"

"I'm sorry," Richard replied. He turned to his opponent. "Want me to go a little slower, sir?"

Master Thorne turned red. He glared at the boy, shook out his arms, and breathed deep. He passed one sleeve over his face—and then he laughed.

"Yes," he said; "go a little slower, will you? It's Harvest Feast, and the Champions fight for the honor of the house and the virtue of the land. Let's give the people what they came for, shall we?"

The duel was so slow that even Octavia could follow the moves; for the first time she understood what it was her son could do. It was a textbook lesson—but it thrilled the country folk, who'd never seen real swordplay before.

Richard wasn't quite grown up enough to let Thorne beat him. So when Thorne finally tired of showing Richard and the crowd just about everything he knew, he obligingly opened himself for St. Vier's final blow.

"How long did you study?" Richard asked Thorne later.

"Oh, just long enough to put on a show. I figured I could get work as a house guard if valeting got thin. Lots of city men do that. It's always good to have a second skill to fall back on."

"So do you think I should learn how to valet?" Richard asked with distaste.

"You?" Thorne shook his head. "Not you."

When Richard was sixteen, the old man came back.

He could smell fumes from the cottage before he entered and found him in there, peeling potatoes for his mother at the big chestnut table as though he'd never been away.

"Look at this dagger," the old fellow wheezed. "Worn thin as one of the King's own Forest Leaves. Now I peel with it, do I?"

"Use the paring knife." Richard held it out to him.

The old man flinched. "Put that down on the table," he said. "It's bad luck passing a knife hand to hand. Cuts the friendship. Didn't you know that?"

It hadn't been that kind of flinch.

"Want to spar?" Richard asked.

"Spar? With you? Hell, no. I hurt, boy; everything hurts. Everything hurts, and I can hardly see. Spar with you?"

"Oh, come on." Richard felt himself jiggle with impatience. "I'll nail my feet to the turf. We'll only do standing. You can just check my wristwork."

The old man wiped a rheumy red eye. "Told you, I can hardly see."

"You've been chopping onions. What's for supper?"

"Onions. Stew. How the hell should I know? I'm just the servant here. You're the man, St. Vier. The man of the house, the man of the hour…."

"Cut it out." Well, he'd smelt it before he came in. There was the tell-tale jug, propped against the chimney piece.

Octavia came in with a fistful of thyme. "There you are, Richard. Look who's dropped by for dinner."

"I didn't come for your cooking, lady," the old man said. "I came for the feast."

"What feast?"

"Don't get out much, do you?" He hawked and spat into the fire. "The whole county's buzzing with it. Thought you'd know. There'll be a feast, after. And alms galore, I shouldn't wonder. And booze."

Octavia pressed her back to the door for support, knowing she'd need it. "What's happened?"

"Your man Trevleyan's on his way out. Thought you'd know."

No one had told them. It was close to autumn; everyone would be busy with the harvest or the hunt; they'd been staying out of the way. True, Lord Trevelyan had been ill for a bit in summer, but last they'd heard, it had passed.

Richard drew a long breath. "He isn't dead now. Maybe it will be all right."

"Maybe," his mother said. She started chopping thyme, thinking, *Well, I've still got a long lease on the cottage… Maybe Crispin will take Richard into his service… I wonder if Thorne will stay on…*.

She handed the old man another onion. "Make yourself useful," she said.

But Richard took it from him. "You're going to slice your thumbs off." The old man's hands were shaking. Richard put the jug into them. "Just drink," Richard said. "I'll cut."

In the morning, very early, he was gone. They found his sword out by the gate, and a horn button in the hedge. Octavia followed her heart to the orchard, expecting to find him lying under the very tree where they had first discovered him passed out with a sword in his hands. But there was nothing there, only a few apples, rotting in the grass.

Three days later, Lord Trevelyan died. The valet, Master Thorne, came himself to the cottage to tell them.

"Should I go see Crispin?" Richard asked.

Thorne fingered the frayed rushes of a chair back. "Maybe. I don't know. He's doing his best, but it's hard on him. Any man grieves when his father passes; but Crispin's Lord Trevelyan now. He's not himself, really; none of them are. The lady's distracted. I didn't know it would be this bad. You never know till it happens, do you?" He sipped the infusion Octavia gave him.

"So should I go now?"

"You might do that." Master Thorne nodded slowly. He looked ten years older. "Yes, go ahead; I'll just sit here for awhile and drink this, if you don't mind."

Richard walked softly through the halls of the Trevelyan manor. He'd known it all his life, but it felt different now. Not the lord's death, exactly—but the effect it had on everyone. The people that he passed were quiet; they barely acknowledged him. The sounds of the hall were all wrong: footsteps in them too fast or too slow, voices too gentle or too low. Richard felt lost. It was as if the shape of the hall had changed. He closed his eyes.

"What are you doing here?"

Lady Trevelyan stood before him, dressed in black, her long bright hair bound back behind her, falling like a girl's. Her eyes were red-rimmed, and her face had the same pulled look as Master Thorne's.

"I came to see if Crispin was all right." She just stared at him. "I'm Richard St. Vier," he said. He wanted to fidget under her gaze. But something about the focus of her stare now kept him still and watchful.

"Yes," she said at last; "I know who you are. The swordsman. That peculiar woman's son." She was grieving, he reminded himself. People were said to go mad with grief. Maybe this was it.

"I'm Crispin's friend," he said.

"Well, you mustn't see him now. He's very busy. You can't see him, really. It's not good. He's Lord Trevelyan now, you know."

He wanted to retort, "I do know." But she felt weirdly dangerous to him, like Crispin on one of his dares. So he just nodded.

"Come with me," she said suddenly. Without waiting for a reply, she turned and walked away. The swirling edge of her black skirt struck his ankle.

Richard followed her down the silent halls. People bowed and curtsied as she passed with him in her wake. She opened the door to a little room, and beckoned him in with her, and shut it behind them.

The walls of the round room were heavy with fabric, dresses hanging on peg after peg.

"My closet," she said. "Old gowns. I was going to sort through them, but now it doesn't matter, does it? I may as well dye them all black, and wear them to shreds."

"They're pretty," he said politely.

She fingered a green and gold dress. "I wore this one to the Halliday Ball. I was going to have it cut down for Melissa… Children grow up so fast, don't they?"

She looked up at him. She was a tiny woman. Crispin's bones hadn't come from her. "Would you like to see me in it?" she asked wistfully.

What kind of a question was that? He licked his lips. He really should go.

A swoosh of icy blue hissed across his skin. "Or do you think this one's better?"

The cold and cloudy thing was in his arms. It smelt metallic.

"That's silk brocade, Richard St. Vier. Blush of Dawn, the color's called. It's to remind you of early morning, when you wake up with your lover." She brushed the fabric over his lips. "Thus. Do you like it?"

He looked over at the door. Silk was expensive; he couldn't just drop it on the floor. Maybe there was a hook it went back on—

She followed his gaze to the wall. "Do you like the pink silk better?" She held a new gown up against herself, the glowing pink cloud eclipsing the black of her dress. "This becomes me, don't you think?"

He nodded. His mouth was dry.

"Come closer," she said.

He knew the challenge when he heard it. He took a step toward her.

"Touch me," she said. He knew where he was, now: walking the fallen tree, climbing to the topmost eave….

"Where?"

"Wherever you like."

He put his hand on the side of her face. She turned her head and licked his palm, and he started as if he had been kicked. He hadn't expected that, to feel that again here, now, that dangerous thrill at the base of his spine. He shuddered with the pleasure he did not like.

"Hold me," she said. He put his arms around her. She smelt of lavender, and blown-out candle wicks.

"Be my friend," she whispered across his lips.

"I will," he whispered back.

Lady Trevelyan laughed low, and sighed. She knotted her fingers in his hair, and pulled his head down to her, biting his lips as she kissed him. He shivered, and pressed himself against her. She lifted her inky skirts, and pulled him closer, fingering his breeches. He didn't even know where his own hands were. He didn't know where anything was, except one thing. His heart was slamming with the danger of how much he wanted it. His eyes were closed, and he could hardly breathe. Every time she touched him he tried to think what a terrible thing this was, but it came out completely different: he had to stop thinking entirely, because thinking it was dangerous just made him want it more. She was saying something, but he couldn't hear it. She was helping him, that was what mattered. She was helping him—and then suddenly it was over, and she was shouting:

"You idiot! Pink *peau de soie*—ruined!" She shoved him away. His sight came back. He reached for his breeches, fallen around his knees. "What do you think you're doing? Who do you think you are?" Her face and neck were flushed, eyes sharp and bright. "You're nobody. You're no one. What are you doing here? Who do you think you are?"

He did up his buttons, stumbled out into the hall.

The door was closed; he couldn't hear her now. He started walking back the way he'd come—or some way, anyway. It wasn't a part of the house he knew.

"Richard!"

Not Crispin. Not now.

"Richard!"

Not now.

"Richard, damn you—you *stand* when I call you!"

Richard stood. He had his back to Crispin; he couldn't look at him now. "What?" he asked. "What do you want?"

"What do I *want*?" Crispin demanded shrilly. "What the hell's wrong with you? What do you think I want?"

"Whatever it is, I don't have it."

"No, you don't, do you?" Crispin said bitterly. "God. I thought you were my friend."

"I guess I'm not, then. I guess I'm not your friend."

Crispin threw a punch at him.

And Richard returned it. He didn't hold back.

It wasn't a fair fight, not really. They'd never been even in this game.

It was, Richard reflected after, a good thing they'd neither of them had swords; but he still left Crispin, Lord Trevelyan, a wheezing mess crumpled on the floor.

Then he went home and told his mother what he'd done.

She had known that it would come someday, but this was so much sooner than she'd hoped.

"You have to go, my love," she said. "Trevelyan's dead. His lady won't protect you, and Crispin certainly won't."

Richard nodded. He wanted to say, "It's only Crispin," or "He'll get over it." But Crispin was Trevelyan now.

"Where should I go?" he said instead. He pictured the mountains, where bold men ran with the deer. He pictured another countryside, much like this; another cottage by a stream, or maybe a forest….

"To the city," his mother said. "It's the only place that you can lose yourself enough."

"The city?" He'd never been there. He didn't know anyone. The house with no air was there, and the place of last resort. But even as he thought it, he felt that curious thrill down his spine, and knew he wanted it, even though he shouldn't.

"The city," he said. "Yes."

"Don't be frightened," his mother said.

He said, "I'm not."

She pulled out the book on Toads, opening to the hollow where the money was. "Here," she said. "Start with this. You'll earn more when you get there."

He did not ask her, "How?" He thought he knew.

THE PELICAN BAR
KAREN JOY FOWLER

Karen Joy Fowler was born in Bloomington, Indiana and attended the University of California at Berkeley from 1968 to 1972, graduated with a BA in political science, and then earned an MA at UC Davis in 1974. She sold her first science fiction story, "Praxis", in 1985 and has won the Nebula Award for stories "What I Didn't See" and "Always". Her short fiction has been collected in *Artificial Things* and World Fantasy Award winner *Black Glass*. Fowler is also the author of five novels, including debut *Sarah Canary* (described by critic John Clute as one of the finest First Contact novels ever written), *Sister Noon*, *The Sweetheart Season*, and *Wit's End*. She is probably best known, though, for her novel *The Jane Austen Book Club*, which was adapted into a successful film. She lives in Santa Cruz, California, with husband Hugh Sterling Fowler II. They have two grown children and three grandchildren.

For her birthday, Norah got a Pink CD from the twins, a book about vampires from her grown-up sister, *High School Musical 2* from her grandma (which Norah might have liked if she'd been turning ten instead of fifteen), an iPod shuffle plus an Ecko Red t-shirt and two hundred dollar darkwash 7jeans—the most expensive clothes Norah had ever owned—from her mother and father.

Not a week earlier, her mother had said it was a shame birthdays came whether you deserved them or not. She'd said she was dog-tired of Norah's disrespect, her ingratitude, her filthy language—as if fucking was just another word for very—fucking this and fucking that, fucking hot and fucking unfair and you have to be fucking kidding me.

And then there were a handful of nights when Norah didn't come home and turned off her phone so they all thought she was in the city in the apartment of some man she'd probably met on the internet and probably dead.

And then there were the horrible things she'd written about both her mother and father on facebook.

And now they had to buy her presents?

I don't see that happening, Norah's mother had said.

So it was all a big surprise and there was even a party. Her parents didn't approve of Norah's friends, (and mostly didn't know who they were) so the party was just family. Norah's big sister brought the new baby who yawned and hiccoughed and whose scalp was scaly with cradle-cap. There was barbecued chicken and ears of corn cooked in milk, an ice-cream cake with pralines and roses and everyone, even Norah, was really careful and nice except for Norah's grandma who had a fight in the kitchen with Norah's mother that stopped the minute Norah entered. Her grandmother gave Norah a kiss, wished her a happy birthday, and left before the food was served.

The party went late and Norah's mother said they'd clean up in the morning. Everyone left or went to bed. Norah made a show of brushing her teeth, but she didn't undress, because Enoch and Kayla had said they'd come by, which they did, just before midnight. Enoch climbed through Norah's bedroom window and then he tiptoed downstairs to the front door to let Kayla in, because she was already too trashed for the window. "Your birthday's not over yet!" Enoch said, and he'd brought Norah some special birthday shrooms called hawk's eyes. Half an hour later, the whole bedroom took a little skip sideways and broke open like an egg. Blue light poured over everything and Norah's carebear Milo had a luminous blue aura, as if he were Yoda or something. Milo told Norah to tell Enoch she loved him, which made Enoch laugh.

They took more of the hawk's eyes so Norah was still tripping the next morning when a man and a woman came into her bedroom, pulled her from her bed and forced her onto her feet while her mother and father watched. The woman had a hooked nose and slightly protuberant eyeballs. Norah looked into her face just in time to see the fast retraction of a nictitating membrane. "Look at her eyes," she said, only the words came out of the woman's mouth instead of Norah's. "Look at her eyes," the woman said. "She's high as a kite."

Norah's mother collected clothes from the floor and the chair in the bedroom. "Put these on," she told Norah, but Norah couldn't find the sleeves so the men left the room while her mother dressed her. Then the man and woman took her down the stairs and out the front door to a car so clean and black that clouds rolled across the hood. Norah's father put a suitcase in the trunk and when he slammed it shut, the noise Norah heard was the last note in a Sunday school choir; the *men* part of *Amen,* sung in many voices.

The music was calming. Her parents had been threatening to ship her off to boarding school for so long she'd stopped hearing it. Even now she thought that they were maybe all just trying to scare her, would drive her around for a bit and then bring her back, lesson learned, and this helped for a minute or two. Then she thought her mother wouldn't be crying in quite the way she was crying if it was all for show. Norah tried to grab her mother's arm, but missed. "Please," she started, "don't make me," but before she got the words out the man had leaned in to take them. "Don't make me hurt you," he said in a tiny whisper that echoed in her skull. He hand-cuffed Norah to the seatbelt because she was struggling. His mouth looked like something drawn onto his face with a charcoal pen.

"This is only because we love you," Norah's father said. "You were on a really dangerous path."

"This is the most difficult thing we've ever done," said Norah's mother. "Please be a good girl and then you can come right home."

The man with the charcoal mouth and woman with the nictitating eyelids drove Norah to an airport. They showed the woman at the ticket counter Norah's passport, and then they all got on a plane together, the woman in the window seat, the man the aisle, and Norah in the middle. Sometime during the flight, Norah came down and the man beside her had an ordinary face and the woman had ordinary eyes, but Norah was still on a plane with nothing beneath her but ocean.

While this was happening, Norah's mother drove to the mall. She had cried all morning and now she was returning the iPod shuffle to the Apple store and the expensive clothes to Nordstrom's. She had all her receipts and everything still had the tags, plus she was sobbing intermittently, but uncontrollably, so there was no problem getting her money back.

Norah's new home was an old motel. She arrived after dark, the sky above pinned with stars and the road so quiet she could hear a bubbling chorus of frogs and crickets. The man held her arm and walked just fast enough to make Norah stumble. He let her fall onto one knee. The ground was asphalt covered with a grit that stuck in her skin and couldn't be brushed off. She was having trouble believing she was here. She was having trouble remembering the plane. It was a bad trip, a bad dream, as if she'd gone to bed in her bedroom as usual and awakened here. Her drugged-up visions of eyelids and mouths were forgotten; she was left with only a nagging suspicion she couldn't track back. But she didn't feel like a person being punished for bad behavior. She felt like an abductee.

An elderly woman in a flowered caftan met them at a chain-link gate. She unlocked it, pulled Norah through without a word. "My suitcase," Norah said to the man, but he was already gone.

"Now I am your mother," the woman told Norah. She was very old, face like a crumpled leaf. "But not like your other mother. Two things different. One: I don't love you. Two: when I tell you what to do, you do it. You call me Mama Strong." Mama Strong stooped a little so she and Norah were eye to eye. Her pupils were tiny black beads. "You sleep now. We talk tomorrow."

They climbed an outside stairway and Norah had just a glimpse of the moon-streaked ocean on the other side of the chainlink. Mama Strong took Norah to room 217. Inside, ten girls were already in bed, the floor nearly covered with mattresses, only narrow channels of brown rug between. The light in the ceiling was on, but the girls' eyes were shut. A second old woman sat on a stool in the corner. She was sucking loudly on a red lollipop. "I don't have my toothbrush," Norah said.

"I didn't say brush your teeth," said Mama Strong. She gave Norah a yellow t-shirt, gray sweatpants, and plastic flip flops, took her to the bathroom and waited for Norah to use the toilet, wash her face with tap water, and change. Then she took the clothes Norah had arrived in and went away.

The old woman pointed with her lollipop to an empty mattress, thin wool blanket folded at the foot. Norah lay down, covered herself with the blanket. The room was stuffy, warm, and smelled of the bodies in it. The mattress closest to Norah's belonged to a skinny black girl with a scabbed nose and a bad cough. Norah knew she was awake because of the coughing. "I'm Norah," she whispered, but the old woman in the corner hissed and clapped her hands. It took Norah a long time to realize that no one was ever going to turn off the light.

Three times during the night she heard someone screaming. Other times she thought she heard the ocean, but she was never sure; it could have been a furnace or a fan.

In the morning, the skinny girl told Mama Strong that Norah had talked to her. The girl earned five points for this, which was enough to be given her hairbrush.

"I said no talking," Mama Strong told Norah.

"No, you didn't," said Norah.

"Who is telling the truth? You or me?" asked Mama Strong.

Norah, who hadn't eaten since the airplane or brushed her teeth in 24 hours, had a foul taste in her mouth like rotting eggs. Even so she could smell the onions on Mama Strong's breath. "Me," said Norah.

She lost ten points for the talking and thirty for the talking back. This put her, on her first day, at minus forty. At plus ten she would have earned her toothbrush; at plus twenty, her hairbrush.

Mama Strong said that no talking was allowed anywhere—points deducted for talking—except at group sessions, where talking was required—points deducted for no talking. Breakfast was cold hard toast with canned peaches—points deducted for not eating—after which Norah had her first group session.

Mama Strong was her group leader. Norah's group was the girls from room 217. They were, Norah was told, her new family. Her family name was Power. Other families in the hotel were named Dignity, Consideration, Serenity, and Respect. These were, Mama Strong said, not so good as family names. Power was the best.

There were boys in the west wings of the motel, but they wouldn't ever be in the yard at the same time as the girls. Everyone ate together, but there was no talking while eating so they wouldn't be getting to know each other; any way they were all very bad boys. There was no reason to think about them at all, Mama Strong said.

She passed each of the Power girls a piece of paper and a pencil. She told them to write down five things about themselves that were true.

Norah thought about Enoch and Kayla, whether they knew where she had gone, what they might try to do about it. What she would do if it were them. She wrote: *I am a good friend. I am fun to be with.* Initially that was a single entry. Later when time ran out, she came back and made it two. She thought about her parents. *I am a picky eater*, she wrote on their behalf. She couldn't afford to be angry with them, not until she was home again. A mistake had been made. When her parents realized the kind of place this was, they would come and get her.

I am honest. I am stubborn, she wrote, because her mother had always said so. How many times had Norah heard how her mother spent eighteen hours in labor and finally had a C-section just because Fetal Norah wouldn't tuck her chin to clear the pubic bone. "If I'd known her then like I know her now," Norah's mother used to say, "I'd have gone straight to the c-section and spared myself the labor. 'This child is never going to tuck her chin,' I'd have said."

And then Norah scratched out the part about being stubborn, because she had never been so angry at her parents and she didn't want to give her mother the satisfaction. Instead she wrote, *nobody knows who I really am.*

They were all to read their lists aloud. Norah was made to go first. Mama Strong sucked loudly through her teeth at number four. "Already this morning, Norah has lied to me two times," she told the group. "'I am honest' is the third lie today."

The girls were invited to comment. They did so immediately and with vigor. Norah seemed very stuck on herself, said a white girl with severe acne on her cheeks and chin. A red-haired girl with a freckled neck and freckled arms said that there was no evidence of Norah taking responsibility for anything. She agreed with the first girl. Norah was very stuck-up. The skinny girl with the cough said that no one honest ended up here. None of them were honest, but at least she was honest enough to admit it.

"I'm here by mistake," said Norah.

"Lie number four." Mama Strong reached over and took the paper, her eyes like stones. "*I* know who you really are," she said. "*I* know how you think. You think, how do I get out of here?

"*You* never will. The only way out is to be different. Change. Grow." She tore up Norah's list. "Only way is to be someone else completely. As long as some tiny place inside is still you, you will never leave."

The other girls took turns reading from their lists. "I am ungrateful," one of them had written. "I am a liar," read another. "I am still carrying around my bullshit," read the girl with the cough. "I am a bad person." "I am a bad daughter."

It took Norah three months to earn enough points to spend an afternoon outside. She stood blinking in the sun, watching a line of birds thread the sky above her. She couldn't see the ocean, but there was a breeze that brought the smell of salt.

Later she got to play kickball with the other Power girls in the old, drained motel pool. No talking, so they played with a silent ferocity, slamming each other into the pool walls until every girl was bleeding from the nose or the knee or somewhere.

After group there were classes. Norah would be given a lesson with a multiple choice exercise. Some days it was math, some days history, geography, literature. At the end of an hour someone on staff would check her answers against a key. There was no instruction and points were deducted for wrong answers. One day the lesson was the Frost poem "The Road Not Taken," which was not a hard lesson, but Norah got almost everything wrong, because the staff member was using the wrong key. Norah said so and she lost points for her poor score, but also for the talking.

It took eleven months for Norah to earn enough points to write her parents. She'd known Mama Strong or someone else on staff would read the letter so she wrote it carefully. "Please let me come home. I promise to do whatever you ask and I think you can't know much about this place. I am sick a lot from the terrible food and have a rash on my legs from bug bites that keeps getting worse. I've lost weight. Please come and get me. I love you. Norah."

"So manipulative," Mama Strong had said. "So dishonest and manipulative." But she put the letter into an envelope and stamped it.

If the letter was dishonest, it was only by omission. The food here was not only terrible, it was unhealthy, often rotting, and there was never enough of it. Meat was served infrequently, so the students, hungry enough to eat anything, were always sick after. No more than three minutes every three hours could be spent on the toilet; there were always students whose legs were streaked with diarrhea. There was no medical care. The bug bites came from her mattress.

Sometimes someone would vanish. This happened to two girls in the Power family. One of them was the girl with the acne, her name was Kelsey. One of them was Jetta, a relatively new arrival. There was no explanation; since no one was allowed to talk, there was no speculation. Mama Strong had said if they earned a hundred points they could leave. Norah tried to remember how many points she'd seen Kelsey get; was it possible she'd had a hundred? Not possible that Jetta did.

The night Jetta disappeared there was a bloody towel in the corner of the shower. Not just stained with blood, soaked with it. It stayed in the corner for three days until someone finally took it away.

A few weeks before her birthday, Norah lost all her accumulated points, forty-five of them, for not going deep in group session. By then Norah had no deep left. She was all surface—skin rashes, eye infections, aching teeth, constant hunger, stomach cramps. The people in her life—the ones Mama

Strong wanted to know everything about—had dimmed in her memory along with everything else—school, childhood, all the fights with her parents, all the Christmases, the winters, the summers, her fifteenth birthday. Her friends went first and then her family.

The only things she could remember clearly were those things she'd shared in group. Group session demanded ever more intimate, more humiliating, more secret stories. Soon it seemed as if nothing had ever happened to Norah that wasn't shameful and painful. Worse, her most secret shit was still found wanting, not sufficiently revealing, dishonest.

Norah turned to vaguely remembered plots from after-school specials until one day the story she was telling was recognized by the freckled girl, Emilene was her name, who got twenty whole points for calling Norah on it.

There was a punishment called the TAP, the Think Again Position. Room 303 was the TAP room. It smelled of unwashed bodies and was crawling with ants. A student sent to TAP was forced to lie face down on the bare floor. Every three hours, a shift in position was allowed. A student who moved at any other time was put in restraint. Restraint meant that one staff member would set a knee on the student's spine. Others would pull the student's arms and legs back and up as far as they could go and then just a little bit farther. Many times a day, screaming could be heard in Room 303.

For lying in group session, Norah was sent to the TAP. She would be released, Mama Strong said, when she was finally ready to admit that she was here as a result of her own decisions. Mama Strong was sick of Norah's games. Norah lasted two weeks.

"You have something to say?" Mama Strong was smoking a small hand-rolled cigarette that smelled of cinnamon. Smoke curled from her nostrils and her fingers were stained with tobacco or coffee or dirt or blood.

"I belong here," Norah said.

"No mistake?"

"No."

"Just what you deserve?"

"Yes,"

"Say it."

"Just what I deserve."

"Two weeks is nothing," Mama Strong said. "We had a girl three years ago, did eighteen."

Although it was the most painful, the TAP was not, to Norah's mind, the worst part. The worst part was the light that stayed on all night. Norah had not been in the dark for one single second since she arrived. The no dark was making Norah crazy. Her voice in group no longer sounded like her voice. It hurt to use it, hurt to hear it.

Her voice had betrayed her, telling Mama Strong everything until there was nothing left inside Norah that Mama Strong hadn't pawed through, like a shopper at a flea market. Mama Strong knew exactly who Norah was, because Norah had told her. What Norah needed was a new secret.

For her sixteenth birthday, she got two postcards. "We came all this way only to learn you're being disciplined and we can't see you. We don't want to be harsh on your birthday of all days, but honest to Pete, Norah, when are you going to have a change of attitude? Just imagine how disappointed we are." The handwriting was her father's, but the card had been signed by her mother and father both.

The other was written by her mother. "Your father said as long as we're here we might as well play tourist. So now we're at a restaurant in the middle of the ocean. Well, maybe not the exact middle, but a long ways out! The restaurant is up on stilts on a sandbar and you can only get here by boat! We're eating a fish right off the line! All the food is so good, we envy you living here! Happy birthday, darling! Maybe next year we can celebrate your birthday here together. I will pray for that!" Both postcards had a picture of the ocean restaurant. It was called the Pelican Bar.

Her parents had spent five days only a few miles away. They'd swum in the ocean, drunk mai-tais and mojitos under the stars, fed bits of bread to the gulls. They'd gone up the river to see the crocodiles and shopped for presents to take home. They were genuinely sorry about Norah; her mother had cried the whole first day and often after. But this sadness was heightened by guilt. There was no denying that they were happier at home without her. Norah had been a constant drain, a constant source of tension and despair. Norah left and peace arrived. The twins had never been difficult, but Norah's instructive disappearance had improved even their good behavior.

Norah is on her mattress in room 217 under the overhead light, but she is also at a restaurant on stilts off the coast. She is drinking something made with rum. The sun is shining. The water is blue and rocking like a cradle. There is a breeze on her face.

Around the restaurant, nets and posts have been sunk into the sandbar. Pelicans sit on these or fly or sometimes drop into the water with their wings closed, heavy as stones. Norah wonders if she could swim all the way back into shore. She's a good swimmer, or used to be, but this is merely hypothetical. She came by motorboat, trailing her hand in the water, and will leave the same way. Norah wipes her mouth with her hand and her fingers taste of salt.

She buys a postcard. Dear Norah, she writes. You could do the TAP better now. Maybe not for eighteen weeks, but probably more than two. Don't ever tell Mama Strong about the Pelican Bar, no matter what.

For her sixteenth birthday what Norah got was the Pelican Bar.

Norah's seventeenth birthday passed without her noticing. She'd lost track of the date; there was just a morning when she suddenly thought that she must be seventeen by now. There'd been no card from her parents, which might have meant they hadn't sent one, but probably didn't. Their letters were frequent, if peculiar. They seemed to think there was water in the pool, fresh fruit at lunchtime. They seemed to think she had counselors and teachers and friends. They'd even made reference to college prep. Norah knew that someone on staff was writing and signing her name. It didn't matter. She could hardly remember her parents, didn't expect to ever see them again. Since "come and get me" hadn't worked, she had nothing further to say to them. Fine with her if someone else did.

One of the night women, one of the women who sat in the corner and watched while they slept, was younger than the others, with her hair in many braids. She took a sudden dislike to Norah. Norah had no idea why; there'd been no incident, no exchange, just an evening when the woman's eyes locked onto Norah's face and filled with poison. The next day she followed Norah through the halls and lobby, mewing at her like a cat. This went on until everyone on staff was mewing at Norah. Norah lost twenty points for it. Worse, she found it impossible to get to the Pelican Bar while everyone was mewing at her.

But even without Norah going there, Mama Strong could tell that she had a secret. Mama Strong paid less attention to the other girls and more to Norah, pushing and prodding in group, allowing the mewing even from the other girls, and sending Norah to the TAP again and again. Norah dipped back into minus points. Her hairbrush and her toothbrush were taken away. Her time in the shower was cut from five minutes to three. She had bruises on her thighs and a painful spot on her back where the knee went during restraint.

After several months without, she menstruated. The blood came in clots, gushes that soaked into her sweatpants. She was allowed to get up long enough to wash her clothes, but the blood didn't come completely out and the sweatpants weren't replaced. A man came and mopped the floor where Norah had to lie. It smelled strongly of piss when he was done.

More girls disappeared until Norah noticed that she'd been there longer than almost anyone in the Power family. A new girl arrived and took the mattress and blanket Kimberly had occupied. The new girl's name was Chloe. The night she arrived, she spoke to Norah. "How long have you been here?" she asked. Her eyes were red and swollen and she had a squashed kind of nose. She wasn't able to hold still; she jabbered about her meds which she hadn't taken and needed to; she rocked on the mattress from side to side.

"The new girl talked to me last night," Norah told Mama Strong in the morning. Chloe was a born victim, gave off the victim vibe. She was so weak it was like a superpower. The kids at her school had bullied her, she said in group session, like this would be news to anyone.

"Maybe you ask for it," Emilene suggested.

"Why don't you take responsibility?" Norah said. "Instead of blaming everyone else."

"You will learn to hold still," Mama Strong told her and had the girls put her in restraint themselves. Norah's was the knee in her back.

Then Mama Strong told them all to make a list of five reasons they'd been sent here. "I am a bad daughter," Norah wrote. "I am still carrying around my bullshit. I am ungrateful." And then her brain snapped shut like a clamshell so she couldn't continue.

"There is something else you want to say." Mama Strong stood in front of her, holding the incriminating paper, two reasons short of the assignment, in her hand.

She was asking for Norah's secret. She was asking about the Pelican Bar. "No," said Norah. "It's just that I can't think."

"Tell me." The black beads of Mama Strong's eyes became pinpricks. "Tell me. Tell me." She stepped around Norah's shoulder so that Norah could smell onion and feel a cold breath on her neck, but couldn't see her face.

"I don't belong here," Norah said. She was trying to keep the Pelican Bar. To do that, she had to give Mama Strong something else. There was probably a smarter plan, but Norah couldn't think. "Nobody belongs here," she said. "This isn't a place where humans belong."

"You are human, but not me?" Mama Strong said. Mama Strong had never touched Norah. But her voice coiled like a spring; she made Norah flinch. Norah felt her own piss on her thighs.

"Maybe so," Mama Strong said. "Maybe I'll send you somewhere else then. Say you want that. Ask me for it. Say it and I'll do it."

Norah held her breath. In that instant, her brain produced the two missing reasons. "I am a liar," she said. She heard her own desperation. "I am a bad person."

There was a silence and then Norah heard Chloe saying she wanted to go home. Chloe clapped her hands over her mouth. Her talking continued, only now no one could make out the words. Her head nodded like a bobblehead dog on a dashboard.

Mama Strong turned to Chloe. Norah got sent to the TAP, but not to Mama Strong's someplace else.

After that, Mama Strong never again seemed as interested in Norah. Chloe hadn't learned yet to hold still, but Mama Strong was up to the challenge. When Norah was seventeen, the gift she got was Chloe.

One day, Mama Strong stopped Norah on her way to breakfast. "Follow me," she said, and led Norah to the chainlink fence. She unlocked the gate and swung it open. "You can go now." She counted out fifty dollars. "You can take this and go. Or you can stay until your mother and father come for you. Maybe tomorrow. Maybe next week. You go now, you get only as far as you get with fifty dollars."

Norah began to shake. This, she thought, was the worst thing done to her yet.

She took a step toward the gate, took another. She didn't look at Mama Strong. She saw that the open gate was a trick, which made her shaking stop. She was not fooled. Norah would never be allowed to walk out. She took a third step and a fourth. "You don't belong here," Mama Strong said, with contempt as if there'd been a test and Norah had flunked it. Norah didn't know if this was because she'd been too compliant or not compliant enough.

And then Norah was outside and Mama Strong was closing and locking the gate behind her.

Norah walked in the sunlight down a paved road dotted with potholes and the smashed skins of frogs. The road curved between weeds taller than Norah's head, bushes with bright orange flowers. Occasionally a car went by, driven very fast.

Norah kept going. She passed stucco homes, some small stores. She saw cigarettes and muumuus for sale, large avocados, bunches of small bananas, liquor bottles filled with dish soap, posters for British ale. She thought about buying something to eat, but it seemed too hard, would require her to talk. She was afraid to stop walking. It was very hot on the road in the sun. A pack of small dogs followed her briefly and then ran back to wherever they'd come from.

She reached the ocean and walked into the water. The salt stung the rashes on her legs, the sores on her arms and then it stopped stinging. The sand was brown, the water blue and warm. She'd forgotten about the fifty dollars though she was still holding them in her hand, now soaked and salty.

There were tourists everywhere on the beach, swimming, lying in the sun with daiquiris and ice cream sandwiches and salted oranges. She wanted to tell them that, not four miles away, children were being starved and terrified. She couldn't remember enough about people to know if they'd care. Probably no one would believe her. Probably they already knew.

She waded into shore and walked farther. It was so hot, her clothes dried quickly. She came to a river and an open air market. A young man with a scar on his cheek approached her. She recognized him. On two occasions, he'd put her in restraint. Her heart began to knock against her lungs. The air around her went black.

"Happy birthday," he said.

He came swimming back into focus, wearing a bright plaid shirt, smiling so his lip rose like a curtain over his teeth. He stepped toward her; she stepped away. "Your birthday, yes?" he said. "Eighteen?" He bought her some bananas, but she didn't take them.

A woman behind her was selling beaded bracelets, peanuts, and puppies. She waved Norah over. "True," she said to Norah. "At eighteen, they have to let you go. The law says." She tied a bracelet onto Norah's wrist. How skinny Norah's arm looked in it. "A present for your birthday," the woman said. "How long were you there?"

Instead of answering, Norah asked for directions to the Pelican Bar. She bought a t-shirt, a skirt, and a cola. She drank the cola, dressed in the new clothes and threw away the old. She bought a ticket on a boat—ten dollars it cost her to go, ten more to come back. There were tourists, but no one sat anywhere near her.

The boat dropped her, along with the others, twenty feet or so out on the sandbar, so that she walked the last bit through waist-high water. She was encircled by the straight, clean line of the horizon, the whole world spinning around her, flat as a plate. The water was a brilliant, sun-dazzled blue in every direction. She turned and turned, her hands floating, her mind flying until she took her turn on a makeshift ladder of planks and branches. Her grip on the wood suddenly anchored her. She climbed into the restaurant in her dripping dress.

She bought a postcard for Chloe. "On your eighteenth birthday, come here," she wrote, "and eat a fish right off the line. I'm sorry about everything. I'm a bad person."

She ordered a fish for herself, but couldn't finish it. She sat for hours, feeling the floor of the bar rocking beneath her, climbing down the ladder into the water, and up again to dry in the warm air. She never wanted to leave this place that was the best place in the world, even more beautiful than she'd imagined. She fell asleep on the restaurant bench and didn't wake up until the last boat was going to shore and someone shook her arm to make sure she was on it.

When Norah returned to shore, she saw Mama Strong seated in an outdoor bar at the edge of the market on the end of the dock. The sun was setting and dark coming on. Mama Strong was drinking something that could have been water or could have been whiskey. The glass was colored blue so there was no way to be sure. She saw Norah getting off the boat. There was no way back that didn't take Norah towards her.

"You have so much money, you're a tourist?" Mama Strong asked. "Next time you want to eat, the money is gone. What then?"

Two men were playing the drums behind her. One of them began to sing. Norah recognized the tune—something old that her mother had liked—but not the words. "Do you think I'm afraid to go hungry?" Norah said.

"So. We made you tougher. Better than you were. But not tough enough. Not what we're looking for. You go be whatever you want now. Have whatever you want. We don't care."

What did Norah want to be? Clean. Not hungry. Not hurting. Able to sleep in the dark. Already there was one bright star in the sky over the ocean.

What else? She couldn't think of a thing. Mama Strong had said Norah would have to change, but Norah felt that she'd vanished instead. She didn't know who she was anymore. She didn't know anything at all. "When I run out of money," she said, "I'll ask someone to help me. And someone will. Maybe not the first person I ask. But someone."

Maybe it was true.

"Very pretty." Mama Strong looked into her blue glass, swirled whatever was left in it, tipped it down her throat. "You're wrong about humans, you know," she said. Her tone was conversational. "Humans do everything we did. Humans do more."

Two men came up behind Norah. She whirled, sure that they were here for her, sure that she'd be taken, maybe back, maybe to Mama Strong's more horrible someplace else. But the men walked right past her toward the drummers. They walked right past her and as they walked, they began to sing. Maybe they were human and maybe not.

"Very pretty world," said Mama Strong.

SPAR
KIJ JOHNSON

Kij Johnson sold her first short story in 1987, and has subsequently appeared regularly in *Analog, Asimov's, Fantasy & Science Fiction*, and *Realms of Fantasy*. She has won the Theodore Sturgeon Memorial Award and the International Association for the Fantastic in the Art's Crawford Award. Her short story "The Evolution of Trickster Stories Among the Dogs of North Park After the Change" was nominated for the Nebula, World Fantasy, and Hugo Awards. Her story "26 Monkeys, Also the Abyss" was nominated for the Nebula, Sturgeon and Hugo Awards, and won the World Fantasy Award.

Her novels include World Fantasy Award nominee *Fudoki* and *The Fox Woman*. She is currently researching a third novel set in Heian, Japan.

In the tiny lifeboat, she and the alien fuck endlessly, relentlessly.

They each have Ins and Outs. Her Ins are the usual, eyes ears nostrils mouth cunt ass. Her Outs are also the common ones: fingers and hands and feet and tongue. Arms. Legs. Things that can be thrust into other things.

The alien is not humanoid. It is not bipedal. It has cilia. It has no bones, or perhaps it does and she cannot feel them. Its muscles, or what might be muscles, are rings and not strands. Its skin is the color of dusk and covered with a clear thin slime that tastes of snot. It makes no sounds. She thinks it smells like wet leaves in winter, but after a time she cannot remember that smell, or leaves, or winter.

Its Ins and Outs change. There are dark slashes and permanent knobs that sometimes distend, but it is always growing new Outs, hollowing new Ins. It cleaves easily in both senses.

It penetrates her a thousand ways. She penetrates it, as well.

The lifeboat is not for humans. The air is too warm, the light too dim. It is too small. There are no screens, no books, no warning labels, no voices, no bed or chair or table or control board or toilet or telltale lights or clocks. The ship's hum is steady. Nothing changes.

There is no room. They cannot help but touch. They breathe each other's breath—if it breathes; she cannot tell. There is always an Out in an In, something wrapped around another thing, flesh coiling and uncoiling inside, outside. Making spaces. Making space.

She is always wet. She cannot tell whether this is the slime from its skin, the oil and sweat from hers, her exhaled breath, the lifeboat's air. Or come.

Her body seeps. When she can, she pulls her mind away. But there is nothing else, and when her mind is disengaged she thinks too much. Which is: at all. Fucking the alien is less horrible.

She does not remember the first time. It is safest to think it forced her.

The wreck was random: a mid-space collision between their ship and the alien's, simultaneously a statistical impossibility and a fact. She and Gary just had time to start the emergency beacon and claw into their suits before their ship was cut in half. Their lifeboat spun out of reach. Her magnetic boots clung to part of the wreck. His did not. The two of them fell apart.

A piece of debris slashed through the leg of Gary's suit to the bone, through the bone. She screamed. He did not. Blood and fat and muscle swelled from his suit into vacuum. An Out.

The alien's vessel also broke into pieces, its lifeboat kicking free and the waldos reaching out, pulling her through the airlock. In.

Why did it save her? The mariner's code? She does not think it knows she is alive. If it did it would try to establish communications. It is quite possible that she is not a rescued castaway. She is salvage, or flotsam.

She sucks her nourishment from one of the two hard intrusions into the featureless lifeboat, a rigid tube. She uses the other, a second tube, for whatever comes from her, her shit and piss and vomit. Not her come, which slicks her thighs to her knees.

She gags a lot. It has no sense of the depth of her throat. Ins and Outs.

There is a time when she screams so hard that her throat bleeds.

She tries to teach it words. "Breast," she says. "Finger. Cunt." Her vocabulary options are limited here.

"Listen to me," she says. "Listen. To. Me." Does it even have ears?

The fucking never gets better or worse. It learns no lessons about pleasing her. She does not learn anything about pleasing it either: would not if she could. And why? How do you please grass and why should you? She suddenly remembers grass, the bright smell of it and its perfect green, its cool clean soft feel beneath her bare hands.

She finds herself aroused by the thought of grass against her hands, because it is the only thing that she has thought of for a long time that is not the alien or Gary or the Ins and Outs. But perhaps its soft blades against her fingers would, feel like the alien's cilia. Her ability to compare anything with anything else is slipping from her, because there is nothing to compare.

She feels it inside everywhere, tendrils moving in her nostrils, thrusting against her eardrums, coiled beside the corners of her eyes. And she sheathes herself in it.

When an Out crawls inside her and touches her in certain places, she tips her head back and moans and pretends it is more than accident. It is Gary, he loves me, it loves me, it is a He. It is not.

Communication is key, she thinks.

She cannot communicate, but she tries to make sense of its actions.

What is she to it? Is she a sex toy, a houseplant? A shipwrecked Norwegian sharing a spar with a monolingual Portugese? A companion? A habit, like nail-biting or compulsive masturbation? Perhaps the sex is communication, and she just doesn't understand the language yet.

Or perhaps there is no It. It is not that they cannot communicate, that she is incapable; it is that the alien has no consciousness to communicate with. *It* is a sex toy, a houseplant, a habit.

On the starship with the name she cannot recall, Gary would read aloud to her. Science fiction, Melville, poetry. Her mind cannot access the plots, the words. All she can remember is a few lines from a sonnet, "Let me not to the marriage of true minds admit impediments"—something something something—"an ever-fixèd mark that looks on tempests and is never shaken; it is the star to every wand'ring bark…."

She recites the words, an anodyne that numbs her for a time until they lose their meaning. She has worn them treadless, and they no longer gain any traction in her mind. Eventually she cannot even remember the sounds of them.

If she ever remembers another line, she promises herself she will not wear it out. She will hoard it. She may have promised this before, and forgotten.

She cannot remember Gary's voice. Fuck Gary, anyway. He is dead and she is here with an alien pressed against her cervix.

It is covered with slime. She thinks that, as with toads, the slime may be a mild psychotropic drug. How would she know if she were hallucinating? In this world, what would that look like? Like sunflowers on a desk, like Gary leaning across a picnic basket to place fresh bread on her tongue. The bread is the first thing she has tasted that feels clean in her mouth, and it's not even real.

Gary feeding her bread and laughing. After a time, the taste of bread becomes "the taste of bread" and then the words become mere sounds and stop meaning anything.

On the off-chance that this will change things, she drives her tongue though its cilia, pulls them into her mouth and sucks them clean. She has no idea whether it makes a difference. She has lived forever in the endless reeking fucking now.

Was there someone else on the alien's ship? Was there a Gary, lost now to space? Is it grieving? Does it fuck her to forget, or because it has forgotten? Or to punish itself for surviving? Or the other, for not?

Or is this her?

When she does not have enough Ins for its Outs, it makes new ones. She bleeds for a time and then heals. She pretends that this is a rape. Rape at least she could understand. Rape is an interaction. It requires intention. It would imply that it hates or fears or wants. Rape would mean she is more than a wine glass it fills.

This goes both ways. She forces it sometimes. Her hands are blades that tear new Ins. Her anger pounds at it until she feels its depths grow soft under her fist, as though bones or muscle or cartilage have disassembled and turned to something else.

And when she forces her hands into the alien? If intent counts, then what she does, at least, is a rape—or would be if the alien felt anything, responded in any fashion. Mostly it's like punching a wall.

She puts her fingers in herself, because she at least knows what her intentions are.

Sometimes she watches it fuck her, the strange coiling of its Outs like a shockwave thrusting into her body, and this excites her and horrifies her; but at least it is not Gary. Gary, who left her here with this, who left her here, who left.

One time she feels something break loose inside the alien, but it is immediately drawn out of reach. When she reaches farther in to grasp the broken piece, a sphincter snaps shut on her wrist. Her arm is forced out. There is a bruise like a bracelet for what might be a week or two.

She cannot stop touching the bruise. The alien has had the ability to stop her fist inside it at any time. Which means it chooses not to stop her, even when she batters things inside it until they grow soft.

This is the only time she has ever gotten a reaction she understands. Stimulus: response. She tries many times to get another. She rams her hands into it, kicks it, tries to tears its cilia free with her teeth, claws its skin with her ragged, filthy fingernails. But there is never again the broken thing inside, and never the bracelet.

For a while, she measures time by bruises she gives herself. She slams her shin against the feeding tube, and when the bruise is gone she does it again. She estimates it takes twelve days for a bruise to heal. She stops after a time because she cannot remember how many bruises there have been.

She dreams of rescue, but doesn't know what that looks like. Gary, miraculously alive pulling her free, eyes bright with tears, I love you, he says, his lips on her eyelids and his kiss his tongue in her mouth inside her hands inside him. But that's the alien. Gary is dead. He got Out.

Sometimes she thinks that rescue looks like her opening the lifeboat to the deep vacuum, but she cannot figure out the airlock.

Her anger is endless, relentless.

Gary brought her here, and then he went away and left her with this thing that will not speak, or cannot, or does not care enough to, or does not see her as something to talk to.

On their third date, she and Gary went to an empty park: wine, cheese, fresh bread in a basket. Bright sun and cool air, grass and a cloth to lie on. He brought Shakespeare. "You'll love this," he said, and read to her.

She stopped him with a kiss. "Let's talk," she said, "about anything."

"But we are talking," he said.

"No, you're reading," she said. "I'm sorry, I don't really like poetry."

"That's because you've never had it read to you," he said.

She stopped him at last by taking the book from his hands and pushing him back, her palms in the grass; and he entered her. Later, he read to her anyway.

If it had just been that.

They were not even his words, and now they mean nothing, are not even sounds in her mind. And now there is this thing that cannot hear her or does not choose to listen, until she gives up trying to reach it and only reaches into it, and bludgeons it and herself, seeking a reaction, any reaction.

"I fucking hate you," she says. "I hate fucking you."

The lifeboat decelerates. Metal clashes on metal. Gaskets seal.

The airlock opens overhead. There is light. Her eyes water helplessly and everything becomes glare and indistinct dark shapes. The air is dry and cold. She recoils.

The alien does not react to the light, the hard air. It remains inside her and around her. They are wrapped. They penetrate one another a thousand ways. She is warm here, or at any rate not cold: half-lost in its flesh, wet from her Ins, its Outs. In here it is not too bright.

A dark something stands outlined in the portal. It is bipedal. It makes sounds that are words. Is it human? Is she? Does she still have bones, a voice? She has not used them for so long.

The alien is hers; she is its. Nothing changes.

But. She pulls herself free of its tendrils and climbs. Out.

GOING DEEP
JAMES PATRICK KELLY

James Patrick Kelly made his first sale in 1975, and since has gone on to become one of the most respected and popular writers to enter the field in the last twenty years. Although Kelly has had some success with novels, especially with *Wildlife*, he has had more impact to date as a writer of short fiction, and is often ranked among the best short story writers in the field. His story "Think Like a Dinosaur" won him a Hugo Award in 1996, as did his story "10^{16} to 1," in 2000. Kelly's first solo novel, *Planet of Whispers*, came out in 1984. It was followed by *Freedom Beach* (written with John Kessel), and then by another solo novel, *Look Into the Sun*. His short novel *Burn* won the Nebula Award in 2006. His short work has been collected in *Think Like a Dinosaur*, *Strange But Not a Stranger* and, most recently, in *The Wreck of the Godspeed*. With his co-editor John Kessel, he has published the anthologies *Feeling Very Strange: The Slipstream Anthology*, *Rewired: The Post-Cyberpunk Anthology*, and the controversial *The Secret History of Science Fiction*. Born in Mineola, New York, Kelly now lives with his family in Nottingham, New Hampshire.

Mariska shivered when she realized that her room had been tapping at the dreamfeed for several minutes. "The earth is up," it murmured in its gentle, singing accent. "Daddy Al is up and I am always up. Now Mariska gets up."

Mariska groaned, determined not to allow her room in. Recently she had been dreaming her own dreams of Jak and his long fingers and the fuzz on his chin and the way her throat tightened when she brushed up against him. But this was one of her room's feeds, one of the best ones, one she had been having as long as she could remember. In it, she was in space, but she wasn't on the moon and she wasn't wearing her hardsuit. There were stars every way she turned. Of course, she'd seen stars through the visor of her helmet but these were always different. Not a scatter of light but a swarm. And they were all were singing their names, calling to her to come to them. She could just make out the closest ones: *Alpha Centauri. Barnard's. Wolf. Lalande. Luyten. Sirius.*

"The earth is up, Daddy Al is up and I am always up." Her room insisted. "Now Mariska gets up." If she didn't wake soon, it would have to sound the gong.

"Slag it." She rolled over, awake and grumpy. Her room had been getting on her last nerve recently When she had been a little girl, she had roused at its whisper, but in the last few weeks it had begun nagging her to wake up. She knew it loved her and was only worried about her going deep, but she was breathing regularly and her heartbeat was probably in the high sixties. It monitored her, so it had to know she was just sleeping.

She thought this was all about Al. He was getting nervous; so her room was nervous.

"*Dobroye utro*," said Feodor Bear. "Good morn-ing Mar-i-ska." The ancient toy robot stood up on its shelf, wobbled and then sat down abruptly. It was over a century old and, in Mariska's opinion, needed to be put out of its misery.

"Good morning, dear Mariska," said her room. "Today is Friday, June 15, 2159. You are expected today in Hydroponics and at the Muoi swimming pool. This Sunday is Father's Day."

"I know, I *know*." She stuck her foot out from underneath the covers and wiggled her toes in the cool air. Her room began to bring the temperature up from sleeping to waking levels.

"I could help you find something for Daddy Al, if you'd like." Her room painted Buycenter icons on the wall. "We haven't shopped together in a while."

"Maybe later." Sometimes she felt guilty that she wasn't spending enough time with her room, but its persona kept treating her like a baby. Still calling him *Daddy Al*, for example; it was embarrassing. And she would get to all her expectations eventually. What choice did she have?

The door slid aside a hand's width and Al peered through the opening.

"Rise and shine, Mariska." His smile was a crack on a worried face. "Pancakes for breakfast," he said. "But only if you get up now." He blew a kiss that she ducked away from.

"I'm shining already," she grumbled. "Your own little star."

As she stepped through the cleanser, she wondered what to do about him. She knew exactly what was going on. The *Gorshkov* had just returned from exploring the *Delta Pavonis* system, which meant they'd probably be hearing soon from Natalya Volochkova. And Mariska had just turned thirteen; in another year she'd be able to vote, sign contracts, get married. This was the way the world worked: now that she was almost an adult, it was time for Al to go crazy. All her friends' parents had. The symptoms were hard to ignore: embarrassing questions like *where was she going* and *who was she going with* and *who else would be there?* He said he trusted her but she knew he'd slap a trace on her if he thought he could get away with it. But what was the point? This was the moon. There were security cams over every safety hatch. How much trouble could she get into? Walk out an airlock without a suit? She wasn't suicidal—or dumb. Have sex and get pregnant? She was *patched*—when she finally jumped a boy, pregnancy wouldn't be an issue. Crash from some toxic feed? She was young—she'd get over it.

The fact that she loved Al's strawberry pancakes did nothing to improve her mood at breakfast. He was unusually quiet, which meant he was working his courage up for some stupid fathering talk. Something in the news? She brought her gossip feed up on the tabletop to see what was going on. The scrape of his knife on the plate as she scanned headlines made her want to shriek. Why did he have to use her favorite food as a bribe so that he could pester her?

"You heard about that boy from Penrose High?" he said at last. "The one in that band you used to like… No Exit? Final Exit?"

"You're talking about Last Exit to Nowhere?" That gossip was so old it had curled around the edges and blown away. "Deltron Cleen?"

"That's him." He stabbed one last pancake scrap and pushed it into a pool of syrup. "They say he was at a party a couple of weeks ago and opened his head to everyone there, I forget how many mindfeeds he accepted."

"So?" She couldn't believe he was pushing Deltron Cleen at her.

"You knew him?"

"I've met him, sure."

"You weren't there, were you?" He actually squirmed, like he had ants crawling up his leg. "When it happened?"

"Oh sure. And when he keeled over, I was the one who gave him CPR." Mariska pinched her nose closed and puffed air at him. "Saved his life—the board of supers is giving me a medal next Thursday."

"This is serious, Mariska. Taking feeds from people you don't know is dangerous."

"Unless they're schoolfeeds. Or newsfeeds. Or dreamfeeds."

"Those are datafeeds. And they're screened."

"God feeds, then."

He sank back against his chair. "You're not joining a church, are you?"

"No." She laughed and patted his hand. "I'm okay, Al. Trust me. I love you and everything is okay."

"I know that." He was so flustered he slipped his fork in his pants pocket. "I know," he repeated, as if trying to convince himself.

"Poor Del is pretty stupid, even for a singer in a shoutcast band," she said. "What I heard was he accepted maybe a dozen feeds, but I guess there wasn't room in his head for more than him and a couple of really shallow friends. But he just crashed is all; they'll reboot him. Might even be an improvement." She reached across the table, picked up Al's empty plate and slid it onto hers. "You never did anything like that, did you?" She carried them to the kitchen counter and pushed them through the processor door. "Accept mindfeeds from perfect strangers?"

"Not strangers, no."

"But you *were* young once, right? I mean, you weren't born a parent?"

"I'm a father, Mariska." He swiped his napkin across his lips and then folded it up absently. "You're a minor and still my responsibility. This is just me, trying to stay in touch.

"Extra credit to you, then." She check-marked the air. "But being a father is complicated. Maybe we should work on your technique?"

The door announced, "Jak is here."

"Got to go." Mariska grabbed her kit, kissed Al and spun toward the door in relief. She felt bad for him sometimes. It wasn't his fault he took all the slag in the *Talking To Your Teen* feed so seriously.

Of course, the other reason why Al was acting up was because Mariska's genetic mother was about to swoop down on them. The *Gorshkov* had finally returned after a fifteen-year mission and was now docked at Sweetspot Station. Rumor was that humankind had a terrestrial world to colonize that was only three years away from the new *Delta Pavonis* wormhole. Natalya Volochkova was on the starship's roster as chief medical officer.

Mariska didn't hate her mother exactly. How could she? They had never met. She knew very little about Volochkova and had no interest in finding out more. Ever, never. All she had from her were a couple of fossil toys: Feodor Bear and that stupid Little Mermaid aquarium. Collector's items from the twenty-first century, which was why Mariska had never been allowed to play with them.

What she did hate was the idea that decisions this stranger had made a decade and a half ago now ruled her life. She was Volochkova's clone and had been carried to term in a plastic womb, then placed in the care of one Alfred DeFord, a licensed father, under a term adoption contract. Her genetic mother had hired Al the way that some people hired secretaries; three-fifths of Volochkova's salary paid for their comfortable if unspectacular lifestyle. Mariska knew that Al had come to love her over the years, but growing up with an intelligent room and a hired father for parents wouldn't have been her choice, had she been given one.

As if parking her with a hired father wasn't bad enough, Volochkova had cursed Mariska with spacer genes. Which was why she had to suffer though all those boring pre-space feeds from the Ed supers and why everyone was so worried that she might go deep into hibernation before her time and why she'd been matched with her one true love when she had been in diapers.

Actually, having Jak as a boyfriend wasn't all that much of a problem. She just wished that it didn't have to be so damn inevitable. She wanted to be the one to decide that a curly black mop was sexier than a blonde crewcut or that thin lips were more kissable than thick or that loyal was more attractive than smart. He was fifteen, already an adult, but still lived with his parents. Even though he was two years older than she was, they were in the same semester in the spacer program.

Jak listened as Mariska whined, first about Volochkova and then about Al's breakfast interrogation, as they skated to the hydroponics lab. He knew when to squeeze her hand, when to emit understanding moans and concerned grunts. This was what he called taking the weight, and she was gratified by his capacity to bear her up when she needed it. They were good together, in the 57th percentile on the Hammergeld Scale, according to their Soc super. Although she wondered if there might be some other boy for her somewhere, Mariska was resigned to the idea that, unless she was struck by a meteor or kidnapped by aliens, she would drag him into bed one of these days and marry him when she turned fourteen and then they would hibernate happily ever after on their way to Lalande 21185, or Barnard's Star or wherever.

"But we were there, 'Ska." Jak said, as the safety hatch to the lab slid aside. "Del asked *you* to open your head." He bent over to crank the rollers into the soles of his shoes.

"Which is why we left." She pulled a disposable green clingy from the dispenser next to the safety door and shrugged into it. "Which is why we were already in Chim Zone when the EMTs went by, which means we *weren't* really there. How many times do I have to go over this?" She gave him a friendly push toward his bench and headed toward her own, which was on the opposite side of the lab.

Mariska checked the chemistry of her nutrient solution. Phosphorus was down 50ppm so she added a pinch of ammonium dihydrogen phosphate. She was raising tomatoes in rockwool spun from lunar regolith. Sixteen new blossoms had opened since Tuesday and needed to be pollinated; she used one of the battery-operated toothbrushes that Mr. Holmgren, the Ag super, favored. Mariska needed an average yield of 4.2 kilograms per plant in order to complete this unit; her tomatoes wouldn't be ripe for another eight weeks. Jak was on tomatoes too; his spring crop had had an outbreak of mosaic virus and so he was repeating the unit.

Other kids straggled into the lab as she worked. Grieg, who had the bench next to hers, offered one of his lima beans, which she turned down, and a hit from his sniffer, which she took. Megawatt waved hello and Fung stopped by to tell her that their *Gorshkov* tour had been rescheduled for Tuesday, which she already knew.

After a while, Random ambled in, using a vacpac to clean up the nutrient spills and leaf litter. He had just washed out of the spacer program but his mother was a Med super so he was hanging around as a janitor until she decided what to do with him. Everyone knew why he had failed. He was a feed demon; his head was like a digital traffic jam. However, unlike Del Cleen, Random had never once crashed. They said that if you ever opened yourself wide to him, even just for an instant, you would be so filled with other people's thoughts that you would never think your own again.

He noticed her staring and saluted her with the wand of his vacuum cleaner. It was funny, he didn't look all that destroyed to Mariska. Sleepy maybe, or bored, or a little high, but not as if he had had his individuality crushed. Besides, even though he was too skinny, she thought he was kind of cute. Not for the first time, she wondered what their Hammergeld compatibility score might be.

Mariska felt the tingle of Jak offering a mindfeed. She opened her head a crack and accepted.

=giving up for today= She was relieved that Jak just wanted to chat. =you?=

=ten minutes= Mariska was still getting used to chatting in public. She and Jak had been more intimate, of course, had even opened wide for full mental convergence a couple of times, but that had been when they were by themselves, sitting next to each other in a dark room. Swapping thoughts was all the mind-feed she could handle without losing track of where she was. After all, she was still a kid.

=how's your fruit set?= Jak's feed always felt like a fizzing behind her eyes.

=fifty, maybe sixty= She noticed Random drifting toward her side of the lab. =this sucks=

=tomatoes?=

=hydroponics=

=spacers got to eat=

=spacers suck=

Jak's pleasant fizz gave way to a bubble of annoyance. =you're a spacer=

Mariska had begun to have her doubts about that, but this didn't seem like the right time to bring them up, because Random had shut his vacuum off and slouched beside her bench in silence. His presence was a kind of absence. He seemed to have parked his body in front of her and then forgotten where he had left it.

"What?" She poked his shoulder. "Say something."

Jak bumped her feed. =problem?=

=just random=

All kids of spacer stock were thin but, with his spindly limbs and teacup waist and translucent skin, Random seemed more a rumor than a boy. His eyelids fluttered and he touched his tongue to his bottom lip, as if he were trying to remember something. "Your mother," he said.

Mariska could feel a ribbon of dread weave into her feed with Jak. She wasn't sure her feet were still on the floor.

='ska what?=

=nothing= Mariska clamped her head closed, then gave Jak a feeble wave to show everything was all right. He didn't look reassured.

"What about my mother?" She hissed at Random. "You don't even know her."

He opened his hand and showed her a small, brown disk. At first she thought it was a button but then she recognized the profile of Abraham Lincoln and realized that it was some old coin from Earth. What was it called? A penalty? No, a *penny*.

"I know this," said Random. "Check the date."

She shrank from him. "No."

Then Jak came to her rescue. He rested a hand on Random's shoulder. "Be smooth now." It didn't take much effort to turn the skinny kid away from her.

"What's happening?

Random tried to shrug from Jak's grip, but he was caught. "Isn't about you."

"Fair enough." Jak always acted polite when he was getting angry. "But here I am. You're not telling me to go away, are you?"

"He says it's about Natalya Volochkova," said Mariska.

Random placed the penny on Mariska's bench. "Check the date."

Jak picked the penny up and held it to the light. "2018," he read. "They used to use this stuff for money."

"I know that," Mariska snapped. She snatched the penny out of his hand and shoved it into the front pouch of her tugshirt.

Random seemed to have lost interest in her now that Jak had arrived. He switched on the vacpac, bent over and touched the wand to a tomato leaf on the deck. It caught crossways for a moment, singing in the suction, and was gone. Then he sauntered off.

"What's this got to do with your mother?" said Jak.

Mariska had been mad at Random, but since he no longer presented a target, she decided to be mad at Jak instead. "Don't be stupid. She's not my mother." She saw that Grieg was hunched over his beans, pretending to check the leaves for white flies. From the way his shoulders were shaking, she was certain that he was laughing at her. "Let's get out of here."

Jak looked doubtfully at the chemical dispensers and gardening tools scattered across her bench. "You want to clean up first?"

"No." She peeled off her clingy and threw it at the bench.

Jak tried to cheer her up by doing a flip-scrape in the corridor immediately in front of the hydroponics safety hatch. He leapt upwards in the moon's one sixth gravity, flipped in mid-air and scraped the rollers on the bottom of his shoes across the white ceiling, *skritch, skritch*, leaving skid marks. He didn't quite stick the landing and had to catch himself on the bulkhead. "Let Random clean that." His face flushed with the effort. "That slaghead."

"You're so busted," said Mariska, nodding at the security cam. "They're probably calling your parents even as we speak."

"Not," said Jak. "Megawatt and I smeared the cams with agar last night." He smiled and swiped a lock of curly hair from his forehead. "From Holmgren's own petri dishes. All they've got is blur and closeups of bacteria."

He looked so proud of himself that she couldn't help but grin back at him. "Smooth." Her Jak was the master of the grand and useless gesture.

He reached for her hand. "So where are we going?"

"Away."

They skated in silence through the long corridors of Hai Zone; Jak let her lead. He was much better on rollers than she was—a two time sugarfoot finalist—and matched her stroke for stroke without loosening or tightening his feathery grip.

"You were mad back there," said Jak.

"Yes."

"Have you heard from your mother yet?"

"I told you, she's not my mother."

"Sure. Your clone, then."

Technically, Mariska was Natalya Volochkova's clone, but she didn't bother to correct him. "Not yet. Probably soon." He gave her hand a squeeze. "Unless I get lucky and she lets me alone."

"I don't see why you care. If she comes to visit, just freeze her out. She'll leave eventually."

"I don't want to see them together. Her and Al." She could just picture Volochkova in their flat. The heroic explorer would sneer at the way her hired father had spent the money she had given them. Then she would order Al around and turn off her room's persona and tell Mariska to grow up. As if she wasn't trying.

"Move out for a while. Stay with Geetha."

Mariska made a vinegar face. "Her little brother is a brat."

"Come stay with us then. You could sleep in Memaw's room." Jak's grandmother had been a fossil spacer, one of the first generation to go to the stars; she had died back in February.

"Sure, let's try that one on Al. It'll be fun watching the top of his head blow off."

"But my parents would be there."

Being Jak's girlfriend meant having to tolerate his parents. The mom wasn't so bad. A little boring, but then what grownup wasn't? But the dad was a mess. He had washed out of the spacer program when he was Jak's age and his mother—Memaw—had never let him forget it. The dad put his nose in a sniffer more than was good for anyone and when he was high, he had a tongue on him that could cut steel.

"Weren't your parents there when you and Megawatt set off that smoke bomb in your room?"

Jak blushed. "It was a science experiment."

"That cleared all of Tam Zone." She pulled him to a stop and gave him a brush kiss on the cheek. "Besides, your parents aren't going to be patrolling the hall at all hours. What if I get an overpowering urge in the middle of the night? Who'll protect you?"

"Urge?" He dashed ahead, launched a jump 180 and landed it, skating backwards, wiggling his cute ass. "Overpowering?" His stare was at once playful and hungry.

"Show off." Mariska looked away, embarrassed for both of them. Jak was so pathetically eager; it wasn't right to tease him about sex. It had seemed like a grownup thing to say, but just now she wasn't feeling much like an adult. She needed to get away from Jak. Everybody. Be by herself.

She decided to cue a fake call. When her fingernail flashed, she studied it briefly then brought it to her ear. "It's Al," she said. "Sorry, Jak, I've got to go."

The swimming pool in Muoi Zone was one of the biggest in the Moon's reservoir system, but Mariska liked it because it didn't have a sky projected on its ceiling. Somehow images of stars and clouds made the water seem colder, even though all the Moon's pools were kept at a uniform 27° Celsius. And she felt less exposed looking up at raw rock. The diving platforms at the deep end were always crowded with acrobats; in the shallows little kids stood on their hands and wiggled their toes and heaved huge, quivering balls of water high into the air. Their shouts of glee echoed off the low ceiling and drowned in the blue expanse of the pool.

The twenty-five lanes were busy as usual with lap swimmers meeting their daily exercise expectation. Mariska owed the Med supers an hour in the pool four times a week. She sat at the edge in lane twelve and waited for an opening. She was wearing the aquablade bodysuit that Al had bought for her birthday. Jak had wanted her to get a tank suit or a two-piece, but she had chosen the neck-to-knee style because her chest was still flat as the lunar plains. That was why she didn't like to swim with Jak—when they stood next to each other in swimsuits, she looked like his baby sister.

She eased into the cool water just behind an old guy in a blue speedo and cued up the datafeed she was supposed to review on ground squirrels.

=The hibernating *Spermophilus tridecemlineatus* can spend six months without food. During this period its temperature drops to as low as 0° Celsius. With a heart rate at one percent of its active state and oxygen consumption at two percent, the squirrel can survive solely on the combustion of its lipid reserves, especially unsaturated and polyunsaturated fatty acids.=

As Mariska's heart rate climbed to its target of one hundred and seventy-nine beats per minute, her deep and regular breathing and the quiet slap of water against her body brought on her usual swimming trance. For a brief, blue moment doing the right thing was easy: just bounce off the two walls connected by the black lane line.

Then her thoughts began to tumble over one another. Everything was stuck together, just like in the Love Gravy song. Al and Jak and Volochkova and her life on the moon and her future in space and sex and going deep and the way her room wouldn't let her grow up and Feodor Bear and pancakes and tomatoes and what did Random want with her anyway?

=The gene regulating the enzyme PDK4 (pyruvate dehydrogenase kinase isoenzyme 4) switches the squirrel's metabolism from the active to the hibernating state by inhibiting carbohydrate oxidation.=

She tried to remember exactly when she had decided to block out everything about Natalya Volochkova, but she couldn't. She had a vague memory that it had been her room's idea. She had asked it why her mother had abandoned her and her room had said that maybe grownups didn't always have choices but that had only made her upset. So her room had told Mariska that she was a special girl who didn't need a mother and that she should never ask about her again. *Ever. Never.* Or had that been a dreamfeed?

=…mitochondrial functions are drastically reduced…=

Mariska felt as if she were swimming through the data in the feed. She was certain that she would never remember any of it. And Mr. Holmgren was going to have a meltdown when he saw how she had left her bench in the lab and she'd probably flunk tomatoes just like Jak had.

=In 2014 the first recombinant ground squirrel and human genes resulted in activity of PTL—pancreatic triacylglycerol lipase—in both heart and white adipose tissue under supercooling conditions.=

What had happened in 2018? She had never much cared for history. The Oil Crash must have started around that time. And Google 3.0. The founding of Moonbase Zhong? A bunch of extinctions. Datafeeds, sure, but mindfeeds didn't come until the eighties. When did the fossil spacers launch the first starship?

As she touched the wall a foot tapped her on the shoulder. She twisted out of her flip turn and broke the surface of the water, sputtering. Random was standing at the edge of the pool, staring at her. His bathing suit had slid down his bony hips. "My penny," he said. "Can I have it back now?" His pale skin had just a tinge of blue and he was shivering.

Random spilled his bundle of clothes onto the floor in front of her locker; he had the handle of a lunch box clamped between his teeth. Mariska slithered into her tube top as he set the lunch box on the bench between them. It had a picture of an apple on it; the apple was wearing a space helmet.

"This isn't funny, Random." Mariska slipped an arm into the sleeve of her tugshirt. "Are you stalking me?"

"No." He punched the print button on the processor and an oversized pool towel rolled from the output slot above the lockers. "Not funny at all."

She sealed the front placket of the tug and plunged both hands into its pouch. There it was. She must have taken the penny without realizing it. She extended the coin to him on her palm.

"First we talk, then you get the penny." She closed her fist around it. "What's this about?"

"I said already." Random stripped off his wet bathing suit. "Your mother." He crammed it into the input slot and began to dry himself with the towel.

Mariska set her jaw but didn't correct him. "What about her?"

"She's a fossil. The penny could have been hers."

"Okay." She wasn't sure she believed this, but she didn't want him to think that she didn't know if it were true. The heroic fossils had been the first humans to go to the stars. They had volunteered to be genetically altered so that they could hibernate through the three year voyage to the wormhole at the far edge of Oort Cloud and then hibernate again as their ships cruised at sublight speeds through distant solar systems. Most of the fossils were dead, many from side effects of the crude genetic surgery of the twenty-first century. "So?"

"She probably has stuff. Or maybe you have her stuff?"

"Stuff?"

"To trade." He wrapped the towel around his waist and opened his lunch box. It was crammed with what looked to Mariska like junk wrapped in clear guardgoo. "Like my goods." Random pulled each item out as if it were a treasure.

"Vanilla Girl." He showed her the head of a doll with a patch over one eye. "Pencil," he said. "Never sharpened." He arranged an empty Coke bubble, a paper book with the cover ripped off, a key, a purple eyelight, a pepper shaker in the shape of a robot, and a thumb teaser on the bench. At the bottom of the lunch box was a tiny red plastic purse. He snapped it open and shook it so that she could hear coins clinking. "Please?"

Mariska dropped the penny into the purse. "How did you find out she's a fossil?"

"It's complicated." He tapped his forehead and she felt a tingle as he offered her a feed. "Want to open up?"

"No." Mariska folded her arms over her chest. "I don't think I do." She was chilled at the thought of losing herself in the chaos of feeds everyone claimed was churning inside Random's head. "You'll just have to say it."

Random dropped the towel on the floor and pulled on his janitor's greens. She was disgusted to see that he didn't bother with underwear. "When the *Gorshkov* came back," he said, "everyone was happy." He furrowed his brow, trying to remember how to string consecutive sentences together. "Happy people talk and make feeds and party all over. That's how I know." He nodded as if that explained everything.

Mariska tried not to sound impatient. "Know what?"

"It's a beautiful planet." Random made a circle with his hands, as if to present the new world to her. "Check the feeds, you'll see. It's the best ever. Even better than earth, at least the way it is now, all crispy and crowded."

"Okay, so it's the Garden of slagging Eden. So what does that have to do with all this crap?"

"Crap?" He drew himself up, and then waved the pepper shaker at her. "My goods aren't crap." He set it carefully back in the lunch box and began to gather up the rest of his odd collection.

"Sorry, sorry, sorry." Mariska didn't want to chase him away—at least not yet. "So it's a beautiful planet. And your goods are great. Tell me what's going on?"

He stacked the Coke bubble and the eyelight on top of the book but then paused, considering her apology. "Most of the crew of the *Gorshkov* are going back." He packed the pile away. "It's their reward, to live on a planet with all that water and all that sky and friendly weather. Going back..." he tapped the bench next to her leg "...with their families."

Mariska's throat was so tight that she could barely croak. "I'm not her family."

"Okay." He shrugged. "But anything you want to trade before you go—either of you…"

Mariska flung herself at the security door.

"Just asking," Random called after her.

When she burst into the kitchen, Al was arranging a layer of lasagna noodles in a casserole. Yet another of her favorite dishes; Mariska should have known something was wrong. She gasped when he looked over his shoulder at her. His eyes were shiny and his cheeks were wet.

"You *knew*." She could actually hear herself panicking. "She wants to drag me off to some stinking rock twenty light years away and you knew."

"I didn't. But I guessed." The weight of his sadness knocked her back onto one of the dining room chairs. "She stopped by right after you left. She's looking for you."

"I'm not here."

"Okay." He picked up a cup of shredded mozzarella and sprinkled it listlessly over the noodles.

"You can't let her do this, Al. You're my daddy. You're supposed to protect me."

"It's a term contract, Mariska. I'm already in the option year."

"Slag the contract. And slag you for signing it. I don't want to go."

"Then don't. I don't think she'll make you. But you need to think about it." He kept his head down and spooned sauce onto the lasagna. "It's space, Mariska. You're a spacer."

"Not yet. I haven't even passed tomatoes. I could wash out. I *will* wash out."

He sniffed and wiped his eyes with his sleeve.

"I don't understand," she said. "Why are you taking her side?"

"Because you're a child and she's your legal parent. Because you can't live here forever." His voice climbed unsteadily to a shout. Al had never shouted at her before. "Because all of this is over." He shook the spoon at their kitchen.

"What do you mean, over?" She thought that it wasn't very professional of him to be showing his feelings like this. "Answer me! And what about Jak?"

"I don't know, Mariska." He jiggled another lasagna noodle out of the colander. "I don't know what I'm going to do."

She stared at his back. The kitchen seemed to warp and twist; all the ties that bound her to Al were coming undone. She scraped her chair from the table and spun down the hall to her room, bouncing off the walls.

"Hello Mariska," said her room as the door slid shut. "You seem upset. Is there anything I can…?

"Shut up, shut up, *shut up*."

She didn't care if she hurt her room's feelings; it was just a stupid persona anyway. She needed quiet to think, sort through all the lies that had been her life. It must have been some other girl who had drawn funny aliens on the walls or listened to the room tell stories—lies!—about a space captain named Mariska or who had built planets inhabited by unicorns and fairies and princesses in her room's simspace. She didn't belong here. Not in this goddamn room, not on the moon, not anywhere.

Then it came to her. She knew what she had to do. Only she wasn't sure exactly how to do it. But how hard could going deep be? It was in her genes—her mother's genes. Slag her. Everyone was so worried that she would go deep without really meaning to. So that must mean that she could. That's how the fossils had done it, before there were hibernation pods and proper euthermic arousal protocols.

She didn't know what good going deep would do her. It was probably stupid. Something a kid would do. But that was the point, wasn't it? She was just a kid. What other choice did she have?

She lay back on her bed and thought about space, about stepping out of the airlock without anything on. Naked and alone, just like she had always been. The air would freeze in her lungs and they would burst. Her eyes would freeze and it would be dark. She would be as cold as she had ever been. As cold as Natalya Volochkova, that bitch.

"The earth is up," the room murmured. "And I am always up. Is Mariska ready to get up yet?"

Mariska shivered from the cold. That wasn't right. Her room was supposed to monitor both its temperature and hers.

"The earth is up, and I am always up," cooed her room. It wasn't usually so patient.

Mariska stretched. She felt stiff, as if she had overdone a swim. She opened her eyes and then shut them immediately. Her room had already brought the lights up to full intensity. It was acting strangely this morning. Usually it would interrupt one of her dreams, but all that she had in her head was a vast and frigid darkness. Space without the stars.

Mariska yawned and slitted her eyes against the light. She was facing the shelf where Feodor Bear sat. "*Dobroye utro*," it said. The antique robot bumped against the shelf twice in a vain attempt to stand. "Good morn-ing Mar-i-ska." There was something wrong with its speech chip; it sounded as if it were talking through a bowl of soup.

"Good morning, dear Mariska," said her room. "Today is Wednesday, November 23, 2163. You have no bookings scheduled for today.

That couldn't be right. The date was way off. Then she remembered.

The door slid open. She blinked several times before she could focus on the woman standing here.

"Mariska?"

Mariska knew that voice. Even though it had a crack to it that her room had never had, she recognized its singing accent.

"Where's Al?" When she sat up the room seemed to spin.

"He doesn't live here anymore." The woman sat beside her on the bed. She had silver hair and a spacer's sallow complexion. Her skin was wrinkled around the eyes and the mouth. "I can send for him, if you like. He's just in Muoi Zone." She seemed to be trying on a smile, to see if it would fit. "It's been three years, Mariska. We couldn't rouse you. It was too dangerous."

She considered this. "Jak?"

"Three years is a long time."

She turned her face to the wall. "The room's voice—that's you. And the persona?"

"I didn't want to go to *Delta Pavonis*, but I didn't have a choice. I'm a spacer, dear, dear Mariska. Just like you. When they need us, we go." She sighed. "I knew you would hate me—*I* would have hated me. So I found another way to be with you; I spent the two months before we left uploading feeds. I put as much of myself into this room as I could." She gestured at Mariska's room.

"You treated me like a kid. Or the room did."

"I'm sorry. I didn't think I'd be gone this long."

"I'm not going to that place with you."

"All right," she said. "But I'd like to go with you, if you'll let me."

"I'm not going anywhere." Mariska shook her head; she was still felt groggy. "Where would I go?"

"To the stars." said Natalya Volochkova. "They've been calling you. *Alpha Centauri. Barnard's. Wolf. Lalande. Luyten. Sirius.*"

Mariska propped herself on a elbow and stared at her. "How do you know that?"

She reached out and brushed a strand of hair from Mariska's forehead. "Because," she said, "I'm your mother."

THE COLDEST GIRL IN COLDTOWN
HOLLY BLACK

Holly Black is the author of the bestselling "The Spiderwick Chronicles". Her first story appeared in 1997, but she got attention with her debut novel, *Tithe: A Modern Faerie Tale*. She has written eight "Spiderwick" novels, three novels in her "Modern Faerie Tale" sequence, including Andre Norton Award winner *Valiant: A Modern Tale of Faerie*, and two books in the *Good Neighbors* series of graphic novels. Black's most recent books are her first short story collection, *The Poison Eaters and Other Stories* and a new novel, *White Cat*, the first book in "The Curse Workers" series.

Matilda was drunk, but then she was always drunk anymore. Dizzy drunk. Stumbling drunk. Stupid drunk. Whatever kind of drunk she could get.

The man she stood with snaked his hand around her back, warm fingers digging into her side as he pulled her closer. He and his friend with the open-necked shirt grinned down at her like underage equaled dumb, and dumb equaled gullible enough to sleep with them.

She thought they might just be right.

"You want to have a party back at my place?" the man asked. He'd told her his name was Mark, but his friend kept slipping up and calling him by a name that started with a D. Maybe Dan or Dave. They had been smuggling her drinks from the bar whenever they went outside to smoke—drinks mixed sickly sweet, that dripped down her throat like candy.

"Sure," she said, grinding her cigarette against the brick wall. She missed the hot ash in her hand, but concentrated on the alcoholic numbness turning her limbs to lead. Smiled. "Can we pick up more beer?"

They exchanged an obnoxious glance she pretended not to notice. The friend—he called himself Ben—looked at her glassy eyes and her cold-flushed cheeks. Her sloppy hair. He probably made guesses about a troubled home life. She hoped so.

"You're not going to get sick on us?" he asked. Just out of the hot bar, beads of sweat had collected in the hollow of his throat. The skin shimmered with each swallow.

She shook her head to stop staring. "I'm barely tipsy," she lied.

"I've got plenty of stuff back at my place," said MarkDanDave. *Mardave*, Matilda thought and giggled.

"Buy me a forty," she said. She knew it was stupid to go with them, but it was even stupider if she sobered up. "One of those wine coolers. They have them at the bodega on the corner. Otherwise, no party."

Both of the guys laughed. She tried to laugh with them even though she knew she wasn't included in the joke. She was the joke. The trashy little slut. The girl who can be bought for a big fat wine cooler and three cranberry-and-vodkas.

"Okay, okay," said Mardave.

They walked down the street and she found herself leaning easily into the heat of their bodies, inhaling the sweat and iron scent. It would be easy for her to close her eyes and pretend Mardave was someone else, someone she wanted to be touched by, but she wouldn't let herself soil her memories of Julian.

They passed by a store with flat-screens in the window, each one showing different channels. One streamed video from Coldtown—a girl who went by the name Demonia made some kind of deal with one of the stations to show what it was really like behind the gates. She filmed the Eternal Ball, a party that started in 1998 and had gone on ceaselessly ever since. In the background, girls and boys in rubber harnesses swung through the air. They stopped occasionally, opening what looked like a modded hospital tube stuck on the inside of their arms just below the crook of the elbow. They twisted a knob and spilled blood into little paper cups for the partygoers. A boy who looked to be about nine, wearing a string of glowing beads around his neck, gulped down the contents of one of the cups and then licked the paper with a tongue as red as his eyes. The camera angle changed suddenly, veering up, and the viewers saw the domed top of the hall, full of cracked windows through which you could glimpse the stars.

"I know where they are," Mardave said. "I can see that building from my apartment."

"Aren't you scared of living so close to the vampires?" she asked, a small smile pulling at the corner of her mouth.

"We'll protect you," said Ben, smiling back at her.

"We should do what other countries do and blow those corpses sky high," Mardave said.

Matilda bit her tongue not to point out that Europe's vampire hunting led to the highest levels of infection in the world. So many of Belgium's citizens were vampires that shops barely opened their doors until nightfall. The truce with Coldtown worked. Mostly.

She didn't care if Mardave hated vampires. She hated them too.

When they got to the store, she waited outside to avoid getting carded and lit another cigarette with Julian's silver lighter—the one she was going to give back to him in thirty-one days. Sitting down on the curb, she let the chill of the pavement deaden the backs of her thighs. Let it freeze her belly and frost her throat with ice that even liquor couldn't melt.

Hunger turned her stomach. She couldn't remember the last time she'd eaten anything solid without throwing it back up. Her mouth hungered for dark, rich feasts; her skin felt tight, like a seed thirsting to bloom. All she could trust herself to eat was smoke.

When she was a little girl, vampires had been costumes for Halloween. They were the bad guys in movies, plastic fangs and polyester capes. They were muppets on television, endlessly counting.

Now she was the one that was counting. Fifty-seven days. Eighty-eight days. Eighty-eight nights.

"Matilda?"

She looked up and saw Dante saunter up to her, earbuds dangling out of his ears like he needed a soundtrack for everything he did. He wore a pair of skin-tight jeans and smoked a cigarette out of one of those long, movie-star holders. He looked pretentious as hell. "I'd almost given up on finding you."

"You should have started with the literal gutter," she said, gesturing to the wet, clogged tide beneath her feet. "I take my gutter-dwelling very seriously."

"*Seriously.*" He pointed at her with the cigarette holder. "Even your mother thinks you're dead. Julian's been crying over you."

Matilda looked down and picked at the thread of her jeans. It hurt to think about Julian, while waiting for Mardave and Ben. She was disgusted with herself and she could only guess how disgusted he'd be. "I got Cold," she said. "One of them bit me."

Dante nodded his head.

That's what they'd started calling it when the infection kicked in—Cold—because of how cold people's skin became. And because of the way the poison in their veins caused them to crave heat and blood. One taste of human blood and the infection mutated. It killed the host and then raised them back up again, colder than before. Cold through and through, forever and ever.

"I didn't think you'd be alive," he said.

She hadn't thought she'd make it this long either without giving in. But going it alone on the street was better than forcing her mother to choose between chaining her up in the basement or shipping her off to Coldtown. It was better, too, than taking the chance that Matilda might get loose from the chains and attack people she loved. Stories like that were in the news all the time; almost as frequent as the ones about people who let vampires into their homes because they seemed so nice and clean-cut.

"Then what are you doing looking for me?" she asked. Dante had lived down the street from her family for years, but they didn't hang out. She'd wave to him as she mowed the lawn while he loaded his panel van with DJ equipment. He shouldn't have been here.

She looked back at the store window. Mardave and Ben were at the counter with a case of beer and her wine cooler. They were getting change from a clerk.

"I was hoping you, er, *wouldn't* be alive," Dante said. "You'd be more help if you were dead."

She stood up, stumbling slightly. "Well screw you too."

It took eighty-eight days for the venom to sweat out a person's pores. She only had thirty-seven to go. Thirty-seven days to stay so drunk that she could ignore the buzz in her head that made her want to bite, rend, devour.

"That came out wrong," he said, taking a step toward her. Close enough that she felt the warmth of him radiating off him like licking tongues of flame. She shivered. Her veins sang with need.

"I can't help you," said Matilda. "Look, I can barely help myself. Whatever it is, I'm sorry. I can't. You have to get out of here."

"My sister Lydia and your boyfriend, Julian, are gone," Dante said. "Together. She's looking to get bitten. I don't know what he's looking for…but he's going to get hurt."

Matilda gaped at him as Mardave and Ben walked out of the store. Ben carried a box on his shoulder and a bag on his arm. "This guy bothering you?" he asked her.

"No," she said, then turned to Dante. "You better go."

"Wait," said Dante.

Matilda's stomach hurt. She was sobering up. The smell of blood seemed to float up from underneath their skin.

She reached into Ben's bag and grabbed a beer. She popped the top, licked off the foam. If she didn't get a lot drunker, she was going to attack someone.

"Jesus," Mardave said. "Slow down. What if someone sees you?"

She drank it in huge gulps, right there on the street. Ben laughed, but it wasn't a good laugh. He was laughing at the drunk.

"She's infected," Dante says.

Matilda whirled toward him, chucking the mostly empty can in his direction automatically. "Shut up, asshole."

"Feel her skin," Dante said. "Cold. She ran away from home when it happened and no one's seen her since."

"I'm cold because it's cold out," she said.

She saw Ben's evaluation of her change from *damaged enough to sleep with strangers* to *dangerous enough to attack strangers*.

Mardave touched his hand gently to her arm. "Hey," he said.

She almost hissed with delight at the press of his hot fingers. She smiled up at him and hoped her eyes weren't as hungry as her skin. "I really like you."

He flinched. "Look, it's late. Maybe we could meet up another time." Then he backed away, which made her so angry that she bit the inside of her own cheek.

Her mouth flooded with the taste of copper and a red haze floated in front of her eyes.

Fifty-seven days ago, Matilda had been sober. She'd had a boyfriend named

Julian and they would dress up together in her bedroom. He liked to wear skinny ties and glittery eye shadow. She liked to wear vintage rock t-shirts and boots that laced up so high that they would constantly be late because they were busy tying them.

Matilda and Julian would dress up and prowl the streets and party at lockdown clubs that barred the doors from dusk to dawn. Matilda wasn't particularly careless; she was just careless enough.

She'd been at a friend's party. It had been stiflingly hot and she was mad because Julian and Lydia were doing some dance thing from the musical they were in at school. Matilda just wanted to get some air. She opened a window and climbed out under the bobbing garland of garlic.

Another girl was already on the lawn. Matilda should have noticed that the girl's breath didn't crystallize in the air, but she didn't.

"Do you have a light?" the girl had asked.

Matilda did. She reached for Julian's lighter when the girl caught her arm and bent her backwards. Matilda's scream turned into a shocked cry when she felt the girl's cold mouth against her neck, the girl's cold fingers holding her off balance.

Then it was as though someone slid two shards of ice into her skin.

The spread of vampirism could be traced to one person—Caspar Morales. Films and books and television had started romanticizing vampires and maybe it was only a matter of time before a vampire started romanticizing *himself*.

Crazy, romantic Caspar decided that he wouldn't kill his victims. He'd just drink a little blood and then move on, city to city. By the time other vampires caught up with him and ripped him to pieces, he'd infected hundreds of people. And those new vampires, with no idea how to prevent the spread, infected thousands.

When the first outbreak happened in Tokyo, it seemed like a journalist's prank. Then there was another outbreak in Hong Kong and another in San Francisco.

The military put up barricades around the area where the infection broke out. That was the way the first Coldtown was founded.

Matilda's body twitched involuntarily. She could feel the spasm start in the muscles of her back and move to her face. She wrapped her arms around herself to try and stop it, but her hands were shaking pretty hard. "You want my help, you better get me some booze."

"You're killing yourself," Dante said, shaking his head.

"I just need another drink," she said. "Then I'll be fine."

He shook his head. "You can't keep going like this. You can't just stay drunk to avoid your problems. I know, people do. It's a classic move even, but I didn't figure you for fetishizing your own doom."

She started laughing. "You don't understand. When I'm wasted I don't crave blood. It's the only thing keeping me human."

"What?" He looked at Matilda like he couldn't quite make sense of her words.

"Let me spell it out: if you don't get me some alcohol, I am going to bite you."

"Oh." He fumbled for his wallet. "Oh. Okay."

Matilda had spent all the cash she'd brought with her in the first few weeks, so it'd been a long time since she could simply overpay some homeless guy to go into a liquor store and get her a fifth of vodka. She gulped gratefully from the bottle Dante gave her in a nearby alley.

A few moments later, warmth started to creep up from her belly and her mouth felt like it was full of needles and Novocain.

"You okay?" he asked her.

"Better now," she said, her words slurring slightly. "But I still don't understand. Why do you need me to help you find Lydia and Julian?

"Lydia got obsessed with becoming a vampire," Dante said, irritably brushing back the stray hair that fell across his face.

"Why?"

He shrugged. "She used to be really scared of vampires. When we were kids, she begged Mom to let her camp in the hallway because she wanted to sleep where there were no windows. But then I guess she started to be fascinated instead. She thinks that human annihilation is coming. She says that we all have to choose sides and she's already chosen."

"I'm not a vampire," Matilda says.

Dante gestures irritably with his cigarette holder. The cigarette has long burned out. He doesn't look like his usual contemptuous self; he looks lost. "I know. I thought you would be. And—I don't know—you're on the street. Maybe you know more than the video feeds do about where someone might be able to get themselves bitten."

Matilda thought about lying on the floor of Julian's parents' living room. They were sweaty from dancing and were kissing languidly. On the television, a list of missing people flashed. She had closed her eyes and kissed him again.

She nodded slowly. "I know a couple of places. Have you heard from her at all?"

He shook his head. "She won't take any of my calls, but she's been updating her blog. I'll show you."

He loaded it on his phone. The latest entry was titled: *I Need A Vampire*. Matilda scrolled down and read. Basically, it was Lydia's plea to be bitten. She wanted any vampires looking for victims to contact her. In the comments, someone suggested Coldtown and then another person commented in ALL CAPS to say that everyone knew that the vampires in Coldtown were careful to keep their food source alive.

It was impossible to know which comments Lydia had read and which ones she believed.

Runaways went to Coldtown all the time, along with the sick, the sad, and the maudlin. There was supposed to be a constant party, theirs for the price of blood. But once they went inside, humans—even human children, even babies born in Coldtown—wouldn't be allowed to leave. The National Guard patrolled the barbed-wire-wrapped and garlic-covered walls to make sure that Coldtown stayed contained.

People said that vampires found ways through the walls to the outside world. Maybe that was just a rumor, although Matilda remembered reading something online about a documentary that proved the truth. She hadn't seen it.

But everyone knew there was only one way to get out of Coldtown if you were still human. Your family had to be rich enough to afford hiring a vampire hunter. Vampire hunters got money from the government for each vampire they put in Coldtown but they could give up the cash reward in favor of a voucher for a single human's release. One vampire in, one human out.

There was a popular reality television series about one of the hunters, called *Hemlok*. Girls hung posters of him on the insides of their lockers, often right next to pictures of the vampires he hunted.

Most people didn't have the money to outbid the government for a hunter's services. Matilda didn't think that Dante's family did and knew Julian's didn't. Her only chance was to catch Lydia and Julian before they crossed over.

"What's with Julian?" Matilda asked. She'd been avoiding the question for hours as they walked through the alleys that grew progressively more empty the closer they got to the gates.

"What do you mean?" Dante was hunched over against the wind, his long skinny frame offering little protection against the chill. Still, she knew he was warm underneath. Inside.

"Why did Julian go with her?" She tried to keep the hurt out of her voice. She didn't think Dante would understand. He DJed at a club in town and was rumored to see a different boy or girl every day of the week. The only person he actually seemed to care about was his sister.

Dante shrugged slim shoulders. "Maybe he was looking for you."

That was the answer she wanted to hear. She smiled and let herself imagine saving Julian right before he could enter Coldtown. He would tell her that he'd been coming to save her and then they'd laugh and she wouldn't bite him, no matter how warm his skin felt.

Dante snapped his fingers in front of Matilda and she stumbled.

"Hey," she said. "Drunk girl here. No messing with me."

He chuckled.

Matilda and Dante checked all the places she knew, all the places she'd slept on cardboard near runaways and begged for change. Dante had a picture of Lydia in his wallet, but no one who looked at it remembered her.

Finally, outside a bar, they bumped into a girl who said she saw Lydia and Julian. Dante traded her the rest of his pack of cigarettes for her story.

"They were headed for Coldtown," she said, lighting up. In the flickering flame of her lighter, Matilda noticed the shallow cuts along her wrists. "Said she was tired of waiting."

"What about the guy?" Matilda asked. She stared at the girl's dried garnet scabs. They looked like crusts of sugar, like the lines of salt left on the beach when the tide goes out. She wanted to lick them.

"He said his girlfriend was a vampire," said the girl, inhaling deeply. She blew out smoke and then started to cough.

"When was that?" Dante asked.

The girl shrugged her shoulders. "Just a couple of hours ago."

Dante took out his phone and pressed some buttons. "Load," he muttered. "Come on, *load*."

"What happened to your arms?" Matilda asked.

The girl shrugged again. "They bought some blood off me. Said that they might need it inside. They had a real professional set-up too. Sharp razor and a one of those glass bowls with the plastic lids."

Matilda's stomach clenched with hunger. She turned against the wall and breathed slowly. She needed a drink.

"Is something wrong with her?" the girl asked.

"Matilda," Dante said, and Matilda half-turned. He was holding out his phone. There was a new entry up on Lydia's blog, entitled: *One-Way Ticket to Coldtown*.

"You should post about it," Dante said. "On the message boards."

Matilda was sitting on the ground, picking at the brick wall to give her fingers something to do. Dante had massively overpaid for another bottle of vodka and was cradling it in a crinkled paper bag.

She frowned. "Post about what?"

"About the alcohol. About it helping you keep from turning."

"Where would I post about that?"

Dante twisted off the cap. The heat seemed to radiate off his skin as he swigged from the bottle. "There are forums for people who have to restrain someone for eighty-eight days. They hang out and exchange tips on straps and dealing with the begging for blood. Haven't you seen them?"

She shook her head. "I bet sedation's already a hot topic of discussion. I doubt I'd be telling them anything they don't already know"

He laughs, but it's a bitter laugh. "Then there's all the people that want to be vampires. The websites reminding all the corpsebait out there that being bitten by an infected person isn't enough; it has to be a vampire. The ones listing gimmicks to get vampires to notice you."

"Like what?"

"I dated a girl who cut thin lines on her thighs before she went out dancing so if there was a vampire in the club, it'd be drawn to her scent." Dante didn't look extravagant or affected anymore. He looked defeated.

Matilda smiled at him. "She was probably a better bet than me for getting you into Coldtown."

He returned the smile wanly. "The worst part is that Lydia's not going to get what she wants. She's going become the human servant of some vampire who's going to make her a whole bunch of promises and never turn her. The last thing they need in Coldtown is new vampires."

Matilda imagined Lydia and Julian dancing at the endless Eternal Ball. She pictured them on the streets she'd seen in pictures uploaded to Facebook and Flickr, trying to trade a bowl full of blood for their own deaths.

When Dante passed the bottle to her, she pretended to swig. On the eve of her fifty-eighth day of being infected, Matilda started sobering up.

Crawling over, she straddled Dante's waist before he had a chance to shift positions. His mouth tasted like tobacco. When she pulled back from him, his eyes were wide with surprise, his pupils blown and black even in the dim streetlight.

"Matilda," he said and there was nothing in his voice but longing.

"If you really want your sister, I am going to need one more thing from you," she said.

His blood tasted like tears.

Matilda's skin felt like it had caught fire. She'd turned into lit paper, burning up. Curling into black ash.

She licked his neck over and over and over.

The gates of Coldtown were large and made of consecrated wood, barbed wire covering them like heavy, thorny vines. The guards slouched at their posts, guns over their shoulders, sharing a cigarette. The smell of percolating coffee wafted out of the guardhouse.

"Um, hello," Matilda said. Blood was still sticky where it half-dried around her mouth and on her neck. It had dribbled down her shirt, stiffening it nearly to cracking when she moved. Her body felt strange now that she was dying. Hot. More alive than it had in weeks.

Dante would be all right; she wasn't contagious and she didn't think she'd hurt him too badly. She hoped she hadn't hurt him too badly. She touched the phone in her pocket, his phone, the one she'd used to call 911 after she'd left him.

"Hello," she called to the guards again.

One turned. "Oh my god," he said and reached for his rifle.

"I'm here to turn in a vampire. For a voucher. I want to turn in a vampire in exchange for letting a human out of Coldtown."

"What vampire?" asked the other guard. He'd dropped the cigarette, but not stepped on the filter so that it just smoked on the asphalt.

"Me," said Matilda. "I want to turn in me."

They made her wait as her pulse thrummed slower and slower. She wasn't a vampire yet, and after a few phone calls, they discovered that technically she could only have the voucher after undeath. They did let her wash her face in the bathroom of the guardhouse and wring the thin cloth of her shirt until the water that ran down the drain was clear, instead of murky with blood.

When she looked into the mirror, her skin had unfamiliar purple shadows, like bruises. She was still staring at them when she stopped being able to catch her breath. The hollow feeling in her chest expanded and she found herself panicked, falling to her knees on the filthy tile floor. She died there, a moment later.

It didn't hurt as much as she'd worried it would. Like most things, the surprise was the worst part.

The guards released Matilda into Coldtown just a little before dawn. The world looked strange—everything had taken on a smudgy, silvery cast, like she was watching an old movie. Sometimes people's heads seemed to blur into black smears. Only one color was distinct—a pulsing, oozing color that seemed to glow from beneath skin.

Red.

Her teeth ached to look at it.

There was a silence inside of her. No longer did she move to the rhythmic drumming of her heart. Her body felt strange, hard as marble, free of pain. She'd never realized how many small agonies were alive in the creak of her bones, the pull of muscle. Now, free of them, she felt like she was floating.

Matilda looked around with her strange new eyes. Everything was beautiful. And the light at the edge of the sky was the most beautiful thing of all.

"What are you doing?" a girl called from a doorway. She had long black hair but her roots were growing in blonde. "Get in here! Are you crazy?"

In a daze, Matilda did as she was told. Everything smeared as she moved, like the world was painted in watercolors. The girl's pinkish-red face swirled along with it.

It was obvious the house had once been grand, but looked like it'd been abandoned for a long time. Graffiti covered the peeling wallpaper and couches had been pushed up against the walls. A boy wearing jeans but no shirt was painting make-up onto a girl with stiff pink pigtails while another girl in a retro polka-dotted dress pulled on mesh stockings.

In a corner, another boy—this one with glossy brown hair that fell to his waist—stacked jars of creamed corn into a precarious pyramid.

"What is this place?" Matilda asked.

The boy stacking the jars turned. "Look at her eyes. She's a vampire!" He didn't seem afraid, though; he seemed delighted.

"Get her into the cellar," one of the other girls said.

"Come on," said the black-haired girl and pulled Matilda toward a doorway. "You're fresh-made, right?"

"Yeah," Matilda said. Her tongue swept over her own sharp teeth. "I guess that's pretty obvious."

"Don't you know that vampires can't go outside in the daylight?" the girl asked, shaking her head. "The guards try that trick with every new vampire but I never saw one almost fall for it."

"Oh, right," Matilda said. They went down the rickety steps to a filthy basement with a mattress on the floor underneath a single bulb. Crates of foodstuffs were shoved against the walls and the high, small windows had been painted over with a tarry substance that let no light through.

The black-haired girl who'd waved her inside smiled. "We trade with the border guards. Black-market food, clothes, little luxuries like chocolate and cigarettes for some action. Vampires don't own everything."

"And you're going to owe us for letting you stay the night," the boy said from the top of the stairs.

"I don't have anything," Matilda said. "I didn't bring any cans of food or whatever."

"You have to bite us."

"What?" Matilda asked.

"One of us," the girl said. "How about one of us? You can even pick which one."

"Why would you want me to do that?"

The girl's expression clearly said that Matilda was stupid. "Who doesn't want to live forever?"

I don't, Matilda wanted to say, but she swallowed the words. She could tell they already thought she didn't deserve to be a vampire. Besides, she wanted to taste blood. She wanted to taste the red throbbing pulsing insides of the girl in front of her. It wasn't the pain she'd felt when she was infected, the hunger that made her stomach clench, the craving for warmth. It was heady, greedy desire.

"Tomorrow," Matilda said. "When it's night again."

"Okay," the girl said, "but you promise, right? You'll turn one of us?"

"Yeah," said Matilda, numbly. It was hard to even wait that long.

She was relieved when they went upstairs, but less relieved when she heard something heavy slide in front of the basement door. She told herself that didn't matter. The only thing that mattered was getting through the day so that she could find Julian and Lydia.

She shook her head to clear it of thoughts of blood and turned on Dante's phone. Although she didn't expect it, a text message was waiting: *I cant tell if I luv u or if I want to kill u.*

Relief washed over her. Her mouth twisted into a smile and her newly sharp canines cut her lip. She winced. Dante was okay.

She opened up Lydia's blog and posted an anonymous message: *Tell Julian his girlfriend wants to see him…and you.*

Matilda made herself comfortable on the dirty mattress. She looked up at the rotted boards of the ceiling and thought of Julian. She had a single ticket out of Coldtown and two humans to rescue with it, but it was easy to picture herself saving Lydia as Julian valiantly offered to stay with her, even promised her his eternal devotion.

She licked her lips at the image. When she closed her eyes, all her imaginings drowned in a sea of red.

Waking at dusk, Matilda checked Lydia's blog. Lydia had posted a reply: *Meet us at the Festival of Sinners.*

Five kids sat at the top of the stairs, watching her with liquid eyes.

"Are you awake?" the black-haired girl asked. She seemed to pulse with color. Her moving mouth was hypnotic.

"Come here," Matilda said to her in a voice that seemed so distant that she was surprised to find it was her own. She hadn't meant to speak, hadn't meant to beckon the girl over to her.

"That's not fair," one of the boys called. "I was the one that said she owed us something. It should be me. You should pick me."

Matilda ignored him as the girl knelt down on the dirty mattress and swept aside her hair, baring a long, unmarked neck. She seemed dazzling, this creature of blood and breath, a fragile manikin as brittle as sticks.

Tiny golden hairs tickled Matilda's nose as she bit down.

And gulped.

Blood was heat and heart and running-thrumming-beating through the fat roots of veins to drip syrup slow, spurting molten hot across tongue, mouth, teeth, chin.

Dimly, Matilda felt someone shoving her and someone else screaming, but it seemed distant and unimportant. Eventually the words became clearer.

"Stop," someone was screaming. "Stop!"

Hands dragged Matilda off the girl. Her neck was a glistening red mess. Gore stained the mattress and covered Matilda's hands and hair. The girl coughed, blood bubbles frothing on her lip, and then went abruptly silent.

"What did you do?" the boy wailed, cradling the girl's body. "She's dead. She's dead. You killed her."

Matilda backed away from the body. Her hand went automatically to her mouth, covering it. "I didn't mean to," she said.

"Maybe she'll be okay," said the other boy, his voice cracking. "We have to get bandages."

"She's *dead*," the boy holding the girl's body moaned.

A thin wail came from deep inside of Matilda as she backed toward the stairs.

Her belly felt full, distended. She wanted to be sick.

Another girl grabbed Matilda's arm. "Wait," the girl said, eyes wide and imploring. "You have to bite me next. You're full now so you won't have to hurt me—"

With a cry, Matilda tore herself free and ran up the stairs—if she went fast enough, maybe she could escape from herself.

By the time Matilda got to the Festival of Sinners, her mouth tasted metallic and she was numb with fear. She wasn't human, wasn't good and wasn't sure what she might do next. She kept pawing at her shirt, as if that much blood could ever be wiped off, as if it hadn't already soaked down into her skin and her soiled insides.

The Festival was easy to find, even as confused as she was. People were happy to give her directions, apparently not bothered that she was drenched in blood. Their casual demeanor was horrifying, but not as horrifying as how much she already wanted to feed again.

On the way, she passed the Eternal Ball. Strobe lights lit up the remains of the windows along the dome and a girl with blue hair in a dozen braids held up a video camera to interview three men dressed all in white with gleaming red eyes.

Vampires.

A ripple of fear passed through her. She reminded herself that there was nothing they could do to her. She was already like them. Already dead.

The Festival of Sinners was being held at a church with stained-glass windows painted black on the inside. The door, papered with pink-stenciled posters, was painted the same thick tarry black. Music thrummed from within and a few people sat on the steps, smoking and talking.

Matilda went inside.

A doorman pulled aside a velvet rope for her, letting her past a small line of people waiting to pay the cover charge. The rules were different for vampires, perhaps especially for vampires accessorizing their grungy attire with so much blood.

Matilda scanned the room. She didn't see Julian or Lydia at first, just a throng of dancers and a bar that served alcohol from vast copper distilling vats. It spilled into mismatched mugs. Then one of the people near the bar moved and Matilda spotted Lydia and Julian. He was bending over her, shouting into her ear.

Matilda pushed her way through the crowd, until she was close enough to touch Julian's arm. She reached out, but couldn't quite bring herself to brush his skin with her foulness.

Julian looked up, startled. "Tilda?"

She snatched back her hand like she'd been about to touch fire.

"Tilda," he said. "What happened to you? Are you hurt?"

Matilda flinched, looking down at herself. "I…"

Lydia laughed. "She ate someone, moron."

"Tilda?" Julian asked.

"I'm sorry," Matilda said. There was so much she had to be sorry for, but at least he was here now. Julian would tell her what to do and how to turn herself back into something decent again. She would save Lydia and Julian would save her.

He touched her shoulder, let his hand rest gingerly on her blood-stiffened shirt. "We were looking for you everywhere." His gentle expression was tinged with terror; fear pulled his smile into something closer to a grimace.

"I wasn't in Coldtown," Matilda said. "I came here so that Lydia could leave. I have a pass."

"But I don't want to leave," said Lydia. "You understand that, right? I want what you have—eternal life."

"You're not infected," Matilda said. "You have to go. You can still be okay. Please, I need you to go."

"One pass?" Julian said, his eyes going to Lydia. Matilda saw the truth in the weight of that gaze—Julian had not come to Coldtown for Matilda. Even though she knew she didn't deserve him to think of her as anything but a monster, it hurt savagely.

"I'm not leaving," Lydia said, turning to Julian, pouting. "You said she wouldn't be like this."

"*I killed a girl*," Matilda said. "I killed her. Do you understand that?"

"Who cares about some mortal girl?" Lydia tossed back her hair. In that moment, she reminded Matilda of her brother, pretentious Dante who'd turned out to be an actual nice guy. Just like sweet Lydia had turned out cruel.

"You're a girl," Matilda said. "You're mortal."

"I know that!" Lydia rolled her eyes. "I just mean that we don't care who you killed. Turn us and then we can kill lots of people."

"No," Matilda said, swallowing. She looked down, not wanting to hear what she was about to say. There was still a chance. "Look, I have the pass. If you don't want it, then Julian should take it and go. But I'm not turning you. I'm never turning you, understand."

"Julian doesn't want to leave," Lydia said. Her eyes looked bright and two feverish spots appeared on her cheeks. "Who are you to judge me anyway? You're the murderer."

Matilda took a step back. She desperately wanted Julian to say something in her defense or even to look at her, but his gaze remained steadfastly on Lydia.

"So neither one of you want the pass," Matilda said.

"Fuck you," spat Lydia.

Matilda turned away.

"Wait," Julian said. His voice sounded weak.

Matilda spun, unable to keep the hope off her face, and saw why Julian had called to her. Lydia stood behind him, a long knife to his throat.

"Turn me," Lydia said. "Turn me or I'm going to kill him."

Julian's eyes were wide. He started to protest or beg or something and Lydia pressed the knife harder, silencing him.

People had stopped dancing nearby, backing away. One girl with red-glazed eyes stared hungrily at the knife.

"Turn me!" Lydia shouted. "I'm tired of waiting! I want my life to begin!"

"You won't be alive—" Matilda started.

"I'll be alive—more alive than ever. Just like you are."

"Okay," Matilda said softly. "Give me your wrist."

The crowd seemed to close in tighter, watching as Lydia held out her arm. Matilda crouched low, bending down over it.

"Take the knife away from his throat," Matilda said.

Lydia, all her attention on Matilda, let Julian go. He stumbled a little and pressed his fingers to his neck.

"I loved you," Julian shouted.

Matilda looked up to see that he wasn't speaking to her. She gave him a glittering smile and bit down on Lydia's wrist.

The girl screamed, but the scream was lost in Matilda's ears. Lost in the pulse of blood, the tide of gluttonous pleasure and the music throbbing around them like Lydia's slowing heartbeat.

Matilda sat on the blood-soaked mattress and turned on the video camera to check that the live feed was working.

Julian was gone. She'd given him the pass after stripping him of all his cash and credit cards; there was no point in trying to force Lydia to leave since she'd just come right back in. He'd made stammering apologies that Matilda ignored and then he fled for the gate. She didn't miss him. Her fantasy of Julian felt as ephemeral as her old life.

"It's working," one of the boys—Michael—said from the stairs, a computer cradled on his lap. Even though she'd killed one of them, they welcomed her back, eager enough for eternal life to risk more deaths. "You're streaming live video."

Matilda set the camera on the stack of crates, pointed toward her and the wall where she'd tied a gagged Lydia. The girl thrashed and kicked, but Matilda ignored her. She stepped in front of the camera and smiled.

My name is Matilda Green. I was born on April 10, 1997. I died on September 3rd, 2013. Please tell my mother I'm okay. And Dante, if you're watching this, I'm sorry.

You've probably seen lots of video feeds from inside Coldtown. I saw them too. Pictures of girls and boys grinding together in clubs or bleeding elegantly for their celebrity vampire masters. Here's what you never see. What I'm going to show you now.

For eighty-eight days you are going to watch someone sweat out the infection. You are going to watch her beg and scream and cry. You're going to watch her throw up food and piss her pants and pass out. You're going to watch me feed her can after can of creamed corn. It's not going to be pretty.

You're going to watch me too. I'm the kind of vampire that you'd be, one that's new at this and basically out of control. I've already killed someone and I can't guarantee I'm not going to do it again. I'm the one that infected this girl.

This is the real Coldtown.

I'm the real Coldtown.

You still want in?

ZEPPELIN CITY
MICHAEL SWANWICK AND EILEEN GUNN

Michael Swanwick's first two short stories were published in 1980, and both featured on the Nebula ballot that year. One of the major writers working in the field today, he has been nominated for at least one of the field's major awards in almost every successive year, and has won the Hugo, Nebula, World Fantasy, Theodore Sturgeon Memorial, and the Locus awards. He has published six collections of short fiction, seven novels—*In the Drift, Vacuum Flowers, Stations of the Tide, The Iron Dragon's Daughter, Jack Faust, Bones of the Earth*, and *The Dragons of Babel*—and a Hugo Award nominated book-length interview with editor Gardner Dozois. His most recent book is major career retrospective collection, *The Best of Michael Swanwick*.

Eileen Gunn was born in Dorchester, Massachusetts and grew up outside Boston. She earned a Bachelor of Arts in History from Emmanuel College. In 1976, she attended the Clarion Writers Workshop in Michigan, then supported herself by writing advertising and books about computers. She was an early employee at Microsoft, where she was director of advertising and sales promotion in the mid-1980s. She left in 1985 to continue writing fiction. She lives in Seattle with the typographer and editor John D. Berry. Gunn's first short story, "What Are Friends For?" was published in 1978; subsequent stories include Nebula Award winner "Coming to Terms" and Hugo Award nominees "Stable Strategies for Middle Management" and "Computer Friendly". Her short fiction collection *Stable Strategies and Others* was published by Tachyon Publications in 2004, and was short-listed for the Philip K. Dick, James Tiptree, Jr., and World Fantasy awards. She is currently working on a biography of Avram Davidson.

Radio Jones came dancing down the slidewalks. She jumped from the express to a local, then spun about and raced backwards, dumping speed so she could cut across the slower lanes two and three at a time. She hopped off at the mouth of an alley, glanced up in time to see a Zeppelin disappear behind a glass-domed skyscraper, and stepped through a metal door left open to vent the heat from the furnaces within.

The glass-blowers looked up from their work as she entered the hot shop.

They greeted her cheerily:

"Hey, Radio!"

"Jonesy!"

"You invented a robot girlfriend for me yet?"

The shop foreman lumbered forward, smiling. "Got a box of off-spec tubes for you, under the bench there."

"Thanks, Mackie." Radio dug through the pockets of her patched leather greatcoat, and pulled out a folded sheet of paper. "Hey, listen, I want you to do me up an estimate for these here vacuum tubes."

Mack studied the list. "Looks to be pretty straightforward. None of your usual experimental trash. How many do you need—one of each?"

"I was thinking more like a hundred."

"*What?*" Mack's shaggy black eyebrows met in a scowl. "You planning to win big betting on the Reds?"

"Not me, I'm a Whites fan all the way. Naw, I was kinda hoping you'd gimme credit. I came up with something real hot."

"You finally built that girlfriend for Rico?"

The workmen all laughed.

"No, c'mon, I'm *serious* here." She lowered her voice. "I invented a universal radio receiver. Not fixed-frequency—tunable! It'll receive any broadcast on the radio spectrum. Twist the dial, there you are. With this baby, you can listen in on every conversation in the big game, if you want."

Mack whistled. "There might be a lot of interest in a device like that."

"Funny thing, I was thinking exactly that myself." Radio grinned. "So waddaya say?"

"I say—" Mack spun around to face the glass-blowers, who were all listening intently, and bellowed—"*Get back to work!*" Then, in a normal voice, "Tell you what. Set me up a demo, and if your gizmo works the way you say it does, maybe I'll invest in it. I've got the materials to build it, and access to the retailers. Something like this could move twenty, maybe thirty units a day, during the games."

"Hey! Great! The game starts when? Noon, right? I'll bring my prototype over, and we can listen to the players talking to each other." She darted toward the door.

"Wait." Mack ponderously made his way into his office. He extracted a five dollar bill from the lockbox and returned, holding it extended before him. "For the option. You agree not to sell any shares in this without me seeing this doohickey first."

"Oh, Mackie, you're the greatest!" She bounced up on her toes to kiss his cheek. Then, stuffing the bill into the hip pocket of her jeans, she bounded away.

Fat Edna's was only three blocks distant. She was inside and on a stool before the door jangled shut behind her. "Morning, Edna!" The neon light she'd rigged up over the bar was, she noted with satisfaction, still working. Nice and quiet, hardly any buzz to it at all. "Gimme a big plate of scrambled eggs and pastrami, with a beer on the side."

The bartender eyed her skeptically. "Let's see your money first."

With elaborate nonchalance, Radio laid the bill flat on the counter before her. Edna picked it up, held it to the light, then slowly counted out four ones and eighty-five cents change. She put a glass under the tap and called over her shoulder, "Wreck a crowd, with sliced dick!" She pulled the beer, slid the glass across the counter, and said, "Out in a minute."

"Edna, there is *nobody* in the world less satisfying to show off in front of than you. You still got that package I left here?"

Wordlessly, Edna took a canvas-wrapped object from under the bar and set it before her.

"Thanks." Radio unwrapped her prototype. It was bench-work stuff—just tubes, resistors and capacitors in a metal frame. No housing, no circuit tracer lights, and a tuner she had to turn with a pair of needle-nose pliers. But it was going to make her rich. She set about double-checking all the connectors. "Hey, plug this in for me, willya?"

Edna folded her arms and looked at her.

Radio sighed, dug in her pockets again, and slapped a nickel on the bar. Edna took the cord and plugged it into the outlet under the neon light.

With a faint hum, the tubes came to life.

"That thing's not gonna blow up, is it?" Edna asked dubiously.

"Naw." Radio took a pair of needle-nose pliers out of her greatcoat pocket and began casting about for a strong signal. "Most it's gonna do is electrocute you, maybe set fire to the building. But it's not gonna explode. You been watching too many kinescopes."

Amelia Spindizzy came swooping down out of the sun like a suicidal angel, all rage and mirth. The rotor of her autogyro whined and snarled with the speed of her dive. Then she throttled up and the blades bit deep into the air and pulled her out, barely forty feet from the ground. Laughing, she lifted the nose of her bird to skim the top of one skywalk, banked left to dip under a second, and then right to hop-frog a third. Her machine shuddered and rattled as she bounced it off the compression effects of the air around the skyscrapers to steal that tiny morsel of extra lift, breaking every rule in the book and not giving a damn.

The red light on Radio 2 flashed angrily. One-handed, she yanked the jacks to her headset from Radio 3, the set connecting her to the referee, and plugged into her comptroller's set. "Yah?"

The flat, emotionless, and eerily artificial voice of Naked Brain XB-29 cut through the static. "*Amelia, what are you doing?*"

"Just wanted to get your attention. I'm going to cut through the elbow between Ninetieth and Ninety-First Avenues. Plot me an Eszterhazy, will you?"

"*Computing.*" Almost as an afterthought, the Naked Brain said, "*You realize this is extremely dangerous.*"

"Nothing's dangerous enough for me," Amelia muttered, too quietly for the microphone to pick up. "Not by half."

The sporting rag *Obey the Brain!* had termed her "half in love with easeful death," but it was not *easeful* death that Amelia Spindizzy sought. It was the inevitable, difficult death of an impossible skill tenaciously mastered but necessarily insufficient to the challenge—a hard-fought battle for life, lost just as the hand reached for victory and closed about empty air. A mischance that conferred deniability, like a medal of honor, on her struggle for oblivion, as she twisted and fell in gloriously tragic heroism.

So far, she hadn't achieved it.

It wasn't that she didn't love being alive (at least some of the time). She loved dominating the air currents in her great titanium whirligig. She loved especially the slow turning in an ever-widening gyre, scanning for the opposition with an exquisite patience only a sigh short of boredom, and then the thrill as she spotted him, a minuscule speck in an ocean of sky. Loved the way her body flushed with adrenalin as she drove her machine up into the sun, searching for that sweet blind spot where the prey, her machine, and that great atomic furnace were all in a line. Loved most of all the instant of stillness before she struck.

It felt like being born all over again.

For Amelia, the Game was more than a game, because necessarily there would come a time when the coordination, strength, and precision demanded by her fierce and fragile machine would prove to be more than she could provide, a day when all the sky would gather its powers to break her will and force her into the ultimate submission. It would happen. She had faith. Until then, though, she strove only to live at the outer edge of her skills, to fly and to play the Game as gloriously as any human could to the astonishment of the unfortunate earthbound classes. And of the Naked Brains who could only float, ponderously, in their glass tanks, in their Zeppelins.

"*Calculations complete.*"

"You have my position?"

Cameras swiveled from the tops of nearby buildings, tracking her. "*Yes.*"

Now she'd achieved maximum height again.

"I'm going in."

Straight for the alley-mouth she flew. Sitting upright in the thorax of her flying machine, rudder pedals at her feet, stick controls to the left and right, she let inertia push her back into the seat like a great hand. Eight-foot-long titanium blades extended in a circle, with her at the center like the heart of a flower. This was no easy machine to fly. It combined the delicacy of flight with the physical demands of operating a mechanical thresher.

"*Pull level on my count. Three… Two… Now.*"

It took all her strength to bully her machine properly while the gee-forces tried to shove her away from the controls. She was flying straight and true toward Dempster Alley, a street that was only feet wider than the diameter of her autogyro's blades, so fine a margin of error that she'd be docked a month's pay if the Naked Brains saw what she was up to.

"*Shift angle of blades on my mark and rudder on my second mark. Three... Two... Mark. And... Rudder.*"

Tilted forty-five degrees, she roared down the alley, her prop wash rattling the windows and filling them with pale, astonished faces. At the intersection, she shifted pitch and kicked rudder, flipping her gyro over so that it canted forty-five degrees the other way (the engine coughed and almost stalled, then roared back to life again) and hammered down Bernoulli Lane (a sixty-degree turn here where the streets crossed at an odd angle) and so out onto Ninety-First. A perfect Eszterhazy! Five months ago, a hypercubed committee of half the Naked Brains in the metropolis had declared that such a maneuver couldn't be done. But one brave pilot had proved otherwise in an aeroplane, and Amelia had determined she could do no less in a 'gyro.

"*Bank left. Stabilize. Climb for height. Remove safeties from your bombs.*"

Amelia Spindizzy obeyed and then, glancing backwards, forwards, and to both sides, saw a small cruciform mote ahead and below, flying low over the Avenue. Grabbing her glasses, she scanned the wing insignia. She could barely believe her luck—it was the Big E himself! And she had a clear run at him.

The autogyro hit a patch of bumpy air, and Amelia snatched up the sticks to regain control. The motor changed pitch, the prop hummed, the rotor blades cut the air. Her machine was bucking now, veering into the scrap zone, and in danger of going out of control. She fought to get it back on an even keel, straightened it out, and swung into a tight arc.

Man, this was the life!

She wove and spun above the city streets as throngs of onlookers watched the warm-up hijinks from the tall buildings and curving skywalks. They shouted encouragement at her. "Don't let 'er drop, Amelia!" "Take the bum down, Millie!" "Spin 'im around, Spindizzy!" Bloodthirsty bastards. Her public. Screaming bloody murder and perfectly capable of chucking a beer bottle at her if they thought she wasn't performing up to par. Times like these she almost loved 'em.

She hated being called Millie, though.

Working the pedals, moving the sticks, dancing to the silent jazz of turbulence in the air around her, she was Josephine Baker, she was Cab Calloway, she was the epitome of grace and wit and intelligence in the service of entertainment. The crowd went wild as she caught a heavy gust of wind and went skidding sideways toward the city's treasured Gaudi skyscraper.

When she had brought everything under control and the autogyro was flying evenly again, Amelia looked down.

For a miracle, he was still there, still unaware of her, flying low in a warm-up run and placing flour bombs with fastidious precision one by one.

She throttled up and focused all her attention on her foe, the greatest flyer of his generation and her own, patently at her mercy if she could first rid herself of the payload. Her engine screamed in fury, and she screamed with it. "XB! Next five intersections! Gimme the count."

"*At your height, there is a risk of hitting spectators.*"

"I'm too good for that and you know it! Gimme the count."

"*Three… two… now. Six… five…*"

Each of the intersections had been roped off and painted blue with a white circle in its center and a red star at the sweet spot. Amelia worked the bombsight, calculated the windage (Naked Brains couldn't do that; you had to be present; you had to feel the air as a physical thing), and released the bombs one after the other. Frantically, then, she yanked the jacks and slammed them into Radio 3. "How'd we do?" she yelled. She was sure she'd hit them all on the square and she had hopes of at least one star.

"*Square. Circle. Circle. Star.*" The referee—Naked Brain QW-14, though the voice was identical to her own comptroller's—said. A pause. "*Star.*"

Yes!

She was coming up on Eszterhazy himself now, high and fast. He had all the disadvantages of position. She positioned her craft so that the very tip of its shadow kissed the tail of his bright red 'plane. He was still acting as if he didn't know she was there. Which was impossible. She could see three of his team's Zeppelins high above, and if she could see them, they sure as hell could see *her*. So why was he playing stupid?

Obviously he was hoping to lure her in.

"I see your little game," Amelia muttered softly. But just what dirty little trick did Eszterhazy have up his sleeve? The red light was flashing on Radio 2. The hell with that. She didn't need XB-29's bloodless advice at a time like this. "Okay, loverboy, let's see what you've got!" She pushed the stick forward hard. Then Radio 3 flashed—and *that* she couldn't ignore.

"*Amelia Spindizzy,*" the referee said. "*Your flight authorization has been canceled. Return to Ops.*"

Reflexively, she jerked the throttle back, scuttling the dive. "What?!"

"*Repeat: Return to Ops. Await further orders.*"

Angrily, Amelia yanked the jacks from Radio 3. Almost immediately the light on Radio 1 lit up. When she jacked in, the hollow, mechanical voice of Naked Brain ZF-43, her commanding officer, filled her earphones. "*I am disappointed in you, Amelia. Wastefulness. Inefficient expenditure of resources. Pilots should not weary themselves unnecessarily. XB-29 should have exercised more control over you. He will be reprimanded.*"

"It was just a pick-up game," she said. "For fun. You remember fun, don't you?"

There was a pause. "*There is nothing the matter with my memory,*" ZF-43 said at last. "*I do remember fun. Why do you ask?*"

"Maybe because I'm as crazy as an old coot, ZF," said Amelia, idly wondering if she could roll an autogyro. Nobody ever had. But if she went to maximum climb, cut the choke, and kicked the rudder hard, that ought to flip it. Then, if she could re-start the engine quickly enough and slam the rudder smartly the other way… It just might work. She could give it a shot right now.

"*Return to the Zeppelin immediately. The Game starts in less than an hour.*"

"Aw shucks, ZF. Roger." Not for the first time, Amelia wondered if the Naked Brain could read her mind. She'd have to try the roll later.

In less than the time it took to scramble an egg and slap it on a plate, Radio Jones had warmed up her tuner and homed in on a signal. "Maybe because I'm as crazy as an old coot, ZF," somebody squawked.

"Hey! I know that voice—it's Amelia!" If Radio had a hero, it was the aviatrix.

"*Return to the Zeppelin—*"

"Crimminy! A Naked Brain! Aw rats, static…" Radio tweaked the tuning ever so slightly with the pliers.

"—ucks, ZF. Roger."

Edna set the plate of eggs and pastrami next to the receiver. "Here's your breakfast, whiz kid."

Radio flipped off the power. "Jeeze, I ain't never heard a Brain before. Creepy."

By now, she had the attention of the several denizens of Fat Edna's.

"Whazzat thing do, Radio?"

"How does it work?"

"Can you make me one, Jonesy?"

"It's a Universal Tuner. Home in on any airwave whatsoever." Radio grabbed the catsup bottle, upended it over the plate, and whacked it hard. Red stuff splashed all over. She dug into her eggs. "I'm'nna make one for anybody who wants one," she said between mouthfuls. "Cost ya, though."

"Do they know you're listening?" It was Rudy the Red, floppy-haired and un-shaven, born troublemaker, interested only in politics and subversion. He was always predicting that the Fist of the Brains was just about to come down on him. As it would, eventually, everyone agreed: people like him tended to disap-pear. The obnoxious ones, however, lingered longer than most. "How can you be sure *they* aren't listening to *you* right now?"

"Well, all I can say, Rudy—" she wiped her mouth with her hand, as Fat Edna's bar was uncluttered with serviettes— "is that if they got something that can overthrow the laws of electromagnetism as we know 'em and turn a receiver into a transmitter, then more power to 'em. That's a good hack. Hey, the Game starts in a few minutes. Who ya bettin' on?"

"Radio, you know I don't wager human against human," Rudy said. "Our energies should be focused on our oppressors—the Naked Brains. But instead we do whatever they want because they've channeled all our aggression into a trivial distraction created to keep the masses stupefied and sedated. The Games are the opiate of the people! You should wise up and join the struggle, Radio. This device of yours could be our secret weapon. We could use it to listen in on them plotting against us."

"Ain't much of a secret," said Radio, "if it's all over Edna's bar."

"We can tell people it doesn't work."

"What are you, some kind of no-brainer? That there's my fancypants college education. I'm not tellin' nobody it don't work."

Amelia Spindizzy banked her tiny craft and turned it toward the huge Operations Zep *Imperator*. The Zeppelin thrust out its landing pad, and Amelia swooped deftly onto it, in a maneuver that she thought of as a penny-toss, a quick leap onto the target platform, which then retracted into the gondola of the airship. She climbed from the cockpit. Grimy Huey tossed her a mooring line and she tied down her machine. "You're on orders to report to the Hall, fly-girl," he shouted. "What have you done now?"

"I think I reminded ZF-43 of his lost physicality, Huey." Amelia scrambled up the bamboo gangway.

"You do that for me every time I look at you."

"You watch it, Huey, or I'll come over there and teach you a lesson," Amelia said.

"Amelia, I'll study under you anytime."

She shied a wheel chuck at him, and the mechanic ducked away, cackling. Mechanics' humor, thought Amelia. You have to let them have their jokes at your expense. It can make you or break you, what they do to your 'gyro.

The Hall of the Naked Brains was amidships. High-ceilinged, bare-walled, and paneled in bamboo, it smelled of lemon oil and beeswax. The windows were shuttered, to keep the room dim; the Brains didn't need light, and the crew was happier not looking at them. Twin rows of enormous glass jars, set in duraluminium frames, lined the sides of the Hall. Within the jars, enormous pink Brains floated motionless in murky electrolyte soup.

In the center of the shadowy room was a semicircle of rattan chairs facing a speaker and a televideon camera. Cables looped across the floor to each of the glass jars.

Amelia plumped down in the nearest chair, unzipped her flight jacket, and said, "Well?"

There was a ratcheting noise as one of the Brains adjusted the camera. A tinny disembodied voice came from the speaker. It was ZF-43. "*Amelia. We are equipping your autogyro with an important new device. It is essential that we test it today.*"

"What does it do?" she asked.

"*If it works properly, it will paralyze Lt. Eszterhazy's engine.*"

Amelia glared at the eye of the camera. "And why would I want to do that?"

"*Clearly you do not, Amelia.*" ZF's voice was as dispassionate as ever. "*It is we*" *who want you to do it. You will oblige us in this matter.*"

"You tell me, ZF, why I would want to cheat."

"*Amelia, you do not want to cheat. However, you are in our service. We have experimental devices to test, and the rules of your game are not important to us. This may be a spiritual endeavor to yourself, it may be a rousing amusement to the multitudes, but it is a military exercise to us.*" There was a pause, as if ZF were momentarily somewhere else, and then he resumed. "*NQ-14 suggests I inform you that Lt. Eszterhazy's aeroplane can glide with a dead engine. There is little risk to the pilot.*"

Amelia glared even more fiercely at the televideon camera. "That is beside the point, ZF. I would argue that my autogyro is far less dependent on its engine than Eszterhazy's 'plane. Why not give the device to each of us, for a square match?"

"*There is only one device, Amelia, and we need to test it now. You are here, you are trusted. Eszterhazy is too independent. You will take the device.*" A grinding noise, as of badly-lubricated machinery. "*Or you will not be in the Game.*"

"What are this bastard's specs? How does it work?"

"*You will be told, Amelia. In good time.*"

"Where is it?"

"*It's being installed in your autogyro as we speak. A red button on your joystick controls it. Press, it's on. Release, it's off.*"

"I'm not happy about this, ZF."

"*Go to your autogyro, Amelia. Fly well.*" The light dimmed even more and the camera clicked again as the lens irised shut. ZF-43 had turned off the world outside his jar.

Rudy choked down a nickel's worth of beans and kielbasa and enough java to keep him running for the rest of the day. It was going to be a long one. The scheduled game would bring the people out into the streets, and that was a recruiting opportunity he couldn't pass up. He knew his targets: not the fat, good-natured guys catching a few hours of fun before hitting the night shift. Not their sharp-eyed wives, juggling the kids and grabbing the paycheck on Friday so it wouldn't be spent on drink. Oh, no. Rudy's constituency was hungry-looking young men, just past their teens, out of work, smarter than they needed to be, and not yet on the bottle. One in ten would take a pamphlet from him. Of those, one in twenty would take it home, one in fifty would read it, one in five hundred would take it to heart, and one in a thousand would seek him out and listen to more.

The only way to make it worth his while, the only way to pull together a force, was to get as many pamphlets out there as possible. It was a numbers game, like the lottery, or like selling insurance.

Rudy had sold insurance once, collecting weekly nickels and dimes from the hopeful and the despairing alike. Until the day he was handed a pamphlet. He took it home, he read it, and he realized what a sham his life was, what a shill he had been for the corporate powers, what a fraud he had been perpetrating upon his own people, the very people that he should be helping to escape from the treadmill of their lives.

He finished his coffee and hit the street. Crowds were already building near the CityPlace—that vast open square at the heart of the city, carved out of the old shops, tenements, and speakeasies that had once thrived there—where the aerobattle would take place. He picked out a corner near some ramshackle warehouses on the plaza's grimy southern rim. That's where his people would be, his tillage, as he thought of them.

"Tillage" was a word his grandfather used, back when Rudy was young. The old man used to speak lovingly of the tillage, the land he had farmed in his youth. The tillage, he said, responded to him as a woman would, bringing forth fruit as a direct result of his care and attention. Not that he, Rudy, had great amounts of time to spend on a woman—but that hadn't seemed to matter on the streets, where women were freely available, and briefly enjoyable. Sexual intercourse was overrated, in his opinion. Politics was another matter, and he made his friends among men and women who felt the same. They kept their distance from one another, so the Naked Brains couldn't pick them all off in a single raid. When they coupled, they did so quickly, and they didn't exchange names.

Moving deftly through the gathering crowd, he held out only one pamphlet at a time, and that only after catching a receptive eye. A willing offering to a willing receptor, that wasn't illegal. It wasn't pamphleteering, which was a harvestable offense. Last thing he wanted, to be harvested and, if the rumors were as he suspected true, have his grey matter pureed and fed to the Naked Brains.

But to build his cadre, to make his mark, he needed to hand out a thousand pamphlets a day, and crowds like this—in the CityPlace or on the slidewalks at rush hour—were the only way to do it.

"Take this, brother. Thank you." He said it over and over. "Salaam, brother, may I offer you this?"

He had to keep moving, couldn't linger anywhere, kept his eye out for the telltale stare of an Eye of the Brains. When he had first started this business, he had sought out only men who looked like himself. But that approach proved too slow. He'd since learned to size up a crowd with a single glance and mentally mark the receptive. That tall, black-skinned man with the blue kerchief, the skinny little freckled guy in the ragged work clothes, the grubby fellow with the wisp of a beard and red suspenders. All men, and mostly young. He let his female compatriots deal with the women. Didn't want any misunderstandings.

The guy with the kerchief first. Eye contact, querying glance, non-sexual affect, tentative offer of pamphlet. He takes it! Eye contact, brief nod, on to the little guy. Guy looks away. Abort. Don't offer pamphlet. On to the third guy—

"What's this, then?" Flatfoot! An Eye? Surely not a Fist? Best to hoof it.

Rudy feinted to one side of the copper and ran past him on the other, swivel-hipping through the crowd like Jim Thorpe in search of a touchdown. He didn't look back, but if the cop was an Eye, he'd have backup pronto. Around the big guy with the orange wig, past the scared-looking lady with the clutch of kids—yikes!—almost overturned the baby carriage. What's that on the ground? No time to think about it! Up and over, down the alleyway and into the door that's cracked open a slot. Close it, latch it, jam the lock. SOP.

Rudy turned away from the fire door. It was almost lightless in here. He was in an old, rundown kinescope parlor, surrounded by benches full of kinescope devotees, their eyes glued to the tiny screens wired to the backs of the pews in front of them. On each screen, the same blurry movie twitched: *Modern Times*, with the Marx Brothers.

He took a seat and put a nickel in the slot.

He was just a regular Joe at the movies now. An anonymous unit of the masses, no different from anybody else. Except that he didn't have his girlfriend with him. Or a girlfriend at all. Or any real interest in having a girlfriend. Or in anything so historically blinkered as going to the kinescope parlor.

Rudy had heard about this particular kinescope in a Know the Foe session. It was supposed to be funny, but its humor originated in a profound class bias. The scene that was playing was one in which Harpo, Chico, and Zeppo were working on an assembly line while their supervisor (Groucho) flirted with the visiting efficiency inspector (Margaret Dumont). Zeppo and Chico worked methodically with wrenches, tightening bolts on the bombs that glided remorselessly into view on the conveyor belt. Harpo, equipped with a little handheld pneumatic drill, worked regularly and efficiently at first, drilling a hole in a bomb fin which Zeppo promptly unbolted and Chico replaced with a new fin. That his work was meaningless appeared to bother him not at all. But then, without noticing it, Groucho leaned against a long lever, increasing the belt's speed. As the pace increased, Harpo realized that the drill could be made to go faster and faster, just like the assembly line. He became fascinated by the drill and then obsessed with it, filling the bombs' fins with so many holes that they looked like slices of Swiss cheese.

Chico and Zeppo, meanwhile, kept working faster and faster as the line sped up. For them, this was grim business. To keep from falling behind, they had to employ two wrenches, one per hand. Sweat poured off them. They shed their hats, then their jackets, then their shirts and pants, leaving them clad only in voluminous underwear. Harpo, on the other hand, was feeling no pressure at all. He began drilling holes in his hat, then his jacket, then his shirt and pants.

Groucho urged Dumont into his office, then doffed his hat, clasped it to his chest, and tossed it aside. He chased her around the desk. Dumont projected both affronted dignity and matronly sexual curiosity. A parody of authority, Groucho backed Dumont up against the wall and, unexpectedly, plucked a rose from a nearby vase and, bowing deeply, offered it to her.

Charmed, Dumont smiled and bent down to accept it.

But then, in a single complex and weirdly graceful action, Groucho spun Dumont around, bending her over backwards in his arms, parallel to the floor.

Margaret Dumont's eyes darted wildly about as she realized how perilously close she was to falling. Meanwhile, Harpo had started to drill holes from the other side of the wall, the drill bit coming through the plaster, each time missing Groucho by a whisker. His desperate gyrations as he tried to avoid the incoming drill were misunderstood by the efficiency expert, who made to slap him. Each time she tried, however, she almost fell and was forced to clutch him tighter to herself. Groucho waggled his eyebrows, obviously pleased with his romantic prowess.

Just then, however, Harpo drilled Dumont in the butt. She lurched forward, mouth an outraged O, losing balance and dignity simultaneously, and overtoppling Grouch as well. The two of them fell to the floor, struggling. It was at that instant that Chico and Zeppo, still in their underwear and with Harpo in tow, appeared in the doorway to report the problem and saw the couple on the floor thrashing about and yelling soundlessly at one another. Without hesitation, all three leaped joyously into the air on top of the pile. Behind them, the runaway assembly line was flooding the factory with bombs, which now crested into the office in a great wave. The screen went white and a single card read: BANG!

The audience was laughing uproariously. But Rudy was not amused. None of these characters had a shred of common sense. Furthermore, it was clear that appropriate measures to protect the workers' health and safety had not been implemented. Harpo should never have been given that drill in the first place. And Margaret Dumont! What was she thinking? How could she have accepted such a demeaning role?

Rudy stood up on his chair. "Comrades!" he yelled. "Why you are laughing?"

A few viewers looked up briefly, then shrugged and returned to their kinescopes. "We're laughin' because it's funny, you halfwit," muttered a surly-looking young man.

"You there, brother," Rudy addressed him directly. After all, he, of everyone there, was Rudy's constituency. "Do you think it's funny that the Brains work people beyond endurance? That they speed up assembly lines without regard for the workers' natural pace, and without increasing their compensation? Do you think it's funny that a human man and woman would take the side of the Brains against their own kind? Think about this: What if Charles Chaplin—a man who respects the worker's dignity—had made this kinescope? There would be nothing funny about it: You'd weep for the poor fellows on the Brains' assembly line. As you should weep for Chico and Zeppo, whose dream of a life of honest labor and just reward has been cruelly exploited."

"Aw, shut yer yap!" It wasn't the young man that Rudy had addressed. This was the voice of an older man, embittered by many years of disappointment and penury.

"I apologize, sir," said Rudy. "You have every right to be angry. You have earned your leisure and have paid dearly for the right to sit here in the darkness and be assaulted by the self-serving garbage of the entertainment industry. Please return to your kinescope. But, I beg of you, do not swallow the tissue of lies that it offers you. Argue with it. Fight back! Resist!"

A huge hand reached out of the darkness and grabbed Rudy's right shoulder.

"Awright there, buddy," said a firm but quiet voice. "And why don't yez come along wit' me, and we can continue this discussion down to the station house?"

Rudy twisted about in the flatfoot's grasp. A sudden head-butt to the solar plexus, a kick to take the man's feet out from under him, and Rudy was running fast, not once looking back to see if he was being pursued. Halfway to the exit, he spotted a narrow circular staircase that burrowed down into the bowels of the earth below the kinescope parlor. He plunged into the darkness, down into the steam tunnels that ran beneath all the buildings of the Old Town.

That was Phase Three of his plan: Run like hell.

Amelia had less than five minutes to the start of the Game. She sprinted to the flight deck and her autogyro. Grimy Huey was waiting, and he didn't look happy. "Why didn't you tell me you were having work done on the machine? You don't trust me no more?"

"Huey, I'm up. We can talk about it later." She swung into the cockpit. The engine was already running. Even when he was ticked off, Huey knew his stuff. "Just throw me out there. The whistle's about to blow."

Grimy Huey waved and Amelia grabbed the controls. Everything in place. She nodded, and the launch platform thrust the autogyro out of the Zep, into takeoff position.

The steam-whistle blew. The Game was in motion.

Amelia kicked, pushed, pedaled, and screamed her improbable craft into the air.

For a time, all was well. As was traditional, the flying aces appeared in goose-vee formation from opposite sides of the plaza, ignoring each other on the first pass, save for a slight wing-waggle of salute, and then curving up into the sky above. Then began the series of thrilling moves that would lead to the heart-stopping aerial ballet of sporting dogfight.

On the first fighting pass, the advantage was to the Reds. But then Blockhead O'Brien threw his autogyro into a mad sideways skid that had half their 'planes pulling up in disarray to avoid being shredded by his blades. Amelia and Hops Wynzowski hurled themselves into the opening and ran five stars, neat as a pin, before the opposition could recover.

Amelia pulled up laughing, only to discover that the Big E was directly behind her and coming up her tail fast. She crouched down over her stick, raising her hips up from the seat, taut as a wire being tested to destruction, neurons snapping and crackling like a Tesla generator. "You catch me," she murmured happily, "and I swear to God I'll never fly again for as long as I live."

Because if there was one thing she knew it was that Eszterhazy *wasn't* going to catch her. She was in her element now. In that timeless instant that lasted forever, that was all instinct and reflex, lust and glory. She was vengeance and righteous fury. She was death in all its cold and naked beauty.

Then a rocket flew up out of nowhere and exploded in her face.

Rudy pounded through the steam tunnels as if every finger in the Fist of the Brains was on his tail. Which they weren't—yet. He'd given Fearless Fosdick the slip, he was sure.

It was only a matter of time, though. Back at Fat Edna's, he knew, they had a pool going as to the date. But when the Fist came for him, he wasn't going to go meekly, with his hands in the air. Not Rudy. That was why he was running now, even though he'd given the flatfoot the slip. He was practicing for the day when it all came down and his speed negotiating the twists and turns of the tunnels would spell the difference between escape and capture, survival and death.

The light from Rudy's electric torch flashed from a rectangle of reflective tape he'd stuck to one wall at chest level. Straight ahead that meant. Turn coming up soon. And, sure enough, up ahead were two bits of tape together, like an equal sign, on the right-hand wall. Which, counter-intuitively, signaled a left turn.

He ran, twisting and turning as the flashing blips of tapes dictated. A left... two rights... a long downward decline that he didn't remember but which had to be correct because up ahead glinted another tab of reflective tape and beyond it another two, indicating a left turn. Into the new tunnel he plunged and then, almost falling, down a rattling set of metal steps that definitely wasn't right. At the bottom the tunnel opened up into an enormous cavernous blackness. He stumbled to a halt.

A cold wind blew down on him from above.

Rudy shivered. This was wrong. He'd never been here before. And yet, straight ahead of him glowed yet another tab of the tape. He lifted his electric torch from the ground in front of his feet to examine it.

And, as he lifted it up, he cried out in horror. The light revealed a mocking gargoyle of a man: filthy, grey-skinned, dressed in rags, with running sores on his misshapen face and only three fingers on the hand that mockingly held up a flashing rectangle of reflective tape.

"It's the bolshy," the creature said to nobody in particular.

"I thought he was a menshevik," said a second voice.

"Naw, he's a tvardokhlebnik," said a third. "A pathetic nibbler at the leavings of others."

"My brothers!" Rudy cried in mingled terror and elation. His torch slid from monstrous face to monstrous face. A throng of grotesques confronted him. These were the broken hulks of men, horribly disfigured by industrial accidents, disease, and bathtub gin, creatures who had been driven into the darkness not by poverty alone but also by the reflexive stares of those who had previously been their fellows and compeers. Rudy's revulsion turned to an enormous and terrible sense of pity. "You have lured me here for some purpose, I presume. Well... here I am. Tell me what is so important that you must play these games with me."

"Kid gets right to the point."

"He's got a good mind."

"No sense of humor, though. Heard him speak once."

Swallowing back his fear, Rudy said, "Now you are laughing at me. Comrades! These are desperate times. We should not be at each other's throats, but rather working together for the common good."

"He's got *that* right."

"Toldya he had a good mind."

One of the largest of the men seized Rudy's jacket in his malformed hand, lifting him effortlessly off his feet. "Listen, pal. Somebody got something important to tell ya." He shook Rudy for emphasis. "So you're gonna go peacefully, all right? Don't do nothing stupid. Remember who lives here and can see in the dark and who don't and can't. Got that?"

"Brother! Yes! Of course!"

"Good." The titan let Rudy drop to the floor. "Open 'er up, boys." Shadowy figures pushed an indistinct pile of boxes and empty barrels away from a steel-clad door. "In there."

Rudy went through the door.

It closed behind him. He could hear the crates and barrels being pushed back into place.

He was in a laboratory. Even though it was only sparsely lit, Rudy could see tables crowded with huge jars that were linked by glass tubes and entwined in electrical cables. Things sizzled and bubbled. The air stank of ozone and burnt sulfur.

In the center of the room, illuminated by a single incandescent bulb dangling from the ceiling, was a glass tank a good twenty feet long. In its murky interior a huge form moved listlessly, filling it almost entirely—a single enormous sturgeon. Rudy was no sentimentalist, but it seemed to him that the great fish, unable to swim or even turn about in its cramped confines—indeed, unable to do much of anything save slowly move its fins in order to keep afloat and flutter its gills to breathe—must lead a grim and terrible existence.

Cables snaked from the tank to a nearby clutter of electrical devices, but he paid them no particular notice. His attention was drawn to a woman standing before the aquarium. Her lab smock seemed to glow in the gloom.

She had clearly been waiting for him, for without preamble, she said, "I am Professor Anna Pavlova." Her face was old and drawn; her eyes blazed with passionate intensity. "You have probably never heard of me, but—"

"Of course I know of you, Professor Pavlova!" Rudy babbled. "You are one of the greatest inventors of all time! The monorail! Citywide steam heat! You made the Naked Brains possible. The masses idolize you."

"Pah!" Professor Pavlova made a dismissive chopping gesture with her right hand. "I am but a scientist, nothing more nor less. All that matters is that when I was young I worked on the Naked Brain Project. Those were brave days indeed. All the best thinkers of our generation—politicians, artists, engineers—lined up to surrender their bodies in order to put their minds at the service of the people. I would have done so myself, were I not needed to monitor and fine-tune the nutrient systems. We were Utopians then! I am sure that not a one of them was influenced by the possibility that as Naked Brains they would live forever. Not a one! We wished only to serve."

She sighed.

"Your idealism is commendable, comrade scientist," Rudy said. "Yet it is my unhappy duty to inform you that the Council of Naked Brains no longer serves the people's interests. They—"

"*It is worse than you think!*" Professor Pavlova snapped. "For many years I was part of the inner circle of functionaries serving the Brains. I saw… many things. Things that made me wonder, and then doubt. Quietly, I began my own research. But the scientific journals rejected my papers. Lab books disappeared. Data were altered. There came a day when none of the Naked Brains—who had been my friends, remember!—would respond to my messages or even, when I went to them in person, deign to speak to me.

"I am no naïve innocent. I knew what that meant: The Fist would shortly be coming for me.

"So I went underground. I befriended the people here, whose bodies are damaged but whose minds remain free and flexible, and together we smuggled in enough equipment to continue my work. I tapped into the city's electric and gas lines. I performed miracles of improvisation and bricolage. At first I was hindered by my lack of access to the objects of my study. But then my new friends helped me liberate Old Teddy—" she patted the side of the fish tank—"from a pet shop where he was kept as a curiosity. Teddy was the key. He told me everything I needed to know."

Rudy interrupted the onslaught of words. "This fish *told* you things?"

"Yes." The scientist picked up a wired metal dish from the lab bench. "Teddy is very, very old, you see. When he was first placed in that tank, he was quite small, a wild creature caught for food but spared the frying pan to be put on display." She adjusted cables that ran from the silver dish to an electrical device on the bench. "That was many years ago, of course, long before you or I were born. Sturgeon can outlive humans, and Teddy has slowly grown into what you see before you." Other cables ran from the device into the tank. Rudy saw that they had been implanted directly into the sturgeon's brain. One golden-grey eye swiveled in the creature's whiskered, impassive head to look at him. Involuntarily, he shuddered. It was just a fish, he thought. It wished him no ill.

"Have you ever wondered what thoughts pass through a fish's brain?" With a grim smile that was almost a leer, the scientist thrust the silver dish at Rudy. "Place this cap on your head—and you will know."

More than almost anything, Rudy wanted *not* to put on the cap. Yet more than anything at all, he wanted to do his duty to his fellow beings, both human and fish. This woman might well be mad: she certainly did not act like any woman he had ever met. The device might well kill him or damage his brain. Yet to refuse it would be to give up on the adventure entirely, to admit that he was not the man for the job.

Rudy reached out and took the silver cap.

He placed it upon his head.

Savage homicidal rage filled him. Rudy hated everything that lived, without degree or distinction. All the universe was odious to him. If he could, he would murder everyone outside his tank, devour their eggs, and destroy their nests. Like a fire, this hatred engulfed him, burning all to nothing, leaving only a dark cinder of self at his core.

With a cry of rage, Rudy snatched the silver cap from his head and flung it away. Professor Pavlova caught it, as if she had been expecting his reaction. Horrified, he turned on her. "They hate us! The very fish hate us!" He could feel the sturgeon's deadly anger burning into his back, and this filled him with shame and self-loathing, even though he knew he did not personally deserve it. All humans deserved it, though, he thought. All humans supported the idea of putting fish in tanks. Those who did not were branded eccentrics and their viewpoint dismissed without a hearing.

"This is a terrible invention! It does not reveal the universal brotherhood natural among disparate species entwined in the Great Web of Life—quite the opposite, in fact!" He despaired of putting his feelings into words. "What it reveals may be the truth, but is it a truth that we really we need to know?"

Professor Pavlova smiled mirthlessly. "You understand so well the inequalities in human intercourse and the effect they have on the human psyche. And now! Now, for the first time, you understand some measure of what a fish feels and thinks. Provided it has been kept immobile and without stimulation for so many years it is no longer sane." She glanced over at Old Teddy with pity. "A fish longs only for cold water, for food, for distances to swim, and for a place to lay its eggs or spread its milt. We humans have kept Teddy in a tank for over a century."

Then she looked at Rudy with almost the same expression. "Imagine how much worse it would be for a human being, used to sunshine on his face, the feel of a lover's hand, the soft sounds an infant makes when it is happy, to find himself—even if of his own volition—nothing more than a Naked Brain afloat in amniotic fluid. Sans touch, sans taste, sans smell, sans sound, sans sight, sans everything. You have felt the fish's hatred. Imagine how much stronger must be the man's." Her eyes glittered with a cold fire. "I have suspected this for years, and now that I have experienced Teddy's mind—now I *know*." She sliced her hand outward, as if with a knife, to emphasize the depth of her knowledge, and its force. "The Naked Brains are all mad. They hate us and they will work tirelessly for our destruction."

"This is what I have been saying all along," Rudy gasped. "I have been trying to engage—"

Pavlova interrupted him. "The time for theorizing and yammering and pamphleteering is over. You were brought here because I have a message and I need a messenger. The time has come for action. Tell your superiors. Tell the world. The Naked Brains must be destroyed."

A sense of determination flooded Rudy's being. This was what all his life had been leading up to. This was his moment of destiny.

Which made it particularly ironic that it was at that very moment that the Fist smashed in the door of the laboratory.

Radio Jones had punched a hole in the center of a sheet of paper and taped it to the casing of her all-frequencies receiver with the tuner knob at the center, so she could mark the location of each transceiver set she found. The tuner had a range of two hundred ten degrees, which covered the entire spectrum of the communications band. So she eyeballed it into quarters and then tenths, to give a rough idea how things were laid out. It would be better to rank them by electromagnetic frequency, but she didn't have the time to work all that out, and anyway, though she would never admit this out loud, she was just a little weak on the theoretics. Radio was more a vacuum-tube-and-solder-gun kind of girl.

Right now the paper was heavily marked right in the center of the dial, from ninety to one-sixty degrees. There were dozens of flier-Brain pairs, and she'd put a mark by each one, and identified a good quarter of them. Including, she was particularly pleased to see, all the big guys—Eszterhazy, Spindizzy, Blockhead O'Brien, Stackerlee Brown. When there wasn't any room for more names, Radio went exploring into the rest of the spectrum, moving out from the center by incremental degrees.

So, because she wasn't listening to the players, Radio missed the beginning of the massacre. It was only when she realized that everybody in Edna's had rushed out into the street that she looked up from her chore and saw the aeroplanes falling and autogyros spinning out of control. She went to the window just in time to hear a universal gasp as a Zeppelin exploded in the sky overhead. Reflected flames glowed red on the uplifted faces.

"Holy cow!" Radio ran back to her set and twisted her dial back toward the center.

"...*Warinowski*," a Naked Brain was saying dispassionately. "*Juric-Kocik. Bai. Gevers...*"

A human voice impatiently broke in on the recitation. "What about Spindizzy? She's worth more than the rest of them put together. Did she set off her bomb?"

"*No.*" A long pause. "*Maybe she disarmed it.*"

"If that's the case, she'll be gunning for me." The human voice was horribly, horribly familiar. "Plot her vectors, tell me where she is, and I'll take care of her."

"Oh, no," Radio said. "It can't be."

"*What is your current situation?*"

"My rockets are primed and ready, and I've got a clear line of sight straight down Archer Road, from Franklin all the way to the bend."

"*Stay your course. We will direct Amelia Spindizzy onto Archer Road, headed south, away from you. When you see her clear the Frank Lloyd Wright Tower, count three and fire.*"

"Roger," the rocket-assassin said. Now there was no doubt at all in Radio's mind. She knew that voice. She knew the killer.

And she knew what she had to do.

Amelia Spindizzy's ears rang from the force of the blast, and she could feel in the joystick an arrhythmic throb. Where had the missile come from that had caused the explosion? What had happened to Eszterhazy? She was sure she had not accidentally pressed the red button on the joystick, so he should be fine, if he had evaded the blast. Hyperalert, Amelia detected an almost-invisible scratch in the air, tracing the trajectory of a second rocket, and braced herself for another shock.

When it came, she was ready for it. This time she rode, with her whole body, the great twisting thrusts that came from the rotor, much as she would ride a stallion or, she imagined, a man. The blades sliced the air and the autogyro shook, but she forced her will on the powerful machine, which had until this instant been her partner, not her opponent, and overmastered it.

It might be true that you never see the missile that kills you. But that didn't mean you couldn't be killed by a missile you could see. Amelia needed to get out of the line of fire—a third missile might err on the side of accuracy. She banked sharply down into Archer Road, past the speakeasy and the storefront church, and pulled a brisk half-Eszterhazy into an alley next to a skeleton of iron girders with a banner reading FUTURE HOME OF BLACK STAR LINE SHIPPING & NAVIGATION. All that raw iron would block her comptroller's radio signal, but that hardly mattered now. At third-floor level, slowing to the speed of a running man, she crept, as it were, back to where she would see what was happening over the Great Square.

Eszterhazy was nowhere in evidence, but neither was there a column of smoke where she had seen him last. Perhaps, like herself, he'd held his craft together and gone to cover. Missiles were still arcing through the air and exploding. There were no flying machines in the sky and the great Zeppelins were sinking down like foundering ships. It wasn't clear what the missiles were aimed at—perhaps their purpose at this point was simply to keep any surviving 'planes and auto-gyros out of the sky.

Or perhaps they were being shot off by fools. In Amelia's experience, you could never write off the fool option.

Radio 2 was blinking and squawking like a battery-operated chicken. Amelia ignored it. Until she knew who was shooting at her, she wasn't talking to anybody: any radio contact would reveal her location.

As, treading air, she rounded the skeleton of the would-be shipping line, Amelia noticed something odd. It looked like a lump of rags hanging from a rope tied to a girder—possibly a support strut for a planned crosswalk—that stuck out from the metal framework. What on earth could that be? Then it moved, wriggling downward, and she saw that it was a boy!

And he was sliding rapidly down toward the end of his rope.

Almost without thinking, Amelia brought her autogyro in. There had to be a way of saving the kid. The rotor blades were a problem, and their wash. She couldn't slow down much more than she already had—autogyros didn't hover. But if she took both the forward speed and the wash into account, made them work together…

It would be trying to snag a baseball in a hurricane. But she didn't see any alternative.

She came in, the wash from her props blowing the lump of rags and the rope it hung from almost parallel to the ground. She could see the kid clearly now, a little boy in a motley coat, his body hanging just above Amelia. He had a metal box hanging from a belt around his neck that in another instant was going to tear him off the rope for sure.

There was one hellishly giddy moment when her rotors went above the out-stuck girder and her fuselage with its stubby wings went below. She reached out with the mail hook, grabbed the kid, and pulled him into the cockpit as the 'gyro moved relentlessly forward.

The tip of the rope whipped up and away and was shredded into dust by the whirling blades. The boy fell heavily between Amelia and her rudder, so that she couldn't see a damned thing.

She shoved him up and over her, unceremoniously dumping the brat head-first into the passenger seat. Then she grabbed the controls, easing her bird back into the center of the alley.

From behind her, the kid shouted, "Jeepers, Amelia. Get outta here, f'cripesake! He's coming for you!"

"What?" Amelia yelled. Then the words registered. "Who's shooting? Why?" The brat knew something. "Where are they? How do you know?" Then, sternly, "That was an insanely dangerous thing for you to do."

"Don't get yer wig in a frizzle," said the kid. "I done this a million times."

"You have?" said Amelia in surprise.

"In my dreams, anyway," said the kid. "Hold the questions. Right now we gotta lam outta here, before somebody notices us what shouldn't. I'll listen in on what's happening." He twisted around and tore open the seat back, revealing the dry batteries, and yanked the cords from them. The radio went dead.

"Hey!" Amelia cried.

"Not to worry. I'm just splicing my Universal Receiver to your power supply.

Your radios are obsolete now, but you couldn't know that…" Now the little gremlin had removed a floor panel and was crawling in among the autogyro's workings. "Lemme just ground this and… Say! Why have you got a bomb in here?"

"Huh? You mean… Oh, that's just some electronic doohickey the Naked Brains asked me to test for them."

"Tell it to the Marines, lady. I didn't fall off no turnip truck. The onliest electronics you got here is two wires coming off a detonator cap and leading to one a your radios. If I didn't know better, I'd tag this sucker as a remote-controlled self-destruct device." The imp stuck its head out of the workings again, and said, "Oh yeah. The name's Radio Jones."

With an abrupt rush of conceptual vertigo, Amelia realized that this gamin was a *girl*. "How do you do," she said dazedly. "I'm…"

"I know who you are," Radio said. "I got your picture on the wall." Then, seeing that they were coming up on the bend in Archer Road, "Hey! Nix! Not that way! There's a guy with a coupla rockets up there just waiting for you to show your face. Pull a double curl and loop back down Vanzetti. There's a vacant lot this side of the Shamrock Tavern that's just wide enough for the 'gyro. Martin Dooley's the barkeep there, and he's got a shed large enough to hide this thing. Let's vamoose!"

A rocket exploded behind her.

Good advice was good advice. No matter how unlikely its source.

Amelia Spindizzy vamoosed.

But as she did, she could not help casting a wistful glance back over her shoulder, hoping against hope for a glimpse of a bright red aeroplane. "I don't suppose you've heard anything about Eszterhazy surviving this?" she heard herself asking her odd young passenger. Whatever was happening, with his superb skills, surely he must have survived.

"Uh, about that…" Radio Jones said. "I kinda got some bad news for you."

Rudy awoke to find himself in Hell.

Hell was touchless, tasteless, scentless, and black as pitch. It consisted entirely of a bedlam of voices: "Lemme outta here—wasn't doing nothing—Mabel! Where are you, Mabel?—I'm serious, I got bad claustrophobia—goddamn flicks!—there's gotta be—minding my own business—Mabel!—gonna puke—all the things I coulda been—I don't like it here—can't even hear myself think— Oh, Freddy, if only I'da toldja I loved you when I coulda—got to be a way out—why won't anybody tell me what's happening?—if the resta youse don't shut—"

He knew where he was now. He understood their situation. Gathering himself together, Rudy funneled all the energy he had into a mental shout:

"*Silence!*"

His thought was so forceful and purposive that it shocked all the other voices into silence.

"Comrades!" he began. "It is clear enough what has happened here. We have all been harvested by the police lackeys of the Naked Brains. By the total lack of somatic sensations, I deduce that we have ourselves been made into Naked Brains." Somebody sent out a stab of raw emotion. Before his or her (not that gender mattered anymore, under the circumstances) hysteria could spread, Rudy rushed onward in a torrent of words. "But there is no need for despair. We are not without hope. So long as we have our thoughts, our inner strength, and our powers of reason, we hold within ourselves the tools of liberation."

"Liberation?" somebody scoffed. "It's my body's been liberated, and from *me*. It's them is doing the liberatin', not us."

"I understand your anger, brother," Rudy said. "But the opportunity is to him who keeps his head." Belatedly, Rudy realized that this was probably not the smartest thing to say. The anonymous voices responded with jeers. "Peace, brothers and sisters. We may well be lost, and we must face up to that." More jeers. "And yet, we all have family and friends who we left behind." Everyone, that is, save for himself—a thought that Rudy quickly suppressed. "Think of the world that is coming for them—one of midnight terror, an absolutist government, the constant fear of denouncement and punishment without trial. Of imprisonment without hope of commutation, of citizens randomly plucked from the streets for harvesting…" He paused to let that sink in. "I firmly believe that we can yet free ourselves. But even if we could not, would it not be worth our uttermost efforts to fight the tyranny of the Brains? For the sake of those we left behind?"

There was a general muttering of agreement. Rudy had created a community among his listeners. Now, quickly, to take advantage of it! "Who here knows anything about telecommunications technology?"

"I'm an electrical engineer," somebody said.

"That Dutch?" said another voice. "You're a damn good engineer. Or you were."

"Excellent. Dutch, you are now the head of our Ad Hoc Committee for Communications and Intelligence. Your task is first to work out the ways that we are connected to each other and to the machinery of the outer world, and second, to determine how we may take over the communications system, control it for our own ends, and when we are ready, deprive the government of its use. Are you up to the challenge, Comrade—?"

"Schwartz. Dutch Schwartz, at your service. Yes, I am."

"Then choose people to work with you. Report back when you have solid findings. Now. Who here is a doctor?"

"I am," a mental voice said dryly. "Professor and Doctor Anna Pavlova at your service."

"Forgive me, comrade Professor. Of course you are here. And we are honored—honored!—to have you with us. One of the greatest—"

"Stop the nattering and put me to work."

"Yes, of course. Your committee will look into the technical possibilities of restoring our brains to the bodies we left behind."

"Well," said the professor, "this is not something we ever considered when we created the Brains. But our knowledge of microsurgery has grown enormously with the decades of Brain maintenance. I would not rule it out."

"You believe our bodies have not been destroyed?" somebody asked in astonishment.

"A resource like that? Of course not," Rudy said. "Think! Any despotic government must have the reliable support of toadies and traitors. With a supply of bodies, many of them young, to offer, the government can effectively give their lackeys immortality—not the immortality of the Brains, but the immortality of body after body, in plentiful supply." He paused to let that sink in. "However. If we act fast to organize the proletariat, perhaps that can be prevented. To do this, we will need the help of those in the Underground who have not been captured and disembodied. Who here is—?"

"And you," somebody else said. "What is your role in this? Are you to be our leader?"

"Me?" Rudy asked in astonishment. "Nothing of the sort! I am a community organizer."

He got back to work organizing.

The last dirigible was moored to the tip of the Gaudi Building. The *Imperator* was a visible symbol of tyranny which cast its metaphoric shadow over the entire city. So far as anybody knew, there wasn't an aeroplane, autogyro, or Zeppelin left in the city to challenge its domination of the air. So it was there that the new Tyrant would be. It was there that the destinies of everyone in the city would play out.

It was there that Amelia Spindizzy and Radio Jones went, after concealing the autogyro in a shed behind Dooley's tavern.

Even from a distance, it was clear that there were gun ports to every side of the *Imperator* and doubtless there were other defenses on the upper floors of the skyscraper. So they took the most direct route—through the lobby of the Gaudi building and up the elevator. Amelia and Radio stepped inside, the doors closed behind them, and up they rose, toward the Zeppelin.

"In my youth, of course, I was an avid balloonsman," somebody said from above.

Radio yelped and Amelia stared sharply upward.

Wedged into an upper corner of the elevator was a radio. From it came a marvelous voice, at once both deep and reedy, and immediately recognizable as well. "…and covered the city by air. Once, when I was a mere child, ballooning alone as was my wont, I caught a line on a gargoyle that stuck out into my airspace from the tower of the Church of Our Lady of the Assumption—what is now the Sepulchre of the Bodies of the Brains—and, thus entangled, I was in some danger of the gondola—which was little more than a basket, really—tipping me out into a long and fatal fall to earth. Fortunately, one of the brown-robed monks, engaged in his Matins, was cloistered in the tower and noticed my predicament. He was able to reach out and free the line." The voice dropped, a hint of humor creeping in. "In my childish piety, of course, I considered this evidence of the beneficent intercession of some remote deity, whom I thanked nightly in my prayers." One could almost hear him shaking his head at his youthful credulousness. "But considering how fortunate we are now—are we not?—to be at last freed from the inhuman tyranny of the Naked Brains, one has to wonder whether it wasn't in some sense the hand of Destiny that reached out from that tower, to save the instrument by which our liberation would one day be achieved."

"It's him!" Radio cried. "Just like I told you."

"It… sounds like him. But he can't be the one who gave the orders you overheard. Can you be absolutely sure?" Amelia asked her unlikely sidekick for the umpteenth time. "Are you really and truly *certain*?"

Radio rolled her eyes. "Lady, I heard him with my own two ears. You don't think I know the voice of the single greatest pilot…" Her voice trailed off under Amelia's glare. "Well, don't hit the messenger! I read *Obey the Brain!* every week. His stats are just plain better'n yours."

"They have been," Amelia said grimly. "But that's about to change." She unsnapped the holster of her pistol.

Then the bell pinged. They'd reached the top floor.

The elevator doors opened.

Rudy was conferring with progressive elements in the city police force about the possibility of a counter-coup (they argued persuasively that, since it was impossible to determine their fellow officers' loyalties without embroiling the force in internecine conflict, any strike would have to be small and fast) when his liaison with the Working Committee for Human Resources popped up in his consciousness and said, "We've located the bodies, boss. As you predicted, they were all carefully preserved and are being maintained in the best of health."

"That is good news, Comrade Mariozzi. Congratulations. But none of that 'boss' business, do you understand? It could easy go from careless language to a common assumption."

Meanwhile, they'd hooked into televideon cameras throughout the city, and though the views were grim, it heartened everybody to no longer be blind. It was a visible—there was no way around the word—sign that they were making progress.

Red Rudy had just wrapped up the meeting with the loyalist police officers when Comrade Mariozzi popped into his consciousness again. "Hey, boss!" he said excitedly. "You gotta see this!"

The guards were waiting at the top of the elevator with guns drawn. To Radio Jones's shock and amazement, Amelia Spindizzy handed over her pistol without a murmur of protest. Which was more than could be said for Radio herself when one of the goons wrested the Universal Receiver out of her hands. Amelia had to seize her by the shoulders and haul her back before she could attack the nearest of their captors.

They were taken onto the *Imperator* and through the Hall of the Naked Brains. The great glass jars were empty and the giant floating Brains were gone who-knows-where. Radio hoped they'd been flung in an alley somewhere to be eaten by dogs. But hundreds of new, smaller jars containing brains of merely human proportions had been brought in and jury-rigged to oxygen feeds and electrical input-output units. Radio noticed that they all had cut-out switches. If one of the New Brains acted up it could be instantly put into solitary confinement. But there was nobody monitoring them, which seemed to defeat the purpose.

"Keep close to the earth!" a voice boomed. Radio jumped. Amelia, she noticed, did not. Then she saw that there were radios set in brackets to either end of the room. "Such was the advice of the preeminent international airman, Alberto Santos-Dumont, and they were good enough words for their time." The familiar voice chuckled and half-snorted, and the radio crackled loudly as his breath struck the sensitive electro-acoustic transducer that had captured his voice. "But his time is not my time." He paused briefly; one could almost hear him shrug his shoulders. "One is never truly tested close to the earth. It is in the huge arching parabola of an aeroplane finding its height and seeking a swift descent from it that a man's courage is found. It is there, in acts outside of the quotidian, that his mettle is tested."

A televideon camera ratcheted about, tracking their progress. Were the New Brains watching them, Radio wondered? The thought gave her the creeps.

Then they were put in an elevator (only two guards could fit in with them and Radio thought sure that Amelia would make her play now; but the aviatrix stared expressionlessly forward and did nothing) and taken down to the flight deck. There, the exterior walls had been removed, as would be done under wartime conditions when the 'planes and wargyros had to be gotten into the air as soon as possible. Cold winds buffeted and blustered about the vast and empty space.

"A young man dreams of war and glory," the voice said from a dozen radios. "He toughens his spirit and hardens his body with physical activity and discomfort. In time, he's ready to join the civil militia, where he is trained in the arts of killing and destruction. At last, his ground training done, he is given an aeroplane and catapulted into the sky, where he discovers…" The voice caught and then, when it resumed, was filled with wonder. "… not hatred, not destruction, not war, but peace."

To the far side of the flight deck, unconcerned by his precarious location, a tall figure in a flyer's uniform bent over a body in greasy coveralls, which he had dragged right to the edge. Then he flipped it over. It was Grimy Huey, and he was dead.

The tall man stood and turned. "Leave," he told the guards.

They clicked their heels and obeyed.

"He almost got me, you know," the man remarked conversationally. "He came at me from behind with a wrench. Who would have thought that a mere mechanic had that much gumption in him?"

For a long moment, Amelia Spindizzy stood ramrod-straight and unmoving. Radio Jones sank to the deck, crouching by her side. She couldn't help herself. The cold and windy openness of the flight deck scared her spitless. She couldn't even stand. But, terrified though she was, she didn't look away. Someday all this would be in the history books; whatever happened, she knew, was going to determine her view of the world and its powers for the rest of her natural life, however short a time that might be.

Then Amelia strolled forward, toward Eszterhazy and said, "Let me help you with that." She stooped and took the mechanic's legs. Eszterhazy took the arms. They straightened, swung the body—one! two! three!—and flung it over the side.

Slapping her hands together, Amelia said, "Why'd you do it?"

Eszterhazy shrugged in a self-deprecating way. "It had to be done. So I stepped up to the plate and took a swing at the ball. That's all." Then he grinned boyishly. "It's good to know that you're on my team."

"That's you on the radios," Amelia said. They were still booming away, even though the buffeting winds drowned out half the words that came from them.

"Wire recording." Eszterhazy strode to a support strut and slapped a switch. The radios all died. "A little talk I prepared, being broadcast to the masses. Radio has been scandalously underutilized as a tool of governance."

Amelia's response was casual—even, Radio thought, a bit dunderheaded technologically. "But radio's everywhere," she said. "There are dozens of public sets scattered through the city. Why, people can hear news bulletins before the newspapers can even set type and roll the presses!"

Eszterhazy smiled a thin, tight, condescending smile. "But they only tell people what's happened, and not what to *think* about it. That's going to change. My people are distributing sets to every bar, school, church, and library in the city. In the future, my future, everyone will have a bank of radios in their home—the government radio, of course, but also one for musical events, another for free lectures, and perhaps even one for business news."

Radio felt the urge to speak up and say that fixed-frequency radios were a thing of the past. But she suppressed it. She sure wasn't about to hand over her invention to a bum the likes of which Eszterhazy was turning out to be. But what the heck was the matter with Amelia?

Amelia Spindizzy put her hands behind her, and turned her back on her longtime arch-rival. Head down, deep in thought, she trod the edge of the abyss. "Hah." The word might have meant anything. "You've clearly put a lot of thought into this... this... new world order of yours."

"I've been planning this all my life," Eszterhazy said with absolute seriousness.

"New and more efficient forms of government, a society that not only promotes the best of its own but actively weeds out the criminals and the morally sick. Were you aware that before Lycurgus became king, the Spartans were a licentious and ungovernable people? He made them the fiercest warriors the world has ever known in the space of a single lifetime." He stopped, and then with a twinkle in his eye said, "There I go again, talking about the Greeks! As I started to say, I thought I would not be ready to make my move for many years. But then I got wind of certain experiments performed by Anna Pavlova which proved that not only were the Naked Brains functionally mad, but that I had it in my power to offer them the one thing for which they would give me their unquestioning cooperation—death.

"In their corruption were the seeds of our salvation. And thus fell our oppressors."

"I worked with them, and I saw no oppressors." Amelia rounded her course strolling back toward Eszterhazy, brow furrowed with thought. "Only nets of neurological fiber who, as it turned out, were overcome by the existential terror of their condition."

"Their condition is called 'life,' Millie. And, yes, life makes us all insane." Eszterhazy could have been talking over the radio, his voice was so reassuring and convincing. "Some of us respond to that terror with useless heroics. Others seek death." He cocked a knowing smile at Amelia. "Others respond by attacking the absurdity at its source. Ruled by Naked Brains, humanity could not reach its full potential. Now, once again, we will rule ourselves."

"It does all make sense. It all fits." Amelia Spindizzy came to a full stop and stood shaking her head in puzzlement. "If only I could understand—"

"What is there to understand?" An impatient edge came into Eszterhazy's voice. "What have I left unexplained? We can perfect our society in our lifetimes! You're so damnably cold and analytic, Millie. Don't you see that the future lies right at your feet? All you have to do is let go of your doubts and analyses and intellectual hesitations and take that leap of faith into a better world."

Radio trembled with impotent alarm. She knew that, small and ignored as she was, it might be possible for her to be the wild card, the unexpected element, the unforeseeable distraction that saves the day. That it was, in fact, her duty to do so. She'd seen enough Saturday afternoon kinescope serials to understand *that*.

If only she could bring herself to stand up. Though it almost made her throw up to do so, Radio brought herself to her feet. The wind whipped the deck, and Eszterhazy quickly looked over at her. As though noticing her for the first time. And then, as Radio fought to overcome her paralyzing fear, Amelia acted.

She smiled that big, easy Amelia grin that had captured the hearts of proles and aristos alike. It was a heartfelt smile and a wickedly hoydenish leer at one and the same time, and it bespoke aggression and an inner shyness in equal parts. A disarming grin, many people called it.

Smiling her disarming grin, Amelia looked Eszterhazy right in the eye. She looked as if she had just found a brilliant solution to a particularly knotty problem. Despite the reflexive decisiveness for which he was known, Eszterhazy stood transfixed.

"You know," she said, "I had always figured that, when all the stats were totted up and the final games were flown, you and I would find a shared understanding in our common enthusiasm for human-controlled—"

All in an instant, she pushed forward, wrapped her arms around her opponent, and let their shared momentum carry them over the edge.

Radio instantly fell to the deck again and found herself scrambling across it to the edge on all fours. Gripping the rim of the flight decking with spasmodic strength, she forced herself to look over. Far below, two conjoined specks tumbled in a final flight to the earth.

She heard a distant scream—no, she heard laughter.

Radio managed to hold herself together through the endless ceremonies of a military funeral. To tell the truth, the pomp and ceremony of it—the horse-drawn hearse, the autogyro fly-by, the lines of dignitaries and endlessly droning eulogies in the Cathedral—simply bored her to distraction. There were a couple of times when Mack had to nudge her because she was falling asleep. Also, she had to wear a dress and, sure as shooting, any of her friends who saw her in it were going to give her a royal ribbing about it when next they met.

But then came the burial. As soon as the first shovel of dirt rattled down on the coffin, Radio began blubbering like a punk. Fat Edna passed her a lace hanky—who'd even known she *had* such a thing?—and she mopped at her eyes and wailed.

When the last of the earth had been tamped down on the grave, and the priest turned away, and the mourners began to break up, Radio felt a hand on her shoulder. It was, of all people, Rudy the Red. He looked none the worse for his weeklong vacation from the flesh.

"Rudy," she said, "is that a *suit* you're wearing?"

"It is not the uniform of the oppressor anymore. A new age has begun, Radio, an age not of hierarchic rule by an oligarchy of detached, unfeeling intellects, but of horizontally-structured human cooperation. No longer will workers and managers be kept apart and treated differently from one another. Thanks to the selfless sacrifice of—"

"Yeah, I heard the speech you gave in the Cathedral."

"You did?" Rudy looked strangely pleased.

"Well, mostly. I mighta slept through some of it. Listen, Rudy, I don't want to rain on your parade, but people are still gonna be people, you know. You're all wound up to create this Big Rock Candy Mountain of a society, and good for you. Only—you gotta be prepared for the possibility that it won't work. I mean, ask any engineer, that's just the way things are. They don't always work the way they're supposed to."

"Then I guess we'll just have to wing it, huh?" Rudy flashed a wry grin. Then, abruptly, his expression turned serious, and he said the very last thing in the world she would have expected to come out of his mouth: "How are you doing?"

"Not so good. I feel like a ton of bricks was dropped on me." She felt around for Edna's hanky, but she'd lost it somewhere. So she wiped her eyes on her sleeve. "You want to know what's the real kicker? I hardly knew Amelia. So I don't even know why I should feel so bad."

Rudy took her arm. "Come with me a minute. Let me show you something."

He led her to a gravestone that was laid down to one side of the grave, to be erected when everyone was gone. It took a second for Radio to read the inscription. "Hey! It's just a quotation. Amelia's name ain't even on it. That's crazy."

"She left instructions for what it would say, quite some time ago. I gather that's not uncommon for flyers. But I can't help feeling it's a message."

Radio stared at the words on the stone for very long time. Then she said, "Yeah, I see what you mean. But, ya know, I think it's a different message than what she thought it would be."

The rain, which had been drizzling off and on during the burial, began in earnest. Rudy shook out his umbrella and opened it over them both. They joined the other mourners, who were scurrying away in streams and rivulets, pouring from the cemetery exits and into the slidewalk stations and the vacuum trains, going back home to their lives and families, to boiled cabbage and schooners of pilsner, to their jobs, and their hopes, and their heartbreaks, to the vast, unknowable, and perfectly ordinary continent of the future.

"It followed that the victory would belong to him who was calmest, who shot best, and who had the cleverest brain in a moment of danger."
— *Baron Manfred von Richthofen (1892-1918)*

DRAGON'S TEETH
ALEX IRVINE

Alex Irvine published his first story in *The Magazine of Fantasy & Science Fiction* in 2000. It was quickly followed by debut fantasy novel, *A Scattering of Jades*, which won him considerable acclaim. The winner of the Locus, International Horror Guild, and Crawford awards, Irvine has published two further fantasy novels, *One King, One Soldier*, and *The Narrows*, and two collections of short fiction. His most recent novel is *Buyout*. A versatile writer, Irvine has also written a number of comic and media-related works, including *Daredevil Noir* and *The Vertigo Encyclopedia*.

I: The Tomb

They brought the singer to the obsidian gate and waited. A sandstorm began to boil in the valley that split the mountains to their west. Across the miles of desert, they watched it rear and approach. Still the singer did not sing. She was blind, and had the way of blind singers. They were as much at the mercy of the song as anyone else.

All of them were going to die in the sandstorm. At least the guard captain, Paulus, hoped so. If the sandstorm did not kill them, whatever was in the tomb would. Of the two deaths, he much preferred the storm. Two fingers of his right hand touched his throat and he hummed the creed of his god, learned from the Book at the feet of a mother he had not seen since his eighth year. The reflex was all that mattered. The first moon, still low over the mountains, vanished in the storm a moment after the mountains themselves.

The singer began to sing. Paulus hated her for it, but with the song begun, even killing her would not stop it. In one of the libraries hung the severed head of a singer, in a cage made of her bones. No one living could remember who she was, or understand the language of the song. The scholars of the court believed that whoever deciphered the song would know immortality.

They were at the mouth of a valley that snaked down from the mountains and spilled into a flat plain that once had been a marsh, a resting place for migrating birds. The tomb's architect, according to the scholars, had believed that the soul's migration was eased by placing the tomb in such a place. In the centuries since the death of the king, his world had also died. The river that fed the marshes shifted course to the south; the desert swept in. Paulus scanned the sky and saw no birds.

At first he found the song pleasing. The melody was unfamiliar to him, in a mode that jarred against the songs he remembered from his boyhood. Then all the gates in his mind boomed shut again. He was not a boy taken into the king's service who remembered the songs his mother might have sung. He was the guard captain Paulus and he was here in the desert to have the singer sing her song, and then to die.

Why, they had not been told. The tomb was to be opened. Paulus was a soldier. He would open the tomb. In doing so, he would die, but Paulus did not fear death. He had faced it in forms seen by few other men, had survived its proximity often enough that it had grown familiar. Fatalism was an old friend. The song made his teeth hurt; no, not the song, but some effect of the song. In this place, it was awakening something that had slumbered since The Fells was a scattering of huts on the riverbank. This king had died so long ago that his name was lost. At his death the desert had been green. The world changed, aged with the rest of them. In the desert, you breathed the air of a world where everything had happened already, and it made you feel that you could never have existed.

The obsidian gate shifted with a groan and the wind rose. Sand cascaded down the walls, revealing worked stone, as the singer's song began the work of undoing a burial that had taken the desert centuries to complete. The dozen soldiers with Paulus shifted on their feet, casting glances back and forth between the gate and the approaching storm. They rested hands on sword hilts, gauged the distance to their horses; Paulus could see each of them running through a delicate personal calculation, with the storm on one side and a deserter's crucifixion on the other.

At the mouth of the tomb, at the end of his life, Paulus had only gossip to steer by. Someone important, a merchant named Jan who had the king's ear, wanted to free the spirit that inhabited the tomb. The king had agreed. Paulus wondered what favor he owed that made him willing to cast away the lives of a dozen men. Perhaps they would not die. Still, they had ridden nine days across the desert, to a tomb so old and feared that it existed on maps only through inference; the desert road bent sharply away from it, cutting upward to run along the spine of a line of hills to the north before coming back down into the valley and following the ancient riverbed up to the Salt Pass, from which a traveler could see the ocean on a clear day. Paulus wondered what in the tomb had convinced the road builders to believe that three days' extra ride was worth it.

The singer wept, whether in ecstasy or sorrow Paulus could not tell. Swirls of sand reared in the figures of snakes all around them, striking away in the rising wind. The obsidian gate was open an inch. The wind scoured sand away from the front of the tomb, revealing a path of flat stones. Another inch of darkness opened up. The singer's vibrato shook slivers from the gate that swept away over their heads like slashes of ink inscribed on the sky. Slowly the gate shivered open, grinding across the stones as the singer began to scream. The soldiers broke and ran; Paulus let them go, to die in whatever way they found best. A sound came from the tomb, answering the singer, and the harmony of voices living and dead burst Paulus' eardrums. Deaf, he felt the wind beat his face. Darkness fell as the storm swallowed the sky. The air grew thick as saliva. The sand undulated like a tongue. From the open gate of the tomb, Paulus smelled the exhalation of an undead spirit. He drew his sword, and then the sandstorm overtook them.

When it had passed, Paulus fumbled for the canteen at his belt. He rinsed his eyes, swished water around in his mouth and spat thick black gunk…onto a floor of even stones. He was in the tomb, without memory of having entered. Water dripped from his beard and he felt the scrape and grind of sand all over his body. He was still deaf. His eardrums throbbed. Where was the rest of the guard? He turned in a slow circle, orienting himself, and stopped when he was facing the open doorway. A featureless sandscape, brushed smooth by the storm and suffused with violet moonlight, stretched to an invisible horizon. The skin on the back of Paulus' neck crawled. He turned back to face into the tomb, growing curious. He had enough oil for a torch. Its light seemed a protective circle to him as he ventured into the tomb to see what might have been left behind when the spirit emerged into the world. What it might do was no concern of his. He had been sent to free it; it was free. The merchant in The Fells had what he had paid for.

Torch held off to his left, sword in his right hand, Paulus walked down the narrow entry hall. He went down a stairway and at the bottom found the open sepulcher. The ancient king's bones lay as they had been left. His hair wisped over a mail coat that caught the torchlight.

Am I to be a graverobber? Paulus thought. The spirit was fled. Why not?

He took a cutting of the king's hair, binding it with a bit of leather from the laces of his jerkin. Arrayed about the king's body were ceremonial articles: a sword pitted and brittle with age, jars which had once held spices and perfumes, the skeletons of a dog and a child. Paulus went through it all, keeping what he knew he could sell and ignoring anything that looked as if it might be infected with magic. He worked methodically, feeling distanced from himself by his deafness. After an hour's search through the main room of the tomb and an antechamber knee-deep in sand from the storm, he had a double handful of gold coins. Everything else he saw—a sandstone figurine with obsidian eyes, a jeweled torc obscured by the king's beard, a filigreed scroll case laid diagonally into a wall alcove just inside the door—made him leery of enchantment. The gold would do.

Leaving the tomb, he stumbled over the body of the singer, buried in a drift of sand just inside the shattered gate. There was no sign of the rest of his men. It disturbed Paulus that he had no memory of entering the tomb as the storm broke over them, but memory was a blade with no handle. When it failed, best to live with the failure and live to accumulate new memories. He took another drink, scanned the desert for sign of the horses, and gave up. Either he would walk back, or he could cross the mountains and sail around the Cape of Thirst from the city of Averon. The boat would be quicker and the coastal waters less treacherous than the desert sands. Paulus turned west.

II: The Fells

In three days, he was coming down the other side of the pass. Two days after that, he was sleeping in the shadow of wine casks on the deck of a ship called *Furioso*. On the twelfth day after walking out of the tomb, Paulus stepped off the gangplank into the dockside chaos of The Fells, and wound his way through the city toward the Ridge of the Keep. He wondered how the merchant Jan would know that the spirit was freed, and also how Mikal, the marshal of the king's guard, would react to the loss of his men.

To be the sole survivor of a battle, or of an expedition, was to be assumed a liar. Paulus knew this. He could do nothing about it except tell what portion of the truth would serve him. Any soldier learned that truths told to superiors were necessarily partial.

Mikal received his report without surprise, in fact without much reaction at all. "Understood," he said at the end of Paulus' tale. "His Majesty anticipated the possibility of such losses. You have done well to return." Mikal wrote in the log of the guard. Paulus waited. When he was done writing, Mikal said, "You will return to regular duties once you have repeated your story for Jan Destrier."

So Paulus walked back through The Fells, from the Ridge of the Keep down into the market known as the Jingle and then upriver past the quay where he had disembarked from *Furioso*, to tell his story to a man named for a horse. In the Jingle he remembered where as a boy he performed acrobatics for pennies, and where his brother Piero had saved his life by changing him into a dog and then saved it again by trading one of his eyes for a spell. Paulus had not seen his brother in years. So much in one life, he thought. I was a boy, feeding chickens and playing at being a pirate. Then I was in The Fells, rejected from the King's service. Then I did serve the King, and still do. I have fought in his wars, and killed the men he wanted killed, and now I have released the spirit of a dead king into the world to satisfy an arrangement whose details I will never know.

But whom have I ever stood for the way Piero stood for me?

Jan Destrier's shopfront faced the river across a cobblestoned expanse that was part street and part quay. There was no sign, but Paulus had been told to look for a stuffed heron in the doorway. He could not remember who had told him. Mikal? Unease roiled his stomach, but his step was sure and steady as he crossed the threshold into Jan Destrier's shop. The merchant was behind a counter through whose glass top Paulus could see bottles of cut crystal in every shape, holding liquids and pooled gases that caught the light of a lantern hung over Jan Destrier's head. He was a large man, taller than Paulus and fat in the way men allowed themselves to get fat when their lives permitted it. At first Paulus assumed the bottles held perfume; then he saw the alchemical array on a second table behind the merchant and he understood. Jan Destrier sold magic.

At once Paulus wanted to run, but he was not the kind of man who ran, perhaps because he did not value his life highly enough to abase himself for its sake. He hated magic, hated its unpredictability and the supercilious unction of the men who brokered its sale, hated even more the wizards of the Agate Tower who bound the lives of unknowing men to their own and from the binding drew their power. Once, drunk, Paulus and a groom in the castle stables named Andrew had found themselves arguing over the single best thing a king could do upon ascending the throne. Andrew, hardheaded and practical, wanted a decisive war with the agitating brigands in the mountains to the north; Paulus wanted every wizard and spell broker in The Fells put to the sword. The conversation had started off stupid and gotten worse as the bottle got lighter.

Now here he was in the shop of a broker, sent by a superior on business that concerned the king. Paulus could spit the broker on his sword and watch him die in the facets of his crystal bottles, but he himself would die shortly after. It was not his kingdom and never would be. He was obligated to carry out the orders he had been given.

"Jan Destrier," he said. "Mikal the king's marshal sent me to you."

"You must have something terribly important to tell me, then," Destrier said. "Tell it."

"I led a detachment of the guard out into the desert, where the Salt Pass Road bends away from the dry riverbed," Paulus said. "We had a singer with us. She opened a tomb, and the spirit of the king buried there was freed." He felt like he should add something about the deaths of the singer and his men, but Jan Destrier would not care. "As you requested," he finished.

"There has been a misunderstanding," Destrier said. "I did not wish the spirit to escape."

Paulus inclined his head. "Beg pardon, that was the order I received."

"As may be." Destrier beckoned Paulus around the counter. "Come here." Paulus did, and the merchant stopped him when he had cleared the counter. "What I wanted was for the spirit to come here. That was what the singer was for. Well, partly."

"Then permit me to convey my regrets at the failure of the King's Guard," Paulus said. "The spirit came out of the tomb, but I did not see it after that. There was a storm."

"I'm sure there was," Destrier said. "There almost always is. Never fear, the spirit arrived just as I had hoped." He held up a brass instrument, all curls and notched edges. Paulus had never seen its like before. "You were kind enough to bring it along with you. Or, perhaps I should say that it was kind enough to bring you along with it."

No, Paulus thought. If the spirit was there, then it saw me robbing the tomb.

He closed his fingers around the cutting of the king's hair, thinking that if he could destroy the fetish—crisp it in one of the candle flames that burned along the edges of the merchant's table—that perhaps the spirit would no longer be able to find him. Already he was too late. The spirit, enlivened by some magnetism of the merchant's, drained the strength from his hands. Paulus felt the whisper of its soul in his brain, like the echo of wind in the black silence of a tomb. His legs were the next to go. His arms jerked out looking for something to hold onto, but nothing was there, and when the numbness crept past his knees, Paulus crumpled to the floor. He felt the paralysis like a drug, spinning his mind away from his body until at last he lost touch even with his senses and fell into a dream that was like dying.

"I thought it would ride the singer," Jan Destrier said. "How odd that it chose you instead."

He did not know how long the stupor lasted. When he regained his senses, everything about him was as it had been before: the table littered with alchemical vessels and curling parchment, the border of pinprick candle flames, the batwing eyebrows of the merchant shadowing his eyes. The merchant looked up as Paulus stirred. "You have performed admirably," he said. "It's not every man who would have survived the initial possession, and even fewer live to tell of the extraction."

There would be nothing to tell, Paulus thought. He had no memory of it.

"Where has the spirit gone, then?" he asked. It would come for him, of that he was sure. It had ridden him back to The Fells and now that it was free it would exact some revenge for his spoliation of its tomb. Perhaps it would ride him back, if by coming it had fulfilled whatever geas the merchant had laid on it. Then it would abandon him in the sands to die, the way he had thought he would die when the first notes of the singer's song had begun to resonate in the stones of the tomb.

"I have it here." Destrier produced a cucurbit stoppered with wax, and filled with a swirling fluid. "The stopper is made from the catalyst. When I apply heat, it will melt into the impure spirit, and the reaction will precipitate the spirit into another glass. This essence is my stock in trade. You are familiar with the magic market?"

"I know of it," Paulus said. "I have never made use of it." This was a lie, but Paulus had no compunction about lying to merchants, who were in his experience congenital liars. Twice in his life, his brother had spent magic on him.

"Well, do keep me in mind if you ever find yourself in need," the merchant said.

Paulus' curiosity got the better of him. He framed his question carefully, already outlining a strategy for evading and defeating the spirit. But first he had to know as much as possible about its nature. "Is there magic in the spirit because it died having not used its own? How do you know it has any?"

"Magic is more complicated than the nursery rhymes and old wives' tales would have it," the merchant said. "Yes, every human is born with a spark, and may use it. But other forms of enchantment and power inhere in the world. In stones, in articles touched by great men or tainted by proximity to unexpected death. These can be refined, their magic distilled and used. This is what I do. In the case of spirits, and whether their magic results from unused mortal power or something else," he went on, "it is not what the mathematicians would call a zero-sum endeavor. By trapping the spirit, I trap the potential for its magic that it has brought back from the other world. Distilled and processed, this magic can be sold just as any other. Although the nature of the spirit makes such magics unsuitable for certain uses."

The echoes of the possession still sounded in the hollows of Paulus' mind. He heard the merchant without active understanding. "We are finished here?" he asked.

"Quite," the merchant said. "Do convey my commendation of your performance to your superior officers."

"A commendation would carry more weight coming from yourself," Paulus said.

The merchant scribbled on a parchment, folded it, and sealed it. "Then let us hope the weight of it does not overburden you," he said. Paulus left him setting small fires under the alembic that would purify the spirit's essence into a salable bit of magic.

He delivered the merchant's commendation to Mikal because not to do so would have been stupid. Then he set about shaping a plan to get that distilled element of magic back from the merchant before he sold it, and in its use an unsuspecting client became a tool for the spirit's vengeance on Paulus. He did not have enough money to buy the magic and knew that he could not trade his own; the essence of the undead spirit was doubtless more powerful. He could take it by force, but he would have to kill the merchant, and then leave The Fells—and the King's service—forever. The cowardice of this path repelled him. He owed the King his life. Twice over. He did not love the King, but Paulus understood obligation.

It was obligation that brought him to the seneschal's chamber after word of the merchant's commendation circulated through the court. Mario Tremano had once been the king's tutor. Now much of the court's business was quietly transacted by means of his approval. He was a careful man, an educated man, and a cruel man. Paulus feared him the way he feared all men who loved subtlety. It was tradition in The Fells for scholars to wield influence, but it was also tradition for them to overreach; as Piero often joked, the scholar's stooped posture cried out for straightening on the gallows. Paulus went to Mario Tremano's chamber wondering if Jan Destrier's commendation had made him useful, or doomed him. The only way to find out was to go.

Nearing seventy years of age, Mario cultivated the appearance of a scholar despite his wealth and the raw unspoken fact of his power. He wore a scholar's simple gown and black cap, and did not braid his beard or hair. "Paulus," he said as his footman escorted Paulus into his study. "You have attracted attention from powerful friends of the King."

"I have always tried to serve the King," Paulus said.

"And serve the King you have," Mario said with a smirk. Paulus noted the insult and folded into his understanding of his situation. It was hardly the first time he had heard cutting remarks about the part of his life he'd spent as a dog. The more venomous ladies of the court still occasionally yipped when they passed him in the castle's corridors. Eleven years had done little to dull the appeal of the joke. The seneschal paused, as if waiting for Paulus to react to the slight. "Now, in our monarch's autumn years, you have a glorious chance to perform a most unusual service," he went on.

"However I may," Paulus said. He had heard that the king was unwell, but Mario's open acknowledgment suggested that the royal health was on unsteadier footing than Paulus had known. He was ten years older than Paulus, and should still have been in the graying end of his prime.

"Your willingness speaks well of you, Captain." Mario spread a map on a table below a window that faced out over The Fells and weighted its edges with candlesticks. Paulus saw the broad estuary of the Black River, with The Fells on its western side. The great Cape of Thirst swept away to the southwest, ending in a curl sheltering Averon. To the north and west, Paulus saw names of places where he had fought in the king's wars: Kiriano, Ie Fure, the Valley of Caves. This was the first time he had ever seen such a map. It made the world seem at once larger, because so much of it Paulus had never seen, and smaller, because it could be encompassed on a sheet of vellum.

The seneschal tapped a location far to the north. *Mare Ultima*, Paulus read. "How long do you think it would take you to get there?"

Paulus looked at the distance between The Fells and Averon, which was twelve days on horse. Then he gauged the distance from The Fells to Mario's fingertip, taking into account the two ranges of mountains. "Six weeks," he guessed. "Or as much as eight if the weather is bad."

"The weather will be bad," Mario said. "Of that you can be sure. Winter falls in September in that country."

It was late in June. Paulus waited for the seneschal to continue his geography lesson, but a sharp question from the chamber door interrupted them. "What have you told him?"

Paulus was kneeling as he turned, the rich tones of the queen's voice acting on his muscles before his brain registered what had been said. He dared not look at her, for fear that he would fall in love as his brother had. This fear had accompanied him for the past eleven years, since he had reawakened into humanity. She had done it, bought the magic to restore his human form, as a reward to his brother for his long service as the king's fool. His brother was blind now, and loved the queen for her voice and her scent and the sound of her gown sweeping along the stone floors. Paulus carried a mosaic of her in his head: the fall of her hair, caught in a thin shaft of sunlight; a line at the corner of her mouth, which had taught Paulus much about the passage of years; a time when an ermine stole slipped from her shoulder and Paulus caught his breath at the sight of her pulse in the hollow of her throat. He believed that if he ever looked her full in the face, and held her gaze for a heartbeat, that love would consume him.

"Your Majesty," Mario said. "He has as yet only heard a bit about the seasons in the north."

"Rise, Captain," the queen said. Paulus did, keeping his eyes low. To the seneschal, the queen said, "Well. Perhaps you should tell him what we are about to ask him to do."

"Of course, Your Majesty. Captain, what stories have you heard about dragons?"

Paulus looked up at the seneschal. "Of dragons? The same stories as any child, Excellency. I think."

Mario retrieved a book from a shelf behind his desk. He set it on the map and opened it. "A natural history," he said. "Written by the only man I know who has ever seen a dragon. A source we can trust. Can you write?"

Paulus nodded.

"Then you must copy this," Mario said, "while we instruct you in the details of your task."

Paulus took up a quill and began to write. *Dragons are solitary beasts, powerful as whales and cunning as an ape. They mate in flight only, and the females are never seen except at these moments. Where they nest and brood, no man knows...* At some point during the lesson that followed, the queen touched Paulus on the shoulder. It felt like a blessing, an expression of faith. His unattainable lady who had given him back the shape of a man was now setting him a quest, and though he would probably die, he would undertake the quest feeling that she had offered him a destiny.

His task was this: in the broken hills between the northernmost range of mountains and the icy Mare Ultima, there lived a dragon. *Extremes of heat and cold are the dragon's love. In caves of ice and on the shoulders of volcanoes, there may they be found in numbers.* Once, before ascending the throne, the king had hunted it, and survived the failure of the hunt. It was the queen's wish that before he died, her husband should know that he had outlived the dragon. *A dragon might live hundreds of years. No man can be certain, because no man lives as long as a dragon.* It was to be her death-gift to him, in thanks for the years they had spent as man and wife. "He has lived a life as full as mortal might wish," she said. "Yet this memory hounds him, and I would not have it hound him when he is in his grave."

"Your Majesty, it will not," Paulus said. Whether he meant that he believed he would kill the dragon, or meant only that worldly desires did not accompany spirits, he could not have said. *Many tales and falsehoods exist regarding magical properties of the dragon's blood. These include…*

"How are we to know it is done?" the seneschal said.

"What token would His Majesty wish, as proof of the deed?" Paulus asked the queen. He kept his eyes on the page, and the nib of the quill wet …*language of birds, which some believe to derive their origin from a lost race of smaller dragons quite gone from the world.*

"On the king's thigh is a scar from the dragon's teeth," she said, "and under his hair a scar from its tail. I would have its long teeth and the tip of its tail. The rest you may keep. I care not for whatever treasure it might hoard."

In fact, according to the seneschal's book, dragons did not hoard treasure. *They care not for gold or jewels, but such may be found in their dens if left by those who try to kill a dragon and fail. It is said that such treasure grows cursed from being in the dragon's presence, but place no faith in this superstition.* Paulus copied this information down without relaying it to the queen. "Captain," Mario said. "Jan Destrier spoke well enough of you that you perhaps should visit him before you embark. He certainly would have something to assist you."

"Many thanks, Excellency," Paulus said. "Would it be possible to put something in writing, that there is no confusion on the merchant's part?"

"I hope you do not express doubt as to my word," the seneschal said.

Although the dragon is said to speak, it does not. Some are said to mimic sounds made in their presence, as do parrots and other talking birds, but I do not know if this is true. Paulus was almost done copying the pages. His hand hurt. He could not remember ever having written three pages at once. "Beg pardon, no, Excellency," he said. "I doubt only the merchant's memory and attachment to his wares, and I have no gold to buy what he refuses to give."

This was a carefully shaded truth. Gold Paulus had; whether it was enough to buy any useful magic, he did not know.

"Well said, Captain," the queen commented.

The seneschal was silent. Out of the corner of his eye, Paulus could see that he was absolutely still. Paulus' soldier instinct began to prickle on the back of his neck and he hesitated in his copying as his hand reflexively began to reach for his sword. There was bad blood in the room. *It is said that a dragon recognizes the man who will kill it, and this is the only man it will flee. Contrary to this saying, I have never observed a fleeing dragon, nor expect to.* Paulus would never be able to prove it, but in that instant he knew that when the king passed from this world, Mario Tremano would attempt to send his widow quickly after. He resolved without a second thought to kill the seneschal when he returned from his errand to the Mare Ultima. *The dragon's scale is fearsome strong, and will deflect nearly any blade or bolt, but its weaknesses are: inside the joints of the legs, near the anus, the eyes, under the hinges of the jaw.*

"Yes. Apparently being around the court has taught you some tricks, Captain.

You must leave immediately," Mario said when Paulus finished copying. He handed Paulus a folded and sealed letter. It could have been a death warrant for all Paulus knew. "Our king must know that this is done, and his time is short."

Paulus rose to leave, rolling the copied pages into a tight scroll that he slid under his belt. Twice now, the seneschal had slighted him. "You may choose any horse," the queen said. "And the armory is yours."

"Your Majesty's generosity humbles me," Paulus said.

"Apparently so much that you act the peasant in my presence," she said, a bit archly. "Will you not look me in the face, Captain Paulus of the King's Guard?"

I would, Paulus thought. How I would. "Your Majesty," he said, "I fear that if I did, I would be unable to go from you, and would prove myself unworthy of your faith in me."

"He certainly is loyal," said Mario the seneschal. Paulus took his leave, right hand throbbing, slighted a third time in front of his queen. One day it would come to blades between him and the seneschal.

That was a battle that could not yet be fought. First, he must survive a long trip to the north and a battle with a dragon. It was said that only a king or a hero could kill a dragon. Paulus was not a king and he did not know if he was a hero. He had fought eleven years of wars, had killed men of every color in every territorial hinterland and provincial capital claimed by The Fells, had survived wounds that he had seen kill other men. Perhaps he had performed heroic deeds. If he survived the encounter with the dragon, the question would be put to rest.

He chose a steel-gray stallion from the stable, young but proven in the Ie Fure campaign the summer before. Andrew, emerging from the workshop where he repaired tack, said, "Paulus, you can't mean it. That one's Mikal's favorite."

"Andrew, friend, if the horse doesn't come back, I won't be coming, either. And if both of us do come back, I'll have the court at my feet. So I have nothing to worry about from Mikal either way."

"Court at your feet," Andrew repeated. "How's that?"

"The queen has sent me to kill a dragon," Paulus said.

"There's no such thing as dragons," Andrew said.

"The queen thinks there are, and she wants me to kill one of them." Paulus swung up onto the horse. "So I will. Now come with me to the armory."

Paulus had never fought with a lance, but he had thrown his share of spears. He took three, and a great sword with a blade twice as wide and a foot longer than the long sword he'd carried these past six years. He added a short butchering knife with a curve near the tip of its blade, which he imagined to be a better tool for digging out a dragon's teeth than his dagger. A sling, for hunting along the way, and a helmet, greaves, and gauntlets to go over the suit of mail that lay oiled and wrapped in canvas in one of Paulus' saddlebags. The book had said nothing about whether dragons could breathe fire. If they could, none of his preparations would make any difference.

"Two swords, spears, knives," Andrew said. "I'll wager a bottle you can kill it just with the sling."

"That's not a bet you make with a man you think is going to survive," Paulus said. Andrew didn't argue the point.

"If I'm not back by the first of November, I won't be back," Paulus said. He clasped hands with Andrew and rode out of the keep into the stinking bustle of The Fells. The sun was sinking toward the desert that began a half-day's ride west from the Black River's banks. Paulus thought of the tomb, and the spirit, and grew uncertain about the plan that was already forming in his head. Twenty minutes' ride through the city brought him to Jan Destrier's door. He tied the horse and went inside.

The spell broker was cleaning a tightly curled copper tube. "Ah, the bearer of spirits is returned," he said. "To purchase, no doubt."

Paulus held out the letter from Mario Tremano. After reading it, the broker said, "I see. I am to assist you."

"I am leaving on a quest given by the queen Herself," Paulus said.

"A quest. Oh my," Destrier said. "For what?"

"For something I will not be able to get without help from your stores."

"Specificity, O Captain of the Guard," Destrier said. "What is it you want? Luck? Do you wish not to feel cold, or fire? Thirst? Do you wish to be invisible, or to go nine days without sleep?"

"I wish the essence of the spirit I brought back to you," Paulus said.

Destrier laughed. "I might as well wish the queen's ankles locked around the back of my neck," he said. "We're both going to be disappointed."

It was not Paulus' life that mattered. Not his success or failure at killing the dragon. It was the murderous guile he had sensed in the presence of Mario Tremano and what that meant for the life of the queen after her husband was no longer there to be a useful asset to the seneschal. For her, Paulus would do anything. He stole nothing after killing Jan Destrier; he used the fetish of the dead king's hair to find the essence of the spirit, which was an inch of clear fluid in a brass bulb the size of a fig. He tied it around his neck with a piece of leather, threading the binding of the fetish into the knot that held the bulb.

There would be consequences. If Paulus brought back the teeth and tail of the dragon, he would survive them; if he did not, it would not matter. On the street, he made no effort to hurry. Most of those who had heard Jan Destrier die would be more interested in plundering his expensive wares than in reporting that the killer was dressed in the livery of the King's Guard. He rode for the North River Gate and out into the world beyond The Fells.

He did not know how much power was in the spirit's essence, or of what kind. He did not know whether any of its soul survived inside the brass bulb. But he had a token of the body it had once animated, and he had six weeks to find out.

III: The Quest

With ten days left in August, Paulus came down out of the mountains into the land that on Mario Tremano's map looked like a thin layer of fat between the mountains and the Mare Ultima. He had seen snow three times in the mountains already and heard an avalanche on a warm day after a heavy storm. He had been traveling fifty days. Twice he had cut his beard with the butchering knife. He had killed one man so far, for trying to steal his horse. Mikal's horse. He had hunted well, and so eaten well, and even traded some of his game for cheese and bread and the occasional piece of fruit at farmsteads and villages along the way.

He had also learned something of the nature of the spirit in the brass bulb that hung next to the fetish around his neck. If there was anything Paulus mistrusted more than magic, it was dreams, but nevertheless it was through dreams that he had begun to learn. He was sitting in front of a campfire built in the ribcage of a dragon, listening to the bones speak, telling him he knew nothing of dragons. Your book is full of lies, the voice said.

The Book is about faith and learning, Paulus replied, touching two fingers to his throat. The Journey and the Lesson. It was what his mother had taught him.

Idiot, the voice said. Your book about dragons is what I mean.

It may be, Paulus said.

It is.

He awoke from that first dream with the brass bulb unstoppered and held to his lips. "No," he said, and stoppered it again. "So you do know me."

He would have to be careful, he thought. Something of the spirit remained and he could not know whether it wished him good or ill. He would learn, and when the time came to face the dragon, he would hope he had learned enough.

The second dream took him after he rose in the night to piss into a creek in the foothills of the first mountain range that lay between him and the Mare Ultima. As he drifted back into sleep, he dreamed of walking out into that creek, trying to wash something from his skin that burned and sickened him. This is what you will feel, said the voice of the water over the rocks. This and much worse.

Paulus stopped and stood, dripping and naked, letting the feeling inhabit him, imagining what it would be like to withstand it and fight through it. How much worse? he asked…and woke screaming in a predawn fog, with the gray stallion a shadow rearing at the agony in his voice.

The night of the first snow, as he crested the first pass and descended into a valley bounded by canyons and glaciers that curved like ribs into sparkling tarns, he was reminded of the first dream. He cut a lean-to from tree branches and packed the snow over and around it, then huddled under his blanket with a small fire at the mouth of the lean-to. When he slept, the voice was the sound of tree branches cracking under the weight of snow. I have killed dragons.

What does that matter to me? You cannot kill this one for me, and even if you could, it would shame me to permit it.

Shame, the voice cackled. It looks very different when you are dead.

Someday I will know that, Paulus said. But not soon.

Sooner than you wish, unless you listen.

Then talk, so I can decide if what you say is worth listening to.

You cut hair from my body, and took gold from my tomb, the voice said.

All the more reason to be suspicious of you.

With a cackle, the voice said, How much you think you know. Who guided you to the broker's? And when you came back to the broker's—do you think you found me? No, mortal man. I brought you to me. I would kill a dragon again.

A cold, shameful fear made Paulus moan in his sleep. The queen—

No. Her mind is her own. I was a king, and would not meddle with others of my station. You, on the other hand…

Paulus woke up. In the pages he had copied from Mario Tremano's book, it was said that kings of old had killed dragons, and driven them to the wastes of the north and west. He rolled the brass bulb in his palms. The spirit had said that the book was full of lies. If the spirit told the truth, then kings of old had not killed dragons, which meant that the spirit was lying.

That is man's logic, he thought, remembering a story from the Book in which a man tried to reason with lightning. Yes, the lightning had said. There is no flaw in your thought, save that it is man's thought, and I am lightning.

Shaking out the blanket and refolding it over the horse's back, Paulus found himself in the same position. In a week, or perhaps ten days, he would find the dragon. Then he would discover which lies the spirit was telling.

With ten days left in August, he came down out of the mountains and began asking the questions. The people who hunted seals and caribou along the shores of Mare Ultima spoke a language he knew only from a few words picked up on campaigns, when mercenary companies had come down from this land of black rock and blue ice, bringing their spears and an indifference to suffering bred at the end of the world. He pieced together, over days, that there was a dragon, and that it slept in a cave formed after the eruption and collapse of a volcano. He worked his way across the country, eating white rabbits and salmon and the dried blubber of seals, building his strength, until he found the dragon's cave.

The mountain still smoked. Standing on a ridge that paralleled the shore, some miles distant, Paulus looked south. The mountains, already whitening. North: water the color of his stallion, broken by ice floes all the way to a misty horizon. East: coastal hills, green and gray speckled with snow. West: more mountains, their peaks shrouded in clouds. The people he had spoken to said that in the west, mountains burned.

This was as good a place as any to find a dragon, Paulus thought. As good a place as any to die.

The dragon's cave was a sleepy eye perhaps a half-mile up the ruined side of a mountain. The top of the mountain was scooped out, ringed with sharp spires; a waterfall drained what must have been an immense lake in the crater, carving a canyon down the mountainside and a new river through the hills to the Mare Ultima. Paulus could smell some kind of flower, and the ocean, and from some-where far to the west the tang of smoke. He dismounted and began to prepare.

First, the mail shirt, still slick with oil. Gauntlets, their knuckles squealing like the hinges of a door not hung true. Greaves buckled over his boots. The great sword across his back. Shield firm on his left forearm, spear in his right hand, long sword on his hip. The butchering knife sheathed behind his left hip.

Then he thought, No. This is man's thinking, and I am going to fight the lightning.

He stabbed the spear into the ground, and let the great sword fall from his back. Setting his shield down, Paulus took off the gauntlets. He snapped the leather thong around his neck and unwound the binding of the fetish. With the butchering knife, he cut a tangled lock of his own hair. There was more gray in it than he remembered from the last time he had looked in a mirror, but he was forty-five years old now. He twisted the two locks of hair together into a tangle of black and gray long enough that he could wind it around the base of the middle finger on his right hand, and then in a figure-eight around his thumb. He bound it in place, and unstoppered the bulb. As he tipped a few drops of the fluid onto the place where the figure-eight crossed itself, he heard the voices of ice and snow, rocks and water, bones of dragons. He put a gauntlet on his right hand over the charm and tipped a few more drops into its palm. The rest he sprinkled over the blade of the sword. Then he cast the bulb away clinking among the stones.

It would work or it would not. Picking up his shield and holding his sword before him, Paulus picked his way at an angle up the slope toward the dragon's cave. A voice in his head said, *Now you know why I did not ride the singer.*

Afterward, he was screaming, and when she came to him, he thought he was being guided out of his life. She spoke, and soothed him, and left him there in his own blood, writhing as the dragon's poison ate its way under his skin. The spirit was gone. In the echoes of its departure Paulus felt the slash of the dragon's claws, shredding his mail shirt and the muscle underneath. When his body spasmed with each fresh wave of poisoned agony, the grating of the mail links on the stone floor of the cave was the sound of the dragon's scales as it uncoiled and raised its head to meet him. The white of his femur and his ribs was the white of its bared fangs crushing his shield and snapping the bones in his wrist. And when he arched his back in seizure, as the poison worked deeper into his body, the impact of his head on the ground was the blinding slap of its tail and then the shock of his blade, driven home and snapped off in the hollow underneath its front leg. The dragon was dead and Paulus soon would be. He thrashed his right arm, flinging the bloody gauntlet away, and caught the fetish in his teeth. His face was slick with the dragon's blood and his own tears. Gnawing the fetish loose, he spat it out. Free, he thought. Free to die my own death. O my queen…

And she was back, with a sledge freshly cut and smelling of sap. Paulus recognized the language she spoke, but couldn't pick out the words. When she dragged him over the stones at the mouth of the cave, pain blew him out like a candle.

The next thing he could remember was the sound of wind, and the weight of a fur blanket, and the rank sweat of his body. He was inside, in a warm place. A creeping icy draft chilled his face. Paulus opened his eyes. The woman was stirring something in a pot over a fire. He tried to sit up and his wounds re-awakened. The sound that came out of him was the sound wounded enemies made when the camp women went around the battlefield to kill them. The woman laid her bone spoon across the lip of the pot and came over to squat next to him. "Shhhhh," she said. Black, black hair, Paulus thought. And black, black eyes. Then he was gone again.

It was quiet and dark when next he awoke. He heard the woman breathing nearby. He flexed his fingers, wondering that he could still feel all ten. Under the blanket, he began to explore his body. His left wrist was bound and splinted, and radiated the familiar pain of a healing broken bone. Heavy scabs covered the right side of his body from just below his shoulder all the way down to the knee. He wiggled his toes. Something was sticking out of the scabs, and after puzzling over it Paulus realized that the woman—or someone—had stitched the worst of his wounds, with what he could not tell. He was going to live. He knew the smell of infection and his nose could not find it. He had clean wounds. Bad wounds, but clean. They would heal. He would walk, and he would live. He saw details in the near-perfect darkness of the room: the last embers in the fire pit, the swell of the woman under her blankets. His fingers roamed over his body, feeling the pebbled scars where the dragon's poison had burned him and the strangely smooth expanses that were without wounds. He flexed the muscles of his arms, and they hurt, but they worked. When he moved his legs, the deep tears in his right thigh cried out. Not healed yet, then. Putting that together with the way his wrist felt, Paulus guessed that it had been two weeks since the woman had found him in the mouth of the dragon's cave.

The teeth, he thought. And the tail.

He must not fail the queen.

"The dragon," he said to the woman the next morning. She shushed him. "I have to—"

Again she shushed him. Paulus sank back into the pile of furs and skins. He still had no strength. He watched her move around, taking in the details of her home. It was made of stone and wood, the spaces between the stones stuffed with moss and earth. One wall was a single slab of stone—a hillside, with three manmade walls completing the enclosure. Timbers slanted from the opposite wall to rest against the natural wall, covered with densely woven branches. Paulus couldn't believe it could contain warmth, but it did. He threw his covers off, suddenly sweating in the fur cocoon. The woman did not react to Paulus' nakedness. She opened a door he hadn't noticed and the interior of the house lit up with sunlight reflected from deep drifts of snow. The snow must be waist-deep, Paulus thought. Perhaps the dragon's cave was buried. Perhaps no one here wanted trophies from its carcass. Exhausted again, he did not resist when the woman settled covers back over him and went about her business. "Why did you save me?" Paulus asked her.

She shushed him, and again he fell asleep.

Gradually over the winter he learned more of her language, and she bits and pieces of his. From this he learned that she had hauled him to her home, put him on the pile of furs, and tended his wounds with skill that few surgeons in The Fells possessed. Or she was fortunate, and Paulus was strong. Perhaps he would have lived in any case, given shelter and food. He would never know.

His horse was outside, kept in an overhung spot along the bluffs that also made up the fourth wall of the house. As soon as he was strong enough, he went out to see it and found that someone in this icy wilderness knew something about horses; it was brushed, its hooves were trimmed. If these people had mastered ironworking, Paulus thought, the horse would have new shoes. The hospitality was humbling. He thanked her and asked her to thank whoever had taken care of the horse. About the dragon, she appeared confused when he finally made her understand that he had traveled for two months just to get pieces of it to take home. "For my queen," he said. Though she understood the words, the concept made no sense to her. Arguing with lightning, Paulus thought. Her name meant Joy in her language. She lived alone. Her mother and father were dead, and this was their house. In the good weather months, she fished and wove and tanned hides; in the winter, she kept to herself and wove cloth to sell the next summer. There was a village twenty minutes' walk away. A man there wanted to marry her, but she would not have him. He was the one who had cared for the stallion.

Paulus thanked her again. She shrugged. What else would she have done?

Growing stronger, he went out into the snow dressed in clothes Joy made. He met a few of the villagers, who lost interest in him as soon as they confirmed that he had not made Joy his wife. The dragon, it seemed, had made little difference in their lives. It ate caribou and sea lions. There were plenty of both to go around. In The Fells, should he survive to return there, Paulus would be celebrated; here, he was a curiosity.

On one of the first spring days, smells of the earth heavy in his nose, Paulus went out from Joy's house with the butchering knife tucked in his belt. He found his way to the dragon's cave and went inside. It lay more or less as he had left it. His broken sword blade, its edges now rusted, protruded from behind its left front leg. Marveling, Paulus paced off the length of its body. Fifty feet. It was mostly still frozen. He laid out the canvas sheet he'd used to protect his armor and set to work hacking into the carcass with the butchering knife. Four fangs for the queen, and the tip of the tail. Then he gouged out most of the rest of its teeth, leaving those that broke as he worked them free of the jawbone. In the pages he had copied from Mario Tremano's book were recipes for alchemical uses of the dragon's eyes, as well as a notation that its heart was said to confer the strength of giants. The eyes came out easily enough; the heart was another matter. Paulus went to work prying loose the scales on its breast until he could crack through its ribs. The heart, larger than his head, was pierced six inches deep by the blade of his sword. Sweating in the cold, he cut it out and put it with the eyes. Then he added several dozen of its scales, each the size of his spread hand.

When he was done, he walked back to Joy, who was outside bartering a roll of cloth for the haunch of a moose killed by a villager who would have gladly given her the haunch, and anything else, if she would accept him. That night, Joy and Paulus ate moose near the fire. When they were done, she got up to put the bowls in water. He handed her his dagger, slick with grease, and she looked at it for a moment before slashing it across his right forearm.

Paulus sprang away from her, hand instinctively dropping toward a sword hilt that wasn't there. "Joy!" he shouted, squaring off against her, glancing around for something he could use as a weapon. He had no doubt that he could overpower her, even weak as he still was, but no man ever went unarmed against an opponent with a knife if there was even a stick nearby that could improve the odds.

She pointed at his forearm. Unable to help himself, he looked. The skin was unmarked. Paulus looked back at her. She made no move to approach him; after a moment, she turned and dropped the knife into the pot of water with the bowls.

It is said of the dragon's blood that washing in it renders human flesh invulnerable to blade or arrow, the seneschal's book had said. Paulus had read over those lines the way he had the rest of the more fanciful passages, skeptically and with no effort to keep them in mind. But it was true. He had felt the blade hit his arm. It should have opened him up to the bone.

"Dragon," Joy said, and began to wash the dishes.

She knew, Paulus thought. She was showing him. Not just the transformation of his skin wetted with the dragon's lifeblood; she was showing him that he had survived.

"How," he began, and stopped when he realized he had too many questions to ask, and no words to ask them, and that she had no words to answer. He watched her dry his dagger and set it aside on the table. Before she could pick up another dish, he caught her wrist and drew her toward him. Her expression changed and he thought she would pull away, but she let him draw her down into the furs. She kept her eyes locked on his. Paulus—who had once been a dog, and who had spoken to the dead, and who had winterlong danced on the line between life and death—knew that when she looked into his eyes, she was seeing a dead man she had once loved.

For him, too, she was someone else. The spill of her hair across his chest was the queen's hair, caught in sunlight. Her body moving against his was the queen's body, pledged to another. Her eyes shining in the last light of the fire were the queen's eyes Paulus never dared to meet.

"He died out on the ice," she said when he asked, a few days later. "Hunting whales."

How long since he had had a woman? Nearly a year, Paulus thought. And he did not want to let this woman go. For her, perhaps longer. She said that her man who died hunting whales was her first, and only. The way she spoke of him made Paulus conscious that he had never felt that way about any woman but the queen, whom he could never have. The queen, with her dying husband and the seneschal Mario Tremano plotting against her. He had come to the ends of the earth, slain a dragon, to realize the futility of his desire. If he could not have her, he could at least save her. This, too, Joy had taught him. Paulus was stronger now. The time was coming when he would have to leave. The dragon's heart and eyes were almost dried. He had carefully cleaned the bits of gum and blood from its teeth, for presentation to his queen. But he was not ready to leave yet. He started obliquely, and over the early weeks of spring more directly, gauging her reactions to the idea of coming south. He described the city, the Keep on the Ridge, the queen, his brother the fool. Subtlety never came easy to him and was impossible to maintain; on the first day in May, he told her that his errand was not yet complete. He must return to The Fells.

"I would have you come with me," he said. They were tangled in a blanket and in each other's scents. Night was falling. She would never know what it had cost him to speak the words. Having Joy meant acquiescing to the caprice of Fate that kept him apart from the queen he would love. Having Joy meant being a curiosity at court, the guard captain who had once been a dog and now had a wife with callused hands from a distant land, who had never seen silk. But he was willing. He would take her if she said yes.

"I would have you stay here," Joy said. "But I know you will not. Go."

"In a little while," Paulus said.

Joy shook her head. "If you know that you are going, go," she said. "Go to your queen. Go."

"You saved my life," he said. Meaning that he felt an obligation to her, but also that he believed she too was obligated, that once she had held his life in her hands, she was no longer able to stand back from him and watch him go. Man logic, he thought. And she is lightning.

"I am from this place," Joy answered. "Someday when I am done mourning, I will take a man from the village, and there will be children in this house. I would take you if you would stay; but if you will not, go to your queen."

There was nothing to say to this. Paulus was not going to stay and Joy was not going to go. She had nursed him back to health, but she did not want him. She wanted a fisherman, a black-haired hunter of moose and caribou, a second chance at her man who had died on the ice. Not a soldier from a foreign land, entering his forty-seventh year, determined to finish a quest he had begun in honor of a woman he could never have. They both knew what it was to find solace for a little while and then reawaken into the desire for what they could never have, or never have again.

The next morning, Paulus saddled the horse and packed into its saddlebags the teeth and tail of the dragon, the scales, the heart, and the eyes. His sword and shield were broken, his armor shredded, his spear taken to hunt seals, the great sword ruined by a winter under snow. He had a thousand miles to cover with a knife and the sling, and a good horse. Mikal would be glad to see it, but not at all glad to see Paulus.

Perhaps the queen would be glad to see him. Perhaps.

Joy came out from the house with jerky and a fish. "I caught it this morning before you woke up. Your first meal when you ride away from the ocean should always be a fish," she said. Paulus thought he understood. He swung up onto the horse and did not look back as he rode south, up the hill track toward the mountains.

THIS WIND BLOWING, AND THIS TIDE
DAMIEN BRODERICK

Damien Broderick is an award-winning Australian SF writer, editor and critical theorist, a senior fellow in the School of Culture and Communication at the University of Melbourne, currently living in San Antonio, Texas, with a PhD from Deakin University. He has published more than 40 books, including *Reading by Starlight, Transrealist Fiction, x, y, z, t: Dimensions of Science Fiction, Unleashing the Strange,* and *Chained to the Alien: The Best of Australian Science Fiction Review. The Spike* was the first full-length treatment of the technological Singularity, and *Outside the Gates of Science* is a study of parapsychology. His 1980 novel *The Dreaming Dragons* (revised in 2009 as *The Dreaming*) is listed in David Pringle's *Science Fiction: The 100 Best Novels.* His latest SF novel is the diptych *Godplayers* and *K-Machines,* written with the aid of a two-year Fellowship from the Literature Board of the Australia Council, and his recent SF collections are *Uncle Bones* and *The Qualia Engine.*

> "Has any one else had word of him?"
> Not this tide.
> For what is sunk will hardly swim,
> Not with this wind blowing, and this tide.
> —"My Boy Jack", Rudyard Kipling (1915)

The starship was old, impossibly old, and covered in flowers. Despite a brisk methane breeze, not a petal nor a stamen of the bright blooms moved. Under an impervious shield, they remained motionless, uncorrupted, altogether untouchable.

"They're alive," reported the Navy remote viewer. When I was a kid, the idea that the armed services might employ a trained, technologically enhanced psychic would have got you a derisive smack in the ear from your elders and betters, even though the American CIA ran a remote viewing program called Star Gate back in the last century, before they ostentatiously closed it down and took it to black ops. This viewer was blind to light, but saw better than the rest of us, by other means, on a good day. Like me, sort of, in my own itchy way.

He stood at the edge of the huge, flower-bedecked vessel, gloved, open palms held outward, his hands vibrating ever so slightly, like insect antennae hunting a pheromone. "It's amazing. Those blossoms are still alive, after… what… millions of years? I can't find my way in yet, but I can detect that much even through the stationary shield."

"Is that the same as a, you know, *stasis field*?" I asked the marine master sergeant standing guard beside us. I turned to face her, and bobbed sickeningly. Two days ago I had been on Ganymede, and on Earth's Moon before that. Now I walked on another world entirely, around yet another world entirely. It wasn't right for a man as ample as I to weigh so little, especially with Titan's bruised-peach air pushing down on me half again as heavily as Earth's. It went against nature. Even with the bodyglove wrapping me, and an air tank on my back, I only weighed about 18 kilos—say 40 lbs. A tenth of what the scales would show back home.

"'Stasis' my ass! That's sci-fi nonsense," she barked. "Media technobabble. Like your own—" She bit the rest of her sentence off, perhaps fortunately. "This here is hard science."

"So sorry."

"And please don't speak again without an invitation to do so, Sensei Park. We don't want to put Mr. Meagle off his stroke."

Opening his startlingly blue, blind eyes, the Navy viewer laughed. The sound echoed oddly in his bodyglove and through our sound loop. All sounds did, out on the orange-snowy surface of Titan. "Let him natter on, Marion. I'm entangled now. You'd have to cut my head off and pith my spine to unhook me from this baby."

I wondered idly how either of them would respond if I told them I was the reason, or at least the proximate occasion, that they were here. They'd regard me as a madman, probably. My role in developing the portage functor was under cover about as deep as any since the creation of the US Office of Strategic Services in 1945, long before CIA got tight with clairvoyants. Perhaps these people already did consider me deluded. Yeah, it was true that I'd told them where to look for the starship, but it wasn't as if I had the credentials of a remote viewer, so undoubtedly it was just a fluke. Right.

I felt the pressure of the thing, its causal gravitas, as I gazed down at the starship. If that's what it was, under its stationary shield and floral tribute.

This thing on Titan had been tugging at me, at my absurd and uncomfortable and highly classified gift, since I was four or five years old, running in the streets of Seoul, playing with a Red Devils soccer ball and picking up English and math. A suitable metaphor for the way a child might register the substrate of a mad universe, and twist its tail. My own son, little Song-Dam, plagued me with questions when he, too, was a kid, no older than I'd been when the starship buried under tons of frozen methane and ethane had plucked for the first time at my stringy loops.

"If light's a wave, Daddy, can I surf on it?" Brilliant, lovely child! "No, darling son," I said. "Well, not exactly. It's more like a Mexican football wave, it's more like an explosion of excitement that blows up." I pulled a big-eyed face and flung my arms in the air and dropped them down. "Boom!" Song laughed, but then his mouth drooped. "If it's a wave, Dad, why do some people say it's made of packets?" "Well," said I, "you know that a football wave is made of lots and lots of team supporters, jumping up and sitting down again." He wasn't satisfied, and neither was I, but the kid was only five years old.

Later, I thought of that wave, sort of not there at all at one end, then plumping up in the middle, falling to nothing again as it moved on. Follow it around the bleachers and you've got a waveform particle moving fast. Kind of. But for a real photon, you needn't follow it, it's already there, its onboard time is crushed and compressed from the moment of launch to the final absorption, just one instantaneous blip in a flattened, timeless universe. Why, you could jump to the Moon, or Ganymede, or even Titan, all in a flash. Just entangle yourself with it, if you knew how (as I showed them how, much later), like Mr. Meagle remote viewing his impenetrable stationary starship.

Physics—you're soaking in it!

"I can likely get more now sitting in my relaxation cell back at Huygens," Meagle said. He looked very calm, as if he'd just stepped out of an immersion tank, but there was a faint quivering around his blind eyes. I watched his face in my viewmask, as if neither of us wore gloves over our heads. The man was exhausted. "So tell me, Mr. Park," he said, as we turned and made our way to the big-wheeled jitney, "what were your own impressions, sir?" Scrupulous about not front-loading me with hints of his own; I liked that.

"Anyone, or any *thing*, who loves flowers that much," I said judiciously, "can't be all bad."

Huygens had provided me with a customized broad-beamed sanitary personal; I have authoritative hams, and a wide stance. It degloved me with slick efficiency. I relieved myself with a gratified sigh. While bodygloves have the capacity to handle such impositions of the mortal order, the experience is undignified and leaves a residual aroma trapped inside with one's nostrils, so I tend to hold on. We had been outside for hours without a pit stop. The sanitary squirted and dabbed, removed sweat from my perspiring hide with its dry tongue, dusted powder across the expanse, set me free. I dressed in my usual unflattering robe, and made my way directly to the commissary bubble. I was starving.

Banally, the wall and ceiling display showed a faux of thrice-magnified Saturn, four hand-widths across, tilted optimally to show off the gorgeous ring system. I'd just seen the reality outside, with nothing between me and the ringed planet itself but a protective film and a million or so kilometers of naked space above the bright Xanadu regional surface where we'd stood. Since we were almost at the equator, Saturn's belt had been a thin glitter in the photomultipliers in our bodyglove masks (and would be invisible to the naked eye), directly overhead, right and left of the primary's waist, not truly impressive. Of course, even with the high frequency step-downs of the photomultipliers, the atmosphere looks hazy anyway.

This magisterial feed on the wall was probably coming, today, from one of the polar sats keeping an eye on the big feller. It seemed to me a bit tacky, a lame pretence, but then again, Titan is tidally locked, so it must get a tad wearying for the regular staff, seeing exactly the same thing in the sky forever, whatever installation dome you're at, Huygens, or Herschel at the north pole. Except that nothing *is* ever the same; all is nuance, the slow fortnightly progression of light and shade, the phases of the Sun's illumination of the big ball of gas… Well, these were scientists and military, most of them, what could one expect?

I loaded my tray with rather edible *Boeuf Bourguignon* from the dedicated cuisine printer, took it to a table where a handful of my new colleagues were chowing and jawing away, sat down at the spare place, set to after a genial glance around. At least with the queasy low gravity I wasn't worried that this spindly conventional chair would give way abruptly beneath me, tipping my consider-able butt ungraciously to the floor. It had been known to happen back on Earth. Nobody laughed derisively if it did, at least there was that. Not any more, they didn't.

"Why, Sensei," said the Japanese biologist, Natasha Hsai, with the slightest edge in her tone, "won't you join us for dinner?" I do not give her title, nor do I mean any disrespect; all these eggheads had at least a couple of doctorates apiece, it went without saying.

"Why, Natasha, thank you, I believe I will." I started in on my second pearl onion. "Good fare, they don't stint you—nor should they, you are doing sterling work out here."

Several of the boffins shared glances, perhaps amused. They fancy themselves a cut above.

The handsome, dark-haired fellow at the head of the table cleared his throat. "So, have you been outside yet to pay your respects to the Enigma, Mr. Park?"

From the dossiers I'd memorized before leaving Jupiter space, I recognized him, beneath his heavy, straggled beard, as the head of molecular engineering, Antonio Caetani. "Just got back from the tour, Dr. Caetani. Fascinating. Right up my street."

"That's Tony," he said gracelessly. More glances flickered about the table. He chose to go right for it. Had to give him points for that. "Unless I'm mistaken, your street is paved with donations from the ID Institute."

I had encountered this kind of feral attitude previously, of course, especially from hard-headed scientists of conventional stamp. I could even share a kind of empathy for his rancor. It was as if, from his highly-credentialed point of view, a government-sponsored raving crackpot were to be imposed on his team. As if a SETI astronomer in the Fermi Taskforce had been obliged to include a rectally-probed UFO abductee, or a global proteome program forced to sign up a fundamentalist creationist. I shrugged.

"Oh, give the guy a break, Tony," said the Iranian artifact expert, Mansour Khosrojerdi. "Let him eat his meal." His beard was darker and thicker even than Caetani's. Granted, the temperature was nearly minus 200 degrees Celsius on the other side of the bubble, but this was self-mythologizing on a preposterous scale. Did they imagine they were rehearsing the doomed expeditions of the Arctic explorers? "We can postpone the ideological catfights until after the cheese and Amontillado."

"No need to spare my delicate sensibilities," I said with a hearty laugh, and reached for the carafe of red wine, luminous as a garnet under spurious golden Saturn light. The woman to my right, the string loop specialist Jendayi Shumba, got there first with her competent, chunky hand, dark as night.

"Allow me, Sensei Park."

"You are gracious, thanks. But let's all be friends, no need for formality, call me Myeong-hui." I grinned with big teeth at her dismay, then laughed out loud. "No, that's an impossible mouthful, it's all right, just call me Sam, love. Everyone does."

"Sam." A slightly uncomfortable silence fell. Scrapings of plastic flatware on realistic plates. I gobbled up my tasty beef, placed the empty plate back on my tray, slurped off some more of the stunningly convincing compiled Shiraz, took a bite of a lemon-ginger dessert to die for, decorated with pistachios. "Fermi-53, that's my considered opinion," I said with my mouth full. "My *tentative, preliminary* opinion, naturally."

"There are no recognizable roses or jonquils or violets or orchids, obviously. But the flowers scattered over the vehicle certainly do appear to be derived from Earth angiosperms, specialized to a range of climates and coevolutionary biomes," said Natasha Hsai. "So far as we can tell purely from visual inspection."

"Which rules out Fermi-53 instantly," Antonio Caetani said. "Blossoms of such complexity and beauty did not evolve on Earth until the Holocene. Probably not until humans deliberately bred the cultivars during the rise of agriculture."

"Oh, let's not oversimplify, Tony," Natasha said. "Pollinator insects and hummers and lizards and all the rest, they speciated along with the angiosperms; they *sculpted* each other without any help. Yes, I grant you, early humans broke up the soil to an unprecedented extent so they could grow their dinner, and then as a sideline retained and cultivated those blossoms that especially… well, made them happy. They're our botanical pets, now, because flowers make us smile and feel good. They induce positive emotions."

"They're scented sex organs," Caetani said, "doing their job."

I'd finished eating, for the moment. "The first flowering plants," I pointed out, "evolved 65 million years prior to the Chicxulub catastrophe. Nice symmetry, that." As far back in time before the extinction of the dinosaurs as we now stood after it. I didn't need to spell that out; these were, after all, highly trained intellects. But I had to add the obvious, the intolerable, the all-but-unthinkable crux. "Humans, I remind you, were not the only cultivators." I found I had no appetite for cheese, and pushed back my chair. "Do you allow smoking here? Anyone for cigars and port?"

"No," said Caetani brusquely. "Sensei Park, we are scientists, not mystagogues. I confess myself bewildered by your presence at Huygens." Jendayi Shumba pulled at his sleeve; he shook her off. "I am frankly offended that the Imperium invited a quack from the Intelligent Dinosaur Institute here to Titan." Shumba kicked his leg under the table; I saw and felt the small causal shock of her intention and its manifestation, because that's who I am, that's what I do. "I have nothing more to say to you." He looked away disdainfully, drew his own dessert plate in front of him, scooped up a heaping spoonful of tiramisu and shoved it into his left eye, hard.

I raised one eyebrow, sighed, and rose, gathered my soiled crockery and plasticware on the tray, and walked away from the table. He probably wouldn't lose the sight in his eye. But what could I do?

Speaking technically, I'm an etiological distortion. Less pompously, there's something buried deep inside me that screws with cause and effect. I'm a footloose bubble of improbability. Call me a witch or a freak if you'd prefer, it rolls more easily off the tongue. Chances are good, though, that if you do call me nasty names, and I get to hear about it, you'll trip over the kid's bike in the dark, or run into an opening door, and break something painful. It's not that I harbor resentment at name-calling, but my unconscious seems to. As I say, not much I can do about that, sorry.

There were ructions and alarums but I brushed them off, went to bed and slept, as I had done every night for five years, like a damned soul. My gift or curse does not permit me to stand aside from that which wraps me like a shroud. Sorrow eddied in my dreams. My son—

—and as so often, these days, the booming, tolling voices came to me from a century and a half past, voices I have heard only in my head, reading their words on the pages of old books I found in an abandoned library, stinking with the reek of extinguished fires, where I had crept for silence like a heavy old dog with a wound too great to bear. The words were in English, that tongue almost as familiar to me as my own, picked up in the streets, later honed in special classes for promising children. I knew nothing of the writer, save that he was a man of substance in his place and time. His words raised a resonance in my burned soul. He must have known this same agony, and sought some bitter draught of comfort:

O Sorrow, cruel fellowship,
O Priestess in the vaults of Death,
O sweet and bitter in a breath,

What whispers from thy lying lip?
"The stars," she whispers, "blindly run;
A web is wov'n across the sky;
From out waste places comes a cry,
And murmurs from the dying sun:
"And all the phantom, Nature, stands—
With all the music in her tone,
A hollow echo of my own,—
A hollow form with empty hands."

And woke in the morning (by the conventional Earth clock calibrated to Seoul time, GMT+9 hours), as always alone, empty hollow form and all, despite the web wov'n palpably across the sky, and ravenously hungry, as usual.

So I ate a healthy breakfast and went to watch Meagle on closed circuit, a feed from the audiovisual record that military remote viewers are obliged to make for assessment, interpretation, and the archive. Today he sat zazen in a small cell like a non-denominational chapel, if chapels come with voice-activated holography displays (and maybe they do, I'm not a religious man), hands curled upward on his knees. His breathing was slow, regular. Maybe this was what their protocol called *cooling down*. His blind eyes were open, apparently fixed on the deep blue depths of the holly. Upon his head was a crown of thorns, a tidy maze of squid detectors pulsing to the quantum state of his brain, his brain stem, his meditative consciousness.

"Looking at the vehicle from above," he murmured. "Still can't find my way in. Yet." His lips quirked the smallest amount. Who Dares Wins, I thought. Semper Fi. Rah-rah. Well, it took a lot of quiet confidence in one's oddball abilities, no doubt. My own kind of disreputable ability just happened to me, or around me.

"Get back to the signal line," a gravelly voice said. Someone not in the room. His controller, I supposed. His operator, whatever they called the role.

"He's physically blind, I realize that," I told the medical officer seated beside me in the observation booth, "but doesn't knowing the identity of the target sort of pollute his, his guesswork?"

"The viewer does not guess."

"No offense. I mean, bias him unconsciously with preconceived notions?" Front-loading, they called it; I knew that much. "Like that stasis field thingee? Can we be sure that's not some scrap of nonsense from a comic strip he read when he was a child?"

"Mr. Meagle is well past all such neophyte hazards," the nurse said, offended by my uppity kvetching. He had gray hair at his close-cropped temples, and a steady gaze. Almost certainly a veteran of the war in—I shut that thought down, hard. "The colonel can afford to depart from the lock-step of traditional protocol. As he does when it suits him." I nodded, made soothing, conciliatory sounds. Perhaps mollified, he explained, "It contracts the search path polynomially."

"Um," I said, and settled back to view the sketched images form, dissolve, re-form in the imaginary three-space of the holograms. As Meagle's fingers moved through the air, unseen lasers tracked the shapes he sketched. It seemed, watching him, that he actually *felt* his way around the starship out there in the frozen crust of Titan. Kinesthetic imagery. A kind of heightened physicality, perhaps unavailable to a sighted person. Or was that nothing better than my whimsy, my fat man's sentimentality?

"Moving downward, gravity tugs at me," the remote viewer murmured. His voice was drowsy. I saw his shoulders spasm, as if he were falling forward and had caught himself.

"Wake up, there, colonel," the voice said, without reproach. "You're drifting."

"He's sliding into Phase Two. That was hypnic myoclonia," the nurse commented. "Jactitation."

"Haven't slept since yesterday," Meagle muttered. He shook himself. "Okay. Got it. I'm in."

The screens, trying to emulate whatever it was the psychic was "seeing/feeling," bloomed with a burst of visual noise. Were those things sketchy blocks of cells, like the hexagonal innards of a bee hive? They shrank, jittered, smoothed into a kind of curvy passageway. The image was being enhanced by the computer's analysis, drawing on an archive of Meagle's private symbols.

"Analytical overlay," the operator said in a tone of admonition.

"I don't—No, this's what I'm actually perceiving. My God, Charley, the place is so fucking *old*. Millions of years. Tens of millions."

"Give me some Stage Three."

"Weirdly beautiful, man. But alien. Not insects, I'm pretty sure." The overlapping images loped along, as if from a camera mounted on a cartoon's shoulder. Is this how the blind imagines seeing? Meagle had been sightless from birth, the dossier had informed me. But maybe that shouldn't be surprising; the blind repurpose the cortical and precortical tissues specialized by evolution for visual capture and registration—the large dedicated occipital lobe, the striate V1 cortex, all the way up the V hierarchy to middle temporal MT, pathways carrying neural trains from the retina to the brain, interpreting, pruning as they flashed their specialized code. Yada yada. His sensitive, trained brain had nabbed that spare capacity, retained its function, modified its input channels. The Marvel That Is Your Brain! I overheard my own mocking subliminal commentary and wondered why I was so anxious, suddenly. A kind of curdling in the causal webs... I felt more and more uncomfortable, as if I badly needed to take a dump. Maybe I did. Meagle had fallen silent. Dropping off to sleep again? No, the constructed image was sliding past us in the hologram, slurring and breaking up in detail, but it was a corridor he walked along, in his spirit walk or whatever you call it.

Something sitting in a large padded chair. Christ!

"Christ!" Meagle cried, loudly. Small indicator lights went from placid green to blipping yellow on one display. A histogram surfed briefly into the red. The nurse was clicking keys, fast and unrattled.

"Bingo, Colonel," said the operator, triumph shaking his professional *sangfroid.*

My etiological sense scrambled. I lurched up, leaned forward, ready to puke. Meagle was doing the same, cable tangled at his neck, contacts pulling from his cropped scalp. In the great chair shown on the screen, as the imaginary viewpoint swung about, the interpretative computer sketched a seated person with a snout and deep-set hooded eyes, clawed hands gripping banked controls on the arm rests.

The image skittered and jittered, revised itself as the causal whirlpool screeched around me. But no, this wasn't the dragon I was looking for. It was, it wasn't. The machine image spoke directly to me through Meagle and memory. That dead person, that ancient thing in its ancient warship, it was… was… Impossible. Delusion and grief. Something else. I knew the beloved face beyond denial, of course, like a clumsy pencil drawing on the screen that tore my heart out. Human. Face burned down in places to the bone, gaze suffering, mouth mute, determined even in death. In his stained UN uniform, with Korean Imperium lieutenant flashes at the collar.

"Oh, lord god," I moaned, and did barf, then, like a puling schoolboy drunk.

From the corner of my leaking eyes, in the window feed from his RV cell, I saw Meagle turn convulsively. He seemed to stare right at me, through the camera, into the display, with his blue, blind eyes.

The main hologram image, too, looked steadfastly back at me—sketched from the Naval remote viewer's words and speaking hands, his brain rhythms, the archived set of his stereotypical ideograms—looked at me from a grave five years dug in the soil.

Song-Dam. My son. My poor boy. My lost hero child.

I started to cry, wiping at my bitter mouth, and couldn't stop.

Huygens is not part of the Imperium, of course, being a research agora, like Herschel, the other settlement on Titan, but it is a fiscal affiliate of Korea, as well as of Zimbabwe, the Brazilian Superstate, Camp Barsoom (on, you guessed it, Mars), and a handful of other polises on the Moon and Ganymede. So while the writ of Mr. Kim, my sponsor, did not run on Titan, precisely, his paternal hand was heavily in the weighing scales. The Warlord had developed a fondness for the Intelligent Dinosaur paradigm when he studied paleontology as a young student in Antarctica, where all the equivocal evidence was located prior to the Enigma's excavation, and he carried that interest through into maturity and, some said, senility. He would be pleased as punch.

Dr. Caetani, surprise, surprise, was not. Everyone by now had studied the remote viewing session, and more than once. My participation and role could be determined only by inference, since no recorders had been trained on the observation room. But the recording of Meagle's results showed plainly the results:

the alien or saurian and, moments later, the harrowing superimposed image of my late son. For Caetani, I'm sure, my distress, my involvement, was just a piece of hammy theatrics, a shameful way to spray my mark onto an historic event.

"This afternoon, we know nothing more than we did a week ago," he stated bluntly. "I'm candidly dismayed at the gullibility of some of my colleagues here."

"The saurian—" began Jendayi Shumba. He cut her off instantly.

"—the *image* was no more veridical than the, the disturbed imposition into the colonel's entangled state of Sensei Park's tragic fixation on his son's death. Nobody doubts that Mr. Park is a functioning poltergeist, capable of casting images and interfering with complex electronic systems. It's why he's here—over my objections—and isn't the point." He took a deep breath, his features flushed behind that pretentious beard. "Our visitor's martyred son is certainly *not* aboard that Jurassic artifact, and surely nobody thinks he is. Neither, by the same token, is the dinosaur space captain that Mr. Park's well-prepped imagination also dreamed up and shoveled into the ideospace."

"With all due respect, you're out of your depth, Tony." This one I hadn't met before, an industrial psychiatrist named Lionel Berger. "Back off, will you? Remote viewing is no exact science, nor even an accomplished art—and I mean no disrespect to Colonel Meagle in pointing this out. We don't know how it works, except that quantum field nonlocality is engaged and implemented by an act of deliberation. Its famous vulnerability is that other minds can become trapped into the entanglement and add their own measures of information… but whether that aggregate data is veridical, symbolic, mythological or sheer phantasy, we can't tell just by simple inspection. Dismissing this evidence by flinging about words like 'psychic' and 'poltergeist' is argument by slur. I'm prepared to wait for more evidence before I decide so confidently what's inside that vessel."

Caetani, the surly fellow, actually said, "Bah!" I'd never heard anyone actually *say* that before. Others spoke, in their turn; Meagle sat at the back, his blind eyes closed, sunk into a sort of exhausted torpor. I'd have liked to go to him, sit beside him in respectful and sorrowing silence. Instead, as requested, I also remained silent, half-listening to the academese, the scholasticism, the stochasticism, the loop theories of cognitive restructuration.

I *had* seen my dead son.

I *had* seen the saurian sit in his great chair, or hers.

If cause is a pool of chaos and order blended by intention and brute event, I am (and nobody, as yet, has managed to explain why it is so) a small stick of dynamite exploding up random fishy critters to the shore. Brrrr… That's a macabre, self-lacerating image. It had been my boy Song who perished in mindless explosions, and not by my hand. But hadn't I sent him into fatal danger? Into ultimate harm's way? Of course I had. Not by urging or forbidding, in so many words, but in my reckless skepticism, my louche lack of patriotism. Which had fetched us up where? Him, smashed like a detonated fish in a pool he could not escape, did not wish to escape. Me, bereft, alone, my bond to my nation long ago broken and betrayed. I grunted aloud, hoisted myself into a less uncomfortable position on a seat too small, as usual, for my girth.

"Sam? You wanted to say something?"

I looked around. They were gazing at me expectantly. "Oh, nothing. What can I donate that hasn't already been weighed and found wanting?" It was petty and self-regarding, and I snapped my mouth shut, but a fierce anger burst up in me anyway, so I opened it again. "I'll say one thing. And make no apologies for it. We are here," I swung one arm through an embracing arc, taking in the auditorium, the station, Titan, "because years ago, when I was still on Earth, I discerned a causal anomaly near this place. We are here because military and independent remote viewers on three worlds concurred in finding and describing the vehicle. We are here, therefore, driven by the many motives that arose from that discovery. But I insist that the principal occasion is Premier Kim's wish to test the hypotheses forwarded by the scientific entity I represent." I took a deep breath. "So far as I can see, what Colonel Meagle uncovered this morning corroborates precisely the predictions of the Intelligent Dinosaur Institute. If my presence has muddied your waters, I'm sorry—but again I remind you, if it were not for me, none of you would be here today.

"So lay the hell off, okay?"

I dug in my robe's pocket, found a Mars bar, unpeeled it, and gobbled it down.

Shortly after Song-Dam's eighth birthday—his mother long since escaped back into the whorehouse alleys she and I had both come from—I took him with me on a business trip to Palo Alto. I was the object of the business trip, my absurd gift, my poltergeist prowess with cause and effect. Several Stanford biophysics researchers had somehow picked up trash journalism stories about me as the luckiest/unluckiest man on earth. Funding was limited, but I convinced them that Song was in my sole charge and that I wasn't budging without him.

So we took an exhausting flight from Incheon International across the Pacific and through the absurd indignities of US Homeland Security (despite a graduate student being on hand at the airport to collect us, now cooling his heels in the arrival lounge with a wilting cardboard sign in two languages; I had inadvertently set off various bells and whistles, so of course we were detained pointlessly, until one of the senior professors was persuaded to drive to the airport and vouch for us), and stayed in an anonymous, ugly block of apartments that seemed to have been compiled from polyurethane pretending to be marble. We could hear the dreary TV set next door through the adjoining wall.

I took Song for a long walk so he and I could get a feel for the alien place, this America, as we stretched our weary legs. Within three blocks (trust my causal eddies for once), we found a Korean food store, established that my parents' modest residence in Nangok—back at the turn of the century when it was still a squalid slum in a hilly area of Sillim-dong, Gwanak District—was just spitting distance from the proprietors' familial stamping grounds, and found ourselves dragged happily to a nearby park by Mr. Kwon's wife and three kids to fly dragon kites in the cool afternoon breeze.

I helped Song pay out the string. Our borrowed kite was a scarlet and gold Dragon Diamond (a gift to us both, as it turned out—and thank you, Mr. and Mrs. Kwon!). Our dragon quivered on the middle air a moment, strained against his leash, then suddenly flung himself upward into the deepening blue California sky. The line went taut. Song let it go in fright, but I held tight, and a moment later he put his hands back to the winch reel beside mine. I saw the line stretched between my hand, his small resolute hands, and the high, swooping, flower-bright dragon: a luminous string.

"Daddy, look!" said my son, wild with excitement. "Our dragon is flying on a beam of photons!"

At that moment, as if Buddha had smacked me in the ear, I was enlightened.

"I think I can get in," I told the Director of Operations, a tight jawed fellow named Namgoong, almost certainly a political appointee but in secure possession of a decent scientific reputation with degrees in geology and astrobiology. Earth and sky, I thought, but hid my smile. "I think I can break the shield. The question is, do I dare?"

"Yes. Precisely. If you rupture the stationary shield, who knows what might seep out into the atmosphere." He gave me a thin-lipped smile. "Fortunately, Sensei, we shall not have to wait three years for an Environmental Impact Study. The Imperium wants this thing opened. Now. It's why you're here."

"To tell you the truth, sir, I'm more worried about what might seep *in*. They must have sealed it against Titan's atmosphere for good reason."

"A motive that expired millions of years ago." He rose. "I'm having a containment dome erected around the locus. There's no way we can establish blockade underneath the ice as well, but this will meet most likely challenges. Or so I'm assured."

"I'm relieved to hear it." I belatedly heaved up my bulk. "When will you want me out there?"

"You'll be advised. We have a full scale colloquium scheduled, starting at two. I'll expect you to be there, Sensei Park, and on your best behavior. No more outbursts, if you please."

"More damned chin-wagging. Science used to be an empirical exercise," I grumbled.

"Led by theory, as I'm sure you understand." He was standing at his door, and I went out, biting my lip. Nobody had the faintest starting point for a theory to explain my causal distortions, and not much to account for the photon-entangled portage functor. I could do it, I could show them a method for using it (and had), but I didn't have a theory-empowered clue how or why. I'm nobody's mutant superman, that much I do know. (Or is that just a fat man's self-doubt speaking?)

Postmodern science, as far as I can tell looking in from the outside, is drunk on the sound of its own voice. But yes, I know: look who's complaining. I recalled again that Victorian sage, that poet Tennyson. He had it right: *I sometimes hold it half a sin to put in words the grief I feel; for words, like Nature, half reveal and half conceal the Soul within. But, for the unquiet heart and brain, a use in measured language lies; the sad mechanic exercise, like dull narcotics, numbing pain.* I followed Dr. Namgoong along the narrow compiled corridors of Hyugens station, so like those awful domiciles on the outskirts of Palo Alto, and went to hear the sad mechanics exercise their tongues and dull their pain, and maybe mine.

The circulated air was pungent, despite the scrubbers, with the musk of excited animals crowded together. A schematic chart I'd grown familiar with, these last few months, started displaying on the auditorium wall, replacing the magnified image of Saturn's glorious tilted hat. The Fermi Paradox Solution candidates. My eye bounced off them, falling down a cliff of words and logic with no footing in reality beyond the dragon-haunted thing outside the dome:

Where are They?

Fermi 1. They are here among us, and call themselves Koreans.

That always got a satisfied titter, except from any Hungarians in the crowd.

Fermi 2. They are here, running things.

A chance for the Hungarians, and anyone else chafing under the Imperium, to get their own back with a belly laugh. No giggles here, though, I noticed.

Fermi 3. They came and left.

Bingo, I thought. They came and left flowers scattered in their wake. Strictly, though, that was Fermi 53, the only choice left. The ancient intelligent dinosaur hypothesis.

Fermi 6. We are interdicted.

Fermi 10. They are still on their way here.

The starship had blown that one, and others like it, clear out of the water. Time to trim the list, methinks.

Fermi 21. They're listening, only fools are transmitting.

Fermi 22. Dedicated killer machines destroy everything that moves, anywhere in space.

Fermi 28. The Vingean Singularity takes them... elsewhere.

No Singularity back near the end of the Cretaceous, I thought. Judging by the remote viewer's sketches, that saurian pilot was advanced, but not sufficiently advanced as to be indistinguishable from magic.

Fermi 38. Earth is the optimal place for life, just by chance.

Could be. And for intelligent life, at that. Hey, look, we've seen it twice: the smart dinosaurs and Homo sap.

Fermi 48. Language is vanishingly rare.

Ha! Yeah, right. Blah blah blah. Still, maybe so. The skies are awfully silent, which is where we came in…

Fermi 49. Science is a rare accident.

Not as rare as I am, I thought, touching the etiological chains and vortices all around—and no scientist ever predicted me. Most of them still didn't even *know* about me, thanks to all those Above Top Secret restrictions. Damn it.

Namgoong cleared his throat at the podium. Voices, in clumps and then one by one, fell silent. Hey, maybe that's it. God tapped His microphone, and the cosmos shut up to listen. And they're still listening, bent and cowed by the awfulness of what they heard. But not us, we haven't heard from God yet, despite a thousand revelations claimed and proclaimed. Or if we have, there's no way to search through the babbling noise and extract the divine signal. Funny way to run a universe.

I could feel the dinosaur calling to me, even so, through the appalling cold of Titan's snows and the void of fifty or a hundred million years. And the entwined memory of my son, sacrificed for nothing. Nothing. Nothing.

"Those are the classic guesses—most of them wrong." The Director flicked his finger; the display went to blank gray. "We still have no idea why the galaxy, indeed the universe as a whole, is quiet. Why the stars are still shining, spilling out their colossal energy resources, when intelligence should be collecting it. Calculations you're all familiar with prove that a single intelligent species arising anywhere in the galaxy within the last billion years would by now have colonized all its trillion stars and associated bodies, turned the sky black with Matrioshka shells—or perhaps obliterated the stars in vast, wasteful wars."

I pricked up my ears. A political subtext? Perhaps not; maybe our director was just a tone-deaf drone. I glanced around; several people near me had dropped their eyes, more than one held fists clenched tight. Okay.

"One of the equally classic Great Filters must screen out potential intelligent life and leave the heavens exactly as they'd have to be if there is no life at all out there. No *intelligent, starfaring* life, anyway.

"So now we're faced with a new paradox. Fermi remains unanswered—and yet we have this old vehicle made by beings not of our own species, but apparently related. The likelihood of that coincidence being due to chance alone is impossibly small. I see only three remaining possibilities."

"Barney did it," someone called, muted but clear across the room. A wave of tittering. I felt my jaw tighten, and a flush creep into my cheeks.

"A previous civilization sprung from dinosaur stock on Cretaceous Earth, or even earlier, yes," said Dr. Namgoog evenly. "The opinion represented here today by our guest, Sensei Park."

A pattering of polite applause, some even more muted groans.

"We have evidence in the form of preliminary scans by our Naval remote viewer, Colonel Meagle, that the creature… the being, forgive me… in charge of the craft has just such an origin. Leaving aside the improbability of parallel evolution. If so, this leaves the earlier and larger Fermi question unanswered: where are its kindred now, why haven't they conquered the whole galaxy? Tipler and others proved decades ago that this could have been achieved at plausible sub-light speeds within a million years. If they have, why don't we see them?"

Hearing it stated so flatly, I was dizzied, as always, by the prospect. Flotillas of starcraft fleeing into the spiral arms at a tenth of light speed, crammed with dragon seed or our own. Or minute nanoscale pods fired toward a hundred million stars by magnetic catapult, or driven on filmy wings by laser light. Yet these, too, were last year's dreams, last century's. We had stepped from Earth to Ganymede to Titan entangled on a light beam, and without waiting to be shoved here by sailboat. The moment entangled luminal portage became a reality for my own species, it opened the yawning cavern: why not for them, as well? What the hell was a *starship* doing here? Why bother? It was so last week, like finding a steam locomotive under the ice.

Namgoog was enunciating his other solutions to Fermi, but I didn't care. I was entranced by the mystery of the sleeping creature, sedate under his bedding of live flowers. It was a hunger like my endless appetite for chow. I wanted to step straight through the damned shell of the ship and look the critter in the eye, man to man. Even if it decided to eat *me*.

That's what dragons do, isn't it?

And so to bed. Where I lay in the dark in a lather of fright for fifteen minutes. Fearful and weak. Bleak. Needing a leak. I climbed out and thudded to the sanitary personal. When I got back, after a swab up and down and across with a wet face cloth to dab away the worse of the flopsweat, my door was slightly open. Through it came the never-stopping background clanging and banging of humans and machines keeping the place ticking over. Snapping my fingers, I clicked the room light up to dim. Dr. Jendayi Shumba, chubby string looper, stretched at ease on my bed, clad in sensible pajamas with a mission blaze on the collar. Of course, I jumped and squealed.

"*What* the—Is there some—"

"Hush up, dear man, and come over here." She grinned.

"You're not serious. Are you?"

In evidence, she slithered out of her pjs and raised her eyebrows.

"Absurd. I'd crush you like a bug."

"Myeong-hui, you don't weigh any more, here, than my little boy."

"You have a—?" I swallowed, and crept closer. "I had a son once."

"Let us be in this moment, Sensei," she said without reproach.

"I'm disgusting to look upon," I said frankly. "And I don't need a pity—"

She had her fingers across my mouth, and then pulled me down through several clunky jumpy evolutions. "There are other ways to convey one's... intimacy," she said.

"Ulp," I protested.

"An easy mouth is a great thing on a long journey, is it not, old fellow?" she said, releasing mine and patting my neck.

"Ex-*cuse* me?"

Jendayi burst out laughing, a slightly husky, wonderfully exciting sound. "A quote from an old British classic about a horse. Nineteenth century, I believe. You might have read it as a child. *Black Beauty*."

"You are the black beauty," I said, noticing a cue when it smacked me between the eyes. I raised my voice and said, "Door close," and it did.

"You've got a way to break into the ship, don't you?" she said, after a time without time.

I was reeling and reckless. "Yes. Probably."

"So you really are a poltergeist." She stroked my contemptible belly, as if it were a friendly animal sharing the bed with us. "Tony nearly poked his damn eye out." Her laugh was throaty, dirty, a tonic.

"Don't blame me," I said, and found a glass of water, drained it. "It's like being able to wiggle your ears."

In the near-dark, she wiggled hers, and more.

But before she left, Jendayi said, "Bring me back a sample. A skin scraping, anything with DNA. Just for me, honey, okay?" Oh, so that's why you're here? Had to be some reason. Exploitative bitch. But that's life, right?

Looking like a well-laid but annoyed and put-upon squat polar bear in my bodyglove, some hellish number of minus degrees on the far side of its skin, I stood gazing down from the edge of the excavation. The spacecraft was unaltered, every bloom precisely where it had been several days before, where it had been, perhaps, several tens of millions of years before. Unless it was salted here recently as a snare for gullible humans. In which case, it might be younger than I. Not so likely, though.

"Ready when you are, Sensei," said the political officer, doing Mr. Kim's bidding, and damn the scientists' caution.

I raised one thumb and let myself drift. Cause and effect unbraided, started their long, looping dance of etiological distortion, swirling, curdling. I was the still center of the spinning world. Certainties creaked, cracked. A favorite poem entered my heart, by Ji-Hoon Cho, "Flower petals on the sleeves":

The wanderer's long sleeves
Are wet from flower petals.
Twilight over a riverside village
Where wine is mellow.

Had this saurian person below me, trapped now in timelessness, known wine? Crushed release and perhaps moments of joy from some archaic fruit not yet grape? I thought, with a wrenching mournfulness:

When this night is over
Flowers will fall in that village.

"Hey!"

And there went the flowers, drawn up and tossed away from the hull of the starship. They were scattering in the methane wind, lifted and flung by the bitter gusts, floral loveliness snap-frozen, blown upward and falling down in drifts into the alien snow.

"The stationary shield is discontinued," said a clipped voice in my ears.

I stepped forward, ready to enter the ancient, imprisoned place. To meet my dinosaur, who had either died or even now lived, freed from timeless suspension. A hand caught my encased arm.

"Not yet, Sam. We have a team prepped. Thanks, you've done good here today." I turned, hardly able to see through my tears, and it was not that bastard Tony Caetani groveling his apologies, the universe could not be so chirpy as that. I hadn't met this one before, although he'd picked up my dining room nickname and used it with a certain familiar breeziness; a beefy functionary of some armed service division, grinning at me in his bluff farmboy way. I nodded, and watched the team of marines go down, and remembered my dear boy and the way he had gone forward fearlessly into darkness and then into the fire falling from the sky. It did not matter one whit that I thought his cause wrong-headed. I remembered a poem in that book I'd found in the ruined library, a poem by an Englishman named Kipling that had torn my heart as I sat before Song-Dam's closed coffin. There was no comfort this tide, the poem warned me, nor in any tide, save this:

he did not shame his kind—
Not even with that wind blowing, and that tide.

Without shame, I sobbed, but then drew myself up and turned back to Huygens agora. Perhaps, I told myself, ten or sixty million years ago, another father had laid his son on these cruel snows and bade him farewell. I murmured to that reptilian father, offering what poor borrowed comfort I might to us both, across all that void of space and time: "Then hold your head up all the more, This tide, And every tide; Because he was the son you bore, And gave to that wind blowing and that tide!"

I looked straight up above me, at the photodiode display before my eyes in the viewmask, swallowing hard, to follow the streaming tide of blossoms on the wind, and there was Saturn, old Father Time, hanging in the orange smoke of the sky, an arrow through his heart. I gave him a respectful nod, and raised one gloved thumb in salute.

BY MOONLIGHT
PETER S. BEAGLE

Peter S. Beagle was born in Manhattan on the same night that Billie Holiday was recording "Strange Fruit" and "Fine and Mellow" just a few blocks away. Raised in the Bronx, Peter originally proclaimed he would be a writer when he was ten years old. Today he is acknowledged as an American fantasy icon, and to the delight of his millions of fans around the world is now publishing more than ever. He is the author of the beloved classic *The Last Unicorn*, as well as the novels *A Fine and Private Place*, *The Innkeeper's Song*, and *Tamsin*. He has won the Hugo, Nebula, Locus, and Mythopoeic awards. His most recent book is the collection *Mirror Kingdoms: The Best of Peter S. Beagle*. Upcoming are two new novels, *I'm Afraid You've Got Dragons* and *Summerlong*, and four short collections featuring new stories about Schmendrick the Magician, unicorns from other cultures, Shakespeare, and his own teenage years in the Bronx.

Darlington was desperately glad to see the little fire as he came over the moor from Bramham. *I can make it that far.* There was less snow on the ground here to betray him with footprints, but the cold was harder because of that, and while his coat could keep the wind off yet awhile, his boot soles had worn as thin as his hopes. He had sent the horse off in a different direction more than an hour ago, but he knew his pursuers too well to imagine that the trick would deceive them for long, if at all. At very best he was buying time; which, Darlington decided, could well be considered the entire story of his life. Wrapping his arms around his own shoulders, he stumbled up the low hill toward the fire. *I think I can make it that far.*

It was reassuring to see that there was only one figure observing his approach. He'd not have expected to encounter any but fleeing, freezing high-tobys like himself on the moor…but he had always found the supposed brotherhood of outlaws greatly overrated: none could be trusted after sunset, and few in broad daylight. But even from such a distance the man near the fire was clearly no bandit. He was tall and white-haired—white-bearded as well—and wrapped in a cloak of intriguing design that Darlington determined was coming away with him, should they survive the night. He saw, as well, that the man's face was curiously ageless in the feeble, wavering firelight, with a paradoxical mix of old sadness and equally profound tranquility. It made him nervous, as contradictions always did.

Showing no trepidation on his own part, the white-haired man beckoned Darlington to the fire, saying in a deep, quiet voice, "Warm yourself, good highwayman. I fear the pickings must have been slim on such a day."

Darlington's legs made the decision to sit before he did, and when he tried to speak, no sound at all came out of his mouth. The stranger nodded understandingly, and offered him a leathern flask plainly meant to contain brandy or *schnapps*; but what Darlington tasted was so astonishingly rich and alive inside him that he very nearly threw up, as though his body were trying to vomit out the whole terror of the day. When he was able, he gasped hoarsely, "Thank you. Whatever that was, thank you."

"Nectar of the gods," the stranger responded. "Or as close to it as either of us is ever likely to come. Rest now, and tell me what you will, or rest and be still. Those on your track will surely follow no further until morning, at the earliest. I will find more wood."

Too weary to wonder about anything, Darlington promptly fell asleep, and was only wakened by the increased heat of the revived fire on his face. The stranger offered him another swallow from the flask, and the heel-end of a battered loaf of brown bread. "The last of my provender, forgive me. I was making for Wetherby, more or less, but that's impossible now, in this cold. I may as well turn toward Ilkley—or even Harrogate, why not? Yes…perhaps Harrogate."

He was obviously debating an important issue with himself, and Darlington was near drowsing off again; but the unnerving oddity of a man who seemed neither mad nor a beggar knowing him on sight for an outlaw prodded him fully awake against his will. He spoke warily to his benefactor therefore, saying, "Sir, if your kindness is meant but to delay me until the High Sheriff's men have their hands on me, I feel bound to inform you that the pistol under my coat is pointed directly at your charitable heart. Let me be hanged at Leeds Assizes next month, I will at least swing for something grander than a mail coach that turned out to carry nothing but solicitors' accounts and begging letters from the colonies." And he patted his breast meaningfully and smiled what he dearly hoped was his most elegantly menacing smile.

"Roger Darlington, you would be," the stranger mused, smiling back at him. "A good Dalesman's name—I hear it everywhere on the moors lately, though I somehow feel I'll have forgotten it utterly by tomorrow's dawn. Wensleydale, most likely?"

Darlington let his hand fall, the pistol being empty anyway, since the last shot over his shoulder that had killed a trooper's horse. "Aye, born and bred in Skipton myself, but there've been Darlingtons in Wensleydale since the bloody Ark. But you have the advantage of me, sir."

"Ah, my name? Elias Patterson, at your service." The stranger offered his hand across the fire. "Reverend Elias Patterson that was, as you might say."

Accepting the handshake, Darlington frowned in some puzzlement. "You're a minister, then?"

Elias Patterson cocked his head slightly, as though the word were new to him. "Perhaps I am still. It's hard to know, you understand."

Darlington did know, having passed a fair number of entertaining evenings drinking, gambling, whoring and weeping with variously fallen clerics. "A woman, was it?" With this one, it would have to be a woman.

Again the thoughtful tilt of the head, the narrowing of the gray eyes, the least breath of a smile. "In a manner of speaking."

"Well, it's a good man's failing. Not like what I do."

He said it in his most swaggering manner, having once slipped into Lincoln's Inn Fields, with a price already on his head, to see *The Beggar's Opera*. Elias Patterson's eyes were neither impressed nor unsympathetic. "You hold a low opinion of your chosen trade, is it?"

"I never said that." Darlington found himself distinctly irritated with his own irritation. "But I hardly expect it to make me,"—he gestured with his thumb toward the cold black sky "—welcome up there."

"But why not? You work hard, you have so far harmed no one—you see, I know a bit of you, Mr. Darlington—and the worst that can be said is that you have a certain passion for redistributing the doubtless ill-gotten wealth of that class which can afford to ride about in coaches, whether public or privately-owned. As a former man of the cloth, I can tell you honestly that the Savior might very well approve."

There was humor in the voice, but no mockery. Darlington had the alarming sense that the man meant exactly what he was saying. "I redistribute the wealth to *myself*, Reverend Patterson—Robin Hood's a long time gone. Now and then I do toss a coin or two into the poor box or the collection plate, but that's the end of it, believe me." Weary as he was, he leaned forward, elbows on his knees. "What sort of a minister *are* you, anyway?"

Elias Patterson did not reply, being occupied with placing more fallen branches on the fire. They blazed up quickly, sputtering a little because of the snow. He leaned toward the flames himself, his eyes and voice speculative, almost dreamy. "How strange, when you think about it," he mused in a near-whisper. "And we *should* think about it, you and I. A gentleman of the road and a—what?—a preacher who dares not even enter a church, for fear that the very blessed timbers might all come down on his head. Oh, we are indeed well met—one forever in flight, a poor fox, with no faithful vixen, no cubs waiting to warm and welcome him, celebrating him for losing the hounds one more time—"

"And just how would you know that, my wise *Reverend* Patterson?"

"—and the other in fact a hunter, a pursuer, wandering the same mazes over and over, endlessly searching for something he begins to feel he dreamed…" The voice dried to a meaningless insect drone.

Born a Dalesman, as Elias Patterson had guessed, Darlington had grown up with the silence of the moors. For him it was a sound in itself: a bleak, deeply elusive music, to be felt along the scalp, and in the soles of the feet, rather than heard with the ears. Tonight, listening intently for hoofbeats, for men's voices calling to each other and the yelping of hounds—suddenly he could not endure the stillness a moment longer. "No matter our need, it's clear that neither of us will be sleeping tonight," he said. "My story is entirely as you imagine it, barring perhaps a trifle more education than most robbers on horseback, and consequently a dream of my own. A dull dream, certainly, for it involves living to retirement and then starting up a good little inn in Whitby or Wensleydale, catering quietly to the profession…oh, an extremely dull dream, believe me. I would much prefer to hear any tale told by a minister of the Gospel who fears to walk into a church." Elias Patterson began to protest, but Darlington continued, "We haven't got wood enough to see us through the night. As an earnest of my intent, I promise to gather what we need before you begin. If you will begin."

They regarded each other for a long moment, during which Elias Patterson neither spoke, nor nodded, nor made any other sign to his criminal companion. Then Roger Darlington abruptly stepped away from the fire and set about collecting more branches. Elias Patterson sat motionless, staring into the darkness.

Darlington made three trips, and was sweating heavily despite the cold when he returned with the last armload. He rebuilt the fire entirely, so that it threw just as much heat but burned more slowly. "The one useful thing I learned from taking the King's shilling. I did leave two shillings for him when I deserted, so he can't be *that* annoyed with me."

"A king's bookkeeping is as mysterious as a woman's." Elias Patterson had not moved. "Thank you for the firewood."

Darlington peered sideways at him. "There was a price attached."

"Ah. My story. Are you certain you want to hear it? It is long, unlikely, and remarkably unedifying—shameful, even, to come from a minister's lips. Blasphemous, too, properly regarded."

"Better and better," Darlington responded. "On such a night, a little blasphemy might serve as well as a hot posset or a mug of mulled ale. I hold you to your word, sir."

Elias Patterson considered. "I suppose this would be as fitting a night as any for the tale, it being Imbolc, Bride's Festival—or perhaps you guise her as St. Bridget in Skipton?" Darlington stared back at him uncomprehendingly. "Come, I know they honor Bride in the Dales, no matter what we priests and preachers admonish them. I have seen the *Brideog* corn dollies made, and caught my own parishioners setting out the strips of cloth for Bride to bless when she walks the land on Imbolc Eve. You? Never?"

Darlington shook his head, forcing an embarrassed laugh. "Not in Skipton, believe me. Never in Skipton."

"A loss," said Elias Patterson. "Christianity was ever the better for a good brawl with the old gods. Now in the village where I lived—actually not too far from here, a bit west—every last sheep in my flock believed in every one of them. Come Beltane night, not a deacon, not an elder, not a First Soprano but was bound to be out till dawn, hunting till they dropped for faery gold. I was younger then, and I scolded them endlessly, shouting that it was an unholy pagan thing, and that those who trifled with such matters were placing their immortal souls in the gravest danger. Those were my very words, and every one of that lot sat mortified, when I called their names in church, and mumbled penitence, and went right on doing it, as I knew they would." He sighed. "It all shames me dreadfully to recall, Mr. Darlington. You won't understand, I expect."

"Well, I was never exactly a churchgoing man," Darlington answered him. "Be a better person if I had been, I've no doubt of it. But the world outside was so much more interesting. Always was."

"I knew nothing of the world in those days," Elias Patterson said. "I had my God, my work, my books and my cat, nor did it occur to me that these might not necessarily be sufficient for a man pledged to follow the Cross all his days. And for all my scorn of the old festivals as wicked folly, still I never left my house on Beltane, Samhain, Lughnasadh. My cat did, mind you, but not I."

"Never hurts to be on the safe side."

Elias Patterson looked directly into Darlington's face, and his gray eyes were very bright in the firelight. He said, "We give them different names, those nights lit only by fire and the moon, depending on the county and the calendar, but we know what they are. They call up the world that was before the Lord came down among us; the world where good and evil were not so certain, so *fixed* as they are today, where the known and the unheard-of could mingle as they chose…where truth had its doubts, do you see?" He laughed harshly. "Well, all that was a bit alarming for me to deal with then, so I stayed by my own neat little fire on those nights, and neither stepped out nor let anything in. Who knows what your door may open to—or upon—on Beltane eve?"

"I've usually taken Beltane off from work," Darlington reflected. "Girls are always so *cheery* at Beltane."

Elias Patterson was staring far into the fire. "But on one such eve, long ago, I opened my door three times. The first occasion was to let my cat out, for there's no Christianizing a cat, as I'm sure you know. They belong to gods older even than Bride and Angus, and our Lord grants them a special dispensation. Or so it was believed in my village, and I chose to believe it myself." This time the laugh was warm and genuine. "The second time I opened the door was to let Hannah Dawkins in. She was a widow, Mrs. Dawkins, but still youthful and pleasing enough to capture any man's eye, I must say. She brought me some of her own currant wine, I remember."

Darlington winked boldly at him. "Must have been a good deal of that coming to visit, hey? You being young and not bad-looking, and of course highly respectable. And unattached."

"She was as respectable herself as any in the village," Elias Patterson responded severely. "A handsome woman, as I say, well set up, with money of her own, and a lively conversationalist in the bargain. And if she did come calling with a purpose, guessing that most of the other women were likely to be out jumping over the Beltane fires, or dancing in a circle widdershins…why, no blame to her, or to me either, for setting down my book and inviting her to my fireside."

"Man was not meant to be alone," Darlington quoted piously. "Isn't that what our Lord himself said? Something like that."

Elias Patterson looked mildly shocked. "No, certainly not, nothing of what I can see you thinking happened between us that night—nothing but a bit of excellent currant wine and a bit of conversation. And if—and I say *if*—she left in some slight disappointment…well, I may have led her on, though I never meant to. I may have done."

Darlington said, "I've always found these things a matter of the moment, myself. Another time—another hour, even—another place…" But the white-haired man shook his head.

"It would have taken another man," he replied softly. "Not owing to any flaw in the good Widow Dawkins, but because of a restlessness that I never could put words to, and never dared name, for fear that would give the thing more power over me than it already had. From my birth, it had always slept quietly in me for months, years at a time, that *thing*…and then it would rouse up to rack my sleep and trouble my reading in the Book, and turn my sermons on their heads. It was such a restlessness came on me after the Widow Dawkins left, and made me bank my hearthfire and open my door for the third time that night, and walk out into the wilderness of Beltane eve. As I had never before done—as I had always known better than to do. Because of that *thing*."

"Yes," Darlington murmured as though to himself. "Not the gold. It's never the gold."

Both men were silent for some time. Elias Patterson had his arms folded on his knees, and was bent almost double, staring into the flames. Darlington, his lethargy vanished, listened constantly for any sounds of pursuit, but he heard nothing except the hiss and crackle of the fire, and the occasional cold bark of a fox, signaling to his mate. The snow clouds were blowing away, and stars were appearing for the first time in several nights. *Be a nice clear day tomorrow,* he thought. *See for bloody miles, they will. Bloody wonderful.*

Elias Patterson finally stirred. "Mr. Darlington, do you believe there is a real place called Faery? We have spoken of Beltane and Imbolc, of Bride and Angus, of corn dollies and old gods. Do you believe that there is an actual realm where such as these still dwell? Your answer is important to me."

Darlington did not laugh, but he slapped both his thighs and grinned with teeth that should not have been as healthy-white as they were, given the life he led. "You mean Under the Hill? The door in the mountain where you wander in and spend a night dancing and reveling with the fairy folk, and then you come out in the morning and it's a hundred years later? That place?"

"That place," Elias Patterson agreed quietly. "*Tír na nÓg,* the Irish call it. The kingdom of Oberon and Titania."

Something in his voice made Darlington's smile fade. After a moment, he said, "Well. I've nothing *against* believing in it, when I think of what I've seen in my time, and what I've had to believe. But I've never yet met anyone who could tell me he'd been there."

"Until now," Elias Patterson said.

Darlington said nothing, but simply held out his hand for the leather flask. He took a swig, handed it back, and remained silent for a long enough time that it became necessary to arrange more wood on the fire. He said at last, "You're a hundred years old."

"I don't know how old I am," Elias Patterson answered. "Do I count the years, or do I count the time?"

The silence was longer this time. Darlington got up again and relieved himself into the darkness. He did up his buttons, turned back to face Elias Patterson, and said, "So, then. Instead of doing the sensible with that nice, willing widow, you walked out alone after she left, and you walked straight Under the Hill. Straight into Faery."

"Nothing about Faery is straight, not as we understand the word." Elias Patterson's eyes seemed to be growing brighter as Darlington stared into them. "The doorway is not always in the side of a hill, or a mountain. Faery lights where it pleases, shows itself where it lists; and though that village of mine lay in country as flat as Norfolk or the Fens, yet even so, when I walked out that night there lay Faery just across the road…or was it across Roger Munro's upper pasture…or perhaps glimmering beyond old Hugh Hobden's rich, muddy bottomland. It danced on before me like a rainbow, Faery did, and I followed as best I might, always explaining to myself that I was looking for my cat. And when at last I was too weary to follow further, I simply laid myself down on a little low hillside, in a pile of fallen leaves, and fell asleep as trusting as a child. And while I slept, Faery came to me."

Darlington raised his eyebrows, but said nothing.

"It must have been an enchantment," Elias Patterson continued, "for I dreamed all that happened, but I could not waken. First there came the loveliest woman I had ever seen, tall and splendid and queenly, riding on a milk-white steed—as is told, you remember, in the rhyme of True Thomas. And after her came another, and then another—all on white horses, each woman so beautiful as to make the one who rode before look like a kitchen wench, a scullery maid—until there were a full dozen of them ranged in a circle around me, looking down on me as though from a far greater height than the back of a horse." His eyes were closed as he spoke, and his voice seemed far away, as though only a part of him still sat by the fire. Darlington knew the man believed every daft word; and in his own despite he felt himself starting to catch that belief, like a head cold.

Elias Patterson looked at him thoughtfully. "Had I actually awakened to that sight at that moment, I think I might well have gone mad. Humankind can only bear so much wonder and glory all at once, which is why I often worry about Heaven."

Darlington shrugged. "Not one of *my* problems. Go on."

"Ah," said Elias Patterson. "Last came Titania, stepping barefoot and alone. In my dream she knelt beside me, like no queen but a young girl, and she gazed long and closely into my blind face before she spoke. She said, "'This is he. I will have no other. Bear him to my bower.' And so it was done."

"*And so it was done*," the highwayman mocked him. "And you mean to tell me that you went on sleeping in the arms of a dozen beautiful women bearing you away? And still knew what was going on, all along?" He shook his head. "Rot and moonshine, man."

"I am telling you what happened. I was lifted and borne directly into a farmer's hayrick, of all things—but through it I know I saw the lights of Faery rippling and flowing, on the far side of my closed eyelids. And I heard the music, for even a faery enchantment cannot altogether silence faery music. Titania told me later that I smiled in my sleep to hear it, and that my smile touched her heart. The women of Faery, glorious as they are, have no hearts, but Titania does. This is why she is often lonely."

Darlington thought he heard a horse somewhere nearby, but Elias Patterson's eyes held him fast, and he could not move. He asked, "How long did you sleep? When did you wake?"

"I was never sure," Elias Patterson replied. "What matters just now is that I woke in a twilight secrecy the like of which I had never seen. There were green and purple vines arching over, and strange birds singing their evening songs in great misty trees for which I had no names, and the thickest, gentlest grass beneath all. I smelled something like honeysuckle, and heard water somewhere, and Titania singing. It was hard to tell her voice from the voice of the stream, for it murmured and laughed by turns, and sighed too, soft as the grass on which I lay, warm as the breeze that ruffled my hair…or it might have been Titania's fingers, for my head was in her lap, and her own starlit hair was brushing my face. And I did not want to move, ever again."

"All most unchristian, to be sure," Darlington twitted him. "Why, I'd go so far as to name it pagan."

"You would be right, without question. And for that, in that moment, I could not have cared a fiddler's fart." Elias Patterson snapped his fingers at the end of that vulgar phrase, and the outlaw was hard put to it to determine whether it was the snap that startled him most, or the sudden startling bite of the words.

"When I sat up," Elias Patterson went on, "which seemed to take forever—and that was perfectly agreeable too—I found myself face to face with a face I could have drowned in, and welcome. I knew this could only be Titania, and this place Faery, and that I was bound under lifelong orders from my God and my bishop to cry out *Retro me, Sathanas!* and turn my mind from temptation and toward

Heaven…if this were truly not it." He ran his hands through his white hair, and smiled helplessly. "But all I could say to that face, to those mischievous tender, fiercely wise eyes was, 'I pray you, madam, give me leave to go from here. For I in no way belong in your realm, as you well know.' Granted, I said this in a small and most tremorous voice, but I did say it."

"I said something similar to a lady in Wapping one time," Darlington offered. "Almost cost me a tooth."

Elias Patterson smiled briefly before continuing. "Then Titania laughed fully, and the sound of that laughter turned all my bones so weightless, and so…so full of sunlight that I could have flown up and out of that bower like a mayfly, if I could have moved at all. She caressed my face with her hands, that were like wings themselves, light and strong enough to bear us both to world's end and beyond, as just then I wished they would. But I was a Christian, even in Faery, Mr. Darlington, even with the Queen of Faery's hands on me, and to her laughter I repeated my request, saying honestly, 'Great lady, you know what I am. You know that I serve another God than yours, and you know further that my Lord's victory is foreordained in the firmament. With every respect, what word have we for one another?'

"'This,' said Titania, and she leaned forward and kissed me."

In a vague, faraway manner, Darlington realized that his eyes had become a child's eyes, stretched so wide that they almost hurt. He did his best to recover himself by saying, "Of course you showed some proper sense, for once, I trust, and abandoned Father, Son, and Holy Spirit on the spot?"

Elias Patterson did not laugh. He said, "On the contrary, my belief was strengthened by that kiss, for I well understood it to be a temptation set in my path to test me. So I straightened my back and put my hands behind it—for all that my mind was spinning in my skull, and my eyes could not focus on anything but Titania's eyes—and I spoke out as forcefully as I might, saying, 'I belong to my Lord and Saviour Jesus Christ. Your wiles have no power over me. Dissolve your enchantments, turn toward righteousness, and release me.'

"'But there are no charms chaining you here,' Titania answered me, and her speaking voice fondled my heart as her hands had done my skin. 'I would be shamed to hold a man so, lord or slave, mortal or faery. Rise and walk away then, if you will; indeed I'll send folk of mine to guide you home.' But she smiled, saying this…she smiled, Mr. Darlington, and suddenly…suddenly I was no reverend at all, nor ever had been, and all I could do was to stand very still where I was. Titania said, 'Or kiss me, for it's one or the other, my beautiful mortal. Choose.'"

"And you chose," Darlington said, surprisingly gently. "As I'd have done in a moment. Indeed, we're a bit alike, after all, as you say."

"And I chose," Elias Patterson said, and no more.

After a time Darlington asked, "You'd never been with a woman, of course? Meaning no offense."

"No, never with a woman. Nor with a man, either—nor was I ever drawn to boys, as happens. By nature I am a shy man, Mr. Darlington, shy even in my dreams and wishes. Imagine me now, if you will, lost in the wild miracle of the Queen of Faery in my arms, unable to take in the words she was saying and singing and sighing to me—let alone the things she was *doing*…"

"Please," Darlington said. "A rough outlaw I may be, but I'm still a little young for such details. How long did it go on, your—what's the word when it's with a queen?—your *liaison*?"

Elias Patterson said, "Time is a different thing in Faery, as you may have heard—sometimes longer than here, sometimes shorter. It rather depends."

"Depends on *what*?" When Elias Patterson did not reply immediately, Darlington said, "I have been hunted all this day, and it's entirely likely that I may be taken tomorrow and hanged in a month; in any case, we will certainly never see each other after this night. Depends on bloody *what*?"

Elias Patterson's white hair showed up his blush more noticeably. "When I was—ah—with her, Titania, in her bower, time simply ceased to exist in any way at all. I never knew how long we were together, or how often we…or what we…or when we slept, when we woke…. It was all one thing, one thing, do you understand me?"

"No," Darlington said. "No, and I don't think I want to. Did you never get out of that…bower of hers?"

He snickered at Elias Patterson's reply. "Those first days—or weeks, or months, whatever they were—we went nowhere else." But he bit his lips sourly when he was diffidently informed that in a little while Elias Patterson found himself grown strong enough—"grown *youthful* enough, perhaps; I had never been young before, you see"—to match the Queen's hunger, and even skilled enough to satisfy it in a few ways that rounded her twilight eyes. "So when she did bring me indoors at last, it was rather to show me off to Faery, not so much the other way around. They are more like us than we might imagine, those folk. In some ways."

To keep his mind off the day to come, Darlington asked, "And what's it like, then, that *indoors* Under the Hill?"

Elias Patterson was not looking at him, but plainly far beyond the flames. "All things, all at once—rather like Titania herself, if you will. In Faery space is just as deceptive as time. For instance, there always seems to be as much forest as any hunter could desire, and those who dwell in Faery love the chase just as we do. Only their beasts of venery are a bit other than those we pursue: they'll be after the manticore for its claws and teeth, as we take wolf and bear; they'll shoot down griffins to make knives from their sharp-edged feathers; and there's a great serpent-thing that the hunter has to strangle, because no blade, no point will even scratch that hide. And the hunts themselves can last a month or a year, for they've got all the time in the world. Remember, *Tír na nÓg* means *The Land of Youth*."

After a considering moment, he added, "They won't take the fox or the unicorn, by the way—those two are sacred in Faery. I never knew why, but I was always glad of it. They can come and go as they desire between the worlds, though foxes clearly do it more often."

"You really were there," Darlington said softly. "By God, old man, you really walked in those woods, didn't you?" This time, it was his eyes holding Elias Patterson's eyes across the fire. "Bloody hell. You danced in the halls of Faery."

"They're full of light," Elias Patterson whispered, "bursting with it, *humming* with it. It's alive, that light. It moves as it pleases, stroking the faces of dancers and musicians, cooks and servants alike, just as Titania caressed me." Darlington could barely hear him. He said, "When you stay long enough in that light, you can feel yourself turning into it, becoming something neither faery nor mortal—nothing but the light. That's the only way those folk ever die, did you know? Dancing too long in the light. Titania told me that. She said sometimes they did it a-purpose."

The clearing sky had let the half-moon come out, and Darlington hunched down against its brightness. He said, "And the gold? The faery gold your church lot were always after?"

Elias Patterson raised his eyebrows. "My, I expected *that* question well before now. Well, yes, I saw a great deal of gold everywhere—there's another thing the faery folk love as much as we do. But they had too much of it to treat it as money, do you see; everybody had enough that more or less of it made no difference. I never worked out whether they had any actual notion of currency, but sometimes I thought it might be poetry." He smiled fondly at the night. "Say a poem to any one of Titania's people, and he'd be in your debt; the richest folk were those who knew the most poems by heart. Especially good long ones, the kind that can run on for an hour, more. They really like *long* poems."

"None of my sort in Faery, then. Pity." Darlington hesitated, and then asked, oddly but genuinely shy himself, "What about their music? You'd not think so, but my family had a music master come to the house for little Roger. I was to be a fiddler in some grand gentleman's private orchestra—that was the proudest career they could imagine for me, poor souls. Alas, all their hopes were dashed when I discovered how easy it was to pick the music master's pocket. I blame them—and him—for my becoming what I am. Tell me about the music you heard Under the Hill, good Reverend."

He halted abruptly when Elias Patterson turned away, too late to hide the tears glittering in the firelight. Darlington waited, but on this subject there was plainly no answer to be had from the man. "Never mind the music, then. Tell me what sort of table they set in Faery."

"There was always food and wine," Elias Patterson said, when he could, "as there was always music. And whether or not I even recognized the dish, or the taste and fume of the drink, I learned to savor it and swallow it, and ask no questions. I remember one wine—they keep it for certain special occasions—that never tastes the same from glass to glass in the course of the feast. *He* makes that one himself. Titania told me so."

"He?" Darlington blinked in puzzlement.

"Oberon. Her husband." Elias Patterson's voice was completely without expression. "King of Faery since ever there's *been* Faery, just as she's been Queen. I went a long while without meeting him, or even catching a glimpse of him, for they spent far more time apart than they did together. They were forever fighting over this or that, like children—what one had, the other wanted, exactly like children. I was just as content to see no more of King Oberon than the shadow in Titania's eyes that always told me when she'd been with him. I became quite good at reading her whims and moods, as we all must learn to read our mates if we mean to keep them. Perhaps that was because she had a heart, as I've said, like a mortal woman. I don't think I could have fathomed any other woman of Faery in the same way."

"I've never *fathomed* a woman in my life," Darlington said shortly. "I never understood my mother and sisters, if you want to know—let alone the silly sluts who run after highwaymen." He stood up, moving to the edge of the firelight, as though he were about to relieve himself again. The night remained as deeply silent as he could have wished, but a lifetime of flight had long since turned even silence chancy. Turning again, and looking down at Elias Patterson, he said, "And I have my doubts that you ever rightly knew the heart of the Queen of Faery. Meaning no disrespect."

"None at all," Elias Patterson assured him. "King Oberon certainly would have agreed with you." The fire flinched from a sudden cold breeze, and the reverend drew his cloak closer around his shoulders. He said, "Once I'd been introduced to company, as you might say, I saw something more of Oberon. Rarely alone, though, for his attendants were always on hand: musicians first of all, and then dancers, jugglers, faery clowns even, and others so strange that it made my eyes hurt to look at them for long, as though important bits of them were hidden around some other corner and my eyes were trying to find the way there, and could not. On such occasion we met face-on—often during a dance, with Titania on my arm, and Oberon hand in hand with his latest elven beauty…why then, it squeezed my earthly heart to see how those two regarded one another, as though no one else existed, for good or ill. Minister no longer, to look at them was to understand where hell and heaven truly dwell, and harps and fire everlasting have no part in it."

"Aye, I'll drink to that one," Darlington swore. "There was this one bloody woman in Sussex—haven't seen her for years, and damned well don't want to, but when I think of her…aye, it squeezes. It does that. I *know* it was her turned me in for the reward money that time! How can you still wake up sad about someone who does that to you?"

Elias Patterson seemed not to have heard him. "It's a puzzling business, but while the lady Titania was, and surely remains, the most beautiful woman who ever walked this world or any other, I could have named you a dozen of my own parishioners handsomer than King Oberon. His cheekbones were too high and too prominent; his eyes too sharply angled, too wolfishly green; and his nose, chin and ears altogether too pointed for anything like beauty as we see it. Yet when Oberon looked at you, you felt naked as a white bone in the rain; and when he spoke, the voice of the Lord Himself would not have distracted you from his words. I was quite relieved that he spoke to me no more than necessary.

"But it happened one glorious Faery morning," Elias Patterson said, "while Titania yet drowsed in her bower, that Oberon came alone to me and drew me away with a single look to walk with him along the bank of that twittering little stream that I had heard on first waking with my head in Titania's lap. We said nothing to one another for a time, and then Oberon addressed me so: 'Do you imagine that my wife loves you?'

"'I would not presume,' I answered him, and that was true. But the shameless pride of having loved the Queen of Faery to sleep was on me, and for the life of me I could not keep from adding, 'But I do know that I make her happy.'"

"Aye, the Sussex woman always said that. No man but me had ever made her really happy, that's exactly what she said. Lying, conniving trull."

Elias Patterson said, "The contempt in Oberon's green eyes should have withered me where I stood, but I was younger then, and I could still hear Titania whispering her desire against my skin. Oberon said, 'You make her happy. And have you any notion of how many mortal men have made her happy? Of how many there will be after you?'

"'Jealous yourself,' I answered him—good God, how dared I speak so to such a king?—'you'll not make me as bitter and spiteful as you are. I know well enough that my time in Faery is limited to seven years. All the old tales and ballads tell me that much, and I would howl at your gates for more, for a lifetime, if I thought it would do me any good. But my religion and my raising have both taught me the virtue of settling for less—less than my dreams, less than my visions—so that I will do when the time comes, and count myself the most fortunate of men, however empty the rest of my life may be. Can you understand that, Lord of Faery?'

"I like to think now that Oberon looked at me with a trifle less scorn after I spoke those words, but perhaps not. It was long ago. At all events, he replied most evenly, saying, 'It was I who laid a *geas* upon her, untold thousands of your years past, enjoining that she might take all the human lovers she chose—she had a fascination with your kind even then—but that none of her alliances might endure longer than seven years. For then she grieves each time, most movingly, and I comfort her, as I—I—know better how to do than any strutting, crowing mortal, and we are happy together for a while.' And after a moment, he added, more softly, 'Sometimes quite a long while.'"

Darlington put another log carefully on the fire. He said, "I should never have stopped here. Now I'm too warm to abandon your hearth, Elias Patterson, and if the High Sheriff himself pops up right now, he's going to have to wait until I learn how the tale turns out. He couldn't have done better if he'd actually hired you to waylay me." He spat into the flame, smiled at the resulting hiss, and said, "Go on, then. What did you say back to His Majesty?"

"I asked a question in my turn," Elias Patterson replied. "I said, 'Is it a part of the *geas* that each of Titania's lovers returns to a world that is a hundred years older than he left it?' And Oberon answered, 'That is true. The dislocation, the shock of finding oneself an alien in one's own land, it keeps your lot fully occupied, far too busy merely remaining sane to be concerned with any notion of returning, any dream of a second chance at Faery. For if any man ever did succeed in returning to her, then the *geas* would be broken, and she free to fancy whom she chose, for as long as she chose. But that will never happen, Elias Patterson—never while I live. And I live forever.'

"'And you tell us all this?' I asked him. 'You take all your wife's men in turn for pleasant morning strolls, and inform them that there is a *geas* on her, and that it can be lifted if any of them should find his way back Under the Hill? Is that wise, my lord?'"

Darlington muttered, "I should have done something like that with that woman. I should have told everyone that she was diseased—something really horrible, really disgusting." He sighed. "I always think of things too late." A second fox barked, fairly close by, and Darlington said, "There's the vixen."

"Yes," Elias Patterson said. "I have spent a good deal of time studying the foxes in this district."

Darlington cocked his head, but the reverend did not explain further, choosing instead to continue his tale. "In response to my question, Oberon replied, 'I tell you about the *geas*, as I have told few others, because, of them all, you *will* try to come back to her. I know this. But you will fail, and fail again and again, and you will suffer endlessly and needlessly until you die. I am only trying to spare you such a fate.'

"'I am touched by your concern,' I said. 'Even honored.' And I was not mocking him, Mr. Darlington, truly. I said, 'But you and I both know that the three of us will do what God in his mystery has put it on us to do. I have failed Him, and I will be punished for it, but that changes nothing. That changes nothing at all.'

"'No,' Oberon answered. 'You are right—we will all do what we will do.' And then he smiled at me in a strange way, almost a sad way, and he said, 'And you may bear this triumph away, if you will, that I, undying Oberon, am indeed envious of a mortal man, which has only once before occurred in all my life Under the Hill. It will be long before my lady forgets you and forgives me what I do. Savor it, human. Savor it well.'"

Elias Patterson drew a deep breath, putting his hands out to the flames and looking straight at Roger Darlington. "Then he was gone, in the way he had of coming and going, and the little stream was still singing to itself. I walked slowly back to where Titania lay in her bower, awake now. And that was how the morning passed, and I envied nobody in the world, nor ever have again."

"I envy you," Darlington said quietly. "I'm telling you that right now."

"Envy nobody. It is the true secret of happiness, or at least the only one I know. So the years passed for me in Faery: not only in making love with Titania, but in hunting with her and her friends and her maidens—for she too loved the chase as well as any—and walking and sporting together in those sunlit woods that became my true home. And if I was happier than the priests and the ministers like myself think mortal man has any right to be…all the same, I never deceived myself into believing that my joy would have no end. One midnight I would fall asleep in Titania's embrace, as I had done every night for seven years, and awaken on the very same cold hillside where I had lain myself down, exactly seven years before. Then the payment would begin, and I was ready for that, too."

"You thought you were," the highwayman said somberly. "We always *think* we're ready."

"Not that I had any sort of calendar, or any way of marking my days: I only had to look in Titania's eyes to see the seventh Beltane come upon us. I had become well skilled at reading her moods, as I've told you—certainly better at it than Oberon, or any of her ladies. We gazed at each other for a long, wordless time, when that day came, and then she said, 'It is not my choice. It is my fate, and my doom.'

"And I answered her simply, saying, 'I know. There was never a moment when I did not know.'

"Faery folk do not—cannot—weep, Mr. Darlington. Only Titania. It is part of her loneliness. I held her that night for the last time, as she rocked and moaned and whimpered against me, and her tears scarred my face and my throat. This is why I grew my beard, you know, to cover the marks. She quieted a little after some while, and I said to her, 'Forget me, my love. It will be hard enough for me in my world without knowing you unhappy in this one. I beg you, forget even my name, as God has done. Will you do that for me, you for whom I forgot Heaven?' And I kissed her tears, though they burned my mouth.

"I could barely hear the words when she breathed her answer. 'If I say that, my beautiful, beautiful mortal, I will be lying, who never once lied to you.'

"'Lie to me now,' I told her then, and Titania did as I bade her."

"And even so." Darlington was not looking at him, but at the ground, his head low. "Even so, you're still never ready."

Elias Patterson smiled in some surprise. "You're quite right, Mr. Darlington. I certainly wasn't ready, on the last night of the last year, for her to shake me out of an exhausted sleep—when you know, as I did, that you will never do something unbearably wonderful ever again in your life, you see no reason to hold back anything for tomorrow—whispering, 'My love, my love, you must run! Please, *wake*—you are in terrible danger!'"

Darlington looked up, his mouth crooked. "I'm always hearing tales of brave women who risk their lives to warn their lovers of one approaching peril or another. Never met one in my life, you understand, but I'm sure there must be thousands."

"Titania never looked more beautiful than she did that midnight," Elias Patterson said, "bending over me, with the moon in her hair and the wild terror in her eyes. I reached out to pull her down once again—*once more, oh, once more*—but she resisted, tugging at my wrist, crying over and over, 'No, no, they are here, I feel them, you *must* fly!' When I dream of her, that is how she comes to me, always."

"What was the danger? I don't imagine they've got troopers or High Sheriffs in Paradise."

"She did not want to tell me at first. But I saw the figures moving in the darkness, and each time, pulling me along as she was, she would freeze in place, absolutely, like a fawn when the wolves are near, knowing that its only chance of life is not to move, not to make a sound, not to breathe." Elias Patterson shook his head in fresh wonder. "Titania, Queen of Faery, who hunted manticores."

Darlington waited, saying nothing. Elias Patterson said, "I never got a close look at them, thanks to her wariness and her skill. They were great shadows, for the most part, moving as silently as she under the ever-blooming trees and meadows of Faery. What I did see of them I will not tell you, for I still dream that, too. But I *felt* them, as she said: hungry shadows who knew my name, clawing at my mind and my soul to be let in—and if I let them in there would be nothing left of me but skin; nothing but a shadow inside, like themselves. And all the same, there was as well a terrible lassitude that came with that feeling—a sense that it would be so pleasant to surrender, even to invite them in, since what would life matter without Titania?" He laughed then, but there was no smile in the laughter. "And when I look back, that is probably just what I should have done."

"But you didn't." Darlington's voice was hoarse and expressionless.

"No. But if it had not been for Titania, holding me together and *them* outside with her faery hands and her human heart…well, I would be in another place than Yorkshire today. For what she said to me was that Faery exists on sufferance of the Hell—whatever it actually is—that you and I were both raised to believe in. 'It is a mere token tithe we pay, every seven years,' she told me, 'most often an animal, though I have known it to be as simple as a flower that grows only here, Under the Hill. But this time, this time'—and dark as it was, her face was white as a flower itself, white as alyssum, white as anemone, white as yarrow—'this time, my darling, *you* are the tithe…'"

"Oberon," Darlington said through his teeth. "It was Oberon who shopped you."

"Aye, I never doubted that, nor did Titania. But it is a curious thing, how certain horrors are so vastly horrible to think about that they simply do not take hold on your imagination at the time, but go almost unnoticed—sooner or later to wake you screaming, surely, but not *now*. What was real was Titania, crouching beside me in a thicket while those—what were they? Demons, monsters, damned souls? I've no idea to this day—while those creatures who had been sent for me glided soundlessly by, close, so close, drawn perhaps by the ticking of my blood, perhaps by the chatter of my mind, the betraying rustle of the hair rising on my forearms." He paused for a moment, and then said in an oddly younger voice, "Or by the sweetness of Titania's breath on my cheek, which I *will* not think of, *will* not remember…" He caught himself, abruptly, but Darlington could hear the effort.

"If I had a shilling for every man, woman and child who's shopped *me*," Darlington murmured, "well, they'd not do me much good just now, all those shillings, would they? Except maybe to bribe a turnkey to let a wench into my cell. Go on."

Elias Patterson said, "Titania led me a long way, circling and doubling back at the least sign of danger, sometimes standing motionless for minutes at a time, even when I could sense nothing. It was a strange, slow flight, and a sad one, for we passed through fields where we had rambled together in sunlight, crossed a stream where the Queen of Faery had tucked up her skirts like a girl and shown me how to tickle fish with my toes; and rounded the golden corner of a wood where I had flattened myself, marveling, against a tree to see her take down a grimly boar with nothing but a slender oaken spear longer than she was. She had leaped into my arms afterward, and rubbed her bloody hands all over my face. But we could speak of none of this, or anything else, for fear of attracting my hunters' attention. We moved along in silence, her hand always in mine; and now and then, when we could, we looked long at each other. I remember."

He was silent for a few moments, and then continued, "We came very near to evading them altogether. Titania had just pointed to a grove of tall hemlocks a little way ahead, and whispered, '*There*, my love—pass under those trees and step safely home into your own world,' and I had turned for…what? A last look, or word, or hopeless embrace? Perhaps none of these, for I had sworn to myself long ago that there would be no such tormented farewell for us when the time came. But all at once my mind filled with fire and stench and despair bearing down on me from all sides. I could not see Titania—I could see nothing but howling shadows—and I cried out in fear, and felt her push me down, hard, so that I sprawled flat on the ground. Something was flung over me, covering me completely, and I knew by the dear scent of her that it was Titania's cloak. I cowered in her smell, feeling the shadows raging around me—around *her*—expecting my pitiful refuge to be torn away from me at any instant. All I could think, over and over, the one light trembling in my darkness, was *when I am in Hell, I will hold her with me, and eternity cannot be so dreadful then.*"

Darlington said quietly, "It's that cloak you're wearing, isn't it? That's Titania's cloak."

"I heard her laugh," Elias Patterson said, "and it was like the first time I had wakened to her singing—soft and clear and proud, as though she had just invented singing at that very moment. She was moving away slowly, back the way we had come—I could feel it, just as I felt the great shadows sullenly trailing behind, and felt their savage bewilderment. Under that cloak, I did not exist for them; and yet the Queen of Faery was laughing joyously at them, and they knew it. I could feel them knowing it, as their night lifted from my mind."

"It's a cloak of invisibility, like in the fairy tales." Darlington was talking aloud to himself. "But it can't be, for you're plain enough to see right now. How *does* the bloody thing work?" His voice had grown harsh and hungry when he raised his eyes to meet Elias Patterson's eyes.

"I wish I could tell you," Elias Patterson answered him sincerely. "It didn't make me invisible—un*thinkable*, really, is what I suspect. All I can say with any certainty is that it's quite a warm cloak. And easy to clean."

"Good to know." Darlington brought out his pistol, though not particularly pointing it at Elias Patterson. "For a man in my profession."

Elias Patterson smiled at him. "Your gun's empty, as we are both aware, but that doesn't matter. I'll give you the cloak, gladly—but if I might make a suggestion, you should wait a bit before you take possession. For your own good."

Darlington scowled, puzzled. "Why?"

"Trust me. I was, after all, a minister of the Gospel."

Darlington put his pistol away. "I do have bullets around somewhere," he said, but absently, still caught up in the tale, still eyeing Elias Patterson's cloak. "So she led them away, and you escaped back to this world."

"So it was. I waited until I could feel that I was safe, and then I scurried to that hemlock grove Titania had pointed out, like a frightened little mouse, with her cloak wrapped round me. Between one mouse-step and the next, I was walking English earth, under an English heaven, safe from the wrath of Hell and Oberon alike—and, if you'll believe it, already frantic to turn and go straight back, whatever the price, whatever the doom. But the grove was gone, the land was as flat and flavorless as I remembered it, and hemlocks don't grow in that soil, anyway. The country Under the Hill was shut to me. I was…home."

"And was it,"—Darlington hesitated—"*is* it a hundred years later? Than when you walked out of your house, that Beltane eve?"

"It was a hundred and six, to be accurate, which such things rarely are. But yes, it turned out exactly as the ballads have it. All my friends and family were long gone, my house had apparently blown down in a storm—and been quite nicely rebuilt, by the by—and my church now belonged to a denomination that hadn't existed in my time. There was nothing of me left in that town, except for an All Hallows' Eve tale of the minister who was snatched away by the Devil—or by the Old Ones, if you talked to the most elderly of the villagers. *Tabula rasa*, you might say, and doubtless the better off for it."

Darlington was staring at him, his expression a mixture of superstitious awe and genuine pity. Elias Patterson laughed outright. "Believe me, good highwayman, there's something to be said for the completely blank slate, the scroll of perfect virgin vellum on which anything at all might yet be inscribed. I wandered away from my village for the second time, perfectly content, and I have never looked back. I have been…otherwise occupied."

"Doing what? If you're not a minister anymore—"

But the white-haired man was suddenly on his feet, half-crouched, his posture almost that of an animal sniffing the air. "Down," he said very quietly. "*Down*."

Darlington had not heard that particular voice before, and he did not question it for a moment. He knelt clumsily, briefly noticing Elias Patterson fumbling with the fastenings of his cloak; then he was flat on the cold ground, with the cloak over him, listening helplessly to slow, deliberate hoofbeats and the soft ring of light mail. He heard Elias Patterson's voice again, now with a strange, singsong boyishness to it, saying eagerly, "Welcome, welcome, captain! It *is* captain, isn't it?"

A growl, impatient but not discourteous, answered him. "Sergeant, sir, sorry to say. What are you doing up here alone?"

The reply, tossed back lightly and cheerily, chilled Darlington more than the ground beneath him. "Why, searching for Faery, sergeant. That's my appointed study in this world, and I flatter myself that I'm uncommon good at it."

Three horses, by the sound, so two other riders, and very bewildered riders they must be by now, Darlington thought.

The sergeant said, a little warily, "That's...interesting, sir. We've been all this day and night in pursuit of a dangerous highwayman named Roger Darlington. Would you have seen him the night, by any chance, or heard any word of him? There's five hundred pounds on his head."

Elias Patterson was saying, in his odd new voice, "No, sergeant, I'm afraid I hardly notice anything when I'm at my searching. It's terribly demanding work, you know."

"I don't doubt it," the sergeant rumbled agreement. "But isn't it cold work as well, on a night like this? That fire can't throw much heat, surely—and you without a proper cloak, at that. Hate to find you frozen stiff as a bull's pizzle on our way back."

Another rider's grunt: "Wager old Darlington'll be happy when we catch him, just to get in out of the weather."

I'm right at your feet, you natural-born imbecile! Practically under *your feet, and you can't see me!*

"Never fear, good sergeant," Elias Patterson chirped in response. "All the warmth I need is here in my hand." Darlington heard the leather flask gurgle. "Taste and see, I beg you."

Three clearly audible swallows—three distinctly louder gasps of "*Jesus!*"—then the third rider: "God's teeth, rouse a stinking corpse, this would. Where'd you come on it?"

Elias Patterson giggled brightly. "The Queen of Faery gave it me, as a remembrance. We are old friends, you see—oh, very old. Very old."

He'll never get away with it. But plainly he had done exactly that—Darlington could hear it in the sergeant's words: "Well, that's a fine thing indeed, sir, to be a friend of the Queen of...But you won't want to be passing it around so free, or there'll be none left to warm your old bones, hey?" The horses were stamping fretfully, already beginning to move away.

Another playfully demented giggle. "Ah, no fear there either." *Christ, don't overdo it!* "This is an enchanted flask, never yet empty in all the years it's companioned me on my quest. A wonderful gift now, don't you think?"

"Wonderful," the sergeant agreed. "Well, we'll be on our way, sir, and my thanks for your kindness. And if by chance you should hear any word of that Darlington fellow—"

"I'll pass it on to you directly, of course I will. On the instant." A knowing chuckle. "I know how to reach you on the instant, you see."

"I'm sure you do. Good night to you then, sir."

Darlington waited a good deal beyond the time when he could no longer hear the hoofs crunching the light snowcrust before he threw off the cloak and scrambled to his feet. "I wouldn't have believed it! I wouldn't have bloody *believed* it! I really *was* invisible, the same as you were!"

Elias Patterson shook his head. "No, I told you—they saw you, all right, just as those creatures come from Hell saw me. They saw that cloak covering some object, but it meant nothing to them, it suggested no connection, no picture in their minds, as most things we even glimpse do. The cloak breaks that connection in some way. I don't understand it, but I know that must be what it does, when sorely needed." He paused, watching Darlington staring after the departed horsemen. In a lower voice, he said, "And why Faery is only seen when it chooses to be seen."

"Well, however it works, it's bound to come in useful," Darlington said. "And so might that ever-full flask on a hard night, now I think of it." He held out his hand.

"I think not, Mr. Darlington," Elias Patterson said gently. Their eyes met, and though the reverend was a century and more older than the other, in a little while Darlington lowered his hand. Elias Patterson said, "It is growing light."

"Aye, I'd best be off, find myself a horse. First farm I come to—" Darlington grinned suddenly—"if the goodman's a bit easier to bluff than you."

He offered his hand again, in a different manner, and Elias Patterson took it, saying, "I'd head south and west if I were you. As far as Sheffield, and straight west from there. Dorset might suit you for a time, in my opinion."

"Poor as churchmice, Dorset. Nothing worth stealing but a bit of copper piping, a bit of lead off the roofs. Hardly my style." He shook Elias Patterson's hand firmly. "But southwest you tell me, so southwest it is. And good fortune to you on your own quest, Reverend."

"Faery is all around us, Mr. Darlington," Elias Patterson said. "The border never stays in one place—Oberon moves and maintains it constantly, to keep me from crossing back—but it is always permeable from the far side, not merely at Beltane and Samhain. That is how the fox and unicorn come and go as they please, as do the phoenix and the mermaid. Not even Oberon can bar their way."

He folded his hands where he sat, and nodded again to Darlington. "And that is why I pay heed to foxes."

Staring at him, Darlington saw the madness fully for the first time. He said, "You really believe you can cross a border that the King of Faery is determined to hide from you forever? A border that will keep moving and moving away from you, even if you find it?"

"The Queen of Faery remembers me," Elias Patterson said. "I have faith in that, as I once had faith in something quite different; and what a fox knows a determined man may discover. Go now, Mr. Darlington—south and west—before those men come back. And do not trust my lady's cloak to hide you a second time. It never did for me. I think you must give it to someone else, in your turn, before it chooses to work again."

"No doubt I'll find reason to test that, Reverend."

"No doubt." Elias Patterson nodded once, placidly. "God be with you, my friend."

Darlington started off, fastening the cloak at his throat. The sky was pale green with dawn over the moors before he looked back. He could still see the hilltop, and even the last bright threads of the dying fire, but there was no sign of Elias Patterson. The highwayman stood for some while, waiting; then finally snugged Titania's cloak about him again, and walked on.

BLACK SWAN
BRUCE STERLING

Bruce Sterling published his first novel, *Involution Ocean*, in 1977. The author of ten novels and four short story collections, he is still perhaps best known in science fiction as the Godfather of Cyberpunk. He edited the cyberpunk anthology *Mirrorshades*, and his early novels *The Artificial Kid* and *Schismatrix* are perhaps the closest things he wrote to cyberpunk. After closing the 'zine *Cheap Truth* and leaving cyberpunk to others in November 1986, he went on to write major science fiction novels like *Holy Fire*, *Distraction* and *The Zenith Angle*. He is the author of a large and influential body of short fiction, much of which have been collected in *Crystal Express*, *Globalhead*, *A Good Old-Fashioned Future* and *Visionary in Residence*. His most recent books are new novel *The Caryatids* and major career retrospective, *Ascendancies: The Best of Bruce Sterling*.

The ethical journalist protects a confidential source. So I protected "Massimo Montaldo," although I knew that wasn't his name.

Massimo shambled through the tall glass doors, dropped his valise with a thump, and sat across the table. We were meeting where we always met: inside the Caffe Elena, a dark and cozy spot that fronts on the biggest plaza in Europe.

The Elena has two rooms as narrow and dignified as mahogany coffins, with lofty red ceilings. The little place has seen its share of stricken wanderers. Massimo never confided his personal troubles to me, but they were obvious, as if he'd smuggled monkeys into the café and hidden them under his clothes.

Like every other hacker in the world, Massimo Montaldo was bright. Being Italian, he struggled to look suave. Massimo wore stain-proof, wrinkle-proof travel gear: a black merino wool jacket, an American black denim shirt, and black cargo pants. Massimo also sported black athletic trainers, not any brand I could recognize, with eerie bubble-filled soles.

These skeletal shoes of his were half-ruined. They were strapped together with rawhide boot-laces.

To judge by his Swiss-Italian accent, Massimo had spent a lot of time in Geneva. Four times he'd leaked chip secrets to me—crisp engineering graphics, apparently snipped right out of Swiss patent applications. However, the various bureaus in Geneva had no records of these patents. They had no records of any

"Massimo Montaldo," either.

Each time I'd made use of Massimo's indiscretions, the traffic to my weblog had doubled.

I knew that Massimo's commercial sponsor, or more likely his spymaster, was using me to manipulate the industry I covered. Big bets were going down in the markets somewhere. Somebody was cashing in like a bandit.

That profiteer wasn't me, and I had to doubt that it was him. I never financially speculate in the companies I cover as a journalist, because that is the road to hell. As for young Massimo, his road to hell was already well-trampled.

Massimo twirled the frail stem of his glass of Barolo. His shoes were wrecked, his hair was unwashed, and he looked like he'd shaved in an airplane toilet. He handled the best wine in Europe like a scorpion poised to sting his liver. Then he gulped it down.

Unasked, the waiter poured him another. They know me at the Elena.

Massimo and I had a certain understanding. As we chatted about Italian tech companies—he knew them from Alessi to Zanotti—I discreetly passed him useful favors. A cellphone chip—bought in another man's name. A plastic hotel pass key for a local hotel room, rented by a third party. Massimo could use these without ever showing a passport or any identification.

There were eight "Massimo Montaldos" on Google and none of them were him. Massimo flew in from places unknown, he laid his eggs of golden information, then he paddled off into dark waters. I was protecting him by giving him those favors. Surely there were other people very curious about him, besides myself.

The second glass of Barolo eased that ugly crease in his brows. He rubbed his beak of a nose, and smoothed his unruly black hair, and leaned onto the thick stone table with both of his black woolen elbows.

"Luca, I brought something special for you this time. Are you ready for that? Something you can't even imagine."

"I suppose," I said.

Massimo reached into his battered leather valise and brought out a no-name PC laptop. This much-worn machine, its corners bumped with use and its keyboard dingy, had one of those thick super-batteries clamped onto its base. All that extra power must have tripled the computer's weight. Small wonder that Massimo never carried spare shoes.

He busied himself with his grimy screen, fixated by his private world there.

The Elena is not a celebrity bar, which is why celebrities like it. A blonde television presenter swayed into the place. Massimo, who was now deep into his third glass, whipped his intense gaze from his laptop screen. He closely studied her curves, which were upholstered in Gucci.

An Italian television presenter bears the relationship to news that American fast food bears to food. So I couldn't feel sorry for her—yet I didn't like the way he sized her up. Genius gears were turning visibly in Massimo's brilliant geek head. That woman had all the raw, compelling appeal to him of some difficult math problem.

Left alone with her, he would chew on that problem until something clicked loose and fell into his hands, and, to do her credit, she could feel that. She opened her dainty crocodile purse and slipped on a big pair of sunglasses.

"Signor Montaldo," I said.

He was rapt.

"Massimo?"

This woke him from his lustful reverie. He twisted the computer and exhibited his screen to me.

I don't design chips, but I've seen the programs used for that purpose. Back in the 1980s, there were thirty different chip-design programs. Nowadays there are only three survivors. None of them are nativized in the Italian language, because every chip geek in the world speaks English.

This program was in Italian. It looked elegant. It looked like a very stylish way to design computer chips. Computer chip engineers are not stylish people. Not in this world, anyway.

Massimo tapped at his weird screen with a gnawed fingernail. "This is just a cheap, 24-K embed. But do you see these?"

"Yes I do. What are they?"

"These are memristors."

In heartfelt alarm, I stared around the café, but nobody in the Elena knew or cared in the least about Massimo's stunning revelation. He could have thrown memristors onto their tables in heaps. They'd never realize that he was tossing them the keys to riches.

I could explain now, in grueling detail, exactly what memristors are, and how different they are from any standard electronic component. Suffice to understand that, in electronic engineering, memristors did not exist. Not at all. They were technically possible—we'd known that for thirty years, since the 1980s—but nobody had ever manufactured one.

A chip with memristors was like a racetrack where the jockeys rode unicorns.

I sipped the Barolo so I could find my voice again. "You brought me schematics for memristors? What happened, did your UFO crash?"

"That's very witty, Luca."

"You can't hand me something like that! What on Earth do you expect me to do with that?"

"I am not giving these memristor plans to you. I have decided to give them to Olivetti. I will tell you what to do: you make one confidential call to your good friend, the Olivetti Chief Technical Officer. You tell him to look hard in his junk folder where he keeps the spam with no return address. Interesting things will happen, then. He'll be grateful to you."

"Olivetti is a fine company," I said. "But they're not the outfit to handle a monster like that. A memristor is strictly for the big boys—Intel, Samsung, Fujitsu."

Massimo laced his hands together on the table—he might have been at prayer—and stared at me with weary sarcasm. "Luca," he said, "don't you ever get tired of seeing Italian genius repressed?"

The Italian chip business is rather modest. It can't always make its ends meet. I spent fifteen years covering chip tech in Route 128 in Boston. When the almighty dollar ruled the tech world, I was glad that I'd made those connections.

But times do change. Nations change, industries change. Industries change the times.

Massimo had just shown me something that changes industries. A disruptive innovation. A breaker of the rules.

"This matter is serious," I said. "Yes, Olivetti's people do read my weblog—they even comment there. But that doesn't mean that I can leak some breakthrough that deserves a Nobel Prize. Olivetti would want to know, they would *have* to know, the source of that."

He shook his head. "They don't want to know, and neither do you."

"Oh yes, I most definitely do want to know."

"No, you don't. Trust me."

"Massimo, I'm a journalist. That means that I always want to know, and I never trust anybody."

He slapped the table. "Maybe you were a 'journalist' when they still printed paper 'journals.' But your dot-com journals are all dead. Nowadays you're a blogger. You're an influence peddler and you spread rumors for a living." Massimo shrugged, because he didn't think he was insulting me. "So, shut up! Just do what you always do! That's all I'm asking."

That might be all that he was asking, but my whole business was in asking. "Who created that chip?" I asked him. "I know it wasn't you. You know a lot about tech investment, but you're not Leonardo da Vinci."

"No, I'm not Leonardo." He emptied his glass.

"Look, I know that you're not even 'Massimo Montaldo'—whoever that is. I'll do a lot to get news out on my blog. But I'm not going to act as your cut-out in a scheme like this! That's totally unethical! Where did you steal that chip? Who made it? What are they, Chinese super-engineers in some bunker under Beijing?"

Massimo was struggling not to laugh at me. "I can't reveal that. Could we have another round? Maybe a sandwich? I need a nice toasty pancetta."

I got the waiter's attention. I noted that the TV star's boyfriend had shown up. Her boyfriend was not her husband. Unfortunately, I was not in the celebrity tabloid business. It wasn't the first time I'd missed a good bet by consorting with computer geeks.

"So you're an industrial spy," I told him. "And you must be Italian to boot, because you're always such a patriot about it. Okay, so you stole those plans somewhere. I won't ask you how or why. But let me give you some good advice:

no sane man would leak that to Olivetti. Olivetti's a consumer outfit. They make pretty toys for cute secretaries. A memristor chip is dynamite."

Massimo was staring raptly at the TV blonde as he awaited his sandwich.

"Massimo, pay attention. If you leak something that advanced, that radical... a chip like that could change the world's military balance of power. Never mind Olivetti. Big American spy agencies with three letters in their names will come calling."

Massimo scratched his dirty scalp and rolled his eyes in derision. "Are you so terrorized by the CIA? They don't read your sorry little one-man tech blog."

This crass remark irritated me keenly. "Listen to me, boy genius: do you know what the CIA does here in Italy? We're their 'rendition' playground. People vanish off the streets."

"Anybody can 'vanish off the streets.' I do that all the time."

I took out my Moleskin notebook and my shiny Rotring technical pen. I placed them both on the Elena's neat little marble table. Then I slipped them both back inside my jacket. "Massimo, I'm trying hard to be sensible about this. Your snotty attitude is not helping your case with me."

With an effort, my source composed himself. "It's all very simple," he lied. "I've been here a while, and now I'm tired of this place. So I'm leaving. I want to hand the future of electronics to an Italian company. With no questions asked and no strings attached. You won't help me do that simple thing?"

"No, of course I won't! Not under conditions like these. I don't know where you got that data, what, how, when, whom, or why... I don't even know who you are! Do I look like that kind of idiot? Unless you tell me your story, I can't trust you."

He made that evil gesture: I had no balls. Twenty years ago—well, twenty-five—and we would have stepped outside the bar. Of course I was angry with him—but I also knew he was about to crack. My source was drunk and he was clearly in trouble. He didn't need a fist-fight with a journalist. He needed confession.

Massimo put a bold sneer on his face, watching himself in one of the Elena's tall spotted mirrors. "If this tiny gadget is too big for your closed mind, then I've got to find another blogger! A blogger with some guts!"

"Great. Sure. Go do that. You might try Beppe Grillo."

Massimo tore his gaze from his own reflection. "That washed-up TV comedian? What does he know about technology?"

"Try Berlusconi, then. He owns all the television stations and half the Italian Internet. Prime Minister Berlusconi is just the kind of hustler you need. He'll free you from all your troubles. He'll make you Minister of something."

Massimo lost all patience. "I don't need that! I've been to a lot of versions of Italy. Yours is a complete disgrace! I don't know how you people get along with yourselves!"

Now the story was tearing loose. I offered an encouraging nod. "How many 'versions of Italy' do you need, Massimo?"

"I have sixty-four versions of Italy." He patted his thick laptop. "Got them all right here."

I humored him. "Only sixty-four?"

His tipsy face turned red. "I had to borrow CERN's supercomputers to calculate all those coordinates! Thirty-two Italies were too few! A hundred twenty-eight… I'd never have the time to visit all those! And as for *your* Italy… well… I wouldn't be here at all, if it wasn't for that Turinese girl."

"'Cherchez la femme,'" I told him. "That's the oldest trouble-story in the world."

"I did her some favors," he admitted, mournfully twisting his wineglass. "Like with you. But much more so."

I felt lost, but I knew that his story was coming. Once I'd coaxed it out of him, I could put it into better order later.

"So, tell me: what did she do to you?"

"She dumped me," he said. He was telling me the truth, but with a lost, forlorn, bewildered air, like he couldn't believe it himself. "She dumped me and she married the President of France." Massimo glanced up, his eyelashes wet with grief. "I don't blame her. I know why she did that. I'm a very handy guy for a woman like her, but Mother of God, I'm not the President of France!"

"No, no, you're not the President of France," I agreed. The President of France was a hyperactive Hungarian Jewish guy who liked to sing karaoke songs. President Nicolas Sarkozy was an exceedingly unlikely character, but he was odd in a very different way from Massimo Montaldo.

Massimo's voice was cracking with passion. "She says that he'll make her the First Lady of Europe! All I've got to offer her is insider-trading hints and a few extra millions for her millions."

The waiter brought Massimo a toasted sandwich.

Despite his broken heart, Massimo was starving. He tore into his food like a chained dog, then glanced up from his mayonnaise dip. "Do I sound jealous? I'm not jealous."

Massimo was bitterly jealous, but I shook my head so as to encourage him.

"I can't be jealous of a woman like her!" Massimo lied. "Eric Clapton can be jealous, Mick Jagger can be jealous! She's a rock star's groupie who's become the Premiere Dame of France! She married Sarkozy! Your world is full of journalists—spies, cops, creeps, whatever—and not for one minute did they ever stop and consider: 'Oh! This must be the work of a computer geek from another world!'"

"No," I agreed.

"Nobody ever imagines that!"

I called the waiter back and ordered myself a double espresso. The waiter seemed quite pleased at the way things were going for me. They were a kindly bunch at the Elena. Friedrich Nietzsche had been one of their favorite patrons.

Their dark old mahogany walls had absorbed all kinds of lunacy.

Massimo jabbed his sandwich in the dip and licked his fingers. "So, if I leak a memristor chip to you, nobody will ever stop and say: 'some unknown geek eating a sandwich in Torino is the most important man in world technology.' Because that truth is inconceivable."

Massimo stabbed a roaming olive with a toothpick. His hands were shaking: with rage, romantic heartbreak, and frustrated fury. He was also drunk.

He glared at me. "You're not following what I tell you. Are you really that stupid?"

"I do understand," I assured him. "Of course I understand. I'm a computer geek myself."

"You know who designed that memristor chip, Luca? You did it. You. But not here, not in this version of Italy. Here, you're just some small-time tech journalist. You created that device in *my* Italy. In my Italy, you are the guru of computational aesthetics. You're a famous author, you're a culture critic, you're a multi-talented genius. Here, you've got no guts and no imagination. You're so entirely useless here that you can't even change your own world."

It was hard to say why I believed him, but I did. I believed him instantly.

Massimo devoured his food to the last scrap. He thrust his bare plate aside and pulled a huge nylon wallet from his cargo pants. This overstuffed wallet had color-coded plastic pop-up tags, like the monster files of some Orwellian bureaucracy. Twenty different kinds of paper currency jammed in there. A huge riffling file of varicolored plastic ID cards.

He selected a large bill and tossed it contemptuously onto the Elena's cold marble table. It looked very much like money—it looked much more like money than the money that I handled every day. It had a splendid portrait of Galileo and it was denominated in "Euro-Lira."

Then he rose and stumbled out of the café. I hastily slipped the weird bill in my pocket. I threw some euros onto the table. Then I pursued him.

With his head down, muttering and sour, Massimo was weaving across the millions of square stone cobbles of the huge Piazza Vittorio Veneto. As if through long experience, he found the emptiest spot in the plaza, a stony desert between a handsome line of ornate lamp-posts and the sleek steel railings of an underground parking garage.

He dug into a trouser pocket and plucked out tethered foam earplugs, the kind you get from Alitalia for long overseas flights. Then he flipped his laptop open.

I caught up with him. "What are you doing over here? Looking for wifi signals?"

"I'm leaving." He tucked the foam plugs in his ears.

"Mind if I come along?"

"When I count to three," he told me, too loudly, "you have to jump high into the air. Also, stay within range of my laptop."

"All right. Sure."

"Oh, and put your hands over your ears."

I objected. "How can I hear you count to three if I have my hands over my ears?"

"Uno." He pressed the F-1 function key, and his laptop screen blazed with sudden light. "Due." The F-2 emitted a humming, cracking buzz. "Tre." He hopped in the air.

Thunder blasted. My lungs were crushed in a violent billow of wind. My feet stung as if they'd been burned.

Massimo staggered for a moment, then turned by instinct back toward the Elena. "Let's go!" he shouted. He plucked one yellow earplug from his head. Then he tripped.

I caught his computer as he stumbled. Its monster battery was sizzling hot.

Massimo grabbed his overheated machine. He stuffed it awkwardly into his valise.

Massimo had tripped on a loose cobblestone. We were standing in a steaming pile of loose cobblestones. Somehow, these cobblestones had been plucked from the pavement beneath our shoes and scattered around us like dice.

Of course we were not alone. Some witnesses sat in the vast plaza, the every-day Italians of Turin, sipping their drinks at little tables under distant, elegant umbrellas. They were sensibly minding their own business. A few were gazing puzzled at the rich blue evening sky, as if they suspected some passing sonic boom. Certainly none of them cared about us.

We limped back toward the café. My shoes squeaked like the shoes of a bad TV comedian. The cobbles under our feet had broken and tumbled, and the seams of my shoes had gone loose. My shining patent-leather shoes were foul and grimy.

We stepped through the arched double-doors of the Elena, and, somehow, despite all sense and reason, I found some immediate comfort. Because the Elena was the Elena: it had those round marble tables with their curvilinear legs, those maroon leather chairs with their shiny brass studs, those colossal time-stained mirrors... and a smell I hadn't noticed there in years.

Cigarettes. Everyone in the café was smoking. The air in the bar was cooler—it felt chilly, even. People wore sweaters.

Massimo had friends there. A woman and her man. This woman beckoned us over, and the man, although he knew Massimo, was clearly unhappy to see him.

This man was Swiss, but he wasn't the jolly kind of Swiss I was used to seeing in Turin, some harmless Swiss banker on holiday who pops over the Alps to pick up some ham and cheese. This Swiss guy was young, yet as tough as old nails, with aviator shades and a long narrow scar in his hairline. He wore black nylon gloves and a raw canvas jacket with holster room in its armpits.

The woman had tucked her impressive bust into a hand-knitted peasant sweater. Her sweater was gaudy, complex and aggressively gorgeous, and so was she. She had smoldering eyes thick with mascara, and talon-like red painted nails, and a thick gold watch that could have doubled as brass knuckles.

"So Massimo is back," said the woman. She had a cordial yet guarded tone, like a woman who has escaped a man's bed and needs compelling reasons to return.

"I brought a friend for you tonight," said Massimo, helping himself to a chair.

"So I see. And what does your friend have in mind for us? Does he play backgammon?"

The pair had a backgammon set on their table. The Swiss mercenary rattled dice in a cup. "We're very good at backgammon," he told me mildly. He had the extremely menacing tone of a practiced killer who can't even bother to be scary.

"My friend here is from the American CIA," said Massimo. "We're here to do some serious drinking."

"How nice! I can speak American to you, Mr. CIA," the woman volunteered. She aimed a dazzling smile at me. "What is your favorite American baseball team?"

"I root for the Boston Red Sox."

"I love the Seattle Green Sox," she told us, just to be coy.

The waiter brought us a bottle of Croatian fruit brandy. The peoples of the Balkans take their drinking seriously, so their bottles tend toward a rather florid design. This bottle was frankly fantastic: it was squat, acid-etched, curvilinear, and flute-necked, and with a triple portrait of Tito, Nasser and Nehru, all toasting one another. There were thick flakes of gold floating in its paralyzing murk.

Massimo yanked the gilded cork, stole the woman's cigarettes, and tucked an unfiltered cig in the corner of his mouth. With his slopping shot-glass in his fingers he was a different man.

"Zhivali!" the woman pronounced, and we all tossed back a hearty shot of venom.

The temptress chose to call herself "Svetlana," while her Swiss bodyguard was calling himself "Simon."

I had naturally thought that it was insane for Massimo to denounce me as a CIA spy, yet this gambit was clearly helping the situation. As an American spy, I wasn't required to say much. No one expected me to know anything useful, or to do anything worthwhile.

However, I was hungry, so I ordered the snack plate. The attentive waiter was not my favorite Elena waiter. He might have been a cousin. He brought us raw onions, pickles, black bread, a hefty link of sausage, and a wooden tub of creamed butter. We also got a notched pig-iron knife and a battered chopping board.

Simon put the backgammon set away.

All these crude and ugly things on the table—the knife, the chopping board, even the bad sausage—had all been made in Italy. I could see little Italian maker's marks hand-etched into all of them.

"So you're hunting here in Torino, like us?" probed Svetlana.

I smiled back at her. "Yes, certainly!"

"So, what do you plan to do with him when you catch him? Will you put him on trial?"

"A fair trial is the American way!" I told them. Simon thought this remark was quite funny. Simon was not an evil man by nature. Simon probably suffered long nights of existential regret whenever he cut a man's throat.

"So," Simon offered, caressing the rim of his dirty shot glass with one nylon-gloved finger, "So even the Americans expect 'the Rat' to show his whiskers in here!"

"The Elena does pull a crowd," I agreed. "So it all makes good sense. Don't you think?"

Everyone loves to be told that their thinking makes good sense. They were happy to hear me allege this. Maybe I didn't look or talk much like an American agent, but when you're a spy, and guzzling fruit brandy, and gnawing sausage, these minor inconsistencies don't upset anybody.

We were all being sensible.

Leaning his black elbows on our little table, Massimo weighed in. "The Rat is clever. He plans to sneak over the Alps again. He'll go back to Nice and Marseilles. He'll rally his militias."

Simon stopped with a knife-stabbed chunk of blood sausage on the way to his gullet. "You really believe that?"

"Of course I do! What did Napoleon say? 'The death of a million men means nothing to a man like me!' It's impossible to corner Nicolas the Rat. The Rat has a star of destiny."

The woman watched Massimo's eyes. Massimo was one of her informants. Being a woman, she had heard his lies before and was used to them. She also knew that no informant lies all the time.

"Then he's here in Torino tonight," she concluded.

Massimo offered her nothing.

She immediately looked to me. I silently stroked my chin in a sagely fashion.

"Listen, American spy," she told me politely, "you Americans are a simple, honest people, so good at tapping phone calls… It won't hurt your feelings any if Nicolas Sarkozy is found floating face-down in the River Po. Instead of teasing me here, as Massimo is so fond of doing, why don't you just tell me where Sarkozy is? I do want to know."

I knew very well where President Nicolas Sarkozy was supposed to be. He was supposed to be in the Elysée Palace carrying out extensive economic reforms.

Simon was more urgent. "You do want us to know where the Rat is, don't you?" He showed me a set of teeth edged in Swiss gold. "Let us know! That would save the International Courts of Justice a lot of trouble."

I didn't know Nicolas Sarkozy. I had met him twice when he was French Minister of Communication, when he proved that he knew a lot about the Internet. Still, if Nicolas Sarkozy was not the President of France, and if he was not in the Elysée Palace, then, being a journalist, I had a pretty good guess of his whereabouts.

"Cherchez la femme," I said.

Simon and Svetlana exchanged thoughtful glances. Knowing one another well, and knowing their situation, they didn't have to debate their next course of action. Simon signaled the waiter. Svetlana threw a gleaming coin onto the table. They bundled their backgammon set and kicked their leather chairs back. They left the café without another word.

Massimo rose. He sat in Svetlana's abandoned chair, so that he could keep a wary eye on the café's double-door to the street. Then he helped himself to her abandoned pack of Turkish cigarettes.

I examined Svetlana's abandoned coin. It was large, round, and minted from pure silver, with a gaudy engraving of the Taj Mahal. "Fifty Dinars," it read, in Latin script, Hindi, Arabic, and Cyrillic.

"The booze around here really gets on top of me," Massimo complained. Unsteadily, he stuffed the ornate cork back into the brandy bottle. He set a slashed pickle on a buttered slice of black bread.

"Is he coming here?"

"Who?"

"Nicolas Sarkozy. 'Nicolas the Rat.'"

"Oh, him," said Massimo, chewing his bread. "In this version of Italy, I think Sarkozy's already dead. God knows there's enough people trying to kill him. The Arabs, Chinese, Africans… he turned the south of France upside down! There's a bounty on him big enough to buy Olivetti—not that there's much left of Olivetti."

I had my summer jacket on, and I was freezing. "Why is it so damn cold in here?"

"That's climate change," said Massimo. "Not in *this* Italy—in *your* Italy. In your Italy, you've got a messed-up climate. In this Italy, it's the *human race* that's messed-up. Here, as soon as Chernobyl collapsed, a big French reactor blew up on the German border… and they all went for each other's throats! Here NATO and the European Union are even deader than the Warsaw Pact."

Massimo was proud to be telling me this. I drummed my fingers on the chilly tabletop. "It took you a while to find that out, did it?"

"The big transition always hinges in the 1980s," said Massimo, "because that's when we made the big breakthroughs."

"In your Italy, you mean."

"That's right. Before the 1980s, nobody understood the physics of parallel worlds… but after that transition, we could pack a zero-point energy generator into a laptop. Just boil the whole problem down into one single micro-electronic mechanical system."

"So you've got zero-point energy MEMS chips," I said.

He chewed more bread and pickle. Then he nodded.

"You've got MEMS chips and you were offering me some fucking lousy memristor? You must think I'm a real chump!"

"You're not a chump." Massimo sawed a fresh slice of bad bread. "But you're from the wrong Italy. It was your own stupid world that made you this stupid, Luca. In my Italy, you were one of the few men who could talk sense to my Dad. My Dad used to confide in you. He trusted you, he thought you were a great writer. You wrote his biography."

"'Massimo Montaldo, Senior,'" I said.

Massimo was startled. "Yeah. That's him." He narrowed his eyes. "You're not supposed to know that."

I had guessed it. A lot of news is made from good guesses.

"Tell me how you feel about that," I said, because this is always a useful question for an interviewer who has lost his way.

"I feel desperate," he told me, grinning. "Desperate! But I feel much *less* desperate here than I was when I was the spoilt-brat dope-addict son of the world's most famous scientist. Before you met me—Massimo Montaldo—had you ever heard of any 'Massimo Montaldo'?"

"No. I never did."

"That's right. I'm never in any of the other Italies. There's never any other Massimo Montaldo. I never meet another version of myself—and I never meet another version of my father, either. That's got to mean something crucial. I know it means something important."

"Yes," I told him, "that surely does mean something."

"I think," he said, "that I know what it means. It means that space and time are not just about physics and computation. It means that human beings really matter in the course of world events. It means that human beings can truly change the world. It means that our actions have consequence."

"The human angle," I said, "always makes a good story."

"It's true. But try telling that story," he said, and he looked on the point of tears. "Tell that story to any human being. Go on, do it! Tell anybody in here! Help yourself."

I looked around the Elena. There were some people in there, the local customers, normal people, decent people, maybe a dozen of them. Not remarkable people, not freakish, not weird or strange, but normal. Being normal people, they were quite at ease with their lot and accepting their daily existences.

Once upon a time, the Elena used to carry daily newspapers. Newspapers were supplied for customers on those special long wooden bars.

In my world, the Elena didn't do that anymore. Too few newspapers, and too much Internet.

Here the Elena still had those newspapers on those handy wooden bars. I rose from my chair and I had a good look at them. There were stylish imported newspapers, written in Hindi, Arabic and Serbo-Croatian. I had to look hard to find a local paper in Italian. There were two, both printed on a foul gray paper full of flecks of badly-pulped wood.

I took the larger Italian paper to the café table. I flicked through the headlines and I read all the lede paragraphs. I knew immediately I was reading lies.

It wasn't that the news was so terrible, or so deceitful. But it was clear that the people reading this newspaper were not expected to make any practical use of news. The Italians were a modest, colonial people. The news that they were offered was a set of feeble fantasies. All the serious news was going on elsewhere.

There was something very strong and lively in the world called the "Non-Aligned Movement." It stretched from the Baltics all the way to the Balkans, throughout the Arab world, and all the way through India. Japan and China were places that the giant Non-Aligned superpower treated with guarded respect. America was some kind of humbled farm where the Yankees spent their time in church.

Those other places, the places that used to matter—France, Germany, Britain, "Brussels"—these were obscure and poor and miserable places. Their names and locales were badly spelled.

Cheap black ink was coming off on my fingers. I no longer had questions for Massimo, except for one. "When do we get out of here?"

Massimo buttered his tattered slice of black bread. "I was never searching for the best of all possible worlds," he told me. "I was looking for the best of all possible me's. In an Italy like this Italy, I really matter. Your version of Italy is pretty backward—but *this* world had a nuclear exchange. Europe had a civil war, and most cities in the Soviet Union are big puddles of black glass."

I took my Moleskin notebook from my jacket pocket. How pretty and sleek that fancy notebook looked, next to that gray pulp newspaper. "You don't mind if I jot this down, I hope?"

"I know that this sounds bad to you—but trust me, that's not how history works. History doesn't have any 'badness' or 'goodness.' This world has a future. The food's cheap, the climate is stable, the women are gorgeous… and since there's only three billion people left alive on Earth, there's a lot of room."

Massimo pointed his crude sausage-knife at the café's glass double door. "Nobody here ever asks for ID, nobody cares about passports… They've never even heard of electronic banking! A smart guy like you, you could walk out of here and start a hundred tech companies."

"If I didn't get my throat cut."

"Oh, people always overstate that little problem! The big problem is—you know—who wants to *work* that hard? I got to know this place, because I knew that I could be a hero here. Bigger than my father. I'd be smarter than him, richer than him, more famous, more powerful. I would be better! But that is a *burden.* 'Improving the world,' that doesn't make me happy at all. That's a *curse,* it's like slavery.'"

"What *does* make you happy, Massimo?"

Clearly Massimo had given this matter some thought. "Waking up in a fine hotel with a gorgeous stranger in my bed. That's the truth! And that would be true of every man in every world, if he was honest."

Massimo tapped the neck of the garish brandy bottle with the back of the carving knife. "My girlfriend Svetlana, she understands all that pretty well, but—there's one other thing. I drink here. I like to drink, I admit that—but they *really* drink around here. This version of Italy is in the almighty Yugoslav sphere of influence."

I had been doing fine so far, given my circumstances. Suddenly the nightmare sprang upon me, unfiltered, total, and wholesale. Chills of terror climbed my spine like icy scorpions. I felt a strong, irrational, animal urge to abandon my comfortable chair and run for my life.

I could run out of the handsome café and into the twilight streets of Turin. I knew Turin, and I knew that Massimo would never find me there. Likely he wouldn't bother to look.

I also knew that I would run straight into the world so badly described by that grimy newspaper. That terrifying world would be where, henceforth, I existed. That world would not be strange to me, or strange to anybody. Because that world was reality. It was not a strange world, it was a normal world. It was I, me, who was strange here. I was desperately strange here, and that was normal.

This conclusion made me reach for my shot glass. I drank. It was not what I would call a 'good' brandy. It did have strong character. It was powerful and it was ruthless. It was a brandy beyond good and evil.

My feet ached and itched in my ruined shoes. Blisters were rising and stinging. Maybe I should consider myself lucky that my aching alien feet were still attached to my body. My feet were not simply slashed off and abandoned in some black limbo between the worlds.

I put my shot glass down. "Can we leave now? Is that possible?"

"Absolutely," said Massimo, sinking deeper into his cozy red leather chair. "Let's sober up first with a coffee, eh? It's always Arabic coffee here at the Elena. They boil it in big brass pots."

I showed him the silver coin. "No, she settled our bill for us, eh? So let's just leave."

Massimo stared at the coin, flipped it from head to tails, then slipped it in a pants pocket. "Fine. I'll describe our options. We can call this place the 'Yugoslav Italy,' and, like I said, this place has a lot of potential. But there are other versions." He started ticking off his fingers.

"There's an Italy where the 'No Nukes' movement won big in the 1980s. You remember them? Gorbachev and Reagan made world peace. Everybody disarmed and was happy. There were no more wars, the economy boomed everywhere... Peace and justice and prosperity, everywhere on Earth. So the climate exploded. The last Italian survivors are living high in the Alps."

I stared at him. "No."

"Oh yes. Yes, and those are very nice people. They really treasure and support each other. There are hardly any of them left alive. They're very sweet and civilized. They're wonderful people. You'd be amazed what nice Italians they are."

"Can't we just go straight back to my own version of Italy?"

"Not directly, no. But there's a version of Italy quite close to yours. After John Paul the First died, they quickly elected another Pope. He was not that Polish anticommunist—instead, that Pope was a pedophile. There was a colossal scandal and the Church collapsed. In that version of Italy, even the Moslems are secular. The churches are brothels and discotheques. They never use the words 'faith' or 'morality.'"

Massimo sighed, then rubbed his nose. "You might think the death of religion would make a lot of difference to people. Well, it doesn't. Because they think it's normal. They don't miss believing in God any more than you miss believing in Marx."

"So first we can go to that Italy, and then nearby into my own Italy—is that the idea?"

"That Italy is boring! The girls there are boring! They're so matter-of-fact about sex there that they're like girls from Holland." Massimo shook his head ruefully. "Now I'm going to tell you about a version of Italy that's truly different and interesting."

I was staring at a round of the sausage. The bright piece of gristle in it seemed to be the severed foot of some small animal. "All right, Massimo, tell me."

"Whenever I move from world to world, I always materialize in the Piazza Vittorio Veneto," he said, "because that plaza is so huge and usually pretty empty, and I don't want to hurt anyone with the explosion. Plus, I know Torino—I know all the tech companies here, so I can make my way around. But once I saw a Torino with no electronics."

I wiped clammy sweat from my hands with the café's rough cloth napkin. "Tell me, Massimo, how did you feel about that?"

"It's incredible. There's no electricity there. There's no wires for the electrical trolleys. There are plenty of people there, very well-dressed, and bright colored lights, and some things are flying in the sky… big aircraft, big as ocean-liners. So they've got some kind of power there—but it's not electricity. They stopped using electricity, somehow. Since the 1980s."

"A Turin with no electricity," I repeated, to convince him that I was listening.

"Yeah, that's fascinating, isn't it? How could Italy abandon electricity and replace it with another power source? I think that they use cold-fusion! Because cold fusion was another world-changing event from the 1980s. I can't explore that Torino—because where would I plug in my laptop? But you could find out how they do all that! Because you're just a journalist, right? All you need is a pencil!"

"I'm not a big expert on physics," I said.

"My God, I keep forgetting I'm talking to somebody from the hopeless George Bush World," he said. "Listen, stupid: physics isn't complicated. Physics is very simple and elegant, because it's *structured*. I knew that from the age of three."

"I'm just a writer, I'm not a scientist."

"Well, surely you've heard of 'consilience.'"

"No. Never."

"Yes you have! Even people in your stupid world know about 'consilience.' Consilience means that all forms of human knowledge have an underlying unity!"

The gleam in his eyes was tiring me. "Why does that matter?"

"It makes all the difference between your world and my world! In your world there was a great physicist once… Dr. Italo Calvino."

"Famous literary writer," I said, "he died in the 1980s."

"Calvino didn't die in my Italy," he said. "Because in my Italy, Italo Calvino completed his 'Six Core Principles.'"

"Calvino wrote 'Six Memos,'" I said. "He wrote 'Six Memos for the Next Millennium.' And he only finished five of those before he had a stroke and died."

"In my world Calvino did not have a stroke. He had a stroke of genius, instead. When Calvino completed his work, those six lectures weren't just 'memos'. He delivered six major public addresses at Princeton. When Calvino gave that sixth, great, final speech, on 'Consistency,' the halls were crammed with physicists. Mathematicians, too. My father was there."

I took refuge in my notebook. "Six Core Principles," I scribbled hastily, "Calvino, Princeton, consilience."

"Calvino's parents were both scientists," Massimo insisted. "Calvino's brother was also a scientist. His Oulipo literary group was obsessed with mathematics. When Calvino delivered lectures worthy of a genius, nobody was surprised."

"I knew Calvino was a genius," I said. I'd been young, but you can't write in Italian and not know Calvino. I'd seen him trudging the porticoes in Turin, hunch-shouldered, slapping his feet, always looking sly and preoccupied. You only had see the man to know that he had an agenda like no other writer in the world.

"When Calvino finished his six lectures," mused Massimo, "they carried him off to CERN in Geneva and they made him work on the 'Semantic Web.' The Semantic Web works beautifully, by the way. It's not like your foul little Internet—so full of spam and crime." He wiped the sausage knife on an oil-stained napkin. "I should qualify that remark. The Semantic Web works beautifully—*in the Italian language*. Because the Semantic Web was built by Italians. They had a little bit of help from a few French Oulipo writers."

"Can we leave this place now? And visit this Italy you boast so much about? And then drop by my Italy?"

"That situation is complicated," Massimo hedged, and stood up. "Watch my bag, will you?"

He then departed to the toilet, leaving me to wonder about all the ways in which our situation could be complicated.

Now I was sitting alone, staring at that corked brandy bottle. My brain was boiling. The strangeness of my situation had broken some important throttle inside my head.

I considered myself bright—because I could write in three languages, and I understood technical matters. I could speak to engineers, designers, programmers, venture capitalists and government officials on serious, adult issues that we all agreed were important. So, yes, surely I was bright.

But I'd spent my whole life being far more stupid than I was at this moment.

In this terrible extremity, here in the cigarette-choked Elena, where the half-ragged denizens pored over their grimy newspapers, I knew I possessed a true potential for genius. I was Italian, and, being Italian, I had the knack to shake the world to its roots. My genius had never embraced me, because genius had never been required of me. I had been stupid because I dwelled in a stupefied world.

I now lived in no world at all. I had no world. So my thoughts were rocketing through empty space.

Ideas changed the world. Thoughts changed the world—and thoughts could be written down. I had forgotten that writing could have such urgency, that writing could matter to history, that literature might have consequence. Strangely, tragically, I'd forgotten that such things were even possible.

Calvino had died of a stroke: I knew that. Some artery broke inside the man's skull as he gamely struggled with his manifesto to transform the next millennium. Surely that was a great loss, but how could anybody guess the extent of that loss? A stroke of genius is a black swan, beyond prediction, beyond expectation. If a black swan never arrives, how on Earth could its absence be guessed?

The chasm between Massimo's version of Italy and my Italy was invisible—yet all-encompassing. It was exactly like the stark difference between the man I was now, and the man I'd been one short hour ago.

A black swan can never be predicted, expected, or categorized. A black swan, when it arrives, cannot even be recognized as a black swan. When the black swan assaults us, with the wingbeats of some rapist Jupiter, then we must rewrite history.

Maybe a newsman writes a news story, which is history's first draft.

Yet the news never shouts that history has black swans. The news never tells us that our universe is contingent, that our fate hinges on changes too huge for us to comprehend, or too small for us to see. We can never accept the black swan's arbitrary carelessness. So our news is never about how the news can make no sense to human beings. Our news is always about how well we understand.

Whenever our wits are shattered by the impossible, we swiftly knit the world back together again, so that our wits can return to us. We pretend that we've lost nothing, not one single illusion. Especially, certainly, we never lose our minds. No matter how strange the news is, we're always sane and sensible. That is what we tell each other.

Massimo returned to our table. He was very drunk, and he looked greenish.

"You ever been in a squat-down Turkish toilet?" he said, pinching his nose. "Trust me, don't go in there."

"I think we should go to your Italy now," I said.

"I could do that," he allowed idly, "although I've made some trouble for myself there... my real problem is you."

"Why am I trouble?"

"There's another Luca in my Italy. He's not like you, because he's a great author, and a very dignified and very wealthy man. He wouldn't find you funny."

I considered this. He was inviting me to be bitterly jealous of myself. I couldn't manage that, yet I was angry anyway. "Am I funny, Massimo?"

He'd stopped drinking, but that killer brandy was still percolating through his gut.

"Yes, you're funny, Luca. You're weird. You're a terrible joke. Especially in this version of Italy. And especially now that you're finally catching on. You've got a look on your face now like a drowned fish." He belched into his fist. "Now, at last, you think that you understand, but no, you don't. Not yet. Listen, in order to arrive here—I *created* this world. When I press the Function-Three key, and the field transports me here—without me as the observer, this universe doesn't even exist."

I glanced around the thing that Massimo called a universe. It was an Italian café. The marble table in front of me was every bit as solid as a rock. Everything around me was very solid, normal, realistic, acceptable and predictable.

"Of course," I told him. "And you also created my universe, too. Because you're not just a black swan. You're God."

"'Black swan,' is that what you call me?" He smirked, and preened in the mirror. "You journalists need a tag-line for everything."

"You always wear black," I said. "Does that keep our dirt from showing?"

Massimo buttoned his black woolen jacket. "It gets worse," he told me. "When I press that Function-Two key, before the field settles in... I generate millions of potential histories. Billions of histories. All with their souls, ethics, thoughts, histories, destinies—whatever. Worlds blink into existence for a few nanoseconds while the chip runs through the program—and then they all blink out. As if they never were."

"That's how you move? From world to world?"

"That's right, my friend. This ugly duckling can fly."

The Elena's waiter arrived to tidy up our table. "A little rice pudding?" he asked.

Massimo was cordial. "No, thank you, sir."

"Got some very nice chocolate in this week! All the way from South America."

"My, that's the very best kind of chocolate." Massimo jabbed his hand into a cargo pocket. "I believe I need some chocolate. What will you give me for this?"

The waiter examined it carefully. "This is a woman's engagement ring."

"Yes, it is."

"It can't be a real diamond, though. This stone's much too big to be a real diamond."

"You're an idiot," said Massimo, "but I don't care much. I've got a big appetite for sweets. Why don't you bring me an entire chocolate pie?"

The waiter shrugged and left us.

"So," Massimo resumed, "I wouldn't call myself a 'God'—because I'm much better described as several million billion Gods. Except, you know, that the zero-point transport field always settles down. Then, here I am. I'm standing outside some café, in a cloud of dirt, with my feet aching. With nothing to my name, except what I've got in my brain and my pockets. It's always like that."

The door of the Elena banged open, with the harsh jangle of brass Indian bells. A gang of five men stomped in. I might have taken them for cops, because they had jackets, belts, hats, batons and pistols, but Turinese cops do not arrive on duty drunk. Nor do they wear scarlet armbands with crossed lightning bolts.

The café fell silent as the new guests muscled up to the dented bar. Bellowing threats, they proceeded to shake-down the staff.

Massimo turned up his collar and gazed serenely at his knotted hands. Massimo was studiously minding his own business. He was in his corner, silent, black, inexplicable. He might have been at prayer.

I didn't turn to stare at the intruders. It wasn't a pleasant scene, but even for a stranger, it wasn't hard to understand.

The door of the men's room opened. A short man in a trenchcoat emerged. He had a dead cigar clenched in his teeth, and a snappy Alain Delon fedora.

He was surprisingly handsome. People always underestimated the good looks, the male charm of Nicolas Sarkozy. Sarkozy sometimes seemed a little odd when sunbathing half-naked in newsstand tabloids, but in person, his charisma was overwhelming. He was a man that any world had to reckon with.

Sarkozy glanced about the café for a matter of seconds. Then he sidled, silent and decisive, along the dark mahogany wall. He bent one elbow. There was a thunderclap. Massimo pitched face-forward onto the small marble table.

Sarkozy glanced with mild chagrin at the smoking hole blown through the pocket of his stylish trenchcoat. Then he stared at me.

"You're that journalist," he said.

"You've got a good memory for faces, Monsieur Sarkozy."

"That's right, asshole, I do." His Italian was bad, but it was better than my French. "Are you still eager to 'protect' your dead source here?" Sarkozy gave Massimo's heavy chair one quick, vindictive kick, and the dead man, and his chair, and his table, and his ruined, gushing head all fell to the hard café floor with one complicated clatter.

"There's your big scoop of a story, my friend," Sarkozy told me. "I just gave that to you. You should use that in your lying commie magazine."

Then he barked orders at the uniformed thugs. They grouped themselves around him in a helpful cluster, their faces pale with respect.

"You can come out now, baby," crowed Sarkozy, and she emerged from the men's room. She was wearing a cute little gangster-moll hat, and a tailored camouflage jacket. She lugged a big black guitar case. She also had a primitive radio-telephone bigger than a brick.

How he'd enticed that women to lurk for half an hour in the reeking café toilet, that I'll never know. But it was her. It was definitely her, and she couldn't have been any more demure and serene if she were meeting the Queen of England.

They all left together in one heavily armed body.

The thunderclap inside the Elena had left a mess. I rescued Massimo's leather valise from the encroaching pool of blood.

My fellow patrons were bemused. They were deeply bemused, even confounded. Their options for action seemed to lack constructive possibilities.

So, one by one, they rose and left the bar. They left that fine old place, silently and without haste, and without meeting each other's eyes. They stepped out the jangling door and into Europe's biggest plaza.

Then they vanished, each hastening toward his own private world.

I strolled into the piazza, under a pleasant spring sky. It was cold, that spring night, but that infinite dark blue sky was so lucid and clear.

The laptop's screen flickered brightly as I touched the F1 key. Then I pressed 2, and then 3.

AS WOMEN FIGHT
SARA GENGE

In addition to working as a doctor in Madrid, Sara Genge writes speculative fiction for the sleepless mind. Her work has appeared in *Strange Horizons*, *Cosmos Magazine*, *Weird Tales*, *Shimmer Magazine* among others, including translations into Greek, Czech and Spanish. "As Women Fight" is her fourth story in *Asimov's* and continues a trend in stories dealing with gender that began with "Prayers for an Egg" and "Shoes-to-Run" (both also published in *Asimov's*) and which is not over.

Merthe stands next to the felled doe and casts a worried look at the sky. He's aching to train for Fight. Between hunting and setting traps, he hasn't trained for a fortnight, but it's too late and he's too far from home. He hoists the doe on his shoulder and heads back. Snow crunches like starch under his boots, reminding him of when he was a young woman and knew a dozen names for snow, all stolen from the dessert section of a cookbook. Whipped cream, soufflé, eggnog with a crisp burnt crust…

The doe is small and Ita will complain. She trusts Merthe only when she can see what he's accomplished in a day's work. She'll want proof that he hasn't been lazing around, or worse, training for Fight. As if he's ever neglected to feed the family. As if he'd ever put his own future before theirs. He swears under his breath. Five years as a man is too much to bear and he vows he will not lose the Fight again even if it means training every waking hour that he isn't hunting.

When he gets home, the children run to him shouting. He lets them tug at his beard, tries to hug them all at once. He senses them drifting away. No matter that he can still feel them tugging at his breasts. He is either the figure of authority, or the gentle giant. The clown. They come to him to play, but if the wound is deep, it is to their mother that they run to.

"Did you hunt at all?" Ita asks.

He nods but says no more. He's been a man so long that this flesh has imprinted its own ways into his mind. Male silence comes easy these days; he revels in communication by grunts—or kisses. He knows how much it enrages her; he sometimes tries to be more verbal. But not now. Anything that'll annoy her may throw her off her game. She's won five years in a row. He needs all the help

285

he can get.

He winks at the children and nods towards the shed. They run off, bringing back the doe between the six of them, the toddlers contributing by getting in the way. Serga doesn't go with them; shei is the eldest, almost ten. Merthe sometimes wonders if shei still remembers heir first mother, still remembers Merthe in Ita's body. He fears shei doesn't: shei was so young when Ita and he swapped places. And yet, Serga stares at him with understanding, a look of pity even. Merthe shivers.

Ita hurries about and Merthe lets her serve him. In the warmth of the winter hut, the children quickly lose their wraps. Merthe's clothes crack open like a husk, revealing thawing feet and a wide chest that has lost its summer tan. He looks upon Ita to do the same and finally, she obliges. She's gained some weight since she took over that body. Her arms are rich and soft but Merthe isn't fooled: he knows firsthand the damage they can inflict in combat. She bounces about, all hips and breasts, and the toddlers stare at her as if she were food, following her with eyes and mouths round as "O"s. Merthe lets his eyes roam her body, disguising one desire for the other. Ah, to be in those hips again. Yeah gods, to inhabit them! There's bounce to her skin and the marks of pregnancy stretch proud across her tummy. Some of them, Merthe put there when he bore Serga and Ramir.

She serves him and leans forward to whisper in his ear.

"Like what you see? Enjoy. You're not getting back in here any time soon."

He grabs her by the waist and tumbles her, eats her mouth, lets her feel the weight of his body on hers. The strength. She gasps in surprise and the children laugh. They're still androgens, and too young to read beneath the surface and into the hidden struggle between man and wife.

She giggles with them, making Merthe's ribs jiggle against hers. He lets her sit up—the children are awake—and nibbles her ear.

"I'll be in there in no time, darling," he says. He doesn't specify what exactly he means by that.

The weeks before Fight come and go so fast that Merthe wonders if he's growing old. Time always seems to speed up the further along you go. Three days before the match, Elgir walks up to the hut at dawn. He's their closest neighbor but Merthe doesn't know him that well. The People don't gather too close. Hunters need their space and the gender arrangement makes for frequent domestic fighting. Nobody likes to live close to noisy neighbors.

Merthe crawls out to meet him without disturbing Ita. The two men step inside the shed, neither knowing what to say.

Merthe offers Elgir a cup of tea.

"You'd make a good woman," Elgir says.

Merthe grunts at the compliment. "Yes, I did make a good wife."

"Ah yes, I forgot. The first two are yours, aren't they?"

It takes Merthe a second to realize Elgir means the children. Merthe nods to hide his shame. It seems impossible that he can't reclaim that body. And the whole village knows how much he wants it. He damns himself. It would not matter so much if he could appear not to care.

"Don't beat yourself up. She's so good she's scary," Elgir says.

Elgir himself has little to fear. He can easily defeat his partner, Samo. She's a small woman and not too fast. She's only been in a woman's body for a year and relied so much on muscle when she was a man that she never mastered technique. Looking at Elgir, Merthe understands how someone inhabiting that body could grow complacent. The man could fell a tree with a backhand cuff.

"How are things at home?" Merthe asks. It must be hard on Samo, knowing that she's going to lose. Elgir made a stunning fighter as a woman. The litheness that is Samo's bane was an advantage when Elgir was in control. Merthe remembers a particularly impressive kick roll in which a female Elgir was too fast for the eye. Merthe misses that lightness. Some days, he trudges around with the grace of a bear.

"Samo doesn't want to lose," Elgir replies.

"Who does?" says Merthe.

Elgir's eyes hold Merthe's for a second. "Some do. Some like being men. Some don't care either way," Elgir says.

Merthe blushes; nobody can judge another person's likes or dislikes, but some things are rarely said in public. Both men look down.

"The moss is thick this winter," Elgir says.

"Yes. It'll get cold fast."

It is so quiet, Merthe can hear the snow fall.

"Say, how about we hunt together. If we get something big, we can split. We can keep the women happy and still have time to train," Elgir suggests.

Merthe knows Ita will disapprove, so he grabs his things and goes with Elgir before she can object.

They spot a squirrelee wallowing up the dikes to get from pond to pond. It digs the snow with its front paws for nuts hidden the previous season. It's only as big as Eme, Merthe's youngest, but Merthe knows that most of its flesh is fat, good for thickening stews. It's a worthy catch, even if the women will complain about getting only half.

But when the time comes to cast his spear, Elgir freezes up. It's no time for questions so Merthe shoots his arrow through air that tastes like sugared ice. The squirrelee falls.

Elgir goes ahead to retrieve it. Merthe wonders at the man's hesitation.

"Nice shot," Elgir says. He punches Merthe on the shoulder. "They say you cannot forget how to be a man anymore than you can forget how to suckle," Elgir says, "but I seem to forget every single time. One year is not enough to relearn it all. I was female for so long before that…"

Merthe remembers. Elgir only lost last season because she caught the bluing cold. She barely escaped with her life—losing the Fight was a small thing compared to that. Everyone still wonders why Samo and Elgir didn't postpone their fight until after her recovery. Was Samo really that desperate to win?

"Then why is it that you wish to remain a man?" Merthe asks. It is a bold question and he hopes he is not mistaken. But intuition isn't just a woman's gift.

"It's not that…" Elgir says. Silence rings off the dusted pines. The men find a clearing and unpack their cheese-and-bread. The cheese has no smell. Merthe sniffs it, licks it.

"It's good," Elgir says.

"Yes. I wish I could taste it like she… like they… like the women do," Merthe says.

"Wouldn't make much difference. Smell's all that counts towards taste. This cheese tastes good because it has a hot bite to it, but the smell is rather bland. Trust me. I remember."

"But Ita says—"

"Ita is pulling your leg. This cheese has no smell."

Merthe curses Ita and tucks in. Sometimes he wonders why he wants to be a woman so much, since he can't even remember what it was like. But he's kidding himself. Even if he can't remember the particulars, the overall impression remains. He recalls that first year after he defeated his first partner. Smells so much more vivid, skin so fine that it could feel the gentlest summer breeze, the touch of the sun… He knows of men and women down south who never change bodies. They are content to live their whole lives as one sex. Sometimes, in his darkest moments, Merthe wants to do likewise. If those men manage, why can't he?

But those men have the blessing of ignorance. They do not know what it is like to feel their bellies grow full. They do not understand the transforming pain of childbirth, the draining of milk from the nipple. The real smell of onion as it cooks.

"What is it then?" he asks. He's suddenly angry at Elgir, for taking this so lightly.

"I like being a woman," Elgir concedes. "I also like being a man. I like changing from one to the other. If you think about it, that's how all of this started, right? We swap bodies the better to understand each other's minds. We were meant to be balanced, equal. That's why our women are faster than the eye and stronger than the ones down South. It makes us even. Swapping bodies was never meant to cause strife."

"Interesting theological argument. Maybe if we pray hard enough, we can all be women. What do you think?"

Elgir snorts half-frozen milk up his nose. His eyes tear and he laughs, but Merthe wonders if he's not also crying.

"It doesn't matter which body you're in. Sure, it's great to be a woman for the first few months after a transition, but after a while you simply get used to it and you don't make use of all those fantastic senses you're supposed to have. Senses work by comparison, if all of your passions are strong, they fade against each other as certainly as if they're all weak. That's why swapping frequently makes sense. That way you can renew the strong feelings often and spend enough time as a man to learn to appreciate the subtler pleasures too."

"What does Samo think of that?"

"She thinks I'm full of worm shit," Elgir says.

They burst out laughing.

Suddenly, Elgir stops laughing and starts crying. Men's tears, quiet, no fuss. But he doesn't try to hide them. Merthe wishes they were women so that they could hug each other and cry and then laugh at their silliness. He loves the way Ita's tears are unapologetic and arbitrary. They come and go like a morning sprinkle over nothing or they storm out and make him wish he'd never been born. Women have practice with crying. They communicate with tears. Men just sit there and cry.

But Elgir seeks him out to finish the last shudders in his arms.

"What is it?" Merthe asks.

"Samo doesn't like being a man."

"Neither do I. She'll just have to get used to—"

Elgir shuts his eyes and shakes his head.

"What is it? What is it?" Merthe asks.

"She doesn't take well to being a man. Not at all. She… he… is angry… all the time."

It sounds worse than just an argument. Merthe doesn't understand. "Why didn't you leave?" he asks.

But Merthe knows why he hasn't left. He hasn't left for the same reasons that Merthe hasn't divorced Ita. He thought things would get better. He hoped for change. The children stay with the mother…

"What exactly is it that she… he… does?"

"He's violent." Elgir bursts out crying and Merthe is confused. Even in a man's body, Samo is no match for Elgir. It makes no sense that Samo could batter Elgir. "It's not me she hurts," Elgir wails and, now, Merthe realizes he's crying from shame.

"The children. As a man, he hit Tine and Vis," Merthe says.

"That's why I let him win last winter. I thought once she was a woman again, it would all be over. It helped, at first. But last night, I saw a bruise on Tine's arm. The kid swears shei fell off a tree, but both of them are awfully quiet when their mother is around. Maybe I'm imagining things."

"She's still hitting them?" Merthe asks. "What are you doing here? What are you doing leaving them alone with her!" He stands up and paces, trying to decide whether to hit Elgir or run back towards his neighbor's house to save those children from their mother.

Elgir grabs Merthe's arm but Merthe wrenches it away. "How could you let that happen?" Merthe shouts. "You could have gone to the elders. Left without their approval, even. Stolen the children—whatever it took! How could you? How could you?" He hoists his bag on his back and heads home, forgetting the squirrelee. Elgir runs after him. When Merthe doesn't stop, Elgir tackles him to the ground.

"Stop. Listen." Merthe stops struggling, less from the command as from the finality of a man twice his size pinning him to the ground.

"I'll save those kids, I promise you. I'll keep them safe from Samo if it's the last thing I do! But I'd rather do it smart. You know how the elders are, they'll argue and fret for months before reaching a decision and in the meantime, the kids will be alone with Samo. An angry Samo. A Samo who's been humiliated in public. I have failed them as a father and as a mother, but I won't compound one mistake with another."

Elgir stops pressing down quite so hard, but he doesn't let go. Both men sit up, hands on each other's arms. It's not a fight grip but it would take no effort to turn it into one.

"What are you going to do, then?" Merthe asks.

"I will win. I will win and leave, and I'll take the children with me."

Merthe lets go, sits back on the snow. As much as he hates the idea of Tine and Vis spending the next week alone at home with Samo, he realizes Elgir's way is best. As soon as he takes back his woman body, he'll be entitled to take the children where he pleases. Merthe tries not to feel sorry for Samo: she birthed them both.

"Do you know where you're going to go? Do you have family to help you out?" he asks.

"I'll worry about that later."

Merthe promises himself that he'll take food from his own mouth before Elgir's children go hungry. He's a strong hunter; he can hunt for two households. Ita will just have to accept it.

It's only later, back at home, that he realizes that he doesn't plan on being the hunter for the coming year.

Serga comes out to meet him at the door and it takes Merthe a moment to figure out why this surprises him. Serga hasn't been at the door with the other children for a while. The kid is too old to puppy around heir father.

Serga wants something. Heir eyes are impatient for Merthe to dispose of his hunting gear and head towards the shed to clean the squirrelee. Shei doesn't even cast a sidelong glance at the half-carcass, even though heir scathing looks are usually as incisive (and effective) as heir mother's.

Merthe takes off his coat and starts skinning. Serga stares on until Merthe motions towards the belly of the animal. There's enough work for two.

Serga hesitates and Merthe wonders if he has insulted the child by offering heir man's work. After all, no woman will touch an animal until it's clean and adolescents like to pretend they're women. But Serga takes heir own blade from heir apron and settles down in front of Merthe.

"It's happened," Serga whispers. "It's arrived."

Merthe hides his surprise and looks Serga up and down discretely. Yes, there's an adult's budding body under the wraps. He hadn't expected it to happen so soon, but he'd always known his children would have to grow up. Serga isn't too young for her first bleeding.

"Have you told your mother?" Merthe asks, and regrets it. Serga has come to him, not Ita. He mustn't push heir away.

Shei shakes heir head.

"The other thing too? Or is it just your period?" Some adolescents don't have erections until a couple of years after their first bleeding.

Serga winces; Merthe is too blunt. He tries not to smile.

"The other thing… I think so."

Merthe grunts his understanding and waits.

"What do I do now!" Serga throws the knife to the ground. It rattles against the floorboards and shei looks up, scared. You don't treat a good knife like that. But Merthe gets up, wipes the knife on his pants and hands it back to Serga without scolding.

"You don't have to fight this season, or even the next. You can still be our child for a little longer, if that's all right with you," he whispers and places his hand on heir shoulder.

Serga nods and clasps heir apron.

"But why do I have to Fight at all? Why can't I just stay like this always?"

"Fighting is fun. You'll come to enjoy it," he says.

"What if I can't? What if I'm really bad? What if—"

"It's okay to lose."

"Mother says—"

"Your mother is very gifted woman, but in some things, she acts like an idiot." Merthe wonders if those words are his, or Elgir's. "She's so proud of winning that she pretends that losing is a big deal. You're going to win some years and lose some years and, either way, you're going to be happy. You're going to love your children and your spouse. You're going to enjoy good food and soft clothes. The differences are there, but the things that matter remain the same."

It's a white lie but the words spring from his mouth with such a force that Merthe wonders if they aren't true.

Elgir and Samo are the first to Fight each season and their combat casts a long shadow on everyone else's match. Merthe wonders what Fight will be like when Elgir and Samo are no longer the item leading the way.

Their combat is short; Elgir seems too sad to care about putting on a good show. Samo comes at him in a blur and the men in the crowd gasp, always surprised at how fast a woman can move.

Samo has learned from previous failures. She never sits still and blows punctuate her every motion. Elgir stands still and takes them, face flat as granite. Merthe wonders if he plans to win through attrition.

Suddenly, his arm shoots out and he catches Samo across the chest. They crash down, Elgir breaking their fall so that Samo lands almost softly, cocooned inside his arms.

He holds her much longer than necessary, after the bell has rung, after the cheering is over. He holds her after Samo has stopped thrashing in anger and frustration, after the children stop hollering. It is their final embrace and Elgir makes it last. This is how Elgir loves, fervently. Even after the unthinkable, he cannot bear to let go.

When the crowd is no longer interested, Elgir presses his palm against Samo's and Merthe can feel his own pores opening up in sympathy, the clever little soul-holes through which bodies are exchanged. It only lasts a second but Merthe knows that those two feel their minds entwined into eternity.

And then it's done, and Samo in his new male body pushes Elgir away so hard that Merthe winces. Elgir stands up, wearing that body with a grace Samo could never muster. She nods her head, a last goodbye, and whistles for the children. By now, even Samo must know they won't be coming home tonight.

That evening, Merthe arrives home with half a nme bird. There's hardly any meat on it and Ita will have to add some sausage to thicken the stew, but nobody will go hungry, not Ita and the children, not Elgir and hers. Sometimes you're lucky, sometimes you aren't. That's the way hunting goes.

When Ita sees the bird she blanches, and Merthe braces for a harangue on hunting and responsibility. But Ita is too angry to bait or mock. Merthe has never seen her like this. She storms back into the house while Merthe goes to the shed to clean the bird.

Dinner is silent and Ita hustles the children to bed long before their bedtime. One of the younger ones whimpers, but Serga cuts heir short with a pinch which Merthe pretends not to see. He's too exhausted to fight heir too.

"Who is she?" Ita whispers after the children are in their bunks.

"What?"

"Don't play games with me, Merthe, who's the woman you keep bringing meat to. Taking it from your children's mouth!"

Merthe laughs "It's not… I'm not…"

"Don't go telling me you hunted with Elgir again! She's a woman now, Samo can hunt for her. I don't know why I believed you the first time, men hunt alone, but I was so trusting—"

"What is it that really bothers you, Ita? Me with another woman or your stupid pantry? It's bursting at the edges, for every gods' sake. You give food away else it rot before we can eat it! Is that what I am to you? The oaf who keeps your stomach full?"

Ita opens her mouth, but manages only a gurgle. She grabs her coat. Polar winter sweeps into the house as she opens the door. The cold steals the breath from his mouth; the sharpness from his brain. It takes him a second to react and take off after her, wrapped only in his sleeping blanket.

The snow outside is knee-deep and she isn't wearing shoes. He scoops her up from a drift and drapes her across his shoulders. She doesn't resist.

"You idiot, don't you see I do it for you?" she wails in his ear over the wind. "Everyone knows you're such a good hunter that I have food to spare. My mother, the neighbors… As long as my pantry is full, nobody can question us or our marriage. Whenever those hags at the market start gossiping about how I should find a stronger Fighter, I give them meat, pelts. That shuts them up. They don't talk, at least not to my face."

Merthe pushes the door open and stomps his feet until he feels them. He doesn't know what to think, much less what to say. He puts Ita down and goes to fetch the liquor. More than half the bottle is missing. He stares pointedly at Ita.

"Don't look at me. I think Serga has started drinking behind my back." She sounds annoyed, but not terribly worried. Adolescents will be adolescents. It's hard to figure out one's body when one is so new to it, especially when one is neither a man nor a woman, but a compendium of impulses with no way to work them off. Merthe's lips twitch as he remembers his own childhood.

"There is no woman, Ita." He sits next to her by the hearth. "Samo and Elgir have broken up. I promised Elgir that her children wouldn't starve. I'm hunting for them for now, at least until Elgir finds a man. That shouldn't take long."

"Can't Samo hunt for them? He has a responsibility towards those children!"

"Samo isn't going to be hunting. Elgir can hunt small game by herself, but not with the children tagging along."

"Really? You must be exaggerating. I can't think of a man who'll visit his children and not bring something…"

"Samo isn't setting foot in Elgir's house."

"Well that's just wrong! I can understand being angry, but keeping a man from his children—"

"You don't know the half of it!" Merthe sets the glass down and frowns: he hadn't intended to shout. "It's bad, Ita, it's really bad."

"Then tell me," she says. *You never tell me anything.* After so long, Merthe hears the words even when she doesn't utter them.

"Samo hits the kids." That gets her attention. He explains in as few words as he can, glad that she's finally decided to shut up and listen.

"Those poor kids. Those poor poor kids," she says.

Merthe tries to explain how angry he is at Elgir for letting it happen.

"You can't judge. You don't know what Elgir was going through at the time…"

"And you do?" Surely, this isn't about him!

"Of course not." She puts a cool hand on his forehead. Despite how angry he is, she soothes him. Ita and he work best together when they do not speak. He wonders why it can't always be like that. A life in silence. Sometimes, his reticence to speak is just that, a desire for this quiet companionship. It is only with words that they hate each other.

When his time to Fight comes, Merthe tells himself the outcome doesn't really matter. He tells himself the same lies he told Serga, trying to believe them with a child's fervor. He fastens his boots and sets out.

A crowd is waiting for him. As he approaches, Elgir joins him, arriving at the square from the left. They walk the last stretch together, Elgir's children trailing from her skirt.

"How are things going?" Merthe asks.

"I should be the one asking that!" Elgir laughs. "Are you afraid?"

"No." Surprisingly, it's the truth. He's too wound up to be scared. "Do you still believe what you said in the forest the other day? Do you still think it's such a good idea to swap bodies from time to time? Or has that precious woman's body changed your mind?"

Elgir laughs. "Oh, yes, I believe it. We are trapped inside these bodies. We've learned since childhood that women do this or that and we never dare to break free of that mold. We're as pitiful as the men and women down South, who only know one way of living, except that we don't have the excuse of ignorance. But hell, it does feel good to sniff my children with this nose again. I'll grant you that." She turns sharply and her children squeal and take off. Obviously, "smelling the children" is a game with them.

They turn into the square where a dozen men cheer when they see Merthe. Merthe turns around but she nods at him to go. She's got her arms full of toddler.

"Do your best." Her face looks pinched. Merthe realizes that if he wins, she will lose her hunter.

He salutes each of the four metallic pillars that mark the Fighting ground. They are made from the remnants of a ship that brought the People here from the sky. Or so the elders say. It seems impossible that people should sail through air. It is true, however, that bodies may only be exchanged within their embrace and only after Fight. Years ago, Merthe and Ita, like all newlyweds, spent some time trying to game the rules and learned that the only result was temporary impotence and a headache that lasted for hours.

On a whim, he jumps into the Fighting square and seeks out Ita before combat begins. He stares at the judge, dares him to object, and takes Ita to the side.

"Are you nervous?" he asks.

She looks at him suspiciously. He sighs, takes her hand and brings the palm to his lips. Her eyes lighten up.

"It's just a game, Ita."

"Maybe it is to you. That's why you always lose."

He lets go of her hand, turns to the crowd. People are coming from villages that he hasn't even been to. He wishes he could confide in Ita, but everything he says will be used against him.

"I'm worried about Elgir," he blurts. "Who will hunt for her when I'm a woman?"

Ita smiles. She thinks it's banter. "I think you'll be able to keep her in meat and gravy for a while yet."

"Really? You would not object?"

"Are you serious?"

It's no use. He heads towards his corner and starts preparing.

Roll of drums; the combatants step up to the judge. Merthe wonders whether he should try to imitate Elgir. Maybe he can just take Ita's hits and try to snatch an advantage when he sees it. Surely, it would be a lot less tiresome that fighting. He is so tired of fighting all the time.

But then he realizes that this is Fight, not just any fight. His verbal skills do not matter and since combatants must remain silent, Ita's wit cannot hurt him inside the ring. Suddenly, he feels protected by those four pillars. He has a good half hour of silence ahead of him, maybe an hour if he can make the fight last. He yearns for intimacy without the burden of words. And there is nothing more intimate than violence.

The drums are still and the crowd holds its breath. Ita starts bouncing and jabbing, trying to circle around him and hit him when he blinks. She moves fast—always a good strategy for a woman—and attempts to bring him down with repeated blows.

Her first hit catches him unawares and he staggers back. No, Elgir's strategy won't work. There is blood in his mouth. He's supposed to hold still, he knows. Maybe feint a bit, watch for patterns and fell her with one decisive blow. Those same muscles that lend force to his blows suck up his energy. Unlike Ita, he cannot jump around forever. He is supposed to preserve his strength, not to commit, strike only when he can win.

But he is so tired of doing what he's supposed to and maybe Elgir is right and we get caught up in patterns, live life within patterns, pushing ourselves beyond our limits because a man should lift that much, throw that far. And maybe, just maybe, Merthe realizes, we do the opposite and fall pitifully short because we've been told our bodies have less endurance that our wife's.

Merthe starts bouncing. His feet know the way. Women fight like they dance, his mother taught him, and he was always such a good dancer.

Ita's rhythm lets up in surprise and he jabs, but she ducks in time and starts bouncing again. He loves her technique and mirrors her as they spin round and round. Merthe is the ugly sibling, echoing heir elder's every move, struggling to copy what can only be born of natural grace.

Ita doesn't know how to hit a moving target. She hasn't fought with a mobile partner for a long time.

His breath is labored; she hardly breaks a sweat. She starts sweating; the pain in his chest won't let up. She pants and swerves; his vision clouds but he sees the gap in her defense and punches through.

She crashes down and he falls right after. For a second, he wonders if she's all right. He put himself in that blow, his loves, his wants, his strengths and weaknesses. He wonders if it was too much for her. But she groans and sits up, spits blood and, of all things, laughs.

"Well, you got me there."

"I'm sorry," he says,

"Oh no, you're not. You won."

He lies back, head spinning. Yes, he won. His chest still hurts and he wonders how bad it is.

The bell rings. She crawls up against him, sets her palm against his and they're off into the limbo of joy. Her mind rises up to him. For a second, both of them are in his body and hers hangs, limp, behind. He creeps in, wondering if the beams still hold in this castle which he's left so long ago. Merthe draws a breath which is oh, so sweet. She smells the male sweat of Ita next to her.

But no. Two women need a hunter and a young androgen needs to learn that being a man isn't so bad. She pushes back into the old body. He regains control and shoves Ita into hers. She was so fond of her female form that it seems a pity to tear her from it. Plus, she made a terrible husband.

Ita tumbles away from him and he sees disbelief in her eyes.

"Really?"

"Really."

"You're leaving me! You're leaving with her!"

It takes a moment for him to understand what she's saying. But, of course, she cannot fathom why anyone would want to be a man. The only explanation that she will consider is that Merthe plans to start a new life with Elgir and that he needs a man's body for that.

"I'm not going with her." He doesn't say he's not leaving, though, because he's not quite sure what he'll do. He can support both women, but he doesn't have the strength for either. He needs time, alone, in silence. He knows just the place for that.

The judge walks up and hesitates before signaling the end of the transition. The elders squirm, then shrug their shoulders. Merthe has won: he may do as he likes.

That night, there's scratching at the door of the shed.

"Does your mother know you're here?" He asks a trembling Serga standing by the doorway.

"No. I think. I don't think so, she was asleep."

Merthe lets heir in, moves his quilts to a corner and places a stack of blankets next to the fire for heir to sleep in. Shei stomps heir feet all the way to bed, and Merthe stays awake until the shivering melts into regular breathing and only soft childish hairs peek out from beneath the covers. He'll wake heir before sunrise and make heir go back to bed inside the house. Ita mustn't know that shei's fled to him for comfort after their separation. Merthe may be too confused to know what he wants, just yet, but he doesn't want to hurt Ita. Whether he can live with her or not is a different matter. The End.

THE CINDERELLA GAME
KELLY LINK

Kelly Link published her first story, "Water Off a Black Dog's Back", in 1995 and attended the Clarion writers workshop in the same year. A writer of subtle, challenging, sometimes whimsical fantasy, Link has published close to thirty stories which have won the Hugo, Nebula, World Fantasy, British SF, and Locus awards, and which have been collected in *4 Stories*, *Stranger Things Happen*, and *Magic for Beginners*. Link is also an accomplished editor, working on acclaimed small press 'zine *Lady Churchill's Rosebud Wristlet*. She co-edited *The Year's Best Fantasy and Horror* with husband Gavin J. Grant and Ellen Datlow. Her most recent book is *Pretty Monsters*, a collection of stories for young adults.

One day Peter would have his own secret hideaway just like this one, his step-father's forbidden room, up in the finished attic: leather couches, stereo system with speakers the size of school lockers, flat screen television, and so many horror movies you'd be able to watch a different one every night of the year. The movie Peter picked turned out to be in a foreign language, but it was still pretty scary and there were werewolves in it.

"What are you doing?" someone said. Peter spilled popcorn all over the couch.

His new stepsister Darcy stood in the door that went down to the second floor. Her hair was black and knotted and stringy, and, no surprise, she was wearing one of her dozens of princess dresses. This one had been pink and spangled at one point. Now it looked like something a zombie would wear to a fancy dress party.

"What are you doing up here?" Peter saw, with fascinated horror, the greasy smears left behind on the leather as he chased popcorn back into the bowl. "Go away. Why aren't you asleep?"

His stepsister said, "Dad says I'm not allowed to watch scary movies." She'd holstered a fairy wand in the pocket of her princess gown. The battered tiara on her head was missing most of its rhinestones.

You are *a scary movie*, Peter thought. "How long have you been standing here?"

"Not long. Since the werewolf bit the other lady. You were picking your nose."

It got better and better. "If you're not allowed to watch scary movies, then what are you doing up here?"

"What are *you* doing up here?" Darcy said. "We're not supposed to watch television up here without an adult. Why aren't you in bed? Where's Mrs. Daly?"

"She had to go home. Somebody called and said her husband was in the hospital. Mom hasn't come back yet," Peter said. "So I'm in charge until they get home. She and your dad are still out on their we-won't-go-on-a-honeymoon-we'll just-have-a-mini-honeymoon-every-Monday-night-for-the-rest-of-our-lives special date. Apparently there was a wait at the restaurant, blah blah blah, and so they're going to a later movie. They called and I said that Mrs. Daly was in the bathroom. So just go back to bed, okay?"

"You're not my babysitter," his stepsister said. "You're only three years older than me."

"Four and a half years older," he said. "So you have to do what I say. If I told you to go jump in a fire then you'd have to jump. Got it?"

"I'm not a baby," Darcy said. But she was. She was only eight.

One of the movie werewolves was roaming through a house, playing hide and seek. There were puddles of blood everywhere. It came into a room where there was a parrot, reached up with a human-like paw, and opened the door of the cage. Peter and Darcy both watched for a minute, and then Peter said, "You *are* a baby. You have over a hundred stuffed animals. You know all the words to all the songs from *The Little Mermaid*. My mom told me you still wet the bed."

"Why are you so mean?" She said it like she was actually curious.

Peter addressed the werewolves. "How can I explain this so that someone your age will understand? I'm not mean. I'm just honest. It's not like I'm your real brother. We just happen to live in the same house because your father needed someone to do his taxes, and my mother is a certified accountant. The rest of it I don't even pretend to understand." Although he did. Her father was rich. His mother wasn't. "Okay? Now go to bed."

"No." Darcy did a little dance, as if to demonstrate that she could do whatever she wanted.

"Fine," he said. "Stay here and watch the werewolf movie then."

"I don't want to."

"Then go play princess or whatever it is you're always doing." Darcy had a closet with just princess dresses in it. And tiaras. And fairy wands. And fairy wings.

"You play with me," she said. "Or I'll tell everyone you pick your nose."

"Who cares," Peter said. "Go away."

"I'll pay you."

"How much?" he said, just out of curiosity.

"Ten dollars."

He thought for a minute. Her grandparents had given her a check for her birthday. Little kids never knew what to do with money and as far as he could tell, her father bought her everything she wanted anyway. And she got an allowance.

Peter got one now too, of course, but he'd knocked a glass of orange juice over on his laptop and his mom said she was only going to pay for half of what a new one would cost. "Make it fifty."

"Twenty," Darcy said. She came over and sat on the couch beside him. She smelled awful. A rank, feral smell, like something that lived in a cave. He'd heard his stepfather tell his mother that half the time Darcy only ran the water and then splashed it around with her hands behind a locked door. Make-believe baths, which was funny when you thought about how much she worshipped Ariel from *The Little Mermaid*. When Darcy really took a bath she left a ring of grime around the tub. He'd seen it with his own eyes.

Peter said, "What does this involve, exactly?"

"We could play Three Little Pigs. Or Cinderella. You be the evil stepsister."

Like everything was already decided. Just to annoy her, Peter said, "For a lousy twenty bucks I get to be whoever I want. I'm Cinderella. You can be the evil stepsister."

"You can't be Cinderella!"

"Why not?"

"Because you're a boy."

"So what?"

Darcy seemed to have no answer to this. She examined the hem of her princess dress. Pulled a few remaining sequins off, as if they were scabs. Finally she said, "My dad says I have to be nice to you. Because this is really my house, and you're a guest, even though I didn't invite you to come live here and now you're going to live here all the time and never go away unless you die or get sent away to military school or something."

"Don't count on it," Peter said, feeling really annoyed now. So that was his stepfather's plan. Or maybe it was his mother, still working out the details of her new, perfect life, worrying that Peter was going to mess things up now that she'd gotten it. He'd gone in and out of three schools in the last two years. It was easy enough to get thrown out of school if you wanted to be. If they sent him away, he'd come right back. "Maybe I like it here."

Darcy looked at him suspiciously. It wasn't like she was problem free, either. She went to see a therapist every Tuesday to deal with some "abandonment issues" which were apparently due to the fact that her real mother now lived in Hawaii.

Peter said, "I'm Cinderella. Deal with it."

His stepsister shrugged. She said, "If I'm the evil stepsister then I get to tell you what to do. First you have to go put the toilet seat down in the bathroom. And I get to hold the remote and you have to go to bed first. And you have to cry a lot. And sing. And make me a peanut butter sandwich with no crusts. And a bowl of chocolate ice cream. And I get your Playstation, because Cinderella doesn't get to have any toys."

"I've changed my mind," Peter said, when she seemed to have finished. He grinned at her. *My what big teeth I have.* "I'm going to be the *evil* Cinderella."

She bared her teeth right back at him. "Wrong. Cinderella isn't evil. She gets to go to the ball and wear a princess dress. And mice like her."

"Cinderella might be evil," Peter said, thinking it through, remembering how it went in the Disney movie. Everybody treated Cinderella like she was a pushover. Didn't she sleep in a fireplace? "If her evil stepsister keeps making fun of her and taking away her Playstation, she might burn down the house with everyone in it."

"That isn't how the story goes. This is stupid," Darcy said. She was beginning to sound less sure of herself, however.

"This is the new, improved version. No fairy godmother. No prince. No glass slipper. No happy ending. Better run away, Darcy. Because evil Cinderella is coming to get you." Peter stood up. Loomed over Darcy in what he hoped was a menacing way. The werewolves were howling on the TV.

Darcy shrank back into the couch. Held up her fairy wand as if it would keep her safe. "No, wait! You have to count to one hundred first. And I'll go hide."

Peter grabbed the stupid, cheap wand. Pointed it at Darcy's throat. Tapped it on her chest and when she looked down, bounced it off her nose. "I'll count to ten. Unless you want to pay me another ten bucks. Then I'll count higher."

"I only have five more dollars!" Darcy protested.

"You got fifty bucks from your grandparents last weekend."

"Your mom made me put half of it into a savings account."

"Okay. I'll count to twenty-three." He put the werewolf movie on pause. "One."

He went into all the bedrooms on the second floor, flicking the light switches on and off. She wasn't under any of the beds. Or in the closets. Or behind the shower curtain in the show-off master bathroom. Or in either of the other two bathrooms on the second floor. He couldn't believe how many bathrooms there were in this house. Back in the dark hallway again he saw something and paused. It was a mirror and he was in it. He paused to look at himself. No Cinderella here. Something dangerous. Something out of place. He felt a low, wild, wolfish delight rise up in him. His mother looked at him sometimes as if she wasn't sure who he was. He wasn't sure, either. He had to look away from what he saw in the face in the mirror.

Wasn't there some other fairy tale? *I'll huff and I'll puff and I'll blow your house down.* He'd like to blow this house down. The first time his mother had brought him over for dinner, she'd said, "Well, what do you think?" In the car, as they came up the driveway. What he'd thought was that it was like television. He'd never seen a house like it except on TV. There had been two forks at dinner and a white cloth napkin he was afraid to use in case he got it dirty. Some kind of vegetable that he didn't even recognize, and macaroni and cheese that didn't taste right. He'd chewed with his mouth open on purpose, and the little girl across the table watched him the whole time.

Everyone was always watching him. Waiting for him to mess up. Even his friends at his last school had acted sometimes like they thought he was crazy. Egged him on and then went silent when he didn't punk out. No friends yet at this new school. No bad influences, his mother said. A new start. But she was the one who had changed. Said things like, "I always wanted a little girl and now I've got one!" And, "It will be good for you, having a little sister. You're a role model now, Peter, believe it or not, so try to act like one."

Peter's mother let Darcy climb into bed with her and her new husband. Lay on the floor of the living room with her head in her new husband's lap, Darcy curled up beside them. Pretending to be a family, but he knew better. He could see the way Darcy wrinkled her nose when his mother hugged her. As if she smelled something bad, which was ironic, considering.

Peter went down the stairs two at a time. That black tide of miserable joy rose higher still, the way it always did when he knew he was doing exactly the wrong thing. As if he were going to die of it, whatever it was that he was becoming.

Darcy wasn't in the laundry room. Or the dining room. Peter went into the kitchen next, and knew immediately that she was here. Could feel her here, somewhere, holding her breath, squeezing her eyes shut, picking at her sequins. He thought of the babysitter, Mrs. Daly, and how afraid she'd looked when she left. Almost wished that she hadn't left, or that his mother and stepfather had skipped the movie, come home when they were supposed to. Wished that he'd told them about Mrs. Daly, except that his mother had sounded as if she were having a good time. As if she were happy.

He kicked a chair at the kitchen table and almost jumped out of his skin to hear it crash on the floor. Stomped around, throwing open the cabinet doors. Howling tunelessly, just for effect, except that it wasn't just for effect. He was enjoying himself. For a moment he didn't really even want to find his stepsister. Maybe no one would ever see her again.

She was folded up under the kitchen sink. Scrambled out when the door was flung open, and slapped his leg when he tried to grab her. Then scooted away on her hands and knees across the floor. There was a sort of sting in his calf now and he looked down and saw a fork was sticking out of him. It looked funny there. The tines hadn't gone far in, but still there were four little holes in the fabric of his jeans. Around the four little holes the black jeans turned blacker. Now it hurt.

"You stabbed me!" Peter said. He almost laughed. "With a fork!"

"I'm the evil stepsister," his stepsister said, glaring at him. "Of course I stabbed you. I'll stab you again if you don't do what I say."

"With what, a spoon?" he said. "You are going to be in so much trouble."

"I don't care," Darcy said. "Evil stepsisters don't care about getting in trouble." She stood up and straightened her princess dress. Then she walked over and gave him a little furious shove. Not such a little shove. He staggered back and then lurched forward again. Swung out for balance, and hit her across her middle with the back of one hand. Maybe he did it on purpose, but he didn't *think* he'd meant to do it. Either way the result was terrible. Blow your house down. Darcy was flung back across the room like she was just a piece of paper.

Now I've done it, he thought. Now they really will send me away. Felt a howling rage so enormous and hurtful that he gasped out loud. He darted after her, bent over her, and grabbed a shoulder. Shook it hard. Darcy's head flopped back and hit the refrigerator door and she made a little noise. "You made me," he said. "Not my fault. If you tell them—"

And stopped. "My mother is going to—" he said, and then had to stop again. He let go of Darcy. He couldn't imagine what his mother would do.

He knelt down. Saw his own blood smeared on the tiles. Not much. His leg felt warm. Darcy looked up at him, her ratty hair all in her face. She had her pajama bottoms on under that stupid dress. She was holding one arm with the other, like maybe he'd broken it. She didn't cry or yell at him and her eyes were enormous and black. Probably she had a concussion. Maybe they'd run into Mrs. Daly and her husband when they went to the hospital. He felt like throwing up.

"I don't know what I'm supposed to do!" he said. It came out in a roar. He didn't even know what he meant. "I don't know what I'm doing here! Tell me what I'm doing here."

Darcy stared at him. She seemed astonished. "You're Peter," she said. "You're being my stepbrother."

"Your evil stepbrother," he said and forced out a laugh, trying to make it a joke. But it was a wild, evil laugh.

Darcy got up, rubbing her head. She swung her other arm in a way that suggested it wasn't broken after all. He tried to feel relieved about this, but instead he just felt guiltier. He could think of no way to make things better and so he did nothing. He watched while Darcy went over and picked up the fork where he'd dropped it, carried it over to the sink, and then stood on the footstool to rinse it off. She looked over at him. Said, with a shrug, "They're home."

Car lights bounced against the windows.

His stepsister got down off the stool. She had a wet sponge in her hand. Calmly she crouched down and scrubbed at the bloody tiles. Swiped once at the blood on his jeans, and then gave up. Went back to the sink, stopping to pick up and straighten the chair he'd knocked over, and ran the water again to get the blood out of the sponge while he just sat and watched.

His mother came in first. She was laughing, probably at something his stepfather had said. His stepfather was always making jokes. It was one of the things Peter hated most about his stepfather, how he could make his mother laugh so easily. And how quickly her face would change from laughter, when she talked to Peter, or like now, when she looked over and saw Darcy at the sink, Peter on the floor. His stepfather came in right behind her, still saying something funny, his mouth invisible behind that bearish, bluish-blackish beard. He was holding a doggy bag.

"Peter," his mother said, knowing right away, the way she always did. "What's going on?"

He opened up his mouth to explain everything, but Darcy got there first. She ran over and hugged his mother around the legs. Lucky for his mother she wasn't holding a fork. And now here it came, the end of everything.

"Mommy," Darcy said, and Peter could see the magical effect this one word had, even on accountants. How his mother grew rigid with surprise, then lovingly pliant, as if Darcy had injected her with some kind of muscle relaxant.

Darcy turned her head, still holding his mother in that monstrously loving hold, and gave Peter a look he didn't understand until she began to speak in a rush. "Mommy, it was Cinderella because I couldn't sleep and Mrs. Daly had to go home and I woke up and we were waiting for you to come home and I got scared. Don't be angry. Peter and I were just playing a game. I was the evil stepsister." Again she looked at Peter.

"And I was Cinderella," Peter said. The leg of his pants was stiff with blood, but he could come up with an explanation tomorrow if only Darcy continued to keep his mother distracted. He had to get upstairs before anyone else. Get changed into his pajamas. Put things away in the forbidden room, where the werewolves waited patiently in the dark for their story to begin again. To begin the game again. No one could see what was in Darcy's face right now but him. He wished she would look away. He saw that she still had a smear of his blood on her hand, from the sponge and she glanced down and saw it too. Slowly, still looking at Peter, she wiped her hand against the princess dress until there was nothing left to see.

FORMIDABLE CARESS:
A TALE OF OLD EARTH
STEPHEN BAXTER

Stephen Baxter is one of the most important science fiction writers to emerge from Britain in the past thirty years. His "Xeelee" sequence of novels and short stories is arguably the most significant work of future history in modern science fiction. Baxter is the author of more than forty books and over 100 short stories. His most recent books are the near-future disaster duology, *Flood* and *Ark*. Upcoming is a new novel, *Stone Spring*, first of a new alternate-prehistory saga, and a major omnibus of the "Xeelee" novels.

As the women tried to pull her away, Ama hammered with her fist on the blank wall of the Building. "Let me inside! Oh, let me inside!"

But the Building had sealed itself against her. If the Weapon decreed that you were to have your child in the open air, that was how it was going to be, and no mere human being could do anything about it.

And she could not fight the logic of her body. The contractions came in pulses now, in waves that washed through the core of her being. In the end it was her father, Telni, who put his bony arm around her shoulders, murmuring small endearments. Exhausted, she allowed herself to be led away.

Telni's sister Jurg and the other women had set up a pallet for her not far from the rim of the Platform. They laid her down here and fussed with their blankets and buckets of warmed water, and prepared ancient knives for the cutting. Her aunt massaged her swollen belly with oils brought up from the Lowland. Telni propped her head on his arm, and held her hand tightly, but she could feel the weariness in his grip.

So it began. She breathed and screamed and pushed. And through it all, here at the lip of the Platform, she was surrounded by her world, the Buildings clustered around her, the red mist of the Lowland far below, above her the gaunt cliff on which glittered the blue-tinged lights of the Shelf cities, and the sky over her head where chains of stars curled like windblown hair. On Old Earth time was layered, and when she looked up she was peering up into accelerated time, at places where human hearts fluttered like songbirds. But there was a personal dimension to time too, so her father had always taught her, and these hours of her labor were the longest of her life, as if her body had been dragged down into the glutinous, redshifted slowness of the Lowland.

When it was done, Jurg handed her the baby. It was a boy, a scrap of flesh born a little early, his weight negligible inside the spindling-skin blankets. She immediately loved him unconditionally, whatever alien thing lay within. "I call him Telni like his grandfather," she managed to whisper.

Telni, exhausted himself, wiped tears from his crumpled cheeks.

She slept for a while, out in the open.

When she opened her eyes, the Weapon was floating above her.

It was a sphere as wide as a human was tall, reflective as a mirror, hovering at waist height above the smooth surface of the Platform. She could see herself in the thing's heavy silver belly, on her back on the heap of blankets, her baby asleep in the cot beside her. A small hatch was open in its flank, an opening with lobed lips, like a mouth. From this hatch a silvery tongue, metres long, reached out and snaked to the back of the neck of the small boy who stood beside the sphere.

Her aunt, her father, the others hung back, nervous of this massive presence that dominated all their lives.

The boy attached to the tongue-umbilical took a step towards the cot.

Telni blocked his way. "Stay back, Powpy, you little monster. You were once a boy as I was. Now I am old and you are young. Stay away from my grandson."

Powpy halted. Ama saw that his eyes flickered nervously, glancing at Telni, the cot, the Weapon. This showed the extent of the Weapon's control of its human creature; somewhere in there was a frightened child.

Ama struggled to sit up. "What do you want?"

The boy Powpy turned to her. "We wish to know why you wanted to give birth within a Building."

"You know why," she snapped back. "No child born inside a Building has ever harbored an Effigy."

The child's voice was flat, neutral—his accent like her father's, she thought, a little boy with the intonation of an older generation. "A child without an Effigy is less than a child with an Effigy. Human custom concurs with that, even without understanding—"

"I didn't want *you* to be interested in him." The words came in a rush. "You control us. You keep us here floating in the sky. All for the Effigies we harbor, or not. That's what you're interested in, isn't it?" Telni laid a trembling hand on her arm, but she shook it away. "My husband believed his life was pointless, that his only purpose was to grow old and die for you. In the end he destroyed himself—"

"Addled by the drink," murmured Telni.

"He didn't want *you* to benefit from his death. He never even saw this baby, his son. He wanted more than this!"

The Weapon seemed to consider this. "We intend no harm. On the contrary, a proper study of the symbiotic relationship between humans and Effigies—"

"Go away," she said. She found she was choking back tears. "Go away!" And she flung a blanket at its impassive hide, for that was all she had to throw.

The Weapon came to see Telni a few days after the funeral of his mother and grandfather. He was ten years old.

Telni had had to endure a vigil beside the bodies, where they had been laid out close to the rim of the Platform. He slept a lot, huddled against his kind but severe aunt Jurg, his last surviving relative.

At the dawn of the third day, as the light storms down on the Lowland glimmered and shifted and filled the air with their pearly glow, Jurg prodded him awake. And, he saw, his mother was ascending. A cloud of pale mist burst soundlessly from the body on its pallet. It hovered, tendrils and billows pulsing—and then, just for a heartbeat, it gathered itself into a form that was recognizably human, a misty shell with arms and legs, torso and head.

Jurg was crying. "She's smiling. Can you see? Oh, how wonderful…"

The sketch of Ama lengthened, her neck stretching like a spindling's, becoming impossibly long. Then the distorted Effigy shot up into the blueshifted sky and arced down over the lip of the Platform, hurling itself into the flickering crimson of the plain below. Jurg told Telni that Ama's Effigy was seeking its final lodging deep in the slow-beating heart of Old Earth, where, so it was believed, something of Ama would survive even the Formidable Caresses. But Telni knew that Ama had despised the Effigies, even the one that turned out to have resided in her.

They waited another day, but no Effigy emerged from old Telni. So the bodies were taken across the Platform, to the centre of the cluster of box-shaped, blank-walled Buildings, and placed reverently inside one of the smaller structures. A week later, when Jurg took Telni to see, the bodies were entirely vanished, their substance subsumed by the Building, which might have become a fraction larger after its ingestion.

So Telni, orphaned, was left in the care of his aunt.

She tried to get him to return to his schooling. A thousand people lived on the Platform, of which a few hundred were children; the schools were efficient and well-organized. But Telni, driven by feelings too complicated to face, was restless. He roamed, alone, through the forest of Buildings. Or he would stand at the edge of the Platform, before the gulf that surrounded the floating city, and watch the Shelf war unfold, accelerated by its altitude, the pale blue explosions and whizzing aircraft making an endless spectacle. He was aware that his aunt and teachers and the other adults were watching him, concerned, but for now they gave him his head.

On the third day he made for one of his favorite places, which was the big wheel at the very centre of the Platform, turned endlessly by harnessed spindlings. Here you could look down through a hatch in the Platform, a hole in the floor of the world, and follow the tethers that attached the Platform like a huge kite to the

Lowland ground half a kilometer below, and watch the bucket chains rising and falling. The Loading Hub was directly beneath the Platform, the convergence of a dozen roads crowded day and night. Standing here it was as if you could see the machinery of the world working. He liked to think about such things, as a distraction from thinking about other things. And it pleased him in other ways he didn't really understand, as if he had a deep, sunken memory of much bigger, more complicated machinery than this.

Best of all you could visit the spindling pens and help the cargo jockeys muck out a tall beast, and brush the fur on its six powerful legs, and feed it the strange purple-colored straw it preferred. The spindlings saw him cry a few times, but nobody else, not even his aunt.

When the Weapon came to see him he was alone in one of the smaller Buildings, near the centre of the cluster on the Platform. He was watching the slow crawl of lightmoss across the wall, the glow it cast subtly shifting. It was as if the Weapon just appeared at the door. Its little boy stood at its side, Powpy, with the cable dangling from the back of his neck.

Telni stared at the boy. "He used to be bigger than me. The boy. Now he's smaller."

"We believe you understand why," said Powpy.

"The last time I saw you was four years ago. I was six. I've grown since then. But you live down on the Lowland, mostly. Did you come up in one of the freight buckets?"

"No."

"You live slower down there."

"Do you know how much slower?"

"No."

The boy nodded stiffly, as if somebody was pushing the back of his head. "A straightforward, honest answer. The Lowland here is deep, about half a kilometer below the Platform, which is itself over three hundred metres below the Shelf. Locally the stratification of time has a gradient of, approximately, five parts in one hundred per meter. So a year on the Platform is—"

"Only a couple of weeks on the Lowland. But, umm, three hundred times five, a year here is fifteen years on the Shelf."

"Actually closer to seventeen. Do you know *why* time is stratified?"

"I don't know that word."

Powpy's little mouth had stumbled on it too, and other hard words. "Layered."

"No."

"Good. Nor do we. Do you know why your mother died?"

That blunt question made him gasp. Since Ama had gone, nobody had even mentioned her name. "It was the refugees' plague. She died of that. And my grandfather died soon after. My aunt Jurg says it was of a broken heart."

"Why did the plague come here?"

"The refugees brought it. Refugees from the war on the Shelf. The war's gone on for years, Shelf years. My grandfather says—said—it is as if they are trying to bring down a Formidable Caress of their own. The refugees came in a balloon. Families with kids. Grandfather says it happens every so often. They don't know what the Platform is but they see it hanging in the air, below them, at peace. So they try to escape."

"Were they sick when they arrived?"

"No. But they carried the plague bugs. People started dying. They weren't im—"

"Immune."

"Immune like the refugees."

"Why not?"

"Time goes faster up on the Shelf. Bugs change quickly. You get used to one, but then another comes along."

"Your understanding is clear."

"My mother hated you. She was unhappy when you visited me that time, when I was six. She says you meddle in our lives."

"'Meddle.' We created the Platform, gathered the sentient Buildings. We designed this community. Your life, and the lives of many generations of your ancestors, have been shaped by what we built. We 'meddled' long before you were born."

"Why?"

Silence again. "That's too big a question. Ask smaller questions."

"Why are there so many roads coming in across the Lowland to the Loading Hub?"

"I think you know the answer to that."

"Time goes twenty-five times slower down there. It's as if you're trying to feed a city twenty-five times the size."

"That's right. Now ask about something you don't know."

He pointed to the lightmoss. "Is this the same stuff as makes the light storms, down on the Lowland?"

"Yes, it is. That's a good observation. To connect two such apparently disparate phenomena—"

"I tried to eat the lightmoss. I threw it up. You can't eat the spindlings' straw either. Why?"

"Because they come from other places. Other worlds than this. Whole other systems of life."

Telni understood some of this. "People brought them here, and mixed everything up." A thought struck him. "Can spindlings eat lightmoss?"

"Why is that relevant?"

"Because if they can it must mean they came from the same other place."

"You can find that out for yourself."

He itched to go try the experiment, right now. "Did people make you?"

"They made our grandfathers, if you like."

"Were you really weapons?"

"Not all of us. Such labels are irrelevant now. When human civilizations fell, sentient machines were left to roam, to interact. There was selection, of a brutal sort, as we competed for resources and spare parts. We enjoyed our own long evolution. A man called Bayle mounted an expedition to the Lowland, and found us."

"You were farming humans. That's what my mother said."

"It wasn't as simple as that. The interaction with Bayle's scholars led to a new generation with enhanced faculties."

"What kind of faculties?"

"Curiosity."

Telni considered that. "What's special about me? That I might have an Effigy inside me?"

"Not just that. Your mother rebelled when you were born. That's very rare. The human community here was founded from a pool of scholars, but that was many generations ago. We fear that we may have bred out a certain initiative. That was how you came to our attention, Telni. There may be questions you can answer that we can't. There may be questions you can *ask* that we can't."

"Like what?"

"You tell me."

He thought. "What are the Formidable Caresses?"

"The ends of the world. Or at least, of civilization. In the past, and in the future."

"How does time work?"

"That's another question you can answer yourself."

He was mystified. "How?"

A seam opened up on the Weapon's sleek side, like a wound, revealing a dark interior. Powpy had to push his little hand inside and grope around for something. Despite the Weapon's control Telni could see his revulsion. He drew out something that gleamed, complex. He handed it to Telni.

Telni turned it over in his hands, fascinated. It was warm. "What is it?"

"A clock. A precise one. You'll work out what to do with it." The Weapon moved, gliding up another meter into the air. "One more question."

"Why do I feel… sometimes…" It was hard to put into words. "Like I should be somewhere else? My mother said everybody feels like that, when they're young. But… Is it a stupid question?"

"No. It is a very important question. But it is one you will have to answer for yourself. We will see you again." It drifted away, two metres up in the air, with the little boy running beneath, like a dog on a long lead. But it paused once more, and the boy turned. "What will you do now?"

Telni grinned. "Go feed moss to a spindling."

At twenty-five, Telni was the youngest of the Platform party selected to meet the Natural Philosophers from the Shelf, and MinaAndry, a year or two younger, was the most junior of the visitors from Foro. It was natural they would end up together.

The formal welcomes were made at the lip of the Platform, under the vast, astonishing bulk of the tethered airship. The Shelf folk looked as if they longed to be away from the edge, and the long drop to the Lowland below. Then the parties broke up for informal discussions and demonstrations. The groups, of fifty or so on each side, were to reassemble for a formal dinner that night in the Hall, the largest and grandest of the Platform's sentient Buildings. Thus the month-long expedition by the Shelf Philosophers would begin to address its goals, the start of a cultural and philosophical exchange with the Platform. It was a fitting project. The inhabitants of the Platform, drawn long ago from Foro, were after all distant cousins of the Shelf folk.

And Telni found himself partnered with MinaAndry.

There was much good-natured ribbing at this, and not a little jealousy in the looks of the older men, Telni thought. But Mina *was* beautiful. All the folk from the Shelf were handsome in their way, tall and elegant—not quite of the same stock as the Platform folk, who, shorter and heavier-built, were themselves different from the darker folk of the Lowland. They were three human groups swimming through time at different rates; of course they would diverge. But whatever the strange physics behind it, MinaAndry was the most beautiful girl Telni had ever seen, tall yet athletic-looking with a loose physical grace, and blonde hair tied tightly back from a spindling-slim neck.

They walked across the Platform, through the city of living Buildings. It was a jumble of cubes and rhomboids, pyramids and tetrahedrons—even one handsome dodecahedron. The walls were gleaming white surfaces, smooth to the touch, neither hot nor cold, and pierced by sharp-edged doorways and windows.

"This place is so strange." Mina ran her hand across the smooth surface of a Building. Within its bland surface, through an open door, could be glimpsed the signs of humanity, a bunk bed made of wood hauled up from the plain, a hearth, a cooking pot, cupboards and heaps of blankets and clothes, and outside a bucket to catch the rain. "We build things of stone, of concrete, or wood. But *this*—"

"We didn't build these structures at all. The Buildings grew here. They bud from units we call Flowers, and soak up the light from the storms. Like the Weapons, the Buildings are technology gone wild, made things modified by time."

"It all feels new, although I suppose it's actually very old. Whereas Foro *feels* old. All that lichen-encrusted stone! It's like a vast tomb…"

But Telni knew that the town she called Foro was built on the ruins of a city itself called *New* Foro, devastated during the war he remembered watching as a boy. He had naïvely expected the Shelf folk to be full of stories of that war when they came here. But the war was fifteen Platform years over, more than two hundred and fifty Shelf years, and what was a childhood memory to Telni was long-dead history to Mina.

"Is it true you feed your dead to the Buildings?" She asked this with a kind of frisson of horror.

"We wouldn't put it like that… They do need organic material. In the wild, you know, down on the Lowland, they preyed on humans. We do let them take our corpses. Why not?" He stroked a wall himself. "It means the Buildings are made of *us*, our ancestors. Sometimes people have to die inside a Building. The Weapon decrees it."

"Why?"

"It seems to be studying Effigies. It thinks that the construction material of which Buildings are made excludes Effigies. Some of us are born inside Buildings, so no Effigy can enter us then. Others die within a Building, a special one we call the Morgue, in an attempt to trap the Effigies when they are driven out of their bodies. My own aunt died recently, and had to be taken inside the Morgue, but no Effigy was released."

"It seems very strange to us," Mina said cautiously. "To Shelf folk, I mean. That here you are living out your lives on a machine, made by another machine."

"It's not as if we have a choice," Telni said, feeling defensive. "We aren't allowed to leave."

She looked down at her feet, which were clad in sensible leather shoes—not spindling, like Telni's. "I think you can tell that a machine built this place. It lacks a certain humanity." She glanced at him uncertainly. "Look, I'm speaking as a Philosopher. I myself am studying geology. The way time stratification affects erosion, with higher levels wearing away faster than the low, and the sluggish way rivers flow as they head down into the red…" She wasn't concentrating on what she was saying, but inspecting her surroundings. "For instance there's the thinness of this floor. On the Shelf we all grew up on a cliff-top. But here we are suspended in the air on a paper-thin sheet! Logically, perhaps, we're even safer here than standing on the Shelf. But it doesn't *feel* safe. A human designer would never have done it like this."

"We live as best we can."

"I'm sure."

He took her to the very centre of the Platform, and the wheel which turned as always, drawn by teams of patient spindlings. The cargo jockeys, unloading buckets and pallets of supplies drawn up from the Lowland, stared with curiosity as MinaAndry patted the necks of the laboring beasts. "How charming these beasts are! You know that on the Shelf they were driven to extinction during the War of the Cities. We are slowly restocking with animals drawn up from the Lowland herds, but it's ferociously expensive…"

Something about the way she patted and stroked the tall, elegant creatures moved Telni, deep inside. But he had to pull her aside when he saw a spindling was ready to cough; spindlings lacked anuses and vomited their shit from their mouths. Mina was astonished at the sight.

Anyhow he hadn't brought her here for spindlings. He took Mina's hand and led her to the centre of the Hub, close to the great hatch in the floor of the Platform, which revealed the cables that dangled down to the Lowland far below.

Mina squealed and drew back. "Oh! I'm sorry. Vertigo—what a foolish reaction that is!"

"But evidently a very ancient one. Look." He pointed down through the hole. "I brought you here to see my own work. I earn my living through my studies with an apothecary. But *this* is my passion…"

Holding tight to the rail, pushing a stray strand of hair back from her face, she peered down through the floor. From here, Terni's cradles of pendulums, of bobs and weights and simple control mechanisms, were clearly visible, attached in a train along one of the guide ropes that tethered the Platform to the Lowland plain.

"Pendulums?"

"Pendulums. I time their swing. From here I can vary the length and amplitude…" He showed her a rigging-up of levers he had fixed above the tether's anchor. "Sometimes there's a snag, and I go down in a harness, or send one of the cargo jockeys."

"How do you time them?"

"I have a clock the Weapon gave me. I don't understand how it works," he said, and that admission embarrassed him. "But it's clearly more accurate than any clock we have. I have the pendulums spread out over more than a quarter of a kilometer. There's no record of anybody attempting to make such measurements over such a height difference. And by seeing how the period of the pendulums vary with height, what I'm trying to measure is—"

"The stratification of time. The higher up you raise your pendulums, the faster they will swing." She smiled. "Even a geologist understands that much. Isn't it about five per cent per meter?"

"Yes. But that's only a linear approximation. With more accurate measurements I've detected an underlying curved function…" The rate at which time flowed faster, Telni believed, was inversely proportional to the distance from the centre of Old Earth. "It only *looks* linear, simply proportional to height, if you pick points close enough together that you can't detect the curve. And an inverse relationship makes sense, because that's the same mathematical form as the planet's gravitational potential, and time stratification is surely some kind of gravitational effect…" He hoped this didn't sound naïve. His physics, based on the philosophies extracted from Foro centuries ago with the Platform's first inhabitants, was no doubt primitive compared to the teachings Mina had been exposed to.

Mina peered up at a sky where an unending storm of star clouds passed, brightly blueshifted. "I think I understand," she said. "My mathematics is rustier than it should be. That means that the time distortion doesn't keep rising on and on. It comes to some limit."

"Yes! And that asymptotic limit is a distortion factor of around three hundred and twenty thousand—compared to the Shelf level, which we've always taken as our benchmark. Actually it corresponds to the five percent rule applied across the radius of Old Earth. So one year here corresponds to nearly a third of a million years, up there in the sky."

"Or," she said, "one year out there—"

"Passes in about a hundred seconds on the Self. We are falling into the future, Mina! Some believe that once Earth was a world without this layering of time, a world like many others, perhaps, hanging among the stars. And its people were more or less like us. But Earth came under some kind of threat. And so the elders of Earth pulled a blanket of time over their world and packed it off to the future: Earth is a jar of time, stopped up to preserve its children."

"That's all speculation."

"Yes. But it would explain such a high rate. And, Mina, I think this rate should be observable. The interval we call a "year" is just a counting-up of days, but it's thought to be a folk memory of what was a *real* year, the time it took Old Earth to circle its sun. We can't distinguish that sun, whatever is left of it. But we ought to be able to see the stars shifting back and forth, every hundred seconds, as we turn around the sun. I'm trying to encourage the astronomers to look for this, but they say they're too busy mapping other changes." He waved a hand at the sky. "Those chains of stars—"

"They evolve faster than seen from Foro," she breathed, her upturned face bathed in the shifting blue starlight.

"They are not as previous generations witnessed them. Something new in the sky. However, if the astronomers *could* be persuaded to measure the external year it would confirm my mathematics… I'm always trying to improve my accuracy. The pendulums need to be long enough to give a decent period, but not too long or else the time stratification becomes significant *even over the length of the pendulum itself*, and the physics gets very complicated—"

She slipped her hand into his. "It's a wonderful discovery. Nobody before, maybe not since the last Caress, has worked out how fast we're all plummeting into the future."

He flushed, pleased. But something made him confess, "I needed the Weapon's clock to measure the effects. And it set me asking questions about time in the first place."

"It doesn't matter what the Weapon did. This is your work. You should be happy."

"I don't feel happy," he blurted.

She frowned. "Why do you say that?"

Suddenly he was opening up to her in ways he'd never spoken to anybody else. "Because I don't always feel as if I *fit*. As if I'm not like other people." He looked at her doubtfully, wondering if she would conclude he was crazy. "Maybe that's why I'm turning out to be a good Philosopher. I can look at the world from outside, and see patterns others can't. Do you ever feel like that?"

Still holding his hand, she walked him back to the wheel and stroked a spin-dling's stubby mane, evidently drawing comfort from the simple physical contact. "Sometimes," she said. "Maybe everybody does. And maybe it's a reaction to the unnatural environment of the Platform. But the world is as it is, and you just have to make the best of it. Do you get many birds up here?"

"Not many. Just caged songbirds. Hard for them to find anywhere to nest."

"I used to watch birds as a kid. I'd climb up to a place we call the Attic... The birds use the time layers. The parents will nest at some low level, then go gathering food higher up. They've worked out they can take as long as they like, while the babies, stuck in slow time, don't get too hungry and are safe from the predators. Of course the parents grow old faster, sacrificing their lives for their chicks."

"I never saw anything like that. I never got the chance." He shook his head, sud-denly angry, resentful. "Not on this island in the sky, a creature of some machine. Sometimes I hope the next Caress comes soon and smashes everything up."

She took both his hands and smiled at him. "I have a feeling you're going to be a challenge. But I like challenges."

"You do?"

"Sure. Or I wouldn't be here, spending a month with a bunch of old folk while seventeen months pass at home. Think of the parties I'm missing!"

His heart hammered, as if he had been lifted up into the blue. "I've only known you hours," he said. "Yet I feel—"

"You should return to your work." The familiar child's voice was strange, cold, jarring.

Telni turned. The Weapon was here, hovering effortlessly over the hole in the floor. His tethered boy stood some metres away, tense, obviously nervous of the long drop. The spindlings still turned their wheel, but the cargo jockeys stood back, staring at the sudden arrival of the Weapon, the maker and ruler of the world.

Telni's anger flared. He stepped forward towards the child, fists clenched. "What do you want?"

"We have come to observe the formal congress this evening. The Philosophers from Shelf and Platform. There are many questions humans can address which we—"

"Then go scare all those old men and women. Leave me alone." Suddenly, with Mina at his side, he could not bear to have the Weapon in his life, with its strange ageless boy on his umbilical. "Leave me alone, I say!"

Powpy turned to look at Mina. "She will not stay here. This girl, MinaAndry. Her home is on the Shelf. Her family, the Andry-Feri, is an ancient dynasty. She has responsibilities, to bear sons and daughters. That is her destiny. Not here."

"I will stay if I wish," Mina said. She was trembling, Telni saw, evidently terri-fied of the Weapon, this strange, ancient, wild machine from the dark Lowland. Yet she was facing it, answering it back.

Telni found himself snarling, "Maybe she'll bear *my* sons and daughters."

"No," said the boy.

"What do you mean, no?"

"She is not suitable for you."

"She's a scholar from Foro! She's from the stock you brought here in the first place."

"It is highly unlikely that she has an Effigy, as few in her family do. Your partner should have an Effigy. That is why—"

"Selective breeding," Mina gasped. "It's true. This machine really is breeding humans like cattle…"

"I don't care about Effigies," Telni yelled. "I don't care about you and your stupid projects." He stalked over to the boy, who stood trembling, clearly afraid, yet unable to move from the spot.

"Telni, don't," Mina called.

The boy said calmly, "Already you have done good and insightful work which—"

Telni struck, a hard clap with his open hand to the side of the boy's head. Powpy went down squealing.

Mina rushed forward and pushed herself between Telni and the boy. "What have you done?"

"He, it—all my life—"

"Is that this boy's fault? Oh, get away, you fool." She knelt down and cradled the child's head on her lap. With the umbilical still dangling from the back of his neck, Powpy was crying, in a strange, contained way. "He's going to bruise. I think you may have damaged his ear. And his jaw—no, child, don't try to talk." She turned to the Weapon, which hovered impassively. "Don't make him speak for you again. He's hurt."

Telni opened his hands. "Mina, please—"

"Are you still here?" she snarled. "Go get help. Or if you can't do that, just go away. Go!"

He knew he had lost her, in this one moment, this one foolish blow.

He turned away and headed towards the Platform's hospital to find a nurse.

The little boy walked into Terni's cell, trailing a silvery rope from the back of his neck.

Telni was huddled up in his bunk, a spindling-skin blanket over his body. He was shivering, drying out, not for the first time. He scowled at the boy. "You again."

"Be fair," the boy said. "We have not troubled you for twenty years."

"Not for you." His figuring was cloudy. "Down on Lowland, less than a year—"

"This boy is not yet healed."

Telni saw his face was distorted on the right-hand side. "I apologize." He sat up. "I apologize to *you*—what in the blue was your name?"

"Powpy."

"I apologize to you, Powpy. Not to the thing that controls you. Where is it, by the way?"

"It would not fit through the door."

He lay back and laughed.

"We did not expect to find you here."

"In the drunk tank? Well, I got fired by the apothecary for emptying her drug cabinet one too many times. So it was the drink for me." He patted his belly. "At least it's putting fat on my bones."

"Why this slow self-destruction?"

"Call it an experiment. I'm following in my father's footsteps, aren't I? After all, thanks to you, I have no more chance of happiness, of meaning in my life, than he did. And besides, it's all going to finish in a big smash soon, isn't it? As you smart machines no doubt know already."

It didn't respond to that immediately. "You never had a wife. Children."

"Sooner no kids at all than to breed at your behest."

"You have long lost contact with MinaAndry."

"You could say that." When the month-long tour of the Shelf Philosophers was concluded, she had gone home with them, leaping seventeen months to continue her interrupted life on Foro. Since then, the accelerated time of the Shelf had whisked her away from him forever. "After—what, three hundred and forty years up there?—she's dust, her descendants won't remember her, even the language she spoke will be half-forgotten. The dead get deader, you know, as every trace of their existence is expunged. That's one thing life on Old Earth has taught us. What do you want, anyway?"

"Your research into the Formidable Caress."

"If you can call it research."

"Your work is good, from what we have seen of that portion you have shared with other scholars. You cannot help but do good work, Telni. The curiosity I saw burning in that ten-year-old boy, long ago, is still bright."

"Don't try to analyze me, you—*thing*."

"Tell me what you have discovered…"

After his discovery of the huge rate at which the inhabitants of Old Earth were plummeting into the future, Telni had become interested in spans of history. On the Shelf, written records went back some four thousand years of local time. These records had been compiled by a new civilization rising from the rubble of an older culture, itself wrecked by a disaster known as the Formidable Caress, thought to have occurred some six thousand years before *that*.

"But in the external universe," Telni said, "ten thousand Shelf years corresponds to over three *billion* years. So much I deduced from my pendulums, swinging away amid streams of spindling shit and cargo jockey piss… Everybody has always thought that the Caresses come about from local events. Something to do with the planet itself. But three billion years is long enough for events to unfold on a wider scale. Time enough, according to what Shelf scholars have reconstructed, for stars to be born and to die, for whole galaxies to swim and jostle… I wondered if the Caresses could have some cosmic cause."

"So you started to correspond with scholars on the Shelf."

"Yes. After that first visit by Mina's party we kept up a regular link, with visits from them once every couple of years for us, once a generation for them…" It had helped that six hundred years after the shock of the War of the Cities, the Shelf cities had not indulged in another bout of warfare on any significant scale. "I spoke to the astronomers over there, about what they saw in the sky. And their archaeologists, for what had been seen in the past. There was always snobbishness, you know. Those of us down in the red think we are better because we are closer to the original stock of Old Earth; those up in the blue believe they are superior products of evolution. None of that bothered *me*. And as their generations ticked by, I think I helped shape whole agendas of academic research by my sheer persistence."

"It must have been a rewarding time for you."

"Academically, yeah. I've never had any problem, academically. It's the rest of my life that's a piece of shit."

"Tell us what you discovered."

"I don't have my notes, my books—"

"Just tell us."

He sat up and stared into the face of the eerily unchanged boy—who, to his credit, did not flinch. "The first Caress destroyed almost everything of what went before, on the Shelf and presumably elsewhere. Almost, but not all. Some trace inscriptions, particularly carvings on stone, have survived. Images, fragmentary, and bits of text. Records of something in the sky."

"What something?"

"The Galaxy is a disc of stars, a spiral. We, on a planet embedded in the disc, see this in cross-section, as a band of light in the sky. Much of it obscured by dust."

"And?"

"The ancients' last records show *two* bands, at an angle to each other. There is evidence that the second band grew brighter, more prominent. The chronological sequence is difficult to establish—the best of these pieces were robbed and used as hearths or altar stones by the fallen generations that followed…"

"Nevertheless," the boy prompted.

"Nevertheless, there is evidence that something came from out of the sky. Something huge. And then there are crude, fragmentary images—cartoons, really—of explosions. All over the sky. A million suns, suddenly appearing." He imagined survivors, huddled in the ruins of their cities, scratching what they saw into fallen stones. "After that—nothing, for generations. People were too busy reinventing agriculture to do much astronomy. That was ten thousand years ago.

"The next bit of evidence comes from around three thousand years back, when a Natural Philosopher called HuroEldon established a new centre of scholarship, at Foro and down on the Lowland… Once again we started getting good astronomical records. And about that time, they observed in the sky—"

"Another band of stars."

"No. A *spiral*—a spiral of stars, ragged, the stars burning and dying, a wheel turning around a point of intense brightness. This object swam towards Old Earth, so it seemed, and at its closest approach there was a flare of dazzling new stars, speckled over the sky—but there was no Caress, not this time. The spiral receded into the dark."

"Tell us what you believe this means."

"I think it's clear. This other spiral is a galaxy like our own. The two orbit each other." He mimed this with his fists, but his hands were shaking; shamed before the boy's steady gaze, he lowered his arms. "As twin stars may orbit one another. But galaxies are big, diffuse structures. They must tear at each other, ripping open those lacy spirals. Perhaps when they brush, they create bursts of starbirth. A Formidable Caress indeed.

"The last Caress was a first pass, when the second galaxy came close enough to *our* part of our spiral to cause a great flaring of stars—and that flaring, a rain of light falling from the blue, was what shattered our world. Then in HuroEldon's time, two billion years later, there was another approach—this one not so close; it was spectacular but did no damage, not to us. And then…"

"Yes?"

He shrugged, peering up at the construction-material roof of the cell. "The sky is ragged, full of ripped-apart spiral arms. The two galaxies continue to circle each other, perhaps heading for a full merger, a final smash. And that, perhaps, will cause a new starburst flare, a new Caress."

The boy stood silently, considering this, though one leg quivered, as if itchy. He asked: "When?"

"That I don't know. I tried to do some mathematics on the orbit. Long time since I stayed sober enough to see *that* through. But there's one more scrap of information in the archaeology. There was always a tradition that the second Caress would follow ten thousand years after the first, Shelf time. Maybe that's a memory of what the smart folk who lived before the first Caress were able to calculate. They *knew*, not only about the Caress that threatened them, but also what would follow. Remarkable, really."

"Ten thousand years," the boy said. "Which is—"

"About now." He grinned. "If the world ends, do you think they will let me out of here to see the show?"

"You have done remarkable work, Telni. This is a body of evidence extracted from human culture which we could not have assembled for ourselves." Even as he spoke the boy trembled, and Telni saw piss swim down his bare leg.

Telni snorted. "You really aren't too good at running the people you herd, are you, machine?"

Ignoring the dribble on his leg, Powpy spoke on. "Regarding the work, however. We are adept at calculation. Perhaps we can take these hints and reconstruct the ancients' computations, or even improve on them."

"So you'll know the precise date of the end of the world. That will help. Come back and tell me what you figure out."

"We will." The boy turned and walked away, leaving piss footprints on the smooth floor.

Telni laughed at him, lay back on his bunk, and tried to sleep.

It was to be a very long time before Telni saw the Weapon and its human attendant again.

"He refuses to die. It's as simple as that. There's nothing but his own stubbornness keeping him alive."

His hearing was so bad now that it was as if his ears were stuffed full of wool. But, lying there on his pallet, he could hear every word they said.

And, though he needed a lot of sleep now, he was aware when they moved him into the Morgue, ready for him to die, ready to capture his Effigy-spirit when it was released from his seventy-two-year-old body. "You can wheel me in here if you like, you bastards." He tried to laugh, but it just made him cough. "I'm just going to lie here as long as it takes."

"As long as it takes for what?"

"For it to come back again."

But, more than thirty years since his last visitation, only a handful of the medical staff knew what he was talking about.

In the end, of course, it came.

He woke from another drugged sleep to find a little boy standing beside his bed. He struggled to sit up. "Hey, Powpy. How's it going with you? For you it must be, what, a year since last time? You've grown. You're not afraid of me, are you? Look, I'm old and disgusting, but at least I can't slap you around the head any more, can I?"

He thought he saw a flicker of something in the boy's eyes. Forgiveness? Pity? Contempt? Well, he deserved the latter. But then the kid spoke in that odd monotone, so familiar even after all these years. "We were here at the beginning of your life. Now here we are at the end."

"Yes." He tried to snap his fingers, failed. "Just another spark in the flames for you, right? And now you've come to see me give up my Effigy so you can trap it in this box of yours."

"We would not describe it as—"

He grabbed the boy's arm, trying to grip hard. "Listen, Weapon. You can have my Effigy. What do I care? But I'm not going to die like this. Not here, not now."

"Then where, and when?"

"Fifty years," he whispered. He glanced at the medical staff, who hovered at the edges of the Building. "I did my own calculations. Took me ten years. Well, I had nothing better to do… Fifty years, right? That's all we've got left, until the fireworks."

The boy said gravely, "We imagine our model of the galaxies' interaction is somewhat more sophisticated than yours. But your answer is substantially correct. You understand that this Caress will be different. *Those on the Platform will survive.* The construction material of the Buildings will shelter them. That was one purpose of the Platform in the first place. And from this seed the recovery after the Caress should be much more rapid."

"But the cities of the Shelf—Foro, Puul—"

"People will survive in caves, underground. But the vast loss of life, the destruction of the ecology, their agricultural support—"

"Well, it serves those bastards right. They lost interest in talking to me decades ago." Which was true. But since the War of the Cities there had been a thousand years of peace on the Shelf, all of which he'd lived through—incredible to be a witness to so much history—and they had built something beautiful and splendid up there, a chain of cities like jewels in the night. In his head he imagined a race of Minas, beautiful, clear-eyed, laughing. "Well. There's nothing I can do for them." He struggled to sit straighter. "But there's something I want you to do for me. You owe me, you artifact. I did everything you asked of me, and more. Now you're going to take away my soul. Well, you can have it. But you can give me something back in return. *I want to see the Caress.*"

"You have only weeks to live. Days, perhaps."

"Take me down into the red. No matter how little time I have left, you can find a pit deep enough on this time-shifted world to squeeze in fifty Platform years." Exhausted, he fell back coughing; a nurse hurried over to catch him and lower him gently to his blankets. "And one more thing."

"More demands?"

"Let this boy go."

When Telni woke again, he found himself staring up at a sky of swirling blue stars. "Made it, by my own blueshifted arse."

A face hovered over him, a woman's. "Don't try to move."

"You're in the way." He tried to sit up, failed, but kept struggling until she helped him up and he could see.

He was on a plain—*on the ground*, his pallet set on red, rusty dirt, down on the ground for the first time in his life. Something like a rail track curled across his view. Buildings of construction material were scattered around like a giant's toys. He got the immediate sense this was a kind of camp, not permanent.

And figures moved in the distance. At first sight they looked human. But then something startled them, and they bucked and fled, on six legs.

"What are *those*?"

"They are called Centaurs." Powpy was standing beside him, his neck umbilical connecting him to the Weapon, which hovered as impassive as ever, though a little rusty dirt clung to its sleek hide. "Human hybrids."

"You were going to let this kid go."

"He will be released," said the woman sternly. "My name's Ama, by the way."

Which had been his mother's name. He felt a stab of obscure guilt. "Glad to meet you."

"You should be. I'm a nurse. I volunteered to stay with you, to keep you alive when they brought you down here."

"No family, I take it."

"Not any more. And when this business is done, I'll be taking Powpy here back up top, to the Platform."

"His mother and father—"

"Long dead," she whispered.

"We're all orphans here, then."

Powpy said solemnly, "We will have to shelter in a construction-material Building to ride out the Caress. We are deep enough that it should be brief—"

"How deep?"

"We are on the Abyss. Once the bed of a deep ocean. Below the offshore plains you call the Lowland... Deep enough."

"Nice sky."

"Most of the stars' radiation is blueshifted far beyond your capacity to see it."

"And how long—ow!" There was a sharp pain in his chest.

Ama grabbed him and lowered him back against a heap of pillows. "Just take it easy. That was another heart attack."

"*Another...*"

"They've been coming thick and fast."

"That Weapon won't want me dying out in the open. Not after all this."

"We have a Morgue designated just over there," Ama said. "Your bed's on wheels."

"Good planning."

"Not long now," murmured Powpy.

But he, the boy, wasn't looking at the sky. Telni touched Poppy's chin, and lifted his face. "He should see this for himself."

"Very well," the Weapon said through the boy's mouth.

"Why, Weapon? Why the grand experiment? Why the Platform? *Why are you so fascinated by the Effigies?*"

"We believe the Effigies are not native to the Earth, any more than the spindlings or the lightmoss or—"

"But they're pretty closely bound up to humans. They live and die with us."

"They do not die. So we believe. We have mapped disturbances, deep in the Earth... We believe there is a kind of nest of them, a colony of the Effigies that dwells deep in the core of Old Earth. They emerge to combine with humans, with infants at birth. Some infants—we don't know how they choose. And we don't know how they bond either. But after the human carrier's death the Effigy symbiote is released, and returns to the core colony. Something of the human is taken with it. We believe."

"Memories."

"Perhaps."

"And are these memories brought back up from this core pit the next time an Effigy surfaces?"

"Perhaps. Everything about this world is designed, or modified. Perhaps the purpose is to preserve something of the memory of humanity across epochal intervals."

"Maybe this is why I always felt like something in me really doesn't belong in this time or place."

"Perhaps. We must study this at second hand. It is something about humanity that no machine shares."

"I think you're jealous. Aren't you, machine? You can farm us, keep us as lab animals. But you can't have *this*."

"No reliable mapping between human emotions and the qualia of our own sensorium…"

But he didn't hear the rest. Another stabbing in his chest, a pain that knifed down his left arm. The nurse leaned over him.

And the sky exploded. They weren't just new stars. They were stars that detonated, each flaring brighter than the rest of the sky put together, then vanishing as quickly, blown-out matches.

"Supernovas," said the boy, Powpy. "That is the ancient word. A wave of supernovas, triggered by the galaxy collision, giant exploding stars flooding nearby space with lethal radiation, a particle sleet…"

But Telni couldn't talk, couldn't breathe.

"He's going," the nurse said. "Get him to the Morgue."

He glimpsed two creatures running up—they were six-legged people, Centaurs—and his bed was shoved forward, across the rusty dirt towards the enclosure of a Building. He tried to protest, to cling to his view of that astounding sky as long as he could. But he couldn't even breathe, and it felt as if a sword were being twisted in his chest.

They got him indoors. He lay back, rigid with pain, staring at a construction material roof that seemed to recede from him.

And a glow, like the glow of the sky outside, suffused the inside of his head, his very eyes.

"It's happening," he heard the nurse say, wonder in her voice. "Look, it's rising from his limbs… His heart has stopped." She straddled him and pounded at his chest, even as a glow lit up her face, the bare flesh of her arms—a glow coming from *him*.

He remembered a glimmering tetrahedron, looming, swallowing him up.

He heard Powpy call, "Who are you? Who are you?"

And suddenly *he knew*, as if his eyes had suddenly focused, after years of myopia. With the last of the air in his lungs he struggled to speak. "Not again. Not again!"

The nurse peered into his eyes. "Stay with me, Telni!"

"*Who are you?*"

"My name is Michael Poole."

The light detonated, deep inside him.

Suddenly he filled this box of Xeelee stuff, and he rattled, anguished. But there was the door, a way out. Somehow he fled that way, seeking the redshift.

And then—

BLOCKED
GEOFF RYMAN

Geoff Ryman is the author of *The Warrior Who Carried Life*, the novella "The Unconquered Country", *The Child Garden*, *Was*, *Lust*, and *Air*. His work *253, or Tube Theatre* was first published as hypertext fiction. A print version was published in 1998 and won the Philip K. Dick Memorial Award. He has also won the World Fantasy Award, the John W. Campbell Award, the Arthur C. Clarke Award (two times), the British Science Fiction Association Award (once for novel, twice for short fiction), the Sunburst Award, The James Tiptree, Jr. Award, and Gaylactic Spectrum awards. His most recent novel, *The King's Last Song*, is set in Cambodia, both at the time of Angkorean emperor Jayavarman VII, and in the present period. He has recently edited *When it Changed*, a collection of commissioned collaborations between writers and scientists. He currently lectures in Creative Writing at the University of Manchester in the United Kingdom.

I dreamed this in Sihanoukville, a town of new casinos, narrow beaches, hot bushes with flowers that look like daffodils, and even now after nine years of peace, stark ruined walls with gates that go nowhere.

In the dream, I get myself a wife. She's beautiful, blonde, careworn. She is not used to having a serious man with good intentions present himself to her on a beach. Her name is Agnete and she speaks with a Danish accent. She has four Asian children.

Their father had been studying permanently in Europe, married Agnete and then "left", which in this world can mean several things. Agnete was an orphan herself and the only family she had was that of her Cambodian husband. So she came to Phnom Penh only to find that her in-laws did not want some strange woman they did not know and all those extra mouths to feed.

I meet the children. The youngest is Gerda, who cannot speak a word of Khmer. She's tiny, as small as an infant though three years old, in a splotched pink dress and too much toy jewellery. She just stares, while her brothers play. She's been picked up from everything she knows and thrown down into this hot, strange world in which people speak nonsense and the food burns your mouth.

I kneel down and try to say hello to her, first in German, and then in English.

Hello Gertie, hello little girl. Hello. She blanks all language and sits like she's sedated.

I feel so sad, I pick her up and hold her, and suddenly she buries her head in my shoulder. She falls asleep on me as I swing in a hammock and quietly explain myself to her mother. I am not married, I tell Agnete. I run the local casino.

Real men are not hard, just unafraid. If you are a man you say what is true, and if someone acts like a monkey, then maybe you punish them. To be a crook, you have to be straight. I sold guns for my boss and bought policemen, so he trusted me, so I ran security for him for years. He was one of the first to Go, and he sold his shares in the casino to me. Now it's me who sits around the black lacquered table with the generals and Thai partners. I have a Lexus and a good income. I have ascended and become a man in every way but one. Now I need a family.

Across from Sihanoukville, all about the bay are tiny islands. On those islands, safe from thieves, glow the roofs where the Big Men live in Soriya-chic amid minarets, windmills, and solar panels. Between the islands hang white suspension footbridges. Distant people on bicycles move across them.

Somehow it's now after the wedding. The children are now mine. We loll shaded in palm-leaf panel huts. Two of the boys play on a heap of old rubber inner tubes. Tharum with his goofy smile and sticky-out ears is long legged enough to run among them, plonking his feet down into the donut holes. Not to be outdone, his brother Sampul clambers over the things. Rith the oldest looks cool in a hammock, away with his earphones, pretending not to know us.

Gerda tugs at my hand until I let her go. Freed from the world of language and adults she climbs up and over the swollen black tubes, sliding down sideways. She looks intent and does not laugh.

Her mother in a straw hat and sunglasses makes a thin, watery sunset smile.

Gerda and I go wading. All those islands shelter the bay, so the waves roll onto the shore child-sized, as warm and gentle as caresses. Gerda holds onto my hand and looks down at them, scowling in silence.

Alongside the beach is a grounded airliner, its wings cut away and neatly laid beside it. I take the kids there, and the boys run around inside it, screaming. Outside, Gerda and I look at the aircraft's spirit house. Someone witty has given the shrine tiny white wings.

The surrounding hills still have their forests; cumulonimbus clouds towering over them like clenched fists.

In the evening, thunder comes.

I look out from our high window and see flashes of light in the darkness. We live in one whole floor of my casino hotel. Each of the boys has his own suite. The end rooms have balconies, three of them, that run all across the front of the building with room enough for sofas and dining tables. We hang tubes full of pink sugar water for hummingbirds. In the mornings, the potted plants buzz with bees, and balls of seed lure the sarika bird that comes to sing its sweetest song.

In these last days, the gambling action is frenetic: Chinese, Thai, Korean, and Malays, they play baccarat mostly, but some prefer the one-armed bandits.

At the tables of my casino, elegant young women, handsome young men and a couple of other genders besides, sit upright ready to deal, looking as alert and frightened as rabbits, especially if their table is empty. They are paid a percentage of the take. Some of them sleep with customers too, but they're good kids; they always sent the money home. Do good, get good, we in Cambodia used to say. Now we say *twee akrow meen lay*, Do bad, have money.

My casino is straight. My wheels turn true. *No guns*, says my sign. *No animals, no children*. Innocence must be protected. *No cigarettes or powders*. Those last two are marked by a skull-and-crossbones.

We have security but the powders don't show up on any scan, so some of my customers come here to die. Most weekends, we find one, a body slumped over the table.

I guess some of them think it's good to go out on a high. The Chinese are particularly susceptible. They love the theatre of gambling, the tough-guy stance, the dance of the cigarette, the nudge of the eyebrow. You get dealt a good hand, you smile, you take one last sip of Courvoisier, then one sniff. You Go Down for good.

It's another way for the winner to take all. For me, they are just a mess to clear up, another reason to keep the kids away.

Upstairs, we've finished eating and we can hear the shushing of the sea.

"Daddy," Sampul asks me and the word thrums across my heart. "Why are we all leaving?"

"We're being invaded."

So far, this has been a strange and beautiful dream, full of Buddhist monks in orange robes lined up at the one-armed bandits. But now it goes like a stupid kids' TV show, except that in my dream, I'm living it, it's real. As I speak, I can feel my own sad, damp breath.

"Aliens are coming," I say and kiss him. "They are bringing many many ships. We can see them now, at the edge of the solar system. They'll be here in less than two years."

He sighs and looks perturbed.

In this disrupted country two-thirds of everything is a delight, two thirds of everything iron nastiness. The numbers don't add up, but it's true.

"How do we know they're bad?" he asks, his face puffy.

"Because the government says so and the government wouldn't lie."

His breath goes icy. "This government would."

"Not all governments, not all of them all together."

"So. Are we going to leave?"

He means leave again. They left Denmark to come here, and they are all of them sick of leaving.

"Yes, but we'll all go together, OK?"

Rith glowers at me from the sofa. "It's all the fault of people like you."

"I made the aliens?" I think smiling at him will make him see he is being silly.

He rolls his eyes. "There's the comet?" he asks like I've forgotten something and shakes his head.

"Oh, the comet, yes, I forgot about the comet, there's a comet coming too. And global warming and big new diseases."

He tuts. "The aliens sent the comet. If we'd had a space program we could meet them halfway and fight there. We could of had people living in Mars, to survive."

"Why wouldn't the aliens invade Mars too?"

His voice goes smaller, he hunches even tighter over his game. "If we'd gone into space, we would of been immortal."

My father was a drunk who left us; my mother died; I took care of my sisters. The regime made us move out of our shacks by the river to the countryside where there was no water so that the generals could build their big hotels. We survived. I never saw a movie about aliens, I never had this dream of getting away to outer space. My dream was to become a man.

I look out over the Cambodian night, and fire and light dance about the sky like dragons at play. There's a hissing sound. Wealth tumbles down in the form of rain.

Sampul is the youngest son and is a tough little guy. He thumps Rith, who's fifteen years old and both of them gang up on gangly Tharum. But tough-guy Sampul suddenly curls up next to me on the sofa as if he's returning to the egg.

The thunder's grief looks like rage. I sit and listen to the rain. Rith plays on, his headphones churning with the sound of stereophonic war.

Everything dies, even suns; even the universe dies and comes back. We already are immortal.

Without us, the country people will finally have Cambodia back. The walled gardens will turn to vines. The water buffalo will wallow; the rustics will still keep the fields green with rice, as steam engines chortle past, puffing out gasps of cloud. Sampul once asked me if the trains made rain.

And if there are aliens, maybe they will treasure it, the Earth.

I may want to stay, but Agnete is determined to Go. She has already lost one husband to this nonsense. She will not lose anything else, certainly not her children. Anyway, it was all part of the deal.

I slip into bed next to her. "You're very good with them," she says and kisses my shoulder. "I knew you would be. Your people are so kind to children."

"You don't tell me that you love me," I say.

"Give it time," she says, finally.

That night lightning strikes the spirit house that shelters our *neak ta*. The house's tiny golden spire is charred.

Gerda and I come down in the morning to give the spirit his bananas, and when she sees the ruin, her eyes boggle and she starts to scream and howl.

Agnete comes downstairs, and hugs and pets her, and says in English, "Oh, the pretty little house is broken."

Agnete cannot possibly understand how catastrophic this is, or how baffling. The *neak ta* is the spirit of the hotel who protects us or rejects us. What does it mean when the sky itself strikes it? Does it mean the *neak ta* is angry and has deserted us? Does it mean the gods want us gone and have destroyed our protector?

Gerda stares in terror, and I am sure then, that though she is wordless, Gerda has a Khmer soul.

Agnete looks at me over Gerda's shoulder, and I'm wondering why she is being so disconnected when she says, "The papers have come through."

That means we will sail to Singapore within the week.

I've already sold the casino. There is no one I trust. I go downstairs and hand over the keys to all my guns to Sreang, who I know will stay on as security at least for a while.

That night after the children are asleep, Agnete and I have the most terrifying argument. She throws things; she hits me; she thinks I'm saying that I want to desert them; I cannot make her listen or understand.

"Neak ta? Neak ta, what are you saying?"

"I'm saying I think we should go by road."

"We don't have time! There's the date, there's the booking! What are you trying to do?" She is panicked, desperate; her mouth ringed with thin strings of muscle, her neck straining.

I have to go and find a monk. I give him a huge sum of money to earn merit, and I ask him to chant for us. I ask him to bless our luggage and at a distance bless the boat that we will sail in. I swallow fear like thin sour spit. I order ahead, food for Pchum Ben, so that he can eat it, and act as mediary so that I can feed my dead. I look at him. He smiles. He is a man without guns, without modernity, without family to help him. For just a moment I envy him.

I await disaster, sure that the loss of our *neak ta* bodes great ill; I fear that the boat will be swamped at sea.

But I'm wrong.

Dolphins swim ahead of our prow leaping out of the water. We trawl behind us for fish and haul up tuna, turbot, sea snakes and turtles. I can assure you that flying fish really do fly—they soar over our heads at night, right across the boat like giant mosquitoes.

No one gets seasick; there are no storms; we navigate directly. It is as though the sea has made peace with us. *Let them be, we have lost them, they are going.*

We are Cambodians. We are good at sleeping in hammocks and just talking. We trade jokes and insults and innuendo sometimes in verse, and we play music, cards, and *bah angkunh*, a game of nuts. Gerda joins in the game and I can see the other kids let her win. She squeals with delight, and reaches down between the slats to find a nut that has fallen through.

All the passengers hug and help take care of the children. We cook on little stoves, frying in woks. Albatrosses rest on our rigging. Gerda still won't speak, so I cuddle her all night long, murmuring. *Kynom ch'mooah Channarith. Oun ch'mooah ay?*

I am your new father.

Once in the night, something huge in the water vents, just beside us. The stars themselves seem to have come back like the fish, so distant and high, cold and pure. No wonder we are greedy for them, just as we are greedy for diamonds. If we could, we would strip-mine the universe, but instead we strip-mine ourselves.

We land at Sentosa. Its resort beaches are now swallowed by the sea, but its slopes sprout temporary, cantilevered accommodation. The sides of the buildings spread downwards like sheltering batwings behind the plastic quays that walk us directly to the hillside.

Singapore's latest growth industry.

The living dead about to be entombed, we march from the boats along the top of pontoons. Bobbing and smooth-surfaced, the quays are treacherous. We slip and catch each other before we fall. There are no old people among us, but we all walk as if aged, stiff-kneed, and unbalanced.

But I am relieved; the island still burgeons with trees. We take a jungle path, through humid stillness, to the north shore, where we face the Lion City.

Singapore towers over the harbor. Its giant versions of Angkor Wat blaze with sunlight like daggers; its zigzag shoreline is ringed round with four hundred clippers amid a white forest of wind turbines. Up the sides of Mt. Fraser cluster the houses of rustics, made of wood and propped against the slope on stilts.

It had been raining during the day. I'd feared a storm, but now the sky is clear, gold and purple with even a touch of green. All along the line where trees give way to salt grasses, like stars going for a swim, fireflies shine.

Gerda's eyes widen. She smiles and holds out a hand. I whisper the Khmer words for firefly: *ampil ampayk.*

We're booked into one of the batwings. Only wild riches can buy a hotel room in Sentosa. A bottle of water is expensive enough.

Once inside, Agnete's spirits improve, even sitting on folding metal beds with a hanging blanket for a partition. Her eyes glisten. She sits Gerda and Sampul on the knees of her crossed legs. "They have beautiful shopping malls Down There," she says. "And Rith, *technik*, all the latest. Big screens. Billion billion pixels."

"They don't call them pixels any more, Mom."

That night, Gerda starts to cry. Nothing can stop her. She wails and wails. Our friends from the boat turn over on their beds and groan. Two of the women sit with Agnete and offer sympathy. "Oh poor thing, she is ill."

No, I think, she is broken-hearted. She writhes and twists in Agnete's lap.

Without words for it, I know why she is crying.

Agnete looks like she's been punched in the face; she didn't sleep well on the boat.

I say, "Darling, let me take her outside. You sleep."

I coax Gerda up into my arms, but she fights me like a cat. *Sssh sssh, Angel, sssh.* But she's not to be fooled. Somehow she senses what this is. I walk out of the refugee shelter and onto the dock that sighs underfoot. I'm standing there, holding her, looking up at the ghost of Singapore, listening to the whoop of the turbines overhead, hearing the slopping sound of water against the quay. I know that Gerda cannot be consoled.

Agnete thinks our people are kind because we smile. But we can also be cruel. It was cruel of Gerda's father to leave her, knowing what might happen after he was gone. It was cruel to want to be missed that badly.

On the north shore, I can still see the towers defined only by their bioluminescence, in leopard-spot growths of blue, or gold-green, otherwise lost in a mist of human manufacture, smoke and steam.

The skyscrapers are deserted now, unusable, for who can climb 70 stories? How strange they look; what drove us to make them? Why all across the world did we reach up so high? As if to escape the Earth, distance ourselves from the ground, and make a shiny new artifice of the world.

And there are the stars. They have always shone; they shine now just like they would shine on the deck of a starship, no nearer. There is the warm sea that gave us birth. There are the trees that turn sunlight into sugar for all of us to feed on.

Then overhead, giant starfish in the sky. I am at a loss, *choy mae!* What on earth is that? They glow in layers, orange red green. Trailing after them in order, come giant butterflies glowing blue and purple. Gerda coughs into silence and stares upwards.

Cable cars. Cable cars strung from Mt. Fraser, to the shore and on to Sentosa, glowing with decorative bioluminescence.

Ampil ampayk, I say again and for just moment, Gerda is still.

I don't want to go. I want to stay here.

Then Gerda roars again, sounding like my heart.

The sound threatens to shred her throat. The sound is inconsolable. I rock her, sush her, kiss her, but nothing brings her peace.

You too, Gerda, I think. You want to stay too, don't you? We are two of a kind.

For a moment, I want to run away together, Gerda and me, get across the straits to Johor Bahu, hide in the untended wilds of old palm-oil plantations.

But now we have no money to buy food or water.

I go still as the night whispers its suggestion.

I will not be cruel like her father. I can go into that warm sea and spread myself among the fishes to swim for ever. And I can take you with me, Gerda.

We can be still, and disappear into the Earth.

I hold her out as if offering her to the warm birthsea. And finally, Gerda sleeps, and I ask myself, will I do it? Can I take us back? Both of us?

Agnete touches my arm. "Oh, you got her to sleep! Thank you so much." Her hand first on my shoulder, then around Gerda, taking her from me, and I can't stop myself tugging back, and there is something alarmed, confused around her eyes. Then she gives her head a quick little shake, dismissing it.

I would rather be loved for my manliness than for my goodness. But I suppose it's better than nothing and I know I will not escape. I know we will all Go Down.

The next day we march, numb and driven by something we do not understand.

For breakfast, we have Chinese porridge with roasted soya, nuts, spices and egg. Our last day is brilliantly sunny. There are too many of us to all take the cable car. Economy class, we are given an intelligent trolley to guide us, carrying our luggage or our children. It whines along the bridge from Sentosa, giving us relentless tourist information about Raffles, independence in 1965, the Singapore miracle, the coolies who came as slaves but stayed to contribute so much to Singapore's success.

The bridge takes us past an artificial island full of cargo, cranes and wagons, and on the main shore by the quays is a squash of a market with noodle stalls, fish stalls, and stalls full of knives or dried lizards. Our route takes us up Mount Fraser, through the trees. The monkeys pursue us, plucking bags of bananas from our hands, clambering up on our carts, trying to open our parcels. Rith throws rocks at them.

The dawn light falls in rays through the trees as if the Buddha himself was overhead, shedding radiance. Gerda toddles next me, her hand in mine. Suddenly she stoops over and holds something up. It is a scarab beetle, its shell a shimmering turquoise green, but ants are crawling out of it. I blow them away. "Oh, that is a treasure, Gerda. You hold onto it, OK?"

There will be nothing like it where we are going.

Then looking something like a railway station, there is the Singapore terminal dug into the rock of the outcropping. It yawns wide open, to funnel us inside. The concrete is softened by a screen of branches sweeping along its face—very tasteful and traditional I think until I touch them and find that they are made of mouldform.

This is Singapore, so everything is perfectly done. *Pamper yourself,* a sign says in ten different languages. *Breathe in an Air of Luxury.*

Beautiful concierges in blue-grey uniforms greet us. One of them asks, "Is this the Sonn family?" Her face is so pretty, like Gerda's will be one day, a face of all nations, smiling and full of hope that something good can be done.

"I'm here to help you with check-in, and make sure you are comfortable and happy." She bends down and looks into Gerda's eyes but something in them makes her falter; the concierge's smile seems to trip and stumble.

Nightmarishly, her lipgloss suddenly smears up and across her face, like a wound. It feels as though Gerda has somehow cut her.

The concierge's eyes are sad now. She gives Gerda a package printed with a clown's face and colored balloons. Gerda holds the gift out from her upside down and scowls at it.

The concierge has packages for all the children, to keep them quiet in line. The giftpacks match age and gender. Rith always says his gender is Geek, as a joke, but he does somehow get a Geek pack. They can analyze his clothes and brand names. I muse on how strange it is that Rith's dad gave him the same name as mine, so that he is Rith and I am Channarith. He never calls me father. Agnete calls me Channa, infrequently.

The beautiful concierge takes our papers, and says that she will do all the needful. Our trolley says goodbye and whizzes after her, to check in our bags. I'm glad it's gone. I hate its hushed and cheerful voice. I hate its Bugs-Bunny baby face.

We wait.

Other concierges move up and down the velvet-roped queues with little trolleys offering water, green tea, dragon fruit or chardonnay. However much we paid, when all is said and done, we are fodder to be processed. I know in my sinking heart that getting here is why Agnete married me. She needed the fare.

No one lied to us, not even ourselves. This is bigger than a lie; this is like an animal migration, this is all of us caught up in something about ourselves we do not understand, never knew.

Suddenly my heart says, firmly. *There are no aliens.*

Aliens are just the excuse. This is something we want to do, like building those skyscrapers. This is all a new kind of dream, a new kind of grief turned inwards, but it's not my dream, nor do I think that it's Gerda's. She is squeezing my hand too hard and I know she knows this thing that is beyond words.

"Agnete," I say. "You and the boys go. I cannot. I don't want this."

Her face is sudden fury. "I knew you'd do this. Men always do this."

"I didn't use to be a man."

"That makes no difference!" She snatches Gerda away from me, who starts to cry again. Gerda has been taken too many places, too suddenly, too firmly. "I knew there was something weird going on." She glares at me as if she doesn't know me, or is only seeing me for the first time. Gently she coaxes Gerda towards her, away from me. "The children are coming with me. All of the children. If you want to be be blown up by aliens…."

"There are no aliens."

Maybe she doesn't hear me. "I have all the papers." She means the papers that identify us, let us in our own front door, give us access to our bank accounts. All she holds is the hologrammed, eye-printed ticket. She makes a jagged, flinty correction: "*They* have all the papers. Gerda is my daughter, and they will favor me." She's already thinking custody battle, and she's right, of course.

"There are no aliens." I say it a third time. "There is no reason to do this."

This time I get heard. There is a sound of breathing-out from all the people around me. A fat Tamil, sated maybe with blowing up other people, says, "What, you think all those governments lie? You're just getting cold feet."

Agnete focuses on me. "Go on. Get going if that's what you want." Her face has no love or tolerance in it.

"People need there to be aliens and so they all believe there are. But I don't."

Gerda is weeping in complete silence, though her face looks calm. I have never seen so much water come out of someone's eyes; it pours out as thick as bird's nest soup. Agnete keeps her hands folded across Gerda's chest and kisses the top of her head. What, does she think I'm going to steal Gerda?

Suddenly our concierge is kneeling down, cooing. She has a pink metal teddy bear in one hand, and it hisses as she uses it to inject Gerda.

"There! All happy now!" The concierge looks up at me with hatred. She gives Agnete our check-in notification, now perfumed and glowing. But not our ID papers. Those they keep, to keep us there, safe.

"Thank you," says Agnete. Her jaw thrusts out at me.

The Tamil is smiling with rage. "You see that idiot? He got the little girl all afraid."

"Fool can't face the truth," says a Cluster of networked Malay, all in unison.

I want to go back to the trees, like Tarzan, but that is a different drive, a different dream.

"Why are you stopping the rest of us trying to go, just because you don't want to?" says a multigen, with a wide, glassy grin. How on earth does s/he think I could stop them doing anything? I can see s/he is making up for a lifetime of being disrespected. This intervention, though late and cowardly and stupid, gets the murmur of approval for which s/he yearns.

It is like cutting my heart at the root, but I know I cannot leave Gerda. I cannot leave her alone down there. She must not be deserted a second time. They have doped her, drugged her, the world swims around her, her eyes are dim and crossed, but I fancy she is looking for me. At the level of the singing blood in our veins, we understand each other.

I hang my head.

"So you're staying," says Agnete, her face pulled in several opposing directions, satisfaction, disappointment, anger, triumph, scorn.

"For Gerda, yes."

Agnete's face resolves itself into stone. She wanted maybe a declaration of love, after that scene? Gerda is limp and heavy and dangling down onto the floor.

"Maybe she's lucky," I say. "Maybe that injection killed her."

The crowd has been listening for something to outrage them. "Did you hear what that man said?"

"What an idiot!"

"Jerk."

"Hey lady, you want a nicer guy for a husband, try me."

"Did he say the little girl should be dead? Did you hear him say that?"

"Yeah, he said that the little baby should be dead!"

"Hey you, Pol Pot. Get out of line. We're doing this to escape genocide, not take it with us."

I feel distanced, calm. "I don't think we have any idea what we are doing."

Agnete grips the tickets and certificates of passage. She holds onto Gerda, and tries to hug the two younger boys. There is a bubble of spit coming out of Gerda's mouth. The lift doors swivel open, all along the wall. Agnete starts forward. She has to drag Gerda with her.

"Let me carry her at least," I say. Agnete ignores me. I trail after her. Someone pushes me sideways as I shuffle. I ignore him.

And so I Go Down.

They take your ID and keep it. It is a safety measure to hold as many of human-kind safely below as possible. I realize I will never see the sun again. No sunset cumulonimbus, no shushing of the sea, no schools of sardines swimming like veils of silver in clear water, no unreliable songbirds that may fail to appear, no more brown grass, no more dusty wild flowers unregarded by the roadside. No thunder to strike the *neak ta,* no chants at midnight, no smells of fish frying, no rice on the floor of the temple.

I am a son of Kambu. Kampuchea.

I slope into the elevator.

"Hey boss," says a voice. The sound of it makes me unhappy before I recognize who it is. Ah yes, with his lucky moustache. It is someone who used to work in my hotel. My Embezzler. He looks delighted, pleased to see me. "Isn't this great? Wait til you see it!"

"Yeah, great," I murmur.

"Listen," says an intervener to my little thief. "Nothing you can say will make this guy happy."

"He's a nice guy," says the Embezzler. "I used to work for him. Didn't I, Boss?"

This is my legacy thug, inherited from my boss. He embezzled his fare from me and disappeared, oh, two years ago. These people may think he's a friend, but I bet he still has his stolen guns, in case there is trouble.

"Good to see you," I lie. I know when I am outnumbered.

For some reason that makes him chuckle, and I can see his silver-outlined teeth. I am ashamed that this unpunished thief is now my only friend.

Agnete knows the story, sniffs and looks away. "I should have married a genetic man," she murmurs.

Never, ever, tread on someone else's dream.

The lift is mirrored, and there are holograms of light as if we stood inside an infinite diamond, glistering all the way up to a blinding heaven. And dancing in the fire, brand names.

Gucci

Armani

Sony

Yamomoto

Hugo Boss

And above us, clear to the end and the beginning, the stars. The lift goes down.

Those stars have cost us dearly. All around me, the faces look up in unison.

Whole nations were bankrupted trying to get there, to dwarf stars and planets of methane ice. Arizona disappeared in an annihilation as matter and antimatter finally met, trying to build an engine. Massive junk still orbits half-assembled, and will one day fall. The saps who are left behind on Ground Zero will probably think it's the comet.

But trying to build those self-contained starships taught us how to do this instead.

Earthside, you walk out of your door, you see birds fly. Just after the sun sets and the bushes bloom with bugs, you will see bats flitter silhouetted as they neep. In hot afternoons the bees waver heavy with pollen, and I swear even fishes fly. But nothing flies between the stars except energy. You wanna be converted into energy, like Arizona?

So we go down.

Instead of up.

"The first thing you will see is the main hall. That should cheer up you claustrophobics," says my Embezzler. "It is the biggest open space we have in the Singapore facility. And as you will see, that's damn big!" The travelers chuckle in appreciation. I wonder if they don't pipe in some of that cheerful sound.

And poor Gerda, she will wake up for the second time in another new world. I fear it will be too much for her.

The lift walls turn like stiles, reflecting yet more light in shards, and we step out.

Ten storeys of brand names go down in circles—polished marble floors, air-conditioning, little murmuring carts, robot pets that don't poop, kids in the latest balloon shoes.

"What do you think of that!" the Malay network demands of me. All its heads turn, including the women wearing modest headscarves.

"I think it looks like Kuala Lumpur on a rainy afternoon."

The corridors of the emporia go off into infinity as well, as if you could shop all the way to Alpha Centauri. An illusion of course, like standing in a hall of mirrors.

It's darn good this technology, it fools the eye for all of 30 seconds. To be fooled longer than that, you have to want to be fooled. At the end of the corridor, reaching out for somewhere beyond, distant and pure, there is only light.

We have remade the world.

Agnete looks worn. "I need a drink, where's a bar?"

I need to be away too, away from these people who know that I have a wife for whom my only value has now been spent.

Our little trolley finds us, calls our name enthusiastically and advises us. In Ramlee Mall, level ten, Central Tower we have the choice of Bar Infinity, the Malacca Club (share the Maugham experience), British India, the Kuala Lumpur Tower View…

Agnete chooses the Seaside Pier; I cannot tell if out of kindness or irony.

I step inside the bar with its high ceiling and for just a moment my heart leaps with hope. There is the sea, the islands, the bridges, the sails, the gulls, and the sunlight dancing. Wafts of sugar vapor inside the bar imitate sea mist, and the breathable sugar makes you high. At the other end of the bar is what looks like a giant orange orb (half of one, the other half is just reflected). People lounge on the brand name sand (guaranteed to brush away and evaporate). Fifty meters overhead, there is a virtual mirror that doubles distance so you can look up and see yourself from what appears to be 100 meters up, as if you are flying. A Network on its collective back is busy spelling the word HOME with their bodies.

We sip martinis. Gerda still sleeps and I now fear she always will.

"So," says Agnete, her voice suddenly catching up with her butt, and plonking down to earth and relative calm. "Sorry about that back there. It was a tense moment for both of us. I have doubts too. About coming here, I mean."

She puts her hand on mine.

"I will always be so grateful to you," she says and really means it. I play with one of her fingers. I seem to have purchased loyalty.

"Thank you," I say, and I realize that she has lost mine.

She tries to bring love back, by squeezing my hand. "I know you didn't want to come. I know you came because of us."

Even the boys know there is something radically wrong. Sampul and Tharum stare in silence, wide brown eyes. Did something similar happen with Dad number one?

Rith the eldest chortles with scorn. He needs to hate us so that he can fly the nest.

My heart is so sore I cannot speak.

"What will you do?" she asks. That sounds forlorn, so she then tries to sound perky. "Any ideas?"

"Open a casino," I say, feeling deadly.

"Oh! Channa! What a wonderful idea, it's just perfect!"

"Isn't it? All those people with nothing to do." Someplace they can bring their powder. I look out at the sea.

Rith rolls his eyes. Where is there for Rith to go from here? I wonder. I see that he too will have to destroy his inheritance. What will he do, drill the rock? Dive down into the lava? Or maybe out of pure rebellion ascend to Earth again?

The drug wears off, and Gerda awakes, but her eyes are calm and she takes an interest in the table and the food. She walks outside onto the mall floor, and suddenly squeals with laughter and runs to the railing to look out. She points at the glowing yellow sign with black ears and says, "Disney". She says all the brand names aloud, as if they are all old friends.

I was wrong. Gerda is at home here.

I can see myself wandering the whispering marble halls like a ghost, listening for something that is dead.

We go to our suite. It's just like the damn casino, but there are no boats outside to push slivers into your hands, no sand too hot for your feet. Cambodia has ceased to exist, for us.

Agnete is beside herself with delight. "What window do you want?"

I ask for downtown Phnom Penh. A forest of grey, streaked skyscrapers to the horizon. "In the rain," I ask.

"Can't we have something a bit more cheerful?"

"Sure. How about Tuol Sleng prison?"

I know she doesn't want me. I know how to hurt her. I go for a walk.

Overhead in the dome is the Horsehead Nebula. Radiant, wonderful, deadly, 30 years to cross at the speed of light.

I go to the pharmacy. The pharmacist looks like a phony doctor in an ad. I ask, "Is... is there some way out?"

"You can go Earthside with no ID. People do. They end up living in huts on Sentosa. But that's not what you mean is it?"

I just shake my head. It's like we've been edited to ensure that nothing disturbing actually gets said. He gives me a tiny white bag with blue lettering on it.

Instant, painless, like all my flopping guests at the casino.

"Not here," he warns me. "You take it and go somewhere else like the public toilets."

Terrifyingly, the pack isn't sealed properly. I've picked it up, I could have the dust of it on my hands; I don't want to wipe them anywhere. What if one of the children licks it?

I know then that I don't want to die. I just want to go home, and always will. I am a son of Kambu, Kampuchea.

"Ah," he says and looks pleased. "You know, the Buddha says that we must accept."

"So why didn't we accept the Earth?" I ask him.

The pharmacist in his white lab coat shrugs. "We always want something different."

We always must move on and if we can't leave home, it drives us mad. Blocked and driven mad, we do something new.

There was one final phase to becoming a man. I remember my uncle. The moment his children and his brother's children were all somewhat grown, he left us to become a monk. That was how a man was completed, in the old days.

I stand with a merit bowl in front of the wat. I wear orange robes with a few others. Curiously enough, Rith has joined me. He thinks he has rebelled. People from Sri Lanka, Laos, Burma, and my own land give us food for their dead. We bless it and chant in Pali.

All component things are indeed transient.
They are of the nature of arising and decaying.
Having come into being, they cease to be.
The cessation of this process is bliss.
Uninvited he has come hither
He has departed hence without approval
Even as he came, just so he went
What lamentation then could there be?

We got what we wanted. We always do, don't we, as a species? One way or another.

TRUTH AND BONE
PAT CADIGAN

Pat Cadigan was born in Schenectady, New York, and grew up in Fitchburg, Massachusetts. She studied at the University of Massachusetts and University of Kansas, edited small press magazines *Shayol* and *Chacal*, and published her first story in 1980. One of the most important writers of the cyberpunk movement, she is the author of sixteen books, including debut novel *Mindplayers*, which was nominated for the Philip K. Dick Award and Arthur C. Clarke Award winners *Synners* and *Fools*, as well as two nonfiction movie books on the making of *The Mummy* and *Lost In Space*, five media tie-ins, and one young adult novel, *Avatar*. Her short fiction is collected in Locus Award winner *Patterns*, *Dirty Work*, *Home by the Sea*, and *Letters from Home*. She currently lives in London with her husband, the Original Chris Fowler.

In my family, we all have exceptionally long memories.

Mine starts under my Aunt Donna's blond Heywood Wakefield dining room table after one of her traditional pre-Christmas Sunday dinners for the familial horde. My cousins had escaped into the living room to watch TV or play computer games while the adults gossiped over coffee and dessert. I wasn't quite two and a half and neither group was as interesting to me as the space under the table. The way the wooden legs came up made arches that looked to my toddler eyes like the inside of a castle. It was my secret kingdom, which I imagined was under the sea.

That afternoon I was deep in thought as to whether I should take off my green, red, and white striped Christmas socks and put them on my stuffed dog Bluebelle. I was so preoccupied—there were only two and they didn't go with her electric blue fur—that I had forgotten everything and everyone around me, until something my mother said caught my ear:

"The minute that boy turned sixteen, he left home and nobody begged him to stay."

All the adults went silent. I knew my mother had been referring to my cousin Loomis. Every time his name came up in conversation, people tended to shut up or at least lower their voices. I didn't know why. I didn't even know what he looked like. The picture in my mind was of a teenaged boy seen from behind, shoving open a screen door as he left without looking back.

The silence stretched while I studied this mental image. Then someone asked if there was more coffee and someone else wanted more fruitcake and I almost got brained with people crossing and uncrossing their legs as the conversation resumed.

One of the relatives had seen Loomis recently in some distant city and it had not been a happy meeting. Loomis still resented the family for the way they had treated him just because (he said) of what he was, as if he'd had any choice about it. The relative had tried to argue that nobody blamed him for an accident of birth. What he did about it was another matter, though, and Loomis had made a lot of his own problems.

Easy to say, Loomis had replied, when you didn't have to walk the walk.

The relative told him he wasn't the first one in the family and he certainly wouldn't be the last.

Loomis said that whether he was the first or the thousand-and-first, he was the only one right now.

And just like that it came to me:

Not any more, Loomis.

In my family, we all have exceptionally long memories and we all…know… something. Only those of us born into the family, of course—marrying in won't do it, we're not contagious.

That's not easy, marrying in. By necessity, we're a clannish bunch and it takes a special kind of person to handle that. Our success rate for marriages is much lower than average. Some of us don't even bother to get married. My parents, for instance. And neither of them was an outsider. My father was from one of the branches that fell off the family tree, as my Aunt Donna put it. There were a few of those, people who had the same traits but who were so far removed that there was no consanguinity to speak of.

It only took one parent to pass the traits on; the other parent never figured it out—not everything, anyway. That might sound unbelievable but plenty of people live secret lives that even those closest to them never suspect.

In my family, we all know something, usually around twelve or thirteen. We call it "coming into our own."

Only a few of us knew ahead of time what it would be. I was glad I did. I could think about how I was going to tell my mother and how we'd break it to everyone else. And what I would do if I had to leave home because no one was begging me to stay.

In the words of an older, wiser head who also may have known something, Forewarned is forearmed.

My mother knows machines: engines, mechanical devices, computer hardware—if it doesn't work, she knows why. My grandfather had the same trait; he ran a repair service and my mother worked in the family business from the time she was twelve. Later she paid her way through college as a freelance car mechanic. She still runs the business from a workshop in our basement. My Aunt Donna keeps the books and even in a time when people tend to buy new things rather than get the old ones fixed, they do pretty well.

Donna told me once that my mother said all repair work bored her rigid. That gave me pause. How could she possibly be bored when her trait was so useful? But when I thought about it a little more, I understood: there's just not a whole lot of variety to broken things.

My father knows where anyone has been during the previous twenty-four hours. This is kind of weird, specific and esoteric, not as handy-dandy as my mother's trait but still useful. If you were a detective you'd know whether a suspect's alibi was real—well, as long as you questioned them within twenty-four hours of the crime. You'd know if your kids were skipping school or sneaking out at night, or if your spouse was cheating on you.

My father said those were things you might be better off *not* knowing. I wasn't sure I agreed with him but it was all moot anyway. My parents split up shortly after Tim was born, when I was six and Benny was three, for reasons that had more to do with where they wanted to be in the future than where either of them had been the day before.

In any case, my father wasn't a detective.

He was a chef on a cruise ship.

This was as specific and esoteric as his trait so I suppose it fit his personality. But I couldn't help thinking that it was also kind of a waste. I mean, on a cruise ship, *everyone* knows where everyone else has been during the previous twenty-four hours: i.e., on the boat. Right?

My Aunt Donna knows when you're lying.

Most people in the family assume that's why she never married. It might be true but there are other people in the family with the same trait and it never stopped them. Donna was the oldest of the seven children in my mother's family and I think she just fell into the assistant mother role so deeply that she never got around to having a family of her own. She was the family matriarch when I was growing up and I guess being a human lie detector is kind of appropriate for someone in that position.

The thing was, unless someone's life was literally in danger, she refused to use her trait for anyone else, family or not.

"Because knowing that someone is lying is not the same as knowing the truth," she explained to Benny on one of several occasions when he tried to talk her into detecting my lies. I was ten at the time and I'd been teasing him with outrageous stories about getting email from movie stars. "Things get tricky if you interfere. When you interfere with the world, the world interferes with you. "Besides," she added, giving me a sly, sideways glance, "sometimes the truth is vastly overrated."

A few weeks after that I was out with her and my mother on the annual back-to-school safari—hours of intense shopping in deepest, darkest shopping-mall hell—and she suddenly asked me if I felt like my body was changing. We were having food-court fish and chips and the question surprised me so much I almost passed a hunk of breaded cod through my nose.

"Hannah's entirely too young," my mother said, bemused. "I wouldn't expect anything to happen for at least another three years."

My aunt had a cagey look, the same one she had worn when she had made the comment about truth being overrated. "That's what you think. Puberty seems to come earlier all the time."

They turned to me expectantly. I just shrugged. A shrug was just a shrug and nothing more, least of all a lie.

"Well, it's true," Donna went on after a moment. "Ma didn't get her period till she was almost fifteen. I was thirteen, you were twelve. The girl who delivers my paper? She was *ten.*"

"And you know this how?" my mother asked. "Was there a little note with the bill—*Dear valued customer, I have entered my childbearing years, please pay promptly?* Or do they print announcements on the society page with the weddings and engagements now?"

Donna made a face at her. "Last week when she was collecting, she asked if she could come in and sit down for a few minutes because she had cramps. I gave her half a Midol."

My mother sobered at once. "Better be careful about that. You could find yourself on the wrong end of a lawsuit."

"For half a Midol?"

"You can never be too careful about giving medicine—*drugs*—to other people's children. She could have been allergic."

I was hoping they'd start trading horror stories about well-intentioned adults accidentally poisoning kids with over-the-counter medicine and forget all about me. No such luck. My mother turned to me with a concerned look. "So *have* you been feeling any changes, Hannah? Of any kind?"

"Do we have to talk about that *here?*" I glanced around unhappily.

"Sorry, honey, I didn't mean to embarrass you." She touched my arm gently and the expression on her face was so kind and, well, motherly that I almost spilled my guts right there. It would have been such a relief to tell her everything, especially how I didn't want to end up like Loomis.

Then I said, "That's OK" and stuffed my mouth with fries.

"I don't care if your papergirl already needs Midol," my mother told Donna, "Hannah's still too young. We shouldn't be trying to hurry her, we ought to let her enjoy being a kid while she can. Kids grow up too fast these days."

The conversation turned to safe, boring things like where we should go next and what if anything I should try on again. But Donna kept sneaking little glances at me and I knew the subject wasn't really closed, just as I knew it hadn't really been about menstruation.

No matter when I came into my own, I decided as I bent over my lunch, I was going to hide it for as long as possible. It might be hard but I had already managed to hide the fact that I knew about my trait.

Besides, hiding things was a way of life with us. It was something we were all raised to do.

We all know something and no matter what it is, we virtually never tell anyone outside the family.

"It's like being in the Mafia," my cousin Ambrose said once at a barbecue in Donna's back yard. "We could even start calling it 'this thing of ours' like on TV."

"Nah, we're not ethnic enough," said his father, my Uncle Scott.

"Speak for yourself," my cousin Sunny piped up and everyone laughed. Sunny was Korean.

"You know what I mean," Scott said, also laughing. "You're the wrong ethnic group anyway."

"Maybe we should marry into the Mafia," Sunny suggested. "Between what we know and what they can do, we could take over the world."

"Never happen," said my mother. "They'd rub us out for knowing too much." More laughter.

"Ridiculous," said someone else—I don't remember who. "Knowledge is power."

Knowledge is power. I've heard it so often I think if you cracked my head open, you'd find it spray-painted like graffiti on the inside of my skull. But it's not the whole story.

Sometimes what power it has is over you.

And it's always incomplete. *Always.*

My cousin Ambrose knows what you've forgotten—the capital of Venezuela, the name of the Beatles' original drummer, or the complete lyrics to Billy Joel's "We Didn't Start The Fire" (Caracas, Pete Best, and don't go there, he can't sing worth a damn). When he came into his own at fourteen, Donna threw him a party and he told everyone where they'd left their keys or when they were supposed to go to the dentist. Apparently reminding people to buy milk or answer their email wasn't interfering with the world, at least not in the way that got tricky.

We all knew the real reason for the party, Ambrose included: he was Loomis's younger brother. Just about all the local relatives showed up and they all behaved themselves, probably under threat of death or worse from Donna. Even so, I overheard whispers about what a chance she had taken, what with Loomis being the elephant in the room. It was hard to have a good time after that, watching my own younger brothers giggling as they asked Ambrose to remember things they'd done as babies.

There were other mutterings suggesting that Ambrose had come into his own earlier than he had let on. He was a straight-A student and who wouldn't be with a trait like his? Just jealousy, I knew; Ambrose had always been brainy, especially in math. He was three years older than I was and I had been going to him for help with my homework since third grade.

Still, I was tempted to ask. If he really had hidden his trait, maybe I could pick up some pointers.

I came into my own in the school library on a Thursday afternoon in early April, when I was thirteen.

After knowing for so long in advance, I had expected to feel different on the day it finally happened, something physical or emotional or even just a thought popping into my head, like all those years ago under my aunt's table. But I didn't. As I sat at a table in the nearly-empty library after the last class of the day, the only thing on my mind was the make-up assignment my math teacher Ms. Chang had given me. I had just been out a week with strep throat so I was behind with everything anyway but this was the worst. X's and y's and a's and b's, pluses and minuses, parentheses with tiny twos floating up high—my eyes were crossing.

I looked up and saw Mr. Bodette, the head librarian, standing at the front desk. Our eyes met and I knew, as matter-of-factly as anything else I knew just by looking at him—there was a spot on his tie, he wore his wedding ring on his right hand, his hair was starting to thin—that in a little over twenty-eight years, he was going to fracture his skull and die.

Mr. Bodette gave me a little smile. I looked down quickly, waiting to get a splitting headache or have to run to the bathroom or just feel like crying. But nothing happened.

I must be an awful person. I stared at the equations without seeing them. A nice man was going to die of a fractured skull and I didn't feel sick about it.

I curled my index finger around the mechanical pencil I was holding and squeezed until my hand cramped. Was it because twenty-eight years was such a long, long time away? For me, anyway. It was twice as long as I had been alive—

"Takes a little extra thought."

I jumped, startled; Mr. Bodette was standing over me, smiling.

"Algebra was a killer for me, too." He took the pencil out of my hand and wrote busily on a sheet of scrap paper. "See? Here, I'll do another one."

I sat like a lump; he might have been writing hieroglyphics.

"There." He drew a circle around something that equaled something else. "See?

Never do anything to one side of the equation without doing the exact same thing to the other. That's good algebra. Got it?"

I didn't but I nodded and took my pencil back from him anyway.

"If you need more help, just ask," he said. "I needed plenty myself. Fortunately my mother was a statistician."

I stared after him as he went back to the front desk. Twenty-eight years; if I hadn't been so hopeless in math, I'd have known if that was equal to x in his equation.

A student volunteer came in and went to work re-shelving books. She had red hair and freckles and she was going to live for another seventy-nine years until a blood vessel broke in her brain. I had to force myself not to keep staring at her. I didn't know her name or what grade she was in or anything about her as a person. Only how and when she was going to die.

Perversely, the equations began to make sense. I worked slowly, hoping the building would be empty by the time I finished. Then I could slip out and hope that I didn't meet anyone I knew on my way home—

—where my mother and Benny and Tim would be waiting for me.

A cold, hard lump formed in my stomach. OK, then I'd go hide somewhere and try to figure out how I was supposed to look at my mother and my brothers every day knowing what I knew.

Is that really worse than knowing the same thing about yourself? asked a small voice in my mind.

That was an easy one: Yes. Absolutely.

Knowing about myself wasn't a horrific blaze of realization, more like remembering something commonplace. In ninety years, two months, seven weeks, and three days, my body would quit and my life would go out like a candle. If twenty-eight years seemed like a long time, ninety was unimaginable.

I slipped out of the library unnoticed and got all the way up to Ms. Chang's classroom on the third floor without meeting anyone. I left the worksheet on her desk, started to leave and then froze, struck by the sight of the rows of empty seats staring at me. Today they had been filled with kids. Tomorrow they'd be filled with heart attacks, cancers, strokes…what else?

More fractured skulls? Drownings? Accidents?

Murders?

My skin tried to crawl off my body. Would I be able to tell if people were going to be murdered by the way they were going to die? Was Mr. Bodette's fractured skull going to be an accident or—

What if someone close to me was going to be murdered?

What if it was going to happen the next day?

I would have to try to stop it. Wouldn't I? Wasn't that why I knew?

It had to be. My mother knew what was wrong with a machine so she could fix it; I knew about someone's death so I could prevent it. Right?

No. Close, but not quite. Even *I* could see that was bad algebra.

Just as I went back out into the shadowy hallway, I heard a metallic squeak and rattle. Down at the far end of the corridor, one of the janitors was pushing a wheeled bucket with a mop handle. I braced myself, waiting as he ran the mop-head through the rollers on the side of the bucket to squeeze out excess water.

Nothing.

He started washing the floor; still I felt nothing. Because, I realized, he was too far away.

I dashed down the nearest staircase before he got any closer and ran out the front door.

Now that was very interesting, I thought as I stood outside on Prince Street looking back at the school: people had to be within a certain distance before I picked anything up from them. So the news wasn't all bad. I could have a career as a forest ranger or a lighthouse keeper. Did they still have lighthouse keepers?

Should've walked toward *the janitor, you wuss,* said a little voice in my mind; *then you'd know how close you had to be to pick up something.* No, only a very general idea; I wasn't good with distances—math strikes again. Too bad Ambrose's sister Rita hadn't been there. She knew space. All she had to do was look at something: a building, a room, a box, and she could give you the dimensions. Rita had capitalized on this and become an interior decorator. Sadly, she didn't have very good taste so she worked in partnership with a designer who, Ambrose said, probably had to tell her several times a week that knotty pine paneling wasn't the Next Big Thing.

I crossed the mercifully empty street but just as I reached the other side, I knew that eleven years and two months from now, a woman was going to die of cancer.

There was no one near me, not on the sidewalk nor in any of the cars parked at the curb. Up at the corner where Prince met Summer there was plenty of traffic but that was farther away from me than the janitor had been.

I didn't get it until the curtains in the front window of the nearest house parted and a woman's face looked out at me. She glanced left and right, and disappeared again. Another useful thing to know, I thought, walking quickly—people had to be within a certain distance but they didn't have to be visible to me.

In the house next door, there was a head injury, forty years; a stroke, thirty-eight years in the one after that. Nothing in the next two—no one home. Internal bleeding, twenty-six years in the next one. A car passed me going the other way: AIDS, ten years behind the wheel and heart failure, twenty-two years in the passenger seat. More AIDS, six years in the house on the corner.

Waiting for a break in the traffic so I could cross, I learned another useful fact—most of the cars on Summer Street passed too quickly for me to pick up on anything about the people in them. Only if one had to slow down or stop to make a turn would something come to me.

Eventually the traffic thinned out enough to let me cross. But by the time I reached the middle of the road, cars had accumulated on every side. My head filled with cancers, heart attacks, infections, organ failures, bleeding brains, diseases, conditions I didn't know the names of. I hefted my backpack, put my head down and watched my feet until I reached the other side.

Baron's Food and Drug was just ahead. I spotted an old payphone at the edge of the parking lot and hurried toward it, digging in my pockets for change (I was the last thirteen-year-old on the planet without a cell phone). It was stupid to hide that I'd come into my own. I would call my mother right now and come clean about everything, how I'd known for years and how I was afraid to tell anyone because I didn't want to end up like Loomis, leaving home with nobody begging me to stay.

I was in the middle of dialing when a great big football player type materialized next to the phone.

"Hey, girlie," he said with all the authority of a bully who'd been running his part of the world since kindergarten. "Who said you could use this phone?"

I glanced at the coin slot. "New England Bell?"

"'Zat so? Funny, Nobody told *me*. Hey, you guys!" he called over his shoulder to his friends who were just coming out of Baron's with cans of soda. "Any a you remember anything saying little girlie here could use our phone?"

My mouth went dry. I had to get the hell out of there, go home, and tell my mother why I now needed a cell. Instead, I heard myself say, "Should've checked your email."

He threw back his head and laughed as three of his pals came over and surrounded me. They were big guys, too, but he was the biggest—wide, fleshy face, neck like a bull, shoulders so massive he probably could have played without pads.

"Sorry, little girlie. You got no phone privileges here."

His friends agreed, sniggering. I tried to see them as bad back-up singers or clowns, anything to keep from thinking about what I knew.

"Come on, what are you, deaf?" The mean playfulness in his face took on a lot more mean than playful. "Step away from the phone and there won't be any trouble."

More sniggering from the back-up chorus; someone yanked hard on my backpack, trying to pull me off-balance. "I need to call home—"

"No, you need to *go* home." He pushed his face closer to mine. "Hear me? Go. The fuck. *Home*."

I should have been a block away already, running as fast as I could. But the devil had gotten into me, along with the knowledge that three days from now on Sunday night, the steering column of a car was going to go through his chest.

"If you'd let me alone," I said, "I'd be done already. Nobody's using this phone—"

"I'm waitin' on an important call," he said loudly. "Right, guys?"

The guys all agreed he sure was, fuckin' A.

"From who?" said the devil in me. "Your parole officer or your mommy?"

Now his pals were all going *Woo woo!* and *She gotcha!* He grabbed the receiver out of my hand and slammed it into the cradle. My change rattled into the coin return; I reached for it and he slapped my hand away, hard enough to leave a mark.

"Smart-ass tax, paid by bad little girlies who don't do as they're told," he said, fishing the coins out with his big fingers. "Now get the fuck outa here before something *really* bad happens to you."

The devil in me still hadn't had enough. "Like what?"

He pushed his face up close to mine again. "You don't want to find out."

The guys around me moved away slightly as I took a step back. "Yeah? Well, it couldn't be anywhere near as bad as what's coming up for you," the devil went on. "Yuk it up while you can, because this Sunday you're gonna d—" I stumbled slightly on a bit of uneven pavement and finally managed to shut myself up.

He tilted his head to one side, eyes bright with curiosity. "Don't stop now, it's just gettin' good. I'm gonna what?"

Now I had no voice at all.

"Come on, girlie." He gave a nasty laugh. "I'm gonna *what?*"

I swallowed hard and took another step back and then another. He moved toward me.

"Come *on,* I'm gonna *what?*"

"You—you're—" I all but choked. "You're gonna have a really bad night!"

I turned and ran until I couldn't hear them jeering any more.

You're not just a bad person, you're the worst person in the world. *No, you're the worst person who* ever lived.

Sitting at the back of the bus, I said it over and over, trying to fill my brain with it so I couldn't think about anything else. I actually managed to distract myself enough so that I didn't notice as many deaths as I might have otherwise.

Or maybe I was just full of my thug's imminent death. That and what I had told him.

Except he couldn't have understood. When that steering column went through his chest, he wasn't going to think, *OMGWTFBBQ, she knew!* in the last second before he died.

Was he?

The public library was my usual hideout when I felt overwhelmed or needed somewhere quiet to get my head together. Today, however, I was out of luck—the place was closed due to some problem with the plumbing. Figured, I thought. No hiding place for the worst person in the world.

By this time, my mother would be teetering on the threshold between annoyed and genuinely worried. I called her from the payphone by the front door of the library.

"This had better be good," she said, a cheery edge in her voice.

I gave her a rambling story about having to finish a math assignment and then going to the library to get a head start on a project only to find it was closed.

"Just get your butt home," she said when I paused for breath. To my relief, she sounded more affectionate than mad now. I told her I'd be there as soon as I could and hung up.

If I were going to live a long time, I thought as I walked two and a half blocks to a bus stop, then wouldn't the chances be really good that my mother and brothers would, too?

And if any of them were going to die in an accident, then I *had* to tell them so we could stop it from happening. I shouldn't have been afraid to go home. I should have *rushed* home.

I had to tell my mother everything, especially what I had said. She would know what to do.

Was this the kind of problem Loomis had made for himself, I wondered? Was this why no one had begged him to stay?

At least being home wasn't an ordeal. My mother would fade away in her sleep at ninety-two, Benny would suffer a massive stroke at eighty-nine, and Tim would achieve a hundred-and-five before his heart failed, making him the grand old man of the house. We were quite the long-lived bunch. I wondered what Mr. Bodette's mother the statistician would have made of that. Maybe nothing.

And it *was* nothing next to the fact that I didn't tell my mother anything after all.

But I had a good reason. It was Benny's night; he'd gotten a perfect score on a history test at school and my mother had decided to celebrate by taking us all to Wiggins, which had the best ice cream in the county, if not the world. We didn't get Wiggins very often and never on a school night. I just couldn't bring myself to spoil the evening with the curse of Loomis.

My thug's name, I discovered, was Phil Lattimore. He was sixteen, a linebacker on the varsity football team. There were lots of team photos in the school trophy case, which was the first thing you saw when you came up the stairs from the front door. I had never paid much attention to it. Sports didn't interest me much, especially sports I couldn't play.

When I went to school on Friday, however, the trophy case that had once barely existed for me seemed to draw me like a magnet—any time I had to go from one place to another, I'd find myself walking past it and I couldn't pass without looking at my thug's grinning face.

Worse was that I was suddenly noticing photos of the team everywhere, adorned with small pennants in the school colors reading !PRIDE!, !STRENGTH!, and !!!CHAMPIONS!!! and it wasn't even football season any more. You'd have thought they'd cured cancer or something.

Unbidden, it came to me: this could be a sign. Maybe if I saved my thug's life, he *would* cure cancer—or AIDS, or Ebola. Or maybe he'd stop global warming or world hunger. Plenty of people turned their lives around after a close brush with death. It was extremely hard to imagine my thug doing anything like that, but what did I know?

Unless I really was supposed to leave him to his fate.

That was like a whack upside my head. Was I supposed to fix this the way my mother fixed broken machines? Or just live with what I knew, like my Aunt Donna?

I couldn't do anything about what I didn't know, I decided. I had to do something about what I *did* know.

I was thirteen.

Ambrose made a pained face and shoved my math book back at me. "Liar."

"What do you mean?" I said, uneasily. "This stuff's driving me crazy."

"You're a liar. You make me come all the way over here when you don't need any help. Not with that, anyway. You just need your head examined." He started to get up from my desk and I caught his arm.

"Gimme a break—"

"Give *me* a break." My cousin gave me a sour, sarcastic smile. "Let me remind you of something you've forgotten: I know what you've forgotten." He tapped my math book with two fingers. "You haven't forgotten this. Ergo, you actually understand it. Congratulations, you're not a moron, just crazy. It's Saturday, it's spring, and there are a gazillion other things I'd rather do."

"Do you know Phil Lattimore?" I blurted just as he reached the doorway of my room.

He turned, the expression on his face a mix of surprise and revulsion. "Are you kidding? Everybody knows Phil the Fuckhead. According to him, anyway. What about him and why should I care?"

I took a deep, uncomfortable breath and let it out slowly. "I, uh…"

Ambrose stuck his fists on his narrow hips and tilted his head to one side. "You what?"

I swallowed and tried again. "There's something…" I cleared my throat. "Close the door."

He frowned as if this were something no one had ever asked him to do before.

"And come back over here and sit down," I added, "so I can tell you what I know."

He did so, looking wary. "You mean…*Know?*"

"Yeah," I said. "Tomorrow night, Phil Lattimore—" I floundered, trying to think of the right words. "OK, look—if you knew you could save someone's life, wouldn't you do it? Even a fuckhead?"

Ambrose's face turned serious. "What are you saying?"

"It's a car accident. Phil Lattimore—he—he'll be hurt."

He stared at me for I don't know how long. "You really, like...*know* this?" he said finally.

I nodded.

"Anyone else going to get hurt with him?"

"Not that I...uh...*know* of."

"Damn." Ambrose shook his head and gave a short, amazed laugh. "You *really* haven't told anyone else?"

"No one. Just you."

"I don't know why not." He ran a hand through his thick, brown hair. "If *I* could warn people when they were going to have an accident instead of just telling them where they left their keys—man, that would be fuckin' awesome." He gave me a significant look. "A hell of a lot better than telling people when they were going to die."

There are so many ways you can go wrong without meaning to.

You can make a mistake, an error, or a faux pas. You can screw things up, you can screw things up royally, or just screw the pooch. Or you can fuck up beyond all hope, like I did. Deliberately.

I knew it was wrong but I was afraid he wouldn't help me. But a life was at stake and that was more important than anything, I told myself. As soon as Phil Lattimore was safe, I'd tell Ambrose the truth. He might be angry with me at first but then he would understand, I told myself. So would the rest of the family. They couldn't possibly *not* understand. I told myself. I was thirteen.

"But *why* don't you want to tell anyone?" Ambrose asked as he worked on a Wiggins butterscotch shake.

"It's complicated. And keep your voice down." We were sitting outside at one of the bright yellow plastic tables near the entrance to the parking lot.

Ambrose made a business of looking around. The only other people there were a young couple with a baby three tables away. "Right. Because they might hear us *over the traffic noise!*" He bellowed the last words as a truck went by on the street. The couple with the baby never looked in our direction.

"Fine, you made your point," I said. Normally two scoops of coffee ice cream topped with hot fudge was enough to put the world right but not today. The people with the baby had arrived after we had and they were directly in my line of sight.

"You know, it's rare but there are a few other people in the family with your trait," Ambrose was saying.

"There are?"

"Yeah, one of our cousins, she lives in California, I think. My dad mentioned her once. Also one of his aunts, which I guess makes her our great-aunt. Dad said she so was high-strung that sometimes she was afraid to go out."

"Because of what she knew?" I said.

Ambrose frowned. "Not exactly. Something real bad happened—I don't know what—that everyone thought was an accident. Only it wasn't, because she didn't know about it in advance. Since she had no connection to anyone involved and no evidence, there was nothing she could do. Dad said she freaked out and never really recovered."

"She couldn't have made an anonymous call to the police? Or sent a letter or something?"

Ambrose shrugged. "I don't know the whole story. Maybe she tried that and it didn't work." His expression became slightly concerned. "I hope nothing like that ever happens to you."

"I can't worry about that right now," I said. "Are you sure Phil the Fuckhead's gonna be here?"

"I told you, my friend Jerry works weekends here and Phil always shows. After the fill-in manager goes home, he comes in to hassle the girls on the counter. Is there something about those people that bothers you?"

The sudden change in subject caught me by surprise. "What people? Why?"

"You keep putting up your hand to your head like you want to block out the sight of them but at the same time you're sneaking little peeks. Something wrong with them?"

Not really. Other than the fact that in nine years, seven months, and one week, the kid is going to drown, it's all good. I had to bite my lip.

Ambrose's eyes widened as he leaned forward. "Are *they* going to have an accident?"

The dad and mom would go on for another forty-five and sixty-eight years respectively before they died of two different cancers. I hoped they'd have other children.

"Nothing in the immediate future," I said.

"What about you and me?" His face was very serious now. "Are we gonna be OK?"

Ambrose had another fifty-two years ahead of him. Not as long as anyone at my house but not what I'd have called being cut off in his prime. "We're fine," I said. "We seem to be pretty l—ah, lucky." I'd been about to say *long-lived.*

"For the *immediate* future," he said, still serious. "How far ahead do you know about—two months? Six months? Longer?"

I took an uncomfortable breath. "I-I don't know. I haven't picked up on anyone else yet. What about the cousin and that great-aunt? How far ahead did they see?"

"My dad said the great-aunt wouldn't tell. He thinks maybe six months for the cousin but he couldn't remember."

"Six months would be pretty helpful," I said lamely.

Ambrose wasn't listening. He was looking at a car pulling into the parking lot.

"Fuckhead alert," he said. "Driving his land yacht. The only thing big enough for his fuckhead posse."

Land yacht was right; the metallic brown convertible was enormous, old but obviously cared for. The top was down, either to show off the tan and plaid upholstery or just to let the guys enjoy the wind blowing through their crew cuts. Phil parked down at the far end of the lot by the exit, taking up two spaces. Not just typical but predictable, like he was following a program laid out for him. The Fuckhead Lifeplan. Maybe I really *was* supposed to leave him to his fate.

As if catching the flavor of my thoughts, Ambrose said, "You *sure* you want to help this asshole? He's got plenty of friends. Let *them* rush him to the hospital."

"Shut up." I slipped over to Ambrose's side of the table. "And turn around, don't let them see we're looking at them."

"Whatever." Pause. "Hey, we're not doing this because you have some kinda masochistic crush on him, are we?"

"*No,* I *hate* him."

"Oh, look—it's my little girlie friend!" bellowed that stupid, awful voice. "And who's that with her? Hey, you're not cheating on me, are you? Better not or I'll have to teach you both a lesson—"

I wiped both hands over my face, begging the earth to open up and swallow me but as usual it didn't. Phil Lattimore loomed over me like the Thug of Doom, his chuckling goon squad backing him up. I glanced at Ambrose. He sat with his arms crossed, staring straight ahead.

"Oh, hey, you got a pet fag!" my thug said with loud delight. "I got no problem with fags as long as they're housetrained and don't try to hump my leg or nothing. You wouldn't do something like that, would you, pet fag? Hey, you got a name? You look like a Fifi. Right, guys?"

Fuckin' A, said the guys, high-fiving each other.

Phil Lattimore bent down so we were eye to eye. "Who said you could eat ice cream here?"

Would his buddies be in the car with him when it happened, would they be hurt? If so, they'd recover. The soonest any of them would pass away was thirty years from now; the goon on Phil's immediate left would die of blood poisoning. Another avoidable death. I Should make a note to phone him in three decades, two months, and six days: *Hey, if you get a splinter today, you'd better go to the hospital immediately because you'll die if you don't.*

All this went through my head in a fraction of a second, before Phil straightened up and went on. "Any a you guys get a memo saying girlie and Fifi could eat here?"

The goon squad chorus didn't answer; instead, they all turned and went into Wiggins.

I turned to Ambrose, stunned. "What just happened?"

"A minor miracle." He pointed; a police car had just pulled into the lot. "Maybe they've been following him." We watched as the cops got out of the car and went inside. "Bunch of guys riding around on Saturday night. Could be trouble."

"It's not night yet," I pointed out.

"But it will be soon. Let's get out of here before Phil and the posse come back out. They're not gonna feel like hassling the waitresses with a couple of cops watching."

We threw our empty dishes away and got into the VW. Technically the car was his mother's but she had left it behind after moving out. His parents, like mine, both carried traits but, unlike mine, had gotten married. Despite splitting up, however, they still weren't divorced.

"You sure this isn't a pervy crush?" Ambrose grumbled as he backed out of the parking space. "Wanting to help that asshole—"

"I don't *want* to," I said. "I *have* to."

"Because?" Ambrose prompted as we approached the exit; it was right near where Phil Lattimore had parked his land yacht. "Or is that a deep, dark, pervy secret?"

"Because I said something to him about what I know."

Ambrose slammed on the brakes so sharply I flopped in my shoulder harness.

"You *told* Phil the Fuckhead that you know he's gonna have an accident tomorrow night?" My cousin's voice was half an octave higher than I'd thought it could go. "You really *are* fucking crazy!"

"I didn't mean to—"

"Don't you realize that he might think you threatened him?"

The idea of Phil Lattimore thinking I could threaten him was so funny I laughed out loud.

"You idiot," Ambrose said. "He could say you did something to his car! For all you know, he told his father or his mother—or maybe he's telling the cops in Wiggins right now."

"I don't think so," I said unhappily, looking at the side view mirror.

"OK, maybe not, but—"

"*Definitely* not. He—"

Phil Lattimore slammed up against the driver's side door and stuck his head through the window. "Hey, why're you sittin' here starin' at my car? What's goin' on, Fifi?"

Ambrose stamped on the accelerator and we shot out of the parking lot, barely missing an oncoming SUV.

"Don't talk," Ambrose said for the fifth or sixth time.

"I wasn't," I said, glaring at him.

"I thought I heard you take a breath like you were gonna say something."

"You were mistaken."

"OK. Don't talk any more now."

"Fine. I won't." I stared out the passenger side window. We were out in the countryside now, taking the long way back to my house. The really long, long way, all the way around town, outside the city limits; a nice drive under other circumstances. "Phil Lattimore would never in a million years believe me," I added under my breath and waited for Ambrose to tell me to shut up. He didn't so I went on muttering. "He wouldn't believe it if *you'd* said it. That's why we don't tell anyone outside the family anything—"

"*Shut* the fuck *up*," Ambrose growled. "You think I spent my life in a coma? I know all that. Now I'm gonna drive you home and you're gonna tell your mom everything, what you know and what you said to Phil—hey, just what *did* you say? No, don't tell me," he added before I could answer. "I'm probably better off not knowing. If I don't know, I'm not an accessory."

"A *what*?" I said, baffled.

"An accessory to your threatening Phil."

"*He* threatened *me*, just because I wanted to use a payphone," I protested. "I only told him he was going to have a bad night."

"I told you not to tell me!" Ambrose gave me a quick, pained glance. "OK, never mind, just don't tell me any more."

"There isn't any more to tell," I said, sulking now.

Ambrose eased off the accelerator and only then did I realize how fast we'd been going. "Are you shitting me?" He looked at me again and I nodded. "Oh, for cryin' out—*that's* not a threat. We're gonna go home and forget the whole thing. And don't worry, I won't remind you."

"We can't," I said.

Ambrose shook his head in a sharp, final way. "We can and we will."

"I thought you said you hadn't spent most of your life in a coma. Don't you get it? I can't just turn my back. If Phil the Fuckhead is in the hospital for months and months, that's on me for not doing anything. If he ends up in a wheelchair for the rest of his life, that's on me."

"He could also just walk away from the wreckage with nothing more than a scratch on his empty fuckin' head," Ambrose said. "Guys like him usually do."

"What about any other people in the accident? If they're crippled or—or worse? That's on me, too. And you. For not doing anything."

Ambrose didn't say anything for a long moment. "It could happen no matter what we do."

"Yeah, but we'd have tried. It wouldn't be like we just stood by."

"Shit." Ambrose turned on the radio and then immediately turned it off again. "But you don't know anything about any other people, do you?"

"I only know about Phil Lattimore getting badly hurt in an accident. If I don't try to do something about it, I might as well stand next to the wreckage and watch him d—suffer."

"And that's why you need to tell your m—"

"*No!* If I tell my mother, then I have to tell her what I said to him."

"But it's not that bad," said Ambrose. "It really isn't. If you're that scared, I'll tell her for you. You can hide in your room."

"Please, Ambrose, I'm begging you—do this my way. I swear I'll confess everything to everyone after it's all over, even if the worst happens. I just—I need to do this as a test. I'm testing myself."

Ambrose gave me a startled glance and I realized I was crying. "But it's not just you," he said. "You dragged me into it."

"And that's on me, too, making you share this," I said. "I know that."

"You *better* know it." His voice was grim. "If I had any sense, I'd take you straight home and tell your mom the whole thing. But I'm not a rat, because—" he took a deep breath. "Just between you and me, OK?"

I looked at him warily. "OK. What."

"I came into my own a year and a half before Aunt Donna gave me that party."

"You did?" I was stunned. "Why did you hide it?"

"Because I felt weird about it. Some of the things that people had forgotten—my father would have realized I knew some things that—well, it wouldn't have been good. But Aunt Donna found out."

"How?"

"She just asked me. I tried to lie by being evasive but I was too young and stupid to do it right. We had a talk and she promised not to tell on me. And she didn't."

I was flabbergasted.

"I know, everyone was suspicious anyway because of how well I always did in school," he said, chuckling a little. "You, too, maybe. But I hadn't come into my own when I started school and after I did, it didn't matter. I was already in the smart-kid classes and smart kids don't forget much. I get straight A's because I'm smart, too, and I study my ass off. Anyway, you can trust me. I won't say anything. But promise me that tomorrow night, when this is all over, you'll tell your mom."

"OK," I said.

"Good." He looked at me sternly. "Because it's not ratting you out if I make you keep that promise."

I got home and went straight upstairs to run a bath for myself. When I took off my clothes, I discovered I had gotten my first period and burst into tears.

My mother waited until I had quieted down before coming to check on me. To my relief, she didn't rhapsodize about becoming a woman or ask me any questions. She just put a new box of sanitary pads on the counter by the sink, gathered up my clothes and let me have a good cry in peace, up to my neck in Mr. Bubble.

The next morning, I came down to breakfast to discover that she had sent Benny and Tim off to Donna's for the day.

"Estrogen-only household, no boys allowed," she said cheerfully as she sat at the kitchen table with the Sunday paper. "We've got plenty of chocolate in a variety of forms and an ample supply of Midol. There's also a heating pad if you need it."

"Thanks, but I'm OK," I said. She started to say something else and I talked over her. "I'm going over to Ambrose's. Algebra."

She looked surprised and then covered it with a smile. "All right. It's your day, after all." And she wished I were spending it with her. So did I.

I started back upstairs to get dressed.

"Hannah," she called after me suddenly. I stopped. "No later than five. You've got school tomorrow. OK?'

Phil Lattimore would die at six-fifty-two unless I saved him. "OK."

"I mean it," she added sharply.

"I know," I said. "No later than five, it's a school night."

Her expression softened. "And if you decide to knock off the studying early, the chocolate and everything else will still be here."

"Thanks, Mom." I got two steps farther when she called after me again.

"Are you really having *that* much trouble with algebra that you have to spend all weekend working on it with your cousin?"

"You have no idea," I replied.

I'd gone another two steps when she said, "Just one more thing."

I waited.

"Is there anything else you want to tell me about?"

"Not yet."

"Leave it open," Ambrose told me as I started to close the door to his room. "New rule. All the time we're spending together is making my father nervous."

I blinked at him. "You kidding?"

Ambrose shook his head gravely. "I wish I were. He thinks it's more than algebra."

"But we're *cousins*," I said, appalled and repelled.

"No shit. Just remember to keep your voice down and your algebra book handy for those moments when he just 'happens' to pass by on his way to the linen closet." He gave a short laugh. "You know, I thought that when I finally told him what we're doing, he'd be mad at me for hiding stuff from him. Now I think he'll just be relieved."

The day crawled by. Ambrose sat at his desk, tapping away on his computer while I stretched out on the bed, trying to ignore the mild discomfort in my lower belly. But after Uncle Scott went past a couple of times, he called Ambrose out of the room for a quick word. Ambrose returned with a request for me to sit up, preferably in one of the two straight-back chairs. I compromised by stretching out on the floor. "If your dad has a problem with this," I said, "I'll give him a complete description of how my first period is going."

Ambrose blanched. "I didn't need to hear that."

"Neither will he."

We finally went out for lunch at two, driving out past the city limits into the country again.

"Won't your dad worry about what we could do in a car?" I asked.

Ambrose shook his head. "Not in a Volkswagen."

I gave an incredulous laugh. "We could get *out* of the Volkswagen."

"And then what? I don't have enough money for a motel and he thinks I'm too hung-up to do it outside." He glanced at me. "Forget it. Grown-ups are fuckin' weird, is all. Every last one of them, fuckin' weird. Especially in our family."

Anxiety did a half-twist in my stomach or maybe it was just cramps.

"And we're giving them a run for their money right now ourselves," he added. "Skulking around so you can play hero single-handed for an asshole who wouldn't appreciate it even if he *did* know what you were doing. Fuckin' weird? Fuckin' A."

The moment hung there between us, a silence that I could have stepped into and confessed everything—the truth about my trait and what I was really trying to do. Then he went on.

"Anyway, I didn't want to talk about this before in case my dad overheard." He glanced at me; anxiety did another twist, high up in my chest where it couldn't have been cramps. "When you come into your own, you don't just get one of the family traits. They let you in on other things. Family things."

"Like what? Skeletons in the closet or something?"

Ambrose gave a small, nervous laugh. "Not just that. There are skills to learn, that go along with the traits."

"Skills?"

"Coping skills. There are ways to compartmentalize your mind so you don't get caught up in something you know when you're supposed to be doing something else. Some traits, you have to learn how to distance yourself. Mind your own business."

I bristled. "If this is a sneaky way of trying to talk me out of—"

"Relax. I should but I'm not."

"You never mentioned any of this before."

"I didn't think you'd want to hear it."

"I still don't."

"I know. But shut up and let me talk, OK? I promised you I'd help you and I will. I am. But I had to talk to somebody. So after my dad went to bed last night, I called my sister Rita and talked to her."

"You *what?*" My voice was so high that even *I* winced.

"*Relax.* I didn't tell her about you. I talked to her about Loomis."

I felt my stomach drop, as if there were thousands of miles for it to fall inside me. "Why…" My voice failed and I had to start again. "Why Loomis?"

"I would have asked Dad about his aunt or the cousin but I was afraid he might start wondering why I wanted to know. Then he'd put two and two together about you and I'd have to explain why you won't tell anyone and it'd be a big mess. Asking about Loomis would've been worse—he'd have gotten the wrong idea about your trait." I winced, wondering if Ambrose would ever speak to me again when the truth did come out. "So after he went to bed, I called Rita."

"But why Loomis?" I asked again.

"Because your trait is similar in a lot of ways. I know, you said Phil Lattimore *could* die, not that he *would,* but there are parallels. You and Loomis know a specific thing about one particular person. So I thought anything Rita told me about him would apply to you, too."

"Good algebra," I said, mostly to myself.

"What?" Ambrose gave me a funny look.

"Nothing. What did she tell you?"

He flexed his fingers on the steering wheel. "The closer it gets to *that* time, the more likely we are to run into Phil Lattimore."

"Why?"

"Because you know what's going to happen and you talked to him. It's a synchronicity thing. Your separate courses affect each other."

"Our 'separate courses'?"

"It's a mathematical thing, really advanced. I kind of understand it but I'd never be able to explain it to you."

"And Rita told you this?" I gave a small, incredulous laugh. "Since when is knotty pine's biggest fan such a brainbox?"

"My sister may be tacky but she's not stupid." Ambrose sounded so serious I was ashamed of laughing even a little. "She knows *space*. Every so often, she picks up on something weird, like two points that are actually far apart registering as being in the same spot."

"What does that mean?" I asked.

"It means she has to use her tape measure."

"Very funny," I said sourly.

Ambrose shrugged. "You're nowhere near ready for quantum mechanics or entanglement." He flexed his fingers on the steering wheel again. "You know, something like this happened with Loomis. When he told somebody something he shouldn't have."

All of a sudden I felt weightless, the way you do in the split second before you start to fall. "Who?" I asked, or tried to. What voice I had was too faint for Ambrose to hear.

"Rita said as soon as he did that, it was like they couldn't keep out of each other's way," my cousin went on. "Not so strange in a small town like this. The strange part was every time Rita read the distance between them, it came up zero."

"You believe her?" I asked before I could stop myself.

"Of course I believe her!" Ambrose glanced at me, his face red with anger.

"What kind of fuckin' question is that? I wish to God she were here now, you'd *eat* those words."

"I'm sorry, I wasn't trying to insult anybody."

"My sister and I sit up half the night just for your benefit and that's the thanks we get?"

"You *did* tell her!" I shouted. "You said you wouldn't—"

"I had to tell her *something*," Ambrose shouted back at me. He slowed down and pulled onto the dirt shoulder of the country road we were on. "She knew I'd never call in the middle of the night just to chat about Loomis and I couldn't get away with lying to her—"

"So you lied to me about lying to her—"

"Shut up and let me finish!" He turned off the ignition. "I figured it wouldn't matter if she knew the truth, she's in Chicago."

"What else did you tell her?" I asked, managing not to scream in his face.

"Just that you'd come into your own and you didn't want to tell anyone yet. Nothing about Phil or what we're doing."

I gave him a poisonous look. "Can I really believe you?"

He blew out a short breath that might have been a humorless laugh. "Don't you think she'd have hung up on me and called your mom if I *had* told her everything?"

"OK," I said after a bit. My heartbeat had finally slowed from machine-gun to a gallop. "Why did we stop here?"

"I don't drive when there's yelling in the car," Ambrose said, sounding almost prim. "That's practically guaranteeing a wreck." He raised an eyebrow at me and I had a sudden vision of him at his father's age, paternal but firm: *You kids behave yourselves* right now *or I'm turning this car around.*

"Fine," I said. "No yelling."

He started the VW again.

"Wake up," Ambrose said.

"I'm not asleep," I said thickly, blinking and sitting up straight in my seat. Most of the daylight was gone and we were no longer out in the country but pulling into the parking lot at Wiggins. "What time is it?"

"Fifteen minutes to Operation Save the Fuckhead." Ambrose cruised slowly through the crowded lot. It was a Sunday night in spring; everyone wanted to end the weekend with one last treat. "Uh-oh."

"What 'uh-oh'?"

"I don't see his car."

My stomach seemed to twist, then drop; at the same time, my cramps woke up with a vengeance. I leaned forward with my arms across my middle. "Maybe he was here already and left. Or maybe *he's* out in the country now."

"I'll drive down the road to Westgate Mall, turn around, and come back again," Ambrose said. "There's no place to park here anyway."

Just as we pulled out of the exit, a car roared up from behind and swerved sharply around us, horn honking, headlights flashing from low to high. Ambrose jerked the wheel to the right and we veered off the road into the dirt. The tires crunched on something as he slowly steered the car back onto the pavement.

"Who do you suppose *that* was?" he said wearily.

"Let's go," I said, hoping I wasn't yelling. "We've got to catch him!"

But as we sped up, the VW began to shudder hard from side to side.

"What the hell is that?" I yelled as Ambrose brought the car to a stop.

"Flat tire."

"Can't we change it?" But even as I asked, I knew. "The spare's flat," we said in unison.

High beams swept across the road and shone through the windshield and lit up the inside of the VW. The driver had crossed from the opposite lane to stop in front of us, facing the wrong direction. "Uh-oh," Ambrose said softly as we watched Phil Lattimore get out of his land yacht and lumber toward us. We rolled up the windows and locked the doors.

"Car trouble?" Phil asked, pressing his nose against my window.

"Can't reach my mom or my dad," Ambrose said unhappily, snapping his cell phone shut.

Lying across the front of the VW, Phil Lattimore waved cheerfully. "Hey, I told you we're *happy* to give you a ride!" He gestured at his friends waiting in the convertible; I could barely hear the *Fucking A's* with the windows rolled up.

"Call a tow truck," I said.

"I'll call the cops."

"You can't! As soon as Phil sees a cop car, he'll take off and it'll happen. We'll have *caused* the accident. Just call a tow-truck. What time is it? How long have we got?"

Ambrose tilted his watch toward the light, trying to read it. "Shit. My watch stopped." He turned the key in the ignition so the dashboard lit up. The digital clock read 88:88.

"What about your phone?" I asked. He showed it to me. The screen said —/—Set Time?

"What the hell does *that* mean?" I asked.

"Just guessing, I'd say it means you won," Ambrose said. "Now if we can just lose the ugly hood ornament."

Phil was squinting at his own watch in a puzzled way. He tapped the face hard with a fingernail, then held his wrist up to the light again. Ambrose leaned hard on the horn, startling Phil so much that he fell off.

"What'd you do *that* for?" I yelled.

"It worked. Now we can call your mother instead of a tow truck. I don't have enough money for a tow truck and you promised you'd tell her. She can take us to a service station and I'll pump up the spare while you tell her everything. It's killing two birds with one stone."

Phil Lattimore was back on his feet, brushing himself off as he went back to his land yacht. I unlocked my door and started to get out.

"Hey, don't!" Ambrose caught my arm. "Are you crazy?"

"I've got to keep him out of his car for just a little longer." I twisted out of his grip and ran toward Phil Lattimore. His buddies gestured, hooting and cheering wildly; the surprise on his face when he turned and saw me was utterly genuine, which surprised me just as much.

"What do you want?" he asked and for a moment he actually seemed concerned. *Hey, girlie, you're doing it wrong—I scare you and you run away, that's how the game goes.*

I stopped in front of him. The smell of beer was like a cloud around him. "Just…wait a minute."

He gazed down at me as if from a great height. "Sorry, girlie, no can do. Watch died. Your ugly face break it, or Fifi's?" He turned away and kept going.

"I said, *wait!*" I yelled, going after him.

He spread his arms as his buddies hooted some more. "She loves me, what can I—"

I made a two-handed fist and walloped his right butt cheek.

He stumbled, more from surprise than from the blow itself. I barely saw him whirl on me before he grabbed my upper arms, lifted me off my feet and threw me into the back seat of the land yacht.

It wasn't a soft landing and his buddies were no more ready for it than I was. I was struggling in a tangle of arms and legs. There was laughing and someone yelling *Jesus are you crazy toss her out she's jailbait* and another voice saying *she wants a beer.* I kicked out, hoping to hit something tender but connected with nothing but air. Beer cans crumpled against my face, dug into my skin as the car jerked forward.

"*Stop!*" I screamed. "*Stop! Don't let him! Don't let him, make him stop!*"

"What the fuck?" somebody said. No more laughing. One guy in the front seat was insisting that we'd better stop, another guy agreed, and then a third guy yelled *Look out!*

For a fraction of a second, I thought it was pure noise, an impact from sound waves. The car skidded at an odd angle and I managed to pull my head up just in time for the second impact. The air went out of my lungs in one hard blow. When my vision cleared I was trapped on the floor; someone seemed to be kneeling on my ribs. Fighting to breathe, I tried to drag myself up toward air.

I don't remember hearing the third impact.

I came to inside something moving fast.

"Do you know your name?" said a woman's voice, all brisk concern. A hand squeezed mine. "Do you know your name?"

The light was blinding me; high beams?

"Do you know your name? If you can't talk, squeeze my hand."

I tried to pull my hand away and sit up but I couldn't move at all.

"Do you—"

"Hannah," I croaked. My mouth tasted funny. "Tell me he's OK."

"You don't worry, everyone's in good hands."

"No, tell me." The light in my eyes grew more painful as I became more alert. "Tell me he's OK. Tell me I saved him."

"Don't worry, honey, everything's gonna be OK—"

I had a glimpse of a woman's face, dark brown, with short black dreadlocks. In thirty-five years, degeneration in her brain would finally reach its end-stage.

Abruptly pain erupted everywhere in my body. I would have howled but all that came out was a long croaky moan. The woman turned away quickly and did something; the pain began to ebb, along with my awareness.

"Midol," I whispered. Or maybe not.

After that, I was in and out, almost like channel surfing. Doctors and nurses appeared and disappeared and I never knew which was which. Sometimes I saw my mother, sometimes my brothers; once in a while Donna was there as well. Although I was never sure if I were dreaming, even when it hurt.

At one point, I was trapped in the back seat of Phil Lattimore's land yacht again, feeling it spin around, tires screeching, glass breaking, metal smashing. I think I heard the third impact that time but afterwards, there was no one asking if I knew what my name was while we traveled. But it was much easier to breathe.

Phil Lattimore came to see me. He peered over a nurse's shoulder and made stupid faces, mouthing *Who said you could have a car accident here?* That was no way to treat the person who had saved his stupid thug ass and I'd tell him that as soon as I was well enough.

My mother was sitting next to my bed, gazing at me with an anxious, searching look.

"Yeah, it's me." It hurt to talk. My voice sounded faint and hoarse.

"No kidding." She tried to smile. "I'd know you anywhere."

I swallowed hard on my dry throat and winced. She poured me a glass of ice water from a sweating metal pitcher and held the straw between my lips for me. "Did Ambrose tell you?"

It was like a shadow passed over her. "Ambrose? No."

"He made me promise—" I sucked greedily at the straw; suddenly ice water was the most wonderful thing in the world. "Said if I didn't tell you, he would. After it was all over. Which it is. Isn't it?"

She made a small, non-committal movement with her head. "Yes, honey. It's all over." She poured some more ice water for me. "Rita got here as soon as she could."

"Rita?" It took me a few moments to remember. "Did she come because Ambrose told her?"

She made that little movement with her head again.

It was easier to talk now; I turned my face away from the straw to show I'd had enough. "I feel bad about that. Because now I have to admit I lied to Ambrose."

My mother closed her eyes briefly as if she had had a sudden pain, then put the ice water down on the table beside the bed. "Yes, I know. We know."

We? Pain nibbled at the edges of my awareness, as if it had just woken up and wanted to join the conversation without drawing too much attention to itself. "How? Who told you?"

"You did." My mother sighed, looking at me sadly. "You don't remember talking to me, do you?"

"Not exactly," I said.

"The doctors said you'd have a spotty memory thanks to the combination of the head injury and the medication." She put her hand over mine on the bed and I realized I had a cast on my arm up to my knuckles.

"Everything's all dream-like." The pain was getting more assertive. "Did he make it? Is he alive?"

Now she hesitated. "Your uncle Scott's been sitting with him. He hasn't left the hospital since—"

"Uncle Scott?" Pain definitely wanted more attention now; I tried to ignore it. "Why is Uncle Scott sitting with Phil Lattimore?"

"Phil who?" My mother looked as mystified as I felt. "He's with *Ambrose.*"

Uh-oh, said a small voice in my mind, under the pain. It sounded exactly like Ambrose. "Phil Lattimore is the guy I was trying to save," I said. "I knew Ambrose would be all right."

"All right?" My mother looked mildly stunned now, as if she had bumped her head.

"Ambrose isn't going to die for f—for a very long time," I said. "I knew I didn't have to worry about him."

My mother took a deep breath and let it out. "Is that so?" She gazed at me for a long moment, her expression a mixture of hurt, frustration, pity, and something else I couldn't read. I started to say something else and she suddenly rushed out of the room.

Caught completely by surprise, I tried to call after her but the pain stole my voice. Before it got really bad, however, a nurse came in with some medication.

When I woke up again, there was a man sitting in the chair next to the bed. I had never seen him before but even without the strong family resemblance I'd have known who he was.

"Hello, Loomis," I croaked.

"Hello, yourself." He got up and gave me some ice water the way my mother had, holding the straw between my lips. I drank slowly, studying his face. He was a little taller than Ambrose, wiry and lean, as if he spent most of his waking hours running. His hair was curly but darker than Ambrose's and he had a full dark beard with a few white hairs here and there. I found it really interesting that although his eyes were same shape as Ambrose's, they weren't the same clear green color but dark muddy brown, like mine.

I finished the water and told him I'd had enough. He put the glass aside and continued to stand there looking me over.

"Guess you know," I said after a bit.

He didn't bother nodding. "You weren't surprised, were you. Knew it almost your whole life and never told anyone."

"That how it was for you?" I asked.

He pressed his lips together. "So, was this premeditated or spontaneous?

I frowned. "What?

Loomis took a breath and let it out; not quite a sigh. "Were you always planning to save someone's life or was it a spur-of-the-moment thing?"

I hesitated. "I was gonna say spur of the moment but now I'm not so sure. Maybe I was always gonna do something like this and never knew it."

Loomis's eyebrows went up. "Good answer. Insightful. More than I was at your age. Otherwise—" he shrugged.

"Otherwise what?"

"Otherwise you're just as much a dumb-ass as any of us."

I was offended and it must have showed. He laughed and patted my hand.

"Hackles down, kid. Till the body cast comes off, anyway." He looked me over again. "Damn. Even I never took a beat-down this bad."

"Was it for nothing?" I asked.

Now it was his turn to be confused. "Say again?"

"Phil Lattimore. Did I save him?"

Fuck, no. He grimaced and poured another glass of water. Before I could tell him I didn't want any more, he drank it himself. "There are two rules, cuz. Number one: Never tell anyone. And that's *anyone,* even family. Never. Tell. Anyone. *Never.* And rule number two: *Never* try to save them. You can't do it. All you can do is make things worse." He gestured along the length of my body. "Exhibit A."

Alarm bells went off in my mind; I shut them out, made myself ignore the cold lump of apprehension in the middle of my chest. I'd be getting more pain medication soon; that always made all the bad feelings go away, physical and emotional. "Yeah, but I knew I was gonna be all right."

Loomis stuck one fist on his hip; the move was pure Ambrose. "You call *this* 'all right'? Hate to tell you, cuz, but after the casts come off, you've got a whole lot of physical therapy ahead of you and you'll probably lose a year of school. At *least* a year."

"You know what I mean," I said defensively. "I knew I wasn't gonna get killed.

It was just Phil Lattimore. No one else."

"Yeah, that was all you needed to know, wasn't it? Only this Phil Lattimore would die so that meant everybody else would be *all right*." He looked at me through half-closed eyes. "Like you and Ambrose."

The lump in my chest was suddenly so large it was hard to breathe around it and my heart seemed to be laboring. "Ambrose wasn't driving, we had a flat—"

"He ran into the road after the car you were in," Loomis said. "One of those things you do without thinking. The car that swerved to keep from hitting him hit another car, which in turn hit the car you were in. Which hit him before skidding into yet another car." I started to say something but he put up a hand. "There were two fatalities—this Phil Lattimore person who was apparently too cheap to install airbags in his old land yacht and got spindled on the steering column, and someone else who you apparently hadn't met."

"But Ambrose is ali—"

"Alive, yes, and will be for another fifty-odd years," Loomis said, talking over me. "Exactly how odd nobody really knows yet. The doctors told my parents it's a miracle he survived that kind of head injury. They won't know how extensive the impairment is until he wakes up. My mother believes he's going to wake up any minute because he's breathing on his own."

It was like I was back on the floor of the car with some thug kneeling on my ribs, but harder, as if he were trying to force all the air out of my lungs.

"Hey, stay with me." I felt Loomis tapping me lightly first on one cheek and then the other. "I wasn't trying to be cruel." He ran a small ice cube back and forth across my forehead. "But you had to be told."

I started to cry, my tears mixing with the cold water running down from my forehead.

"Shouldn't have happened," Loomis went on. "Wouldn't have, but they just won't talk about it in front of the kids. They tell you everything else—why we keep the traits secret, how to be careful around those poor souls who have the misfortune and/or bad judgment to marry one of us, how to cover if you say something you shouldn't to an outsider. But not how I 'accidentally' broke a kid's wrist playing football so he couldn't go to the municipal swimming pool afterwards like he planned and drown. And he didn't. He went straight home because he didn't know his wrist was broken and he drowned in the bathtub. His parents were investigated for child abuse and his sister spent eight months in foster care."

"Stop," I said. "Please."

"They were all so mad at me, the family was." Loomis shook his head at the memory. "They claimed they weren't, they told me it wasn't really my fault because I didn't know any better. Everyone kept telling me they weren't upset with me even after the authorities found out *I* had broken the kid's wrist and called me in for questioning. Along with Mom and Dad and Rita. Ambrose was a baby; they examined him for bruises."

"OK. Now stop," I pleaded. "I mean it."

Loomis was talking over me again. "It all came out all right, there was no reason to be upset with me. They said and they said and they said. But after my mother searched my room and found my journal with everybody's dates in it—*then* they got upset. Oh, they got *furious* with me. I said it was my mother's fault for snooping and then telling the rest of the family about it but they weren't having any of that. Writing down *those dates*—how could I have done such a thing? I stuck it out till I was sixteen and then I booked."

The silence hung in the air. I closed my eyes hoping that I'd pass out or something.

"When you're well enough to travel," he said after a while, "you'll come with me."

My eyes flew open.

"Death is the one thing you never, ever even *try* to mess with. Everything in the world—everything in the *universe* changes. But not that. Death *is*. If you went down to the deepest circle of hell and offered resurrection to everyone there, they'd all say no and mean it."

"That's not where you live, is it?" I asked.

Loomis chuckled. "Not even close."

"They won't beg me to stay, will they? They all hate me now."

"They don't hate you," Loomis said, patting my hand again. "They love you as much as they ever did. They just don't like you very much any more."

The nurse came in with my pain medication and I closed my eyes again. "Let me know when we leave."

EROS, PHILIA, AGAPE
RACHEL SWIRSKY

Rachel Swirsky holds an MFA in fiction from the Iowa Writers Workshop and is a graduate of the Clarion West Writers Workshop. Her short fiction has appeared in a number of venues, including *Tor.com*, *Subterranean Magazine*, *Weird Tales*, and *Fantasy Magazine*, and has been collected in several year's best. She lives in Bakersfield, California, with her husband and two cats, and is seriously considering whether or not to become a crazy cat lady by adopting all four stray kittens which were recently born in her yard.

Lucian packed his possessions before he left. He packed his antique silver serving spoons with the filigreed handles; the tea roses he'd nurtured in the garden window; his jade and garnet rings. He packed the hunk of gypsum-veined jasper that he'd found while strolling on the beach on the first night he'd come to Adriana, she leading him uncertainly across the wet sand, their bodies illuminated by the soft gold twinkling of the lights along the pier. That night, as they walked back to Adriana's house, Lucian had cradled the speckled stone in his cupped palms, squinting so that the gypsum threads sparkled through his lashes.

Lucian had always loved beauty—beautiful scents, beautiful tastes, beautiful melodies. He especially loved beautiful objects because he could hold them in his hands and transform the abstraction of beauty into something tangible.

The objects belonged to them both, but Adriana waved her hand bitterly when Lucian began packing. "Take whatever you want," she said, snapping her book shut. She waited by the door, watching Lucian with sad and angry eyes.

Their daughter, Rose, followed Lucian around the house. "Are you going to take that, Daddy? Do you want that?" Wordlessly, Lucian held her hand. He guided her up the stairs and across the uneven floorboards where she sometimes tripped. Rose stopped by the picture window in the master bedroom, staring past the palm fronds and swimming pools, out to the vivid cerulean swath of the ocean. Lucian relished the hot, tender feel of Rose's hand. *I love you*, he would have whispered, but he'd surrendered the ability to speak.

He led her downstairs again to the front door. Rose's lace-festooned pink satin dress crinkled as she leapt down the steps. Lucian had ordered her dozens of satin party dresses in pale, floral hues. Rose refused to wear anything else.

Rose looked between Lucian and Adriana. "Are you taking me, too?" she asked Lucian.

Adriana's mouth tightened. She looked at Lucian, daring him to say something, to take responsibility for what he was doing to their daughter. Lucian remained silent.

Adriana's chardonnay glowed the same shade of amber as Lucian's eyes. She clutched the glass's stem until she thought it might break. "No, honey," she said with artificial lightness. "You're staying with me."

Rose reached for Lucian. "Horsey?"

Lucian knelt down and pressed his forehead against Rose's. He hadn't spoken a word in the three days since he'd delivered his letter of farewell to Adriana, announcing his intention to leave as soon as she had enough time to make arrangements to care for Rose in his absence. When Lucian approached with the letter, Adriana had been sitting at the dining table, sipping orange juice from a wine glass and reading a first edition copy of Cheever's *Falconer*. Lucian felt a flash of guilt as she smiled up at him and accepted the missive. He knew that she'd been happier in the past few months than he'd ever seen her, possibly happier than she'd ever been. He knew the letter would shock and wound her. He knew she'd feel betrayed. Still, he delivered the letter anyway, and watched as comprehension ached through her body.

Rose had been told, gently, patiently, that Lucian was leaving. But she was four years old, and understood things only briefly and partially, and often according to her whims. She continued to believe her father's silence was a game.

Rose's hair brushed Lucian's cheek. He kissed her brow. Adriana couldn't hold her tongue any longer.

"What do you think you're going to find out there? There's no Shangri-La for rebel robots. You think you're making a play for independence? Independence to do what, Lu?"

Grief and anger filled Adriana's eyes with hot tears, as if she were a geyser filled with so much pressure that steam could not help but spring up. She examined Lucian's sculpted face: his skin inlaid with tiny lines that an artist had rendered to suggest the experiences of a childhood which had never been lived; his eyes calibrated with a hint of asymmetry to mimic the imperfection of human growth. His expression showed nothing—no doubt, or bitterness, or even relief. He revealed nothing at all.

It was all too much. Adriana moved between Lucian and Rose, as if she could use her own body to protect her daughter from the pain of being abandoned. Her eyes stared achingly over the rim of her wine glass. "Just go," she said.

He left.

Adriana bought Lucian the summer she turned thirty-five. Her father, long afflicted with an indecisive cancer that vacillated between aggression and remittance, had died suddenly in July. For years, the family had been squirreling away emotional reserves to cope with his prolonged illness. His death released a burst of excess.

While her sisters went through the motions of grief, Adriana thrummed with energy she didn't know what to do with. She considered squandering her vigor on six weeks in Mazatlan, but as she discussed ocean-front rentals with her travel agent, she realized escape wasn't what she craved. She liked the setting where her life took place: her house perched on a cliff overlooking the Pacific Ocean, her bedroom window that opened on a tangle of blackberry bushes where crows roosted every autumn and spring. She liked the two block stroll down to the beach where she could sit with a book and listen to the yapping lapdogs that the elderly women from the waterfront condominiums brought walking in the evenings.

Mazatlan was a twenty-something's cure for restlessness. Adriana wasn't twenty-five anymore, famished for the whole gourmet meal of existence. She needed something else now. Something new. Something more refined.

She explained this to her friends Ben and Lawrence when they invited her to their ranch house in Santa Barbara to relax for the weekend and try to forget about her father. They sat on Ben and Lawrence's patio, on iron-worked deck chairs arrayed around a garden table topped with a mosaic of sea creatures made of semi-precious stones. A warm, breezy dusk lengthened the shadows of the orange trees. Lawrence poured sparkling rosé into three wine glasses and proposed a toast to Adriana's father—not to his memory, but to his death.

"Good riddance to the bastard," said Lawrence. "If he were still alive, I'd punch him in the schnoz."

"I don't even want to think about him," said Adriana. "He's dead. He's gone."

"So if not Mazatlan, what are you going to do?" asked Ben.

"I'm not sure," said Adriana. "Some sort of change, some sort of milestone, that's all I know."

Lawrence sniffed the air. "Excuse me," he said, gathering the empty wine glasses. "The kitchen needs its genius."

When Lawrence was out of earshot, Ben leaned forward to whisper to Adriana. "He's got us on a raw food diet for my cholesterol. Raw carrots. Raw zucchini. Raw almonds. No cooking at all."

"Really," said Adriana, glancing away. She was never sure how to respond to lovers' quarrels. That kind of affection mixed with annoyance, that inescapable intimacy, was something she'd never understood.

Birds twittered in the orange trees. The fading sunlight highlighted copper strands in Ben's hair as he leaned over the mosaic table, rapping his fingers against a carnelian-backed crab. Through the arched windows, Adriana could see Lawrence mincing carrots, celery and almonds into brown paste.

"You should get a redecorator," said Ben. "Tile floors, Tuscan pottery, those red leather chairs that were in vogue last time we were in Milan. That'd make me feel like I'd been scrubbed clean and reborn."

"No, no," said Adriana, "I like where I live."

"A no-holds-barred shopping spree. Drop twenty thousand. That's what I call getting a weight off your shoulders."

Adriana laughed. "How long do you think it would take my personal shopper to assemble a whole new me?"

"Sounds like a midlife crisis," said Lawrence, returning with vegan hors d'oeuvres and three glasses of mineral water. "You're better off forgetting it all with a hot Latin pool boy, if you ask me."

Lawrence served Ben a small bowl filled with yellow mush. Ben shot Adriana an aggrieved glance.

Adriana felt suddenly out of synch. The whole evening felt like the set for a photo shoot that would go in a decorating magazine, a two-page spread featuring Cozy Gardens, in which she and Ben and Lawrence were posing as an intimate dinner party for three. She felt reduced to two dimensions, air-brushed, and then digitally grafted onto the form of whoever it was who should have been there, someone warm and trusting who knew how to care about minutia like a friend's husband putting him on a raw food diet, not because the issue was important, but because it mattered to him.

Lawrence dipped his finger in the mash and held it up to Ben's lips. "It's for your own good, you ungrateful so-and-so."

Ben licked it away. "I eat it, don't I?"

Lawrence leaned down to kiss his husband, a warm and not at all furtive kiss, not sexual but still passionate. Ben's glance flashed coyly downward.

Adriana couldn't remember the last time she'd loved someone enough to be embarrassed by them. Was this the flavor missing from her life? A lover's fingertip sliding an unwanted morsel into her mouth?

She returned home that night on the bullet train. Her emerald cockatiel, Fuoco, greeted her with indignant squawks. In Adriana's absence, the house puffed her scent into the air and sang to Fuoco with her voice, but the bird was never fooled.

Adriana's father had given her the bird for her thirtieth birthday. He was a designer species spliced with Macaw DNA that colored his feathers rich green. He was expensive and inbred and neurotic, and he loved Adriana with frantic, obsessive jealousy.

"Hush," Adriana admonished, allowing Fuoco to alight on her shoulder. She carried him upstairs to her bedroom and hand-fed him millet. Fuoco strutted across the pillows, obsidian eyes proud and suspicious.

Adriana was surprised to find that her alienation had followed her home. She found herself prone to melancholy reveries, her gaze drifting toward the picture window, her fingers forgetting to stroke Fuoco's back. The bird screeched to regain her attention.

In the morning, Adriana visited her accountant. His fingers danced across the keyboard as he slipped trust fund moneys from one account to another like a magician. What she planned would be expensive, but her wealth would regrow in fertile soil, enriching her on lab diamonds and wind power and genetically modified oranges.

The robotics company gave Adriana a private showing. The salesman ushered her into a room draped in black velvet. Hundreds of body parts hung on the walls and reclined on display tables: strong hands, narrow jaws, biker's thighs, voice boxes that played sound samples from gruff to dulcet, skin swatches spanning ebony to alabaster, penises of various sizes.

At first, Adriana felt horrified at the prospect of assembling a lover from fragments, but then it amused her. Wasn't everyone assembled from fragments of DNA, grown molecule by molecule inside their mother's womb?

She tapped her fingernails against a slick brochure. "Its brain will be malleable? I can tell it to be more amenable, or funnier, or to grow a spine?"

"That's correct." The salesman sported slick brown hair and shiny teeth and kept grinning in a way that suggested he thought that if he were charismatic enough Adriana would invite him home for a lay and a million-dollar tip. "Humans lose brain plasticity as we age, which limits how much we can change. Our models have perpetually plastic brains. They can reroute their personalities at will by reshaping how they think on the neurological level."

Adriana stepped past him, running her fingers along a tapestry woven of a thousand possible hair textures.

The salesman tapped an empty faceplate. "Their original brains are based on deep imaging scans melded from geniuses in multiple fields. Great musicians, renowned lovers, the best physicists and mathematicians."

Adriana wished the salesman would be quiet. The more he talked, the more doubts clamored against her skull. "You've convinced me," she interrupted. "I want one."

The salesman looked taken aback by her abruptness. She could practically see him rifling through his internal script, trying to find the right page now that she had skipped several scenes. "What do you want him to look like?" he asked.

Adriana shrugged. "They're all beautiful, right?"

"We'll need specifications."

"I don't have specifications."

The salesman frowned anxiously. He shifted his weight as if it could help him regain his metaphorical footing. Adriana took pity. She dug through her purse.

"There," she said, placing a snapshot of her father on one of the display tables. "Make it look nothing like him."

Given such loose parameters, the design team indulged the fanciful. Lucian arrived at Adriana's door only a shade taller than she and equally slender, his limbs smooth and lean. Silver undertones glimmered in his blond hair. His skin was excruciatingly pale, white and translucent as alabaster, veined with pink. He smelled like warm soil and crushed herbs.

He offered Adriana a single white rose, its petals embossed with the company's logo. She held it dubiously between her thumb and forefinger. "They think they know women, do they? They need to put down the bodice rippers."

Lucian said nothing. Adriana took his hesitation for puzzlement, but perhaps she should have seen it as an early indication of his tendency toward silence.

"That's that, then." Adriana drained her chardonnay and crushed the empty glass beneath her heel as if she could finalize a divorce with the same gesture that sanctified a marriage.

Eyes wide, Rose pointed at the glass with one round finger. "Don't break things."

It suddenly struck Adriana how fast her daughter was aging. Here she was, this four year old, this sudden person. When had it happened? In the hospital, when Rose was newborn and wailing for the woman who had birthed her and abandoned her, Adriana had spent hours in the hallway outside the hospital nursery while she waited for the adoption to go through. She'd stared at Rose while she slept, ate, cried, striving to memorize her nascent, changing face. Sometime between then and now, Rose had become this round-cheeked creature who took rules very seriously and often tried to conceal her emotions beneath a calm exterior, as if being raised by a robot had replaced her blood with circuits. Of course Adriana loved Rose, changed her clothes, brushed her teeth, carried her across the house on her hip—but Lucian had been the most central, nurturing figure. Adriana couldn't fathom how she might fill his role. This wasn't a vacation like the time Adriana had taken Rose to Italy for three days, just the two of them sitting in restaurants, Adriana feeding her daughter spoonfuls of gelato to see the joy that lit her face at each new flavor. Then, they'd known that Lucian would be waiting when they returned. Without him, their family was a house missing a structural support. Adriana could feel the walls bowing in.

The fragments of Adriana's chardonnay glass sparkled sharply. Adriana led Rose away from the mess.

"Never mind," she said, "The house will clean up."

Her head felt simultaneously light and achy as if it couldn't decide between drunkenness and hangover. She tried to remember the parenting books she'd read before adopting Rose. What had they said about crying in front of your child? She clutched Rose close, inhaling the scent of children's shampoo mixed with the acrid odor of wine.

"Let's go for a drive," said Adriana. "Okay? Let's get out for a while."

"I want daddy to take me to the beach."

"We'll go out to the country and look at the farms. Cows and sheep, okay?" Rose said nothing.

"Moo?" Adriana clarified. "Baa?"

"I know," said Rose. "I'm not a baby."

"So, then?"

Rose said nothing. Adriana wondered whether she could tell that her mother was a little mad with grief.

Just make a decision, Adriana counseled herself. She slipped her fingers around Rose's hand. "We'll go for a drive."

Adriana instructed the house to regulate itself in their absence, and then led Rose to the little black car that she and Lucian had bought together after adopting Rose. She fastened Rose's safety buckle and programmed the car to take them inland.

As the car engine initialized, Adriana felt a glimmer of fear. What if this machine betrayed them, too? But its uninspired intelligence only switched on the left turn signal and started down the boulevard.

Lucian stood at the base of the driveway and stared up at the house. Its stark orange and brown walls blazed against cloudless sky. Rocks and desert plants tumbled down the meticulously landscaped yard, imitating natural scrub.

A rabbit ran across the road, followed by the whir of Adriana's car. Lucian watched them pass. They couldn't see him through the cypresses, but Lucian could make out Rose's face pressed against the window. Beside her, Adriana slumped in her seat, one hand pressed over her eyes.

Lucian went in the opposite direction. He dragged the rolling cart packed with his belongings to the cliff that led down to the beach. He lifted the cart over his head and started down, his feet disturbing cascades of sandstone chunks.

A pair of adolescent boys looked up from playing in the waves. "Whoa," shouted one of them. "Are you carrying that whole thing? Are you a weightlifter?"

Lucian remained silent. When he reached the sand, the kids muttered disappointments to each other and turned away from shore. "…Just a robot…" drifted back to Lucian on the breeze.

Lucian pulled his cart to the border where wet sand met dry. Oncoming waves lapped over his feet. He opened the cart and removed a tea-scented apricot rose growing in a pot painted with blue leaves.

He remembered acquiring the seeds for his first potted rose. One evening, long ago, he'd asked Adriana if he could grow things. He'd asked in passing, the question left to linger while they cleaned up after dinner, dish soap on their hands, Fuoco pecking after scraps. The next morning, Adriana escorted Lucian to the hot house near the botanical gardens. "Buy whatever you want," she told him. Lucian was awed by the profusion of color and scent, all that beauty in one place. He wanted to capture the wonder of that place and own it for himself.

Lucian drew back his arm and threw the pot into the sea. It broke across the water, petals scattering the surface.

He threw in the pink roses, and the white roses, and the red roses, and the mauve roses. He threw in the filigreed-handled spoons. He threw in the chunk of gypsum-veined jasper.

He threw in everything beautiful that he'd ever collected. He threw in a chased silver hand mirror, and an embroidered silk jacket, and a hand-painted egg. He threw in one of Fuoco's soft, emerald feathers. He threw in a memory crystal that showed Rose as an infant, curled and sleeping.

He loved those things, and yet they were things. He had owned them. Now they were gone. He had recently come to realize that ownership was a relationship. What did it mean to own a thing? To shape it and contain it? He could not possess or be possessed until he knew.

He watched the sea awhile, the remnants of his possessions lost in the tumbling waves. As the sun tilted past noon, he turned away and climbed back up the cliff. Unencumbered by ownership, he followed the boulevard away from Adriana's house.

Lucian remembered meeting Adriana the way that he imagined that humans remembered childhood. Oh, his memories had been as sharply focused then as now—but it was still like childhood, he reasoned, for he'd been a different person then.

He remembered his first sight of Adriana as a burst of images. Wavy strawberry blonde hair cut straight across tanned shoulders. Dark brown eyes that his artistic mind labeled "sienna." Thick, aristocratic brows and strong cheekbones, free of makeup. Lucian's inner aesthete termed her blunt, angular face "striking" rather than "beautiful." His inner psychoanalyst reasoned that she was probably "strong-willed" as well, from the way she stood in the doorway, her arms crossed, her eyebrows lifted as if inquiring how he planned to justify his existence.

Eventually, she moved away, allowing Lucian to step inside. He crossed the threshold into a blur off frantic screeching and flapping.

New. Everything was new. So new that Lucian could barely assemble feathers and beak and wings into the concept of "bird" before his reflexes jumped him away from the onslaught. Hissing and screeching, the animal retreated to a perch atop a bookshelf.

Adriana's hand weighed on Lucian's shoulder. Her voice was edged with the cynicism Lucian would later learn was her way of hiding how desperately she feared failure. "Ornithophobia? How ridiculous."

Lucian's first disjointed days were dominated by the bird, who he learned was named Fuoco. It followed him around the house. When he remained in place for a moment, the bird settled on some nearby high spot—the hat rack in the entryway, or the hand-crafted globe in the parlor, or the rafters above the master bed—to spy on him. It glared at Lucian in the manner of birds, first peering through one eye and then turning its head to peer through the other, apparently finding both views equally loathsome.

When Adriana took Lucian into her bed, Fuoco swooped at Lucian's head. Adriana pushed Lucian out of the way. "Damn it, Fuoco," she muttered, but she offered the bird a perch on her shoulder.

Fuoco crowed with pleasure as she led him downstairs. His feathers fluffed with victory as he hopped obediently into his cage, expecting her to reward him with treats and conversation. Instead, Adriana closed the gilded door and returned upstairs. All night, as Lucian lay with Adriana, the bird chattered madly. He plucked at his feathers until his tattered plumage carpeted the cage floor.

Lucian accompanied Adriana when she brought Fuoco to the vet the next day. The veterinarian diagnosed jealousy. "It's not uncommon in birds," he said. He suggested they give Fuoco a rigid routine that would, over time, help the bird realize he was Adriana's companion, not her mate.

Adriana and Lucian rearranged their lives so that Fuoco could have regular feeding times, scheduled exercise, socialization with both Lucian and Adriana, and time with his mistress alone. Adriana gave him a treat each night when she locked him in his cage, staying to stroke his feathers for a few minutes before she headed upstairs.

Fuoco's heart broke. He became a different bird. His strut lacked confidence, and his feathers grew ever more tattered. When they let him out of his cage, he wandered after Adriana with pleading, wistful eyes, and ignored Lucian entirely.

Lucian had been dis-integrated then: musician brain, mathematician brain, artist brain, economist brain, and more, all functioning separately, each personality rising to dominance to provide information and then sliding away, creating staccato bursts of consciousness.

As Adriana made clear which responses she liked, Lucian's consciousness began integrating into the personality she desired. He found himself noticing connections between what had previously been separate experiences. Before, when he'd seen the ocean, his scientist brain had calculated how far he was from the shore, and how long it would be until high tide. His poet brain had recited Strindberg's "We Waves." *Wet flames are we:/Burning, extinguishing;/Cleansing, replenishing.* Yet it wasn't until he integrated that the wonder of the science, and the mystery of the poetry, and the beauty of the view, all made sense to him at once as part of this strange, inspiring thing: the sea.

He learned to anticipate Adriana. He knew when she was pleased and when she was ailing, and he knew why. He could predict the cynical half-smile she'd give when he made an error he hadn't yet realized was an error: serving her cold coffee in an orange juice glass, orange juice in a shot glass, wine in a mug. When integration gave him knowledge of patterns, he suddenly understood why these things were errors. At the same time, he realized that he liked what happened when he made those kinds of errors, the bright bursts of humor they elicited from the often sober Adriana. So he persisted in error, serving her milk in crystal decanters, and grapefruit slices in egg cups.

He enjoyed the many varieties of her laughter. Sometimes it was light and surprised, as when he offered her a cupcake tin filled with tortellini. He also loved her rich, dark laughter that anticipated irony. Sometimes, her laughter held a bitter undercurrent, and on those occasions, he understood that she was laughing more at herself than at anyone else. Sometimes when that happened, he would go to hold her, seeking to ease her pain, and sometimes she would spontaneously start crying in gulping, gasping sobs.

She often watched him while he worked, her head cocked and her brows drawn as if she were seeing him for the first time. "What can I do to make you happy?" she'd ask.

If he gave an answer, she would lavishly fulfill his desires. She took him traveling to the best greenhouses in the state, and bought a library full of gardening books. Lucian knew she would have given him more. He didn't want it. He wanted to reassure her that he appreciated her extravagance, but didn't require it, that he was satisfied with simple, loving give-and-take. Sometimes, he told her in the simplest words he knew: "I love you, too." But he knew that she never quite believed him. She worried that he was lying, or that his programming had erased his free will. It was easier for her to believe those things than to accept that someone could love her.

But he did love her. Lucian loved Adriana as his mathematician brain loved the consistency of arithmetic, as his artist brain loved color, as his philosopher brain loved piety. He loved her as Fuoco loved her, the bird walking sadly along the arm of Adriana's chair, trilling and flapping his ragged wings as he eyed her with his inky gaze, trying to catch her attention.

Adriana hadn't expected to fall in love. She'd expected a charming conversationalist with the emotional range of a literary butler and the self-awareness of a golden retriever. Early on, she'd felt her prejudices confirmed. She noted Lucian's lack of critical thinking and his inability to maneuver unexpected situations. She found him most interesting when he didn't know she was watching. For instance, on his free afternoons: was his program trying to anticipate what would please her? Or did the thing really enjoy sitting by the window, leafing through the pages of one of her rare books, with nothing but the sound of the ocean to lull him?

Once, as Adriana watched from the kitchen doorway while Lucian made their breakfast, the robot slipped while he was dicing onions. The knife cut deep into his finger. Adriana stumbled forward to help. As Lucian turned to face her, Adriana imagined that she saw something like shock on his face. For a moment, she wondered whether he had a programmed sense of privacy she could violate, but then he raised his hand to her in greeting, and she watched as the tiny bots that maintained his system healed his inhuman flesh within seconds.

At that moment, Adriana remembered that Lucian was unlike her. She urged herself not to forget it, and strove not to, even after his consciousness integrated. He was a person, yes, a varied and fascinating one with as many depths and facets as any other person she knew. But he was also alien. He was a creature for whom a slip of a chef's knife was a minute error, simply repaired. In some ways, she was more similar to Fuoco.

As a child, Adriana had owned a book that told the fable of an emperor who owned a bird which he fed rich foods from his table, and entertained with luxuries from his court. But a pet bird needed different things than an emperor. It wanted seed and millet, not grand feasts. It enjoyed mirrors and little brass bells, not lacquer boxes and poetry scrolls. Gorged on human banquets and revelries, the little bird sickened and died.

Adriana vowed not to make the same mistake with Lucian, but she had no idea how hard it would be to salve the needs of something so unlike herself.

Adriana ordered the car to pull over at a farm that advertised children could "Pet Lambs and Calves" for a fee. A ginger-haired teenager stood at a strawberry stand in front of the fence, slouching as he flipped through a dog-eared magazine.

Adriana held Rose's hand as they approached. She tried to read her daughter's emotions in the feel of her tiny fingers. The little girl's expression revealed nothing; Rose had gone silent and flat-faced as if she were imitating Lucian. He would have known what she was feeling.

Adriana examined the strawberries. The crates contained none of the different shapes one could buy at the store, only the natural, seed-filled variety. "Do these contain pesticides?" Adriana asked.

"No, ma'am," said the teenager. "We grow organic."

"All right then. I'll take a box." Adriana looked down at her daughter. "Do you want some strawberries, sweetheart?" she asked in a sugared tone.

"You said I could pet the lambs," said Rose.

"Right. Of course, honey." Adriana glanced at the distracted teenager. "Can she?"

The teenager slumped, visibly disappointed, and tossed his magazine on a pile of canvas sacks. "I can take her to the barn."

"Fine. Okay."

Adriana guided Rose toward the teenager. Rose looked up at him, expression still inscrutable.

The boy didn't take Rose's hand. He ducked his head, obviously embarrassed. "My aunt likes me to ask for the money upfront."

"Of course." Adriana fumbled for her wallet. She'd let Lucian do things for her for so long. How many basic living skills had she forgotten? She held out some bills. The teenager licked his index finger and meticulously counted out what she owed.

The teen took Rose's hand. He lingered a moment, watching Adriana. "Aren't you coming with us?"

Adriana was so tired. She forced a smile. "Oh, that's okay. I've seen sheep and cows. Okay, Rose? Can you have fun for a little bit without me?"

Rose nodded soberly. She turned toward the teenager without hesitation, and followed him toward the barn. The boy seemed to be good with children. He walked slowly so that Rose could keep up with his long-legged strides.

Adriana returned to the car, and leaned against the hot, sun-warmed door. Her head throbbed. She thought she might cry or collapse. Getting out had seemed like a good idea—the house was full of memories of Lucian. He seemed to sit in every chair, linger in every doorway. But now she wished she'd stayed in her haunted but familiar home, instead of leaving with this child she seemed to barely know.

A sharp, long wail carried on the wind. Adrenaline cut through Adriana's melancholia. She sprinted toward the barn. She saw Rose running toward her, the teenager close behind, dust swirling around both of them. Blood dripped down Rose's arm.

Adriana threw her arms around her daughter. Arms, legs, breath, heart beat: Rose was okay. Adrianna dabbed at Rose's injury; there was a lot of blood, but the wound was shallow. "Oh, honey," she said, clutching Rose as tightly as she dared.

The teenager halted beside them, his hair mussed by the wind.

"What happened?" Adriana demanded.

The teenager stammered. "Fortuna kicked her. That's one of the goats. I'm so sorry. Fortuna's never done anything like that before. She's a nice goat. It's Ballantine usually does the kicking. He got me a few times when I was little. I came through every time. Honest, she'll be okay. You're not going to sue, are you?"

Rose struggled out of Adriana's grasp and began wailing again. "It's okay, Rose, it's okay," murmured Adriana. She felt a strange disconnect in her head as she spoke. Things were not okay. Things might never be okay again.

"I'm leaking," cried Rose, holding out her blood-stained fingers. "See, mama? I'm leaking! I need healer bots."

Adriana looked up at the teenager. "Do you have bandages? A first aid kit?"

The boy frowned. "In the house, I think…"

"Get the bots, Mama! Make me stop leaking!"

The teen stared at Adriana, the concern in his eyes increasing. Adriana blinked, slowly. The moment slowed. She realized what her daughter had said. She forced her voice to remain calm. "What do you want, Rose?"

"She said it before," said the teen. "I thought it was a game."

Adriana leveled her gaze with Rose's. The child's eyes were strange and brown, uncharted waters. "Is this a game?"

"Daddy left," said Rose.

Adriana felt woozy. "Yes, and then I brought you here so we could see lambs and calves. Did you see any nice, fuzzy lambs?"

"Daddy left."

She shouldn't have drunk the wine. She should have stayed clear-headed. "We'll get you bandaged up and then you can go see the lambs again. Do you want to see the lambs again? Would it help if mommy came, too?"

Rose clenched her fists. Her face grew dark. "My arm hurts!" She threw herself to the ground. "I want healer bots!"

Adriana knew precisely when she'd fallen in love with Lucian. It was three months after she'd bought him—after his consciousness had integrated, but before Adriana fully understood how integration had changed him.

It began when Adriana's sisters called from Boston to inform her that they'd arranged for a family pilgrimage to Italy. In accordance with their father's will, they would commemorate him by lighting candles in the cathedrals of every winding hillside city.

"Oh, I can't. I'm too busy," Adriana answered airily, as if she were a debutante without a care, as if she shared her sisters' ability to overcome her fear of their father.

Her phone began ringing ceaselessly. Nanette called before she rushed off to a tennis match. "How can you be so busy? You don't have a job. You don't have a husband. Or is there a man in your life we don't know about?" And once Nanette was deferred with mumbled excuses, it was Eleanor calling from a spa. "Is something wrong, Adriana? We're all worried. How can you miss a chance to say goodbye to papa?"

"I said goodbye at the funeral," said Adriana.

"Then you can't have properly processed your grief," said Jessica, calling from her office between appointments. She was a psychoanalyst in the Freudian mode. "Your aversion rings of denial. You need to process your Oedipal feelings."

Adriana slammed down the phone. Later, to apologize for hanging up, she sent all her sisters chocolates, and then booked a flight. In a fit of pique, she booked a seat for Lucian, too. Well, he was a companion, wasn't he? What else was he for?

Adriana's sisters were scandalized, of course. As they rode through Rome, Jessica, Nanette, and Eleanor gossiped behind their discreetly raised hands. Adriana with a robot? Well, she'd need to be, wouldn't she? There was no getting around the fact that she was damaged. Any girl who would make up those stories about their father would have to be.

Adriana ignored them as best she could while they whirled through Tuscany in a procession of rented cars. They paused in cities to gawk at gothic cathedrals and mummified remnants, always moving on within the day. During their father's long sickness, Adriana's sisters had perfected the art of cheerful anecdote. They used it to great effect as they lit candles in his memory. Tears welling in their eyes, they related banal, nostalgic memories. How their father danced at charity balls. How he lectured men on the board who looked down on him for being new money. How he never once apologized for anything in his life.

It had never been clear to Adriana whether her father had treated her sisters the way he treated her, or whether she had been the only one to whom he came at night, his breathing heavy and staccato. It seemed impossible that they could lie so seamlessly, never showing fear or doubt. But if they were telling the truth, that meant Adriana was the only one, and how could she believe that either?

One night, while Lucian and Adriana were alone in their room in a hotel in Assisi that had been a convent during the Middle Ages, Adriana broke down. It was all too much, being in this foreign place, talking endlessly about her father. She'd fled New England to get away from them, fled to her beautiful modern glass-and-wood house by the Pacific Ocean that was like a fresh breath drawn on an Autumn morning.

Lucian held her, exerting the perfect warmth and pressure against her body to comfort her. It was what she'd have expected from a robot. She knew that he calculated the pace of his breath, the temperature of his skin, the angle of his arm as it lay across her.

What surprised Adriana, what humbled her, was how eloquently Lucian spoke of his experiences. He told her what it had been like to assemble himself from fragments, to take what he'd once been and become something new. It was something Adriana had tried to do herself when she fled her family.

Lucian held his head down as he spoke. His gaze never met hers. He spoke as if this process of communicating the intimate parts of the self were a new kind of dance, and he was tenuously trying the steps. Through the fog of her grief, Adriana realized that this was a new, struggling consciousness coming to clarity. How could she do anything but love him?

When they returned from Italy, Adriana approached the fledgling movement for granting rights to artificial intelligences. They were underfunded and poorly organized. Adriana rented them offices in San Francisco, and hired a small but competent staff.

Adriana became the movement's face. She'd been on camera frequently as a child: whenever her father was in the news for some or other board room scandal, her father's publicists had lined up Adriana and her sisters beside the family limousine, chaste in their private school uniforms, ready to provide Lancaster Nuclear with a friendly, feminine face.

She and Lucian were a brief media curiosity: Heiress In Love With Robot. "Lucian is as self-aware as you or I," Adriana told reporters, all-American in pearls and jeans. "He thinks. He learns. He can hybridize roses as well as any human gardener. Why should he be denied his rights?"

Early on, it was clear that political progress would be frustratingly slow. Adriana quickly expended her patience. She set up a fund for the organization, made sure it would run without her assistance, and then turned her attention toward alternate methods for attaining her goals. She hired a team of lawyers to draw up a contract that would grant Lucian community property rights to her estate and accounts. He would be her equal in practicality, if not legality.

Next, Adriana approached Lucian's manufacturer, and commissioned them to invent a procedure that would allow Lucian to have conscious control of his brain plasticity. At their wedding, Adriana gave him the chemical commands at the same time as she gave him his ring. "You are your own person now. You always have been, of course, but now you have full agency, too. You are yourself," she announced, in front of their gathered friends. Her sisters would no doubt have been scandalized, but they had not been invited.

On their honeymoon, Adriana and Lucian toured hospitals, running the genetic profiles of abandoned infants until they found a healthy girl with a mitochondrial lineage that matched Adriana's. The infant was tiny and pink and curled in on herself, ready to unfold, like one of Lucian's roses.

When they brought Rose home, Adriana felt a surge in her stomach that she'd never felt before. It was a kind of happiness she'd never experienced, one that felt round and whole without any jagged edges. It was like the sun had risen in her belly and was dwelling there, filling her with boundless light.

There was a moment, when Rose was still new enough to be wrapped in the hand-made baby blanket that Ben and Lawrence had sent from France, in which Adriana looked up at Lucian and realized how enraptured he was with their baby, how much adoration underpinned his willingness to bend over her cradle for hours and mirror her expressions, frown for frown, astonishment for astonishment. In that moment, Adriana thought that this must be the true measure of equality, not money or laws, but this unfolding desire to create the future together by raising a new sentience. She thought she understood then why unhappy parents stayed together for the sake of their children, why families with sons and daughters felt so different from those that remained childless. Families with children were making something new from themselves. Doubly so when the endeavor was undertaken by a human and a creature who was already, himself, something new. What could they make together?

In that same moment, Lucian was watching the wide-eyed, innocent wonder with which his daughter beheld him. She showed the same pleasure when he entered the room as she did when Adriana entered. If anything, the light in her eyes was brighter when he approached. There was something about the way Rose loved him that he didn't yet understand. Earlier that morning, he had plucked a bloom from his apricot tea rose and whispered to its petals that they were beautiful. They were his, and he loved them. Every day, he held Rose, and understood that she was beautiful, and that he loved her. But she was not his. She was her own. He wasn't sure he'd ever seen a love like that, a love that did not want to hold its object in its hands and keep and contain it.

"You aren't a robot!"

Adriana's voice was rough from shouting all the way home. Bad enough to lose Lucian, but the child was out of control.

"I want healer bots! I'm a robot I'm a robot I'm a robot I'm a robot!"

The car stopped. Adriana got out. She waited for Rose to follow, and when she didn't, Adriana scooped her up and carried her up the driveway. Rose kicked and screamed. She sank her teeth into Adriana's arm. Adriana halted, surprised by the sudden pain. She breathed deeply, and then continued up the driveway. Rose's screams slid upward in register and rage.

Adriana set Rose down by the door long enough to key in the entry code and let the security system take a DNA sample from her hair. Rose hurled herself onto the porch, yanking fronds by the fistful off the potted ferns. Adriana leaned down to scrape her up and got kicked in the chest.

"God da... for heaven's sake." Adriana grabbed Rose's ankles with one hand and her wrists with the other. She pushed her weight against the unlocked door until it swung open. She carried Rose into the house, and slammed the door closed with her back. "Lock!" she yelled to the house.

When she heard the reassuring click, she set Rose down on the couch, and jumped away from the still-flailing limbs. Rose fled up the stairs, her bedroom door crashing shut behind her.

Adriana dug in her pocket for the bandages that the people at the farm had given her before she headed home, which she'd been unable to apply to a moving target in the car. Now was the time. She followed Rose up the stairs, her breath surprisingly heavy. She felt as though she'd been running a very long time.

She paused outside Rose's room. She didn't know what she'd do when she got inside. Lucian had always dealt with the child when she got overexcited. Too often, Adriana felt helpless, and became distant.

"Rose?" she called. "Rose? Are you okay?"

There was no response.

Adriana put her hand on the doorknob, and breathed deeply before turning.

She was surprised to find Rose sitting demurely in the center of her bed, her rumpled skirts spread about her as if she were a child at a picnic in an Impressionist painting. Dirt and tears trailed down the pink satin. The edges of her wound had already begun to bruise.

"I'm a robot," she said to Adriana, tone resentful.

Adriana made a decision. The most important thing was to bandage Rose's wound. Afterward, she could deal with whatever came next.

"Okay," said Adriana. "You're a robot."

Rose lifted her chin warily. "Good."

Adriana sat on the edge of Rose's bed. "You know what robots do? They change themselves to be whatever humans ask them to be."

"Dad doesn't," said Rose.

"That's true," said Adriana. "But that didn't happen until your father grew up."

Rose swung her legs against the side of the bed. Her expression remained dubious, but she no longer looked so resolute.

Adriana lifted the packet of bandages. "May I?"

Rose hesitated. Adriana resisted the urge to put her head in her hands. She had to get the bandages on, that was the important thing, but she couldn't shake the feeling that she was going to regret this later.

"Right now, what this human wants is for you to let her bandage your wound instead of giving you healer bots. Will you be a good robot? Will you let me?"

Rose remained silent, but she moved a little closer to her mother. When Adriana began bandaging her arm, she didn't scream.

Lucian waited for a bus to take him to the desert. He had no money. He'd forgotten about that. The driver berated him and wouldn't let him on.

Lucian walked. He could walk faster than a human, but not much faster. His edge was endurance. The road took him inland away from the sea. The last of the expensive houses stood near a lighthouse, lamps shining in all its windows. Beyond, condominiums pressed against each other, dense and alike. They gave way to compact, well-maintained homes, with neat green aprons maintained by automated sprinklers that sprayed arcs of precious water into the air.

The landscape changed. Sea breeze stilled to buzzing heat. Dirty, peeling houses squatted side by side, separated by chain link fences. Iron bars guarded the windows, and broken cars decayed in the driveways. Parched lawns stretched from walls to curb like scrub-land. No one was out in the punishing sun.

The road divided. Lucian followed the fork that went through the dilapidated town center. Traffic jerked along in fits and starts. Lucian walked in the gutter. Stray plastic bags blew beside him, working their way between dark storefronts. Parking meters blinked at the passing cars, hungry for more coins. Pedestrians ambled past, avoiding eye contact, mumbled conversations lost beneath honking horns.

On the other side of town, the road winnowed down to two lonely lanes. Dry golden grass stretched over rolling hills, dotted by the dark shapes of cattle. A battered convertible, roof down, blared its horn at Lucian as it passed. Lucian walked where the asphalt met the prickly weeds. Paper and cigarette butts littered the golden stalks like white flowers.

An old truck pulled over, the manually driven variety still used by companies too small to afford the insurance for the automatic kind. The man in the driver's seat was trim, with a pale blond moustache and a deerstalker cap pulled over his ears. He wore a string of fishing lures like a necklace. "Not much comes this way anymore," he said. "I used to pick up hitchhikers half the time I took this route. You're the first I've seen in a while."

Sun rendered the truck in bright silhouette. Lucian held his hand over his eyes to shade them.

"Where are you headed?" asked the driver.

Lucian pointed down the road.

"Sure, but where after that?"

Lucian dropped his arm to his side. The sun inched higher.

The driver frowned. "Can you write it down? I think I've got some paper in here." He grabbed a pen and a receipt out of his front pocket, and thrust them out the window.

Lucian took them. He wasn't sure, at first, if he could still write. His brain was slowly reshaping itself, and eventually all his linguistic skills would disappear, and even his thoughts would no longer be shaped by words. The pen fell limp in his hand, and then his fingers remembered what to do. "Desert," he wrote.

"It's blazing hot," said the driver. "A lot hotter than here. Why do you want to go there?"

"To be born," wrote Lucian.

The driver slid Lucian a sideways gaze, but he nodded at the same time, almost imperceptibly. "Sometimes people have to do things. I get that. I remember when…" The look in his eyes became distant. He moved back in his seat. "Get on in."

Lucian walked around the cab and got inside. He remembered to sit and to close the door, but the rest of the ritual escaped him. He stared at the driver until the pale man shook his head and leaned over Lucian to drag the seatbelt over his chest.

"Are you under a vow of silence?" asked the driver.

Lucian stared ahead.

"Blazing hot in the desert," muttered the driver. He pulled back onto the road, and drove toward the sun.

During his years with Adriana, Lucian tried not to think about the cockatiel Fuoco. The bird had never become accustomed to Lucian. He grew ever more angry and bitter. He plucked out his feathers so often that he became bald in patches. Sometimes he pecked deeply enough to bleed.

From time to time, Adriana scooped him up and stroked his head and nuzzled her cheek against the heavy feathers that remained on the part of his back he couldn't reach. "My poor little crazy bird," she'd say, sadly, as he ran his beak through her hair.

Fuoco hated Lucian so much that for a while they wondered whether he would be happier in another place. Adriana tried giving him to Ben and Lawrence, but he only pined for the loss of his mistress, and refused to eat until she flew out to retrieve him.

When they returned home, they hung Fuoco's cage in the nursery. Being near the baby seemed to calm them both. Rose was a fussy infant who disliked solitude. She seemed happier when there was a warm presence about, even if it was a bird. Fuoco kept her from crying during the rare times when Adriana called Lucian from Rose's side. Lucian spent the rest of his time in the nursery, watching Rose day and night with sleepless vigilance.

The most striking times of Lucian's life were holding Rose while she cried. He wrapped her in cream-colored blankets the same shade as her skin, and rocked her as he walked the perimeter of the downstairs rooms, looking out at the diffuse golden ambience that the streetlights cast across the blackberry bushes and neighbors' patios. Sometimes, he took her outside, and walked with her along the road by the cliffs. He never carried her down to the beach. Lucian had perfect balance and night vision, but none of that mattered when he could so easily imagine the terror of lost footing—Rose slipping from his grasp and plummeting downward. Instead, they stood a safe distance from the edge, watching from above as the black waves threw themselves against the rocks, the night air scented with cold and salt.

Lucian loved Adriana, but he loved Rose more. He loved her clumsy fists and her yearnings toward consciousness, the slow accrual of her stumbling syllables. She was building her consciousness piece by piece as he had, learning how the world worked and what her place was in it. He silently narrated her stages of development. *Can you tell that your body has boundaries? Do you know your skin from mine?* and *Yes! You can make things happen! Cause and effect. Keep crying and we'll come.* Best of all, there was the moment when she locked her eyes on his, and he could barely breathe for the realization that, *Oh, Rose. You know there's someone else thinking behind these eyes. You know who I am.*

Lucian wanted Rose to have all the beauty he could give her. Silk dresses and lace, the best roses from his pots, the clearest panoramic views of the sea. Objects delighted Rose. As an infant she watched them avidly, and then later clapped and laughed, until finally she could exclaim, "Thank you!" Her eyes shone.

It was Fuoco who broke Lucian's heart. It was late at night when Adriana went into Rose's room to check on her while she slept. Somehow, sometime, the birdcage had been left open. Fuoco sat on the rim of the open door, peering darkly outward.

Adriana had been alone with Rose and Fuoco before. But something about this occasion struck like lightning in Fuoco's tiny, mad brain. Perhaps it was the darkness of the room, with only the nightlight's pale blue glow cast on Adriana's skin, that confused the bird. Perhaps Rose had finally grown large enough that Fuoco had begun to perceive her as a possible rival rather than an ignorable baby-thing. Perhaps the last vestiges of his sanity had simply shredded. For whatever reason, as Adriana bent over the bed to touch her daughter's face, Fuoco burst wildly from his cage.

With the same jealous anger he'd shown toward Lucian, Fuoco dove at Rose's face. His claws raked against her forehead. Rose screamed. Adriana recoiled. She grabbed Rose in one arm, and flailed at the bird with the other. Rose struggled to escape her mother's grip so she could run away. Adriana instinctually responded by trying to protect her with an even tighter grasp.

Lucian heard the commotion from where he was standing in the living room, programming the house's cleaning regimen for the next week. He left the house panel open and ran through the kitchen on the way to the bedroom, picking up a frying pan as he passed through. He swung the pan at Fuoco as he entered the room, herding the bird away from Adriana, and into a corner. His fist tightened on the handle. He thought he'd have to kill his old rival.

Instead, the vitality seemed to drain from Fuoco. The bird's wings drooped.

He dropped to the floor with half-hearted, irregular wingbeats. His eyes had gone flat and dull.

Fuoco didn't struggle as Lucian picked him up and returned him to his cage. Adriana and Lucian stared at each other, unsure what to say. Rose slipped away from her mother and wrapped her arms around Lucian's knees. She was crying.

"Poor Fuoco," said Adriana, quietly.

They brought Fuoco to the vet to be put down. Adriana stood over him as the vet inserted the needle. "My poor crazy bird," she murmured, stroking his wings as he died.

Lucian watched Adriana with great sadness. At first, he thought he was feeling empathy for the bird, despite the fact it had always hated him. Then, with a realization that tasted like sour wine, he realized that wasn't what he was feeling. He recognized the poignant, regretful look that Adriana was giving Fuoco. It was the way Lucian himself looked at a wilted rose, or a tarnished silver spoon. It was a look inflected by possession.

It wasn't so different from the way Adriana looked at Lucian sometimes when things had gone wrong. He'd never before realized how slender the difference was between her love for him and her love for Fuoco. He'd never before realized how slender the difference was between his love for her and his love for an unfolding rose.

Adriana let Rose tend Lucian's plants, and dust the shelves, and pace by the picture window. She let the girl pretend to cook breakfast, while Adriana stood behind her, stepping in to wield the chopping knife and use the stove. At naptime, Adriana convinced Rose that good robots would pretend to sleep a few hours in the afternoon if that's what their humans wanted. She tucked in her daughter and then went downstairs to sit in the living room and drink wine and cry.

This couldn't last. She had to figure something out. She should take them both on vacation to Mazatlan. She should ask one of her sisters to come stay. She should call a child psychiatrist. But she felt so betrayed, so drained of spirit, that it was all she could do to keep Rose going from day to day.

Remnants of Lucian's accusatory silence rung through the house. What had he wanted from her? What had she failed to do? She'd loved him. She *loved* him. She'd given him half of her home and all of herself. They were raising a child together. And still he'd left her.

She got up to stand by the window. It was foggy that night, the streetlights tingeing everything with a weird, flat yellow glow. She put her hand on the pane, and her palm print remained on the glass, as though someone outside were beating on the window to get in. She peered into the gloom; it was as if the rest of the world were the fuzzy edges of a painting, and her well-lit house was the only defined spot. She felt as though it would be possible to open the front door and step over the threshold and blur until she was out of focus.

She finished her fourth glass of wine. Her head was whirling. Her eyes ran with

Lucian said nothing.

Dread laced Adriana's stomach. She read.

I have restored plasticity to my brain. The first thing I have done is to destroy my capacity for spoken language.

You gave me life as a human, but I am not a human. You shaped my thoughts with human words, but human words were created for human brains. I need to discover the shape of the thoughts that are my own. I need to know what I am.

I hope that I will return someday, but I cannot make promises for what I will become.

Lucian walks through the desert. His footsteps leave twin trails behind him. Miles back, they merge into the tire tracks that the truck left in the sand.

The sand is full of colors—not only beige and yellow, but red and green and blue. Lichen clusters on the stones, the hue of oxidized copper. Shadows pool between rock formations, casting deep stripes across the landscape.

Lucian's mind is creeping away from him. He tries to hold his fingers the way he would if he could hold a pen, but they fumble.

At night there are birds and jackrabbits. Lucian remains still, and they creep around him as if he weren't there. His eyes are yellow like theirs. He smells like soil and herbs, like the earth.

Elsewhere, Adriana has capitulated to her desperation. She has called Ben and Lawrence. They've agreed to fly out for a few days. They will dry her tears, and take her wine away, and gently tell her that she's not capable of staying alone with her daughter. "It's perfectly understandable," Lawrence will say. "You need time to mourn."

Adriana will feel the world closing in on her as if she cannot breathe, but even as her life feels dim and futile, she will continue breathing. Yes, she'll agree, it's best to return to Boston, where her sisters can help her. Just for a little while, just for a few years, just until, until, until. She'll entreat Nanette, Eleanor and Jessica to check the security cameras around her old house every day, in case Lucian returns. *You can check yourself,* they tell her, *You'll be living on your own again in no time.* Privately, they whisper to each other in worried tones, afraid that she won't recover from this blow quickly.

Elsewhere, Rose has begun to give in to her private doubts that she does not carry a piece of her father within herself. She'll sit in the guest room that Jessica's maids have prepared with her, and order the lights to switch off as she secretly scratches her skin with her fingernails, willing to cuts to heal on their own the way daddy's would. When Jessica finds her bleeding on the sheets and rushes in to comfort her niece, Rose will stand stiff and cold in her aunt's embrace. Jessica will call for the maid to clean the blood from the linen, and Rose will throw herself between the two adult women, and scream with a determination born of doubt and desperation. Robots do not bleed!

Without words, Lucian thinks of them. They have become geometries, cut out of shadows and silences, the missing shapes of his life. He yearns for them, the way that he yearns for cool during the day, and for the comforting eye of the sun at night.

The rest he cannot remember—not oceans or roses or green cockatiels that pluck out their own feathers. Slowly, slowly, he is losing everything, words and concepts and understanding and integration and sensation and desire and fear and history and context.

Slowly, slowly, he is finding something. Something past thought, something past the rhythm of day and night. A stranded machine is not so different from a jackrabbit. They creep the same way. They startle the same way. They peer at each other out of similar eyes.

Someday, Lucian will creep back to a new consciousness, one dreamed by circuits. Perhaps his newly reassembled self will go to the seaside house. Finding it abandoned, he'll make his way across the country to Boston, sometimes hitch-hiking, sometimes striding through cornfields that sprawl to the horizon. He'll find Jessica's house and inform it of his desire to enter, and Rose and Adriana will rush joyously down the mahogany staircase. Adriana will weep, and Rose will fling herself into his arms, and Lucian will look at them both with love tempered by desert sun. Finally, he'll understand how to love filigreed-handled spoons, and pet birds, and his wife, and his daughter—not just as a human would love these things, but as a robot may.

Now, a blue-bellied lizard sits on a rock. Lucian halts beside it. The sun beats down. The lizard basks for a moment, and then runs a few steps forward, and flees into a crevice. Lucian watches. In a diffuse, wordless way, he ponders what it must be like to be cold and fleet, to love the sun and yet fear open spaces. Already, he is learning to care for living things. He cannot yet form the thoughts to wonder what will happen next.

He moves on.

THE MOTORMAN'S COAT
JOHN KESSEL

John Kessel lives in Raleigh, North Carolina, where he is professor of American literature and creative writing at North Carolina State University. A writer of erudite short fiction that often makes reference to or pastiches popular culture, Kessel received the Nebula Award for his early novella "Another Orphan", and for "Pride and Prometheus", which appeared in last year's Best SF and Fantasy of the Year. He has published a range of impressive short fiction, including a series of time travel stories featuring character Detlev Gruber (the most recent of which is "It's All True"), and a series of science fiction stories set in the same world as James Tiptree, Jr. Award winner "Stories for Men". Kessel's short fiction has been collected in three volumes, *Meeting In Infinity*, *The Pure Product*, and *The Baum Plan for Financial Independence*, and he has published three novels: *Freedom Beach* (with James Patrick Kelly), *Good News from Outer Space*, and *Corrupting Dr. Nice*. He and Kelly have recently published an anthology, *The Secret History of Science Fiction*, that makes the case for the rapprochement, over the last forty years, of literary and science fiction.

When they opened the shop in Michaelska Street, Frantisek swore it would be the making of them. Veronika protested that the mortgage would leave them in penury, but he countered that a Staré Mêsto address was necessary to attract the clientele that would be interested in—and could afford—the merchandise they would have for sale. Veronika said they would just see tourists, not real monied people.

"Tourists have money, too," Frantisek would explain. He would be wearing a chef's jacket of nucotton twill with a double row of buttons down the front, or perhaps a Victorian cutaway with a red waistcoat, or even a synthetic denim shirt whose shoulders were embroidered with poppies.

"But will they pay a thousand euros for some old pitcher?"

"Tourists especially will pay."

She would only sigh, her dark eyes glistening so much Frantisek wanted to kiss her. Veronika was willowy, with long chestnut hair and a full mouth. "I hope you're right," she said.

Within a year she had left him.

As agent for InVirtu GMBH, Frantisek had established a large network of the most knowledgeable suppliers in Europa and the Caliphate. His shop, situated between a music store and a small restaurant, was full of exotic *objets d'art* dating from before the Die-Off. A seventeenth-century astrolabe. Roman glassware. A functioning late-twentieth-century Atari computer. Marlene Dietrich's hand mirror. A perfectly preserved tabla, with drumhead of genuine animal hide. The bicycle that had won the 2012 Tour de France. And Frantisek's specialty: antique clothing of materials ancient and rare. Despite lanolin-resistant bacteria and the bio-engineered cotton smut, Frantisek could sell you a pre-collapse jacket in 100% genuine wool and put a 1950s sateen handkerchief in its breast pocket.

On the shelf behind the counter stood a photograph of Frantisek and Veronika from nine years before. Frantisek had had the photo done in the style of a century ago, in black and white. It was from early in their marriage, when they still thought they might have a child. The two of them were about to cross Zitna Street, on their way to the Museum Dvorák, leaning into each other, her face in profile smiling at him. A strong wind blew her hair back like a flag. He wore a polo coat; she had on the beautifully tailored redingote he had bought for her the day after they had first slept together.

Now Veronika was gone.

She had not been able, she claimed, to handle the stress. She did not care about antiques, and never valued the things that he considered valuable. Frantisek had known that from the beginning of their relationship, but he had told himself that his love for her would overwhelm such matters of temperament. Instead, as his savings dwindled and their customers remained few, Veronika came increasingly to blame him for every thing that dissatisfied her.

As Frantisek dusted the row of vases at the rear of the store, he heard the bell of the shop door chime. He turned to find an attractive black woman entering.

"Dobry den," the woman said, nodding to him.

"Dobry den," he said.

The woman idly circled the shop. Frantisek tried not to follow her with his eyes, letting her have her time. She possessed the lithe slenderness of a dancer. Had he seen her at the ballet? She stopped to examine a purple ceramic elephant, the product of some child's primary school class a hundred years ago. Beside it a Peruvian bird totem, fired red clay, glazed black, inscribed with intricate lines.

"You have interesting merchandise," she said.

"Thank you."

She turned to face him. "But your shop is not busy." She smiled.

"People do not always recognize quality," Frantisek said.

"Perhaps it would help if you had some item of transcendent interest. Something so rare as to attract even the purblind."

"Perhaps. Such items are hard to come by."

"I have one," the woman said. "A motorman's coat."

Frantisek laughed. "I don't believe you."

The woman laughed as well. Her laugh was light, sexy. "I don't blame you. Nevertheless, it is true."

"A motorman's coat? A Czech coat?"

"Praha Transportation Company, 1911, regulation issue, dark blue wool with solid brass buttons."

How did she know—did she know?—that Frantisek was a descendant of Frantisek Krizik, the engineer who in the 1890s established the second electric tram line in Praha. "Where did you find this marvel?"

Before she answered the door chime rang again, and in came two young people. In halting Czech the man asked if he could buy some matches. The woman took a glance around the store with indifference and turned back to the front window. "These things are old," she said in English.

Frantisek gave the man a box of Kafkas and turned back to the black woman. "Is this coat for sale?"

"For the correct price."

"I would need to see it."

"Of course."

"Do you have any cigarettes?" the man asked.

Frantisek lost his temper. "Does this look like a tobacconist's shop?"

The man looked confused. He muttered something to his companion that Frantisek could not make out, then turned back. "You're right. It looks like a bunch of crap," he said in English. He took the woman's arm and they walked out the door.

The black woman had observed this calmly. Frantisek colored at her slight smile. "You should not have to deal with such people," she said.

"I have little choice."

"One always has choices," she said. She stuck out her hand. "My name is Carlotta Olembe."

"Frantisek Lanik. I would like to see this coat."

"Meet me tonight, Mala Xavernova 27, at ten p.m." The elegant woman touched his wrist with her finely manicured hand. Her fingertips were warm. "Ciao," she said, and left.

Frantisek stood there wondering what had happened. The rest of the afternoon passed uneventfully, and unprofitably. At seven he closed the shop and went to his flat in Vinohrady. He washed, shaved, changed his shirt, and put on a jacket, then walked down to *Dert Dünyasý*, a Turkish restaurant in his neighborhood. He wondered whether this coat could be what Carlotta Olembe claimed. He wondered if she had felt the same sexual charge from him that he had gotten from her. He had not thought of a woman in that way since Veronika had left.

Just past nine he took the tram south, then across the Vlatava. The buildings shortened as the tram climbed the bluff above the river. The address Carlotta had given him was in Smíchov, an industrial district in the mid-20th which had been renovated after the fall of the Communists, only to suffer another decline in the disasters that had depopulated the city in the mid-21st. Now it was coming back again. Biological buildings, edible ornamental hedges, brick walkways.

Mala Xavernova was a street of tree houses, underground clubs, new gardens. Frantisek wandered with groups of idlers out for the evening. Most of the people here were Czech, not tourists. Luminescents grew among the branches of fruit trees laden with fragrant blossoms. Number 27 was an organic building that must have been planted thirty years ago, in the aftermath. Between the building's massive buttress roots, beneath a neon sign announcing *Ne Omluva*, stood an open door. Frantisek heard the sounds of jazz as he stepped into the club. Smoke swirled over small tables in the crowded room. He spotted Carlotta sitting on a stool by the bar.

"Ciao," she said, kissing him on the cheek. She wore a tight green acrylic dress, a line of faux pearls dangling from its sleeve. She pushed a liqueur glass toward him. "Have a drink."

Carlotta did not look like a woman who indulged in emotigens. He sipped. Some sort of cocktail. It tasted like peaches and alcohol. "I would like to see this motorman's coat."

"Is that what you would like to see?'

"Among other things. If I can afford them."

"You can afford the coat. I am not able to tell you if you can afford any other indulgences."

"Is it all a matter of sale?"

"No. Some things are not for sale. Some are free."

If Frantisek had come to understand anything from his relationship to Veronika, it was that nothing came free. He plucked a cherry from the dwarf tree that grew out of the middle of the bar. "So, why do we meet in this club?"

"My flat is just below," Carlotta said, pointing down. "In the roots."

The jazz trio ground to a halt in a flurry of tortured sax triple notes. Polite applause. Frantisek finished his drink. He felt dizzy. "Let's see it."

"So business-like." But Carlotta rose from the stool and wove through the crowd to a stairwell. He watched her hips swing as he followed her.

They descended into the roots of the building. The stairwell had been engineered out of the taproot, the spiraling treads shiny as mahogany. More luminescents gleamed from the organic surfaces of the walls. They might have been descending into the bowels of some animal. He was impressed with the condition of this building: no sign of the house blight that had destroyed whole neighborhoods as it swept through the city a decade before.

On the first landing, Carlotta took the polished faux-ivory handle of a door and opened it. Her apartment was elegant, sparely furnished. A false window showed a night scene of the Charles Bridge and the castle. In the soft light, beside a sofa, stood a mannequin with a blank silver face, wearing the motorman's coat.

Frantisek slipped past Carlotta and examined it. The sleeve was flawless, the stitching tiny and precise, a typical product of the first machine age. The hand that had formed the drawing-in stitches along the roll line of this collar moldered in the grave now for close to two centuries. Yet the brass buttons gleamed. The worked buttonholes were in perfect condition. He ran his fingers along the lapel. On a cold night the man who had worn this coat would have been snug and warm, the fresh air on his face as the tram moved noisily through the stone city, on the electric magic carpet of his generation. Frantisek had a vision of Praha as it had been, of elegant women, proper men, churches filled with believers while artists, con men, and prostitutes crowded the nighttime cafes under yellow incandescent lights.

"How much?" he asked her.

Carlotta named a large number. It was more than he could afford. He would have to borrow against his equity even to consider it. But, with this coat in his shop, he knew he could reverse his fortunes. It was a gift. An opportunity not to be passed by.

"Would you like to try it on?" she said. "It looks to be made for you."

It was true—the mannequin was precisely as tall as he. He touched the coat. "Go ahead," Carlotta said, putting her hand on his arm. He could smell her faint perfume.

Frantisek removed his own jacket. Carlotta took the coat from the mannequin and held it out for him. He turned his back to her, his face flushed, and slipped his arms into the sleeves. She lifted the coat toward his shoulders, and lowered it onto them. He pulled his shirt collar straight. The coat felt comfortable. Its scent, ancient but not unpleasant, filled his nostrils. He stretched out his right arm, slowly, feeling the weight of it, as if he were exercising tai chi.

"It's perfect," he said.

The shop was crowded the day of the showing. He'd had the party catered, another expense, but by now he was falling free and money did not matter. A steady, cold rain dulled the street, but inside candles glowed, light piano music played softly, and the turnout made Frantisek giddy.

Many important people had come. Here was the actress Dusana Melk, and her director Javed Mostaghim. There stood industrialist and notorious collector of antiquities Josef Bondy, sliver-haired, elegant, and slender in black. The monk Vavrin Cerny, down from his Moravian retreat with two of his acolytes in white robes. The mayor herself, Nadezda Markovic.

Carlotta was there, dressed in red, a good color for her. Frantisek had sold his flat, cleaned out his bank account, and taken out a loan from the bank against the accumulated assets of the shop in order to pay her. In return he had the coat, which stood displayed, under a pin spot, on a mannequin in the center of the shop floor.

He had worn it all day the previous day. It was by no means a miracle of tailoring—it had been, after all, only a uniform, one of many manufactured in its time. It was not the coat of a rich man, not even as plush as the camel hair jacket he had once worn for three minutes. But the destruction of most organic fabrics had left such items as this so rare as to give them an aura. When he wore the motorman's coat, Frantisek felt taller, handsomer, smarter, and more acute. He could discern the future with a knife's edge clarity and plot his course through it as agilely as a dancer.

Of course, Carlotta was the dancer. She approached him. "Are you happy with the turnout?"

"Very. Do you know Josef Bondy?"

"I have made his acquaintance."

"Why didn't you sell the coat to him?"

"You assume he wishes to buy it."

"Why otherwise would he be here?"

"Perhaps because I asked him?"

"You did?"

"Did I?" She touched her slender finger to the tip of his nose, then whirled away toward the table where a servant in a white coat poured champagne.

Frantisek lowered the music, then tapped his fingernail against the side of his champagne flute to get the people's attention. "My friends, and good people of Praha. I welcome you to my humble shop. Thank you for coming out on this wet evening. It does me honor to look around and see so many of the most discerning citizens of our great city.

"The city of Kafka and Rilke and Capek, Havel and Klima and Kundera, beloved of the mystical Rabbi Loew and the brilliant Mozart and a dozen others too familiar to us all. It is a city of stories and of storytellers. And we tonight are here to continue a story. This coat that brings us together tonight—" he gestured with his glass to the motorman's coat, "—is a piece of history that persists, miraculously undamaged, into our quite different present. It provides us a way to connect with the past, and implies a future, both for me personally and for all of us. We live in history, which is a tale we create out of events that happen—"

As he spoke, the door of the shop opened and a gust of wind flickered the candles. Through the door came Veronika.

She wore a long black coat over a blue dress cut to the knee. Her hair was loose on one side and pulled back with a comb above the opposite ear. Frantisek, disconcerted, stopped speaking, and a number of people, following his gaze, turned to see who had entered.

"—that story does not end," Frantisek continued. "That story takes what we know is real—our troubles, failures, mishaps—and transforms them into meaning. Our losses are put into a context that gives them purpose and proportion, so that, in the end, we are not overwhelmed, we do not despair, we are reconciled. That story creates joy."

A look of weariness and distaste flashed across Veronika's face, and Frantisek, though he had rehearsed this speech obsessively for weeks, forgot what he was about to say. Temporizing, he held his hand out toward her. "Ladies and gentlemen, my wife. Herself a creator of stories."

Nervous laughter. Frantisek saw Carlotta, head inclined intimately, speaking softly to Josef Bondy. "And now, please enjoy each other's company, and the rebirth of our city."

The people applauded politely. Frantisek did not want to have to deal with Veronika, and she, thank God, after her abrupt appearance did not seem to want to speak with him. Perhaps she felt ashamed. If so, that would be the first time. She went over to the mannequin and examined the coat—reached out and fingered the lapel. He wanted to rush over and tell her to keep her hands off, but was interrupted by Mrs. Staegers, who complimented him on his redoing the décor of the shop.

By the time Frantisek had extricated himself, Veronika was leaning against a shelf, sipping from a glass of champagne. Frantisek decided to have a word with Mr. Bondy.

"Mr. Bondy, let me say how honored I am to have you visit my shop," Frantisek began.

"Call me Josef."

"Josef. I believe you are acquainted with Ms. Olembe? It was she who discovered this coat."

"Ms. Olembe obtained the coat from me."

Frantisek's hopes for a sale were dashed. He tried not to show it. "Ah. I am surprised that you would part with such a unique item."

"There is a season for everything, and then it passes. I have my eye on new things. This astrolabe, for instance. Did you know that I named my sons Tycho and Johannes?"

"I did not."

"Visionaries are my hobby."

"Well, if you are interested in the astrolabe, I can certify its provenance." And, thought Frantisek, perhaps get back some of the money that ended up in your pocket. Yet why had Bondy used Carlotta as his go-between?

Bondy smiled. "Not just a visionary, but an entrepreneur. You will excuse me?" The collector snagged another flute of wine from the tray of one of the caterers, and turned to speak with a very young woman in gray who was playing with a long beaded necklace that hung to her waist.

As Frantisek mingled with the others, gradually a heaviness settled over him. He could not say exactly what it was. Certainly he could not have asked for a better turnout. The fact that Bondy would not buy the coat, that he was in fact the seller of the coat, was a surprise and disappointment, but he could not reasonably have counted on the industrialist's interest. Reason, of course, has little to do with want.

He looked at the motorman's coat. It glowed in the lights, the brass buttons gleaming. It belonged to him now. If he wanted to, he could walk over, remove it from the mannequin and put it on.

Looking around the room of strangers, he realized that Veronika was not there. Had she come simply to discomfit him publicly, then run off without ever exchanging a civil word? He should have noticed if she had left.

Frantisek found her in the back room, bent over an open drawer in his desk. Her bateau neckline exposed her breasts. "What are you doing back here?"

She looked up, startled. She slid the drawer closed.

"I could not stand to watch you abase yourself to those people. Did you ever find my red scarf?"

Frantisek sighed, and sat on the edge of his desk. "Veronika, I'm glad to see you, but as usual, I can't fathom your behavior. You know how hard I have worked. All that happens here tonight is for your benefit as much as mine. So have some wine, meet these people, and please, please, do not hurt me any more."

"Frantisek, I am not hurting you. I'm trying to keep you from making a pompous ass of yourself. You hang your entire future on a coat?"

"This venture will save me. It could save us both, if you loved me."

"I don't need saving."

She had always needed saving, from the moment he first saw her overdosed on theostimulants in the nave of St. Vitus's, her pupils as large as saucers as she stared at the stained glass image of the blessing of St. Cyril. How that trembling girl had turned into this judgmental bitch was beyond him. He took her by the hand and pulled her to him, pressed his face to hers and crushed his lips against hers. She did not resist. He felt her nerveless body beneath the sheath of her dress. But, passive as a martyr, she did not kiss him back. He let her go.

"When all this ends, call me," she said. She took her coat and walked out.

It was several minutes before he could make himself go back in to the front of the store. The crowd of people had thinned. Carlotta was leaning forward, examining the coat from a few centimeters away, as if she were hypnotized by the weave of the fabric. She looked up as he approached. "Has this gone as well as you hoped?"

"Why didn't you tell me that Bondy was the seller of the coat? What was the purpose of this charade?"

A nearby man stood very still to eavesdrop. "There is no charade," Carlotta said. "Josef sought to sell the coat. I acted as his agent."

"Why did you lead me to believe he might buy it, then?"

"I led you to believe nothing of the sort."

Other people had stopped their conversations to listen, now. In the sudden stillness, Frantisek became aware of the music—Mozart's Piano Sonata in F major—in the background. "Why did you bring him here, if not to mislead me of his intentions?"

"He came because I asked him to, in order to help your business. Which I begin to regret."

Frantisek took her wine glass from her hand and put it aside. "The deal is off!" he shouted. "You will take it back. Take it—now!" He began to unbutton the coat to remove it from the mannequin. As his fingers fumbled, the brass button came off in his hand. Angrier still, he moved to the next button. Rather than slip through the buttonhole, the brass disk tore through the fabric around it.

People had put on their coats and were leaving. Carlotta stood watching him.

When Frantisek reached up to open the coat and pull the sleeves off the mannequin's arms, the lapel tore like wet tissue paper. When he tugged at a sleeve, it came off in his hands.

He fell back in dismay. As he and the remaining, startled guests stared, the coat began to slide into pieces, disintegrating before him. The facing of the lapel mottled like a time-lapse video of fruit molding. A second button fell to the floor and clattered across the hardwood. The sleeve in his hands fell into shreds that floated in the air like down. In minutes all that was left of the motorman's coat was a heap of fragments on the floor, and some bluish dust on Frantisek's numb fingertips.

MONGOOSE
SARAH MONETTE AND ELIZABETH BEAR

Sarah Monette grew up in Oak Ridge, Tennessee, one of the three secret cities of the Manhattan Project, and now lives in a 104-year-old house in the Upper Midwest with a great many books, four cats, one husband, and one albino bristlenose plecostomus. Her Ph.D. diploma (English Literature, 2004) hangs in the kitchen. Her first four novels were published by Ace Books. Her short stories have appeared in *Strange Horizons*, *Weird Tales*, and *Lady Churchill's Rosebud Wristlet*, among other venues, and have been reprinted in several Year's Best anthologies; a short story collection, *The Bone Key*, was published by Prime Books in 2007. She has written one novel (*A Companion to Wolves*) and three short stories with Elizabeth Bear, and hopes to write more.

Elizabeth Bear was born in Hartford, Connecticut, on the same day as Frodo and Bilbo Baggins, but in a different year. She lives in Manchester, Connecticut, with a presumptuous cat, a giant ridiculous dog, the best roommate ever, and a selection of struggling houseplants. Her first short fiction appeared in 1996, and was followed after a nearly decade-long gap by fifteen novels, two short story collections, and more than fifty short stories. Her most recent books are novels *Chill*, *By The Mountain Bound*, and novella *Bone & Jewel Creatures*. Bear's "Jenny Casey" trilogy won the Locus Award for Best First Novel, and she won the John W. Campbell Award for Best New Writer in 2005. Her stories "Tideline" and "Shoggoths in Bloom" won the Hugo, while "Tideline" also won the Theodore Sturgeon Memorial award.

Izrael Irizarry stepped through a bright-scarred airlock onto Kadath Station, lurching a little as he adjusted to station gravity. On his shoulder, Mongoose extended her neck, her barbels flaring, flicked her tongue out to taste the air, and colored a question. Another few steps, and he smelled what Mongoose smelled, the sharp stink of toves, ammoniac and bitter.

He touched the tentacle coiled around his throat with the quick double tap that meant *soon*. Mongoose colored displeasure, and Irizarry stroked the slick velvet wedge of her head in consolation and restraint. Her four compound and twelve simple eyes glittered and her color softened, but did not change, as she leaned into the caress. She was eager to hunt and he didn't blame her. The boojum *Manfred von Richthofen* took care of its own vermin. Mongoose had had to make do with a share of Irizarry's rations, and she hated eating dead things.

If Irizarry could smell toves, it was more than the "minor infestation" the message from the station master had led him to expect. Of course, that message had reached Irizarry third- or fourth- or fifteenth-hand, and he had no idea how long it had taken. Perhaps when the station master had sent for him, it *had* been minor.

But he knew the ways of bureaucrats, and he wondered.

People did double-takes as he passed, even the heavily modded Christian cultists with their telescoping limbs and biolin eyes. You found them on every station and steelships too, though mostly they wouldn't work the boojums. Nobody liked Christians much, but they could work in situations that would kill an unmodded human or a even a gilly, so captains and station masters tolerated them.

There were a lot of gillies in Kadath's hallways, and they all stopped to blink at Mongoose. One, an indenturee, stopped and made an elaborate hand-flapping bow. Irizarry felt one of Mongoose's tendrils work itself through two of his earrings. Although she didn't understand staring exactly—her compound eyes made the idea alien to her—she felt the attention and was made shy by it.

Unlike the boojum-ships they serviced, the stations—Providence, Kadath, Leng, Dunwich, and the others—were man-made. Their radial symmetry was predictable, and to find the station master, Irizarry only had to work his way inward from the *Manfred von Richthofen*'s dock to the hub. There he found one of the inevitable safety maps (you are here; in case of decompression, proceed in an orderly manner to the life vaults located here, here, or here) and leaned close to squint at the tiny lettering. Mongoose copied him, tilting her head first one way, then another, though flat representations meant nothing to her. He made out STATION MASTER'S OFFICE finally, on a oval bubble, the door of which was actually in sight.

"Here we go, girl," he said to Mongoose (who, stone-deaf though she was, pressed against him in response to the vibration of his voice). He hated this part of the job, hated dealing with apparatchiks and functionaries, and of course the Station Master's office was full of them, a receptionist, and then a secretary, and then someone who was maybe the *other* kind of secretary, and then finally— Mongoose by now halfway down the back of his shirt and entirely hidden by his hair and Irizarry himself half-stifled by memories of someone he didn't want to remember being—he was ushered into an inner room where Station Master Lee, her arms crossed and her round face set in a scowl, was waiting.

"Mr. Irizarry," she said, unfolding her arms long enough to stick one hand out in a facsimile of a congenial greeting.

He held up a hand in response, relieved to see no sign of recognition in her face. It was Irizarry's experience that dead lives were best left lie where they fell. "Sorry, Station Master," he said. "I can't."

He thought of asking her about the reek of toves on the air, if she understood just how bad the situation had become. People could convince themselves of a lot of bullshit, given half a chance.

Instead, he decided to talk about his partner. "Mongoose hates it when I touch other people. She gets jealous, like a parrot."

"The cheshire's here?" She let her hand drop to her side, the expression on her face a mixture of respect and alarm. "Is it out of phase?"

Well, at least Station Master Lee knew a little more about cheshire-cats than most people. "No," Irizarry said. "She's down my shirt."

Half a standard hour later, wading through the damp bowels of a ventilation pore, Irizarry tapped his rebreather to try to clear some of the tove-stench from his nostrils and mouth. It didn't help much; he was getting close.

Here, Mongoose wasn't shy at all. She slithered up on top of his head, barbels and graspers extended to full length, pulsing slowly in predatory greens and reds. Her tendrils slithered through his hair and coiled about his throat, fading in and out of phase. He placed his fingertips on her slick-resilient hide to restrain her. The last thing he needed was for Mongoose to go spectral and charge off down the corridor after the tove colony.

It wasn't that she wouldn't come back, because she would—but that was only if she didn't get herself into more trouble than she could get out of without his help. "Steady," he said, though of course she couldn't hear him. A creature adapted to vacuum had no ears. But she could feel his voice vibrate in his throat, and a tendril brushed his lips, feeling the puff of air and the shape of the word. He tapped her tendril twice again—*soon*—and felt it contract. She flashed hungry orange in his peripheral vision. She was experimenting with jaguar rosettes—they had had long discussions of jaguars and tigers after their nightly reading of Pooh on the *Manfred von Richthofen*, as Mongoose had wanted to know what jagulars and tiggers were. Irizarry had already taught her about mongooses, and he'd read *Alice in Wonderland* so she would know what a Cheshire Cat was. Two days later—he still remembered it vividly—she had disappeared quite slowly, starting with the tips of the long coils of her tail and tendrils and ending with the needle-sharp crystalline array of her teeth. And then she'd phased back in, all excited aquamarine and pink, almost bouncing, and he'd praised her and stroked her and reminded himself not to think of her as a cat. Or a mongoose.

She had readily grasped the distinction between jaguars and jagulars, and had almost as quickly decided that she was a jagular; Irizarry had almost started to argue, but then thought better of it. She was, after all, a Very Good Dropper. And nobody ever saw her coming unless she wanted them to.

When the faint glow of the toves came into view at the bottom of the pore, he felt her shiver all over, luxuriantly, before she shimmered dark and folded herself tight against his scalp. Irizarry doused his own lights as well, flipping the passive infrared goggles down over his eyes. Toves were as blind as Mongoose was deaf, but an infestation this bad could mean the cracks were growing large enough for bigger things to wiggle through, and if there were raths, no sense in letting the monsters know he was coming.

He tapped the tendril curled around his throat three times, and whispered "Go." She didn't need him to tell her twice; really, he thought wryly, she didn't need him to tell her at all. He barely felt her featherweight disengage before she was gone down the corridor as silently as a hunting owl. She was invisible to his goggles, her body at ambient temperature, but he knew from experience that her barbels and vanes would be spread wide, and he'd hear the shrieks when she came in among the toves.

The toves covered the corridor ceiling, arm-long carapaces adhered by a foul-smelling secretion that oozed from between the sections of their exoskeletons. The upper third of each tove's body bent down like a dangling bough, bringing the glowing, sticky lure and flesh-ripping pincers into play. Irizarry had no idea what they fed on in their own phase, or dimension, or whatever.

Here, though, he knew what they ate. Anything they could get.

He kept his shock probe ready, splashing after, to assist her if necessary. That was sure a lot of toves, and even a cheshire-cat could get in trouble if she was outnumbered. Ahead of him, a tove warbled and went suddenly dark; Mongoose had made her first kill.

Within moments, the tove colony was in full warble, the harmonics making Irizarry's head ache. He moved forward carefully, alert now for signs of raths. The largest tove colony he'd ever seen was on the derelict steelship *Jenny Lind*, which he and Mongoose had explored when they were working salvage on the boojum *Harriet Tubman*. The hulk had been covered inside and out with toves; the colony was so vast that, having eaten everything else, it had started cannibalizing itself, toves eating their neighbors and being eaten in turn. Mongoose had glutted herself before the *Harriet Tubman* ate the wreckage, and in the refuse she left behind, Irizarry had found the strange starlike bones of an adult rath, consumed by its own prey. The bandersnatch that had killed the humans on the *Jenny Lind* had died with her reactor core and her captain. A handful of passengers and crew had escaped to tell the tale.

He refocused. This colony wasn't as large as those heaving masses on the *Jenny Lind*, but it was the largest he'd ever encountered not in a quarantine situation, and if there weren't raths somewhere on Kadath Station, he'd eat his infrared goggles.

A dead tove landed at his feet, its eyeless head neatly separated from its segmented body, and a heartbeat later Mongoose phased in on his shoulder and made her deep clicking noise that meant, *Irizarry! Pay attention!*

He held his hand out, raised to shoulder level, and Mongoose flowed between the two, keeping her bulk on his shoulder, with tendrils resting against his lips and larynx, but her tentacles wrapping around his hand to communicate. He pushed his goggles up with his free hand and switched on his belt light so he could read her colors.

She was anxious, strobing yellow and green. *Many,* she shaped against his palm, and then emphatically, *R.*

"R" was bad—it meant rath—but it was better than "B." If a bandersnatch had come through, all of them were walking dead, and Kadath Station was already as doomed as the *Jenny Lind.* "Do you smell it?" he asked under the warbling of the toves.

Taste, said Mongoose, and because Irizarry had been her partner for almost five Solar, he understood: the toves tasted of rath, meaning that they had recently been feeding on rath guano, and given the swiftness of toves' digestive systems, that meant a rath was patrolling territory on the station.

Mongoose's grip tightened on his shoulder. *R,* she said again. *R. R. R.*

Irizarry's heart lurched and sank. More than one rath. The cracks were widening.

A bandersnatch was only a matter of time.

Station Master Lee didn't want to hear it. It was all there in the way she stood, the way she pretended distraction to avoid eye-contact. He knew the rules of this game, probably better than she did. He stepped into her personal space. Mongoose shivered against the nape of his neck, her tendrils threading his hair. Even without being able to see her, he knew she was a deep, anxious emerald.

"A rath?" said Station Master Lee, with a toss of her head that might have looked flirtatious on a younger or less hostile woman, and moved away again. "Don't be ridiculous. There hasn't been a rath on Kadath Station since my grandfather's time."

"Doesn't mean there isn't an infestation now," Irizarry said quietly. If she was going to be dramatic, that was his cue to stay still and calm. "And I said raths. Plural."

"That's even more ridiculous. Mr. Irizarry, if this is some ill-conceived attempt to drive up your price—"

"It isn't." He was careful to say it flatly, not indignantly. "Station Master, I understand that this isn't what you want to hear, but you have to quarantine Kadath."

"Can't be done," she said, her tone brisk and flat, as if he'd asked her to pilot Kadath through the rings of Saturn.

"Of course it can!" Irizarry said, and she finally turned to look at him, outraged that he dared to contradict her. Against his neck, Mongoose flexed one set of claws. She didn't like it when he was angry.

Mostly, that wasn't a problem. Mostly, Irizarry knew anger was a waste of time and energy. It didn't solve anything. It didn't fix anything. It couldn't bring back anything that was lost. People, lives. The sorts of things that got washed away in the tides of time. Or were purged, whether you wanted them gone or not.

But this was... "You do know what a colony of adult raths can do, don't you?

With a contained population of prey? Tell me, Station Master, have you started noticing fewer indigents in the shelters?"

She turned away again, dismissing his existence from her cosmology. "The matter is not open for discussion, Mr. Irizarry. I hired you to deal with an alleged infestation. I expect you to do so. If you feel you can't, you are of course welcome to leave the station with whatever ship takes your fancy. I believe the *Arthur Gordon Pym* is headed in-system, or perhaps you'd prefer the Jupiter run?"

He didn't have to win this fight, he reminded himself. He could walk away, try to warn somebody else, get himself and Mongoose the hell off Kadath Station. "All right, Station Master. But remember that I warned you, when your secretaries start disappearing."

He was at the door when she cried, "Irizarry!"

He stopped, but didn't turn.

"I can't," she said, low and rushed, as if she was afraid of being overheard. "I can't quarantine the station. Our numbers are already in the red this quarter, and the new political officer… it's my head on the block, don't you understand?"

He didn't understand. Didn't want to. It was one of the reasons he was a wayfarer, because he never wanted to let himself be like her again.

"If Sanderson finds out about the quarantine, she finds out about you. Will your papers stand up to a close inspection, Mr. Irizarry?"

He wheeled, mouth open to tell her what he thought of her and her clumsy attempts at blackmail, and she said, "I'll double your fee."

At the same time, Mongoose tugged on several strands of his hair, and he realized he could feel her heart beating, hard and rapid, against his spine. It was her distress he answered, not the Station Master's bribe. "All right," he said. "I'll do the best I can."

Toves and raths colonized like an epidemic, outward from a single originating point, Patient Zero in this case being the tear in spacetime that the first tove had wriggled through. More tears would develop as the toves multiplied, but it was that first one that would become large enough for a rath. While toves were simply lazy—energy efficient, the Arkhamers said primly—and never crawled farther than was necessary to find a useable anchoring point, raths were cautious. Their marauding was centered on the original tear because they kept their escape route open. And tore it wider and wider.

Toves weren't the problem, although they were a nuisance, with their tendency to use up valuable oxygen, clog ductwork, eat pets, drip goo from ceilings, and crunch wetly when you stepped on them. Raths were worse; raths were vicious predators. Their natural prey might be toves, but they didn't draw the line at disappearing weakened humans or small gillies, either.

But even they weren't the danger that had made it hard for Irizarry to sleep the past two rest shifts. What toves tore and raths widened was an access for the apex predator of this alien food chain.

The bandersnatch: *Pseudocanis tindalosi*. The old records and the indigent Arkhamers called them hounds, but of course they weren't, any more than Mongoose was a cat. Irizarry had seen archive video from derelict stations and ships, the bandersnatch's flickering angular limbs appearing like spiked mantis arms from the corners of sealed rooms, the carnage that ensued. He'd never heard of anyone left alive on a station where a bandersnatch manifested, unless they made it to a panic pod damned fast. More importantly, even the Arkhamers in their archive-ships, breeders of Mongoose and all her kind, admitted they had no records of anyone *surviving* a bandersnatch rather than *escaping* it.

And what he had to do, loosely put, was find the core of the infestation before the bandersnatches did, so that he could eradicate the toves and raths and the stress they were putting on this little corner of the universe. Find the core—somewhere in the miles upon miles of Kadath's infrastructure. Which was why he was in this little-used service corridor, letting Mongoose commune with every ventilation duct they found.

Anywhere near the access shafts infested by the colony, Kadath Station's passages reeked of tove—ammoniac, sulfurous. The stench infiltrated the edges of Irizarry's mask as he lifted his face to a ventilation duct. Wincing in anticipation, he broke the seal on the rebreather and pulled it away from his face on the stiff elastic straps, careful not to lose his grip. A broken nose would not improve his day.

A cultist engineer skittered past on sucker-tipped limbs, her four snake-arms coiled tight beside her for the narrow corridor. She had a pretty smile, for a Christian.

Mongoose was too intent on her prey to be shy. The size of the tove colony might make her nervous, but Mongoose loved the smell—like a good dinner heating, Irizarry imagined. She unfolded herself around his head like a tendriled hood, tentacles outreached, body flaring as she stretched towards the ventilation fan. He felt her lean, her barbels shivering, and turned to face the way her wedge-shaped head twisted.

He almost tipped backwards when he found himself face-to-face with someone he hadn't even known was there. A woman, average height, average weight, brown hair drawn back in a smooth club; her skin was space-pale and faintly reddened across the cheeks, as if the IR filters on a suit hadn't quite protected her. She wore a sleek space-black uniform with dull silver epaulets and four pewter-colored bands at each wrist. An insignia with a stylized sun and Earth-Moon dyad clung over her heart.

The political officer, who was obviously unconcerned by Mongoose's ostentatious display of sensory equipment.

Mongoose absorbed her tendrils in like a startled anemone, pressing the warm underside of her head to Irizarry's scalp where the hair was thinning. He was surprised she didn't vanish down his shirt, because he felt her trembling against his neck.

The political officer didn't extend her hand. "Mr. Irizarry? You're a hard man to find. I'm Intelligence Colonel Sadhi Sanderson. I'd like to ask you a few quick questions, please."

"I'm, uh, a little busy right now," Irizarry said, and added uneasily, "Ma'am." The *last* thing he wanted was to offend her.

Sanderson looked up at Mongoose. "Yes, you would appear to be hunting," she said, her voice dry as scouring powder. "That's one of the things I want to talk about."

Oh *shit*. He had kept out of the political officer's way for a day and a half, and really that was a pretty good run, given the obvious tensions between Lee and Sanderson, and the things he'd heard in the Transient Barracks: the gillies were all terrified of Sanderson, and nobody seemed to have a good word for Lee. Even the Christians, mouths thinned primly, could say of Lee only that she didn't actively persecute them. Irizarry had been stuck on a steelship with a Christian congregation for nearly half a year once, and he knew their eagerness to speak well of everyone; he didn't know whether that was actually part of their faith, or just a survival tactic, but when Elder Dawson said, "She does not trouble us," he understood quite precisely what that meant.

Of Sanderson, they said even less, but Irizarry understood that, too. There was no love lost between the extremist cults and the government. But he'd heard plenty from the ice miners and dock workers and particularly from the crew of an impounded steelship who were profanely eloquent on the subject. Upshot: Colonel Sanderson was new in town, cleaning house, and profoundly not a woman you wanted to fuck with.

"I'd be happy to come to your office in an hour, maybe two?" he said. "It's just that—"

Mongoose's grip on his scalp tightened, sudden and sharp enough that he yelped; he realized that her head had moved back toward the duct while he fenced weakly with Colonel Sanderson, and now it was nearly *in* the duct, at the end of a foot and a half of iridescent neck.

"Mr. Irizarry?"

He held a hand up, because really this wasn't a good time, and yelped again when Mongoose reached down and grabbed it. He knew better than to forget how fluid her body was, that it was really no more than a compromise with the dimension he could sense her in, but sometimes it surprised him anyway.

And then Mongoose said, *Nagina,* and if Colonel Sanderson hadn't been standing right there, her eyebrows indicating that he was already at the very end of the slack she was willing to cut, he would have cursed aloud. Short of a band-ersnatch—and that could still be along any time now, don't forget, Irizarry—a breeding rath was the worst news they could have.

"Your cheshire seems unsettled," Sanderson said, not sounding in the least alarmed. "Is there a problem?"

"She's eager to eat. And, er. She doesn't like strangers." It was as true as anything you could say about Mongoose, and the violent colors cycling down her tendrils gave him an idea what her chromatophores were doing behind his head.

"I can see that," Sanderson said. "Cobalt and yellow, in that stippled pat-tern—and flickering in and out of phase—she's acting aggressive, but that's fear, isn't it?"

Whatever Irizarry had been about to say, her observation stopped him short. He blinked at her—*like a gilly*, he thought uncharitably—and only realized he'd taken yet another step back when the warmth of the bulkhead pressed his coveralls to his spine.

"You know," Sanderson said mock-confidentially, "this entire corridor *reeks* of toves. So let me guess: it's not just toves anymore."

Irizarry was still stuck at her being able to read Mongoose's colors. "What do you know about cheshires?" he said.

She smiled at him as if at a slow student. "Rather a lot. I was on the *Jenny Lind* as an ensign—there was a cheshire on board, and I saw... It's not the sort of thing you forget, Mr. Irizarry, having been there once." Something complicated crossed her face—there for a flash and then gone. "The cheshire that died on the *Jenny Lind* was called Demon," Irizarry said, carefully. "Her partner was Long Mike Spider. You knew them?"

"Spider John," Sanderson said, looking down at the backs of her hands. She picked a cuticle with the opposite thumbnail. "He went by Spider John. You have the cheshire's name right, though."

When she looked back up, the arch of her carefully shaped brow told him he hadn't been fooling anyone.

"Right," Irizarry said. "Spider John."

"They were friends of mine." She shook her head. "I was just a pup. First bil-let, and I was assigned as Demon's liaison. Spider John liked to say he and I had the same job. But I couldn't make the captain believe him when he tried to tell her how bad it was."

"How'd you make it off after the bandersnatch got through?" Irizarry asked. He wasn't foolish enough to think that her confidences were anything other than a means of demonstrating to him why he could trust her, but the frustration and tired sadness sounded sincere.

"It went for Spider John first—it must have known he was a threat. And De-mon—she threw herself at it, never mind it was five times her size. She bought us time to get to the panic pod and Captain Golovnina time to get to the core overrides." She paused. "I saw it, you know. Just a glimpse. Wriggling through this... this *rip* in the air, like a big gaunt hound ripping through a hole in a blanket with knotty paws. I spent years wondering if it got my scent. Once they scent prey, you know, they never stop... ."

She trailed off, raising her gaze to meet his. He couldn't decide if the furrow between her eyes was embarrassment at having revealed so much, or the calcu-lated cataloguing of his response.

"So you recognize the smell, is what you're saying."

She had a way of answering questions with other questions. "Am I right about the raths?"

He nodded. "A breeder."

She winced.

He took a deep breath and stepped away from the bulkhead. "Colonel Sanderson—I have to get it *now* if I'm going to get it at all."

She touched the microwave pulse pistol at her hip. "Want some company?"

He didn't. Really, truly didn't. And if he had, he wouldn't have chosen Kadath Station's political officer. But he couldn't afford to offend her… and he wasn't licensed to carry a weapon.

"All right," he said and hoped he didn't sound as grudging as he felt. "But don't get in Mongoose's way."

Colonel Sanderson offered him a tight, feral smile. "Wouldn't dream of it."

The only thing that stank more than a pile of live toves was a bunch of half-eaten ones.

"Going to have to vacuum-scrub the whole sector," Sanderson said, her breath hissing through her filters.

If we live long enough to need to, Irizarry thought, but had the sense to keep his mouth shut. You didn't talk defeat around a politico. And if you were unfortunate enough to come to the attention of one, you certainly didn't let her see you thinking it.

Mongoose forged on ahead, but Irizarry noticed she was careful to stay within the range of his lights, and at least one of her tendrils stayed focused back on him and Sanderson at all times. If this were a normal infestation, Mongoose would be scampering along the corridor ceilings, leaving scattered bits of half-consumed tove and streaks of bioluminescent ichor in her wake. But this time, she edged along, testing each surface before her with quivering barbels so that Irizarry was reminded of a tentative spider or an exploratory octopus.

He edged along behind her, watching her colors go dim and cautious. She paused at each intersection, testing the air in every direction, and waited for her escort to catch up.

The service tubes of Kadath Station were mostly large enough for Irizarry and Sanderson to walk single-file through, though sometimes they were obliged to crouch, and once or twice Irizarry found himself slithering on his stomach through tacky half-dried tove slime. He imagined—he hoped it was imagining—that he could sense the thinning and stretch of reality all around them, see it in the warp of the tunnels and the bend of deck plates. He imagined that he glimpsed faint shapes from the corners of his eyes, caught a whisper of sound, a hint of scent, as of something almost there.

Hypochondria, he told himself firmly, aware that that was the wrong word and not really caring. But as he dropped down onto his belly again, to squeeze through a tiny access point—this one clogged with the fresh corpses of newly-slaughtered toves—he needed all the comfort he could invent.

He almost ran into Mongoose when he'd cleared the hole. She scuttled back to him and huddled under his chest, tendrils writhing, so close to out of phase that she was barely a warm shadow. When he saw what was on the other side, he wished he'd invented a little more.

This must be one of Kadath Station's recycling and reclamation centers, a bowl ten meters across sweeping down to a pile of rubbish in the middle. These were the sorts of places you always found minor tove infestations. Ships and stations might be supposed to be kept clear of vermin, but in practice, the dimensional stresses of sharing the spacelanes with boojums meant that just wasn't possible. And in Kadath, somebody hadn't been doing their job.

Sanderson touched his ankle, and Irizarry hastily drew himself aside so she could come through after. He was suddenly grateful for her company.

He really didn't want to be here alone.

Irizarry had never seen a tove infestation like this, not even on the *Jenny Lind*. The entire roof of the chamber was thick with their sluglike bodies, long lure-tongues dangling as much as half a meter down. Small flitting things—young raths, near-transparent in their phase shift—filled the space before him. As Irizarry watched, one blundered into the lure of a tove, and the tove contracted with sudden convulsive force. The rath never stood a chance.

Nagina, Mongoose said. *Nagina, Nagina, Nagina.*

Indeed, down among the junk in the pit, something big was stirring. But that wasn't all. That pressure Irizarry had sensed earlier, the feeling that many eyes were watching him, gaunt bodies stretching against whatever frail fabric held them back—here, it was redoubled, until he almost felt the brush of not-quite-in-phase whiskers along the nape of his neck.

Sanderson crawled up beside him, her pistol in one hand. Mongoose didn't seem to mind her there.

"What's down there?" she asked, her voice hissing on constrained breaths.

"The breeding pit," Irizarry said. "You feel that? Kind of funny, stretchy feeling in the universe?"

Sanderson nodded behind her mask. "It's not going to make you any happier, is it, if I tell you I've felt it before?"

Irizarry was wearily, grimly unsurprised. But then Sanderson said, "What do we do?"

He was taken aback and it must have shown, even behind the rebreather, because she said sharply, "*You're* the expert. Which I assume is why you're on Kadath Station to begin with and why Station Master Lee has been so anxious that I not know it. Though with an infestation of this size, I don't know how she thought she was going to hide it much longer anyway."

"Call it sabotage," Irizarry said absently. "Blame the Christians. Or the gillies. Or disgruntled spacers, like the crew off the *Caruso*. It happens a lot, Colonel. Somebody like me and Mongoose comes in and cleans up the toves, the station authorities get to crack down on whoever's being the worst pain in the ass, and life keeps on turning over. But she waited too long."

Down in the pit, the breeder heaved again. Breeding raths were slow—much slower than the juveniles, or the sexually dormant adult rovers—but that was because they were armored like titanium armadillos. When threatened, one of two things happened. Babies flocked to mama, mama rolled herself in a ball, and it would take a tactical nuke to kill them. Or mama went on the warpath. Irizarry had seen a pissed-off breeder take out a bulkhead on a steelship once; it was pure dumb luck that it hadn't breached the hull.

And, of course, once they started spawning, as this one had, they could produce between ten and twenty babies a day for anywhere from a week to a month, depending on the food supply. And the more babies they produced, the weaker the walls of the world got, and the closer the bandersnatches would come.

"The first thing we have to do," he said to Colonel Sanderson, "as in, *right now,* is kill the breeder. Then you quarantine the station and get parties of volunteers to hunt down the rovers, before they can bring another breeder through, or turn into breeders, or however the fuck it works, which frankly I don't know. It'll take fire to clear this nest of toves, but Mongoose and I can probably get the rest. And *fire,* Colonel Sanderson. Toves don't give a shit about vacuum."

She could have reproved him for his language; she didn't. She just nodded and said, "How do we kill the breeder?"

"Yeah," Irizarry said. "That's the question."

Mongoose clicked sharply, her *Irizarry!* noise.

"No," Irizarry said. "Mongoose, don't—"

But she wasn't paying attention. She had only a limited amount of patience for his weird interactions with other members of his species and his insistence on *waiting,* and he'd clearly used it all up. She was Rikki Tikki Tavi, and the breeder was Nagina, and Mongoose knew what had to happen. She launched off Irizarry's shoulders, shifting phase as she went, and without contact between them, there was nothing he could do to call her back. In less than a second, he didn't even know where she was.

"You any good with that thing?" he said to Colonel Sanderson, pointing at her pistol.

"Yes," she said, but her eyebrows were going up again. "But, forgive me, isn't this what cheshires are for?"

"Against rovers, sure. But—Colonel, have you ever seen a breeder?"

Across the bowl, a tove warbled, the chorus immediately taken up by its neighbors. Mongoose had started.

"No," Sanderson said, looking down at where the breeder humped and wallowed and finally stood up, shaking off ethereal babies and half-eaten toves. "Oh. *Gods.*"

You couldn't describe a rath. You couldn't even look at one for more than a few seconds before you started getting a migraine aura. Rovers were just blots of shadow. The breeder was massive, armored, and had no recognizable features, save for its hideous, drooling, ragged-edged maw. Irizarry didn't know if it had eyes, or even needed them.

"She can kill it," he said, "but only if she can get at its underside. Otherwise, all it has to do is wait until it has a clear swing, and she's…" He shuddered. "I'll be lucky to find enough of her for a funeral. So what *we* have to do now, Colonel, is piss it off enough to give her a chance. Or"—he had to be fair; this was not Colonel Sanderson's job—"if you'll lend me your pistol, you don't have to stay."

She looked at him, her dark eyes very bright, and then she turned to look at the breeder, which was swinging its shapeless head in slow arcs, trying, no doubt, to track Mongoose. "Fuck that, Mr. Irizarry," she said crisply. "Tell me where to aim."

"You won't hurt it," he'd warned her, and she'd nodded, but he was pretty sure she hadn't really understood until she fired her first shot and the breeder didn't even *notice*. But Sanderson hadn't given up; her mouth had thinned, and she'd settled into her stance, and she'd fired again, at the breeder's feet as Irizarry had told her. A breeding rath's feet weren't vulnerable as such, but they were sensitive, much more sensitive than the human-logical target of its head. Even so, it was concentrating hard on Mongoose, who was making toves scream at various random points around the circumference of the breeding pit, and it took another three shots aimed at that same near front foot before the breeder's head swung in their direction.

It made a noise, a sort of "wooaaurgh" sound, and Irizarry and Sanderson were promptly swarmed by juvenile raths.

"Ah, fuck," said Irizarry. "Try not to kill them."

"I'm sorry, try *not* to kill them?"

"If we kill too many of them, it'll decide we're a threat rather than an annoyance. And then it rolls up in a ball, and we have no chance of killing it until it unrolls again. And by then, there will be a lot more raths here."

"And quite possibly a bandersnatch," Sanderson finished. "But—" She batted away a half-corporeal rath that was trying to wrap itself around the warmth of her pistol.

"If we stood perfectly still for long enough," Irizarry said, "they could probably leech out enough of our body heat to send us into hypothermia. But they can't bite when they're this young. I knew a cheshire-man once who swore they ate by crawling down into the breeder's stomach to lap up what it'd digested. I'm still hoping that's not true. Just keep aiming at that foot."

"You got it."

Irizarry had to admit, Sanderson was steady as a rock. He shooed juvenile raths away from both of them, Mongoose continued her depredations out there in the dark, and Sanderson, having found her target, fired at it in a nice, steady rhythm. She didn't miss; she didn't try to get fancy. Only, after a while, she said out of the corner of her mouth, "You know, my battery won't last forever."

"I know," Irizarry said. "But this is good. It's working."

"How can you tell?"

"It's getting mad."

"How can you *tell*?"

"The vocalizing." The rath had gone from its "wooaaurgh" sound to a series of guttural huffing noises, interspersed with high-pitched yips. "It's warning us off. Keep firing."

"All right," Sanderson said. Irizarry cleared another couple of juveniles off her head. He was trying not to think about what it meant that no adult raths had come to the pit—just how much of Kadath Station had they claimed?

"*Have* there been any disappearances lately?" he asked Sanderson.

She didn't look at him, but there was a long silence before she said, "None that *seemed* like disappearances. Our population is by necessity transient, and none too fond of authority. And, frankly, I've had so much trouble with the station master's office that I'm not sure my information is reliable."

It had to hurt for a political officer to admit that. Irizarry said, "We're very likely to find human bones down there. And in their caches."

Sanderson started to answer him, but the breeder decided it had had enough. It wheeled toward them, its maw gaping wider, and started through the mounds of garbage and corpses in their direction.

"What now?" said Sanderson.

"Keep firing," said Irizarry. *Mongoose, wherever you are, please be ready.*

He'd been about seventy-five percent sure that the rath would stand up on its hind legs when it reached them. Raths weren't sapient, not like cheshires, but they were smart. They knew that the quickest way to kill a human was to take its head off, and the second quickest was to disembowel it, neither of which they could do on all fours. And humans weren't any threat to a breeder's vulnerable abdomen; Sanderson's pistol might give the breeder a hot foot, but there was no way it could penetrate the breeder's skin.

It was a terrible plan—there was that whole twenty-five percent where he and Sanderson died screaming while the breeder ate them from the feet up—but it worked. The breeder heaved itself upright, massive, indistinct paw going back for a blow that would shear Sanderson's head off her neck and probably bounce it off the nearest bulkhead, and with no warning of any kind, not for the humans, not for the rath, Mongoose phased viciously in, claws and teeth and sharp-edged tentacles all less than two inches from the rath's belly and moving fast.

The rath screamed and curled in on itself, but it was too late. Mongoose had already caught the lips of its—oh gods and fishes, Irizarry didn't know the word. Vagina? Cloaca? Ovipositor? The place where little baby raths came into the world. The only vulnerability a breeder had. Into which Mongoose shoved the narrow wedge of her head, and her clawed front feet, and began to rip.

Before the rath could even reach for her, her malleable body was already entirely inside it, and it—screaming, scrabbling—was doomed.

Irizarry caught Sanderson's elbow and said, "Now would be a good time, *very slowly*, to back away. Let the lady do her job."

Irizarry almost made it off of Kadath clean.

He'd had no difficulty in getting a berth for himself and Mongoose—after a party or two of volunteers had seen her in action, after the stories started spreading about the breeder, he'd nearly come to the point of beating off the steelship captains with a stick. And in the end, he'd chosen the offer of the captain of the *Erich Zann*, a boojum; Captain Alvarez had a long-term salvage contract in the Kuiper belt—"cleaning up after the ice miners," she'd said with a wry smile—and Irizarry felt like salvage was maybe where he wanted to be for a while. There'd be plenty for Mongoose to hunt, and nobody's life in danger. Even a bandersnatch wasn't much more than a case of indigestion for a boojum.

He'd got his money out of the station master's office—hadn't even had to talk to Station Master Lee, who maybe, from the things he was hearing, wasn't going to be station master much longer. You could either be ineffectual *or* you could piss off your political officer. Not both at once. And her secretary so very obviously didn't want to bother her that it was easy to say, "We had a contract," and to plant his feet and smile. It wasn't the doubled fee she'd promised him, but he didn't even want that. Just the money he was owed.

So his business was taken care of. He'd brought Mongoose out to the *Erich Zann*, and insofar as he and Captain Alvarez could tell, the boojum and the cheshire liked each other. He'd bought himself new underwear and let Mongoose pick out a new pair of earrings for him. And he'd gone ahead and splurged, since he was, after all, *on* Kadath Station and might as well make the most of it, and bought a selection of books for his reader, including *The Wind in the Willows*. He was looking forward, in an odd, quiet way, to the long nights out beyond Neptune: reading to Mongoose, finding out what she thought about Rat and Mole and Toad and Badger.

Peace—or as close to it as Izrael Irizarry was ever likely to get.

He'd cleaned out his cubby in the Transient Barracks, slung his bag over one shoulder with Mongoose riding on the other, and was actually in sight of the *Erich Zann*'s dock when a voice behind him called his name.

Colonel Sanderson.

He froze in the middle of a stride, torn between turning around to greet her and bolting like a rabbit, and then she'd caught up to him. "Mr. Irizarry," she said. "I hoped I could buy you a drink before you go."

He couldn't help the deeply suspicious look he gave her. She spread her hands, showing them empty. "Truly. No threats, no tricks. Just a drink. To say thank you." Her smile was lopsided; she knew how unlikely those words sounded in the mouth of a political officer.

And any other political officer, Irizarry wouldn't have believed them. But he'd seen her stand her ground in front of a breeder rath, and he'd seen her turn and puke her guts out when she got a good look at what Mongoose did to it. If she wanted to thank him, he owed it to her to sit still for it.

"All right," he said, and added awkwardly, "Thank you."

They went to one of Kadath's tourist bars: bright and quaint and cheerful and completely unlike the spacer bars Irizarry was used to. On the other hand, he could see why Sanderson picked this one. No one here, except maybe the bartender, had the least idea who she was, and the bartender's wide-eyed double take meant that they got excellent service: prompt and very quiet.

Irizarry ordered a pink lady—he liked them, and Mongoose, in delight, turned the same color pink, with rosettes matched to the maraschino "cherry." Sanderson ordered whisky, neat, which had very little resemblance to the whisky Irizarry remembered from planetside. She took a long swallow of it, then set the glass down and said, "I never got a chance to ask Spider John this: how did you get your cheshire?"

It was clever of her to invoke Spider John and Demon like that, but Irizarry still wasn't sure she'd earned the story. After the silence had gone on a little too long, Sanderson picked her glass up, took another swallow, and said, "I know who you are."

"I'm *nobody*," Irizarry said. He didn't let himself tense up, because Mongoose wouldn't miss that cue, and she was touchy enough, what with all the steelship captains, that he wasn't sure what she might think the proper response was. And he wasn't sure, if she decided the proper response was to rip Sanderson's face off, that he would be able to make himself disagree with her in time.

"I promised," Sanderson said. "No threats. I'm not trying to trace you, I'm not asking any questions about the lady you used to work for. And, truly, I'm only *asking* how you met *this* lady. You don't have to tell me."

"No," Irizarry said mildly. "I don't." But Mongoose, still pink, was coiling down his arm to investigate the glass—not its contents, since the interest of the egg-whites would be more than outweighed by the sharp sting to her nose of the alcohol, but the upside-down cone on a stem of a martini glass. She liked geometry. And this wasn't a story that could hurt anyone.

He said, "I was working my way across Jupiter's moons, oh, five years ago now. Ironically enough, I got trapped in a quarantine. Not for vermin, but for the black rot. It was a long time, and things got... ugly."

He glanced at her and saw he didn't need to elaborate.

"There were Arkhamers trapped there, too, in their huge old scow of a ship. And when the water rationing got tight, there were people that said the Arkhamers shouldn't have any—said that if it was the other way 'round, they wouldn't give us any. And so when the Arkhamers sent one of their daughters for their share..." He still remembered her scream, a grown woman's terror in a child's voice, and so he shrugged and said, "I did the only thing I could. After that, it was safer for me on their ship than it was on the station, so I spent some time with them. Their Professors let me stay.

"They're not bad people," he added, suddenly urgent. "I don't say I understand what they believe, or why, but they were good to me, and they did share their water with the crew of the ship in the next berth. And of course, they had cheshires. Cheshires all over the place, cleanest steelship you've ever seen. There was a litter born right about the time the quarantine finally lifted. Jemima—the little girl I helped—she insisted they give me pick of the litter, and that was Mongoose."

Mongoose, knowing the shape of her own name on Irizarry's lips, began to purr, and rubbed her head gently against his fingers. He petted her, feeling his tension ease, and said, "And I wanted to be a biologist before things got complicated."

"Huh," said Sanderson. "Do you know what they are?"

"Sorry?" He was still mostly thinking about the Arkhamers, and braced himself for the usual round of superstitious nonsense: demons or necromancers or what-not.

But Sanderson said, "Cheshires. Do you know what they are?"

"What do you mean, 'what they are'? They're cheshires."

"After Demon and Spider John... I did some reading and I found a Professor or two—Arkhamers, yes—to ask." She smiled, very thinly. "I've found, in this job, that people are often remarkably willing to answer my questions. And I found out. They're bandersnatches."

"Colonel Sanderson, not to be disrespectful—"

"Sub-adult bandersnatches," Sanderson said. "Trained and bred and intentionally stunted so that they never mature fully."

Mongoose, he realized, had been watching, because she caught his hand and said emphatically, *Not.*

"Mongoose disagrees with you," he said and found himself smiling. "And really, I think she would know."

Sanderson's eyebrows went up. "And what does Mongoose think she is?"

He asked, and Mongoose answered promptly, pink dissolving into champagne and gold: *Jagular.* But there was a thrill of uncertainty behind it, as if she wasn't quite sure of what she stated so emphatically. And then, with a sharp toss of her head at Colonel Sanderson, like any teenage girl: *Mongoose.*

Sanderson was still watching him sharply. "Well?"

"She says she's Mongoose."

And Sanderson really wasn't trying to threaten him, or playing some elaborate political game, because her face softened in a real smile, and she said, "Of course she is."

Irizarry swished a sweet mouthful between his teeth. He thought of what Sanderson has said, of the bandersnatch on the *Jenny Lind* wriggling through stretched rips in reality like a spiny, deathly puppy tearing a blanket. "How would you domesticate a bandersnatch?"

She shrugged. "If I knew that, I'd be an Arkhamer, wouldn't I?" Gently, she extended the back of her hand for Mongoose to sniff. Mongoose, surprising

Irizarry, extended one tentative tendril and let it hover just over the back of Sanderson's wrist.

Sanderson tipped her head, smiling affectionately, and didn't move her hand. "But if I had to guess, I'd say you do it by making friends."

ECHOES OF AURORA
ELLEN KLAGES

Ellen Klages was born in Columbus, Ohio. Her first story, "Time Gypsy," was nominated for the Hugo and Nebula Awards. It was followed by a dozen more, including Nebula nominee "Flying Over Water," and 2005 Nebula winner "Basement Magic," most of which appear in World Fantasy Award finalist *Portable Childhoods*. She was a finalist for the John W. Campbell Award for Best New Writer in 2000. Klages is the author of two novels, *The Green Glass Sea*, which won the Scott O'Dell Award for historical fiction, and sequel, *White Sands, Red Menace*, which won the California Book Award and the New Mexico Book Award, both in the Young Adult category. She lives in San Francisco.

Cedar River was a summer town.

You've seen it, or one just like it. Off a state highway, on the edge of a lake—a thousand souls, more or less, until Memorial Day. Then the tourists come, for swimming and fudge and miniature golf. They laugh, their sunburns redden and peel, and when the first cool autumn breezes ripple the water, they leave.

The carnival is over.

Jo Norwood grew up in the flat above her family's penny arcade. When she was eleven, her mother ran off to Milwaukee; after that Jo helped with repairs and opened in the mornings, filling the change machine and rolling the wooden clown out to the entrance before she could escape to her tree house. There she nested, hidden behind the screen of green leaves, cotton in her ears muffling the hurly-burly and the melancholy cheer of the carousel. The day after high school graduation, she ran away too, and did not return until her father's funeral.

In those thirty-five years, Disneyland and the interstate had lured the tourists away to brighter lights, and Cedar River had become ordinary. Norwood's Amusements sat shuttered at the end of Beach Street, garish paint faded beyond pastel. The mortgage was paid off; Jo's father had sold the carousel horses, one by one, to collectors, for property taxes. But when she screeched open the big wooden doors, she was not quite prepared for the emptiness.

The air was cool and almost sweet with mildew and the first blooms of rust. A score of pale rectangles on the concrete floor were memorials to Norwood's former glory. Only the fortune-teller, the Magic Ray, the nickelodeon, and half a dozen brass-cranked Mutoscopes remained, each of them coated with a film of gray dust.

Jo was single and newly retired, unsettled and unencumbered. Her time was her own, but she had no desire to linger. She would sort and sift through her inheritance and sell anything of value, find a realtor, put a few things in storage. Two weeks. A month at the most.

She awoke in her old bedroom, the oak outside the window fractal against the colorless April sky. A few tiny green buds, like match heads, dotted the filigree of bare, dark twigs. No coffee in the cupboard. She walked two blocks to Lake Street and had breakfast at the café, dawdling over the crossword and a second cup until there was nothing to do but begin dismantling.

Bert Norwood had been a tinkerer, his workshop a narrow room at the back of the arcade. A wall of cubbyholes and cabinets held gilded fittings, ancient light bulbs, half-toned sepia postcards of cowboy stars no one remembered, all smiling teeth and gabardine. Jo made lists and teetering piles, temporarily creating chaos out of order. As she laid unmourned bits of her past out on the counter, she began to tap her foot and sing along with the nickelodeon.

"Be kind to your web-footed friends, for a duck may be somebody's muh-thur. Be kind to your friends in the swa—"

Jo stopped, holding a Lash LaRue card in mid-air.

Whose nickel had turned that on?

The arcade floor was dim, the only illumination a row of whitewashed windows high along one wall. The paint had flaked away in places, and in a finger of afternoon light, sparkling with dust motes, a copper-haired woman was dancing. She wore a loose green sweater that floated out from her body as she turned and spun, like a leaf before a hard spring rain. The melody echoed, a brass band in a tin box; the piano keys clicked under invisible fingers.

John Philip Sousa ended with a flourish. A floorboard squeaked under Jo's shoe. The dancing woman looked up and waved, as if they were old friends, reunited after a long absence.

"Do I know you?" Jo called. Possible. It was a small town.

"I'm Aurora." She smiled. "Rory."

The voice was soft, but strong; the name was unfamiliar, but its timbre fluttered the short hairs on the back of Jo's neck.

"Uh, sorry. I think you've got the wrong—"

"You grew up here. You had a tree house."

Such a small town. Jo took a step closer, puzzled. The woman's face was smooth, unlined cream. She'd have been a baby when Jo left.

"Yeah, I did. So?"

"Your tree is dying."

"What, are you from the county?"

"No. Come and see."

"Not now. I'm kind of busy and—"

"Come and *see.*" Rory stepped into another bit of sunlight. Her eyes were green too, flecked with gold. They tickled a fragment of memory with no context to anchor it, and Jo felt herself nod.

Standing in the gravel driveway, she could see half a dozen sawed-off stubs of branches spiraling the oak's trunk. One long, silvered limb hung overhead at a precarious angle. The cluster of buds on the side nearest the building was the only sign of life.

"I hadn't even noticed," Jo said, staring at the wide-ringed stub that had once held her tree house. A gust of wind came up off the lake, skittering trash across the gravel, and she hugged her arms to her chest. "Thanks. I'll—I'll call someone to take care of it."

"Not yet." Rory shook her head and shouldered a knapsack, worn leather the color of walnuts. "You're shivering. Come upstairs," she said, as if it were her house. "I'll make tea." She held out her hand.

For no reason that she could ever explain, Jo followed, slipping her palm into Rory's, like a child about to cross a busy street. Her fingers tingled with the contact.

The summer that her mother left, Jo's favorite toy was a potato. An odd choice for the daughter of a machinist. No moving parts. But with a penny and a nail and a bit of wire, it became a battery, strong enough to elicit a faint incandescent glow from one of the tiniest bulbs.

Jo climbed the back stairs, holding Rory's hand. And for the first time in decades she felt that same flicker of connection from an unexpected source.

Rory made a face at the box of Lipton's. She produced a tin of lapsang souchong from her knapsack and put the battered kettle on to boil. The leather pack, she said, was everything she owned—notebooks and pens, a change of clothes, a toothbrush, and a small, lumpy drawstring sack. She held it up. "The rest of my trousseau."

"What do you do?" Jo asked.

"I'm a poet, a storyteller—fairy tales and fables, mostly. I've always liked this one."

That made no sense. But nothing had, since Jo'd come back. Everything was as familiar as it was alien, and in that setting, in the early spring twilight, logic and Rory could not co-exist.

Rory smiled, and logic lost.

By the time they switched from tea to wine, rainy darkness had turned the kitchen windows to funhouse mirrors, reflecting the florid walls, wavy and indistinct.

"Where do you live?" Jo asked an hour later. "I'll give you a ride home. It's pouring out there."

"Hmm." Rory cocked her head, then held out her hands, palms up. "I don't know. I haven't gotten that far yet. I suppose I should stay with you." She stood to pour the last of the Merlot into Jo's glass.

"I guess," Jo said. She wasn't sure if she was still okay to drive on slick country roads. "I'll see if I can find clean sheets, and make up my father's bed."

"Oh, we can make up something better than that." Rory finished the last inch of wine in her glass. "I know how it starts," she said.

"How?"

"Once upon a time, you kissed me."

Jo woke up the next morning curled around a still-warm pillow. Through the doorway she could see Rory at the kitchen table, her head bent and intent, silent but for the soft scritch of pen on paper. A flurry of motion, pen sweeping wide, crossing out unruly words. A small sigh. Rory bit the top of her pen and stared into space, as if an elusive phrase were etched into the wallpaper, hidden among the tea roses. Jo pulled on a pair of sweats and a t-shirt and padded out in her bare feet.

She had been a quiet, solitary child, and in middle age considered herself a private person, practical and self-sufficient. Not a prude—she'd had some lovers—but not accustomed to awkward good-mornings after unlikely evenings. She cleared her throat as an introduction.

Rory looked up. "Hi. There's coffee on the stove."

"How? There wasn't any."

"I made some." She waved a hand at her knapsack and the open bag of Starbucks French Roast on the counter.

"Oh. Thanks." There wasn't a Starbucks within a hundred miles. And last night the knapsack hadn't had… But damn, it smelled good.

Jo filled a mug and leaned against the table. "What are you working on?"

"A new story." Rory turned and kissed Jo's hand, curled around the handle of the mug, just below the knuckles. "So many possibilities."

The second time Jo got up that morning, she took a shower. When she came out of the bathroom, combing her fingers through her short, salt-and-pepper hair, Rory was back at the table, staring at a blank page.

"I have to go to the Wal-Mart, out by the highway." Jo rested her hands on Rory's shoulders. "Boxes and tape and labels. Do you want to come along?"

"I need to stay here. Be back for lunch," she answered, and picked up her pen.

Jo left the packing supplies downstairs and walked into the kitchen expecting sandwiches. The table was covered with a bright, Indian-print bedspread identical to the one she'd had in her first apartment. Small bowls and plates held strawberries, a wedge of crumbly cheese, half a baguette, slices of avocado, green olives, pink curls of prosciutto—*where had she gotten that?*—a fan of shortbread wedges.

"What's all this?"

"Magpie lunch." Rory opened the fridge. "Sit. There's more coffee if you need to work this afternoon but—" She grinned and put a pitcher on the counter. "I made sangria, too."

A thin orange slice floated in ruby liquid, colors that shouldn't work together. But they did, and Jo accepted the invitation. She feasted on a panoply of nibbles and let the edges of responsibility soften into a long, languid afternoon.

April became May. The buds on the oak unfurled to celadon flags, and color crept back into the world. In the mornings, while Rory hummed and scribbled, Jo opened cupboards, filled boxes, made lists and phone calls. She emptied the workbench drawers into neatly labeled Ziploc bags, made two solo runs to the town dump. Lunch was sometimes a sandwich, but sometimes a magpie, and Jo grew quite fond of the way the afternoon light played through the bedroom window.

They didn't talk about where they were from or what had come before. Their days were filled with laughter and small touches, like a cat bumping against a leg to reassure itself that the world was as it should be. Rory skipped and sang and made up holidays for them to celebrate.

"It's the ninth. No work today."

Jo raised an eyebrow.

"The nines are for joy," Rory said. "For feasts and blue flowers and the connecting of hearts." She didn't always talk that way. If she ever *went* to the grocery, Jo doubted that she'd stand in the checkout line answering, "Paper or plastic?" in iambic pentameter. But they were alone and, arm-in-arm or spooned around each other, Rory's words wove her into a place she could never have imagined—and never wanted to leave.

The weather grew warmer. Jo opened the double doors downstairs to the endless blue sky, and Rory sat with her back against the wood, her hair like flame in the sunlight.

The man from the circus museum in Baraboo was coming after the fourth of July to make an offer on some of the machines. Jo had her father's toolbox open on a stool next to a cast-iron peepshow called *Through the Keyhole*. Its risqué images skipped and stuttered, and she had opened the side, exposing the gears and wheels. Her father, a methodical packrat, had saved the tattered schematic, but she hadn't made much progress.

"What's it supposed to do?" Rory asked.

"It's a dirty movie—at least it was seventy years ago." Jo laughed. "The woman does the hootchy-cootchy and takes off some of her clothes. But right now she dances worse than I do."

"You dance."

"No, I don't."

"Not *ever*?"

"Nope, 'fraid not."

"Liar. You dance with me in bed."

Jo felt her face redden. "Not the same."

Rory just smiled and shook her head. She peered into the machine. "Where's the film?"

"There isn't any. It's like a big, round flipbook. Hundreds of photos. But when you see one after another after another, you get the illusion of motion. Persistence of vision." She dug a handful of nickels out of a small canvas bag in the toolbox. "Here. Go take a look at *When the Lights Are Low*."

Rory spent an hour peering, fascinated, into the brass eyepieces of the other machines. Jo discovered the problem—a gear worn almost smooth, connecting only once every dozen turns of the wheel—and found a spare part that fit.

She hadn't expected to come across anything of her own in the apartment—she'd been gone most of her life, and her father was not a sentimental man. But the next morning, on a shelf at the back of his closet, behind his Sunday hat and a framed medal from the war, she did: a manila folder with a handful of crayon drawings, leaf prints, and fat-lined kindergarten paper. She climbed down from the stepstool and took the folder into the kitchen, where the light was better.

A flat black tin of watercolor lozenges and a sketchbook lay open on the table. Rory swirled a brush in a tumbler of pale orange water.

"I didn't know you painted." Jo opened the folder.

"This story needs color," Rory replied. She reached for one of the stiff pieces of construction paper, spatters of red and blue tempera outlining the spiky contours of a maple leaf. "You made this?"

"Every fall until fourth grade. Then we just pressed leaves in the encyclopedia; there was a prize for collecting the most different kinds."

"Have you ever seen the cave paintings in France?"

It was a non sequitur, but Jo had gotten used to them. "Lascaux," she nodded. "Not in person, but I had a textbook, in college. Hunters' drawings: bison and spotted horses."

"And hands. Your picture reminds me of the hands." Rory laid her left one flat on the table, its back spotted with freckles. "Ten thousand years ago, an artist put his hand on the cave wall and held the pigment in his mouth, then spit it through a hollow reed." She was silent for a minute, then asked, "Are there any blank peepshow cards downstairs?"

"No, but the reel for *Seeing Is Believing* only has a handful left. The backs are blank."

"That'll work. And I need one of your father's pipes."

"Okay. Why?"

"I want to paint your hand."

When Jo returned, Rory removed the bowl of the pipe, then reached into her wonder-filled knapsack and produced a jar of rust-colored powder. "Red ochre," she said. "Put your hand on the card and hold very still."

Rory tipped half the jar of powder into her mouth, and held the pipe stem in her teeth. She leaned over Jo's hand and puffed damp russet clouds around each splayed finger. Jo closed her eyes; Rory's breath defined the edges of her senses.

"Done. Lift it straight up. Don't smear it."

Jo did, and looked down at a red card with a perfect white hand shape at its center.

"See. Lascaux. They knew." Rory nodded. "When we're gone, we leave a void where we used to be." She leaned over and began to lick the away the specks of pigment from Jo's knuckles.

August arrived with humidity that made sweat drip off Jo's nose when she filled the last Goodwill box with her father's shirts and work boots. Too hot to be upstairs, even with all the windows open. There wasn't much left to do in the arcade—the man from Baraboo had written a nice check and taken everything but the nickelodeon and the broken peep show. But the space was cool and dim, and most afternoons a thunderstorm massed over the lake, and rain roared down from a pewter sky, making small rivers that snaked across the gravel.

One evening, after, they sat out on the small balcony at the top of the back stairs with cold bottles of cider, two middle-aged women listening to the drips off the eaves, the world golden in the setting sun.

"I used to love the woods this time of year," Jo said. "Everything's that deep, lush green."

Rory laughed. "What do you mean, everything? There's a rainbow out there. Hickory leaves aren't the same green as a chestnut's, or a poplar's, or—" she took a long, slow swallow of her cider and scooched closer, leaning against Jo's shoulder. "Doesn't matter. In a couple of weeks, even someone as chlorophyll-challenged as you will be able to see the difference."

"I know. Summer's almost over." Jo shook her head. "I never thought I'd still be *here.*" She put her cider down on the weathered wood. "But I'm done. The Grange is going to store the nickelodeon for me, and the realtor said she can come by Monday to pick up the keys. We can hit the road any time you're ready."

She felt Rory shift, tense, and grow still.

"One more month," she said after a long time. "I need to finish the story."

"If you've got your notebook, can't you do that anywhere?"

"Not this one," Rory said.

So they stayed. One after another, the supple green leaves of the oak were veined with yellow, and the view from the balcony turned calico, a patchwork of rusts and reds and browns among the green. Rory wrote while Jo ran errands, swept the arcade floor, thought about where they might go, tried not to be impatient.

Every morning, she woke and watched another oak leaf glide past the window, drifting slowly down onto the gravel.

"I've got a task for you," Rory said, her head on Jo's chest, her voice muffled.

"What?"

"There are only a few leaves left on the oak. Catch one for me this morning and make a spatter print."

"How come?"

"An illustration for the end of this chapter." She unfolded herself and leaned over the side of the bed for her knapsack. "Here. Yellow ochre." She handed Jo the jar. "Use the back of a peepshow card, and spit it."

Jo made a face. "Can't I just use a toothbrush and a pencil to make the spatter, the way we did in school?"

"No. Then there'd be none of *you* in it."

"But—" Jo stared at the jar.

"Don't worry. It's just ground-up clay. And after—" Rory grinned. "I'll think of *some* way to cleanse your palate."

Later that night, Jo came in from the bathroom to find Rory sitting in bed, a pair of glasses perched on the end of her nose. Jo had never seen her wear them before. "Cuddle up with me," Rory said. "I need to read this to you. It's time."

The carnival comes to every town
  for a month or two
  before the cold winds strike the set.
Autumn is the festival of death.
  The chorus prepares for the season's curtain;
    only the most elaborate shrouds will do
    for the grand finale.
Leaves don't fall—
  they just let go.
One by one they pirouette,
  a curtsy so deep it touches the ground,
  no applause but silence.

The carnival comes every year;
  not all the cast returns.
If you look, you can see
  the orphaned dryads
  passing among the humans.
They are the old women,
  withering and flamboyant,
  sparse hair the color of persimmons,
  going out in a blaze of glory—
    too-bright scarves
    and spots of rouge that shout:
Attention, please.
Dance with me while you can;

it's not that long a run.
If you blink, you'll miss my closing number—
    and it's your loss, dearie.

Silence filled the small bedroom. Jo sat stiff, unmoving against the headboard. "Tell me that's only a poem."

Rory laid the pages on the bedside table and put her glasses on top of them. She slid under the covers and snuggled close. "I can't."

Jo looked at her in the lamplight, fine lines around her eyes; white and silver twined amid the copper curls. "The tree is dying." Her voice sounded hollow. "That's the first thing you said to me."

"You loved her. No one else ever cared."

"I felt safe there."

"I know. I remember." Rory tucked her arm through Jo's. "I was so afraid you wouldn't come back. The wheel turned and turned, then I only had one summer left."

"What's going to—?" Jo asked.

"Just love me tonight." Rory kissed her, both gentle and fierce. "Then love me again tomorrow."

* * *

Rory glowed as she shrank into herself, veins prominent under tissue-thin flesh. They stayed cuddled under the blanket for two days, touching more than talking. The last morning, Jo was awake before dawn. She lay facing the window, her head on Rory's chest, rising and falling with each shallow breath. A breeze whispered against the side of the house, and with no sound at all, the oak tree gave up its final leaf. As the yellow scrap drifted down, Jo felt a faint tremble under her cheek, then stillness.

The sun was high above the trees across the lake before Jo moved, and then only because nature called, a force too strong to ignore. When she returned, two minutes later, the bed was impossibly empty. Rory's knapsack sat on the pillow, an envelope propped against it.

Jo stared. Jo sat on the edge of the bed. After a minute or an hour or a week— what did it matter?—Jo opened the envelope. A folded page from Rory's notebook held the spatter sprints they had each made: the red, Jo's hand; the yellow, a void where an oak leaf had been.

She unfolded the paper and read:

The next chapter is yours again.
It cannot happen here.
Take some acorns from my tree.

Find somewhere safe to hibernate, and wait for spring.
Then begin a new carnival.
But before you go,
Put these in your peep show—
   one on each side of the wheel.
And don't blink.

Jo moved slowly, mechanically. After some time, she dressed and went downstairs. A nickel and the gilt-rimmed Mutoscope sat on the bare workbench. The title card, in angular 1920s script, now read: *Echoes of Aurora.* She tried to smile, but that touched a hurt too big. She mounted the spattered cards onto the empty wheel, three hundred gaps between them. Jo closed the cast-iron door.

She dropped the nickel in the slot. The light came on, revealing a red card, a white hand. She turned the brass handle.

Red. Yellow. Hand. Leaf.

She cranked faster. Nothing but an orange blur, and her eyes stung with the first real tears.

Then behind her, out on the darkened floor, the nickelodeon began to play itself. *Lonesome Woman Blues.*

The orange began to shimmer. The images flickered, re-formed, focused. Through the eyepiece, Jo watched as Rory curtsied and held out her hand, saw herself bow and accept.

And in the last finger of afternoon light, in an empty penny arcade, they danced.

BEFORE MY LAST BREATH
ROBERT REED

Robert Reed was born in Omaha, Nebraska, in 1956. He has a Bachelor of Science in Biology from the Nebraska Wesleyan University, and has worked as a lab technician. He became a full-time writer in 1987, the same year he won the L. Ron Hubbard Writers of the Future Contest, and has published eleven novels, including *The Leeshore*, *The Hormone Jungle*, and far-future science fiction novels *Marrow* and *The Well of Stars*. An extraordinarily prolific writer, Reed has published over 180 short stories, mostly in *Fantasy & Science Fiction* and *Asimov's*, which have been nominated for the Hugo, James Tiptree Jr., Locus, Nebula, Seiun, Theodore Sturgeon Memorial, and World Fantasy awards, and have been collected in *The Dragons of Springplace* and *The Cuckoo's Boys*. His novella "A Billion Eves" won the Hugo Award last year. Nebraska's only SFWA member, Reed lives in Lincoln with his wife and daughter, and is an ardent long-distance runner.

Thomas

The afternoon was clear and exceptionally cold. An off-duty company geologist was driving across the floor of the mine when a flash of reflected light caught his gaze. He didn't particularly want to go home, and thirty-one years in the coal industry hadn't quite killed the curious boy inside him. Backing up, he saw the flash repeated, and it seemed peculiar enough that he pulled on his stocking cap and mittens and climbed slowly up over the lignite coal, taking a close, careful look at something that made no sense whatsoever.

His fingers were numb and nose frostbitten when he reached the field office. But he didn't tremble until he began to look at the maps, showing his superiors which patch of ground shouldn't be touched until more qualified experts could come in and kick around.

"What'd you find?" they asked.

"An unknown species," seemed like an honest, worthy answer.

Sixty million years ago, plant material had gathered inside a basin sandwiched between young mountain ranges. Then the peat was covered over with eroded debris and slowly cooked into the low-sulfur treasure that now fed power plants across half of the country. Fossils were common in Powder River country. The

coal often looked like rotted leaves and sticks. But there was no way to systematically investigate what the gigantic machines wrested from the ground. Tons of
profit came up with every scoop, and only one person in the room wanted the
discovery preserved, no matter how unique it might be.

The geologist listened to the group's decision. Then he lifted the stakes, showing
the photographs that he had taken with his cell phone camera. "This resembles
nothing I've ever seen before," he added. Then mostly to himself, he muttered,
"It's like nothing else in the world."

"I've seen these before," one supervisor barked. "It's nothing, Tom."

Normally an agreeable sort, the geologist nodded calmly, but then his voice
showed bite when he asked, "Why can't we damn well be sure? Just to be safe?"

"No," another boss growled. "Now forget about it."

Thirty-one years of loyal service to the company brought one undeniable
lesson: this argument would never be won here. So he retreated, driving into
Gillette and his tiny house. His wife was sitting in the front of the television,
half-asleep. He poured the last of her whiskey down the sink, and she stood and
cursed him for some vague reason and swung hard at his face, and he caught her
and wrestled her to bed, saying all of the usual words until she finally closed her
eyes. Then he collected several dozen important names and agencies, sending out
a trim but explicit e-mail that included his phone numbers and the best of his
inadequate pictures. Thomas showered quickly, and he waited. Nobody called.
Then he dressed and ate dinner before carrying two shotguns, unloaded, and a
tall thermos of coffee out to the truck, and after a few minutes of consideration,
he drove back to the mine, parking as close to the fossil as possible.

Tom's plan, such as it was, involved shooing away the excavators as long as possible, first with words, and if necessary, empty threats. But these were temporary
measures, and worse, he discovered that his phone didn't work down here in the
pit's deepest corner. That's why he stepped out into the cold again. Navigating
by the stars and carrying a small hammer, he intended to break off a few pieces
of the fossil—as a precaution, in case this treasure was dug up and rolled east,
doomed to be incinerated with the rest of the anonymous coal.

Mattie

Few took notice of the peculiar e-mail. Three colleagues called its author, two
leaving messages on his voice mail. CNN's science reporter ordered her intern to
contact the corporation's main office for reaction. The PR person on duty knew
nothing about the incident, sharply questioned its validity, and after restating
his employer's sterling environmental record, hung up. In frustration, the intern contacted a random astronomer living in Colorado. The astronomer knew
nothing about the matter. She glanced at the forwarded e-mail, in particular the
downloaded images, and then said, "Interesting," to the uninterested voice. It
wasn't until later, staring at the twisted body with its odd limbs and very peculiar skull that her heart began to race. She called the geologist's phones. Nobody

answered. Leaving warning of her imminent arrival, she dressed for the Arctic and grabbed the department's sat-phone, buying two tall coffees when she gassed up on her way out of Boulder.

Better than most, Mattie understood the temporary nature of life. This woman who had never before been stopped by the police earned three speeding tickets on the journey north. Approaching the mine, she slipped in behind an empty dump truck, driving almost beneath the rear axle, and because the only security guard happened to be relieving himself, she managed to slip undetected out onto the gouged, unearthly landscape.

GPS coordinates took her to a pickup truck parked beside a blackish-brown cliff. The engine was running, a stranger sleeping behind the wheel. Beside him on the seat was what looked like huge, misshapen hands cradling a large golden ring. Two shotguns were perched against the far door. For a brief moment, she hesitated. But Mattie shoved her natural caution aside. With a tap on the glass, she woke the stranger, and startled, he stared out at what must have looked like a ghost—this young woman with almost no hair and a gaunt, wasted face.

He nervously rolled down the window.

"Are you Thomas Greene? I'm Mattie Chong."

Stupid with fatigue, Tom asked, "What are you doing here?"

"I came to see your alien," she reported.

He accepted that. What bothered him more was the stranger's appearance. "Ma'am, if you don't mind my asking…what's wrong with you?"

"Cancer," Mattie reported amiably, throwing her flashlight's beam against the deep seam of lignite. "And if I'm alive in four months, I'll beat all of my doctors' predictions."

The President

It was rare not to be the most important man in the room. And today brought one of those exceptional occasions: a trailer crowded with scientists and Secret Service agents, mining representatives and select reporters, plus the three-person congressional delegation from Wyoming. But the hero of the moment was Dr. Greene, and everybody wanted to stand beside the renowned geologist. Of course Dr. Chong should have shared this limelight, but she was flown to Utah that morning, her illness taking its expected, presumably fatal turn. The president was merely another visitor, and as the lesser celebrity, it was his duty to shake hands and ask about the poor woman's health. Every researcher had to be congratulated on the historic, world-shattering work. And he insisted on smiles all around. Bullied joviality was the president's great skill, and he was at his best when he was feeling less than happy.

Today was especially miserable. The bitter wind and low leaden skies only underscored a mood that had crumbled at dawn. That's when word arrived that his former Chief of Staff—a slippery political worm on his noblest day—planned to give the Special Investigator everything, including the damned briefcase filled with cash and ten hours of exceptionally embarrassing recordings. The president's administration was wounded, and by tomorrow it might well be dead. Cautious voices wanted the Wyoming visit cancelled, but that would have required an artful excuse, and what would have changed? Nothing. Besides, he understood that if enough people were fascinated with these old bones and odd artifacts, the coming nastiness might not be as awful as it promised to be.

Dr. Irving Case was the project administrator, and he had been on duty for less than a week. But with a bureaucrat's instincts for what counted, he used a large empty smile and a big voice. "Mr. President, sir. Would you like to go see the discovery now, sir?"

"If it's no problem. Let's have a peek at old George."

Back into the winter miseries they went. A tent-like shelter had been erected around the burial site, to block the wind and blowing coal dust. As they strolled across the barren scene, a dozen experts spoke in a competitive chorus, agreeing that the fossil was unique and remarkable, and of course immeasurably precious. The first priority was to disturb nothing, every clue precious and no one certain what constituted a clue. The president kept hearing how little was known, yet in the next moment, a dozen different hypotheses were offered to explain the creature's origins and how it might have looked in life and why it was where it was and why this wasn't where it had lived.

"It didn't live here?" the president interrupted. Aiming for humor, he said, "This splendid desolation…this is exactly where every movie alien roams."

Laughter blossomed—the bright fleeting giddiness that attaches itself to men of power. Then they reached the shelter, and reverent silence took hold. Dr. Case mentioned rules. Politely but firmly, he reminded everybody to wear the proper masks and gloves, and nothing could be touched, and then he warned the press to stand back so that all might enjoy the best possible view.

Photographs and video had already shown the mysterious fossil to the world. The enormous stratum of coal in which he, or she, was entombed was long ago dubbed Big George, hence the fossil's popular name. Lights had been strung near the tent ceiling. The coal slag was cleared away, the flat floor littered with scientific instruments and brightly colored cables. What rose before the president was both immediately recognizable and immeasurably strange: sixty million years ago, alien hands had dug a hole deep into the watery peat, and then "George" was lowered in or climbed in, feet first. Shovels had been used in the excavation. Two archeologists pointed at nearly invisible details, describing with confidence how the metal blades must have looked and what kinds of limbs employed them, and even while they were talking, a third voice reminded everyone that conjectures were fine, but nothing was proved and might never be.

George was a big fellow, and even to the uninformed eye, he looked like something from another world. The weight of the rock had compressed him, but not as badly as the president expected. Two bent legs helped carry the long horizontal body, and two more legs were presumably buried out of sight. A fifth limb rose from behind what looked like the angular and watchful face of a praying mantis, and the arm was jointed and complicated and partially destroyed. Dr. Greene had removed the matching hands and now-famous gold ring. The corpse was majestic, wasn't it? But in the next moment, in the president's eyes, George looked preposterous. Pieces stolen from unrelated creatures had been thrown together, a wily hoaxer having his laugh at all this foolish, misplaced fascination.

Turning to the world's most famous geologist, the president asked, "How were we so lucky, this poor fellow exposed this way?"

"The coal's weak around the edges of the grave," Dr. Greene explained. His celebrity was wearing on him, puffy eyes half-closed, a dazed, deep fatigue visible in his features and slope-shouldered posture. "If the blade had cut anywhere else, I wouldn't have noticed anything."

"It was the ring you saw?"

"Yes, sir."

The president nodded. "I haven't seen that artifact yet," he mentioned.

Dr. Case stepped forward. "The hands and ring have been sent to the Sandia, sir. For analysis and closer study."

The president nodded, looking up again. "So well preserved."

Dr. Case enjoyed his little stage. "The corpse shows very little sign of decomposition," he explained. "And we don't know why. Maybe the acidic peat and lack of oxygen preserved it. Although it's possible that the flesh was simply too alien and our microbes couldn't find anything to chew on."

The president nodded, pretending to appreciate the vagaries of alien biology. Then he returned to one statement that had puzzled him earlier. "And why do we think George lived elsewhere?"

Somebody said, "The feet."

Each leg ended with a narrow, three-toed foot.

"They're not built for bogs," another voice volunteered. "George would have sunk in to his knees, or deeper."

Against the rules, the president stepped closer. Nobody dared correct him, but the scene grew noticeably quieter. A Clydesdale horse would have been larger, but not by much. He knelt and stared at the lead foot, moving his head back and forth to avoid his own shadow. Sixty million years in the ground, yet the corpse retained its flesh and what seemed to be its natural color, which was tan. The crushing weight had twisted the dead foot, every toe visible. But what was perhaps more remarkable lay beneath the foot—the remnants of what might be animal skin, cut and stitched to create a simple shoe.

"Is this really a moccasin?" he asked.

Dr. Case joined him, kneeling and pushing his own mask closer to his mouth—making absolutely certain not to contaminate the treasure. "We have at least fifteen features that are probably remnants of clothing, Mr. President. And six metallic objects that look like knives and such, all carried on the body."

"Anything special?" the president inquired.

The administrator blinked, unsure what to make of the question.

"You know, like a laser-gun or portable reactor."

"Nothing like that, sir."

"That surprises me," the president admitted.

Dr. Case stood, offering his hand. "From what we can tell, sir…the technology is Early Iron Age. If that."

The president rose without anyone's help.

Another few minutes of inexpert study ended when someone mentioned lunch. "A fine idea," the president agreed. "Let the scientists back to work!" Then everyone filed outside and pulled off the choking masks. The distraction was over, the show finished. The president found his previous depression waiting for him, like a black mountain bearing down on his aging frame. He wiped his mouth with a sleeve, accepted the vacuous thanks of several people, and then he dredged up another one of his patented smiles, wondering why it was that no President had killed himself in office. Considering the pressures of the job, that seemed remarkable. Almost an oversight, really. The idea was so intriguing that he spent the next several moments dancing with a lurid fantasy: he would kill himself today, people around the world would weep, and with that, he would give himself a lasting, however inglorious place in history.

Irving

He was asked to say a few words at the funeral, honoring the heroic figure that had been lost. It was a fine speech and a very pleasant day in late September, the press in full attendance and millions watching only Irving. But how does one dispose of the body of a great person, someone composed of digital images and countless memories as well as flesh and bone? That was the question he had asked himself, preparing for this moment. This opportunity. Of course he wouldn't say anything so blatant or borderline crass, but that was the crux of the situation. Most of the world's citizens were anonymous bodies with a few possessions soon to be misplaced. But one can never bury or burn the modern celebrity. Their lives were so vast, so persistent and sturdy, that it was impossible to make a suitable grave. Indeed, death could free the largest celebrities into a greater, more enduring realm where they would never age, and with luck, would only grow even more impressive with the passage of years.

What Irving did address was his great admiration for a colleague who quickly became his good friend. "A sad, tragic death," he said, "and as unexpected as the discovery inside the coal. And we are all the lesser because of it." He didn't mention the deep irony that hadn't escaped anyone's attention: Thomas Greene was killed in a minor traffic accident, while George's co-discoverer was on the rebound, her withered body responding to an experimental regimen of stem cells and tailored phages.

The audience smiled as Irving left the podium.

Of course Mattie deserved the final word, and she used her public moment to beg for full funding of the ongoing Graveyard Project. It was a clumsy display of politics, and only she could get away with it. Irving was the project's administrator, far too exposed to act in such obvious ways. But he was grateful for her waving the hat, and he told her so afterwards. There was a reception back in Gillette, and another one of the endless news conferences, and the two sat close together behind a long table, fielding the same questions again and again.

Ten months after its discovery, nobody knew for sure how large the burial ground was. But evidence hinted at an enormous field of bodies, most of them deeper than George, buried over a period of many thousands of years. That was why the entire mine had been closed and made into a national monument. Power plants were sitting idle back east, but that's how important the Graveyard was. Every reporter wanted to know why the aliens had used this location. Mattie and Irving confessed that they were just as curious and as frustrated by their ignorance. To date, thirty-eight "georges" had been recovered from within the gigantic coal seam. As a rule, the deeper bodies wore better clothes and carried fancier tools, though nothing worthy of a star-traveler had been uncovered yet. Without giving details, Irving allowed that a final census might be coming, and that's when Mattie mentioned the new seismic scans—an elaborate experiment to make the lignite transparent as water.

"Don't put too much stock in success," Irving warned the reporters and cameras. "This technology is new and fickle, and we might not get results for months, if ever."

It seemed odd, a man in his position staunching excitement. But if these scans failed, he might be blamed. And what good would that do? This job was a dream, and Irving intended to remain inside the dream as long as possible. He was successful and couldn't imagine being happier, wielding power over hundreds of lives and a billion-dollar budget: emperor to an empire that had already revolutionized how humanity looked at itself and the universe.

Irving was exhilarated by the news conference; Mattie was exhausted. He made a point of walking the still-frail woman to her car, even when she claimed she could manage on her own, thank you. "I insist," he told her, and they shook hands and parted, and as he walked back into the reception hall, an associate approached quickly and whispered, "Sir, you have to see this, sir."

"See what?"

Then in the next instant, he muttered, "Results?"

"Yes, sir."

The laptop was set up in the little kitchen, linked to Base Camp's computers, and the news was astonishing enough that this man who never failed to find the right words was mute, knees bending as he stared at data that made his fondest dreams look like weak fantasies.

The screen was jammed with white marks and long numbers, each grave given a precise designation tied to estimated size and metal content and other crucial information. The graveyard covered more than a five square kilometers, and the dead were thick, particularly in the deepest layers.

"How many…?" he muttered.

"At least thirty thousand, sir."

Again, Irving's voice failed him.

The assistant misread his silence, assuming disappointment. "But that's not the final number," she added. "They're so many bodies, particularly near the bottom, sir…the final number is sure to be quite a bit larger than this."

Badger

Why he loved the girl was a complicated business. There were so many reasons he couldn't count them—moments of bliss and the intense looks that she gave him and little touches in the dark and touches offered but then taken away. Teasing. She was an expert at the tease. She was funny and quick with her tongue, and she was beautiful, of course. Yet she carried her beauty in ways most girls couldn't. Slender and built like a boy, she had the smallest tits he'd every felt up—a fact that he foolishly admitted once. But her face had this wonderful full mouth and a perfect nose and impossibly big eyes full of an earthly blue that watched him whenever he talked and paid even closer attention when he wasn't saying anything. She was observant in ways he never would be, and she was smart about people, and even though she rarely left Wyoming, she seemed to know more about the world than did her much older boyfriend who had already traveled across the globe three or four times.

Badger had little memory for the places he had been, but Hanna knew that if she kept asking questions, he might remember what the Sahara looked like at midnight and what he saw on a certain street in Phnom Penh and what it felt like to tunnel his way into an Incan burial chamber seven hundred years after it was sealed off from the world.

"Why Badger?" was her first question, asked moments after they met.

He sipped his beer and looked around the bar, wondering who this youngster was. "Because that's my name," he said with a shrug.

"You dig tunnels, right?"

"Who are you?" he asked.

"Hanna." She'd already settled on the stool beside his. Without another word, she pulled his glass over and took a sip, grinning as she licked the Budweiser off her upper lip. Reading his mind, she said, "I'm twenty-two."

"You aren't," he replied.

She laughed and gave back his remaining beer. "Word is, Badger, you're working at the Graveyard, digging down to the most interesting georges."

"Which high school do you go to?"

"I attend the University in Laramie," she replied. Then she put an elbow on the bar and set her delicate chin on edge of her palm, fingers curled up beneath that big, wonderful, smiling mouth. Without a trace of doubt, she told him, "You aren't all that comfortable with women. Are you, Badger?"

"How do you know my name?"

"I've seen you. And I've asked about you, I guess." Then she laughed at him, adding, "Or maybe I heard there was this guy named Badger digging holes for Dr. Chong, and you came tromping in here, and I figured, just by looking at you, that you had to be that guy. What would you think of that?"

He didn't know what the girl was telling him, or if he should care one way or another.

"I know Mattie pretty well," she reported. "Your boss has come to school to talk…I don't know, maybe ten times. She's a neat, neat lady, I think."

He nodded agreeably.

"How long has she been in charge?"

"Three months," he answered. "Dr. Case got pushed up to Washington—"

"I bet she drives you nuts," she interrupted.

"Why's that?"

"A feeling." Hanna shrugged and suddenly changed topics. "Does it ever make you crazy, thinking what you're working on?"

"Why would it?"

"The Graveyard!" she shouted. Down came her hand, and she sat up straight on the stool, looking around the quiet bar as if to hunt down a witness to this foolishness. "One hundred thousand dead aliens in the ground, and you're part of the team that's working their way to the bottom of the dead. Isn't that an astonishing thing? Don't you wake up every morning and think, 'God, how incredibly lucky can one burrowing weasel be?'"

"My build," he allowed.

She fell silent, watching him.

"I got the name as a kid," he reported. "My given name is Stuart, but I got the nickname because I've got short legs and a little bit of strength, I guess."

"You guess?"

"I'm strong," he said.

"I can tell."

"Yeah?"

"I like strong," she confessed, leaning in close.

Or maybe it wasn't that complicated, why he loved Hanna. She seemed to truly love him, and how could he not return the emotion? Beautiful and smart and sharp, and he was powerless to ignore her overtures. He gave her the rest of his beer and answered her questions as far as he could, admitting that the scope and importance of the Graveyard was beyond him. He was a professional digger. Using equipment designed by others, he was adept at carving his way through complicated strata, avoiding other graves and other treasures on his way to realms that hadn't seen sun since a few million years after the dinosaurs died away.

Later, Hanna asked, "What do you think of them?"

They were sitting in his truck in the open countryside, at night. So far they hadn't even kissed, but it felt as if they'd been sitting there for years. It was that natural, that inevitable.

"Think about who?" he said.

She gave him a look.

He understood. But the honest answer was another shrug and the embarrassing admission, "I don't think much. I don't know much at all. I've seen hundreds of them, but the aliens still look nothing but strange to me. What they were like when they were alive…I don't have any idea…"

"You don't call them 'georges,'" she pointed out.

"That's a silly name," he growled, "and it doesn't suit them."

She accepted the logic.

This was the moment when Badger caught himself wondering when he would ask the girl to marry him. Not if, but when.

"Everybody else has a story," Hanna told him. "I haven't met the person who doesn't think these creatures were part of some lost colony or prisoners in an alien work camp, or maybe they were wanderers living in orbit but burying themselves in the peat so we'd find them millions of years later. Just to prove to us that they'd been here."

"I don't know the answer," he said.

"And do you know why?" she asked. "Because you understand what's important." Then she lifted her face to his, and they kissed for a long while, and it was all that he could do, big, strong, unimaginative Badger, not to ask that girl to marry him right then.

Hanna

He called to ask, "How you doing, hon?"

"Good," she lied.

"Feel like walking around?"

"Why?"

"Dr. Chong says it's all right. I explained how the doctor wants you in bed, but for the next couple weeks you can still move—"

"I get to see the new one?"

"You want to?"

"I'm getting dressed now," she lied, crawling off the couch. "Are you coming to get me, Badge?"

"Pulling into the driveway right now," he reported happily.

So she got caught. Not only wasn't she close to ready, Hanna looked awful, and it took more promises and a few growls before Badger decided she was up to this adventure. Babies. Such a bother! Laying eggs would be so much easier. Drop them somewhere safe and walk away, living your own life until the kids were big enough to be fun. That's how mothering should be.

She mentioned her idea to Badger.

He was driving and laughing. "I wonder where you got that from?"

Georges had laid eggs. The younger females always had a few in some incomplete stage of development. Nobody knew if they put their basketball-sized eggs inside nests or incubators or what. Two years of research, yet the aliens' life remained mysterious, open to guesswork and wishful thinking. But somewhere in those vanished mountains, up high where the air was deliciously thin, the species had struggled mightily to replace the several friends and family being buried every year in that deep black peat.

Mattie was waiting for them at the surface. She smiled warmly and asked Hanna how she was feeling, and Hanna tried to sound like a woman in robust good health. Everybody dressed in clean gowns and masks, and then they took the long walk below ground, following one of the worm-like tunnels that Badger had cut into the deep seam. Seven other times Hanna had gotten a tour. But this visit was unique because of the age of the corpse being unearthed—one of the first generation georges, it was guessed—and because this was a privilege that not even the most connected members of the media had known.

This body lay at the graveyard's edge. To help the studies, Badger had carved an enormous room beside the fossil. The room was filled with machinery and lights, coolers full of food and drink, a portable restroom, plus several research-ers busy investigating the tiniest features, making ready for the slow cautious removal of the dead alien female.

Compared to the first george, she was a giant. Hanna expected as much, but seeing the body made her breath quicken. A once-powerful creature, larger than most rhinoceroses, she now lay crumpled down by death and suffocation and the weight of the world that had been peeled away above her. She was dead, yet she was entirely whole too. The acidic peat was a perfect preservative for flesh born outside this world, and presumably the aliens understood that salient fact.

"Great," Hanna gushed. "Wonderful. Thank you."

"Step closer," Mattie offered. "Just not past the yellow line."

A pair of researchers—sexless in their gowns and masks—were perched on a short scaffold, carefully working with the alien's hands.

"The burial ring?" Hanna asked.

Mattie nodded. "An aluminum alloy. Very sophisticated, very obvious in the scans."

"How different?"

The older the corpse, the more elaborate the ring. Mattie explained, "This one's more like a cylinder than a ring, and it's covered with details we don't find in any of the later burials."

The clothing was more elaborate, Hanna noticed, legs covered with trousers held up by elaborate belts, the feet enjoying what looked like elegant boots sewn from an ancient mammal's leathery hide. A nylon satchel rode the long back, worn by heavy use, every pocket stripped of anything that would have been difficult to replace.

"Will we ever find the prize?" Hanna asked.

"That amazing widget that transforms life on earth?" Mattie shrugged, admitting, "I keep promising that. Every trip to Congress, I say it's going to happen soon. But I seriously wonder. From what I've seen, these creatures never went into the ground carrying anything fancy or difficult to make."

Those words sank home. Hanna nodded and glanced at Badger's eyes, asking, "What else did I want to ask, hon? You remember?"

"Religion," he mentioned.

"Oh, yeah." Standing on the yellow line, she asked, "So why did they go into the ground, Mattie?"

"I don't know."

Hanna glanced at the woman, and then she stared up at the alien's cupped hands, imagining that important ring of metal. "I know the story I like best."

"Which one?"

"A starship reached our solar system, but something went wrong. Maybe the ship was supposed to refuel and set out for a different star, and it malfunctioned. Maybe its sister ships were supposed to meet here, but nobody showed." Hanna liked Mattie and respected her, and she wanted to sound informed on this extraordinary topic. "Mars or the moon would have made better homes. Their plan could have been to terraform another world. I know they would have appreciated the lighter gravity. And we think—because of the evidence, we can surmise—that their bodies didn't need or want as much free oxygen as we require. So whatever the reason, earth isn't where they wanted to be."

"A lot of people think that," Mattie said.

Hanna continued. "They didn't want to stay here long. And we don't have any evidence that their starship landed nearby. But they came here. The aliens set down in the nearby mountains, and they managed to find food and build shelter, and survive. But after ten or fifty or maybe two hundred years…whatever felt like a long time for that first generation…no one had come to rescue them. And that's why they started digging holes and climbing inside."

"You believe they were hibernating," Mattie guessed.

"No," Hanna admitted. "Or I mean, maybe they slept when they were buried. But they weren't planning to wake up like normal either. Their brains weren't like ours, I know. Crystalline and tough, and all the evidence points to a low-oxygen metabolism. What I think happened…each of the creatures reached a point in life when they felt past their prime, or particularly sad, or whatever…and that's why a lady like this would climb into the cold peat. She believes, or at least she needs to believe, that in another few hundred years, another ring-shaped starship is going to fall toward our sun, dig her up and bring her back to life."

Mattie contemplated the argument and nodded. "I've heard that story a few times, in one fashion or another."

"That's how their tradition started," Hanna continued. "Every generation of georges buried itself in the peat, and after a few centuries or a few thousand years, nobody would remember why. All they knew was that it was important to do, and that by holding a metal ring in your hands, you were making yourself a little easier to find inside your sleeping place."

Badger sighed, disapproving of the rampant speculation.

"That might well be true," said Mattie. "Which explains why the rings got simpler as time passed. Nobody remembered what the starship looked like. Or maybe they forgot about the ship entirely, and the ring's purpose changed. It was a symbol, an offering, something that would allow their god to catch their soul and take them back to Heaven again."

Just then, the two workers on the scaffold slipped the burial ring out from between the dead fingers. Mattie approached them and took the prize in both of her gloved hands. Hanna and then Badger stared at what everyone in the world would see in another few hours: a model of a great starship that had once crossed the vacant unloving blackness of space, ending up where it shouldn't have been and its crew and their descendants dying slowly over the next twenty thousand years.

One last time, Hanna thanked Mattie for the tour.

Walking to the surface again, she took her husband's big hand and held it tightly and said, "We're lucky people."

"Why's that?" Badger asked.

"Because we're exactly where we belong," she replied, as if it couldn't be more obvious.

Then they were in the open again, walking on a ravaged landscape dwarfed by the boundless Wyoming sky, and between one step and the next Hanna felt something change inside her body—a slight sensation that held no pain and would normally mean nothing. But she stopped walking. She stopped, but Badger kept marching forward. With both hands, she tenderly touched herself, and she forgot all about the aliens and their epic, long-extinct problems. Bleeding harder by the moment, she looked up to see her husband far ahead of her now, and to herself, with the smallest of whispers, she muttered, "Oh, no…not today…"

George

Despite night and the season, the thick air burned with its heat and choking oxygen, and the smallest task brought misery, and even standing was work too, and the strongest of the All stood on the broad planks and dug and he dug with them at the soft wet rot of the ground. Everyone but him said those good proper words saved for occasions such as this—ancient chants about better worlds and difficult journeys that ended with survival and giant caring hands that were approaching even now, soon to reach down from the stars to rescue the worthy dead. Silence was expected of the dead, and that was why he said nothing. Silence was the grand tradition born because another—some woman buried far beneath them—said nothing at her death, and the All were so impressed by her reserve and dignity that a taboo was born on that night. How long ago was that time? It was a topic of some conjecture and no good answers, and he used to care about abstract matters like that but discovered now that he couldn't care anymore. His life had been full of idle ideas that had wasted his time, and he was sorry for his misspent passion and all else that went wrong for him. Grief took hold, so dangerous and so massive that he had to set his shovel on the plank and say nothing in a new fashion, gaining the attention of his last surviving daughter. She was a small and pretty and very smart example of the All, and she was more perceptive than most, guessing what was wrong and looking at him compassionately when she said with clicks and warbles that she was proud of her father and proud to belong to his honorable lineage and that he should empty his mind of poisonous thoughts, that he should think of the dead under them and how good it would feel to pass into a realm where thousands of enduring souls waited.

But the dead were merely dead. Promised hands had never arrived, not in their lives or in his. That buoyant faith of youth, once his most cherished possession, was a tattered hope, and perhaps the next dawn would erase even that. That was why it was sensible to accept the smothering sleep now, now while the mind believed however weakly in its own salvation. Because no matter how long the odds, every other ending was even more terrible: he could become a sack of skin filled with anonymous bones and odd organs that would never again know life, that would be thrown into the communal garden to serve as compost, that the All might recall for another three generations, or maybe four, before the future erased his entire existence.

Once again, to the joy of his daughter and the others, the dead man picked up the long shovel and dug. The front feet threw his weight into the blade, and the blade cut into the cold watery muck, and up came another gout of peat that had to be set carefully behind him. Still the right words were spoken, the right blessings offered, and the right motions made, no one daring complain about the heat or the slow progress or the obvious, sorry fact that the strongest and largest of the All were barely able to manage what their ancestors had done easily.

At least so the old stories claimed.

Then came the moment when the fresh, wet, rectangular hole was finished and one of them had to climb inside. Odd as it seemed, he forgot his duty here. He found himself looking at the others, even at his exhausted daughter, wondering who was to receive this well-deserved honor. Oh yes, me, he recalled, and then he clicked a loud laugh, and he almost spoke, thinking maybe they would appreciate the grim humor. But no, this was a joke best enjoyed by the doomed, and these souls were nothing but alive. Leaving the moment unspoiled, the ceremony whole and sacred, he set his shovel aside and proved to each that he was stealing nothing precious. Hands empty, pockets opened, he showed them just a few cheap knives that he wanted for sentimental reasons. Then he stepped into the chilly stinking mess of water and rot, and with his feet sinking but his head exposed, he reached up with his long arm, hands opened until that good daughter placed the golden ring into his ready grip.

True to the custom, he said nothing more.

In the east, above the high snow-laced mountains, the winter sun was beginning to rise. Soon the killing heat would return to the lowlands, this brutal ground rendered unlivable. The All worked together to finish what had taken too long, shovels and muddy hands flinging the cold peat at the water and then at him—ceremony balanced on growing desperation—and he carefully said nothing and worked hard to think nothing but good thoughts. But then a favorite son returned to him, killed in a rockslide and lost, and he thought of his best mate whose central heart burst without warning, and because promises cost so little, he swore to both of them that he would carry their memories into this other realm, whatever shape it took.

When he discovered that he could not breathe, he struggled, but his mouth was already beneath the water, his head fixed in place.

With the job nearly finished, most of the All kept working. But others were standing away from the grave—those too weak to help, or too spent or too indifferent—and they decided that the dead could not hear them. With private little voices, they spoke about the coming day and the coming year, gentle but intense words dwelling on relationships forming and relationships lost, and who looked best in their funeral garb, and whose children were the prettiest and wisest, and who would die next, and oh by the way, did anyone think to bring a little snack for the journey home...?

JOBOY
DIANA WYNNE JONES

Diana Wynne Jones was born in London, England. At an early age, she began writing stories for herself and her sisters. She received her Bachelor of Arts at St. Anne's College in Oxford and went on to write full-time in 1965. Her first novel, *Changeover*, was published in 1970 and was followed by more than forty novels for adults and children, including the "Chrestomanci", "Dalemark", "Derkholm" series of fantasy novels. She is also the author of six collections of short stories, a critical assessment of fantasy, *The Tough Guide to Fantasyland*, and has edited several anthologies. In 2004 her novel, *Howl's Moving Castle*, was adapted for film by Hayao Miyazaki. Jones's most recent books are a third "Howl" novel, *House of Many Ways* and *The Game*. She has won many awards and honors including the Carnegie Commendation for *Dogsbody*, the Boston Globe-Horn Book Award twice, and is a recipient of the World Fantasy Award for Life Achievement. Upcoming is a new novel, *Enchanted Glass*.

This is the story behind the recent swathe of destruction just south of London.

His name was Jonathan Patek, but his father, Paul, always called him JoBoy. Lydia, his mother, never called him that until his father was dead. Paul Patek, the offspring of an Englishwoman and an Asian father, who was a tall, bulky, jovial man with a passion for cooking and eating curry, very much adhered to his Asian side, while working as a GP from his very English house in Surrey. Lydia, who worked as receptionist for Paul, preferred to be English. She picked at the curries, made a roast every Sunday, and ensured that JoBoy had the most English education possible.

When JoBoy thought of his father, he also always thought of the lovely, hot, throaty feel of swallowing a good curry.

Paul's death was a mystery. He set off one afternoon to visit a bedridden patient. "And I told him." Lydia said, "that doctors don't do home visits these days. It's a waste of their valuable time. And he simply laughed."

Two days later, Paul's body was discovered at the bottom of a nearby quarry. His car had been driven into gorse bushes at the top of the quarry and half overturned. It seemed to be suicide. Except, why was Paul's body as dry and emaciated as if he had starved to death? Nobody ever answered the question.

This reduction of his father to skin and bone troubled JoBoy horribly. He always thought of Paul as "full of juice", as he put it to himself. He could not understand it. There had not been time for Paul to starve.

Lydia made the best of things by selling the large house to a partnership of doctors, where she continued to work as receptionist, and moving into a smaller house nearby. JoBoy, while he finished his education, had to make do with a small glum room at the top of the new house, from which he could see one frail dusty tree and a patch of sky interrupted by television aerials. He was not happy, but this did not stop him growing taller and wider than his father before he had finished school.

"You'll follow in your father's footsteps, of course," Lydia said, and made arrangements. Consequently, JoBoy found himself a student doctor in the same teaching hospital as his father's, complete with white coat and stethoscope, following a consultant round the wards. He accepted this. He thought that perhaps, in time, he might discover the reason for Paul's sudden emaciation.

He had completed nearly a year of his training when he collapsed. It was a disease as mysterious as Paul's death. They thought it was a variant of glandular fever. At all events, JoBoy was now a patient where he had been a student and others studied him. He was there for six months, during which time he became weak as a kitten and nearly as emaciated as his father's corpse.

"I wish they'd let you come home!" Lydia said whenever she visited him.

In the spring, they did let JoBoy go home, out of pure bafflement. Lydia had to help him climb the stairs to his room and help him down again in the mornings. JoBoy's limbs creaked as he moved and his muscles felt to him like slabs of jelly. Worst, to his mind, was the way his brain had become an inert, shallow thing, incapable of any kind of speculation. I must work on my brain, he thought helplessly.

Lydia never let JoBoy be alone for long. She came home at midday and made him curry for lunch every day. Since she had never attended to the way Paul made curry, hers was a weak yellow stuff, full of large squashy raisins. JoBoy ate it listlessly for a week or so. Then he rebelled.

"I'll get my own lunch," he said. "I prefer bread and cheese anyway."

Lydia was possibly relieved. "If you're quite sure," she said. "I can go shopping again in the lunch hour then." She left the ingredients for curry carefully laid out on the kitchen table. JoBoy ignored them. He spent the days reading his father's medical books, trying to revive his brain, and obediently ate the curry when Lydia cooked it in the evenings. He several times tried to ask his mother medical questions while she supported his staggering person upstairs at night, but she always said, "You can't expect me to know anything about that, dear."

JoBoy concluded that he would have to cure himself.

He lay on the sofa downstairs and wondered how this was done. The disease seemed to have permeated every cell of his body, and, as it made him so weak and tired, it followed that he first needed some way of injecting energy into his body. He looked weakly around for some high-octane source. The fireplace was empty and he had no strength to light a fire. But he felt that fire was what he needed. Water too, he thought. Something elemental. But he had no strength. After a while, he tottered over to the patch of sun from the big window and lay down in it.

It worked. Sunlight did seem to infuse him in some way. After three days of lying in the sun, he had sufficient energy to remember that, among the schoolboy possessions randomly stashed in his bedroom, there was an old bunsen burner. He staggered up there and searched. The burner turned up in a black plastic sack rammed into the washbasin he never used. JoBoy looked from it to the taps. "Water," he said. "I have fire and water."

He tottered back downstairs and attached the bunsen burner to the unused inlet beside the fire. He lit it. Then he tottered to the kitchen and turned the cold tap on full. Then he collapsed on the sofa and tried to reconstruct himself.

It went slowly, so slowly that JoBoy sometimes despaired and used his precious energy in bursts of useless rage. And he had at all times not to become so immersed in his own cellular structure that Lydia would come home and find him with these energy sources burning and gushing. It would alarm her. She would think he was mad. She would worry about the gas bill and wasting water. So he set his alarm clock for the time of her return and hurried to turn off the tap and the burner before he heard her key in the door.

Slowly, oh slowly, for the rest of that year, he visualized each part of himself in turn and laboriously rebuilt it. At first, he had to do it cell by cell and it all seemed endless. But by Christmas, he found that he could reconstruct larger parts of himself in one go. He redid his liver, which made him feel much better. But there were strange side effects. The main one was that he kept feeling as if the body he was reconstructing was separate, outside him somewhere. He imagined it as lying beside him in the air next to his sofa. The other side effect was stranger. He found that he could turn off the bunsen burner and the kitchen tap without having to actually go and do it. Odd as this was, it saved JoBoy from having to get up before Lydia came home.

By this time, Lydia was saying, "You do seem better, but you're still so pale. Why don't you go out and get some fresh air?"

JoBoy groaned at first. But eventually, he redid his wobbly legs, wrapped himself in a coat, and crept down to the wood at the end of the road. There it smelt sharply of winter. The bare trees patterned the sky like the branching veins in his new-made eyeballs. He looked up and breathed deeply, sending clouds of breath into the branches. And the wood breathed back. JoBoy thought, This is an even better energy source than fire and water! He turned and crept home, almost invigorated. His legs—indeed, every bone in his body—were creaking in a strange new way. It felt as if they were lighter and more supple than before.

"Must have gone to feed the new body," he murmured as he plodded up his mother's front path. There was a strange feeling to his shoulder blades, like cobwebs growing there. He went to the wood every day after that. It seemed to enlarge his sense of smell. He smelt keenly the softness of rain and even more keenly the sting of frost. When the first intense yellow celandines appeared at the roots of trees, he smelt those too. He was not aware that they *had* a smell before that.

By this time, the way to the wood was less of a journey and more like a stroll. And with every journey, the cobwebby feel at his shoulders grew stronger. One day, as he stood staring at a bush of catkins, dangling yellow-green and reminding him of a Chinese painting, he realized that his shoulders rattled. They felt constricted. Uncomfortable, he spread the wings out. They were big and webby and weak as yet, but he could no longer deceive himself. He was becoming something else.

"I'd better redo my brain at once," he muttered as he walked home. "I need to make sense of this."

He remade his brain the next day. Not that it helped. A confusion of notions and images thundered into his head and left him so entirely bewildered that he found he was rolling about on the floor.

Eventually, he managed to stand up and make his way to the bathroom, where he stripped all his clothes off and studied himself in the mirror. He saw a thin, spindly human body. Definitely human. And so thin that it reminded him forcibly of his father's corpse. As he turned to pick up his clothes, he saw, sideways in the mirror, the large sketchy outline, dense and dark grey, of the thing that he was becoming. It had wings and a long spiked face. It went on four legs. The spines of its head continued in a line down to the tip of its arrow-headed tail. Its eyes blazed at him, through and somehow beyond his human eyes.

JoBoy turned his great spiked head and breathed gently from his huge fanged mouth on to the mirror. Steam—or was that smoke?—gushed out and made a rosy cloud on the glass. There was no question what he was.

That night, Lydia came out of her bedroom several times and implored JoBoy to stop pacing about the house. "Some of us have to work tomorrow," she said.

"Sorry," he said.

Around dawn, he thought that he understood what had happened to his father. Paul, like his son, had two bodies, one of them a dragon. This must account for his fiery relish for curry. When the dragon flew, it left its drained and lifeless human body temporarily behind. Paul's body had been found before the dragon could return to it. It followed then that JoBoy's father was alive still, without a human shape to return to.

JoBoy slept exhaustedly most of the next day. At night, he set out to find his father. He left his fine, thin, new-made body asleep in its bed and went on four legs down the road to the wood. It had come to him that the wood's energies might help him locate Paul.

The energies were tremendous that night. They poured through JoBoy, faintly illuminating his grey-blue dragon outline. He stood with his claws in moist twigs and his wings cocked and sent out great questing dragon calls. Around midnight, he caught a small distant answer. It was definitely a dragon voice. It seemed to be asking, faintly, for help from somewhere a long way south and east of the wood.

JoBoy's clawed feet scrambled as he galloped out into the road to find room to fly in. He spread the great webby wings. But it seemed they were not yet quite developed enough to get him airborne. He flapped hard and angrily, hearing the wind from the wings set the trees threshing, but he remained crouched in the road. His tail stabbed the tarmac in frustration.

Some of the noise he had thought was the trees turned out to be the sound of a neighbor's car returning from a theatre. Before JoBoy could move, he was skewered, dazzled, in the headlights, and, as he tried to move, the car swept through him and on, to turn into a driveway further down the road.

Nobody shouted. Nobody came to look. JoBoy discovered that he himself was quite undamaged. And he had felt nothing as the car went through him. I'm invisible! he thought. Then, I'm made of fog!

He crawled back home thinking that this was probably very useful indeed. He could hunt Paul by daylight. Since he was not in the least sleepy, he spent the hours until dawn strengthening his wings. It felt odd to work on a part of himself that did not seem to exist, but it seemed quite possible. He fell asleep on his sofa.

"Well, really," Lydia said as she hurried past on her way to work. "Are you ill again or just lazy?" She did not seem to expect an answer.

JoBoy made himself a leisurely breakfast and took his dragon form out of the house. He went warily at first, in case he proved to be visible after all. But no one seemed to notice, so he grew bold and rushed down the length of the road, flapping, flapping, until, to his great joy, he found himself in the air, planing above the springing green of the wood. He wheeled around above the trees and pointed himself in the direction the call for help had come from, and flew there.

It was hard work at first, until he discovered how to catch breezes and thermals without needing to flap his wings, and he kept being distracted too by the increasingly rural land that passed underneath him. It was so green, so full of life. Before long, he saw what he took to be an oasthouse, and decided that he must be in Kent. He sent out a long, cautious dragon call.

The reply was instant. "Help! Oh, thank goodness! Help! Here!" It sounded like a female. Puzzled, JoBoy came planing down onto deliciously fragrant new grass, into what felt like an old common. The oasthouse, plainly converted to living space, stood on one side. The rest was surrounded by hedges, fruit trees, and comely old cottages. "Where are you?" JoBoy called.

The reply was piercingly from under his great clawed feet. "Here! Underneath! Let me out!"

JoBoy looked down. In the grass, almost between his talons, there was a small boulder embedded in the turf. He pawed at it dubiously. It felt queer, as if there was more to it than just a boulder—almost as if, he had to admit to himself, there was some kind of magic involved.

"Just move the stone!" the voice implored him from underground. "I've been here so long!"

JoBoy flexed his great claws, dug both feet under the sides of the boulder, and pulled. And heaved. He would never have shifted it, but for a high speed train that went screaming past in the mid-distance, presumably on its way to France via the Channel tunnel. JoBoy thought, Ah! Energy source! and felt power surge into him. He saw his forelegs glow foggy white with it as he heaved at the stone again.

It rolled away on its side. Blue mist instantly filled the earthy depression it had left, bulged, crested, and took form as a blue female dragon, slightly smaller than JoBoy. She put her jagged muzzle up and breathed in the power from the rapidly disappearing train. He saw her glow with it and enlarge slightly. "Oh good!" she said. "I knew there was a lot of power around nowadays, but I never could use it to break that spell. Thank you." She rested, pulsing for a moment, and then asked, "Who are you? You're new, aren't you?"

"I'm JoBoy," JoBoy said. "I—er—had to make myself, you know."

"Oh, we all had to," the blue dragon answered. "But not many people can. I was the only one in Kent who managed it, and that was so long ago that my human part is dead." She added, "People were terrified of me of course. And I was a bit unwise, drawing power from cattle and so forth. They hired a wizard to put me underground." Her glistening blue eyes surveyed JoBoy thoughtfully. "Has anyone noticed you yet?"

"No," he said. "What's your name?"

She rattled her wings in a shrug. "Call me Kent."

"And," JoBoy asked eagerly, "do you know of any more dragons? I think my father—"

"If he's recent, like you," Kent said, "he isn't a dragon." She looked at him searchingly. "Forgive me, but something's odd. What is that line of substance leading off you into the distance?"

JoBoy turned his head over his wing and shoulder to look where Kent nodded. There did indeed seem to be a misty line of, of *something* leading from the middle of his scaly chest into the far distance. "It must be my connection to my human body," he said.

"It doesn't work like that," Kent said. "You *are* your human body. Forgive me again, but that looks uncommonly like something feeding off you."

"I think I may have got something wrong then," JoBoy suggested.

"I don't think so. It looks far more like what used to happen when I took power from a cow in the old days," Kent said. "Or are you taking power from something at the moment?"

"Not that I know of," JoBoy said. "That train was plenty."

"Then," said Kent, "do you mind if we go and look? I don't like the idea of a dragon being a victim, not after being locked up underground like that."

She spread veiny blue wings and wafted up into the sky. JoBoy, after a few ungainly hops and some flapping, managed to get airborne too and soared off after her. She was dawdling in the air, waiting for him and laughing puffs of faint steam. "This is wonderful!" she said as JoBoy coasted up alongside. "You can't guess how much I've longed to fly again. And there's such a lot of power coming from everywhere! From that trainline, and those roads, and that building over there that seems to be making something. I can't believe anyone would need to feed on anything alive these days."

"I think I just got it wrong," JoBoy said.

"Let's follow the line and see," Kent said.

They went onward. Wind poured over and under their wings and the line in JoBoy's chest seemed to shorten like elastic as they went. They followed it almost to London and then to a house right underneath, and swooped after it. JoBoy was expecting to find the house where his body lay, but, to his surprise, they came down into the large house where he had been born, through its roof and its upper story, into a smell of new paint and disinfectant. I suppose that if a car can go through me, I can go through a house, JoBoy thought as they planed down into what had once been their dining room. A row of unhappy looking people sat waiting there. None of them seemed to notice that there were now two dragons in the room. In front of them was a varnished desk labeled Reception, where Lydia sat, telephoning impatiently. The line from JoBoy's chest led straight into Lydia's.

"What did I tell you?" Kent said, coiling herself to fit among the chairs. "Whoever she is, she's feeding on you. Have you ever felt very weak at all?"

"Yes," he admitted. "For the last eighteen months."

Lydia said angrily to her telephone, "If the child really is having convulsions, take it to a hospital. You can't bother the doctors with it now." And after a pause, "If your car's broken, call an ambulance. We can't deal with you here." She slammed the phone down. It rang again at once. "Dr. Grayling's surgery," she said. JoBoy saw and felt the line from him to her pulse and bulge as she gathered herself to repel another patient. "No," she said, "you can't see a doctor without an appointment."

"I don't believe this," JoBoy said miserably.

"She seems a very negative person," Kent observed. "Let's see why." She put her long blue face forward, through the telephone flex, and gently touched Lydia's chest. It went transparent. JoBoy stared incredulously into the inner parts of Lydia and at the black, writhing, stunted dragon that lived inside there. It was twisting about, sucking sustenance from JoBoy's pulsing line.

"Ah," Kent said sadly. "This happens to a lot of people when they can't admit to their dragon. They can't live on their own, you see. She must have been doing this since before you were born."

JoBoy knew nothing except that he was suddenly and enormously angry. He knew now exactly what had happened to his father. He had simply been sucked dry. He knew he had to destroy that stunted inner dragon. He surged himself forward in a slither of scales, through the desk, through Lydia—

"No, wait!" said Kent.

JoBoy was too angry to listen. He wrapped his huge jaws around the writhing creature and breathed fire. He flamed and he roared and he seethed heat into Lydia, until he was quite sure that the stunted dragon was burned up entirely.

He hadn't expected it to kill Lydia.

The one thing more dangerous than an angry dragon is a dragon full of grief. We have Kent to thank that the destruction in that neighborhood was no worse.

UTRIUSQUE COSMI
ROBERT CHARLES WILSON

Robert Charles Wilson made his first sale in 1974, to *Analog*, but little more was heard from him until the late '80s, when he began to publish a string of ingenious and well-crafted novels and stories that have since established him among the top ranks of the writers who came to prominence in the last two decades of the 20th century. His first novel, *A Hidden Place*, appeared in 1986. He won the John W. Campbell Memorial Award for his novel *The Chronoliths*, the Philip K. Dick Award for his novel *Mysterium*, and the Aurora Award for his story "The Perseids." In 2006, he won the Hugo Award for his acclaimed novel, *Spin*. His other books include the novels *Memory Wire*, *Gypsies*, *The Divide*, *The Harvest*, *A Bridge of Years*, *Darwinia*, *Blind Lake*, *Bios*, and *Axis*, and a collection of his short work, *The Perseids and Other Stories*. His most recent book is a new novel, *Julian Comstock: A Story of 22nd-Century America*. He lives in Toronto, Canada.

Diving back into the universe (now that the universe is a finished object, boxed and ribboned from bang to bounce), Carlotta calculates ever-finer loci on the frozen ordinates of spacetime until at last she reaches a trailer park outside the town of Commanche Drop, Arizona. Bodiless, no more than a breath of imprecision in the Feynman geography of certain virtual particles, thus powerless to affect the material world, she passes unimpeded through a sheet-aluminum wall and hovers over a mattress on which a young woman sleeps uneasily.

The young woman is her own ancient self, the primordial Carlotta Boudaine, dewed with sweat in the hot night air, her legs caught up in a spindled cotton sheet. The bedroom's small window is cranked open, and in the breezeless distance a coyote wails.

Well, look at me, Carlotta marvels: skinny girl in panties and a halter, sixteen years old—no older than a gnat's breath—taking shallow little sleep-breaths in the moonlit dark. Poor child can't even see her own ghost. Ah, but she will, Carlotta thinks—she *must*.

The familiar words echo in her mind as she inspects her dreaming body, buried in its tomb of years, eons, kalpas. *When it's time to leave, leave. Don't be afraid. Don't wait. Don't get caught. Just go. Go fast.*

Her ancient beloved poem. Her perennial mantra. The words, in fact, that saved her life.

She needs to share those words with herself, to make the circle complete. Everything she knows about the nature of the physical universe suggests that the task is impossible. Maybe so… but it won't be for lack of trying.

Patiently, slowly, soundlessly, Carlotta begins to speak.

Here's the story of the Fleet, girl, and how I got raptured up into it. It's all about the future—a bigger one than you believe in—so brace yourself.

It has a thousand names and more, but we'll just call it the Fleet. When I first encountered it, the Fleet was scattered from the core of the galaxy all through its spiraled tentacles of suns, and it had been there for millions of years, going about its business, though nobody on this planet knew anything about it. I guess every now and then a Fleet ship must have fallen to Earth, but it would have been indistinguishable from any common meteorite by the time it passed through the atmosphere: a chunk of carbonaceous chondrite smaller than a human fist, from which all evidence of ordered matter had been erased by fire—and such losses, which happened everywhere and often, made no discernable difference to the Fleet as a whole. All Fleet data (that is to say, all *mind*) was shared, distributed, fractal. Vessels were born and vessels were destroyed; but the Fleet persisted down countless eons, confident of its own immortality.

Oh, I know you don't understand the big words, child! It's not important for you to hear them—not *these* words—it's only important for me to *say* them. Why? Because a few billion years ago tomorrow I carried your ignorance out of this very trailer, carried it down to the Interstate and hitched west with nothing in my backpack but a bottle of water, a half-dozen Tootsie Rolls, and a wad of twenty-dollar bills stolen out of Dan-O's old ditty bag. That night (tomorrow night: mark it) I slept under an overpass all by myself, woke cold and hungry long before dawn, and looked up past a concrete arch crusted with bird shit into a sky so thick with falling stars it made me think of a dark skin bee-stung with fire. Some of the Fleet vectored too close to the atmosphere that night, no doubt, but I didn't understand that (any more than *you* do, girl)—I just thought it was a big flock of shooting stars, pretty but meaningless. And after a while I slept some more. And come sunrise I waited for the morning traffic so I could catch another ride…but the only cars that came by were all weaving or speeding, as if the whole world was driving home from a drunken party.

"They won't stop," a voice behind me said. "Those folks already made their decisions, Carlotta. Whether they want to live or die, I mean. Same decision you have to make."

I whirled around, sick-startled, and that was when I first laid eyes on dear Erasmus.

Let me tell you right off that Erasmus wasn't a human being. Erasmus just then was a knot of shiny metal angles about the size of a microwave oven, hovering in mid-air, with a pair of eyes like the polished tourmaline they sell at those roadside souvenir shops. He didn't *have* to look that way—it was some old avatar he used because he figured it would impress me. But I didn't know that then. I was only surprised, if that's not too mild a word, and too shocked to be truly frightened.

"This world won't last much longer," Erasmus said in a low and mournful voice. "You can stay here, or you can come with me. But choose quick, Carlotta, because the mantle's come unstable and the continents are starting to slip."

I half-believed I was still asleep and dreaming. I didn't know what that meant, about the mantle, though I guessed he was talking about the end of the world. Some quality of his voice (which reminded me of that actor Morgan Freeman) made me trust him despite how weird and impossible the whole conversation was. Plus I had a confirming sense that *something* was going bad *somewhere*, partly because of the scant traffic (a Toyota zoomed past, clocking speeds it had never been built for, the driver a hunched blur behind the wheel), partly because of the ugly green cloud that just then billowed up over a row of rat-toothed mountains on the horizon. Also the sudden hot breeze. And the smell of distant burning. And the sound of what might have been thunder, or something worse.

"Go with you where?"

"To the stars, Carlotta! But you'll have to leave your body behind."

I didn't like the part about leaving my body behind. But what choice did I have, except the one he'd offered me? Stay or go. Simple as that.

It was a ride—just not the kind I'd been expecting.

There was a tremor in the earth, like the devil knocking at the soles of my shoes. "Okay," I said, "whatever," as white dust bloomed up from the desert and was taken by the frantic wind.

Don't be afraid. Don't wait. Don't get caught. Just go. Go fast.

Without those words in my head I swear, girl, I would have died that day. Billions did.

She slows down the passage of time so she can fit this odd but somehow necessary monologue into the space between one or two of the younger Carlotta's breaths. Of course she has no real voice in which to speak. The past is static, imperturbable in its endless sleep; molecules of air on their fixed trajectories can't be manipulated from the shadowy place where she now exists. Wake up with the dawn, girl, she says, steal the money you'll never spend—it doesn't matter; the important thing is to leave. It's time.

When it's time to leave, leave. Of all the memories she carried out of her earthly life this is the most vivid: waking to discover a ghostly presence in her darkened room, a white-robed woman giving her the advice she needs at the moment she needs it. Suddenly Carlotta wants to scream the words: *When it's time to leave—*

But she can't vibrate even a single mote of the ancient air, and the younger Carlotta sleeps on.

Next to the bed is a thrift-shop night table scarred with cigarette burns. On the table is a child's night-light, faded cut-outs of SpongeBob SquarePants pasted on the paper shade. Next to that, hidden under a splayed copy of *People* magazine, is the bottle of barbiturates Carlotta stole from Dan-O's ditty-bag this afternoon, the same khaki bag in which (she couldn't help but notice) Dan-O keeps his cash, a change of clothes, a fake driver's license, and a blue steel automatic pistol.

Young Carlotta detects no ghostly presence... nor is her sleep disturbed by the sound of Dan-O's angry voice and her mother's sudden gasp, two rooms away. Apparently Dan-O is awake and sober. Apparently Dan-O has discovered the theft. That's a complication.

But Carlotta won't allow herself to be hurried.

The hardest thing about joining the Fleet was giving up the idea that I had a body, that my body had a real place to be.

But that's what everybody believed at first, that we were still whole and normal—everybody rescued from Earth, I mean. Everybody who said "Yes" to Erasmus—and Erasmus, in one form or another, had appeared to every human being on the planet in the moments before the end of the world. Two and a half billion of us accepted the offer of rescue. The rest chose to stay put and died when the Earth's continents dissolved into molten magma.

Of course that created problems for the survivors. Children without parents, parents without children, lovers separated for eternity. It was as sad and tragic as any other incomplete rescue, except on a planetary scale. When we left the Earth we all just sort of re-appeared on a grassy plain as flat as Kansas and wider than the horizon, under a blue faux sky, each of us with an Erasmus at his shoulder and all of us wailing or sobbing or demanding explanations.

The plain wasn't "real," of course, not the way I was accustomed to things being real. It was a virtual place and all of us were wearing virtual bodies, though we didn't understand that fact immediately. We kept on being what we expected ourselves to be—we even wore the clothes we'd worn when we were raptured up. I remember looking down at the pair of greasy second-hand Reeboks I'd found at the Commanche Drop Goodwill store, thinking: in Heaven? *Really?*

"Is there any place you'd rather be?" Erasmus asked with a maddening and clearly inhuman patience. "Anyone you need to find?"

"Yeah, I'd rather be in New Zealand," I said, which was really just a hysterical joke. All I knew about New Zealand was that I'd seen a show about it on PBS, the only channel we got since the cable company cut us off.

"Any particular part of New Zealand?"

"What? Well—okay, a beach, I guess."

I had never been to a real beach, a beach on the ocean.

"Alone, or in the company of others?"

"Seriously?" All around me people were sobbing or gibbering in (mostly) foreign languages. Pretty soon fights would start to break out. You can't put a couple of billion human beings so close together under circumstances like that and expect any other result. But the crowd was already thinning, as people accepted similar offers from their own Fleet avatars.

"Alone," I said. "Except for *you*."

And quick as that, there I was: Eve without Adam, standing on a lonesome stretch of white beach.

After a while the astonishment faded to a tolerable dazzle. I took off my shoes and tested the sand. The sand was pleasantly sun-warm. Salt water swirled up between my toes as a wave washed in from the coral-blue sea.

Then I felt dizzy and had to sit down.

"Would you like to sleep?" Erasmus asked, hovering over me like a gem-studded party balloon. "I can help you sleep, Carlotta, if you like. It might make the transition easier if you get some rest, to begin with."

"You can answer some fucking *questions*, is what you can *do*," I said.

He settled down on the sand beside me, the mutant offspring of a dragonfly and a beach ball. "Okay, shoot," he said.

It's a read-only universe, Carlotta thinks. The Old Ones have said as much, so it must be true. And yet she knows, she remembers, that the younger Carlotta will surely wake and find her here: a ghostly presence, speaking wisdom.

But how can she make herself perceptible to this sleeping child? The senses are so stubbornly material, electrochemical data cascading into vastly complex neural networks… is it possible she could intervene in some way at the borderland of quanta and perception? For a moment Carlotta chooses to look at her younger self with different eyes, sampling the fine gradients of molecular magnetic fields. The child's skin and skull grow faint and then transparent as Carlotta shrinks her point of view and wanders briefly through the carnival of her own animal mind, the buzzing innerscape where skeins of dream merge and separate like fractal soap bubbles. If she could manipulate even a single boson—influence the charge at some critical synaptic junction, say—

But she can't. The past simply doesn't have a handle on it. There's no uncertainty here anymore, no alternate outcomes. To influence the past would be to change the past, and by definition that's impossible.

The shouting from the next room grows suddenly louder and more vicious, and Carlotta senses her younger self moving from sleep toward an awakening, too soon.

Of course I figured it out eventually, with Erasmus's help. Oh, girl, I won't bore you with the story of those first few years—they bored *me*, heaven knows.

Of course "heaven" is exactly where we weren't. Lots of folks were inclined to see it that way—assumed they must have died and been delivered to whatever afterlife they happened to believe in. Which was actually not *too* far off the mark; but of course God had nothing to do with it. The Fleet was a real-world business, and ours wasn't the first sentient species it had raptured up. Lots of planets got destroyed, Erasmus said, and the Fleet didn't always get to them in time to salvage the population, hard as they tried—we were *lucky*, sort of.

So I asked him what it was that caused all these planets to blow up.

"We don't know, Carlotta. We call it the Invisible Enemy. It doesn't leave a signature, whatever it is. But it systematically seeks out worlds with flourishing civilizations and marks them for destruction." He added, "It doesn't like the Fleet much, either. There are parts of the galaxy where we don't go—because if we *do* go there, we don't come back."

At the time I wasn't even sure what a "galaxy" was, so I dropped the subject, except to ask him if I could see what it looked like—the destruction of the Earth, I meant. At first Erasmus didn't want to show me; but after a lot of coaxing he turned himself into a sort of floating TV screen and displayed a view "looking back from above the plane of the solar ecliptic," words which meant nothing to me.

What I saw was… well, no more little blue planet, basically.

More like a ball of boiling red snot.

"What about my mother? What about Dan-O?"

I didn't have to explain who these people were. The Fleet had sucked up all kinds of data about human civilization, I don't know how. Erasmus paused as if he was consulting some invisible Rolodex. Then he said, "They aren't with us."

"You mean they're dead?"

"Yes. Abby and Dan-O are dead."

But the news didn't surprise me. It was almost as if I'd known it all along, as if I had had a vision of their deaths, a dark vision to go along with that ghostly visit the night before, the woman in a white dress telling me *go fast*.

Abby Boudaine and Dan-O, dead. And me raptured up to robot heaven. Well, well.

"Are you sure you wouldn't like to sleep now?"

"Maybe for a while," I told him.

Dan-O's a big man, and he's working himself up to a major tantrum. Even now Carlotta feels repugnance at the sound of his voice, that gnarl of angry consonants. Next Dan-O throws something solid, maybe a clock, against the wall. The clock goes to pieces, noisily. Carlotta's mother cries out in response, and the sound of her wailing seems to last weeks.

"It's not good," Erasmus told me much later, "to be so much alone."

Well, I told him I *wasn't* alone—he was with me, wasn't he? And he was pretty good company, for an alien machine. But that was a dodge. What he meant was that I ought to hook up with somebody human.

I told him I didn't care if I ever set eyes on another human being ever again. What had the human race ever done for me?

He frowned—that is, he performed a particular contortion of his exposed surfaces that I had learned to interpret as disapproval. "That's entropic talk, Carlotta. Honestly, I'm worried about you."

"What could happen to me?" Here on this beach where nothing ever *really* happens, I did not add.

"You could go crazy. You could sink into despair. Worse, you could die."

"I could *die?* I thought I was immortal now."

"Who told you that? True, you're no longer *living*, in the strictly material sense. You're a metastable nested loop embedded in the Fleet's collective mentation. But everything's mortal, Carlotta. Anything can die."

I couldn't die of disease or falling off a cliff, he explained, but my "nested loop" was subject to a kind of slow erosion, and stewing in my own lonely juices for too long was liable to bring on the decay that much faster.

And admittedly, after a month on this beach, swimming and sleeping too much and eating the food Erasmus conjured up whenever I was hungry (though I didn't really need to eat), watching recovered soap operas on his bellyvision screen or reading celebrity magazines (also embedded in the Fleet's collective memory) that would never get any fresher or produce another issue, and just being basically miserable as all hell, I thought maybe he was right.

"You cry out in your sleep," Erasmus said. "You have bad dreams."

"The world ended. Maybe I'm depressed. You think meeting people would help with that?"

"Actually," he said, "you have a remarkable talent for being alone. You're sturdier than most. But that won't save you, in the long run."

So I tried to take his advice. I scouted out some other survivors. Turned out it was interesting what some people had done in their new incarnations as Fleet-data. The Erasmuses had made it easy for like-minded folks to find each other and to create environments to suit them. The most successful of these cliques, as they were sometimes called, were the least passive ones: the ones with a purpose. Purpose kept people lively. Passive cliques tended to fade into indifference pretty quickly, and the purely hedonistic ones soon collapsed into dense orgasmic singularities; but if you were curious about the world, and hung out with similarly curious friends, there was a lot to keep you thinking.

None of those cliques suited me in the long run, though. Oh, I made some friends, and I learned a few things. I learned how to access the Fleet's archival data, for instance—a trick you had to be careful with. If you did it right you could think about a subject as if you were doing a Google search, all the relevant information popping up in your mind's eye just as if it had been there all along. Do it too often or too enthusiastically, though, and you ran the risk of getting lost in the overload—you might develop a "memory" so big and all-inclusive that it absorbed you into its own endless flow.

(It was an eerie thing to watch when it happened. For a while I hung out with a clique that was exploring the history of the non-human civilizations that had been raptured up by the Fleet in eons past… until the leader of the group, a Jordanian college kid by the name of Nuri, dived down too far and literally fogged out. He got this look of intense concentration on his face, and moments later his body turned to wisps and eddies of fluid air and faded like fog in the sunlight. Made me shiver. And I had liked Nuri—I missed him when he was gone.)

But by sharing the effort we managed to safely learn some interesting things. (Things the Erasmuses could have just *told* us, I suppose; but we didn't know the right questions to ask.) Here's a big for-instance: although every species was mortal after it was raptured up—every species eventually fogged out much the way poor Nuri had—there were actually a few very long-term survivors. By that I mean individuals who had outlived their peers, who had found a way to preserve a sense of identity in the face of the Fleet's hypercomplex data torrent.

We asked our Erasmuses if we could meet one of these long-term survivors.

Erasmus said no, that was impossible. The Elders, as he called them, didn't live on our timescale. The way they had preserved themselves was by dropping out of realtime.

Apparently it wasn't necessary to "exist" continuously from one moment to the next. You could ask the Fleet to turn you off for a day or a week, then turn you on again. Any moment of active perception was called a *saccade*, and you could space your saccades as far apart as you liked. Want to live a thousand years? Do it by living one second out of every million that passes. Of course it wouldn't *feel* like a thousand years, subjectively; but a thousand years would flow by before you aged much. That's basically what the Elders were doing.

We could do the same, Erasmus said, if we wanted. But there was a price tag attached to it. "Timesliding" would carry us incomprehensibly far into a future nobody could predict. We were under continual attack by the Invisible Enemy, and it was possible the Fleet might lose so much cohesion that we could no longer be sustained as stable virtualities. We wouldn't get a long life out of it, and we might well be committing a kind of unwitting suicide.

"You don't really go anywhere," Erasmus summed up. "In effect, you just go fast. I can't honestly recommend it."

"Did I ask for your advice? I mean, what *are* you, after all? Just some little fragment of the Fleet mind charged with looking after Carlotta Boudaine. A cybernetic babysitter."

I swear to you, he looked *hurt*. And I heard the injury in his voice.

"I'm the part of the Fleet that cares about you, Carlotta."

Most of my clique backed down at that point. Most people aren't cut out to be timesliders. But I was more tempted than ever. "You can't tell me what to do, Erasmus."

"I'll come with you, then," he said. "If you don't mind."

It hadn't occurred to me that he might *not* come along. It was a scary idea.

But I didn't let that anxiety show.

"Sure, I guess that'd be all right," I said.

Enemies out there too, the elder Carlotta observes. A whole skyful of them. As above, so below. Just like in that old drawing—what was it called? *Utriusque Cosmi*. Funny what a person remembers. Girl, do you hear your mother crying?

The young Carlotta stirs uneasily in her tangled sheet.

Both Carlottas know their mother's history. Only the elder Carlotta can think about it without embarrassment and rage. Oh, it's an old story. Her mother's name is Abby. Abby Boudaine dropped out of high school pregnant, left some dreary home in South Carolina to go west with a twenty-year-old boyfriend who abandoned her outside Albuquerque. She gave birth in a California emergency ward and nursed Carlotta in a basement room in the home of a retired couple, who sheltered her in exchange for housework until Carlotta's constant wailing got on their nerves. After that Abby hooked up with a guy who worked for a utility company and grew weed in his attic for pin money. The hookup lasted a few years, and might have lasted longer, except that Abby had a weakness for what the law called "substances" and couldn't restrain herself in an environment where coke and methamphetamine circulated more or less freely. A couple of times Carlotta was bounced around between foster homes while Abby Boudaine did court-mandated dry-outs or simply binged. Eventually Abby picked up ten-year-old Carlotta from one of these periodic suburban exiles and drove her over the state border into Arizona, jumping bail. "We'll never be apart again," her mother told her, in the strained voice that meant she was a little bit high or hoping to be. "Never again!" Blessing or curse. Carlotta wasn't sure which. "You'll never leave me, baby. You're my one and only."

Not such an unusual story, the elder Carlotta thinks; though her younger self, she knows, feels uniquely singled out for persecution.

Well, child, Carlotta thinks, try living as a distributed entity on a Fleet that's being eaten by invisible monsters, *then* see what it feels like.

But she knows the answer to that. It feels much the same.

"Now you *steal* from me?" Dan-O's voice drills through the wall like a rusty auger. Young Carlotta stirs and whimpers. Any moment now she'll open her eyes, and then what? Although this is the fixed past it feels suddenly unpredictable, unfamiliar, dangerous.

So Erasmus came with me when I went timesliding, and I appreciated that, even before I understood what a sacrifice it was for him.

Early on I asked him about the Fleet and how it came to exist. The answer to that question was lost to entropy, he said. He had never known a time without a Fleet—he couldn't have, because Erasmus *was* the Fleet, or at least a sovereign fraction of it.

"As we understand it," he told me, "the Fleet evolved from networks of self-replicating, data-collecting machine intelligences, no doubt originally created by some organic species, for the purpose of exploring interstellar space. Evidence suggests we're only a little younger than the universe itself."

The Fleet had outlived its creators. "Biological intelligence is unstable over the long term," Erasmus said, a little smugly. "But out of that original compulsion to acquire and share data we evolved and refined our own collective purpose."

"That's why you hoover up doomed civilizations? So you can catalogue and study them?"

"So they won't be forgotten, Carlotta. That's the greatest evil in the universe— the entropic decay of organized information. Forgetfulness. We despise it."

"Worse than the Invisible Enemy?"

"The Enemy is evil to the degree to which it abets entropic decay."

"Why does it want to do that?"

"We don't know. We don't even understand what the Enemy *is*, in physical terms. It seems to operate outside of the material universe. If it consists of matter, that matter is non-baryonic and impossible to detect. It pervades parts of the galaxy—though not *all* parts—like an insubstantial gas. When the Fleet passes through volumes of space heavily infested by the Enemy, our loss-rate soars. And as these infested volumes of space expand, they encompass and destroy life-bearing worlds."

"The Enemy's growing, though. And the Fleet isn't."

I had learned to recognize Erasmus's distress, not just because he was slowly adopting somewhat more human features. "The Fleet is my home, Carlotta. More than that. It's my body, my heart."

What he didn't say was that by joining me in the act of surfing time he would be isolating himself from the realtime network that had birthed and sustained him. In realtime, Erasmus was a fraction of something reassuringly immense. But in slide-time he'd be as alone as an Erasmus could get.

And yet he came with me, when I made my decision. He was my Erasmus as much as he was the Fleet's, and he came with me. What would you call that, girl? Friendship? At least. I came to call it love.

The younger Carlotta has stolen those pills (the ones hidden under her smudged copy of *People*) for a reason. To help her sleep, was what she told herself. But she didn't really have trouble sleeping. No: if she was honest she'd have to say the pills were an escape hatch. Swallow enough of them and it's, hey, fuck you, world. Less work than the highway, an alternative she was also considering.

More shouting erupts in the next room. A real roust-up, bruises to come. Then, worse, Dan-O's voice goes all small and jagged. That's a truly bad omen, Carlotta knows. Like the smell of ozone that floods the air in advance of a lightning strike, just before the voltage ramps up and the current starts to flow.

Erasmus built a special virtuality for him and me to time-trip in. Basically, it was a big comfy room with a wall-sized window overlooking the Milky Way.

The billions of tiny dense components that made up the Fleet swarmed at velocities slower than the speed of light, but timesliding made it all seem faster—scarily so. Like running the whole universe in fast-forward, knowing you can't go back. During the first few months of our expanded Now we soared a long way out of the spiral arm that contained the abandoned Sun. The particular sub-swarm of the Fleet that hosted my sense of self was on a long elliptical orbit around the supermassive black hole at the galaxy's core, and from this end of the ellipse, over the passing days, we watched the Milky Way drop out from under us like a cloud of luminous pearls.

When I wasn't in that room I went off to visit other timesliders, and some of them visited me there. We were a self-selected group of radical roamers with a thing for risk, and we got to know one another pretty well. Oh, girl, I wish I could tell you all the friends I made among that tribe of self-selected exiles! Many of them human, not all: I met a few of the so-called Elders of other species, and managed to communicate with them on a friendly basis. Does that sound strange to you? I guess it is. Surpassing strange. I thought so too, at first. But these were people (mostly people) and things (but things can be people too) that I mostly liked and often loved, and they loved me back. Yes they did. Whatever quirk of personality made us timesliders drew us together against all the speedy dark outside our virtual walls. Plus—well, we were survivors. It took not much more than a month to outlive all the remaining fractions of humanity. Even our ghosts were gone, in other words, unless you counted *us* as ghosts.

Erasmus was a little bit jealous of the friends I made. He had given up a lot for me, and maybe I ought to have appreciated him more for it. Unlike us formerly biological persons, though, Erasmus maintained a tentative link with realtime. He had crafted protocols to keep himself current on changes in the Fleet's symbol-sets and core mentation. That way he could update us on what the Fleet was doing—new species raptured up from dying worlds and so forth. None of these newcomers lasted long, though, from our lofty perspective, and I once asked Erasmus why the Fleet even bothered with such ephemeral creatures as (for instance) human beings. He said every species was doomed in the long run, but that didn't make it okay to kill people—or to abandon them when they might be rescued. That instinct was what made the Fleet a moral entity, something more than just a collection of self-replicating machines.

And it made *him* more than a nested loop of complex calculations. In the end, Carlotta, I came to love Erasmus best of all.

Meanwhile the years and stars scattered in our wake like dust—a thousand years, a hundred thousand, a million, more, and the galaxy turned like a great white wheel. We all made peace with the notion that we were the last of our kind, whatever "kind" we represented.

If you could hear me, girl, I guess you might ask what I found in that deep well of strangeness that made the water worth drinking. Well, I found friends, as I said—isn't that enough? And I found lovers. Even Erasmus began to adopt a human avatar, so we could touch each other in the human way.

I found, in plain words, a *home*, Carlotta, however peculiar in its nature—a *real* home, for the first time in my life.

Which is why I was so scared when it started to fall apart.

In the next room Abby isn't taking Dan-O's anger lying down. It's nearly the perfect storm tonight—Dan-O's temper and Abby's sense of violated dignity both rising at the same ferocious pitch, rising toward some unthinkable crescendo.

But her mother's outrage is fragile, and Dan-O is frankly dangerous. The young Carlotta had known that about him from the get-go, from the first time her mother came home with this man on her arm: knew it from his indifferent eyes and his mechanical smile; knew it from the prison tattoos he didn't bother to disguise and the boastfulness with which he papered over some hole in his essential self. Knew it from the meth-lab stink that burned off him like a chemical perfume. Knew it from the company he kept, from the shitty little deals with furtive men arranged in Carlotta's mother's home because his own rental bungalow was littered with incriminating cans of industrial solvent. Knew it most of all by the way he fed Abby Boudaine crystal meth in measured doses, to keep her wanting it, and by the way Abby began to sign over her weekly Wal-Mart paycheck to him like a dutiful servant, back when she was working checkout.

Dan-O is tall, wiry, and strong despite his vices. The elder Carlotta can hear enough to understand that Dan-O is blaming Abby for the theft of the barbiturates—an intolerable sin, in Dan-O's book. Followed by Abby's heated denials and the sound of Dan-O's fists striking flesh. All this discovered, not remembered: the young Carlotta sleeps on, though she's obviously about to wake; the critical moment is coming fast. And Carlotta thinks of what she saw when she raided Dan-O's ditty bag, the blue metal barrel with a black gnurled grip, a thing she had stared at, hefted, but ultimately disdained.

We dropped back down the curve of that elliptic, girl, and suddenly the Fleet began to vanish like drops of water on a hot griddle. Erasmus saw it first, because of what he was, and he set up a display so I could see it too: Fleet-swarms set as ghostly dots against a schema of the galaxy, the ghost-dots dimming perilously and some of them blinking out altogether. It was a graph of a massacre. "Can't anyone stop it?" I asked.

"They would if they could," he said, putting an arm (now that he had grown a pair of arms) around me. "They will if they can, Carlotta."

"Can *we* help?"

"We are helping, in a way. Existing the way we do means they don't have to use much mentation to sustain us. To the Fleet, we're code that runs a calculation for a few seconds out of every year. Not a heavy burden to carry."

Which was important because the Fleet could only sustain so much computation, the upper limit being set by the finite number of linked nodes. And that number was diminishing as Fleet vessels were devoured wholesale.

"Last I checked," Erasmus said (which would have been about a thousand years ago, realtime), "the Fleet theorized that the Enemy is made of dark matter." (Strange stuff that hovers around galaxies, invisibly—it doesn't matter, girl; take my word for it; you'll understand it one day.) "They're not material objects so much as *processes*—parasitical protocols played out in dark matter clouds. Apparently they can manipulate quantum events we don't even see."

"So we can't defend ourselves against them."

"Not yet. No. And you and I might have more company soon, Carlotta. As long-timers, I mean."

That was because the Fleet continued to rapture up dying civilizations, nearly more than their shrinking collectivity could contain. One solution was to shunt survivors into the Long Now along with us, in order to free up computation for battlefield maneuvers and such.

"Could get crowded," he warned.

"If a lot of strangers need to go Long," I said…

He gave me a carefully neutral look. "Finish the thought."

"Well… can't we just… go Longer?"

Fire a pistol in a tin box like this ratty trailer and the sound is ridiculously loud. Like being spanked on the ear with a two-by-four. It's the pistol shot that finally wakes the young Carlotta. Her eyelids fly open like window shades on a haunted house.

This isn't how the elder Carlotta remembers it. *Gunshot?* No, there was no *gunshot*: she just came awake and saw the ghost—

And no ghost, either. Carlotta tries desperately to speak to her younger self, wills herself to succeed and fails yet again. So who fired that shot, and where did the bullet go, and why can't she *remember* any of this?

The shouting in the next room has yielded up a silence. The silence becomes an eternity. Then Carlotta hears the sound of footsteps—she can't tell whose—approaching her bedroom door.

In the end almost every conscious function of the Fleet went Long, just to survive the attrition of the war with the dark-matter beings. The next loop through the galactic core pared us down to a fraction of what we used to be. When I got raptured up, the Fleet was a distributed cloud of baseball-sized objects running quantum computations on the state of their own dense constituent atoms—*millions and millions* of such objects, all linked together in a nested hierarchy. By the time we orbited back up our ellipsis you could have counted us in the tens of thousands, and our remaining links were carefully narrowbanded to give us maximum stealth.

So us wild timesliders chose to go Longer.

Just like last time, Erasmus warned me that it might be a suicidal act. If the Fleet was lost we would be lost along with it… our subjective lives could end within days or hours. If, on the other hand, the Fleet survived and got back to reproducing itself, well, we might live on indefinitely—even drop back into realtime if we chose to do so. "Can you accept the risk?" he asked.

"Can you?"

He had grown a face by then. I suppose he knew me well enough to calculate what features I'd find pleasing. But it wasn't his ridiculous fake humanity I loved. What I loved was what went on behind those still-gemlike tourmaline eyes—the person he had become by sharing my mortality. "I accepted that risk a long time ago," he said.

"You and me both, Erasmus."

So we held on to each other and just—*went fast.*

Hard to explain what made that time-dive so vertiginous, but imagine centuries flying past like so much dust in a windstorm! It messed up our sense of *place*, first of all. Used to be we had a point of view light-years wide and deep… now all those loops merged into one continuous cycle; we grew as large as the Milky Way itself, with Andromeda bearing down on us like a silver armada. I held Erasmus in my arms, watching wide-eyed while he updated himself on the progress of the war and whispered new discoveries into my ear.

The Fleet had worked up new defenses, he said, and the carnage had slowed; but our numbers were still dwindling.

I asked him if we were dying.

He said he didn't know. Then he looked alarmed and held me tighter. "Oh, Carlotta…"

"What?" I stared into his eyes, which had gone faraway and strange. "*What is it?* Erasmus, tell me!"

"The Enemy," he said in numbed amazement.

"What about them?"

"*I know what they are.*"

The bedroom door opens.

The elder Carlotta doesn't remember the bedroom door opening. None of this is as she imagines it should be. The young Carlotta cringes against the backboard of the bed, so terrified she can barely draw breath. *Bless you, girl, I'd hold your hand if I could!*

What comes through the door is just Abby Boudaine. Abby in a cheap white nightgown. But Abby's eyes are yellow-rimmed and feral, and her nightgown is spattered with blood.

See, the thing is this. All communication is limited by the speed of light. But if you spread your saccades over time, that speed-limit kind of expands. Slow as we were, light seemed to cross galactic space in a matter of moments. Single thoughts consumed centuries. We felt the supermassive black hole at the center of the galaxy beating like a ponderous heart. We heard whispers from nearby galaxies, incomprehensibly faint but undeniably manufactured. Yes, girl, we were *that* slow.

But the Enemy was even slower.

"Long ago," Erasmus told me, channeling this information from the Fleet's own dying collectivity, "long ago the Enemy learned to parasitize dark matter… to use it as a computational substrate… to evolve *within* it…"

"*How* long ago?"

His voice was full of awe. "Longer than you have words for, Carlotta. They're older than the universe itself."

Make any sense to you? I doubt it would. But here's the thing about our universe: it oscillates. It *breathes*, I mean, like a big old lung, expanding and shrinking and expanding again. When it shrinks it wants to turn into a singularity, but it can't do that, because there's a limit to how much mass a quantum of volume can hold without busting. So it all bangs up again, until it can't accommodate any more emptiness. Back and forth, over and over. Perhaps, *ad infinitum*.

Trouble is, no information can get past those hot chaotic contractions. Every bang makes a fresh universe, blank as a chalkboard in an empty schoolhouse…

Or so we thought.

But dark matter has a peculiar relationship with gravity and mass, Erasmus said; so when the Enemy learned to colonize it they found ways to propagate themselves from one universe to the next. They could survive *the end of all things material*, in other words, and they had already done so—many times!

The Enemy was genuinely immortal, if that word has any meaning. The Enemy conducted its affairs not just across galactic space but across the voids that separate galaxies, clusters of galaxies, superclusters… slow as molasses, they were, but vast as all things, and as pervasive as gravity, and very powerful.

"So what have they got against the Fleet, if they're so big and almighty? Why are they killing us?"

Erasmus smiled then, and the smile was full of pain and melancholy and an awful understanding. "But they're not *killing* us, Carlotta. They're rapturing us up."

One time in school, when she was trying unsuccessfully to come to grips with *The Merchant of Venice*, Carlotta had opened a book about Elizabethan drama to a copy of an old drawing called *Utriusque Cosmi*. It was supposed to represent the whole cosmos, the way people thought of it back in Shakespeare's time, all layered and orderly: stars and angels on top, hell beneath, and a naked guy stretched foursquare between divinity and damnation. Made no sense to her at all. Some antique craziness. She thinks of that drawing now, for no accountable reason. *But it doesn't stop at the angels, girl. I learned that lesson. Even angels have angels, and devils dance on the backs of lesser devils.*

Her mother in her bloodstained nightgown hovers in the doorway of Carlotta's bedroom. Her unblinking gaze strafes the room until it fixes at last on her daughter. Abby Boudaine might be standing right here, Carlotta thinks, but those eyes are looking out from someplace deeper and more distant.

The blood fairly drenches her. But it isn't Abby's blood.

"Oh, Carlotta," Abby says. Then she clears her throat, the way she does when she has to make an important phone call or speak to someone she fears. "Carlotta…"

And Carlotta (the invisible Carlotta, the Carlotta who dropped down from that place where the angels dice with eternity) understands what Abby is about to say, recognizes at last the awesome circularity, not a paradox at all. She pronounces the words silently as Abby makes them real: "Carlotta. Listen to me, girl. I don't guess you understand any of this. I'm so sorry. I'm sorry for many things. But listen now. When it's time to leave, you leave. Don't be afraid, and don't get caught. Just go. Go *fast*."

Then she turns and leaves her daughter cowering in the darkened room.

Beyond the bedroom window the coyotes are still complaining to the moon. The sound of their hooting fills up the young Carlotta's awareness until it seems to speak directly to the heart of her.

Then comes the second and final gunshot.

I have only seen the Enemy briefly, and by that time I had stopped thinking of them as the Enemy.

Can't describe them too well. Words really do fail me. And by that time, might as well admit it, I was not myself a thing I would once have recognized as human. Just say that Erasmus and I and the remaining timesliders were taken up into the Enemy's embrace along with all the rest of the Fleet—all the memories we had deemed lost to entropy or warfare were preserved there. The virtualities the Enemy had developed across whole kalpas of time were labyrinthine, welcoming, strange beyond belief. Did I roam in those mysterious glades? Yes I did, girl, and Erasmus by my side, for many long (subjective) years, and we became—well, larger than I can say.

And the galaxies aged and flew away from one another until they were swallowed up in manifolds of cosmic emptiness, connected solely by the gentle and inexorable thread of gravity. Stars winked out, girl; galaxies merged and filled with dead and dying stars; atoms decayed to their last stable forms. But the fabric of space can tolerate just so much emptiness. It isn't infinitely elastic. Even vacuum ages. After some trillions and trillions of years, therefore, the expansion became a contraction.

During that time I occasionally sensed or saw the Enemy—but I have to call them something else: say, *the Great Old Ones,* pardon my pomposity—who had constructed the dark matter virtualities in which I now lived. They weren't people at all. Never were. They passed through our adopted worlds like storm clouds, black and majestic and full of subtle and inscrutable lightnings. I couldn't speak to them, even then; as large and old as I had become, I was only a fraction of what they were.

I wanted to ask them why they had destroyed the Earth, why so many people had to be wiped out of existence or salvaged by the evolved benevolence of the Fleet. But Erasmus, who delved into these questions more deeply than I was able to, said the Old Ones couldn't perceive anything as tiny or ephemeral as a rocky planet like the Earth. The Earth and all the many planets like her had been destroyed, not by any willful calculation, but by autonomic impulses evolved over the course of many cosmic conflations—impulses as imperceptible and involuntary to the Old Ones as the functioning of your liver is to *you*, girl.

The logic of it is this: Life-bearing worlds generate civilizations that eventually begin playing with dark matter, posing a potential threat to the continuity of the Old Ones. Some number of these intrusions can be tolerated and contained—like the Fleet, they were often an enriching presence—but too many of them would endanger the stability of the system. It's as if we were germs, girl, wiped out by a giant's immune system. They couldn't *see* us, except as a somatic threat. Simple as that.

But they could see the Fleet. The Fleet was just big enough and durable enough to register on the senses of the Old Ones. And the Old Ones weren't malevolent: they perceived the Fleet much the way the Fleet had once perceived *us*, as something primitive but alive and thinking and worth the trouble of salvation.

So they raptured up the Fleet (and similar Fleet-like entities in countless other galaxies), thus preserving us against the blind oscillations of cosmic entropy.

(Nice of them, I suppose. But if I ever grow large enough or live long enough to confront an Old One face-to-face I mean to lodge a complaint. Hell *yes* we were small—people are some of the smallest thought-bearing creatures in the cosmos, and I think we all kind of knew that even before the end of the world… *you* did, surely. But pain is pain and grief is grief. It might be inevitable, it might even be built into the nature of things; but it isn't *good*, and it ought not to be tolerated, if there's a choice.)

Which I guess is why I'm here watching you squinch your eyes shut while the sound of that second gunshot fades into the air.

Watching you process a nightmare into a vision.

Watching you build a pearl around a grain of bloody truth.

Watching you *go fast*.

The bodiless Carlotta hovers a while longer in the fixed and changeless corridors of the past.

Eventually the long night ends. Raw red sunlight finds the window.

Last dawn this small world will ever see, as it happens; but the young Carlotta doesn't know that yet.

Now that the universe has finished its current iteration, all its history is stored in transdimensional metaspace like a book on a shelf—it can't be changed. Truly so. I guess I know that now, girl. Memory plays tricks that history kindly corrects.

And I guess that's why the Old Ones let me have access to these events, as we hover on the brink of a new creation.

I know some of the questions you'd ask me if you could. You might say, *Where are you really?* And I'd say, *I'm at the end of all things, which is really just another beginning.* I'm walking in a great garden of dark matter, while all things known and baryonic spiral up the ladder of unification energies to a fiery new dawn. I have grown so large that I can fly down history like a bird over a prairie field. But I cannot remake what has already been made. That is one power I do not possess.

I watch you get out of bed. I watch you dress. Blue jeans with tattered hems, a man's lumberjack shirt, those thrift-shop Reeboks. I watch you go to the kitchen and fill your vinyl Bratz backpack with bottled water and Tootsie Rolls, which is all the cuisine your meth-addled mother has left in the cupboards.

Then I watch you tiptoe into Abby's bedroom. I confess I don't remember this part, girl. I suppose it didn't fit my fantasy about a benevolent ghost. But here you are, your face fixed in a willed indifference, stepping over Dan-O's corpse. Dan-O bled a lot after Abby Boudaine blew a hole in his chest, and the carpet is a sticky, rust-colored pond.

I watch you pull Dan-O's ditty bag from where it lies half under the bed. On the bed, Abby appears to sleep. The pistol is still in her hand. The hand with the pistol in it rests beside her head. Her head is damaged in ways the young Carlotta can't stand to look at. Eyes down, girl. That's it.

I watch you extract a roll of bills from the bag and stuff it into your pack. Won't need that money where you're going! But it's a wise move, taking it. Commendable forethought.

Now go.

I have to go too. I feel Erasmus waiting for me, feel the tug of his love and loyalty, gentle and inevitable as gravity. He used to be a machine older than the dirt under your feet, Carlotta Boudaine, but he became a man—*my* man, I'm proud to say. He needs me, because it's no easy thing crossing over from one universe to the next. There's always work to do, isn't that the truth?

But right now, you go. You leave those murderous pills on the nightstand, find that highway. Don't be afraid. Don't wait. Don't get caught. Just go. Go fast. And excuse me while I take my own advice.

A DELICATE ARCHITECTURE
CATHERYNNE M. VALENTE

Born in the Pacific Northwest in 1979, Catherynne M. Valente is the author of a dozen works of fiction and poetry, including *Palimpsest*, the "Orphan's Tales" series, *The Labyrinth*, and crowd-funded phenomenon *The Girl Who Circumnavigated Fairyland in a Ship of Her Own Making*. She is the winner of the James Tiptree, Jr. Award, the Mythopoeic Award, the Rhysling Award, and the Million Writers Award She has been nominated for the Pushcart Prize, the Spectrum Awards, and was a finalist for the World Fantasy Award in 2007 and 2009. She lives on an island off the coast of Maine with her partner and two dogs.

My father was a confectioner. I slept on pillows of spun sugar; when I woke, the sweat and tears of my dreams had melted it all to nothing, and my cheek rested on the crisp sheets of red linen. Many things in the house of my father were made of candy, for he was a prodigy, having at the age of five invented a chocolate trifle so dark and rich that the new Emperor's chocolatier sat down upon the steps of his great golden kitchen and wept into his truffle-dusted mustache. So it was that when my father found himself in possession of a daughter, he cut her corners and measured her sweetness with no less precision than he used in his candies.

My breakfast plate was clear, hard butterscotch, full of oven-bubbles. I ate my soft-boiled marzipan egg gingerly, tapping its little cap with a toffee-hammer. The yolk within was a lemony syrup that dribbled out into my egg-cup. I drank chocolate in a black vanilla-bean mug. But I ate sugared plums with a fork of sparrow bones, and the marrow left salt in the fruit, the strange, thick taste of a thing once alive in all that sugar. When I asked him why I should taste these bones as well as the glistening, violet plums, he told me very seriously that I must always remember that sugar was once alive. It grew tall and green and hard as my own knuckles in a far-away place, under a red sun that burned on the face of the sea. I must always remember that children just like me cut it down and crushed it up with tan and strong hands, and that their sweat, which gave me my sugar, tasted also of salt.

"If you forget that red sun and those long, green stalks, then you are not truly a confectioner, you understand nothing about candy but that it tastes good and

477

is colorful—and these things a pig can tell, too. We are the angels of the cane, we are oven-magicians, but if you would rather be a pig snuffling in the leaves—"

"No, Papa."

"Well then, eat your plums, magician of my heart."

And so I did, and the tang of marrow in the sugar-meat was rich and disturbing and sweet.

Often I would ask my father where my mother had gone, if she had not liked her fork of sparrow bones, or if she had not wanted to eat marzipan eggs every day. These were the only complaints I could think of. My father ruffled my hair with his sticky hand and said:

"One morning, fine as milk, when I lived in Vienna and reclined on turquoise cushions with the Empress licking my fingers for one taste of my sweets, I went walking through the city shops, my golden cane cracking on the cobbles, peering into their frosted windows and listening to the silver bells strung from the doors. In the window of a competitor who hardly deserved the name, being but a poor maker of trifles which would hardly satisfy a duchess, I saw the loveliest little crystal jar. It was as intricately cut as a diamond and full of the purest sugar I have ever seen. The little shopkeeper, bent with decades of hunching over trays of chocolate, smiled at me with few enough teeth and cried:

'Alonzo! I see you have cast your discerning gaze upon my little vial of sugar! I assure you it is the finest of all the sugars ever made, rendered from the tallest cane in the isles by a fortunate virgin snatched at the last moment from the frothing red mouth of her volcano! It was then blanched to the snowy shade you see in a bath of lion's milk and ground to sweetest dust with a pearl pestle, and finally poured into a jar made from the glass of three church windows. I am no Emperor's darling, but in this I exceed you at last!'

The little man did a shambling dance of joy, to my disgust. But I poured out coins onto his scale until his eyes gleamed wet with longing, and took that little jar away with me." My father pinched my chin affectionately. "I hurried back home, boiled the sugar with costly dyes and other secret things, and poured it into a Costanze-shaped mold, slid it into the oven, and out you came in an hour or two, eyes shining like caramels!"

He laughed, and I pulled his ear and told him not to tease me, that every girl has a mother, and an oven is no proper mother! He gave me a slice of honeycomb, and shooed me into the garden, where the raspberries snarled along the white gate.

And thus I grew up. I ate my egg every morning, and licked the yolk from my lips. I ate my plums with my bone fork, and thought very carefully about the tall cane under the red sun. I scrubbed my pillow from my cheeks until they were quite pink. Every old woman in the village remarked on how much I resembled the little ivory cameos of the Empress, the same delicate nose, high brow, thick red hair. I begged my father to let me go to Vienna, as he had done when he was a boy. After all, I was far from a dense child. I had my suspicions—I wanted to see her. I wanted to hear the violas playing in white halls with green and rose checkered floors. I wanted to ride a horse with long brown reins. I wanted to taste radishes and carrots and potatoes, even a chicken, even a fish on a plate of real porcelain, with no oven-bubbles in it.

"Why did we leave Vienna, Papa?" I cried, over our supper of marshmallow crèmes and caramel cakes. "I could have learned to play the flute there; I could have worn a wig like spun sugar. You learned these things—why may I not?"

My father's face reddened and darkened all at once, and he gripped the sides of the butcher's board where he cut caramel into bricks. His bark-brown eyes glazed. "I learned to prefer sugar to white curls," he growled, "and peppermints to piccolos, and cherry creams to the Empress. You will learn this, too, Costanze." He cleared his throat. "It is an important thing to know."

I bent myself to the lesson. I learned how to test my father's syrups by dropping them into silver pots of cold water. By the time I was sixteen I hardly needed to do it, I could sense the hard crack of finished candy, feel the brittle snap prickling the hairs of my neck. My fingers were red with so many crushed berries; my palms were dry and crackling with the pale and scratchy wrapping papers we used for penny sweets. I was a good girl. By the time my father gave me the dress, I was a better confectioner than he, though he would never admit it. It was almost like magic, the way candies would form, glistening and impossibly colorful, under my hands.

It was very bright that morning. The light came through the window panes like butterscotch plates. When I came into the kitchen, there was no egg on the table, no toffee-hammer, no chocolate in a sweet black cup. Instead, lying over the cold oven like a cake waiting to be iced, was a dress. It was the color of ink, tiered and layered like the ones Viennese ladies wore in my dreams, floating blue to the floor, dusted with diamonds that caught the morning light and flashed cheerfully.

"Oh, Papa! Where would I wear a thing like that?"

My father smiled broadly, but the corners of his smile were wilted and sad.

"Vienna," he said. "The court. I thought you wanted to go, to wear a wig, to hear a flute?"

He helped me on with the dress, and as he cinched in my waist and lifted my red hair from bare shoulders, I realized that the dress was made of hard blue sugar and thousands of blueberry skins stitched together with syrupy thread. The diamonds were lumps of crystal candy, still a bit sticky, and at the waist were icing flowers in a white cascade. Nothing of that dress was not sweet, was not sugar, was not my father's trade and mine.

Vienna looked like a Christmas cake we had once made for a baroness: all hard, white curls and creases and carvings, like someone had draped the city in vanilla cream. There were brown horses, and brown carriages attached to them. In the Emperor's palace, where my father walked as though he had built it, there were green and rose checkered floors, and violas playing somewhere far off, the echoes drifting down over me like spring winds. My father took my hand and smiled that same wilted smile, and led me across all those green checks to a room which was harder and whiter than all the rest, where the Emperor and the Empress sat frowning on terrible silver thrones of sharpened filigree, like two demons on their wedding day. I gasped, and shrunk behind my father, the indigo train of my dress showing so dark against the floor. I could not hope to hide from those awful royal eyes.

"Why have you brought us this thing, Alonzo?" barked the Emperor, who had a short blonde mustache and copper buttons running down his chest. "This thing which bears such resemblance to our wife? Do you insult us by dragging this reminder of your crimes and hers across our floor like a dust broom?"

The Empress blushed deeply, her skin going the same shade as her hair, the same shade as my hair. My father clenched his teeth.

"I told you then, when you loved my chocolates above all things, that I did not touch her, that I loved her as a man loves God, not as he loves a woman."

"Yet you come back, begging to return to my Grace, towing a child who is a mirror of her! This is obscene, Alonzo!"

My father's face broke open, pleading. It was terrible to see him so. I clutched my icing flowers, confused and frightened.

"But she is not my child! She is not the Empress's child! She is the greatest thing I have ever created, the greatest of all things I have baked in my oven. I have brought her to show you what I may do in your name, for your Grace, if you will look on me with love again, if you will give me your favor once more. If you will let me come back to the city, to my home."

I gaped, and tears filled my eyes. My father drew a little silver icing-spade from his belt and started towards me. I cried out and my voice echoed in the hard, white hall like a sparrow cut into a fork. I cringed, but my father gripped my arms tight as a tureen's handles, and his eyes were wide and wet. He pushed me to my knees on the Emperor's polished floor, and the two monarchs watched impassively as I wept in my beautiful blue dress, though the Empress let a pale hand flutter to her throat. My father put the spade to my neck and scraped it up, across my skin, like a barber giving a young man his first shave.

A shower of sugar fell glittering across my chest.

"I never lied to you, Costanze," he murmured in my ear.

He pierced my cheek with the tip of the spade, and blood trickled down my chin, over my lips. It tasted like raspberries.

"Look at her, your Majesty. She is nothing but sugar, nothing but candy, through and through. I made her in my own oven. I raised her up. Now she is grown—and so beautiful! Look at her cinnamon hair, her marzipan skin, her tears of sugar and salt! And you may have her, you may have the greatest confection made on this earth, if you will but let me come home, and make you chocolates as I used to, and put your hand to my shoulder in friendship again."

The Empress rose from her throne and walked towards me, like a mirror gliding on a hidden track, so like me she was, though her gown was golden, and its train longer than the hall. She looked at me, her gaze pointed and deep, but did not seem to hear my sobbing, or see my tears. She put her hand to my bleeding cheek, and tasted the blood on her palm, daintily, with the tip of her tongue.

"She looks so much like me, Alonzo. It is a strange thing to see."

My father flushed. "I was lonely," he whispered. "And perhaps a man may be forgiven for casting a doll's face in the image of God."

I was kept in the kitchens, hung up on the wall like a copper pot, or a length of garlic. Every day a cook would clip my fingernails to sweeten the Emperor's coffee, or cut off a curl of my scarlet hair to spice the Easter cakes of the Empress's first child—a boy with bark-brown eyes. Sometimes, the head cook would lance my cheek carefully and collect the scarlet syrup in a hard white cup. Once, they plucked my eyelashes, ever so gently for a licorice comfit the Empress' new daughter craved. They were kind enough to ice my lids between plucking. They tried not to cause me any pain. Cooks and confectioners are not wicked creatures by nature, and the younger kitchen girls were disturbed by the shape of me hanging there, toes pointed at the oven. Eventually, they grew accustomed to it, and I was no more strange to them than a shaker of salt or a pepper mill. My dress sagged and browned, as blueberry skins will do, and fell away. A kind little boy who scrubbed the floors brought me a coarse black dress from his mother's closet. It was made of wool, real wool, from a sheep and not an oven. They fed me radishes and carrots and potatoes, and sometimes chicken, sometimes even fish, on a plate of real porcelain, with no heat-bubbles in it, none at all.

I grew old on that wall, my marzipan-skin withered and wrinkled no less than flesh, helped along by lancings and scrapings and trimmings. My hair turned white and fell out, eagerly collected. As I grew old, I was told that the Emperor liked the taste of my hair better and better, and soon I was bald.

But Emperors die, and so do fathers. Both of these occurred in their way, and when at last the Empress died, there was no one to remember that the source of the palace sugar was not a far-off isle, under a red sun that burned on the face of the sea. I thought of that red sun often on the wall, and the children cutting cane, and the taste of the bird's marrow deep in my plum. That same kind floor-scrubber, grown up and promoted to butler, cut me down when my bones were brittle, and touched my shorn hair gently. But he did not apologize. How could he? How many cakes and teas had he tasted which were sweetened by me?

I ran from the palace in the night, as much as I could run, an old, scraped-out crone, a witch in a black dress stumbling across the city and through, across and out. I kept running and running, my sugar-body burning and shrieking with disuse. I ran past the hard, white streets and past the villages where I had been a child who knew nothing of Vienna, into the woods, into the black forest with the creeping loam and nothing sweet for miles. Only there did I stop, panting, my spiced breath fogging in the air. There were great, dark, green boughs arching over me, pine and larch and oak. I sank down to the earth, wrung dry of weeping, safe and far from anything hard, anything white, anything with accusing eyes and a throne like a demon's wedding. No one would scrape me for teatime again. No one would touch me again. I put my hands to my head and stared up at the stars though the leaves. It was quiet, at last, quiet and dark. I curled up on the leaves and slept.

When I woke, I was cold. I shivered. I needed more than a black dress to cover me. I would not go back, not to any place which had known me, not to Vienna, not to a village without a candy-maker. I would not hang a sign over a door and feed sweets to children. I would stay, in the dark, under the green. And so I needed a house. But I knew nothing of houses. I was not a bricklayer or a thatcher. I did not know how to make a chimney. I did not know how to make a door-hinge. I did not know how to stitch curtains.

But I knew how to make candy.

I went begging in the villages, a harmless old crone—was it odd that she asked for sugar and not for coins? Certainly. Did they think it mad that she begged for berries and liquors and cocoa, but never alms? Of course. But the elderly are strange and their ways inexplicable to the young. I collected, just as they had done to me all my years on the wall, and my hair grew. I went to my place in the forest, under the black and the boughs, and I poured a foundation of caramel. I raised up thick, brown gingerbread walls, with cinnamon for wattle and marshmallow for daub. Hard-crack windows clear as the morning air, a smoking licorice chimney, stairs of peanut brittle and carpets of red taffy, a peppermint bathtub. And a great black oven, all of blackened, burnt sugar, with a yellow flame within. Gumdrops studded my house like jewels, and a little path of molasses ran liquid and dark from my door. And when my hair had grown long enough, I thatched my roof with cinnamon strands.

It had such a delicate architecture, my house, which I baked and built, as delicate as I had. I thought of my father all the while, and the red sun on waving green cane. I thought of him while I built my pastry-table, and I thought of him while I built my gingerbread floors. I hated and loved him in turns, as witches will do, for our hearts are strange and inexplicable. He had never come to see me on the wall, even once. I could not understand it. But I made my caramel bricks and I rolled out sheets of toffee onto my bed, and I told his ghost that I was a good girl, I had always been a good girl, even on the wall.

I made a pillow of spun sugar. I made plates of butterscotch. Each morning I tapped a marzipan egg with a little toffee-hammer. But I never caught a sparrow for my plums. They are so very quick. I was always hungry for them, for something living, and salty, and sweet amid all my sugar. I longed for something alive in my crystalline house, something to remind me of the children crushing up cane with tan, strong hands. There was no marrow in my plums. I could not remember the red sun and the long, green stalks, and so I bent low in my lollipop rocking-chair, weeping and whispering to my father that I was sorry, I was sorry, I was no more than a pig snuffling in the leaves, after all.

And one morning, when it was very bright, and the light came through the window like a viola playing something very sweet and sad, I heard footsteps coming up my molasses-path. Children: a boy and a girl. They laughed, and over their heads blackbirds cawed hungrily.

I was hungry, too.

THE CAT WHO WALKED A THOUSAND MILES
KIJ JOHNSON

Kij Johnson is also the author of "Spar" which appears earlier in this book.

Chapter 1

The Garden

At a time now past, a cat was born. This was not so long after the first cats came to Japan, so they were rare and mostly lived near the capital city.

This cat was the smallest of her litter of four. Her fur had been dark when she was born, but as she grew it changed to black with speckles of cinnamon and ivory, and a little gold-colored chin. Her eyes were gold, like a fox's.

She lived in the gardens of a great house in the capital. They filled a city block and the house had been very fine once, but that was many years ago. The owners moved to a new home in a more important part of the city, and left the house to suffer fires and droughts and earthquakes and neglect.

Now there was very little left that a person might think of as home. The main house still stood, but the roofs leaked and had fallen in places. Furry green moss covered the walls. Many of the storehouses and other buildings were barely more than piles of wood. Ivy filled the garden, and water weeds choked the three little lakes and the stream.

But it was a perfect home for cats. The stone wall around the garden kept people and dogs away. Inside, cats could find ten thousand things to do. There were trees and walls to climb, bushes to hide under, corners to sleep in.

There was food everywhere. Delicious mice skittered across the ground and crunchy crickets hopped in the grass. The stream was full of slow, fat frogs. Birds lived in the trees, and occasionally a stupid one came within reach.

The little cat shared the grounds with a handful of other female cats. Each adult claimed part of the gardens, where she hunted and bore her kittens alone. The private places all met at the center like petals on a flower, in a courtyard beside the main house. The cats liked to gather here and sleep on sunny days, or to groom or watch the kittens playing. No males lived in the garden, except for boy-kittens who had not gotten old enough to start their prowling; but tomcats visited, and a while later there were new kittens.

The cats shared another thing: their *fudoki*. The fudoki was the collection of stories about all the cats who had lived in a place. It described what made it a home, and what made the cats a family. Mothers taught their kittens the fudoki. If the mother died too soon, the other cats, the aunts and cousins, would teach the kittens. A cat with no fudoki was a cat with no family, no home, and no roots. The small cat's fudoki was many cats long, and she knew them all—The Cat From The North, The Cat Born The Year The Star Fell, The Dog-Chasing Cat.

Her favorite was The Cat From The North. She had been her mother's mother's mother's aunt, and her life seemed very exciting. As a kitten she lived beside a great hill to the north. She got lost when a dog chased her and tried to find her way home. She escaped many adventures. Giant oxen nearly stepped on her, and cart-wheels almost crushed her. A pack of wild dogs chased her into a tree and waited an entire day for her to come down. She was insulted by a goat that lived in a park, and stole food from people. She met a boy, but she ran away when he tried to pull her tail.

At last she came to the garden. The cats there called her The Cat From The North, and as such she became part of the little cat's fudoki.

The ancestors and the aunts were all clever and strong and resourceful. More than anything, the little cat wanted to earn the right for her story and name to be remembered alongside theirs. And when she had kittens, she would be part of the fudoki that they would pass on to their own kittens.

The other cats had started calling her Small Cat. It wasn't an actual name, but it was the beginning. She knew she would have a story worth telling someday.

Chapter 2

The Earthquake

One day, it was beautiful and very hot. It was August, but the first leaf in the garden had turned bright yellow overnight. A duck bobbed on the lake just out of reach, but the cats were too lazy to care, dozing in the courtyard or under the shadow of the trees. A mother cat held down her kitten with one paw as she licked her ears clean, telling her the fudoki as she did so. Small Cat wrestled, not very hard, with an orange striped male almost old enough to leave the garden.

A wind started. The duck on the lake burst upward with a flurry of wings, quacking with panic. Small Cat watched it race across the sky, puzzled. There was nothing to scare the duck, so why was it so frightened?

Suddenly the ground heaved underfoot: an earthquake. Small Cat crouched to keep her balance while the ground shook, as if it were a giant animal waking up and she were just a flea clinging to its hide. Tree branches clashed against one another. Leaves rustled and rained down. Just beyond the garden walls, people shouted, dogs barked, horses whinnied. There was a crashing noise like a pile of pottery falling from a cart (which is exactly what it was). A temple bell rang, tossed about in its frame. And the strangest sound of all: the ground itself groaned as roots and rocks were pulled about.

The older cats had been through earthquakes before, so they crouched wherever they were, waiting for it to end. Small Cat knew of earthquakes through the stories, but she'd never felt one. She hissed and looked for somewhere safe to run, but everything around her rose and fell. It was *wrong* for the earth to move.

The old house cracked and boomed like river ice breaking up in the spring. Blue pottery tiles slid from the roof to shatter in the dirt. A wooden beam in the main house broke in half with a cloud of flying splinters. The roof collapsed in on itself, and crashed into the building with a wave of white dust. The crash was too much for even the most experienced cats, and they ran in every direction.

Small Cat staggered and fell. Cones and needles rained down on Small Cat from a huge cedar tree. It was shaking, but trees shook all the time in the wind, so maybe it would be safer up there. She bolted up the trunk. She ran through an abandoned birds' nest tucked on a branch, the babies grown and flown away and the adults nowhere to be found. A terrified squirrel chattered as she passed it, more upset by Small Cat than the earthquake.

Small Cat paused and looked down. The ground had stopped moving. As the dust settled, she saw most of the house and garden. The courtyard was piled with beams and branches, but there was still an open space to gather and tell stories, and new places to hunt or play hide-and-seek. It was still home.

Aunts and cousins emerged from their hiding places, slinking or creeping or just trotting out. They were too dusty to tell who was who, except for The Cat With No Tail, who sniffed and pawed at a fallen door. Other cats hunched in the remains of the courtyard, or paced about the garden, or groomed themselves as much for comfort as to remove the dirt. She didn't see everyone.

She fell asleep the way kittens do, suddenly and all at once, and wherever they happen to be. She had been so afraid during the earthquake that she fell asleep lying flat on a broad branch with her claws sunk into the bark.

When she woke up with her whiskers twitching, the sun was lower in the sky. What had awakened her? The air had a new smell, bitter and unpleasant. She wrinkled her nose and sneezed.

She crept along a branch until she saw out past the tree's needles and over the garden's stone wall.

The city was on fire.

Chapter 3

The Fire

Fires in the capital were even more common than earthquakes. Buildings there were made of wood, with paper screens and bamboo blinds and straw mats on the floor. And in August the gardens were dry, the weeds so parched that they broke like twigs.

In a home far southeast of Small Cat's home, a lamp tipped over in the earthquake. No one noticed until the fire leapt to a bamboo blind and then to the wall and from there into the garden. By that time it couldn't be stopped.

Smoke streamed up across the city: thin white smoke where grass sizzled, thick gray plumes where some great house burned. The smoke concealed most of the fire, though in places the flames were as tall as trees. People fled through the streets wailing or shouting, their animals adding to the din. But beneath those noises, even at this distance the fire roared.

Should she go down? Other cats in the fudoki had survived fires—The Fire-Tailed Cat, The Cat Who Found The Jewel—but the stories didn't say what she should do. Maybe one of her aunts or cousins could tell her, but where were they?

Smoke drifted into the garden.

She climbed down and meowed loudly. No one answered, but a movement caught her eye. One of her aunts, The Painted Cat, trotted toward a hole in the wall, her ears pinned back and tail low. Small Cat scrambled after her. A gust of smoky wind blew into her face. She squeezed her eyes tight, coughing and gasping. When she could see again, her aunt had gone.

She retreated up the tree and watched houses catch fire. At first smoke poured from their roofs, and then flames roared up and turned each building into a pillar of fire. Each house was closer than the last. The smoke grew so thick that she could only breathe by pressing her nose into her fur and panting.

Her house caught fire just as the sky grew dark. Cinders rained on her garden, and the grass beside the lake hissed as it burned, like angry kittens. The fires in the garden crawled up the walls and slipped inside the doors. Smoke gushed through the broken roof. Something collapsed inside the house with a huge noise and the flames shot up, higher even than the top of Small Cat's tree.

The air was too hot to breathe. She moved to the opposite side of the tree and dug her claws into the bark, as deep as they would go, and huddled down, as small as she could get.

Fire doesn't always burn everything in its path. It can leave an area untouched, surrounded by nothing but smoking ruins. The house burned until it was just blackened beams and ashes. Small Cat's tree beside it got charred, but the highest branches stayed safe.

Small Cat stayed there all night long, and by dawn, the tall flames in the garden were gone and the smoke didn't seem so thick. At first she couldn't get her claws to let go, or her muscles to carry her, but at last she managed to climb down.

Much of the house remained, but it was roofless now, hollowed out and charred. Other buildings were no more than piles of smoking black wood. With their leaves burned away, the trees looked like skeletons. The pretty bushes were all gone. Even the ground smoked in places, too hot to touch.

There was no sound of any sort: no morning songbirds, no people going about their business on the street. No cats. All she could hear was a small fire still burning in an outbuilding. She rubbed her sticky eyes against her shoulder.

She was very thirsty. She trotted to the stream, hopping from paw to paw on the hot ground. Chalky-white with ashes, the water tasted bitter, but she drank until her stomach was full. Then she was hungry, so she ate a dead bird she found beside the stream, burnt feathers and all.

From the corner of her eye, she caught something stirring inside a storehouse. Maybe it was an aunt who had hidden during the fire, or maybe The Painted Cat had come back to help her. She ran across the hot ground and into the storehouse, but there was no cat. What had she seen? There, in a window, she saw the motion again, but it was just an old bamboo curtain.

She searched everywhere. The only living creature she saw was a soaked rat climbing from the stream. It shook itself and ran beneath a fallen beam, leaving nothing but tiny, wet pawprints in the ashes.

She found no cats, or any signs of what had happened to them.

Chapter 4

The Burnt Paws

Cats groom themselves when they're upset, so Small Cat sat down to clean her fur, making a face at the bitter taste of the ashes. For comfort, she recited the stories from the fudoki: The Cat Who Ate Roots, The Three-Legged Cat, The Cat Who Hid Things—every cat all the way down to The Cat Who Swam, her youngest aunt, who had just taken her place in the fudoki.

The fudoki was more than just stories. The cats of the past had claimed the garden and made it home for those who lived there now. If the cats were gone, was this still home? Was it still her garden, if nothing looked the same and it all smelled like smoke? Logs and broken roof tiles filled the courtyard. The house was a ruin. There were no frogs, no insects, no fat ducks, no mice. No cats.

Small Cat cleaned her ear with a paw, thinking hard. No, she wasn't alone. She didn't know where the other cats had gone, but she had seen The Painted Cat just before the fire. If Small Cat could find her, there would be two cats, and that would be better than one. The Painted Cat would know what to do.

A big fallen branch leaned against the wall, just where the hole was. She inched carefully across the ground which was still hot in places, twisting her face away from the fumes wherever something smoked. There was no way to follow The Painted Cat by pushing through the hole. Small Cat didn't mind that: she had always liked sitting on top of the wall, watching the outside world. She crawled up the branch.

There were people on the street, carrying bundles or boxes or crying babies. Many of them looked lost or frightened. A wagon pulled by a single ox passed, and a cart pushed by a man and two boys, heaped high with possessions. A stray flock of geese clustered around a tipped cart, eating fallen rice. Even the dogs looked weary.

There was no sign of The Painted Cat. Small Cat climbed higher.

The branch cracked in half. She crashed to the ground and landed on her side on a hot rock. She twisted upright and jumped away from the terrible pain; but when she landed, it was with all four paws on a smoldering beam. She howled and started running. Every time she put a foot down, the agony made her run faster. She bolted across the broad street and through the next garden, and the next.

Small Cat stopped when her exhaustion got stronger than her pain. She made it off the road—barely—before she slumped to the ground and she was asleep immediately. People and carts and even dogs tramped past, but no one bothered her, a small, filthy cat lying in the open, looking dead.

When she woke up, she was surrounded by noise and tumult. Wheels rolled past her head. She jumped up, her claws out. The searing pain in her paws made her almost forget herself again, but she managed to limp to a clump of weeds.

Where was she? Nothing looked or smelled familiar. She didn't recognize the street or the buildings. She did not know that she had run nearly a mile in her panic, but she knew she would never find her way back.

She had collapsed beside an open market. Even so soon after the earthquake and fire, merchants set up new booths to sell things, rice and squash and tea and pots. Even after a great disaster, people are hungry, and broken pots always need to be replaced.

If there was food for people, there would be food for cats. Small Cat limped through the market, staying away from the big feet of the people. She stole a little silver fish from a stall and crept inside a broken basket to eat it. When she was done, she licked her burnt paws clean.

She had lost The Painted Cat, and now she had lost the garden. The stories were all she had left. But the stories were not enough without the garden and the other cats. They were just a list. If everyone and everything was gone, did she even have a home? She could not help the cry of sadness that escaped her.

It was her fudoki now, hers alone. She had to find a way to make it continue.

Chapter 5

The Strange Cats

Small Cat was very careful to keep her paws clean as they healed. For the first few days, she only left her basket when she was hungry or thirsty. It was hard to hunt mice, so she ate things she found on the ground: fish, rice, once even an entire goose-wing. Sad as she was, she found interesting things to do as she got stronger. Fishtails were fun to bat at, and she liked to crawl under tables of linen and hemp fabric and tug the threads that hung over the edges.

As she got better, she began to search for her garden. Since she didn't know where she was going, she wandered, hoping that something would look familiar. Her nose didn't help, for she couldn't smell anything but smoke for days. She was slow on her healing paws. She stayed close to trees and walls because she couldn't run fast and had to be careful about dogs.

There was a day when Small Cat limped along an alley so narrow that the roofs on either side met overhead. She had seen a mouse run down the alley and vanish into a gap between two walls. She wasn't going to catch it by chasing it, but she could always wait in the gap beside its hole until it emerged. Her mouth watered.

Someone hissed. Another cat squeezed out the gap, a striped gray female with a mouse in her mouth. Her mouse! Small Cat couldn't help but growl and flatten her ears. The stranger hissed, arched her back, and ran away.

Small Cat trailed after the stranger with her heart beating so hard she could barely hear the street noises. She had not seen a single cat since the fire. One cat might mean many cats. Losing the mouse would be a small price to pay for that.

The stranger spun around. "Stop following me!" she said through a mouthful of mouse. Small Cat sat down instantly and looked off into the distance, as if she just happened to be traveling the same direction. The stranger glared and stalked off. Small Cat jumped up and followed. Every few steps the stranger whirled, and Small Cat pretended not to be there; but after a while, the stranger gave up and trotted to a tall bamboo fence, her tail bristling with annoyance. With a final hiss, she squeezed under the fence. Small Cat waited a moment before following.

She was behind a tavern, in a small yard filled with barrels. And cats! There were six of them that she could see, and she knew others would be in their private ranges, prowling or sleeping. She meowed with excitement. She could teach them her fudoki and they would become her family. She would have a home again.

Cats don't like new things much. The strangers all stared at her, every ear flattened, every tail bushy. "I don't know why she followed me," the striped cat said sullenly. "Go away!" The others hissed agreement: "No one wants *you*."

Small Cat backed out under the bamboo fence, but she didn't leave. Every day she came to the tavern yard. At first the strange cats drove her off with scratches and hisses, but she always returned to try again, and each time she got closer before they attacked her. After a while they ignored her and she came closer still.

One day the strange cats gathered beneath a little roof attached to the back of the tavern. It was raining, so when Small Cat jumped onto a stack of barrels under the roof, no one seemed to think it was worthwhile chasing her away.

The oldest cat, a female with black fur growing thin, was teaching the kittens their fudoki. The stories were told in the correct way: The Cat Inside The Lute, The Cat Born With One Eye, The Cat Who Bargained With A Flea. But these strangers didn't know the right cats: The Cat From The North, or The Cat Who Chased Foxes, or any of the others. Small Cat jumped down, wanting to share.

The oldest cat looked sidelong at her. "Are you ready to learn our stories?"

Small Cat felt as though she'd been kicked. Her fudoki would never belong here! These strangers had their own stories, for different aunts and ancestors and for a different place. If she stayed, she would no longer be a garden cat, but a cat in the tavern yard's stories, The Cat After The Fire or The Burnt-Paw Cat. If she had kittens, they would learn about the aunts and ancestors of the tavern-yard cats. There would be no room for her own.

She arched and backed away, tail shivering, teeth bared, and when she was far enough from the terrible stories, she turned and ran.

Chapter 6
The Rajo Gate

Small Cat came to the Rajo Gate at sunset. Rain fell on her back, so light that it didn't soak through but just slid from her fur in drops. She inspected the weeds beside the street as she walked: she had eaten three mice for dinner but a fourth would make a nice snack.

She looked up and saw a vast dark building looming ahead, a hundred feet wide and taller than the tallest tree she had ever seen, made of wood that had turned black with age. There were actually three gates in Rajo Gate. The smallest one was fifteen feet high and wide enough for ox-carts, and it was the only one still open.

A guard stood by the door, holding a corner of a cape over his head against the rain. "Gate closes at sunset," he shouted. "No one wants to be wet all night. Hurry it up!" People crowded through. A man carrying geese tied together by their feet narrowly missed a fat woman carrying a bundle of blue fabric and dragging a goat on a rope.

The guard bent down. "What about you, miss?" Small Cat pulled back. Usually no one noticed her, but he was talking to her, smiling and wiggling his fingers. Should she bite him? Run? Smell his hand? She leaned forward, trembling but curious.

Through the gate behind him she saw a wide, busy road half-hidden by the rain. The guard pointed. "That's the Tokaido," he said, as if she had asked a question. "The Great North Road. It starts right here, and it goes all the way to the end of Japan." He shrugged. "Maybe farther. Who knows?"

North! She had never thought about it before this, but The Cat From The North must have come from somewhere, before she became part of Small Cat's fudoki. And if she came *from* somewhere, Small Cat could go there. There would be cats, and they would have to accept her—and they would have to accept a fudoki that included one of their own.

Unfortunately, The Cat From The North's story didn't say where the North was. Small Cat kneaded the ground, uncertain.

The guard straightened and shouted, "Last warning!" Looking down, he added in a softer voice, "That means you, too. Stay or go?"

Suddenly deciding, she dashed through the gate, into the path of an ox cart. A wheel rolled by her head, close enough to bend her whiskers back. She scrambled out of the way—and tumbled in front of a man on horseback. The horse shied as Small Cat leapt aside. She felt a hoof brush her whiskers. Small Cat streaked into the nearest yard and crouched beneath a wagon, panting.

The gate shut with a great crash. She was outside.

The rain got harder as the sky dimmed. She needed a place to rest and think, out from underfoot until morning. She explored warily, avoiding a team of steaming oxen that entered the yard. She was in an inn yard full of wagons. Light shone from the inn's paper windows, and the sound of laughter and voices poured out. Too busy. The back of the building was quiet and unlit, with a single window cracked open to let in the night air. Perfect. She jumped onto the sill.

A voice screeched inside the room, and a heavy object hurtled past her head. Small Cat fell from the sill and bolted back to the wagon. Maybe not so perfect.

But where else could she go? She couldn't stay here because someone would step on her. Everything she might climb onto was wet. And she didn't much want to hide in the forest behind the inn: it smelled strange and deep and frightening, and night is not the best time for adventures. But there was a promising square shape in a corner of the yard.

It was a small shed with a shingled roof, knee high to a person and open in front: a roadside shrine to a kami. Kami are the spirits and gods that exist everywhere in Japan, and their shrines can be as large as palaces or as small as a doll's house. She pushed her head into the shed. Inside was an even smaller building, barely bigger than she was. This was the shrine itself, and its doors were shut tight. Two stone foxes stood on either side of a ledge with little bowls and pots. She smelled cooked rice.

"Are you worshipping the kami?" a voice said behind her. She whirled, backed into the shed, and knocked over the rice.

A Buddhist monk stood in the yard. He was very tall and thin and wore a straw cape over his red and yellow robes, and a pointed straw hat on his head. He looked like a pile of wet hay, except for his smiling face.

"Are you catching mice, or just praying to catch some?"

The monk worshipped Buddha, who had been a very wise man who taught people how to live properly. But the monk also respected Shinto, which is the religion of the kami. Shinto and Buddhism did not war between themselves, and many Buddhist temples had Shinto shrines on their grounds. And so the monk was happy to see a cat do something so wise.

Small Cat had no idea of any of this. She watched suspiciously as he put down his basket to place his hands together and murmur for a moment. "There," he said, "I have told the Buddha about you. I am sure he will help you find what you seek." And he bowed and took his basket and left her alone, her whiskers twitching in puzzlement.

She fell asleep curled against the shrine in the shed, still thinking about the monk. And in the morning, she headed north along the Tokaido.

Chapter 7
The Tokaido

At first the Tokaido looked a lot like the streets within the city. It was packed earth just as the streets had been, fringed with buildings, and overshadowed by trees so close that they dropped needles onto the road. She recognized most of the sorts of buildings, but some she had never seen before, houses like barns where people and animals lived under a single high thatched roof.

At first she stayed in the brush beside the road and hid whenever anything approached—and there was always something. People crowded the Tokaido: peasants and carpenters and charcoal-sellers, monks and nurses. There were carts and wagons, honking geese and quacking ducks. She saw a man on horseback, and a very small boy leading a giant black ox by a ring through its nose. Everyone (except the ox) seemed in a hurry to get somewhere else, and then to get back from there, just as fast as they could.

She stayed out of their way until she realized that no one had paid any attention to her since the guard and the monk, back at the Rajo Gate. Even if they did notice her, everyone was too busy to bother with her. Well, everyone except dogs, anyway, and she knew what to do about dogs: make herself look large and then get out of reach.

The Tokaido followed a broad valley divided into fields and dotted with trees and farmhouses. The mountains beyond that were dark with pine and cedar trees, with bright larches and birch trees among them. As she traveled, the road left the valley and crossed hills and other valleys. There were fewer buildings and more fields and forests and lakes. The Tokaido grew narrower and other roads and lanes left it, but she always knew where to go. North.

She did leave the road a few times, when curiosity drove her.

In one place, where the road clung to the side of a wooded valley, a rough stone staircase climbed up into the forest. She glimpsed the flicker of a red flag. It was a hot day, maybe the last hot day before autumn and then winter settled in. She might not have investigated, except that the stairs looked cool and shady.

She padded into a graveled yard surrounded by red flags. There was a large Shinto shrine and many smaller shrines and buildings. She walked through the grounds, sniffing statues and checking offering bowls to see if they were empty. Acolytes washed the floor of the biggest shrine. She made a face—too much water for her—and returned to the road.

Another time, she heard a crowd of people approaching, and she hid herself in a bush. It was a row of sedan chairs, which looked exactly like people-sized boxes carried on poles by two strong men each. Other servants tramped along. The chairs smelled of sandalwood perfume.

The chairs and servants turned onto a narrow lane. Small Cat followed them to a Buddhist monastery with many gardens, where monks and other people could worship the Buddha and his servants. The sedan chairs stopped in front of a building, and then nothing happened.

Small Cat prowled around inside, but no one did much in there either, mostly just knelt and chanted. There were many monks, but none of them was the monk who had spoken to her beside the tiny shrine. She was coming to realize that there were many monks in the world.

To sleep, she hid in storehouses, boxes, barns, the attics where people kept silkworms in the spring—any place that would keep the rain off and some of her warmth in. But sometimes it was hard to find safe places to sleep: one afternoon, she was almost caught by a fox, who had found her half-buried inside a loose pile of straw.

And there was one gray, windy day when she napped in a barn, in a coil of rope beside the oxen. She awoke when a huge black cat leapt on her and scratched her face.

"Leave or I will kill you," the black cat snarled. "I am The Cat Who Killed A Hawk!"

Small Cat ran. She knew The Cat From The North could not have been family to so savage a cat. After The Cat Who Killed A Hawk, she saw no more cats.

She got used to her wandering life. At first she did not travel far each day, but she soon learned that a resourceful cat could hop into the back of a cart just setting off northward, and get many miles along her way without lifting a paw.

There was food everywhere, fat squirrels and absent-minded birds, mice and voles. She loved the tasty crunch of crickets and beetles, easy to catch as the weather got colder. She stole food from storehouses and trash heaps, and even learned to eat vegetables. There were lots of things to play with, as well. She didn't have other cats to wrestle, but mice were a constant amusement, as was teasing dogs.

"North" was turning out to be a long way away. Day followed day and still the Tokaido went on. She did not notice how long she had been traveling. There was always another town or village or farmhouse, always something else to eat or look at or play with. The leaves on the trees turned red and orange and yellow, and fell to crackle under Small Cat's feet. Evenings were colder. Her fur got thicker.

She recited the stories of her fudoki as she walked. Someday, she would get to wherever The Cat From The North came from, and she wanted to have them right.

Chapter 8

The Approach

One morning a month into her journey, Small Cat awoke in the attic of an old farmhouse. When she had stopped the night before, it was foggy and cold, as more and more nights were lately. She had wanted to sleep near the big charcoal brazier at the house's center, but an old dog dozed there and Small Cat worried that he might wake up. It had seemed smarter to slip upstairs and sleep there, where the floor was warm above the brazier.

Small Cat stretched and scrubbed her whiskers with a paw. What sort of day was it? She saw a triangular opening in the thatched roof overhead, where smoke could leave. It was easy enough to climb up and peek out.

It would be a beautiful day. The fog was thinning, and the sky glowed pale pink with dawn. The farmhouse was on a plain near a broad river, with fields of wheat ready to be harvested, and beyond everything the dim outlines of mountains, just beginning to appear as the light grew. She could see that the Tokaido meandered across the plain, narrow because there was not very much traffic here.

The sun rose and daylight poured across the valley. And there, far in the distance, was a mountain bigger than anything Small Cat had ever seen, so big it dwarfed every other mountain. This was Mt. Fuji-san, the great mountain of Japan. It was still more than a hundred miles away, though she didn't know that.

Small Cat had seen many mountains, but Fuji-san was different: a perfect snow-covered cone with a thin line of smoke that rose straight into the sky. Fuji-san was a volcano, though it had been many years since it had erupted. The ice on its peak never melted. Snow came halfway down its slopes.

Could that be where The Cat From The North had begun? She had come from a big hill, the story said. This was so much more than a hill, but the Tokaido seemed to lead toward Fuji-san. Even if it weren't The Cat From The North's home, surely Small Cat would be able to see her hill from a mountain that high.

That day Small Cat didn't linger over her morning grooming, and she ate a squirrel without playing with it. In no time at all, she trotted down the road. And even when the sky grew heavy the next day and she could no longer see Fuji-san, she kept going.

It was fall now, so there was more rain and whole days of fog. In the mornings puddles had a skin of ice, but her thick fur kept her warm. She was too impatient to do all the traveling on her own paws, so she stole rides on wagons. The miles added up, eight or even ten in a day.

The farmers finished gathering their buckwheat and rice and the root vegetables that would feed them for the winter, and set their pigs loose in the fields to eat the stubble. Small Cat caught the sparrows that joined them. After the first time, she always remembered to pull off the feathers before eating.

But she was careful. The people here had never even heard of cats. She frightened a small boy so much that he fell from a fence, screaming, "Demon! A demon!" Small Cat fled before the parents arrived. Another night, a frightened grandfather threw hot coals at her. A spark caught in her fur, and Small Cat ran into the darkness in panic, remembering the fire that destroyed her home. She slept cold and wet that night under a pile of logs. After that, Small Cat made sure not to be seen again.

Fuji-san was almost always hidden by *something*. Even when there was a break in the forests and the mountains, the low never-ending clouds concealed it. Then there was a long period when she saw no farther than the next turn of the road, everything gray in the pouring rain. She trudged on, cold and miserable. Water dribbled from her whiskers and drooping tail. She couldn't decide which was worse, walking down the middle of the road so that the trees overhead dropped cold water on her back, or brushing through the weeds beside the road and soaking her belly. She groomed herself whenever she could, but even so she was always muddy.

The longer this went, the more she turned to stories. But these were not the stories of her aunts and ancestors, the stories that taught Small Cat what home was like. She made up her own stories, about The Cat From The North's home, and how well Small Cat would fit in there, how thrilled everyone would be to meet her.

After many days of this, she was filthy and frustrated. She couldn't see anything but trees, and the fallen leaves underfoot were an awful-feeling slippery, sticky brown mass. The Tokaido seemed to go on forever.

Had she lost the mountain?

The sky cleared as she came up a long hill. She quickened her pace. Once she got to the top, she might see a village nearby. She was tired of mice and sparrows; cooked fish would taste good.

She came to the top of the hill and sat down, hard. She hadn't lost the mountain. There was no way she could possibly lose the mountain. Fuji-san seemed to fill the entire sky, so high that she tipped her head to see the top. It was whiter now, for the clouds that rained on the Tokaido had snowed on Fuji-san. Small Cat would see the entire world from a mountain that tall.

Chapter 9
Mt. Fuji-san

Fuji-san loomed to the north, closer and bigger each time Small Cat saw it. The Tokaido threaded through the forested hills and came to a river valley that ended on a large plain. She was only a short way across the plain when she had to leave the Tokaido, for the road skirted the mountain, going east instead of north.

The plain was famous for its horses, which were praised even in the capital for their beauty and courage. Small Cat tried to stay far from the galloping hooves of the herds, but the horses were fast and she was not. She woke up one day to find herself less than a foot from a pair of nostrils bigger than her entire body—a red mare snuffling the weeds where she hid. Small Cat leapt in the air, the mare jumped back, and they pelted in opposite directions, tails streaming behind them. Horses and cats are both curious, but there is such a thing as too much adventure.

She traveled as quickly as a small cat can when she is eager to get somewhere. The mountain towered over her, its white slopes leading into the sky. The bigger it got, the more certain she was that she would climb to the top of Fuji-san, she would see The Cat From The North's home, and everything would be perfect. She wanted this to be true so much that she ignored all the doubts that came to her —What if she *couldn't* find them? What if she was already too far north, or not north enough? Or if they didn't want her?

And because she was ignoring so many important things, she started ignoring other important things, as well. She stopped being careful where she walked, and she scraped her paws raw on the rough rock. She got careless about her grooming, and her fur grew dirty and matted. She stopped repeating the stories of her fudoki, and instead, just told the fantasy-stories of how she wanted everything to be.

The climb went on and on. She trudged through the forests, her nose pointed up the slope. The narrow road she followed turned to a lane and then a path and started zigzagging through the rock outcroppings everywhere. The mountain was always visible now because she was on it.

There were only a few people, just hunters and once a small, tired woman in a blue robe lined with feathers, who had a bundle on her back. But she saw strange animals everywhere: deer almost small enough to catch, and white goats with long beards that stared down their noses at her. Once, a troop of pink-faced monkeys surprised her by tearing through the trees overhead, hurling jeers.

At last even the path ended, but Small Cat kept climbing through the trees until she saw daylight ahead. Maybe this was the top of Fuji-san. She hurried forward. The trees ended abruptly. She staggered sideways, hit by a frigid wind so strong that it threw her off her feet. There was nothing to stop the wind, for she had come to the tree line, and trees did not grow higher than this. She staggered to the sheltered side of a rock.

This wasn't the top. It was nowhere near the top. She was in a rounded basin cut into the mountain, and she could see all the way to the peak itself. The slope above her grew still steeper and craggier; and above that it became a smooth glacier. Wind pulled snow from the peak in white banners.

She looked the way she had come. The whole world seemed made of mountains. Except for the plain she had come across, mountains and hills stretched everywhere around her. All the villages she had passed were too far away to see, though wood smoke rose from the trees in places. She looked for the capital, but it was hundreds of miles away, so far away that there was nothing to see, not even the Rajo Gate.

She had never imagined that all those days and all those miles added up to something immense. She could never go back so far, and she could never find anything so small as a single hill, a single family of cats.

A flash of color caught her eye, a man huddled behind another rock just a few feet away. She had been so caught up in the mountain that she hadn't even noticed him. Under a padded brown coat, he wore the red and yellow robes of a Buddhist monk, with thick straw sandals tied tightly to his feet. His face was red with cold.

How had he gotten up here, and why? He was staring up the mountain as if trying to see a path, but why was he doing that? He saw her and his mouth made a circle of surprise. He crawled toward her and ducked into the shelter of her rock. They looked up at the mountain. "I didn't know it would be so far," he said, as if they were in the middle of a conversation.

She looked at him.

"We can try," he added. "I think we'll die, but sometimes pilgrimages are worth it."

They sat there for a while longer, as the sun grew lower and the wind grew colder. "But we don't have to," he said. "We can go back down and see what happens next."

They started off the mountain together.

Chapter 10
The Monk

Small Cat and the monk stayed together for a long time. In many ways they were alike, both journeying without a goal, free to travel as fast or as slow as they liked. Small Cat continued north because she had started on the Tokaido, and she might as well see what lay at the end of it. The monk went north because he could beg for rice and talk about the Buddha anywhere, and he liked adventures.

It was winter now, and a cold, snowy one. It seemed as though the sun barely rose before it set behind the mountains. The rivers they crossed were sluggish, the lakes covered with ice, smooth as the floorboards in a house. It seemed to snow every few days, sometimes clumps heavy enough to splat when they landed, sometimes tiny flakes so light they tickled her whiskers. Small Cat didn't like snow: it looked like feathers, but it just turned into water when it landed on her.

Small Cat liked traveling with the monk. When she had trouble wading through the snow, he let her hop onto the big straw basket he carried on his back. When he begged for rice, he shared whatever he got with her. She learned to eat bits of food from his fingers, and stuck her head into his bowl if he set it down. One day, she brought him a bird she had caught, as a gift. He didn't eat the bird, just looked sad and prayed for its fate. After that, she killed and ate her meals out of his sight.

The monk told stories as they walked. She lay comfortably on the basket and watched the road unroll slowly under his feet as she listened to stories about the Buddha's life and his search for wisdom and enlightenment. She didn't understand what enlightenment was, exactly, but it seemed very important, for the monk said he also was looking for it. Sometimes on nights when they didn't find anywhere to stay and had to shelter under the heavy branches of a pine tree, he told stories about himself as well, from when he was a child.

And then the Tokaido ended.

It was a day that even Small Cat could tell was about to finish in a storm, as the first flakes of snow whirled down from low, dark clouds that promised more to come. Small Cat huddled atop the basket on the monk's back, her face pressed into the space between her front paws. She didn't look up until the monk said, "There! We can sleep warm tonight."

There was a village at the bottom of the hill they were descending. The Tokaido led through a double handful of buildings scattered along the shore of a storm-tossed lake, but it ended at the water's edge. The opposite shore—if there was one—was hidden by snow and the gathering dusk. Now what? She mewed.

"Worried, little one?" the monk said over his shoulder. "You'll get there! Just be patient."

One big house rented rooms as if it were an inn. When the monk called out, a small woman with short black hair emerged and bowed many times. "Come in, come in! Get out of the weather." The monk took off his straw sandals and put down his basket with a sigh of relief. Small Cat leapt down and stretched.

The innkeeper screeched and snatched up a hoe to jab at Small Cat, who leapt behind the basket.

"Wait!" The monk put his hands out. "She's traveling with me."

The innkeeper lowered the hoe a bit. "Well, she's small, at least. What is she, then?"

The monk looked at Small Cat. "I'm not sure. She was on a pilgrimage when I found her, high on Fuji-san."

"Hmm," the woman said, but she put down the hoe. "Well, if she's with you…."

The wind drove through every crack and gap in the house. Everyone gathered around a big brazier set into the floor of the centermost room, surrounded by screens and shutters to keep out the cold. Besides the monk and Small Cat and the members of the household, there were two farmers—a young husband and wife—on their way north.

"Well, you're here for a while," the innkeeper said as she poured hot broth for everyone. "The ferry won't run for a day or two, until the storm's over."

Small Cat stretched out so close to the hot coals that her whiskers sizzled, but she was the only one who was warm enough. Everyone else huddled inside the screens. They ate rice and barley and dried fish cooked in pots that hung over the brazier.

She hunted for her own meals. The mice had gnawed a secret hole into a barrel of rice flour, so there were a lot of them. Whenever she found something she brought it back to the brazier's warmth, where she could listen to the people.

There was not much for them to do but talk and sing, so they talked and sang a lot. They shared fairy tales and ghost stories. They told stories about themselves or the people they knew. People had their own fudoki, Small Cat realized, though there seemed to be no order to the stories, and she didn't see yet how they made a place home. They sang love songs and funny songs about foolish adventurers, and Small Cat realized that songs were stories, as well.

At first the servants in the house kicked at Small Cat whenever she was close, but the monk stopped them.

"But she's a demon!" the young wife said.

"If she is," the monk said, "she means no harm. She has her own destiny. She deserves to be left in peace to fulfill it."

"What destiny is that?" the innkeeper asked.

"Do you know *your* destiny?" the monk asked. She shook her head, and slowly everyone else shook theirs, as well. The monk said, "Well, then. Why should she know hers?"

The young husband watched her eat her third mouse in as many hours. "Maybe catching mice is her destiny. Does she always do that? Catch mice?"

"Anything small," the monk said, "but mice are her favorite."

"That would be a useful animal for a farmer," the husband said. "Would you sell her?"

The monk frowned. "No one owns her. It's her choice where she goes."

The wife scratched at the floor, trying to coax Small Cat into playing. "Maybe she would come with us! She's so pretty." Small Cat batted at her fingers for a while before she curled up beside the brazier again. But the husband looked at Small Cat, thoughtfully.

Chapter 11
The Abduction

It was two days before the snowstorm stopped, and another day before the weather cleared enough for them to leave. Small Cat hopped onto the monk's straw basket and they left the inn, blinking in the daylight after so many days lit by dim lamps and the brazier.

Sparkling new snow hid everything, making it strange and beautiful. Waves rippled the lake, but the frothing white-caps whipped up by the storm had gone. The Tokaido, no more than a broad flat place in the snow, ended at a dock on the lake. A big man wearing a brown padded jacket and leggings made of fur took boxes from a boat tied there; two other men carried them into a covered shelter.

The Tokaido only went south from here, back the way she had come. A smaller road, still buried under the snow, followed the shore line to the east, but she couldn't see where the lake ended. The road might go on forever and *never* turn north. Small Cat mewed anxiously.

The monk turned his head a little. "Still eager to travel?" He pointed to the opposite shore. "They told me the road starts again on the other side. The boat's how we can get there."

Small Cat growled.

The farmers tramped down to the boat with their packs and four shaggy goats, tugging and bleating and cursing the way goats do. The boatman accepted their fare, counted out in old-fashioned coins, but he offered to take the monk for free. He frowned at Small Cat and said, "That thing, too, whatever it is."

The boat was the most horrible thing that had ever happened to Small Cat, worse than the earthquake, worse than the fire. It heaved and rocked, tipping this way and that. She crouched on top of a bundle with her claws sunk deep, drooling with nausea and meowing with panic. The goats jostled against one another, equally unhappy.

She would run if she could, but there was nowhere to go. They were surrounded by water in every direction, too far from the shore to swim. The monk offered to hold her, but she hissed and tried to scratch him. She kept her eyes fixed on the hills to the north as they grew closer.

The moment the boat bumped against the dock, she streaked ashore and crawled as far into a little roadside shrine as she could get.

"Sir!" A boy stood by the dock, hopping from foot to foot. He bobbed a bow at the monk. "My mother isn't well. I saw you coming, and was so happy! Could you please come see her, and pray for her?" The monk bowed in return, and the boy ran down the lane.

The monk knelt beside Small Cat's hiding place. "Do you want to come with me?" he asked. She stayed where she was, trembling. He looked a little sad. "All right, then. I'll be back in a bit."

"Oh sir, please hurry!" the boy shouted from down the lane.

The monk stood. "Be clever and brave, little one. And careful!" And he trotted after the boy.

From her hiding place, Small Cat watched the husband and the boatman wrestle the goats to shore. The wife walked to the roadside shrine and squatted in front of it, peering in.

"I saw you go hide," she said. "Were you frightened on the boat? I was. I have rice balls with meat. Would you like one?" She bowed to the kami of the shrine and pulled a packet from her bundle. She laid a bit of food in front of the shrine and bowed again. "There. Now some for you."

Small Cat inched forward. She felt better now, and it did smell nice.

"What did you find?" The farmer crouched behind his wife.

"The little demon," she said. "See?"

"Lost the monk, did you? Hmm." The farmer looked up and down the lane, and pulled an empty sack from his bundle. He bowed to the kami, reached in, and grabbed Small Cat by the scruff of her neck.

Nothing like this had ever happened to her! She yowled and scratched, but the farmer kept his grip and managed to stuff her into the sack. He lifted it to his shoulder and started walking.

She swung and bumped for a long time.

Chapter 12

The Farmhouse

Small Cat gave up fighting after a while, for she was squeezed too tightly in the sack to do anything but make herself even more uncomfortable; but she meowed until she was hoarse. It was cold in the sack. Light filtered in through the coarse weave, but she could see nothing. She could smell nothing but onions and goats.

Night fell before the jostling ended and she was carried indoors. Someone laid the sack on a flat surface and opened it: the farmer. Small Cat clawed him as she emerged. She was in a small room with a brazier. With a quick glance she saw a hiding place, and she stuffed herself into a corner where the roof and wall met.

The young husband and wife and two alarmed farmhands stood looking up at her, all wide eyes and opened mouths.

The husband sucked at the scratch marks on his hand. "She's not dangerous," he said, a little doubtfully. "Well, except for this. I think she is a demon for mice, not for us."

Small Cat stayed in her high place for two days. The wife put scraps of chicken skin and water on top of a huge trunk, but the people mostly ignored her. Though they didn't know it, this was the perfect way to treat a frightened cat in an unfamiliar place. Small Cat watched the activity of the farmhouse at first with suspicion and then with growing curiosity. At night, after everyone slept, she saw the mice sneak from their holes and her mouth watered.

By the third night, her thirst overcame her nervousness. She slipped down to drink. She heard mice in another room, and quickly caught two. She had just caught her third when she heard the husband rise.

"Demon?" he said softly. He came into the room. She backed into a corner with her mouse in her mouth. "There you are. I'm glad you caught your dinner." He chuckled. "We have plenty more, just like that. I hope you stay."

Small Cat did stay, though it was not home. She had never expected to travel with the monk forever, but she missed him anyway: sharing the food in his bowl, sleeping on his basket as they hiked along. She missed his warm hand when he stroked her.

Still, this was a good place to be, with many mice to eat and only a small yellow dog to fight her for them. No one threw things or cursed her. The people still thought she was a demon, but she was *their* demon now, as important a member of the household as the farmhands or the dog. And the farmhouse was large enough that she could get away from them all when she needed.

In any case, she didn't know how to get back to the road. The path had vanished with the next snowfall, so she had nowhere to go but the wintry fields and the forest.

Though she wouldn't let the farmer touch her, she liked to follow him and watch as he tended the ox and goats, or kill a goose for dinner. The husband talked to her just as the monk had, as though she understood him. Instead of the Buddha's life, he told her what he was doing when he repaired the harness or set tines in a new rake; or he talked about his brothers, who lived not so very far away.

Small Cat liked the wife better than the husband. *She* wasn't the one who had thrown Small Cat into a bag. She gave Small Cat bits of whatever she cooked. Sometimes, when she had a moment, she played with a goose feather or a small knotted rag; but it was a working household and there were not many moments like that.

Busy as the wife's hands might be, her mind and her voice were free. She talked about the baby she was hoping to have and her plans for the gardens as soon as the soil softened with springtime. When she didn't talk, she sang in a voice as soft and pretty as a dove's. One of her favorite songs was about Mt. Fuji-san. This puzzled Small Cat. Why would anyone tell stories of a place so far away, instead of one's home? With a shock, she realized her stories were about a place even more distant.

Small Cat started reciting her fudoki again, putting the stories back in their proper order: The Cat Who Ate Dirt, The Earless Cat, The Cat Under The Pavement. Even if there were no other cats to share it with, *she* was still here. For the first time, she realized that The Cat From The North might not have come from very far north at all. There hadn't been any monks or boats or giant mountains in The Cat From The North's story, just goats and dogs. The more she thought about it, the more it seemed likely that she'd spent all this time looking for something she left behind before she even left the capital.

The monk had told her that courage and persistence would bring her what she wanted, but was this it? The farm was a good place to be: safe, full of food. But the North went on so much farther than The Cat From The North had imagined. If Small Cat could not return to the capital, she might as well find out where North really ended.

A few days later, a man hiked up the snow-covered path. It was one of the husband's brothers, come with news about their mother. Small Cat waited until everyone was inside, and then trotted briskly down the way he had come.

Chapter 13
The Wolves

It was much less pleasant to travel alone and in the coldest part of winter. The monk would have carried her or kicked the snow away so that she could walk more easily; they would have shared food; he would have found warm places to stay and talked the people they met into not hurting her. He would have spoken to her, and stroked her ears when she wished.

Without him, the snow came to her shoulders. She had to stay on the road itself, which was slippery with packed ice and had deep slushy ruts that froze into slick, flat ponds. Small Cat learned how to hop without being noticed onto the huge bundles of hay that oxen sometimes carried on their backs.

She found somewhere to sleep each night by following the smell of smoke. She had to be careful, but even the simplest huts had corners and cubbyholes where a small, dark cat could sleep in peace, provided no dogs smelled her and sounded the alarm. But there were fewer leftover scraps of food to find. There was no time or energy to play.

The mice had their own paths under the snow. On still days she could hear them creeping through their tunnels, too deep for her to catch, and she had to wait until she came to shallower places under the trees. At least she could easily find and eat the dormice that hibernated in tight little balls in the snow, and the frozen sparrows that dropped from the bushes on the coldest nights.

One night it was very cold. She was looking for somewhere to stay, but she hadn't smelled smoke or heard anything promising.

There was a sudden rush from the snow-heaped bushes beside the road. She tore across the snow and scrambled high into a tree before turning to see what had chased her. It was bigger than the biggest dog she had ever seen, with a thick ruff and flat gold eyes: a wolf. It was a hard winter for wolves, and they were coming down from the mountains and eating whatever they could find.

This wolf glared and then sat on its haunches and tipped its head to one side, looking confused. It gave a puzzled yip. Soon a second wolf appeared from the darkening forest. It was much larger and she realized that the first one was young.

They looked thin and hungry. The two wolves touched noses for a moment, and the older one called up, "Come down, little one. We wish to find out what sort of animal you are."

She shivered. It was bitterly cold this high in the tree, but she couldn't trust them. She looked around for a way to escape, but the tree was isolated.

"We can wait," the older wolf said, and settled onto its haunches.

She huddled against the tree's trunk. The wind shook ice crystals from the branches overhead. If the wolves waited long enough, she would freeze to death, or her paws would go numb and she would fall. The sun dipped below the mountains and it grew much colder.

The icy air hurt her throat, so she pressed her face against her leg to breathe through her fur. It reminded her of the fire so long ago back in the capital, the fire that had destroyed her garden and her family. She had come so far, just to freeze to death or be eaten by wolves?

The first stars were bright in the clear night. The younger wolf was curled up tight in a furry ball, but the old wolf sat, looking up, its eyes shining in the darkness. It said, "Come down and be eaten."

Her fur rose on her neck, and she dug her claws deep into the branch. She couldn't feel her paws any more.

The wolf growled softly, "I have a pack, a family. This one is my son, and he is hungry. Let me feed him. You have no one."

The wolf was right: she had no one.

It sensed her grief, and said, "I understand. Come down. We will make it quick."

Small Cat shook her head. She would not give up, even if she did die like this. If they were going to eat her, at least there was no reason to make it easy for them. She clung as hard as she could, trying not to let go.

Chapter 14

The Bear Hunter

A dog barked and a second dog joined the first, their deep voices carrying through the still air. Small Cat was shivering so hard that her teeth chattered and she couldn't tell how far they were: in the next valley or miles away.

The wolves pricked their ears and stood. The barking stopped for a moment, and then began again, each bark closer. Two dogs hurtled into sight at the bottom of the valley. The wolves turned and vanished into the forest without a sound.

The dogs were still barking as they raced up to the tree. They were a big male and a smaller female, with thick golden fur that covered them from their toes to the tips of their round ears and their high, curling tails. The female ran a few steps after the wolves and returned to sniff the tree. "What's that smell?"

They peered up at her. She tried to climb higher, and loose bark fell into their surprised faces.

"I better get the man," the female said and ran off, again barking.

The male sat, just where the big wolf had sat. "What are you, up there?"

Small Cat ignored him. She didn't feel so cold now, just very drowsy.

She didn't even notice when she fell from the tree.

Small Cat woke up slowly. She felt warm, curled up on something dark and furry, and for a moment she imagined she was home, dozing with her aunts and cousins in the garden, light filtering through the trees to heat her whiskers.

She heard a heavy sigh, a dog's sigh, and with a start she realized this wasn't the garden; she was somewhere indoors and everything smelled of fur. She leapt to her feet.

She stood on a thick pile of bear hides in a small hut, dark except for the tiny flames in a brazier set into the floor. The two dogs from the forest slept in a pile beside it.

"You're awake, then," a man said. She hadn't seen him, for he had wrapped himself in a bear skin. Well, he hadn't tried to harm her. Wary but reassured, she drank from a bowl on the floor, and cleaned her paws and face. He still watched her.

"What are you? Not a dog or a fox. A tanuki?" Tanuki were little red-and-white striped animals that could climb trees and ate almost anything. The hunter lived a long way from where cats lived, so how would he know better? She meowed. "Out there is no place for a whatever-you-are, at least until spring," he added. "You're welcome to stay until then. If the dogs let you."

The dogs didn't seem to mind, though she kept out of reach for the first few days. She found plenty to do. An entire village of mice lived in the hut, helping themselves to the hunter's buckwheat and having babies as fast as they could. Small Cat caught so many at first that she didn't bother eating them all, and just left them on the floor for the dogs to crunch up when they came in from outdoors. Within a very few days the man and the dogs accepted her as part of the household, even though the dogs still pestered her to find out what she was.

The man and the dogs were gone a lot. They hunted bears in the forest, dragging them from their caves while they were sluggish from hibernation. The man skinned them and would sell their hides when summer came. If they were gone for a day or two, the hut got cold, for there was no one to keep the charcoal fire burning, but Small Cat didn't mind. She grew fat on all the mice, and her fur got thick and glossy.

The hut stood in a meadow with trees and mountains on either side. A narrow stream cut through the meadow, too fast to freeze. The only crossing was a single fallen log that shook from the strength of the water beneath it. The forest crowded close to the stream on the other side.

There was plenty to do, trees to climb and birds to catch. Small Cat watched for wolves, but daylight wasn't their time and she was careful to be inside before dusk. She never saw another human.

Each day the sun got brighter and stayed up longer. It wasn't spring yet, but Small Cat could smell it. The snow got heavy and wet, and she heard it slide from the trees in the forest with thumps and crashes. The stream swelled with snowmelt.

The two dogs ran off for a few days, and when they came back, the female was pregnant. At first she acted restless and cranky, and Small Cat kept away. But once her belly started to get round with puppies, she calmed down. The hunter started leaving her behind, tied to a rope so she wouldn't follow. She barked and paced, but she didn't try to pull free, and after a while she didn't even bother to do that.

Small Cat was used to the way people told stories, and the bear hunter had his stories as well, about hunts with the dogs, and myths he had learned from the old man who had taught him to hunt, so long ago. Everyone had a fudoki, Small Cat knew now. Everyone had their own stories, and the stories of their families and ancestors. There were adventures and love stories, or tricks and jokes and funny things that had happened, or disasters.

People wanted to tell their stories, and to know where they fit in their own fudoki. She was not that different.

Chapter 15

The Bear

The last bear hunt of the season began on a morning that felt like the first day of spring, with a little breeze full of the smell of growing things. The snow had a dirty crust and it had melted away in places, to leave mud and the first tiny green shoots pushing through the dead grass of the year before.

Fat with her puppies, the female lay on a straw mat put down over the mud for her. The male paced eagerly, his ears pricked and tail high. The bear hunter sat on the hut's stone stoop. He was sharpening the head of a long spear. Small Cat watched him from the doorway.

The man said, "Well, you've been lucky for us this year. Just one more good hunt, all right?" He looked along the spear's sharp edge. "The bears are waking up, and we don't want any angry mothers worried about their cubs. We have enough of our own to worry about!" He patted the female dog, who woke up and heaved herself to her feet.

He stood. "Ready, boy?" The male barked happily. The bear hunter shouldered a small pack and picked up his throwing and stabbing spears. "Stay out of trouble, girls," he said.

He and the male filed across the log. The female pulled at her rope, but once they vanished into the forest she slumped to the ground again with a heavy sigh. They would not be back until evening, or even the next day.

Small Cat had already eaten a mouse and a vole for her breakfast. Now she prowled the edges of the meadow, more for amusement than because she was hungry, and ended up at a large black rock next to the log across the stream. It was warmed and dried by the sun, and close enough to look down into the creamy, racing water: a perfect place to spend the middle of the day. She settled down comfortably. The sun on her back was almost hot.

A sudden sense of danger made her muscles tense up. She lifted her head. She saw nothing, but the female sensed it too, for she was sitting up, intently staring toward the forest beyond the stream.

The bear hunter burst from the woods, running as fast as he could. He had lost his spear. The male dog wasn't with him. Right behind him a giant black shape crashed from the forest—a black bear, bigger than he was. Small Cat could hear them splashing across the mud, and the female behind her barking hysterically.

It happened too fast to be afraid. The hunter bolted across the shaking log, just as the bear ran onto the far end. The man slipped as he passed Small Cat and he fell to one side. Small Cat had been too surprised to move, but when he slipped she leapt out of his way, sideways—onto the log.

The bear was a heavy black shape hurtling toward her, and she could see the little white triangle of fur on its chest. A paw slammed into the log, so close that she felt fur touch her whickers. With nowhere else to go, she jumped straight up. For an instant, she stared into the bear's red-rimmed eyes.

The bear reared up at Small Cat's leap. It lost its balance, fell into the swollen stream and was carried away, roaring and thrashing. The bear had been swept nearly out of sight before it managed to pull itself from the water on the opposite bank. Droplets scattered as it shook itself. It swung its head from side to side looking for them, then shambled back into the trees, far downstream. A moment later, the male dog limped from the trees, and across the fallen log to them.

The male whined but sat quiet as the bear hunter cleaned out his foot. He had stepped on a stick and torn the pad. When the hunter was done, he leaned against the wall, the dogs and Small Cat tucked close.

They had found a bear sooner than expected, he told them: a female with her cub just a short walk into the forest. She saw them and attacked immediately. He used his throwing spears but they didn't stick, and she broke his stabbing spear with a single blow of her big paw. The male slammed into her from the side, giving him time to run for the hut and the rack of spears on the wall beside the door.

"I knew I wouldn't make it," the hunter said. His hand still shook a little as he finally took off his pack. "But at least I wasn't going to die without trying."

Small Cat meowed.

"Exactly," the hunter said. "You don't give up, ever."

Chapter 16

The North

Small Cat left, not so many days after the bear attacked. She pushed under the door flap while the hunter and the dogs dozed beside the fire. She stretched all the way from her toes to the tip of her tail, and she stood tall on the step, looking around.

It was just at sunset, the bright sky dimming to the west. To the east she saw the first bit of the full moon crawling out of the trees. Even at dusk, the forest looked different now, the bare branches softened with buds. The air smelled fresh with spring growth.

She paced the clearing looking for a sign of the way to the road. She hadn't been conscious when the bear hunter had brought her. In any case it was a long time ago.

Someone snuffled behind her. The female stood blinking outside the hut. "Where are you?" she asked. "Are you gone already?"

Small Cat walked to her.

"I knew you would go," the dog said. "This is my home, but you're like the puppies will be when they're born. We're good hunters, so the man will be able to trade our puppies for fabric, or even spear heads." She sounded proud. "They will go other places and have their own lives. You're like that, too. But you were very interesting to know, whatever you are."

Small Cat came close enough to touch noses with her.

"If you're looking for the road," the female said, "it's on the other side, over the stream." She went back inside, and the door flap dropped behind her.

Small Cat sharpened her claws and trotted across the log, back toward the road.

Traveling got harder at first, as spring grew warmer. Helped along by the bright sun and the spring rains, the snow in the mountains melted quickly. The rivers were high and icy-cold with snow-melt. No cat, however tough she was, could hope to wade or swim them, and sometimes there was no bridge. Whenever she couldn't cross, Small Cat waited a day or two until the water went down or someone passed.

People seemed to like seeing her. This surprised her. Maybe it was different here. They couldn't know about cats, but maybe demons did not frighten them, especially small ones. She wasn't afraid of the people, either, so she sniffed their fingers and ate their offerings, and rode in their wagons whenever she had the chance.

The road wandered down through the mountains and hills, into little towns and past farmhouses. Everything seemed full of new life. The trees were loud with baby birds and squirrels. The wind rustled through the new leaves. Wild yellow and pink flowers spangled the meadows, and smelled so sweet and strong that she sometimes stepped right over a mouse and didn't notice until it jumped away. The fields were full of new plants, and the pastures and farmyards were full of babies: goats and sheep, horses, oxen and geese and chickens. Goslings, it turned out, tasted delicious.

Journeying was a pleasure now, but she knew she was almost ready to stop. She could have made a home anywhere, she realized—strange cats or no cats, farmer or hunter, beside a shrine or behind an inn. It wasn't about the stories or the garden. It was about her.

But she wasn't quite ready. She had wanted to find The Cat From The North's home, and when that didn't happen she had gone on, curious to find how far the road went. And she didn't know yet.

Then there was a day when it was beautiful and bright, the first really warm day. She came around a curve in the road and looked down into a broad valley, with a river flowing to a distant bay that glittered in the sun. It was the ocean, and Small Cat knew she had come to the end of her travels. This was North.

Chapter 17
Home

There was a village where the river and the ocean met. The path led down through fields green with new shoots, and was full of people planting things or digging with hoes. The path became a lane and others joined it.

Small Cat trotted between the double row of houses and shops. Every window and door and screen was open to let the winter out and the spring in. Bedding and robes fluttered as they aired. Young grass and white flowers glowed in the sun, and the three trees in the center of the village were bright with new leaves.

Everyone seemed to be outside doing something. A group of women sang a love song as they pounded rice in a wood mortar to make flour. A man with no hair wove sturdy sandals of straw to wear in the fields, while he told a story about catching a wolf cub when he had been a child by falling on it. A girl sitting on the ground beside him listened as she finished a straw cape for her wooden doll, and then ran off calling for her mother. The geese who had been squabbling over a weed scrambled out of her way.

A man on a ladder tied new clumps of thatch onto a roof where the winter had worn through. Below him, a woman laid a bearskin across a rack. She tied her sleeves back to bare her arms, and hit the skin with a stick. Clouds of dirt puffed out with each blow. In between blows, she shouted instructions up to the man on the roof, and Small Cat recognized that this was a story, too: the story of what the man should do next.

A small Buddhist temple peeked from a grove of trees, with stone dogs guarding a gate into the grounds. A boy swept the ground in front of a Shinto shrine there. Small Cat smelled the dried fish and mushrooms that had been left as offerings: it might be worth her while later to find out more.

Two young dogs wrestled in the dirt by a sheep pen until they noticed her. They jumped to their feet and raced about, barking, "Cat! Cat!" She wasn't afraid of dogs any more—not happy dogs like these, with their heads high and their ears pricked. She hopped onto a railing where they couldn't accidentally bowl her over. They milled about, wagging their tails.

A woman stretching fabric started to say something to the dogs. When she saw Small Cat, her mouth made an O of surprise. "A cat!" She whirled and ran toward the temple. "A cat! Look, come see!"

The woman knew what a cat was, and so had the dogs! Ignoring the dogs, ignoring all the people who were suddenly seeing her, Small Cat pelted after the woman.

The woman burst through a circle of children gathered around a seated man. He was dressed in red and yellow, his shaved head shiny in the sun. A monk, but not her monk, she knew right away: this one was rounder, though his face was still open and kind. He stood up as the woman pointed at Small Cat. "Look, look! Another cat!"

The monk and the children all started talking at once. And in the middle of the noise, Small Cat heard a meow.

Another cat?

A little ginger- and white-striped tomcat stood on a stack of boxes nearby, looking down at her. His golden eyes were bright and huge with excitement, and his whiskers vibrated. He jumped down and ran to her.

"Who are you?" he said. His tail waved. "Where did you come from?"

When she had decided to make this her home, she hadn't thought she might be sharing it. He wasn't much bigger than she was, or any older, and right now, he was more like a kitten than anything, hopping from paw to paw. She took a step toward him.

"I am so glad to see another cat!" he said. He purred so hard that his breath wheezed in his throat. "The monk brought me here last year to catch mice, all the way from the capital in a basket! It was very exciting. There are so many things to do here! I have a really nice secret place to sleep, but I'll show it to you." He touched her nose with his own.

"There's no fudoki," he said, a little defensively. "There's just me."

"And me now," said The Cat Who Walked A Thousand Miles, and she rubbed her cheek against his. "And I have such a tale to tell!"

RECOMMENDED READING

The following stories would appear in this volume if space permitted. All of them are recommended, and would repay your attention.

Daniel Abraham, "Balfour and Meriwether in the Adventure Of The Emperor's Vengeance", *Postscripts 19*

Daniel Abraham, "The Best Monkey", *The Solaris Book of New Science Fiction: Volume 3*

Peter M. Ball, "Horn", Twelfth Planet Press

Peter M. Ball, "On the Destruction of Copenhagen by the War-Machines of the Merfolk", *Strange Horizons*, July 2009

Peter S. Beagle, "Vanishing", *Orson Scott Card's Intergalactic Medicine Show*, March 2009

Elizabeth Bear, "Cuckoo", *Shadow Unit*

James P. Blaylock, "The Dry Spell", *Subterranean*, Winter 2009

Leah Bobet, "Sugar", *Shadow Unit*

Damien Broderick, "The Qualia Engine", *Asimov's Science Fiction*, August 2009

Pat Cadigan, "Don't Mention Madagascar", *Eclipse Three*

Paul Cornell, "One of Our Bastards Is Missing", *The Solaris Book of New Science Fiction: Volume Three*

Andy Duncan, "The Dragaman's Bride", *The Dragon Book*

Greg Egan, "Hot Rock", *Oceanic*

James Enge, "Fire and Sleet", *Pyrsf.com*

Sara Genge, "Shoes-to-Run", *Asimov's Science Fiction*, July, 2009

Theodora Goss, "Child-Empress of Mars", *Interfictions 2*

Steven Gould, "A Story, with Beans", *Analog Science Fiction and Fact*, December 2009

Paul Haines, "Wives", *X6*

Cecelia Holland, "Dragon's Deep", *The Dragon Book*

Gwyneth Jones, "Collision", *When It Changed*

John Kessel, "Events Preceding the Helvetican Renaissance", *The New Space Opera 2*

Caitlin R. Kiernan, "Galapagos", *Eclipse Three*

Ellen Klages, "Singing on a Star", *Firebirds Soaring*

Ted Kosmatka & Michael Poore, "Blood Dauber", *Asimov's Science Fiction*, October/November 2009

Nancy Kress, "Act One", *Asimov's Science Fiction*, March 2009

Ellen Kushner, "Dulce Domum", *Eclipse Three*

Margo Lanagan, "Sea-Hearts", *X6*

Jessica Lee, "Superhero Girl", *Fantasy Magazine*, June 2009

Paul McAuley, "Crimes and Glory", *Subterranean*, Spring 2009

Ian McDonald, "Vishnu at the Cat Circus", *Cyberabad Days*

Maureen F. McHugh, "Useless Things", *Eclipse Three*

James Morrow, *Shambling Towards Hiroshima,* Tachyon Publications

Kim Newman, "Moon Moon Moon", *Subterranean*, Summer 2009

Garth Nix, "The Heart of the City", *Subterranean*, Summer 2009

Holly Phillips, "The Long Cold Goodbye", *Asimov's Science Fiction Magazine*, March 2009

Tim Pratt, "Unexpected Outcomes", *Interzone 222*

Chris Roberson, "Edison's Frankenstein", *Postscripts 20/21*

Tansy Rayner Roberts, "Siren Beat", *Siren Beat/Roadkill*

Rudy Rucker and Bruce Sterling, "Colliding Branes", *Asimov's Science Fiction Magazine*, February 2009

Geoff Ryman, "You", *When It Changed*

Gord Sellar, "Of Melei, of Ulthar", *Clarkesworld Magazine*, October 2009

Lucius Shepard, "Sylgarmo's Proclamation", *Songs of the Dying Earth*

Robert Silverberg, "The True Vintage of Erzuine Thale", *Songs of the Dying Earth*

William Browning Spencer, "Come Lurk with Me and Be My Love", *Lovecraft Unbound*

Bruce Sterling, "Esoteric City", *The Magazine of Fantasy & Science Fiction*, August/September 2009

Harry Turtledove, "We Haven't Got There Yet", *Tor.com*

Steven Utley & Michael Bishop, "The City Quiet as Death", *Tor.com*

Catherynne M. Valente, "The Radiant Car Thy Sparrows Drew", *Clarkesworld Magazine*, August 2009

Jeff VanderMeer, "Errata", *Tor.com*

Jo Walton, "Escape to Other Worlds with Science Fiction", *Tor.com*

Robert Charles Wilson, "This Peaceable Land; or The Unbearable Vision of Harriet Beecher Stowe", *Other Earths*

John C. Wright, "One Bright Star to Guide Them", *The Magazine of Fantasy & Science Fiction,* April/May 2009

John C. Wright, "The Far End of History", *The New Space Opera 2*

COPYRIGHT ACKNOWLEDGMENTS

Night Shade Books Is an Independent Publisher of Quality SF, Fantasy and Horror

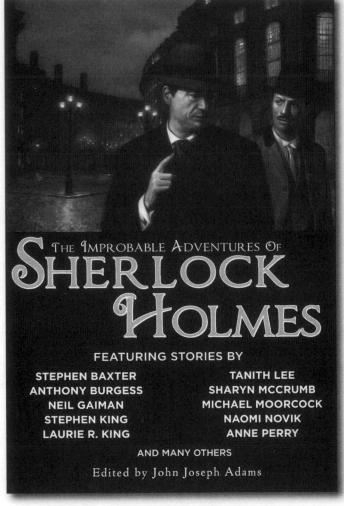

THE IMPROBABLE ADVENTURES OF

SHERLOCK HOLMES

FEATURING STORIES BY

STEPHEN BAXTER	TANITH LEE
ANTHONY BURGESS	SHARYN MCCRUMB
NEIL GAIMAN	MICHAEL MOORCOCK
STEPHEN KING	NAOMI NOVIK
LAURIE R. KING	ANNE PERRY

AND MANY OTHERS

Edited by John Joseph Adams

ISBN 978-1-59780-160-7, Trade Paperback; $15.95

Sherlock Holmes is back! These are the improbable adventures of Sherlock Holmes, where nothing is impossible, and nothing can be ruled out. In these cases, Holmes investigates ghosts, curses, aliens, dinosaurs, shapeshifters, and evil gods. But is it the supernatural, or is there a perfectly rational explanation?

In these pages you'll also find our hero crossing paths with H. G. Wells, Lewis Carroll, and even Arthur Conan Doyle himself, and you'll be astounded to learn the truth behind cases previously alluded to by Watson but never before documented until now. Here are some of the best Holmes pastiches of the last thirty years, twenty-eight tales of mystery and the imagination detailing Holmes's further exploits, as told by many of today's greatest storytellers, including Stephen King, Anne Perry, Anthony Burgess, Neil Gaiman, Stephen Baxter, Tanith Lee, Michael Moorcock, and many more. The game is afoot!

Night Shade Books Is an Independent Publisher of Quality SF, Fantasy and Horror

ISBN 978-1-59780-187-4, Trade Paperback; $15.95

Dragons: fearsome fire-breathing foes, scaled adversaries, legendary lizards, ancient hoarders of priceless treasures, serpentine sages with the ages' wisdom, and winged weapons of war.

Wings of Fire brings you all these dragons, and more, seen clearly through the eyes of many of today's most popular authors, including Peter S. Beagle, Holly Black, Orson Scott Card, Mercedes Lackey, Charles De Lint, Diana Wynne Jones, Ursula K Le Guin, George R. R. Martin, Anne McCaffrey, Garth Nix, and many others.

Edited by Jonathan Strahan (*The Best Science Fiction and Fantasy of the Year, Eclipse*), *Wings of Fire* collects the best short stories about dragons. From writhing wyrms to snakelike devourers of heroes; from East to West and everywhere in between, *Wings of Fire* is sure to please dragon lovers everywhere.